KU-441-108

PUFFIN BOOKS

White Fang

Born in the primitive, frozen wilds of north-west Canada, White Fang is destined for a life of hardship, where only the strong survive. The fiercest cub in the litter, only he manages to endure the cold and hunger which kill his brothers and sisters.

White Fang's is a remarkable story. Through his eyes we experience every one of his adventures; his triumphant first kill, his discovery of mankind, his harsh time as a sledge dog, his rescue from cruel slavery . . .

We also witness White Fang's growing awareness of the world around him, and watch his development from a ferocious, savage creature of the Wild into one who learns to love and trust his human master.

Written in 1905, this remarkable, moving story spans the life-time of a fiercely independent creature of the Wild – one of the most famous and impressive of all animal characters in fiction. It is now the subject of a stunning Walt Disney film.

Jack London was born in San Francisco in 1876. He joined the goldrush to the Klondike in 1897, from which experience came many of his books, including *The Call of the Wild*, published in Puffin Classics, complete and unabridged. *White Fang* is his most famous and best-loved story.

Jack London

WHITE FANG

PUFFIN BOOKS

PUFFIN BOOKS

Published by the Penguin Group
Penguin Books Ltd, 27 Wrights Lane, London W8 5TZ, England
Penguin Books USA Inc., 375 Hudson Street, New York, New York 10014, USA
Penguin Books Australia Ltd, Ringwood, Victoria, Australia
Penguin Books Canada Ltd, 3801 John Street, Markham, Ontario, Canada L3R 1B4
Penguin Books (NZ) Ltd, 182–190 Wairau Road, Auckland 10, New Zealand
Penguin Books Ltd, Registered Offices: Harmondsworth, Middlesex, England

First published 1905
Published in Puffin Books 1985
9 10

Printed in England by Clays Ltd, St Ives plc
Set in Palatino by
Rowland Phototypesetting Ltd
Bury St Edmunds, Suffolk

Library of Congress catalog card number: 85-42971
(CIP data available)

Except in the United States of America,
this book is sold subject to the condition
that it shall not, by way of trade or otherwise,
be lent, re-sold, hired out, or otherwise circulated
without the publisher's prior consent in any form of
binding or cover other than that in which it is
published and without a similar condition
including this condition being imposed
on the subsequent purchaser

CONTENTS

PART V

PART I

CHAPTER

1

THE TRAIL OF THE MEAT

Dark spruce forest frowned on either side the frozen waterway. The trees had been stripped by a recent wind of their white covering of frost, and they seemed to lean toward each other, black and ominous, in the fading light. A vast silence reigned over the land. The land itself was a desolation, lifeless, without movement, so lone and cold that the spirit of it was not even that of sadness. There was a hint in it of laughter, but of a laughter more terrible than any sadness – a laughter that was mirthless as the smile of the sphinx, a laughter cold as the frost and partaking of the grimness of infallibility. It was the masterful and incommunicable wisdom of eternity laughing at the futility of life and the effort of life. It was the Wild – the savage, frozen-hearted Northland Wild.

But there *was* life, abroad in the land and defiant. Down the frozen waterway toiled a string of wolfish dogs. Their bristly fur was rimed with frost. Their breath froze in the air as it left their mouths, spouting forth in spumes of vapour that settled upon the hair of their bodies and formed into crystals of frost. Leather harness was on the dogs, and leather traces attached them to a sled which dragged along behind. The sled was without runners. It was made of stout birch-bark, and its full surface rested on the snow. The front end of the sled was turned up, like a scroll, in order to force down and under the bore of soft snow that surged like a wave before it. On the sled, securely lashed, was a long and narrow oblong box. There were other things on the sled – blankets, an axe, and a coffee-pot and frying-pan; but prominent, occupying most of the space, was the long and narrow oblong box.

In advance of the dogs, on wide snowshoes, toiled a man. At the rear of the sled toiled a second man. On the sled, in the box, lay a third man whose toil was over – a man whom the Wild had conquered and beaten down until he would never move nor struggle again. It is not the way of the Wild to like movement. Life is an offence to it, for life is movement; and the Wild aims always to destroy movement. It freezes the water to prevent it running to the sea; it drives the sap out of the trees till they are frozen to their mighty hearts; and most ferociously and terribly of all does the Wild harry and crush into submission man – man who is the most restless of life, ever in revolt against the dictum that all movement must in the end come to the cessation of movement.

But at front and rear, unawed and indomitable, toiled the two men who were not yet dead. Their bodies were covered with fur and soft tanned leather. Eyelashes and cheeks and lips were so coated with the crystals from their frozen breath that their faces were not discernible. This gave them the seeming of ghostly masques, undertakers in a spectral world at the funeral of some ghost. But under it all they were men, penetrating the land of desolation and mockery and silence, puny adventurers bent on colossal adventure, pitting themselves against the might of a world as remote and alien and pulseless as the abysses of space.

They travelled on without speech, saving their breath for the work of their bodies. On every side was the silence, pressing upon them with a tangible presence. It affected their minds as the many atmospheres of deep water affect the body of the diver. It crushed them with the weight of unending vastness and unalterable decree. It crushed them into the remotest recesses of their own minds, pressing out of them, like juices from the grape, all the false ardours and exaltations and undue self-values of the human soul, until they perceived themselves finite and small, specks and motes, moving with weak cunning and little wisdom amidst the play and inter-play of the great blind elements and forces.

An hour went by, and a second hour. The pale light of the short sunless day was beginning to fade, when a faint far cry arose on the still air. It soared upward with a swift rush, till it reached its topmost note, where it persisted, palpitant and tense, and then slowly died away. It might have been a lost soul wailing, had it not been invested with a certain sad fierceness and hungry eagerness. The front man turned his head until his eyes met the eyes of the man behind. And then, across the narrow oblong box, each nodded to the other.

A second cry arose, piercing the silence with needle-like shrillness. Both men located the sound. It was to the rear, somewhere in the snow expanse they had just traversed. A third and answering cry arose, also to the rear and to the left of the second cry.

'They're after us, Bill,' said the man at the front.

His voice sounded hoarse and unreal, and he had spoken with apparent effort.

'Meat is scarce,' answered his comrade. 'I ain't seen a rabbit sign for days.'

Thereafter they spoke no more, though their ears were keen for the hunting-cries that continued to rise behind them.

At the fall of darkness they swung the dogs into a cluster of spruce trees on the edge of the waterway, and made a camp. The coffin, at the side of the fire, served for seat and table. The wolf-dogs, clustered on the far side of the fire, snarled and bickered among themselves, but evinced no inclination to stray off into the darkness.

'Seems to me, Henry, they're stayin' remarkable close to camp,' Bill commented.

Henry, squatting over the fire and settling the pot of coffee with a piece of ice, nodded. Nor did he speak till he had taken his seat on the coffin and begun to eat.

'They know where their hides is safe,' he said. 'They'd sooner eat grub than be grub. They're pretty wise, them dogs.'

Bill shook his head. 'Oh, I don't know.'

His comrade looked at him curiously. 'First time I ever heard you say anything about their not bein' wise.'

'Henry,' said the other, munching with deliberation the beans he was eating, 'did you happen to notice the way them dogs kicked up when I was a-feedin' 'em?'

'They did cut up more 'n usual,' Henry acknowledged.

'How many dogs've we got, Henry?'

'Six.'

'Well, Henry . . .' Bill stopped for a moment, in order that his words might gain greater significance. 'As I was sayin', Henry, we've got six dogs. I took six fish out of the bag. I gave one fish to each dog, an', Henry, I was one fish short.'

'You counted wrong.'

'We've got six dogs,' the other reiterated dispassionately. 'I took out six fish. One Ear didn't get no fish. I came back to the bag afterward an' got 'm his fish.'

'We've only got six dogs,' Henry said.

'Henry,' Bill went on, 'I won't say they was all dogs, but there was seven of 'm that got fish.'

Henry stopped eating to glance across the fire and count the dogs.

'There's only six now,' he said.

'I saw the other one run off across the snow,' Bill announced with cool positiveness. 'I saw seven.'

Henry looked at him commiseratingly and said: 'I'll be almighty glad when this trip's over.'

'What d' ye mean by that?' Bill demanded.

'I mean that this load of ourn is gettin' on your nerves, an' that you're beginnin' to see things.'

'I thought of that,' Bill answered gravely. 'An' so, when I saw it run off across the snow, I looked in the snow an' saw its tracks. Then I counted the dogs, an' there was still six of 'em. The tracks is there in the snow now. D' ye want to look at 'em? I'll show 'em to you.'

Henry did not reply, but munched on in silence, until, the meal finished, he topped it with a final cup of coffee. He wiped his mouth with the back of his hand and said:

'Then you're thinkin' as it was – '

A long wailing cry, fiercely sad, from somewhere in the darkness, had interrupted him. He stopped to listen to it, then he finished his sentence with a wave of his hand toward the sound of the cry, '– one of them?'

Bill nodded. 'I'd a blame sight sooner think that than

anything else. You noticed yourself the row the dogs made.'

Cry after cry, and answering cries, were turning the silence into a bedlam. From every side the cries arose, and the dogs betrayed their fear by huddling together and so close to the fire that their hair was scorched by the heat. Bill threw on more wood, before lighting his pipe.

'I'm thinking you're down in the mouth some,' Henry said.

'Henry . . .' He sucked meditatively at his pipe for some time before he went on. 'Henry, I was a-thinkin' what a blame sight luckier he is than you an' me'll ever be.'

He indicated the third person by a downward thrust of the thumb to the box on which they sat.

'You an' me, Henry, when we die, we'll be lucky if we get enough stones over our carcases to keep the dogs off of us.'

'But we ain't got people an' money an' all the rest, like him,' Henry rejoined. 'Long-distance funerals is somethin' you an' me can't exactly afford.'

'What gets me, Henry, is what a chap like this, that's a lord or something in his own country, and that's never had to bother about grub nor blankets – why he comes a-buttin' round the God-forsaken ends of the earth – that's what I can't exactly see.'

'He might have lived to a ripe old age if he'd stayed to home,' Henry agreed.

Bill opened his mouth to speak, but changed his mind. Instead, he pointed toward the wall of darkness that pressed about them from every side. There was no suggestion of form in the utter blackness; only could be seen a pair of eyes gleaming like live coals. Henry indicated with his head a second pair, and a third. A circle of the gleaming eyes had drawn about their camp. Now and again a pair of eyes moved, or disappeared to appear again a moment later.

The unrest of the dogs had been increasing, and they stampeded, in a surge of sudden fear, to the near side of the fire, cringing and crawling about the legs of the men. In the scramble one of the dogs had been overturned on the edge of the fire, and it had yelped with pain and fright as the smell of its singed coat possessed the air. The commotion caused the circle of eyes to shift restlessly for a moment and even to withdraw a bit, but it settled down again as the dogs became quiet.

'Henry, it's a blame misfortune to be out of ammunition.'

Bill had finished his pipe and was helping his companion spread the bed of fur and blanket upon the spruce boughs which he had laid over the snow before supper. Henry grunted, and began unlacing his moccasins.

'How many cartridges did you say you had left?' he asked.

'Three,' came the answer. 'An' I wisht 'twas three hundred. Then I'd show 'em what for, damn 'em!'

He shook his fist angrily at the gleaming eyes, and began securely to prop his moccasins before the fire.

'An' I wisht this cold snap'd break,' he went on. 'It's ben fifty below for two weeks now. An' I wisht I'd never started on this trip, Henry. I don't like the looks of it. I don't feel right, somehow. An' while I'm wishin', I wisht the trip was over an' done with, an' you an' me a-sittin' by the fire in Fort M'Gurry just about now, an' playin' cribbage – that's what I wisht.'

Henry grunted and crawled into bed. As he dozed off he was aroused by his comrade's voice.

'Say, Henry, that other one that come in an' got a fish – why didn't the dogs pitch into it? That's what's botherin' me.'

'You're botherin' too much, Bill,' came the sleepy response. 'You was never like this before. You jes' shut up now, an' go to sleep, an' you'll be all hunkydory in the mornin'. Your stomach's sour – that's what's botherin' you.'

The men slept, breathing heavily, side by side, under the one covering. The fire died down, and the gleaming eyes drew closer the circle they had flung about the camp. The dogs clustered together in fear, now and again snarling menacingly as a pair of eyes drew close. Once their uproar became so loud that Bill woke up. He got out of bed carefully, so as not to disturb the sleep of his comrade, and threw more wood on the fire. As it began to flame up, the circle of eyes drew farther back. He glanced casually at the huddling dogs. He rubbed his eyes and looked at them more sharply. Then he crawled back into the blankets.

'Henry,' he said. 'Oh, Henry!'

Henry groaned as he passed from sleep to waking, and demanded: 'What's wrong now?'

'Nothin',' came the answer; 'only there's seven of 'em again. I just counted.'

Henry acknowledged receipt of the information with a grunt that slid into a snore as he drifted back into sleep.

In the morning it was Henry who awoke first and routed his companion out of bed. Daylight was yet three hours away, though it was already six o'clock; and in the darkness Henry went about preparing breakfast, while Bill rolled the blankets and made the sled ready for lashing.

'Say, Henry,' he asked suddenly, 'how many dogs did you say we had?'

'Six.'

'Wrong,' Bill proclaimed triumphantly.

'Seven again?' Henry queried.

'No, five; one's gone.'

'The hell!' Henry cried in wrath, leaving the cooking to come and count the dogs.

'You're right, Bill,' he concluded. 'Fatty's gone.'

'An' he went like greased lightnin' once he got started. Couldn't 've seen 'm for smoke.'

'No chance at all,' Henry concluded. 'They jus' swallowed 'm alive. I bet he was yelpin' as he went down their throats, damn 'em!'

'He always was a fool dog,' said Bill.

'But no fool dog ought to be fool enough to go off an' commit suicide that way.' He looked over the remainder of the team with a speculative eye that summed up instantly the salient traits of each animal. 'I bet none of the others would do it.'

'Couldn't drive 'em away from the fire with a club,' Bill agreed. 'I always did think there was somethin' wrong with Fatty anyway.'

And this was the epitaph of a dead dog on the Northland trail – less scant than the epitaph of many another dog, of many a man.

CHAPTER
2

THE SHE-WOLF

Breakfast eaten and the slim camp-outfit lashed to the sled, the men turned their backs on the cheery fire and launched out into the darkness. At once began to rise the cries that were fiercely sad – cries that called through the darkness and cold to one another and answered back. Conversation ceased. Daylight came at nine o'clock. At midday the sky to the south warmed to rose-colour, and marked where the bulge of the earth intervened between the meridian sun and the northern world. But the rose-colour swiftly faded. The grey light of day that remained lasted until three o'clock, when it too faded, and the pall of the Arctic night descended upon the lone and silent land.

As darkness came on, the hunting-cries to right and left and rear drew closer – so close that more than once they sent surges of fear through the toiling dogs, throwing them into short-lived panics.

At the conclusion of one such panic, when he and Henry had got the dogs back in the traces, Bill said:

'I wisht they'd strike game somewheres, an' go away an' leave us alone.'

'They do get on the nerves horrible,' Henry sympathized.

They spoke no more until camp was made.

Henry was bending over and adding ice to the bubbling pot of beans when he was startled by the sound of a blow, an exclamation from Bill, and a sharp snarling cry of pain from among the dogs. He straightened up in time to see a dim form disappearing across the snow into the shelter of the dark. Then he saw Bill, standing amid the dogs, half triumphant, half crestfallen, in one hand a stout club, in the other the tail and part of the body of a sun-cured salmon.

'It got half of it,' he announced; 'but I got a whack at it jes' the same. D' ye hear it squeal?'

'What'd it look like?' Henry asked.

'Couldn't see. But it had four legs an' a mouth an' hair an' looked like any dog.'

'Must be a tame wolf, I reckon.'

'It's damned tame, whatever it is, comin' in here at feedin' time an gettin' its whack of fish.'

That night, when supper was finished and they sat on the oblong box and pulled at their pipes, the circle of gleaming eyes drew in even closer than before.

'I wisht they'd spring up a bunch of moose or something, an' go away an' leave us alone,' Bill said.

Henry grunted with an intonation that was not all sympathy, and for a quarter of an hour they sat on in silence, Henry staring at the fire, and Bill at the circle of eyes that burned in the darkness just beyond the firelight.

'I wisht we was pullin' into M'Gurry right now,' he began again.

'Shut up your wishin' and your croakin',' Henry burst

out angrily. 'Your stomach's sour. That's what's ailin' you. Swallow a spoonful of sody, an' you'll sweeten up wonderful an' be more pleasant company.'

In the morning Henry was aroused by fervid blasphemy that proceeded from the mouth of Bill. Henry propped himself up on an elbow and looked to see his comrade standing among the dogs beside the replenished fire, his arms raised in objurgation, his face distorted with passion.

'Hello!' Henry called. 'What's up now?'

'Frog's gone,' came the answer.

'No.'

'I tell you yes.'

Henry leaped out of the blankets and to the dogs. He counted them with care, and then joined his partner in cursing the powers of the Wild that had robbed them of another dog.

'Frog was the strongest dog of the bunch,' Bill pronounced finally.

'An' he was no fool dog neither,' Henry added.

And so was recorded the second epitaph in two days.

A gloomy breakfast was eaten, and the four remaining dogs were harnessed to the sled. The day was a repetition of the days that had gone before. The men toiled without speech across the face of the frozen world. The silence was unbroken save by the cries of their pursuers, that, unseen, hung upon their rear. With the coming of night in the mid-afternoon, the cries sounded closer as the pursuers drew in according to their custom; and the dogs grew excited and frightened, and were guilty of panics that tangled the traces and further depressed the two men.

'There, that'll fix you fool critters,' Bill said with satisfaction that night, standing erect at completion of his task.

Henry left his cooking to come and see. Not only had his partner tied the dogs up, but he had tied them, after the Indian fashion, with sticks. About the neck of each dog he had fastened a leather thong. To this, and so close to the neck that the dog could not get his teeth to it, he had tied a stout stick four or five feet in length. The other end of the stick, in turn, was made fast to a stake in the ground by means of a leather thong. The dog was unable to gnaw through the leather at his own end of the stick. The stick prevented him from getting at the leather that fastened the other end.

Henry nodded his head approvingly.

'It's the only contraption that'll ever hold One Ear,' he said. 'He can gnaw through leather as clean as a knife an' jes' about half as quick. They all'll be here in the mornin' hunkydory.'

'You jes' bet they will,' Bill affirmed. 'If one of 'em turns up missin', I'll go without my coffee.'

'They jes' know we ain't loaded to kill,' Henry remarked at bedtime, indicating the gleaming circle that hemmed them in. 'If we could put a couple of shots into 'em, they'd be more respectful. They come closer every night. Get the firelight out of your eyes an' look hard – there! Did you see that one?'

For some time the two men amused themselves with watching the movement of vague forms on the edge of the firelight. By looking closely and steadily at where a pair of eyes burned in the darkness, the form of the animal would slowly take shape. They could even see these forms move at times.

A sound among the dogs attracted the men's attention.

One Ear was uttering quick, eager whines, lunging at the length of his stick toward the darkness, and desisting now and again in order to make frantic attacks on the stick with his teeth.

'Look at that, Bill,' Henry whispered.

Full into the firelight, with a stealthy, sidelong movement, glided a doglike animal. It moved with commingled mistrust and daring, cautiously observing the men, its attention fixed on the dogs. One Ear strained the full length of the stick toward the intruder and whined with eagerness.

'That fool One Ear don't seem scairt much,' Bill said in a low tone.

'It's a she-wolf,' Henry whispered back, 'an' that accounts for Fatty an' Frog. She's the decoy for the pack. She draws out the dog an' then all the rest pitches in an' eats 'm up.'

The fire crackled. A log fell apart with a loud spluttering noise. At the sound of it the strange animal leaped back into the darkness.

'Henry, I'm a-thinkin',' Bill announced.

'Thinkin' what?'

'I'm thinkin' that was the one I lambasted with the club.'

'Ain't the slightest doubt in the world,' was Henry's response.

'An' right here I want to remark', Bill went on, 'that that animal's familiarity with camp-fires is suspicious an' immoral.'

'It knows for certain more'n a self-respectin' wolf ought to know,' Henry agreed. 'A wolf that knows enough to come in with the dogs at feedin' time has had experiences.'

'Ol' Villan had a dog once that run away with the wolves,' Bill cogitated aloud. 'I ought to know. I shot it out of the pack in a moose pasture over on Little Stick. An' Ol' Villan cried like a baby. Hadn't seen it for three years, he said. Ben with the wolves all that time.'

'I reckon you've called the turn, Bill. That wolf's a dog, an' it's eaten fish many's the time from the hand of man.'

'An' if I get a chance at it, that wolf that's a dog'll be jes' meat,' Bill declared. 'We can't afford to lose no more animals.'

'But you've only got three cartridges,' Henry objected.

'I'll wait for a dead sure shot,' was the reply.

In the morning Henry renewed the fire and cooked breakfast to the accompaniment of his partner's snoring.

'You was sleepin' jes' too comfortable for anything,' Henry told him, as he routed him out for breakfast. 'I hadn't the heart to rouse you.'

Bill began to eat sleepily. He noticed that his cup was empty, and started to reach for the pot. But the pot was beyond arm's length and beside Henry.

'Say, Henry,' he chided gently, 'ain't you forgot somethin'?'

Henry looked about with great carefulness and shook his head. Bill held up the empty cup.

'You don't get no coffee,' Henry announced.

'Ain't run out?' Bill asked anxiously.

'Nope.'

'Ain't thinkin' it'll hurt my digestion?'

'Nope.'

A flush of angry blood pervaded Bill's face.

'Then it's jes' warm an' anxious I am to be hearin' you explain yourself,' he said.

'Spanker's' gone,' Henry answered.

Without haste, with the air of one resigned to misfortune, Bill turned his head, and from where he sat counted the dogs.

'How'd it happen?' he asked apathetically.

Henry shrugged his shoulders. 'Don't know. Unless One Ear gnawed 'm loose. He couldn't a-done it himself, that's sure.'

'The darned cuss.' Bill spoke gravely and slowly, with no hint of the anger that was raging within. 'Jes' because he couldn't chew himself loose, he chews Spanker loose.'

'Well, Spanker's troubles is over anyway; I guess he's digested by this time, an' cavortin' over the landscape in the bellies of twenty different wolves,' was Henry's epitaph on this, the latest lost dog. 'Have some coffee, Bill.'

But Bill shook his head.

'Go on,' Henry pleaded, elevating the pot.

Bill shoved his cup aside. 'I'll be ding-dong-danged if I do. I said I wouldn't if ary dog turned up missin', an' I won't.'

'It's darn good coffee,' Henry said enticingly.

But Bill was stubborn, and he ate a dry breakfast, washed down with mumbled curses at One Ear for the trick he had played.

'I'll tie 'em up out of reach of each other tonight,' Bill said, as they took the trail.

They had travelled little more than a hundred yards when Henry, who was in front, bent down and picked up something with which his snowshoe had collided. It was dark, and he could not see it, but he recognized it by the touch. He flung it back, so that it struck the sled and bounced along until it fetched up on Bill's snowshoes.

'Mebbe you'll need that in your business,' Henry said.

Bill uttered an exclamation. It was all that was left of Spanker – the stick with which he had been tied.

'They ate 'm hide an' all,' Bill announced. 'The stick's as clean as a whistle. They've ate the leather offen both ends. They're damn hungry, Henry, an' they'll have you an' me guessin' before this trip's over.'

Henry laughed defiantly. 'I ain't been trailed this way by wolves before, but I've gone through a whole lot worse an' kept my health. Takes more'n a handful of them pesky critters to do for yours truly, Bill, my son.'

'I don't know, I don't know,' Bill muttered ominously.

'Well, you'll know all right when we pull into M'Gurry.'

'I ain't feelin' special enthusiastic,' Bill persisted.

'You're off colour; that's what's the matter with you,' Henry dogmatized. 'What you need is quinine, an' I'm goin' to dose you up stiff as soon as we make M'Gurry.'

Bill grunted his disagreement with the diagnosis, and lapsed into silence. The day was like all the days. Light came at nine o'clock. At twelve o'clock the southern horizon was warmed by the unseen sun; and then began the cold grey of afternoon that would merge, three hours later, into night.

It was just after the sun's futile effort to appear that Bill slipped the rifle from under the sled-lashings and said:

'You keep right on, Henry; I'm goin' to see what I can see.'

'You'd better stick by the sled,' his partner protested. 'You've only got three cartridges, an' there's no tellin' what might happen.'

'Who's croaking now?' Bill demanded triumphantly.

Henry made no reply, and plodded on alone, though often he cast anxious glances back into the grey solitude where his partner had disappeared. An hour later, taking advantage of the cut-offs around which the sled had to go, Bill arrived.

'They're scattered an' rangin' along wide,' he said, 'keeping up with us an' lookin' for game at the same time. You see, they're sure of us, only they know they've got to wait to get us. In the meantime they're willin' to pick up anything eatable that comes handy.'

'You mean they *think* they're sure of us,' Henry objected pointedly.

But Bill ignored him. 'I seen some of them. They're pretty thin. They ain't had a bite in weeks, I reckon, outside of Fatty an' Frog an' Spanker; an' there's so many of 'em that that didn't go far. They're remarkable thin. Their ribs is like wash-boards, an' their stomachs is right up against their backbones. They're pretty desperate, I can tell you. They'll be goin' mad yet, an' then watch out.'

A few minutes later, Henry, who was now travelling behind the sled, emitted a low, warning whistle. Bill turned and looked, then quietly stopped the dogs. To the rear, from around the last bend and plainly into view, on the very trail they had just covered, trotted a furry, slinking form. Its nose was to the trail, and it trotted with a peculiar, sliding, effortless gait. When they halted, it halted, throwing up its head and regarding them steadily with nostrils that twitched as it caught and studied the scent of them.

'It's the she-wolf,' Bill answered.

The dogs had lain down in the snow, and he walked past them to join his partner in the sled. Together they watched the strange animal that had pursued them for days and that had already accomplished the destruction of half their dog-team.

After a searching scrutiny, the animal trotted forward a few steps. This it repeated several times, till it was a short hundred yards away. It paused, head up, close by a clump of spruce trees, and with sight and scent studied the outfit of the watching men. It looked at them in a strangely wistful way, after the manner of a dog; but in its wistfulness there was none of the dog affection. It was a wistfulness bred of hunger, as cruel as its own fangs, as merciless as the frost itself.

It was large for a wolf, its gaunt frame advertising the lines of an animal that was among the largest of its kind.

'Stands pretty close to two feet an' a half at the shoulders,' Henry commented. 'An' I'll bet it ain't far from five feet long.'

'Kind of strange colour for a wolf,' was Bill's criticism. 'I never seen a red wolf before. Looks almost cinnamon to me.'

The animal was certainly not cinnamon-coloured. Its coat was the true wolf-coat. The dominant colour was grey, and yet there was to it a faint reddish hue – a hue that was baffling, that appeared and disappeared, that was more like an illusion of the vision, now grey, distinctly grey, and again giving hints and glints of a vague redness of colour not classifiable in terms of ordinary experience.

'Looks for all the world like a big husky sled-dog,' Bill said. 'I wouldn't be s'prised to see it wag its tail.'

'Hello, you husky!' he called. 'Come here, you, whatever your name is.'

'Ain't a bit scairt of you,' Henry laughed.

Bill waved his hand at it threateningly and shouted loudly; but the animal betrayed no fear. The only change in it that they could notice was an accession of alertness. It still regarded them with the merciless wistfulness of hunger. They were meat, and it was hungry; and it would like to go in and eat them if it dared.

'Look here, Henry,' Bill said, unconsciously lowering his voice to a whisper because of what he meditated. 'We've got three cartridges. But it's a dead shot. Couldn't miss it. It's got away with three of our dogs, an' we oughter put a stop to it. What d' ye say?'

Henry nodded his consent. Bill cautiously slipped the gun from under the sled-lashing. The gun was on the way to his shoulder, but it never got there, for in that instant the she-wolf leaped sidewise from the trail into the clump of spruce trees, and disappeared.

The two men looked at each other. Henry whistled long and comprehendingly.

'I might have knowed it,' Bill chided himself aloud as he replaced the gun. 'Of course a wolf that knows enough to come in with the dogs at feedin' time'd know all about shooting-irons. I tell you right now, Henry, that critter's the cause of all our trouble. We'd have six dogs at the present time, 'stead of three, if it wasn't for her. An' I tell you right now, Henry, I'm goin' to get her. She's too smart to be shot in the open. But I'm goin' to lay for her. I'll bushwhack her as sure as my name is Bill.'

'You needn't stray off too far in doin' it,' his partner admonished. 'If that pack ever starts to jump you, them three cartridges'd be wuth no more 'n three whoops in hell. Them animals is damn hungry, an' once they start in, they'll sure get you, Bill.'

They camped early that night. Three dogs could not

drag the sled so fast nor for so long hours as could six, and they were showing unmistakable signs of playing out. And the men went early to bed, Bill first seeing to it that the dogs were tied out of gnawing reach of one another.

But the wolves were growing bolder, and the men were aroused more than once from their sleep. So near did the wolves approach, that the dogs became frantic with terror, and it was necessary to replenish the fire from time to time in order to keep the adventurous marauders at safer distance.

'I've hearn sailors talk of sharks followin' a ship,' Bill remarked, as he crawled back into the blankets after one such replenishing of the fire. 'Well, them wolves is land sharks. They know their business better 'n we do, an' they ain't a-holdin' our trail this way for their health. They're goin' to get us. They're sure goin' to get us, Henry.'

'They've half got you a'ready, a-talkin' like that,' Henry retorted sharply. 'A man's half licked when he says he is. An' you're half eaten from the way you're goin' on about it.'

'They've got away with better men than you an' me,' Bill answered.

'Oh, shet up your croakin'. You make me all-fired tired.'

Henry rolled over angrily on his side, but was surprised that Bill made no similar display of temper. This was not Bill's way, for he was easily angered by sharp words. Henry thought long over it before he went to sleep, and as his eyelids fluttered down and he dozed off, the thought in his mind was: 'There's no mistakin' it; Bill's almighty blue. I'll have to cheer him up tomorrow.'

CHAPTER

3

THE HUNGER-CRY

The day began auspiciously. They had lost no dogs during the night, and they swung out upon the trail and into the silence, the darkness, and the cold with spirits that were fairly light. Bill seemed to have forgotten his forebodings of the previous night, and even waxed facetious with the dogs when, at midday, they overturned the sled on a bad piece of trail.

It was an awkward mix-up. The sled was upside-down and jammed between a tree-trunk and a huge rock, and they were forced to unharness the dogs in order to straighten out the tangle. The two men were bent over the sled and trying to right it, when Henry observed One Ear sidling away.

'Here, you, One Ear!' he cried, straightening up and turning around on the dog.

But One Ear broke into a run across the snow, his traces trailing behind him. And there, out in the snow of their back track, was the she-wolf waiting for him. As he neared her, he became suddenly cautious. He slowed down to an alert and mincing walk and then stopped. He regarded her carefully and dubiously, yet desirefully. She seemed to smile at him, showing her teeth in an ingratiating rather than a menacing way. She moved toward him a few steps, playfully, and then halted. One Ear drew near to her, still alert and cautious, his tail and ears in the air, his head held high.

He tried to sniff noses with her, but she retreated playfully and coyly. Every advance on his part was accompanied by a corresponding retreat on her part. Step by step she was alluring him away from the security of his human companionship. Once, as though a warning had in vague ways flitted through his intelligence, he turned his head and looked back at the overturned sled, at his team-mates, and at the two men who were calling to him.

But whatever idea was forming in his mind was dissipated by the she-wolf, who advanced upon him, sniffed noses with him for a fleeting instant, and then resumed her coy retreat before his renewed advances.

In the meantime, Bill had bethought himself of the rifle. But it was jammed beneath the overturned sled, and by the time Henry had helped him to right the load One Ear and the she-wolf were too close together and the distance too great to risk a shot.

Too late, One Ear learned his mistake. Before they saw the cause, the two men saw him turn and start to run back toward them. Then, approaching at right angles to the trail and cutting off his retreat, they saw a dozen wolves, lean and grey, bounding across the snow. On the instant, the she-wolf's coyness and playfulness disappeared. With a snarl she sprang upon One Ear. He thrust her off with his shoulder, and, his retreat cut off and still intent on regaining the sled, he altered his course in an attempt to circle around to it. More wolves were appearing every moment and joining in the chase.

The she-wolf was one leap behind One Ear and holding her own.

'Where are you goin'?' Henry suddenly demanded, laying his hand on his partner's arm.

Bill shook it off. 'I won't stand it,' he said. 'They ain't a-goin' to get any more of our dogs if I can help it.'

Gun in hand, he plunged into the underbrush that lined the side of the trail. His intention was apparent enough. Taking the sled as the centre of the circle that One Ear was making, Bill planned to tap that circle at a point in advance of the pursuit. With his rifle, in the broad daylight, it might be possible for him to awe the wolves and save the dog.

'Say, Bill!' Henry called after him. 'Be careful! Don't take no chances!'

Henry sat down on the sled and watched. There was nothing else for him to do. Bill had already gone from sight; but now and again, appearing and disappearing amongst the underbrush and the scattered clumps of spruce, could be seen One Ear. Henry judged his case to be hopeless. The dog was thoroughly alive to its danger, but it was running on the outer circle while the wolf-pack was running on the inner and shorter circle. It was vain to think of One Ear so outdistancing his pursuers as to be able to cut across their circle in advance of them and to regain the sled.

The different lines were rapidly approaching a point. Somewhere out there in the snow, screened from his sight by trees and thickets, Henry knew that the wolf-pack, One Ear, and Bill were coming together. All too quickly, far more quickly than he had expected, it happened. He heard a shot, then two shots in rapid succession, and he knew that Bill's ammunition was gone.

Then he heard a great outcry of snarls and yelps. He recognized One Ear's yell of pain and terror, and he heard a wolf-cry that bespoke a stricken animal. And that was all. The snarls ceased. The yelping died away. Silence settled down again over the lonely land.

He sat for a long while upon the sled. There was no need for him to go and see what had happened. He knew it as though it had taken place before his eyes. Once he roused with a start and hastily got the axe out from underneath the lashings. But for some time longer he sat and brooded, the two remaining dogs crouching and trembling at his feet.

At last he arose in a weary manner, as though all the resilience had gone out of his body, and proceeded to fasten the dogs to the sled. He passed a rope over his shoulder, a man-trace, and pulled with the dogs. He did not go far. At the first hint of darkness he hastened to make a camp, and he saw to it that he had a generous supply of firewood. He fed the dogs, cooked and ate his supper, and made his bed close to the fire.

But he was not destined to enjoy that bed. Before his eyes closed the wolves had drawn too near for safety. It no longer required an effort of the vision to see them. They were all about him and the fire, in a narrow circle, and he could see them plainly in the firelight, lying down, sitting up, crawling forward on their bellies, or slinking back and forth. They even slept. Here and there he could see one curled up in the snow like a dog, taking the sleep that was now denied himself.

He kept the fire brightly blazing, for he knew that it alone intervened between the flesh of his body and their hungry fangs. His two dogs stayed close by him, one on either side, leaning against him for protection, crying and whimpering, and at times snarling desperately when a wolf approached a little closer than usual. At such moments, when his dogs snarled, the whole circle would be agitated, the wolves coming to their feet and pressing tentatively forward, a chorus of snarls and eager yelps rising about him. Then the circle would lie down again, and here and there a wolf would resume its broken nap.

But this circle had a continuous tendency to draw in upon him. Bit by bit, an inch at a time, with here a wolf bellying forward, and there a wolf bellying forward, the circle would narrow until the brutes were almost within springing distance. Then he would seize brands from the fire and hurl them into the pack. A hasty drawing back always resulted, accompanied by angry yelps and frightened snarls when a well-aimed brand struck and scorched a too-daring animal.

Morning found the man haggard and worn, wide-eyed from want of sleep. He cooked breakfast in the darkness, and at nine o'clock, when, with the coming of daylight, the wolf-pack drew back, he set about the task he had planned through the long hours of the night. Chopping down young saplings, he made them crossbars of a scaffold by lashing them high up to the trunks of standing trees. Using the sled-lashing for a heaving rope, and with the aid of the dogs, he hoisted the coffin to the top of the scaffold.

'They got Bill, an' they may get me, but they'll sure never get you, young man,' he said, addressing the dead body in its tree sepulchre.

Then he took the trail, the lightened sled bounding along behind the willing dogs; for they, too, knew that safety lay open in the gaining of Fort M'Gurry. The wolves were now more open in their pursuit, trotting sedately behind and ranging along on either side, their red tongues lolling out, their lean sides showing the undulating ribs with every movement. They were very lean, mere skin-bags stretched over bony frames, with strings for muscles – so lean that Henry found it in his mind to marvel that they still kept their feet and did not collapse forthright in the snow.

He did not dare travel until dark. At midday, not only did the sun warm the southern horizon, but it even thrust its upper rim, pale and golden, above the skyline. He received it as a sign. The days were growing longer. The sun was returning. But scarcely had the cheer of its light departed, than he went into camp. There were still several hours of grey daylight and sombre twilight, and he utilized them in chopping an enormous supply of firewood.

With night came horror. Not only were the starving wolves growing bolder, but lack of sleep was telling upon Henry. He dozed despite himself, crouching by the fire, the blankets about his shoulders, the axe between his knees, and on either side a dog pressing close against him. He awoke once and saw in front of him, not a dozen feet away, a big grey wolf, one of the largest of the pack. And even as he looked, the brute deliberately stretched himself after the manner of a lazy dog, yawning full in his face and looking upon him with a possessive eye, as if, in truth, he were merely a delayed meal that was soon to be eaten.

This certitude was shown by the whole pack. Fully a score he could count, staring hungrily at him or calmly sleeping in the snow. They reminded him of children gathered about a spread table and awaiting permission to begin to eat. And he was the food they were to eat! He wondered how and when the meal would begin.

As he piled wood on the fire he discovered an appreciation of his own body which he had never felt before. He watched his moving muscles and was interested in the cunning mechanism of his fingers. By the light of the fire he crooked his fingers slowly and repeatedly, now one at a time, now all together, spreading them wide or making quick, gripping movements. He studied the nail-formation, and prodded the finger-tips, now sharply, and again softly, gauging the while the nerve-sensations produced. It fascinated him, and he grew suddenly fond of this subtle flesh of his that worked so beautifully and smoothly and delicately. Then he would cast a glance of fear at the wolf-circle drawn expectantly about him, and like a blow the realization would strike him that this wonderful body of his, this living flesh, was no more than so much meat, a quest of ravenous animals, to be torn and slashed by their hungry fangs, to be sustenance to them as the moose and the rabbit had often been sustenance to him.

He came out of a doze that was half nightmare to see the red-hued she-wolf before him. She was not more than half a dozen feet away, sitting in the snow and wistfully regarding him. The two dogs were whimpering and snarling at his feet, but she took no notice of them. She was looking at the man, and for some time he returned her look. There was nothing threatening about her. She looked at him merely with a great wistfulness, but he knew it to be the wistfulness of an equally great hunger. He was the food, and the sight of him excited in her the gustatory sensations. Her mouth opened, the saliva drooled forth, and she licked her chops with the pleasure of anticipation.

A spasm of fear went through him. He reached hastily for a brand to throw at her. But even as he reached, and before his fingers had closed on the missile, she sprang back into safety; and he knew that she was used to having things thrown at her. She had snarled as she sprang away, baring her white fangs to their roots, all her wistfulness vanishing, being replaced by a carnivorous malignity that made him shudder. He glanced at the hand that held the brand, noticing the cunning delicacy of the fingers that gripped it, how they adjusted themselves to all the inequalities of the surface, curling over and under and about the rough wood, and one little finger, too close to the burning portion of the brand, sensitively and automatically writhing back from the hurtful heat to a cooler gripping-place; and in the same instant he seemed to see a vision of those same sensitive and delicate fingers being crushed and torn by the white teeth of the she-wolf. Never had he been so fond of this body of his as now when his tenure of it was so precarious.

All night, with burning brands, he fought off the hungry pack. When he dozed, despite himself, the whimpering and snarling of the dogs aroused him. Morning came, but for the first time the light of day failed to scatter the wolves. The man waited in vain for them to go. They remained in a circle about him and his fire, displaying an arrogance of possession that shook his courage born of the morning light.

He made one desperate attempt to pull out on the trail. But the moment he left the protection of the fire, the boldest wolf leaped for him, but leaped short. He saved himself by springing back, the jaws snapping together a scant six inches from his thigh. The rest of the pack was now up and surging upon him, and a throwing of firebrands right and left was necessary to drive them back to a respectful distance.

Even in the daylight he did not dare to leave the fire to chop fresh wood. Twenty feet away towered a huge dead spruce. He spent half the day extending his camp-fire to the tree, at any moment a half-dozen burning faggots ready at hand to fling at his enemies. Once at the tree, he studied the surrounding forest in order to fell the tree in the direction of the most fire-wood.

The night was a repetition of the night before, save that the need for sleep was becoming overpowering. The snarling of his dogs was losing its efficacy. Besides, they were snarling all the time, and his benumbed and drowsy senses no longer took note of changing pitch and intensity. He awoke with a start. The she-wolf was less than a yard from him. Mechanically, at short range, without letting go of it, he thrust a brand full into her open and snarling mouth. She sprang away, yelling with pain, and while he took delight in the smell of burning flesh and hair, he watched her shaking her head and growling wrathfully a score of feet away.

But this time, before he dozed again, he tied a burning pine-knot to his right hand. His eyes were closed but few minutes when the burn of the flame on his flesh awakened him. For several hours he adhered to this programme. Every time he was thus awakened he drove back the wolves with flying brands, replenished the fire, and rearranged the pine-knot on his hand. All worked well, but there came a time when he fastened the pine-knot insecurely. As his eyes closed it fell away from his hand.

He dreamed. It seemed to him that he was in Fort M'Gurry. It was warm and comfortable, and he was playing cribbage with the Factor. Also, it seemed to him that the fort was besieged by wolves. They were howling at the very gates, and sometimes he and the Factor paused from the game to listen and laugh at the futile efforts of the wolves to get in. And then, so strange was the dream, there was a crash. The door was burst open. He could see the wolves flooding into the big living-room of the fort. They were leaping straight for him and the Factor. With the bursting open of the door, the noise of their howling had increased tremendously. This howling now bothered him. His dream was merging into something else – he knew not what; but through it all, following him, persisted the howling.

And then he awoke to find the howling real. There was a great snarling and yelping. The wolves were rushing him. They were all about him and upon him. The teeth of one had closed upon his arm. Instinctively he leaped into the fire, and as he leaped he felt the sharp slash of teeth that tore through the flesh of his leg. Then began a fire fight. His stout mittens temporarily protected his hands, and he scooped live coals into the air in all directions, until the camp-fire took on the semblance of a volcano.

But it could not last long. His face was blistering in the heat, his eyebrows and lashes were singed off, and the heat was becoming unbearable to his feet. With a flaming brand in each hand, he sprang to the edge of the fire. The wolves had been driven back. On every side, wherever the live coals had fallen, the snow was sizzling, and every little while a retiring wolf, with wild leap and snort and snarl, announced that one such live coal had been stepped upon.

Flinging his brands at the nearest of his enemies, the man thrust his smouldering mittens into the snow and stamped about to cool his feet. His two dogs were missing, and he well knew that they had served as a course in the protracted meal which had begun days before with Fatty, the last course of which would likely be himself in the days to follow.

'You ain't got me yet!' he cried, savagely shaking his fist at the hungry beasts; and at the sound of his voice the whole circle was agitated, there was a general snarl, and the she-wolf slid up close to him across the snow and watched him with hungry wistfulness.

He set to work to carry out a new idea that had come to him. He extended the fire into a large circle. Inside this circle he crouched, his sleeping outfit under him as a protection against the melting snow. When he had thus disappeared within his shelter of flame, the whole pack came curiously to the rim of the fire to see what had become of him. Hitherto they had been denied access to the fire, and they now settled down in a close-drawn circle, like so many dogs, blinking and yawning and stretching their lean bodies in the unaccustomed warmth. Then the she-wolf sat down, pointed her nose at a star, and began to howl. One by one the wolves joined her, till the whole pack, on haunches, with noses pointed skyward, was howling its hunger-cry.

Dawn came, and daylight. The fire was burning low. The fuel had run out, and there was need to get more. The man attempted to step out of his circle of flame, but the wolves surged to meet him. Burning brands made them spring aside, but they no longer sprang back. In vain he strove to drive them back. As he gave up and stumbled inside his circle, a wolf leaped for him, missed, and landed with all four feet in the coals. It cried out with terror, at the same time snarling, and scrambled back to cool its paws in the snow.

The man sat down on his blankets in a crouching position. His body leaned forward from the hips. His shoulders, relaxed and drooping, and his head on his knees advertised that he had given up the struggle. Now and again he raised his head to note the dying down of the fire. The circle of flame and coals was breaking into segments with openings in between. These openings grew in size, the segments diminished.

'I guess you can come an' get me any time,' he mumbled. 'Anyway, I'm goin' to sleep.'

Once he wakened, and in an opening in the circle, directly in front of him, he saw the she-wolf gazing at him.

Again he awakened, a little later, though it seemed hours to him. A mysterious change had taken place – so mysterious a change that he was shocked wider awake. Something had happened. He could not understand at first. Then he discovered it. The wolves were gone. Remained only the trampled snow to show how closely they had pressed him. Sleep was welling up and gripping him again, his head was sinking down upon his knees, when he roused with a sudden start.

There were cries of men, the churn of sleds, the creaking of harnesses, and the eager whimpering of straining dogs. Four sleds pulled in from the river bed to the camp among the trees. Half a dozen men were about the man who crouched in the centre of the dying fire. They were shaking and prodding him into consciousness. He looked at them like a drunken man and maundered in strange, sleepy speech:

'Red she-wolf . . . Come in with the dogs at feedin' time . . . First she ate the dog-food . . . Then she ate the dogs . . . An' after that she ate Bill . . .'

'Where's Lord Alfred?' one of the men bellowed in his ear, shaking him roughly.

He shook his head slowly. 'No, she didn't eat him . . . He's roostin' in a tree at the last camp.'

'Dead?' the man shouted.

'An' in a box,' Henry answered. He jerked his shoulder petulantly away from the grip of his questioner. 'Say, you lemme alone . . . I'm jes' plump tuckered out . . . Goo' night, everybody.'

His eyes fluttered and went shut. His chin fell forward on his chest. And even as they eased him down upon the blankets his snores were rising on the frosty air.

But there was another sound. Far and faint it was, in the remote distance, the cry of the hungry wolf-pack as it took the trail of other meat than the man it had just missed.

Part II

CHAPTER

1

THE BATTLE OF THE FANGS

It was the she-wolf who had first caught the sound of men's voices and the whining of the sled-dogs, and it was the she-wolf who was first to spring away from the cornered man in his circle of dying flame. The pack had been loath to forego the kill it had hunted down, and it lingered for several minutes, making sure of the sounds, and then it, too, sprang away on the trail made by the she-wolf.

Running at the forefront of the pack was a large grey wolf – one of its several leaders. It was he who directed the pack's course on the heels of the she-wolf. It was he who snarled warningly at the younger members of the pack or slashed at them with his fangs when they ambitiously tried to pass him. And it was he who increased the pace when he sighted the she-wolf, now trotting slowly across the snow.

She dropped in alongside by him, as though it were her appointed position, and took the pace of the pack. He did not snarl at her, nor show his teeth, when any leap of hers chanced to put her in advance of him. On the contrary, he seemed kindly disposed toward her – too kindly to suit her, for he was prone to run near to

her, and when he ran too near it was she who snarled
and showed her teeth. Nor was she above slashing his
shoulder sharply on occasion. At such times he betrayed
no anger. He merely sprang to the side and ran stiffly
ahead for several awkward leaps, in carriage and conduct
resembling an abashed country swain.

This was his one trouble in the running of the pack;
but she had other troubles. On her other side ran a gaunt
old wolf, grizzled and marked with the scars of many
battles. He ran always on her right side. The fact that he
had but one eye, and that the left eye, might account for
this. He, also, was addicted to crowding her, to veering
toward her till his scarred muzzle touched her body, or
shoulder, or neck. As with the running mate on the left,
she repelled these attentions with her teeth; but when
both bestowed their attentions at the same time, she was
roughly jostled, being compelled, with quick snaps to
either side, to drive both lovers away, and at the same
time to maintain her forward leap with the pack and see
the way of her feet before her. At such times her running
mates flashed their teeth and growled threateningly
across at each other. They might have fought, but even
wooing and its rivalry waited upon the more pressing
hunger-need of the pack.

After each repulse, when the old wolf sheered abruptly away from the sharp-toothed object of his desire,
he shouldered against a young three-year-old that ran
on his blind right side. This young wolf had attained
his full size; and, considering the weak and famished
condition of the pack, he possessed more than the average vigour and spirit. Nevertheless, he ran with his head
even with the shoulder of his one-eyed elder. When he
ventured to run abreast of the older wolf (which was

seldom), a snarl and a snap sent him back even with the shoulder again. Sometimes, however, he dropped cautiously and slowly behind and edged in between the old leader and the she-wolf. This was doubly resented, even triply resented. When she snarled her displeasure, the old leader would whirl on the three-year-old. Sometimes she whirled with him. And sometimes the young leader on the left whirled too.

At such times, confronted by three sets of savage teeth, the young wolf stopped precipitately, throwing himself back on his haunches, with fore-legs stiff, mouth menacing, and mane bristling. This confusion in the front of the moving pack always caused confusion in the rear. The wolves behind collided with the young wolf, and expressed their displeasure by administering sharp nips on his hind-legs and flanks. He was laying up trouble for himself, for lack of food and short tempers went together; but with the boundless faith of youth he persisted in repeating the manoeuvre every little while, though it never succeeded in gaining anything for him but discomfiture.

Had there been food, love-making and fighting would have gone on apace, and the pack-formation would have been broken up. But the situation of the pack was desperate. It was lean with long-standing hunger. It ran below its ordinary speed. At the rear limped the weak members – the very young and the very old. At the front were the strongest. Yet all were more like skeletons than full-bodied wolves. Nevertheless, with the exception of the ones that limped, the movements of the animals were effortless and tireless. Their stringy muscles seemed founts of inexhaustible energy. Behind every steel-like contraction of a muscle lay another steel-like contraction, and another, and another, apparently without end.

They ran many miles that day. They ran through the night. And the next day found them still running. They were running over the surface of a world frozen and dead. No life stirred. They alone moved through the vast inertness. They alone were alive, and they sought for other things that were alive in order that they might devour them and continue to live.

They crossed low divides and ranged a dozen small streams in a lower-lying country before their quest was rewarded. Then they came upon moose. It was a big bull they first found. Here was meat and life, and it was guarded by no mysterious fires nor flying missiles of flame. Splay hoofs and palmated antlers they knew, and they flung their customary patience and caution to the wind. It was a brief fight and fierce. The big bull was beset on every side. He ripped them open or split their skulls with shrewdly-driven blows of his great hoofs. He crushed them and broke them on his large horns. He stamped them into the snow under him in the wallowing struggle. But he was foredoomed, and he went down with the she-wolf tearing savagely at his throat, and with other teeth fixed everywhere upon him, devouring him alive, before ever his last struggles ceased or his last damages had been wrought.

There was food in plenty. The bull weighed over eight hundred pounds – fully twenty pounds of meat per mouth for the forty-odd wolves of the pack. But if they could fast prodigiously, they could feed prodigiously, and soon a few scattered bones were all that remained of the splendid live brute that had faced the pack a few hours before.

There was now much resting and sleeping. With full stomachs, bickering and quarrelling began among the younger males, and this continued through the few days that followed before the breaking-up of the pack. The famine was over. The wolves were now in the country of game, and though they still hunted in pack, they hunted more cautiously, cutting out heavy cows or crippled old bulls from the small moose-herds they ran across.

There came a day, in this land of plenty, when the wolf-pack split in half and went in different directions. The she-wolf, the young leader on her left, and the one-eyed elder on her right, led their half of the pack down to the Mackenzie River and across into the lake country to the east. Each day this remnant of the pack dwindled. Two by two, male and female, the wolves were deserting. Occasionally a solitary male was driven out by the sharp teeth of his rivals. In the end there remained only four – the she-wolf, the young leader, the one-eyed one, and the ambitious three-year-old.

The she-wolf had by now developed a ferocious temper. Her three suitors all bore the marks of her teeth. Yet they never replied in kind, never defended themselves against her. They turned their shoulders to her most savage slashes, and with wagging tails and mincing steps strove to placate her wrath. But if they were all mildness toward her, they were all fierceness toward one another. The three-year-old grew too ambitious in his fierceness. He caught the one-eyed elder on his blind side and ripped his ear into ribbons. Though the grizzled old fellow could see only on one side, against the youth and vigour of the other he brought into play the wisdom of long years of experience. His lost eye and his scarred muzzle bore evidence to the nature of his experience. He had survived too many battles to be in doubt for a moment about what to do.

The battle began fairly, but it did not end fairly. There was no telling what the outcome would have been, for the third wolf joined the elder, and together, old leader and young leader, they attacked the ambitious three-year-old and proceeded to destroy him. He was beset on either side by the merciless fangs of his erstwhile comrades. Forgotten were the days they had hunted together, the game they had pulled down, the famine they had suffered. That business was a thing of the past. The business of love was at hand – ever a sterner and crueller business than that of food-getting.

And in the meanwhile the she-wolf, the cause of it all, sat down contentedly on her haunches and watched. She was even pleased. This was her day – and it came not often – when manes bristled, and fang smote fang or ripped and tore the yielding flesh, all for the possession of her.

And in the business of love the three-year-old, who had made this his first adventure upon it, yielded up his life. On either side of his body stood his two rivals. They were gazing at the she-wolf, who sat smiling in the snow. But the elder leader was wise, very wise, in love even as in battle. The younger leader turned his head to lick a wound on his shoulder. The curve of his neck was turned toward his rival. With his one eye the elder saw the opportunity. He darted in low and closed with his fangs. It was a long, ripping slash, and deep as well. His teeth, in passing, burst the wall of the great vein of the throat. Then he leaped clear.

The young leader snarled terribly, but his snarl broke

midmost into a tickling cough. Bleeding and coughing, already stricken, he sprang at the elder and fought while life faded from him, his legs going weak beneath him, the light of day dulling on his eyes, his blows and springs falling shorter and shorter.

And all the while the she-wolf sat on her haunches and smiled. She was made glad in vague ways by the battle, for this was the love-making of the Wild, the sex-tragedy of the natural world that was tragedy only to those that died. To those that survived it was not tragedy, but realization and achievement.

When the young leader lay in the snow and moved no more, One Eye stalked over to the she-wolf. His carriage was one of mingled triumph and caution. He was plainly expectant of a rebuff, and he was just as plainly surprised when her teeth did not flash out at him in anger. For the first time she met him with a kindly manner. She sniffed noses with him, and even condescended to leap about and frisk and play with him in quite puppyish fashion. And he, for all his grey years and sage experience, behaved quite as puppyishly and even a little more foolishly.

Forgotten already were the vanquished rivals and the love-tale red-written on the snow. Forgotten, save once, when old One Eye stopped for a moment to lick his stiffening wounds. Then it was that his lips half writhed into a snarl, and the hair of his neck and shoulders involuntarily bristled, while he half crouched for a spring, his claws spasmodically clutching into the snow-surface for firmer footing. But it was all forgotten the next moment as he sprang after the she-wolf, who was coyly leading him a chase through the woods.

After that they ran side by side, like good friends who

have come to an understanding. The days passed by, and they kept together, hunting their meat and killing and eating it in common. After a time the she-wolf began to grow restless. She seemed to be searching for something that she could not find. The hollows under fallen trees seemed to attract her, and she spent much time nosing about among the larger snow-piled crevices in the rocks and in the caves of overhanging banks. Old One Eye was not interested at all, but he followed her good-naturedly in her quest, and when her investigations in particular places were unusually protracted, he would lie down and wait until she was ready to go on.

They did not remain in one place, but travelled across country until they regained the Mackenzie River, down which they slowly went, leaving it often to hunt game along the small streams that entered it, but always returning to it again. Sometimes they chanced upon other wolves, usually in pairs; but there was no friendliness of intercourse displayed on either side, no gladness at meeting, no desire to return to the pack-formation. Several times they encountered solitary wolves. These were always males, and they were pressingly insistent on joining with One Eye and his mate. This he resented, and when she stood shoulder to shoulder with him, bristling and showing her teeth, the aspiring solitary ones would back off, turn tail, and continue on their lonely way.

One moonlight night, running through the quiet forest, One Eye suddenly halted. His muzzle went up, his tail stiffened, and his nostrils dilated as he scented the air. One foot also he held up, after the manner of a dog. He was not satisfied, and he continued to smell the air, striving to understand the message borne upon it to him. One careless sniff had satisfied his mate, and she trotted on to reassure him. Though he followed her, he was still dubious, and he could not forbear an occasional halt in order more carefully to study the warning.

She crept out cautiously on the edge of a large open space in the midst of the trees. For some time she stood alone. Then One Eye, creeping and crawling, every sense on the alert, every hair radiating infinite suspicion, joined her. They stood side by side, watching and listening and smelling.

To their ears came the sounds of dogs wrangling and scuffling, the guttural cries of men, the sharper voices of scolding women, and once the shrill and plaintive cry of a child. With the exception of the huge bulks of the skin-lodges, little could be seen save the flames of the fire, broken by the movements of intervening bodies, and the smoke rising slowly on the quiet air. But to their nostrils came the myriad smells of an Indian camp, carrying a story that was largely incomprehensible to One Eye, but every detail of which the she-wolf knew.

She was strangely stirred, and sniffed and sniffed with an increasing delight. But old One Eye was doubtful. He betrayed his apprehension, and started tentatively to go. She turned and touched his neck with her muzzle in a reassuring way, then regarded the camp again. A new wistfulness was in her face, but it was not the wistfulness of hunger. She was thrilling to a desire that urged her to go forward, to be in closer to that fire, to be squabbling with the dogs, and to be avoiding and dodging the stumbling feet of men.

One Eye moved impatiently beside her; her unrest

came back upon her, and she knew again her pressing need to find the thing for which she searched. She turned and trotted back into the forest, to the great relief of One Eye, who trotted a little to the fore until they were well within the shelter of the trees.

As they slid along, noiseless as shadows, in the moonlight, they came upon a run-way. Both noses went down to the footprints in the snow. These footprints were very fresh. One Eye ran ahead cautiously, his mate at his heels. The broad pads of their feet were spread wide, and in contact with the snow were like velvet. One Eye caught sight of a dim movement of white in the midst of the white. His sliding gait had been deceptively swift, but it was as nothing to the speed at which he now ran. Before him was bounding the faint patch of white he had discovered.

They were running along a narrow alley flanked on either side by a growth of young spruce. Through the trees the mouth of the alley could be seen, opening out on a moonlit glade. Old One Eye was rapidly overhauling the fleeing shape of white. Bound by bound he gained. Now he was upon it. One leap more and his teeth would be sinking into it. But that leap was never made. High in the air, and straight up, soared the shape of white, now a struggling snowshoe rabbit that leaped and bounded, executing a fantastic dance there above him in the air and never once returning to earth.

One Eye sprang back with a snort of sudden fright, then shrank down to the snow and crouched, snarling threats at this thing of fear he did not understand. But the she-wolf coolly thrust past him. She poised for a moment, then sprang for the dancing rabbit. She, too, soared high, but not so high as the quarry, and her teeth clipped emptily together with a metallic snap. She made another leap, and another.

Her mate had slowly relaxed from his crouch and was watching her. He now evinced displeasure at her repeated failures, and himself made a mighty spring upward. His teeth closed upon the rabbit, and he bore it back to earth with him. But at the same time there was a suspicious crackling movement beside him, and his astonished eye saw a young spruce sapling bending down above him to strike him. His jaws let go their grip, and he leaped backward to escape this strange danger, his lips drawn back from his fangs, his throat snarling, every hair bristling with rage and fright. And in that moment the sapling reared its slender length upright, and the rabbit soared dancing in the air again.

The she-wolf was angry. She sank her fangs into her mate's shoulder in reproof; and he, frightened, unaware of what constituted this new onslaught, struck back furiously and in still greater fright, ripping down the side of the she-wolf's muzzle. For him to resent such reproof was equally unexpected to her, and she sprang upon him in snarling indignation. Then he discovered his mistake and tried to placate her; but she proceeded to punish him roundly, until he gave over all attempts at placation, and whirled in a circle, his head away from her, his shoulders receiving the punishment of her teeth.

In the meantime the rabbit danced above them in the air. The she-wolf sat down in the snow, and old One Eye, now more in fear of his mate than of the mysterious sapling, again sprang for the rabbit. As he sank back with it between his teeth, he kept his eye on the sapling. As before, it followed him back to earth. He crouched down under the impending blow, his hair bristling, but his teeth still keeping tight hold of the rabbit. But the blow did not fall. The sapling remained bent above him. When he moved it moved, and he growled at it through his clenched jaws; when he remained still, it remained still, and he concluded it was safer to continue remaining still. Yet the warm blood of the rabbit tasted good in his mouth.

It was his mate who relieved him from the quandary in which he found himself. She took the rabbit from him, and while the sapling swayed and teetered threateningly above her, she calmly gnawed off the rabbit's head. At once the sapling shot up, and after that gave no more trouble, remaining in the decorous and perpendicular position in which nature had intended it to grow. Then, between them, the she-wolf and One Eye devoured the game which the mysterious sapling had caught for them.

There were other run-ways and alleys where rabbits were hanging in the air, and the wolf-pair prospected them all, the she-wolf leading the way, old One Eye following and observant, learning the method of robbing snares – a knowledge destined to stand him in good stead in the days to come.

2

THE LAIR

For two days the she-wolf and One Eye hung about the Indian camp. He was worried and apprehensive, yet the camp lured his mate, and she was loath to depart. But when, one morning, the air was rent with the report of a rifle close at hand, and a bullet smashed against a tree-trunk several inches from One Eye's head, they hesitated no more, but went off on a long, swinging lope that put quick miles between them and the danger.

They did not go far – a couple of days' journey. The she-wolf's need to find the thing for which she searched had now become imperative. She was getting very heavy, and could run but slowly. Once, in the pursuit of a rabbit, which she ordinarily would have caught with ease, she gave over and lay down and rested. One Eye came to her; but when he touched her neck gently with his muzzle, she snapped at him with such quick fierceness that he tumbled over backward and cut a ridiculous figure in his effort to escape her teeth. Her temper was now shorter than ever; but he had become more patient than ever and more solicitous.

And then she found the thing for which she sought. It was a few miles up a small stream that in the summer time flowed into the Mackenzie, but that then was frozen over and frozen down to its rocky bottom – a dead stream of solid white from source to mouth. The she-wolf was trotting wearily along, her mate well in advance, when she came upon the overhanging high clay-bank. She turned aside and trotted over to it. The wear and tear of spring storms and melting snows had underwashed the bank, and in one place had made a small cave out of a narrow fissure.

She paused at the mouth of the cave and looked the wall over carefully. Then, on one side and the other, she ran along the base of the wall to where its abrupt bulk merged from the softer-lined landscape. Returning to the cave, she entered its narrow mouth. For a short three feet she was compelled to crouch, then the walls widened and rose higher in a little round chamber nearly six feet in diameter. The roof barely cleared her head. It was dry and cosy. She inspected it with painstaking care, while One Eye, who had returned, stood in the entrance and patiently watched her. She dropped her head, with her nose to the ground and directed toward a point near to her closely bunched feet, and around this point she circled several times; then, with a tired sigh that was almost a grunt, she curled her body in, relaxed her legs, and dropped down, her head toward the entrance. One Eye, with pointed, interested ears, laughed at her, and beyond, outlined against the white light, she could see the brush of his tail waving good-naturedly. Her own ears, with a snuggling movement, laid their sharp points backward and down against the head for a moment, while her mouth opened and her tongue lolled peaceably out, and in this way she expressed that she was pleased and satisfied.

One Eye was hungry. Though he lay down in the entrance and slept, his sleep was fitful. He kept awakening and cocking his ears at the bright world without, where the April sun was blazing across the snow. When he dozed, upon his ears would steal the faint whispers of hidden trickles of running water, and he would rouse and listen intently. The sun had come back, and all the awakening Northland world was calling to him. Life was stirring. The feel of spring was in the air, the feel of growing life under the snow, of sap ascending in the trees, of buds bursting the shackles of the frost.

He cast anxious glances at his mate, but she showed no desire to get up. He looked outside, and half a dozen snow-birds fluttered across his field of vision. He started to get up, then looked back to his mate again, and settled down and dozed. A shrill and minute singing stole upon his hearing. Once, and twice, he sleepily brushed his nose with his paw. Then he woke up. There, buzzing in the air at the tip of his nose, was a lone mosquito. It was a full-grown mosquito, one that had lain frozen in a dry log all winter and that had now been thawed out by the sun. He could resist the call of the world no longer. Besides, he was hungry.

He crawled over to his mate and tried to persuade her to get up. But she only snarled at him, and he walked out alone into the bright sunshine to find the snow-surface soft under foot and the travelling difficult. He went up the frozen bed of the stream, where the snow, shaded by the trees, was yet hard and crystalline. He was gone eight hours, and he came back through the darkness hungrier than when he had started. He had found game, but he had not caught it. He had broken through the melting snow-crust, and wallowed, while the snowshoe rabbits had skimmed along on top lightly as ever.

He paused at the mouth of the cave with a sudden shock of suspicion. Faint, strange sounds came from within. They were sounds not made by his mate, and yet they were remotely familiar. He bellied cautiously inside, and was met by a warning snarl from the she-wolf. This he received without perturbation, though he obeyed it by keeping his distance; but he remained interested in the other sounds – faint, muffled sobbings and slubberings.

His mate warned him irritably away, and he curled up and slept in the entrance. When morning came and a dim light pervaded the lair, he again sought after the source of the remotely familiar sounds. There was a new note in his mate's warning snarl. It was a jealous note, and he was very careful in keeping a respectful distance. Nevertheless, he made out, sheltering between her legs against the length of her body, five strange little bundles of life, very feeble, very helpless, making tiny whimpering noises, with eyes that did not open to the light. He was surprised. It was not the first time in his long and successful life that this thing had happened. It had happened many times, yet each time it was as fresh a surprise as ever to him.

His mate looked at him anxiously. Every little while she emitted a low growl, and at times, when it seemed to her he approached too near, the growl shot up in her throat to a sharp snarl. Of her own experience she had no memory of the thing happening; but in her instinct, which was the experience of all the mothers of wolves, there lurked a memory of fathers that had eaten their new-born and helpless progeny. It manifested itself as a fear strong within her, that made her prevent One Eye from more closely inspecting the cubs he had fathered.

But there was no danger. Old One Eye was feeling the urge of an impulse, that was, in turn, an instinct that had come down to him from all the fathers of wolves. He did not question it, nor puzzle over it. It was there, in the fibre of his being; and it was the most natural thing in the world that he should obey it by turning his back on his new-born family, and by trotting out and away on the meat-trail whereby he lived.

Five or six miles from the lair, the stream divided, its forks going off among the mountains at a right angle. Here, leading up the left fork, he came upon a fresh track. He smelled it and found it so recent that he crouched swiftly, and looked in the direction in which it disappeared. Then he turned deliberately and took the right fork. The footprint was much larger than the one his own feet made, and he knew that in the wake of such a trail there was little meat for him.

Half a mile up the right fork, his quick ears caught the sound of gnawing teeth. He stalked the quarry and found it to be a porcupine, standing upright against a tree and trying his teeth on the bark. One Eye approached carefully but hopelessly. He knew the breed, though he had never met it so far north before; and never in his long life had porcupine served him for a meal. But he had long since learned that there was such a thing as chance, or opportunity, and he continued to draw near. There was never any telling what might happen, for with live things events were somehow always happening differently.

The porcupine rolled itself into a ball, radiating long, sharp needles in all directions that defied attack. In his youth One Eye had once sniffed too near a similar, apparently inert ball of quills, and had the tail flick out suddenly in his face. One quill he had carried away in his muzzle, where it had remained for weeks, a rankling flame, until it finally worked out. So he lay down, in a comfortable crouching position, his nose fully a foot away, and out of the line of the tail. Thus he waited, keeping perfectly quiet. There was no telling. Something might happen. The porcupine might unroll. There might be opportunity for a deft and ripping thrust of paw into the tender, unguarded belly.

But at the end of half an hour he arose, growled wrathfully at the motionless ball, and trotted on. He had waited too often and futilely in the past for porcupines to unroll, to waste any more time. He continued up the right fork. The day wore along, and nothing rewarded his hunt.

The urge of his awakened instinct of fatherhood was strong upon him. He must find meat. In the afternoon he blundered upon a ptarmigan. He came out of a thicket and found himself face to face with the slow-witted bird. It was sitting on a log, not a foot beyond the end of his nose. Each saw the other. The bird made a startled rise, but he struck it with his paw, and smashed it down to earth, then pounced upon it, and caught it in his teeth as it scuttled across the snow trying to rise in the air again. As his teeth crunched through the tender flesh and fragile bones, he began naturally to eat. Then he remembered, and, turning on the back-track, started for home, carrying the ptarmigan in his mouth.

A mile above the forks, running velvet-footed as was his custom, a gliding shadow that cautiously prospected each new vista of the trail, he came upon later imprints of the large tracks he had discovered in the early morning. As the track led his way, he followed, prepared to meet the maker of it at every turn of the stream.

He slid his head around a corner of rock, where began an unusually large bend in the stream, and his quick eyes made out something that sent him crouching swiftly down. It was the maker of the track, a large female lynx. She was crouching as he had crouched once that day, in front of her the tight-rolled ball of quills. If he had been a gliding shadow before, he now became the ghost of such a shadow, as he crept and circled around, and came up well to leeward of the silent, motionless pair.

He lay down in the snow, depositing the ptarmigan beside him, and with eyes peering through the needles of a low-growing spruce he watched the play of life before him – the waiting lynx and the waiting porcupine, each intent on life; and, such was the curiousness of the game, the way of life for one lay in the eating of the other, and the way of life for the other lay in being not eaten. While old One Eye, the wolf, crouching in the covert, played his part, too, in the game, waiting for some strange freak of chance, that might help him on the meat-trail which was his way of life.

Half an hour passed, an hour; and nothing happened. The ball of quills might have been a stone for all it moved; the lynx might have been frozen to marble; and old One Eye might have been dead. Yet all three animals were keyed to a tenseness of living that was almost painful, and scarcely ever would it come to them to be more alive than they were in their seeming petrification.

One Eye moved slightly and peered forth with increased eagerness. Something was happening. The porcupine had at last decided that its enemy had gone away. Slowly, cautiously, it was unrolling its ball of impregnable armour. It was agitated by no tremor of anticipation. Slowly, slowly, the bristling ball straightened out and lengthened. One Eye, watching, felt a sudden moistness in his mouth and a drooling of saliva, involuntary, excited by the living meat that was spreading itself like a repast before him.

Not quite entirely had the porcupine unrolled when it discovered its enemy. In that instant the lynx struck. The blow was like a flash of light. The paw, with rigid claws curving like talons, shot under the tender belly and came back with a swift ripping movement. Had the porcupine been entirely unrolled, or had it not discovered its enemy a fraction of a second before the blow was struck, the paw would have escaped unscathed; but a side-flick of the tail sank sharp quills into it as it was withdrawn.

Everything had happened at once – the blow, the counter-blow, the squeal of agony from the porcupine, the big cat's squall of sudden hurt and astonishment. One Eye half arose in his excitement, his ears up, his tail straight out and quivering behind him. The lynx's bad temper got the best of her. She sprang savagely at the thing that had hurt her. But the porcupine, squealing and grunting, with disrupted anatomy trying feebly to roll up into its ball-protection, flicked out its tail again, and again the big cat squalled with hurt and astonishment. Then she fell to backing away and sneezing, her nose bristling with quills like a monstrous pin-cushion. She brushed her nose with her paws, trying to dislodge the fiery darts, thrust it into the snow, and rubbed it against twigs and branches, and all the time leaping about, ahead, sidewise, up and down, in a frenzy of pain and fright.

She sneezed continually, and her stub of a tail was doing its best toward lashing about by giving quick, violent jerks. She quit her antics, and quieted down for a long minute. One Eye watched. And even he could not repress a start and an involuntary bristling of hair along his back when she suddenly leaped, without warning, straight up in the air, at the same time emitting a long and most terrible squall. Then she sprang away, up the trail, squalling with every leap she made.

It was not until her racket had faded away in the distance and died out that One Eye ventured forth. He walked as delicately as though all the snow were carpeted with porcupine quills, erect and ready to pierce the soft pads of his feet. The porcupine met his approach with a furious squealing and a clashing of its long teeth. It had managed to roll up in a ball again, but it was not quite the old compact ball; its muscles were too much torn for that. It had been ripped almost in half, and was still bleeding profusely.

One Eye scooped out mouthfuls of the blood-soaked snow, and chewed and tasted and swallowed. This served as a relish, and his hunger increased mightily; but he was too old in the world to forget his caution. He waited. He lay down and waited, while the porcupine grated its teeth and uttered grunts and sobs and occasional sharp little squeals. In a little while, One Eye noticed that the quills were drooping and that a great quivering had set up. The quivering came to an end suddenly. There was a final defiant clash of the long teeth. Then all the quills drooped quite down, and the body relaxed and moved no more.

With a nervous, shrinking paw, One Eye stretched out the porcupine to its full length, and turned it over on its back. Nothing had happened. It was surely dead. He studied it intently for a moment, then took a careful grip with his teeth, and started off down the stream, partly carrying, partly dragging the porcupine, with head turned to the side so as to avoid stepping on the prickly mass. He recollected something, dropped the burden, and trotted back to where he had left the ptarmigan. He did not hesitate a moment. He knew clearly what was to be done, and this he did by promptly eating the ptarmigan. Then he returned and took up his burden.

When he dragged the result of his day's hunt into the cave, the she-wolf inspected it, turned her muzzle to him, and lightly licked him on the neck. But the next instant she was warning him away from the cubs with a snarl that was less harsh than usual and that was more apologetic than menacing. Her instinctive fear of the father of her progeny was toning down. He was behaving as a wolf-father should, and manifesting no unholy desire to devour the young lives she had brought into the world.

3

THE GREY CUB

He was different from his brothers and sisters. Their hair already betrayed the reddish hue inherited from their mother, the she-wolf; while he alone, in this particular, took after his father. He was the one little grey cub of the litter. He had bred true to the straight wolf-stock – in fact, he had bred true to old One Eye himself, physically, with but a single exception, and that was – he had two eyes to his father's one.

The grey cub's eyes had not been open long, yet already he could see with steady clearness. And while his eyes were still closed, he had felt, tasted, and smelled. He knew his two brothers and his two sisters very well. He had begun to romp with them in a feeble, awkward way, and even to squabble, his little throat vibrating with a queer rasping noise (the forerunner of the growl), as he worked himself into a passion. And long before his eyes had opened, he had learned by touch, taste, and smell to know his mother – a fount of warmth and liquid food and tenderness. She possessed a gentle, caressing tongue that soothed him when it passed over his soft little body, and that impelled him to snuggle close against her and to doze off to sleep.

Most of the first month of his life had been passed thus in sleeping; but now he could see quite well, and he stayed awake for longer periods of time, and he was coming to learn his world quite well. His world was gloomy; but he did not know that, for he knew no other world. It was dim-lighted; but his eyes had never had to adjust themselves to any other light. His world was very small. Its limits were the walls of the lair; but as he had no knowledge of the wide world outside, he was never oppressed by the narrow confines of his existence.

But he had early discovered that one wall of his world was different from the rest. This was the mouth of the cave and the source of light. He had discovered that it was different from the other walls long before he had any thoughts of his own, any conscious volitions. It had been an irresistible attraction before ever his eyes opened and looked upon it. The light from it had beat upon his sealed lids, and the eyes and the optic nerves had pulsated to little, sparklike flashes, warm-coloured and strangely pleasing. The life of his body and of every fibre of his body, the life that was the very substance of his body and that was apart from his own personal life, had yearned toward this light, and urged his body toward it in the same way that the cunning chemistry of a plant urges it toward the sun.

Always, in the beginning, before his conscious life dawned, he had crawled toward the mouth of the cave. And in this his brothers and sisters were one with him. Never, in that period, did any of them crawl toward the dark corners of the back wall. The light drew them as if they were plants; the chemistry of the life that composed them demanded the light as a necessity of being; and their little puppet-bodies crawled blindly and chemically, like the tendrils of a vine. Later on, when each developed individuality and became personally conscious of impulsions and desires, the attraction of the light increased. They were always crawling and sprawling toward it, and being driven back from it by their mother.

It was in this way that the grey cub learned other attributes of his mother than the soft, soothing, tongue. In his insistent crawling toward the light, he discovered in her a nose that with a sharp nudge administered rebuke, and later, a paw, that crushed him down and rolled him over and over with swift, calculating stroke. Thus he learned hurt; and on top of it he learned to avoid hurt – first, by not incurring the risk of it; and second, when he had incurred the risk, by dodging and by retreating. These were conscious actions, and were the results of his first generalizations upon the world. Before that he had recoiled automatically from hurt, as he had crawled automatically toward the light. After that he recoiled from hurt because he *knew* that it was hurt.

He was a fierce little cub. So were his brothers and sisters. It was to be expected. He was a carnivorous animal. He came of a breed of meat-killers and meat-eaters. His father and mother lived wholly upon meat. The milk he had sucked with his first flickering life was milk transformed directly from meat; and now, at a month old, when his eyes had been open for about a week, he was beginning himself to eat meat – meat half digested by the she-wolf and disgorged for the five growing cubs that already made too great demand upon her breast.

But he was, further, the fiercest of the litter. He could make a louder rasping growl than any of them. His tiny rages were much more terrible than theirs. It was he that first learned the trick of rolling a fellow-cub over with a cunning paw-stroke. And it was he that first gripped another cub by the ear and pulled and tugged and growled through jaws tight-clenched. And certainly it was he that caused the mother the most trouble in keeping her litter from the mouth of the cave.

The fascination of the light for the grey cub increased from day to day. He was perpetually departing on yard-long adventures toward the cave's entrance, and as perpetually being driven back. Only he did not know it for an entrance. He did not know anything about entrances – passages whereby one goes from one place to another place. He did not know any other place, much less of a way to get there. So to him the entrance of the cave was a wall – a wall of light. As the sun was to the outside dweller, this wall was to him the sun of his world. It attracted him as a candle attracts a moth. He was always striving to attain it. The life that was so swiftly expanding within him urged him continually toward the wall of light. The life that was within him knew that it was the one way out, the way he was predestined to tread. But he himself did not know anything about it. He did not know there was any outside at all.

There was one strange thing about this wall of light. His father (he had already come to recognize his father as the one other dweller in the world, a creature like his mother, who slept near the light and was a bringer of meat) – his father had a way of walking right into the white far wall and disappearing. The grey cub could not understand this. Though never permitted by his mother to approach that wall, he had approached the other walls, and encountered hard obstruction on the end of his tender nose. This hurt. And after several such adventures, he left the walls alone. Without thinking about it, he accepted this disappearing into the wall as a peculiarity of his father, as milk and half-digested meat were peculiarities of his mother.

In fact, the grey cub was not given to thinking – at least, to the kind of thinking customary of men. His brain worked in dim ways. Yet his conclusions were as sharp and distinct as those achieved by men. He had a method of accepting things without questioning the why and wherefore. In reality, this was the act of classification. He was never disturbed over *why* a thing happened. *How* it happened was sufficient for him. Thus, when he had bumped his nose on the back wall a few times, he accepted that he would not disappear into walls. In the same way he accepted that his father could disappear into walls. But he was not in the least disturbed by desire to find out the reason for the difference between his father and himself. Logic and physics were no part of his mental make-up.

Like most creatures of the Wild, he early experienced famine. There came a time when not only did the meat-supply cease, but the milk no longer came from his mother's breast. At first, the cubs whimpered and cried, but for the most part they slept. It was not long before they were reduced to a coma of hunger. There were no more spats and squabbles, no more tiny rages nor attempts at growling; while the adventures toward the far white wall ceased altogether. The cubs slept, while the life that was in them flickered and died down.

One Eye was desperate. He ranged far and wide, and slept but little in the lair that had now become cheerless and miserable. The she-wolf, too, left her litter and went out in search of meat. In the first days after the birth of the cubs, One Eye had journeyed several times back to the Indian camp and robbed the rabbit snares; but, with the melting of the snow and the opening of the streams, the Indian camp had moved away, and that source of supply was closed to him.

When the grey cub came back to life and again took interest in the far white wall, he found that the population of his world had been reduced. Only one sister remained to him. The rest were gone. As he grew stronger, he found himself compelled to play alone, for the sister no longer lifted her head nor moved about. His little body rounded out with the meat he now ate; but the food had come too late for her. She slept continuously, a tiny skeleton flung round with skin, while the flame flickered lower and lower and at last went out.

Then there came a time when the grey cub no longer saw his father appearing and disappearing in the wall, nor lying down asleep in the entrance. This had happened at the end of a second and less severe famine. The she-wolf knew why One Eye never came back, but there was no way by which she could tell what she had seen to the grey cub. Hunting herself for meat, up the left fork of the stream where lived the lynx, she had followed a day-old trail of One Eye. And she had found him, or what remained of him, at the end of the trail. There were many signs of the battle that had been fought, and of the lynx's withdrawal to her lair after having won the victory. Before she went away, the she-wolf had found this lair, but the signs told her that the lynx was inside, and she had not dared to venture in.

After that, the she-wolf in her hunting avoided the

left fork. For she knew that in the lynx's lair was a litter of kittens, and she knew the lynx for a fierce, bad-tempered creature and a terrible fighter. It was all very well for half a dozen wolves to drive a lynx, spitting and bristling, up a tree; but it was quite a different matter for a lone wolf to encounter a lynx – especially when the lynx was known to have a litter of hungry kittens at her back.

But the Wild is the Wild, and motherhood is motherhood, at all times fiercely protective whether in the Wild or out of it; and the time was to come when the she-wolf, for her grey cub's sake, would venture the left fork, and the lair in the rocks, and the lynx's wrath.

CHAPTER

4

THE WALL OF THE WORLD

By the time his mother began leaving the cave on hunting expeditions, the cub had learned well the law that forbade his approaching the entrance. Not only had this law been forcibly and many times impressed on him by his mother's nose and paw, but in him the instinct of fear was developing. Never, in his brief cave-life, had he encountered anything of which to be afraid. Yet fear was in him. It had come down to him from a remote ancestry through a thousand thousand lives. It was a heritage he had received directly from One Eye and the she-wolf; but to them, in turn, it had been passed down through all the generations of wolves that had gone before. Fear! – that legacy of the Wild which no animal may escape nor exchange for pottage.

So the grey cub knew fear, though he knew not the stuff of which fear was made. Possibly he accepted it as one of the restrictions of life. For he had already learned that there were such restrictions. Hunger he had known; and when he could not appease his hunger he had felt restriction. The hard obstruction of the cave-wall, the sharp nudge of his mother's nose, the smashing stroke of her paw, the hunger unappeased of several famines, had borne in upon him that all was not freedom in the world – that to life there were limitations and restraints. These limitations and restraints were laws. To be obedient to them was to escape hurt and make for happiness.

He did not reason the question out in this man fashion. He merely classified the things that hurt and the things that did not hurt. And after such classification he avoided the things that hurt – the restrictions and restraints – in order to enjoy the satisfactions and the remunerations of life.

Thus it was that in obedience to the law laid down by his mother, and in obedience to the law of that unknown and nameless thing, fear, he kept away from the mouth of the cave. It remained to him a white wall of light. When his mother was absent, he slept most of the time, while during the intervals that he was awake he kept very quiet, suppressing the whimpering cries that tickled in his throat and strove for noise.

Once, lying awake, he heard a strange sound in the white wall. He did not know that it was a wolverine, standing outside, all a-trembling with its own daring, and cautiously scenting out the contents of the cave. The cub knew only that the sniff was strange, a something unclassified, therefore unknown and terrible – for the unknown was one of the chief elements that went into the making of fear.

The hair bristled up on the grey cub's back, but it bristled silently. How was he to know that this thing that sniffed was a thing at which to bristle? It was not born of any knowledge of his, yet it was the visible expression of the fear that was in him, and for which, in his own life, there was no accounting. But fear was accompanied by another instinct – that of concealment.

The cub was in a frenzy of terror, yet he lay without movement or sound, frozen, petrified into immobility, to all appearances dead. His mother, coming home, growled as she smelt the wolverine's track, and bounded into the cave and licked and nozzled him with undue vehemence of affection. And the cub felt that somehow he had escaped a great hurt.

But there were other forces at work in the cub, the greatest of which was growth. Instinct and law demanded of him obedience. But growth demanded disobedience. His mother and fear impelled him to keep away from the white wall. Growth is life, and life is for ever destined to make for light. So there was no damming up the tide of life that was rising within him – rising with every mouthful of meat he swallowed, with every breath he drew. In the end, one day, fear and obedience were swept away by the rush of life, and the cub straddled and sprawled toward the entrance.

Unlike any other wall with which he had had experience, this wall seemed to recede from him as he approached. No hard surface collided with the tender little nose he thrust out tentatively before him. The substance of the wall seemed as permeable and yielding as light. And as condition, in his eyes, had the seeming of form, so he entered into what had been wall to him, and bathed in the substance that composed it.

It was bewildering. He was sprawling through solidity. And ever the light grew brighter. Fear urged him to go back, but growth drove him on. Suddenly he found himself at the mouth of the cave. The wall, inside which he had thought himself, as suddenly leaped back before him to an immeasurable distance. The light had become painfully bright. He was dazzled by it. Likewise he was made dizzy by this abrupt and tremendous extension of space. Automatically, his eyes were adjusting themselves to the brightness, focusing themselves to meet the increased distance of objects. At first, the wall had leaped beyond his vision. He now saw it again; but it had taken upon itself a remarkable remoteness. Also, its appearance had changed. It was now a variegated wall, composed of the trees that fringed the stream, the opposing mountain that towered above the trees, and the sky that out-towered the mountain.

A great fear came upon him. This was more of the terrible unknown. He crouched down on the lip of the cave and gazed out on the world. He was very much afraid. Because it was unknown, it was hostile to him. Therefore the hair stood up on end along his back, and his lips wrinkled weakly in an attempt at a ferocious and intimidating snarl. Out of his puniness and fright he challenged and menaced the whole wide world.

Nothing happened. He continued to gaze, and in his interest he forgot to snarl. Also, he forgot to be afraid. For the time, fear had been routed by growth, while growth had assumed the guise of curiosity. He began to notice near objects – an open portion of the stream that flashed in the sun, the blasted pine-tree that stood at the base of the slope, and the slope itself, that ran right up to him and ceased two feet beneath the lip of the cave on which he crouched.

Now the grey cub had lived all his days on a level floor. He had never experienced the hurt of a fall. He did not know what a fall was. So he stepped boldly out upon the air. His hind-legs still rested on the cave-lip, so he fell forward head downward. The earth struck him a harsh blow on the nose that made him yelp. Then he began rolling down the slope, over and over. He was in a panic of terror. The unknown had caught him at last. It had gripped savagely hold of him and was about to wreak upon him some terrific hurt. Growth was now routed by fear, and he ki-yi'd like any frightened puppy.

The unknown bore him on he knew not to what frightful hurt, and he yelped and ki-yi'd unceasingly. This was a different proposition from crouching in frozen fear while the unknown lurked just alongside. Now the unknown had caught tight hold of him. Silence would do no good. Besides, it was not fear, but terror, that convulsed him.

But the slope grew more gradual, and its base was grass-covered. Here the cub lost momentum. When at last he came to a stop, he gave one last agonized yelp and then a long, whimpering wail. Also, and quite as a matter of course, as though in his life he had already made a thousand toilets, he proceeded to lick away the dry clay that soiled him.

After that he sat up and gazed about him, as might the first man of the earth who landed upon Mars. The cub had broken through the wall of the world, the unknown had let go its hold of him, and here he was without hurt. But the first man on Mars would have experienced less unfamiliarity than did he. Without any antecedent knowledge, without any warning whatever that such existed, he found himself an explorer in a totally new world.

Now that the terrible unknown had let go of him, he forgot that the unknown had any terrors. He was aware only of curiosity in all the things about him. He inspected the grass beneath him, the moss-berry plant just beyond, and the dead trunk of the blasted pine that stood on the edge of an open space among the trees. A squirrel, running around the base of the trunk, came full upon him, and gave him a great fright. He cowered down and snarled. But the squirrel was as badly scared. It ran up the tree, and from a point of safety chattered back savagely.

This helped the cub's courage, and though the woodpecker he next encountered gave him a start, he proceeded confidently on his way. Such was his confidence, that when a moose-bird impudently hopped up to him, he reached out at it with a playful paw. The result was a sharp peck on the end of his nose that made him cower down and ki-yi. The noise he made was too much for the moose-bird, who sought safety in flight.

But the cub was learning. His misty little mind had already made an unconscious classification. There were live things and things not alive. Also, he must watch out for the live things. The things not alive remained always in one place; but the live things moved about, and there was no telling what they might do. The thing to expect of them was the unexpected, and for this he must be prepared.

He travelled very clumsily. He ran into sticks and things. A twig that he thought a long way off would the next instant hit him on the nose or rake along his ribs. There were inequalities of surface. Sometimes he overstepped and stubbed his nose. Quite as often he understepped and stubbed his feet. Then there were the pebbles and stones that turned under him when he trod upon them; and from them he came to know that the things not alive were not all in the same state of stable equilibrium as was his cave; also, that small things not alive were more liable than large things to fall down or turn over. But with every mishap he was learning. The longer he walked, the better he walked. He was adjusting himself. He was learning to calculate his own muscular movements, to know his physical limitations, to measure distances between objects, and between objects and himself.

His was the luck of the beginner. Born to be a hunter of meat (though he did not know it), he blundered upon meat just outside his own cave-door on his first foray into the world. It was by sheer blundering that he chanced upon the shrewdly hidden ptarmigan nest. He fell into it. He had essayed to walk along the trunk of a fallen pine. The rotten bark gave way under his feet, and with a despairing yelp he pitched down the rounded descent, smashed through the leafage and stalks of a small bush, and in the heart of the bush, on the ground, fetched up in the midst of seven ptarmigan chicks.

They made noises, and at first he was frightened at them. Then he perceived that they were very little, and he became bolder. They moved. He placed his paw on one, and its movements were accelerated. This was a source of enjoyment to him. He smelled it. He picked it up in his mouth. It struggled and tickled his tongue. At the same time he was made aware of a sensation of hunger. His jaws closed together. There was a crunching of fragile bones, and warm blood ran in his mouth. The taste of it was good. This was meat, the same as his mother gave him, only it was alive between his teeth and therefore better. So he ate the ptarmigan. Nor did he stop till he had devoured the whole brood. Then he licked his chops in quite the same way his mother did, and began to crawl out of the bush.

He encountered a feathered whirlwind. He was confused and blinded by the rush of it and the beat of angry wings. He hid his head between his paws and yelped. The blows increased. The mother-ptarmigan was in a fury. Then he became angry. He rose up, snarling, striking out with his paws. He sank his tiny teeth into one of the wings and pulled and tugged sturdily. The ptarmigan struggled against him, showering blows upon him with her free wing. It was his first battle. He was elated. He forgot all about the unknown. He was fighting, tearing at a live thing that was striking at him. Also this live thing was meat. The lust to kill was on him. He had just destroyed little live things. He would now destroy a big live thing. He was too busy and happy to know that he was happy. He was thrilling and exulting in ways new to him and greater to him than any he had known before.

He held on to the wing and growled between his tight-clenched teeth. The ptarmigan dragged him out of the bush. When she turned and tried to drag him back into the bush's shelter, he pulled her away from it and on into the open. And all the time she was making outcry and striking with her free wing, while feathers were flying like a snowfall. The pitch to which he was aroused was tremendous. All the fighting blood of his breed was up in him and surging through him. This was living, though he did not know it. He was realizing his own meaning in the world; he was doing that for which he was made – killing meat and battling to kill it. He was justifying his existence, than which life can do no greater; for life achieves its summit when it does to the uttermost that which it was equipped to do.

After a time the ptarmigan ceased her struggling. He

still held her by the wing, and they lay on the ground and
looked at each other. He tried to growl threateningly,
ferociously. She pecked on his nose, which by now,
what of previous adventures, was sore. He winced but
held on. She pecked him again and again. From wincing
he went to whimpering. He tried to back away from her,
oblivious to the fact that by his hold on her he dragged
her after him. A rain of pecks fell on his ill-used nose.
The flood of fight ebbed down in him, and, releasing his
prey, he turned tail and scampered off across the open
in inglorious retreat.

He lay down to rest on the other side of the open,
near the edge of the bushes, his tongue lolling out, his
chest heaving and panting, his nose still hurting him
and causing him to continue to whimper. But as he
lay there, suddenly there came to him a feeling as of
something terrible impending. The unknown with all its
terrors rushed upon him, and he shrank back instinctively into the shelter of the bush. As he did so, a draught
of air fanned him, and a large, winged body swept
ominously and silently past. A hawk, driving down out
of the blue, had barely missed him.

While he lay in the bush, recovering from this fright
and peering fearfully out, the mother-ptarmigan on the
other side of the open space fluttered out of the ravaged
nest. It was because of her loss that she paid no attention
to the winged bolt of the sky. But the cub saw, and it
was a warning and a lesson to him – the swift downward
swoop of the hawk, the short skim of its body, just above
the ground, the strike of its talons in the body of the
ptarmigan, the ptarmigan's squawk of agony and fright,
and the hawk's rush upward into the blue, carrying the
ptarmigan away with it.

It was a long time before the cub left his shelter. He had learned much. Live things were meat. They were good to eat. Also, live things, when they were large enough, could give hurt. It was better to eat small live things like ptarmigan chicks, and to let alone large live things like ptarmigan hens. Nevertheless he felt a little prick of ambition, a sneaking desire to have another battle with that ptarmigan hen – only the hawk had carried her away. Maybe there were other ptarmigan hens. He would go and see.

He came down a shelving bank to the stream. He had never seen water before. The footing looked good. There were not inequalities of surface. He stepped boldly out on it, and went down, crying with fear, into the embrace of the unknown. It was cold, and he gasped, breathing quickly. The water rushed into his lungs instead of the air that had always accompanied his act of breathing. The suffocation he experienced was like the pang of death. To him it signified death. He had no conscious knowledge of death, but like every animal of the Wild, he possessed the instinct of death. To him it stood as the greatest of hurts. It was the very essence of the unknown, it was the sum of the terrors of the unknown – the one culminating and unthinkable catastrophe that could happen to him, about which he knew nothing and about which he feared everything.

He came to the surface, and the sweet air rushed into his open mouth. He did not go down again. Quite as though it had been a long-established custom of his, he struck out with all his legs and began to swim. The near bank was a yard away; but he had come up with his back to it, and the first thing his eyes rested upon was the opposite bank, toward which he immediately began to swim. The stream was a small one, but in the pool it widened out to a score of feet.

Midway in the passage, the current picked up the cub and swept him down-stream. He was caught in the miniature rapid at the bottom of the pool. Here was little chance for swimming. The quiet water had become suddenly angry. Sometimes he was under, sometimes on top. At all times he was in violent motion, now being turned over or around, and again, being smashed against a rock. And with every rock he struck he yelped. His progress was a series of yelps, from which might have been adduced the number of rocks he encountered.

Below the rapid was a second pool, and here, captured by the eddy, he was gently borne to the bank and as gently deposited on a bed of gravel. He crawled frantically clear of the water and lay down. He had learned some more about the world. Water was not alive. Yet it moved. Also, it looked as solid as the earth, but was without any solidity at all. His conclusion was that things were not always what they appeared to be. The cub's fear of the unknown was an inherited distrust, and it had now been strengthened by experience. Thenceforth, in the nature of things, he would possess an abiding distrust of appearances. He would have to learn the reality of a thing before he could put his faith into it.

One other adventure was destined for him that day. He had recollected that there was such a thing in the world as his mother. And then there came to him a feeling that he wanted her more than all the rest of the things in the world. Not only was his body tired with the adventures it had undergone, but his little brain was equally tired. In all the days he had lived it had not worked so hard as on this one day. Furthermore, he was sleepy. So he started out to look for the cave and his mother, feeling at the same time an overwhelming rush of loneliness and helplessness.

He was sprawling along between some bushes, when he heard a sharp, intimidating cry. There was a flash of yellow before his eyes. He saw a weasel leaping swiftly away from him. It was a small live thing, and he had no fear. Then, before him, at his feet, he saw an extremely small live thing, only several inches long – a young weasel, that, like himself, had disobediently gone out adventuring. It tried to retreat before him. He turned it over with his paw. It made a queer, grating noise. The next moment the flash of yellow reappeared before his eyes. He heard again the intimidating cry, and at the same instant received a severe blow on the side of the neck, and felt the sharp teeth of the mother-weasel cut into his flesh.

While he yelped and ki-yi'd and scrambled backward, he saw the mother-weasel leap upon her young one and disappear with it into the neighbouring thicket. The cut of her teeth in his neck still hurt, but his feelings were hurt more grievously, and he sat down and weakly whimpered. This mother-weasel was so small and so savage! He was yet to learn that for size and weight the weasel was the most ferocious, vindictive, and terrible of all the killers of the Wild. But a portion of this knowledge was quickly to be his.

He was still whimpering when the mother-weasel reappeared. She did not rush him, now that her young one was safe. She approached more cautiously, and the cub had full opportunity to observe her lean, snake-like body, and her head, erect, eager, and snake-like itself. Her sharp, menacing cry sent the hair bristling along his back, and he snarled warningly at her. She came closer and closer. There was a leap, swifter than his unpractised sight, and the lean, yellow body disappeared for a moment out of the field of his vision. The next moment she was at his throat, her teeth buried in his hair and flesh.

At first he snarled and tried to fight; but he was very young, and this was only his first day in the world, and his snarl became a whimper, his fight a struggle to escape. The weasel never relaxed her hold. She hung on, striving to press down with her teeth to the great vein where his life-blood bubbled. The weasel was a drinker of blood, and it was ever her preference to drink from the throat of life itself.

The grey cub would have died, and there would have been no story to write about him, had not the she-wolf come bounding through the bushes. The weasel let go the cub and flashed at the she-wolf's throat, missing, but getting a hold on the jaw instead. The she-wolf flirted her head like the snap of a whip, breaking the weasel's hold and flinging it high in the air. And, still in the air, the she-wolf's jaws closed on the lean, yellow body, and the weasel knew death between the crunching teeth.

The cub experienced another access of affection on the part of his mother. Her joy at finding him seemed greater even than his joy at being found. She nozzled him, and caressed him, and licked the cuts made in him by the weasel's teeth. Then, between them, mother and cub, they ate the blood-drinker, and after that went back to the cave and slept.

CHAPTER

5

THE LAW OF MEAT

The cub's development was rapid. He rested for two days, and then ventured forth from the cave again. It was on this adventure that he found the young weasel whose mother he had helped eat, and he saw to it that the young weasel went the way of its mother. But on this trip he did not get lost. When he grew tired, he found his way back to the cave and slept. And every day thereafter found him out and ranging a wider area.

He began to get accurate measurement of his strength and his weakness, and to know when to be bold and when to be cautious. He found it expedient to be cautious all the time, except for the rare moments when, assured of his own intrepidity, he abandoned himself to petty rages and lusts.

He was always a little demon of fury when he chanced upon a stray ptarmigan. Never did he fail to respond savagely to the chatter of the squirrel he had first met on the blasted pine. While the sight of a moose-bird almost invariably put him into the wildest of rages, for he never forgot the peck on the nose he had received from the first of that ilk he encountered.

But there were times when even a moose-bird failed

to affect him, and those were times when he felt himself to be in danger from some other prowling meat-hunter. He never forgot the hawk, and its moving shadow always sent him crouching into the nearest thicket. He no longer sprawled and straddled, and already he was developing the gait of his mother, slinking and furtive, apparently without exertion, yet sliding along with a swiftness that was as deceptive as it was imperceptible.

In the matter of meat, his luck had been all in the beginning. The seven ptarmigan chicks and the baby weasel represented the sum of his killings. His desire to kill strengthened with the days, and he cherished hungry ambitions for the squirrel that chattered so volubly and always informed all wild creatures that the wolf-cub was approaching. But as birds flew in the air, squirrels could climb trees, and the cub could only try to crawl unobserved upon the squirrel when it was on the ground.

The cub entertained a great respect for his mother. She could get meat, and she never failed to bring him his share. Further, she was unafraid of things. It did not occur to him that this fearlessness was founded upon experience and knowledge. Its effect on him was that of an impression of power. His mother represented power; and as he grew older he felt this power in the sharper admonishment of her paw; while the reproving nudge of her nose gave place to the slash of her fangs. For this, likewise, he respected his mother. She compelled obedience from him, and the older he grew the shorter grew her temper.

Famine came again, and the cub with clearer consciousness knew once more the bite of hunger. The she-wolf ran herself thin in the quest for meat. She rarely slept any more in the cave, spending most of her time on the meat-trail, and spending it vainly. This famine was not a long one, but it was severe while it lasted. The cub found no more milk in his mother's breast, nor did he get one mouthful of meat for himself.

Before, he had hunted in play, for the sheer joyousness of it; now he hunted in deadly earnestness, and found nothing. Yet the failure of it accelerated his development. He studied the habits of the squirrel with greater carefulness, and strove with greater craft to steal upon it and surprise it. He studied the wood-mice, and tried to dig them out of their burrows; and he learned much about the ways of moose-birds and woodpeckers. And there came a day when the hawk's shadow did not drive him crouching into the bushes. He had grown stronger, and wiser, and more confident. Also, he was desperate. So he sat on his haunches, conspicuously in an open space, and challenged the hawk down out of the sky. For he knew that there, floating in the blue above him, was meat – the meat his stomach yearned after so insistently. But the hawk refused to come down and give battle, and the cub crawled away into a thicket and whimpered his disappointment and hunger.

The famine broke. The she-wolf brought home meat. It was strange meat, different from any she had ever brought before. It was a lynx kitten, partly grown, like the cub, but not so large. And it was all for him. His mother had satisfied her hunger elsewhere, though he did not know that it was the rest of the lynx litter that had gone to satisfy her. Nor did he know the desperateness of her deed. He knew only that the velvet-furred kitten was meat, and he ate and waxed happier with every mouthful.

A full stomach conduces to inaction, and the cub lay in the cave, sleeping against his mother's side. He was aroused by her snarling. Never had he heard her snarl so terribly. Possibly in her whole life it was the most terrible snarl she ever gave. There was reason for it, and none knew it better than she. A lynx's lair is not despoiled with impunity. In the full glare of the afternoon light, crouching in the entrance of the cave, the cub saw the lynx-mother. The hair rippled up along his back at the sight. Here was fear, and it did not require his instinct to tell him of it. And if sight alone were not sufficient, the cry of rage the intruder gave, beginning with a snarl and rushing abruptly upward into a hoarse screech, was convincing enough in itself.

The cub felt the prod of the life that was in him, and stood up and snarled valiantly by his mother's side. But she thrust him ignominiously away and behind her. Because of the low-roofed entrance the lynx could not leap in, and when she made a crawling rush of it the she-wolf sprang upon her and pinned her down. The cub saw little of the battle. There was a tremendous snarling and spitting and screeching. The two animals threshed about, the lynx ripping and tearing with her claws and using her teeth as well, while the she-wolf used her teeth alone.

Once the cub sprang in and sank his teeth into the hind leg of the lynx. He clung on, growling savagely. Though he did not know it, by the weight of his body he clogged the action of the leg and thereby saved his mother much damage. A change in the battle crushed him under both their bodies and wrenched loose his hold. The next moment the two mothers separated, and before they rushed together again the lynx lashed out at the cub with a huge forepaw that ripped his shoulder open to the bone and sent him hurtling sidewise against the wall. Then was added to the uproar the cub's shrill yelp of pain and fright. But the fight lasted so long that he had time to cry himself out and to experience a second burst of courage; and the end of the battle found him again clinging to a hind-leg and furiously growling between his teeth.

The lynx was dead. But the she-wolf was very weak and sick. At first she caressed the cub and licked his wounded shoulder; but the blood she had lost had taken with it her strength, and for all of a day and a night she lay by her dead foe's side, without movement, scarcely breathing. For a week she never left the cave, except for water, and then her movements were slow and painful. At the end of that time the lynx was devoured, while the she-wolf's wounds had healed sufficiently to permit her to take the meat-trail again.

The cub's shoulder was stiff and sore, and for some time he limped from the terrible slash he had received. But the world now seemed changed. He went about in it with greater confidence, with a feeling of prowess that had not been his in the days before the battle with the lynx. He had looked upon life in a more ferocious aspect; he had fought; he had buried his teeth in the flesh of a foe, and he had survived. And because of all this, he carried himself more boldly, with a touch of defiance that was new in him. He was no longer afraid of minor things and much of his timidity had vanished, though the unknown never ceased to press upon him with its mysteries and terrors, intangible and ever-menacing.

He began to accompany his mother on the meat-trail, and he saw much of the killing of meat, and began to play his part in it. And in his own dim way he learned the law of meat. There were two kinds of life – his own kind and the other kind. His own kind included his mother and himself. The other kind included all live things that moved. But the other kind was divided. One portion was what his own kind killed and ate. This portion was composed of the non-killers and the small killers. The other portion killed and ate his own kind, or was killed and eaten by his own kind. And out of this classification arose the law. The aim of life was meat. Life itself was meat. Life lived on life. There were the eaters and the eaten. The law was: EAT, OR BE EATEN. He did not formulate the law in clear, set terms and moralize about it. He did not even think the law; he merely lived the law without thinking about it at all.

He saw the law operating around him on every side. He had eaten the ptarmigan chicks. The hawk had eaten the ptarmigan mother. The hawk would also have eaten him. Later, when he had grown more formidable, he wanted to eat the hawk. He had eaten the lynx kitten. The lynx-mother would have eaten him had she not herself been killed and eaten. And so it went. The law was being lived about him by all live things, and he himself was part and parcel of the law. He was a killer. His only food was meat, live meat, that ran away swiftly before him, or flew into the air, or climbed trees, or hid in the ground, or faced him and fought with him, or turned the tables and ran after him.

Had the cub thought in man-fashion, he might have epitomized life as a voracious appetite and the world as a place wherein ranged a multitude of appetites, pursuing and being pursued, hunting and being hunted, eating and being eaten, all in blindness and confusion, with violence and disorder, a chaos of gluttony and slaughter, ruled over by chance, merciless, planless, endless.

But the cub did not think in man-fashion. He did not look at things with wide vision. He was single-purposed, and entertained but one thought or desire at a time. Besides the law of meat, there were a myriad other and lesser laws for him to learn and obey. The world was filled with surprise. The stir of the life that was in him, the play of his muscles, was an unending happiness. To run down meat was to experience thrills and elations. His rages and battles were pleasures. Terror itself, and the mystery of the unknown led to his living.

And there were easements and satisfactions. To have a full stomach, to doze lazily in the sunshine – such things were remuneration in full for his ardours and toils, while his ardours and toils were in themselves self-remunerative. They were expressions of life, and life is always happy when it is expressing itself. So the cub had no quarrel with his hostile environment. He was very much alive, very happy, and very proud of himself.

PART III

CHAPTER

1

THE MAKERS OF FIRE

The cub came upon it suddenly. It was his own fault.
He had been careless. He had left the cave and run down
to the stream to drink. It might have been that he took
no notice because he was heavy with sleep. (He had
been out all night on the meat-trail, and had but just
then awakened.) And his carelessness might have been
due to the familiarity of the trail to the pool. He had
travelled it often, and nothing had ever happened on it.

He went down past the blasted pine, crossed the open
space, and trotted in amongst the trees. Then, at the
same instant, he saw and smelt. Before him sitting silently on their haunches were five live things, the like of
which he had never seen before. It was his first glimpse
of mankind. But at the sight of him the five men did not
spring to their feet, nor show their teeth, nor snarl. They
did not move, but sat there, silent and ominous.

Nor did the cub move. Every instinct of his nature
would have impelled him to dash wildly away, had there
not suddenly and for the first time arisen in him another
and counter instinct. A great awe descended upon him.
He was beaten down to movelessness by an overwhelming sense of his own weakness and littleness. Here was

mastery and power – something far and away beyond him.

The cub had never seen man, yet the instinct concerning man was his. In dim ways he recognized in man the animal that had fought itself to primacy over the other animals of the Wild. Not alone out of his own eyes, but out of the eyes of all his ancestors was the cub now looking upon man – out of eyes that had circled in the darkness around countless winter camp-fires, that had peered from safe distances and from the hearts of thickets at the strange, two-legged animal that was lord over living things. The spell of the cub's heritage was upon him, the fear and the respect born of the centuries of struggle and the accumulated experience of the generations. The heritage was too compelling for a wolf that was only a cub. Had he been full-grown, he would have run away. As it was, he cowered down in a paralysis of fear, already half proffering the submission that his kind had proffered from the first time a wolf came in to sit by man's fire and be made warm.

One of the Indians arose and walked over to him and stooped above him. The cub cowered closer to the ground. It was the unknown, objectified at last, in concrete flesh and blood, bending over him and reaching down to seize hold of him. His hair bristled involuntarily; his lips writhed back, and his little fangs were bared. The hand, poised like doom above him, hesitated, and the man spoke, laughing, 'Wabam wabisca ip pit tah.' (Look! The white fangs!)

The other Indians laughed loudly, and urged the man on to pick up the cub. As the hand descended closer and closer, there raged within the cub a battle of the instincts. He experienced two great impulsions – to yield and to fight. The resulting action was a compromise. He did both. He yielded till the hand almost touched him. Then he fought, his teeth flashing in a snap that sank them into the hand. The next moment he received a clout alongside the head that knocked him over on his side. Then all fight fled out of him. His puppyhood and the instinct of submission took charge of him. He sat up on his haunches and ki-yi'd. But the man whose hand he had bitten was angry. The cub received a clout on the other side of his head. Whereupon he sat up and ki-yi'd louder than ever.

The four Indians laughed more loudly, while even the man who had been bitten began to laugh. They surrounded the cub and laughed at him, while he wailed out his terror and his hurt. In the midst of it he heard something. The Indians heard it, too. But the cub knew what it was, and with a last, long wail that had in it more of triumph than grief, he ceased his noise and waited for the coming of his mother – of his ferocious and indomitable mother who fought and killed all things and was never afraid. She was snarling as she ran. She had heard the cry of her cub and was dashing to save him.

She bounded in amongst them, her anxious and militant motherhood making her anything but a pretty sight. But to the cub the spectacle of her protective rage was pleasing. He uttered a glad little cry and bounded to meet her, while the man-animals went back hastily several steps. The she-wolf stood over against her cub, facing the men, with bristling hair, a snarl rumbling deep in her throat. Her face was distorted and malignant with menace, even the bridge of the nose wrinkling from tip to eyes, so prodigious was her snarl.

Then it was that a cry went up from one of the men.

'Kiche!' was what he uttered. It was an exclamation of surprise. The cub felt his mother wilting at the sound.

'Kiche!' the man cried again, this time with sharpness and authority.

And then the cub saw his mother, the she-wolf, the fearless one, crouching down till her belly touched the ground, whimpering, wagging her tail, making peace signs. The cub could not understand. He was appalled. The awe of man rushed over him again. His instinct had been true. His mother verified it. She, too, rendered submission to the man-animals.

The man who had spoken came over to her. He put his hand upon her head, and she only crouched closer. She did not snap, nor threaten to snap. The other men came up, and surrounded her, and felt her, and pawed her, which actions she made no attempt to resent. They were greatly excited, and made many noises with their mouths. These noises were not indications of danger, the cub decided, as he crouched near his mother, still bristling from time to time, but doing his best to submit.

'It is not strange,' an Indian was saying. 'Her father was a wolf. It is true her mother was a dog; but did not my brother tie her out in the woods all of three nights in the mating season? Therefore was the father of Kiche a wolf.'

'It is a year, Grey Beaver, since she ran away,' spoke a second Indian.

'It is not strange, Salmon Tongue,' Grey Beaver answered. 'It was the time of the famine, and there was no meat for the dogs.'

'She has lived with the wolves,' said a third Indian.

'So it would seem, Three Eagles,' Grey Beaver

answered, laying his hand on the cub; 'and this be the sign of it.'

The cub snarled a little at the touch of the hand, and the hand flew back to administer a clout. Whereupon the cub covered its fangs, and sank down submissively; while the hand, returning, rubbed behind his ears and up and down his back.

'This be the sign of it,' Grey Beaver went on. 'It is plain that his mother is Kiche. But his father was a wolf. Wherefore is there in him little dog and much wolf. His fangs be white, and White Fang shall be his name. I have spoken. He is my dog. For was not Kiche my brother's dog? And is not my brother dead?'

The cub, who had thus received a name in the world, lay and watched. For a time the man-animals continued to make their mouth-noises. Then Grey Beaver took a knife from a sheath that hung around his neck, and went into the thicket and cut a stick. White Fang watched him. He notched the stick at each end, and in the notches fastened strings of raw hide. One string he tied around the throat of Kiche. Then he led her to a small pine, around which he tied the other string.

White Fang followed and lay down beside her. Salmon Tongue's hand reached out to him and rolled him over on his back. Kiche looked on anxiously. White Fang felt fear mounting in him again. He could not quite suppress a snarl, but he made no offer to snap. The hand, with fingers crooked and spread apart, rubbed his stomach in a playful way and rolled him from side to side. It was ridiculous and ungainly lying there on his back with legs sprawling in the air. Besides, it was a position of such utter helplessness that White Fang's whole nature revolted against it. He could do nothing to defend himself.

If this man-animal intended harm, White Fang knew that he could not escape it. How could he spring away with his four legs in the air above him? Yet submission made him master his fear, and he only growled softly. This growl he could not suppress; nor did the man-animal resent it by giving him a blow on the head. And furthermore, such was the strangeness of it, White Fang experienced an unaccountable sensation of pleasure as the hand rubbed back and forth. When he was rolled on his side he ceased to growl; when the fingers pressed and prodded at the base of his ears the pleasurable sensation increased; and when, with a final rub and scratch, the man left him alone, and went away, all fear had died out of White Fang. He was to know fear many times in his dealings with man; yet it was a token of the fearless companionship with man that was ultimately to be his.

After a time White Fang heard strange noises approaching. He was quick in his classification, for he knew them at once for man-animal noises. A few minutes later the remainder of the tribe, strung out as it was on the march, trailed in. There were more men and many women and children – forty souls of them – and all heavily burdened with camp equipage and outfit. Also there were many dogs; and these, with the exception of the part-grown puppies, were likewise burdened with camp outfit. On their backs, in bags that fastened tightly around underneath, the dogs carried from twenty to thirty pounds of weight.

White Fang had never seen dogs before, but at sight of them he felt that they were his own kind, only somehow different. But they displayed little difference from the wolf when they discovered the cub and his mother.

There was a rush. White Fang bristled and snarled and snapped in the face of the open-mouthed oncoming wave of dogs, and went down and under them, feeling the sharp slash of teeth in his body, himself biting and tearing at the legs and bellies above him. There was a great uproar. He could hear the snarl of Kiche as she fought for him; and he could hear the cries of the man-animals, the sound of clubs striking upon bodies, and the yelps of pain from the dogs so struck.

Only a few seconds elapsed before he was on his feet again. He could now see the man-animals driving back the dogs with clubs and stones, defending him, saving him from the savage teeth of his kind that somehow was not his kind. And though there was no reason in his brain for a clear conception of so abstract a thing as justice, nevertheless, in his own way, he felt the justice of the man-animals, and he knew them for what they were – makers of law and executors of law. Also, he appreciated the power with which they administered the law. Unlike any animals he had ever encountered, they did not bite nor claw. They enforced their live strength with the power of dead things. Dead things did their bidding. Thus, sticks and stones, directed by these strange creatures, leaped through the air like living things, inflicting grievous hurts upon the dogs.

To his mind this was power unusual, power inconceivable and beyond the natural, power that was god-like. White Fang, in the very nature of him, could never know anything about gods – at the best he could know only things that were beyond knowing; but the wonder and awe that he had of these man-animals in ways resembled what would be the wonder and awe of man at sight of some celestial creature, on a mountain top, hurling thunderbolts from either hand at an astonished world.

The last dog had been driven back; the hubbub died down; and White Fang licked his hurts and meditated upon this his first taste of pack-cruelty and his introduction to the pack. He had never dreamed that his own kind consisted of more than One Eye, his mother, and himself. They had constituted a kind apart; and here, abruptly, he had discovered many more creatures apparently of his own kind. And there was a subconscious resentment that these, his kind, at first sight had pitched upon him and tried to destroy him. In the same way he resented his mother being tied with a stick, even though it was done by the superior man-animals. It savoured of the trap, of bondage. Yet of the trap and of bondage he knew nothing. Freedom to roam and run and lie down at will had been his heritage, and here it was being infringed upon. His mother's movements were restricted to the length of a stick, and by the length of that same stick was he restricted, for he had not yet got beyond the need of his mother's side.

He did not like it. Nor did he like it when the man-animals arose and went on with their march, for a tiny man-animal took the other end of the stick and led Kiche captive behind him, and behind Kiche followed White Fang, greatly perturbed and worried by this new adventure he had entered upon.

They went down the valley of the stream, far beyond White Fang's widest ranging, until they came to the end of the valley, where the stream ran into the Mackenzie River. Here, where canoes were cached on poles high in the air and where stood fish-racks for the drying of fish, camp was made; and White Fang looked on with wondering eyes. The superiority of these man-animals increased with every moment. There was their mastery over all these sharp-fanged dogs. It breathed of power. But greater than that, to the wolf-cub, was their mastery over things not alive; their capacity to communicate motion to unmoving things; their capacity to change the very face of the world.

It was this last that especially affected him. The elevation of frames of poles caught his eye; yet this in itself was not so remarkable, being done by the same creatures that flung sticks and stones to great distances. But when the frames of poles were made into tepees by being covered with cloth and skins, White Fang was astounded. It was the colossal bulk of them that impressed him. They arose around him, on every side, like some monstrous quick-growing form of life. They occupied nearly the whole circumference of his field of vision. He was afraid of them. They loomed ominously above him; and when the breeze stirred them into huge movements, he cowered down in fear, keeping his eyes warily upon them, and prepared to spring away if they attempted to precipitate themselves upon him.

But in a short while his fear of the tepees passed away. He saw the women and children passing in and out of them without harm, and he saw the dogs trying often to get into them, and being driven away with sharp words and flying stones. After a time, he left Kiche's side and crawled cautiously toward the wall of the nearest tepee. It was the curiosity of growth that urged him on – the necessity of learning and living and doing that brings experience. The last few inches to the wall of the tepee were crawled with painful slowness and precaution. The day's events had prepared him for the unknown to manifest itself in most stupendous and unthinkable ways. At last his nose touched the canvas. He waited; nothing happened. Then he smelled the strange fabric, saturated with the man-smell. He closed on the canvas with his teeth and gave a gentle tug. Nothing happened, though the adjacent portions of the tepee moved. He tugged harder. There was a greater movement. It was delightful. He tugged still harder, and repeatedly, until the whole tepee was in motion. Then the sharp cry of a squaw inside sent him scampering back to Kiche. But after that he was afraid no more of the looming bulks of the tepees.

A moment later he was straying away again from his mother. Her stick was tied to a peg in the ground, and she could not follow him. A part-grown puppy, somewhat larger and older than he, came toward him slowly, with ostentatious and belligerent importance. The puppy's name, as White Fang was afterward to hear him called, was Lip-lip. He had had experience in puppy fights, and was already something of a bully.

Lip-lip was White Fang's own kind, and, being only a puppy, did not seem dangerous; so White Fang prepared to meet him in friendly spirit. But when the stranger's walk became stiff-legged and his lips lifted clear of his teeth, White Fang stiffened too, and answered with lifted lips. They half circled about each other, tentatively, snarling and bristling. This lasted several minutes, and White Fang was beginning to enjoy it, as a sort of game. But suddenly, with remarkable swiftness, Lip-lip leaped in, delivered a slashing snap, and leaped away again. The snap had taken effect on the shoulder that had been hurt by the lynx and that was still sore deep down near the bone. The surprise and hurt of it brought a yelp out of White Fang; but the next moment, in a rush of anger, he was upon Lip-lip and snapping viciously.

But Lip-lip had lived his life in camp and had fought many puppy fights. Three times, four times, and half a dozen times, his sharp little teeth scored on the new-comer, until White Fang, yelping shamelessly, fled to the protection of his mother. It was the first of the many fights he was to have with Lip-lip, for they were enemies from the start, born so, with natures destined perpetu-ally to clash.

Kiche licked White Fang soothingly with her tongue, and tried to prevail upon him to remain with her. But his curiosity was rampant, and several minutes later he was venturing forth on a new quest. He came upon one of the man-animals, Grey Beaver, who was squatting on his hams and doing something with sticks and dry moss spread before him on the ground. White Fang came near to him and watched. Grey Beaver made mouth-noises which White Fang interpreted as not hostile, so he came still nearer.

Women and children were carrying more sticks and branches to Grey Beaver. It was evidently an affair of moment. White Fang came in until he touched Grey Beaver's knee, so curious was he, and already forgetful that this was a terrible man-animal. Suddenly he saw a strange thing like mist beginning to arise from the sticks and moss beneath Grey Beaver's hands. Then, amongst the sticks themselves, appeared a live thing, twisting and turning, of a colour like the colour of the sun in the sky. White Fang knew nothing about fire. It drew him as the light in the mouth of the cave had drawn him in his early puppyhood. He crawled the several steps to-ward the flame. He heard Grey Beaver chuckle above him, and he knew the sound was not hostile. Then his nose touched the flame, and at the same instant his little tongue went out to it.

For a moment he was paralysed. The unknown, lurking in the midst of the sticks and moss, was savagely clutching him by the nose. He scrambled backward, bursting out in an astonished explosion of ki-yi's. At the sound, Kiche leaped, snarling, to the end of her stick, and there raged terribly because she could not come to his aid. But Grey Beaver laughed loudly, and slapped his thighs, and told the happening to all the rest of the camp, till everybody was laughing uproariously. But White Fang sat on his haunches and ki-yi'd and ki-yi'd, a forlorn and pitiable little figure in the midst of the man-animals.

It was the worst hurt he had ever known. Both nose and tongue had been scorched by the live thing, sun-coloured, that had grown up under Grey Beaver's hands. He cried and cried interminably, and every fresh wail was greeted by bursts of laughter on the part of the man-animals. He tried to soothe his nose with his tongue, but the tongue was burnt too, and the two hurts coming together produced greater hurt; whereupon he cried more hopelessly and helplessly than ever.

And then shame came to him. He knew laughter and the meaning of it. It is not given us to know how some animals know laughter, and know when they are being laughed at; but it was this same way that White Fang knew it. And he felt shame that the man-animals should be laughing at him. He turned and fled away, not from the hurt of the fire, but from the laughter that sank even deeper, and hurt in the spirit of him. And he fled to

Kiche, raging at the end of her stick like an animal gone mad – to Kiche, the one creature in the world who was not laughing at him.

Twilight drew down and night came on, and White Fang lay by his mother's side. His nose and tongue still hurt, but he was perplexed by a greater trouble. He was homesick. He felt a vacancy in him, a need for the hush and quietude of the stream and the cave in the cliff. Life had become too populous. There were so many of the man-animals – men, women, and children – all making noises and irritations. And there were the dogs, ever squabbling and bickering, bursting into uproars and creating confusions. The restful loneliness of the only life he had known was gone. Here the very air was palpitant with life. It hummed and buzzed unceasingly. Continually changing its intensity, and abruptly variant in pitch, it impinged on his nerves and senses, made him nervous and restless, and worried him with a perpetual imminence of happening.

He watched the man-animals coming and going and moving about the camp. In fashion distantly resembling the way men look upon the gods they create, so looked White Fang upon the man-animals before him. They were superior creatures, of a verity gods. To his dim comprehension they were as much wonder-workers as gods are to men. They were creatures of mastery, possessing all manner of unknown and impossible potencies; overlords of the alive and the not alive, making obey that which moved, imparting movement to that which did not move, and making life, sun-coloured and biting life, to grow out of dead moss and wood. They were fire-makers! They were gods!

CHAPTER

2

THE BONDAGE

The days were thronged with experience for White Fang. During the time that Kiche was tied by the stick, he ran about over all the camp, inquiring, investigating, learning. He quickly came to know much of the ways of the man-animals, but familiarity did not breed contempt. The more he came to know them, the more they vindicated their superiority, the more they displayed their mysterious powers, the greater loomed their godlikeness.

To man has been given the grief, often, of seeing his gods overthrown and his altars crumbling; but to the wolf and the wild dog that have come in to crouch at man's feet this grief has never come. Unlike man, whose gods are of the unseen and the overguessed, vapours and mists of fancy eluding the garmenture of reality, wandering wraiths of desired goodness and power, intangible out-croppings of self into the realm of spirit – unlike man, the wolf and the wild dog that have come in to the fire find their gods in the living flesh, solid to the touch, occupying earth-space and requiring time for the accomplishment of their ends and their existence. No effort of faith is necessary to believe in such a god; no effort of will can possibly induce disbelief in such a god. There is no getting away from it. There it stands, on its two hind-legs, club in hand, immensely potential, passionate and wrathful and loving, god and mystery and power all wrapped up and around by flesh that bleeds when it is torn and that is good to eat like any flesh.

And so it was with White Fang. The man-animals were gods unmistakable and unescapable. As his mother, Kiche, had rendered her allegiance to them at the first cry of her name, so he was beginning to render his allegiance. He gave them the trail as a privilege indubitably theirs. When they walked he got out of their way. When they called he came. When they threatened he cowered down. When they commanded him to go he went away hurriedly. For behind any wish of theirs was power to enforce that wish, power that hurt, power that expressed itself in clouts and clubs, in flying stones and stinging lashes of whips.

He belonged to them as all dogs belonged to them. His actions were theirs to command. His body was theirs to maul, to stamp upon, to tolerate. Such was the lesson that was quickly borne in upon him. It came hard, going as it did counter to much that was strong and dominant in his own nature; and while he disliked it in the learning of it, unknown to himself he was learning to like it. It was a placing of his destiny in another's hands, a shifting of the responsibilities of existence. This in itself was compensation, for it is always easier to lean upon another than to stand alone.

But it did not all happen in a day, this giving over of himself, body and soul, to the man-animals. He could not immediately forego his wild heritage and his memories of the Wild. There were days when he crept to the edge of the forest and stood and listened to something calling him far away. And always he returned, restless and uncomfortable, to whimper softly and wistfully at Kiche's side, and to lick her face with eager, questioning tongue.

White Fang learned rapidly the ways of the camp. He knew the injustice and greediness of the older dogs when meat or fish was thrown out to be eaten. He came to know that men were more just, children more cruel, and women more kindly and more likely to toss him a bit of meat or bone. And after two or three painful adventures with the mothers of part-grown puppies, he came into the knowledge that it was always good policy to let such mothers alone, to keep away from them as far as possible, and to avoid them when he saw them coming.

But the bane of his life was Lip-lip. Larger, older, and stronger, Lip-lip had selected White Fang for his special object of persecution. White Fang fought willingly enough, but he was outclassed. His enemy was too big. Lip-lip became a nightmare to him. Whenever he ventured away from his mother, the bully was sure to appear, trailing at his heels, snarling at him, picking upon him, and watchful of an opportunity, when no man-animal was near, to spring upon him and force a fight. As Lip-lip invariably won, he enjoyed it hugely. It became his chief delight in life, as it became White Fang's chief torment.

But the effect upon White Fang was not to cow him. Though he suffered most of the damage and was always defeated, his spirit remained unsubdued. Yet a bad effect was produced. He became malignant and morose. His temper had been savage by birth, but it became more savage under this unending persecution. The genial, playful, puppyish side of him found little expression. He never played and gambolled about with the other puppies of the camp. Lip-lip would not permit it. The moment White Fang appeared near them, Lip-lip was upon him, bullying and hectoring him, or fighting with him until he had driven him away.

The effect of all this was to rob White Fang of much of his puppyhood, and to make him in his comportment older than his age. Denied the outlet, through play, of his energies, he recoiled upon himself and developed his mental processes. He became cunning; he had idle time in which to devote himself to thoughts of trickery. Prevented from obtaining his share of meat and fish when a general feed was given to the camp-dogs, he became a clever thief. He had to forage for himself, and he foraged well, though he was ofttimes a plague to the squaws in consequence. He learned to sneak about camp, to be crafty, to know what was going on everywhere, to see and to hear everything and to reason accordingly, and successfully to devise ways and means of avoiding his implacable persecutor.

It was early in the days of his persecution that he played his first really big crafty game, and got therefrom his first taste of revenge. As Kiche, when with the wolves, had lured out to destruction dogs from the camps of men, so White Fang, in manner somewhat similar, lured Lip-lip into Kiche's avenging jaws. Retreating before Lip-lip, White Fang made an indirect flight that led in and out and around the various tepees of the camp. He was a good runner, swifter than any puppy of his size, and swifter than Lip-lip. But he did not run his best in this chase. He barely held his own – one leap ahead of his pursuer.

Lip-lip, excited by the chase and by the persistent nearness of his victim, forgot caution and locality. When he remembered locality it was too late. Dashing at top speed around a tepee, he ran full tilt into Kiche lying at the end of her stick. He gave one yelp of consternation, and then her punishing jaws closed upon him. She was tied, but he could not get away from her easily. She rolled him off his legs so that he could not run, while she repeatedly ripped and slashed him with her fangs.

When at last he succeeded in rolling clear of her, he crawled to his feet, badly dishevelled, hurt both in body and in spirit. His hair was standing out all over him in tufts where her teeth had mauled. He stood where he had arisen, opened his mouth, and broke out the long, heart-broken puppy wail. But even this he was not allowed to complete. In the middle of it, White Fang, rushing in, sank his teeth into Lip-lip's hind-leg. There was no fight left in Lip-lip, and he ran away shamelessly, his victim hot on his heels and worrying him all the way back to his own tepee. Here the squaws came to his aid, and White Fang, transformed into a raging demon, was finally driven off only by a fusillade of stones.

Came the day when Grey Beaver, deciding that the liability of her running away was past, released Kiche. White Fang was delighted with his mother's freedom. He accompanied her joyfully about the camp; and, so long as he remained close by her side, Lip-lip kept a respectful distance. White Fang even bristled up to him and walked stiff-legged, but Lip-lip ignored the challenge. He was no fool himself, and whatever vengeance he desired to wreak, he could wait until he caught White Fang alone.

Later on that day, Kiche and White Fang strayed into

the edge of the woods next to the camp. He had led his mother there, step by step; and now, when she stopped, he tried to inveigle her farther. The stream, the lair, and the quiet woods were calling to him, and he wanted her to come. He ran on a few steps, stopped, and looked back. She had not moved. He whined pleadingly, and scurried playfully in and out of the underbrush. He ran back to her, licked her face, and ran on again. And still she did not move. He stopped and regarded her, all of an intentness and eagerness, physically expressed, that slowly faded out of him as she turned her head and gazed back at the camp.

There was something calling to him out there in the open. His mother heard it too. But she heard also that other and louder call – the call of the fire and of man – the call which has been given alone of all animals to the wolf to answer – to the wolf and the wild dog, who are brothers.

Kiche turned and slowly trotted back toward camp. Stronger than the physical restraint of the stick was the clutch of the camp upon her. Unseen and occultly, the gods still gripped with their power and would not let her go. White Fang sat down in the shadow of a birch and whimpered softly. There was a strong smell of pine, and subtle wood fragrances filled the air, reminding him of his old life of freedom before the days of his bondage. But he was still only a part-grown puppy, and stronger than the call either of man or of the Wild was the call of his mother. All the hours of his short life he had depended upon her. The time was yet to come for independence. So he arose and trotted forlornly back to camp, pausing once or twice to sit down and whimper and to listen to the call that still sounded in the depths of the forest.

In the Wild the time of a mother with her young is short, but under the dominion of man it is sometimes even shorter. Thus it was with White Fang. Grey Beaver was in the debt of Three Eagles. Three Eagles was going away on a trip up the Mackenzie to the Great Slave Lake. A strip of scarlet cloth, a bearskin, twenty cartridges, and Kiche went to pay the debt. White Fang saw his mother taken aboard Three Eagles's canoe, and tried to follow her. A blow from Three Eagles knocked him backward to the land. The canoe shoved off. He sprang into the water and swam after it, deaf to the sharp cries of Grey Beaver to return. Even a man-animal, a god, White Fang ignored – such was the terror he was in of losing his mother.

But gods are accustomed to being obeyed, and Grey Beaver wrathfully launched a canoe in pursuit. When he overtook White Fang, he reached down, and by the nape of the neck lifted him clear of the water. He did not deposit him at once in the bottom of the canoe. Holding him suspended with one hand, with the other hand he proceeded to give him a beating. And it *was* a beating. His hand was heavy. Every blow was shrewd to hurt, and he delivered a multitude of blows.

Impelled by the blows that rained upon him, now from this side, now from that, White Fang swung back and forth like an erratic and jerky pendulum. Varying were the emotions that surged through him. At first he had known surprise. Then came a momentary fear, when he yelped several times to the impact of the hand. But this was quickly followed by anger. His free nature asserted itself, and he showed his teeth and snarled fearlessly in the face of the wrathful god. This but served to make the god more wrathful. The blows came faster, heavier, more shrewd to hurt.

Grey Beaver continued to beat, White Fang continued to snarl. But this could not last for ever. One or the other must give over, and that one was White Fang. Fear surged through him again. For the first time he was being really man-handled. The occasional blows of sticks and stones he had previously experienced were as caresses compared with this. He broke down and began to cry and yelp. For a time each blow brought a yelp from him; but fear passed into terror, until finally his yelps were voiced in unbroken succession, unconnected with the rhythm of the punishment.

At last Grey Beaver withheld his hand. White Fang, hanging limply, continued to cry. This seemed to satisfy his master, who flung him down roughly in the bottom of the canoe. In the meantime the canoe had drifted down the stream. Grey Beaver picked up the paddle. White Fang was in his way. He spurned him savagely with his foot. In that moment White Fang's free nature flashed forth again, and he sank his teeth into the mocca-sined foot.

The beating that had gone before was as nothing compared with the beating he now received. Grey Beaver's wrath was terrible; likewise was White Fang's fright. Not only the hand, but the hard wooden paddle was used upon him; and he was bruised and sore in all his small body when he was again flung down in the canoe. Again, and this time with purpose, did Grey Beaver kick him. White Fang did not repeat his attack on the foot. He had learned another lesson of his bondage. Never, no matter what the circumstance, must he dare to bite the god who was lord and master over him; the body of the lord and master was sacred, not to be defiled by the teeth of such as he. That was evidently the crime of crimes, the one offence there was no condoning nor overlooking.

When the canoe touched the shore, White Fang lay whimpering and motionless, waiting the will of Grey Beaver. It was Grey Beaver's will that he should go ashore, for ashore he was flung, striking heavily on his side and hurting his bruises afresh. He crawled tremblingly to his feet and stood whimpering. Lip-lip, who had watched the whole proceeding from the bank, now rushed upon him, knocking him over and sinking his teeth into him. White Fang was too helpless to defend himself, and it would have gone hard with him had not Grey Beaver's foot shot out, lifting Lip-lip into the air with its violence, so that he smashed down to earth a dozen feet away. This was the man-animal's justice; and even then, in his own pitiable plight, White Fang experienced a little grateful thrill. At Grey Beaver's heels he limped obediently through the village to the tepee. And so it came that White Fang learned that the right to punish was something the gods reserved for themselves and denied to the lesser creatures under them.

That night, when all was still, White Fang remembered his mother and sorrowed for her. He sorrowed too loudly, and woke up Grey Beaver, who beat him. After that he mourned gently when the gods were around. But sometimes, straying off to the edge of the woods by himself, he gave vent to his grief, and cried it out with loud whimperings and wailings.

It was during this period that he might have hearkened to the memories of the lair and the stream and run back to the Wild. But the memory of his mother held him. As the hunting man-animals went out and came back, so she would come back to the village some time. So he remained in his bondage waiting for her.

But it was not altogether an unhappy bondage. There was much to interest him. Something was always happening. There was no end to the strange things these gods did, and he was always curious to see. Besides, he was learning how to get along with Grey Beaver. Obedience, rigid, undeviating obedience, was what was exacted of him; and in return he escaped beatings, and his existence was tolerated.

Nay, Grey Beaver himself sometimes tossed him a piece of meat, and defended him against the other dogs in the eating of it. And such a piece of meat was of value. It was worth more, in some strange way, than a dozen pieces of meat from the hand of a squaw. Grey Beaver never petted nor caressed. Perhaps it was the weight of his hand, perhaps his justice, perhaps the sheer power of him, and perhaps it was all these things that influenced White Fang; for a certain tie of attachment was forming between him and his surly lord.

Insidiously, and by remote ways, as well as by the power of stick and stone and clout of hand, were the shackles of White Fang's bondage being riveted upon him. The qualities in his kind that in the beginning made it possible for them to come in to the fires of men were qualities capable of development. They were developing in him, and the camp-life, replete with misery as it was, was secretly endearing itself to him all the time. But White Fang was unaware of it. He knew only grief for the loss of Kiche, hope for her return, and a hungry yearning for the free life that had been his.

CHAPTER

3

THE OUTCAST

Lip-lip continued so to darken his days that White Fang became wickeder and more ferocious than it was his natural right to be. Savageness was a part of his make-up, but the savageness thus developed exceeded his make-up. He acquired a reputation for wickedness amongst the man-animals themselves. Wherever there was trouble and uproar in camp, fighting and squabbling, or the outcry of a squaw over a bit of stolen meat, they were sure to find White Fang mixed up in it and usually at the bottom of it. They did not bother to look after the causes of his conduct. They saw only the effects, and the effects were bad. He was a sneak and a thief, a mischief-maker, a fomenter of trouble; and irate squaws told him to his face, the while he eyed them alert and ready to dodge any quick-flung missile, that he was a wolf and worthless and bound to come to an evil end.

He found himself an outcast in the midst of the populous camp. All the young dogs followed Lip-lip's lead. There was a difference between White Fang and them. Perhaps they sensed his wild-wood breed, and instinctively felt for him the enmity that the domestic dog feels for the wolf. But be that as it may, they joined with

Lip-lip in the persecution. And, once declared against him, they found good reason to continue declared against him. One and all, from time to time, they felt his teeth; and to his credit, he gave more than he received. Many of them he could whip in single fight; but single fight was denied him. The beginning of such a fight was a signal for all the young dogs in camp to come running and pitch upon him.

Out of this pack-persecution he learned two important things: how to take care of himself in a mass-fight against him; and how, on a single dog, to inflict the greatest amount of damage in the briefest space of time. To keep one's feet in the midst of the hostile mass meant life, and this he learnt well. He became cat-like in his ability to stay on his feet. Even grown dogs might hurtle him backward or sideways with the impact of their heavy bodies; and backward or sideways he would go, in the air or sliding on the ground, but always with his legs under him and his feet downward to the mother earth.

When dogs fight there are usually preliminaries to the actual combat – snarlings and bristlings and stiff-legged struttings. But White Fang learned to omit these preliminaries. Delay meant the coming against him of all the young dogs. He must do his work quickly and get away. So he learnt to give no warning of his intention. He rushed in and snapped and slashed on the instant, without notice, before his foe could prepare to meet him. Thus he learned how to inflict quick and severe damage. Also he learned the value of surprise. A dog taken off its guard, its shoulder slashed open or its ear ripped in ribbons before it knew what was happening, was a dog half whipped.

Furthermore, it was remarkably easy to overthrow a

dog taken by surprise; while a dog thus overthrown invariably exposed for a moment the soft underside of its neck – the vulnerable point at which to strike for its life. White Fang knew this point. It was a knowledge bequeathed to him directly from the hunting generation of wolves. So it was that White Fang's method when he took the offensive was: first, to find a young dog alone; second, to surprise it and knock it off its feet; and third, to drive in with his teeth at the soft throat.

Being but partly grown, his jaws had not yet become large enough nor strong enough to make his throat-attack deadly; but many a young dog went around camp with a lacerated throat in token of White Fang's intention. And one day, catching one of his enemies alone on the edge of the woods, he managed, by repeatedly overthrowing him and attacking the throat, to cut the great vein and let out the life. There was a great row that night. He had been observed, the news had been carried to the dead dog's master, the squaws remembered all the instances of stolen meat, and Grey Beaver was beset by many angry voices. But he resolutely held the door of his tepee, inside which he had placed the culprit, and refused to permit the vengeance for which his tribes-people clamoured.

White Fang became hated by man and dog. During this period of his development he never knew a moment's security. The tooth of every dog was against him, the hand of every man. He was greeted with snarls by his kind, with curses and stones by his gods. He lived tensely. He was always keyed up, alert for attack, wary of being attacked, with an eye for sudden and unexpected missiles, prepared to act precipitately and coolly, to leap in with a flash of teeth, or to leap away with a menacing snarl.

As for snarling, he could snarl more terribly than any dog, young or old, in camp. The intent of the snarl is to warn or frighten, and judgment is required to know when it should be used. White Fang knew how to make it and when to make it. Into his snarl he incorporated all that was vicious, malignant, and horrible. With nose serrulated by continuous spasms, hair bristling in recurrent waves, tongue whipping out like a red snake and whipping back again, ears flattened down, eyes gleaming hatred, lips wrinkled back, and fangs exposed and dripping, he could compel a pause on the part of almost any assailant. A temporary pause, when taken off his guard, gave him the vital moment in which to think and determine his action. But often a pause so gained lengthened out until it evolved into a complete cessation from the attack. And before more than one of the grown dogs White Fang's snarl enabled him to beat an honourable retreat.

An outcast himself from the pack of the part-grown dogs, his sanguinary methods and remarkable efficiency made the pack pay for its persecution of him. Not permitted himself to run with the pack, the curious state of affairs obtained that no member of the pack could run outside the pack. White Fang would not permit it. What of his bushwhacking and waylaying tactics, the young dogs were afraid to run by themselves. With the exception of Lip-lip, they were compelled to hunch together for mutual protection against the terrible enemy they had made. A puppy alone by the river bank meant a puppy dead or a puppy that aroused the camp with its shrill pain and terror as it fled back from the wolf-cub that had waylaid it.

But White Fang's reprisals did not cease, even when

the young dogs had learned thoroughly that they must stay together. He attacked them when he caught them alone, and they attacked him when they were bunched. The sight of him was sufficient to start them rushing after him, at which times his swiftness usually carried him into safety. But woe the dog that outran his fellows in such pursuit! White Fang had learned to turn suddenly upon the pursuer that was ahead of the pack and thoroughly to rip him up before the pack could arrive. This occurred with great frequency, for, once in full cry, the dogs were prone to forget themselves in the excitement of the chase, while White Fang never forgot himself. Stealing backward glances as he ran, he was always ready to whirl around and down the over-zealous pursuer that outran his fellows.

Young dogs are bound to play, and out of the exigencies of the situation they realized their play in this mimic warfare. Thus it was that the hunt of White Fang became their chief game – a deadly game, withal, and at all times a serious game. He, on the other hand, being the fastest-footed, was unafraid to venture anywhere. During the period that he waited vainly for his mother to come back, he led the pack many a wild chase through the adjacent woods. But the pack invariably lost him. Its noise and outcry warned him of its presence; while he ran alone, velvet-footed, silently, a moving shadow among the trees, after the manner of his father and mother before him. Further, he was more directly connected with the Wild than they; and he knew more of its secrets and stratagems. A favourite trick of his was to lose his trail in running water, and then lie quietly in a nearby thicket while their baffled cries arose around him.

Hated by his kind and by manhood, indomitable, perpetually warred upon and himself waging perpetual war, his development was rapid and one-sided. This was no soil for kindliness and affection to blossom in. Of such things he had not the faintest glimmering. The code he learned was to obey the strong and to oppress the weak. Grey Beaver was a god, and strong. Therefore White Fang obeyed him. But the dog younger or smaller than himself was weak – a thing to be destroyed. His development was in the direction of power. In order to face the constant danger of hurt and even of destruction, his predatory and protective faculties were unduly developed. He became quicker of movement than the other dogs, swifter of foot, craftier, deadlier, more lithe, more lean with ironlike muscle and sinew, more enduring, more cruel, more ferocious, and more intelligent. He had to become all these things, else he would not have held his own nor survived the hostile environment in which he found himself.

CHAPTER

4

THE TRAIL OF THE GODS

In the fall of the year, when the days were shortening and the bite of the frost was coming into the air, White Fang got his chance for liberty. For several days there had been a great hubbub in the village. The summer camp was being dismantled, and the tribe, bag and baggage, was preparing to go off to the fall hunting. White Fang watched it all with eager eyes, and when the tepees began to come down and the canoes were loading at the bank, he understood. Already the canoes were departing, and some had disappeared down the river.

Quite deliberately he determined to stay behind. He waited his opportunity to slink out of camp to the woods. Here, in the running stream where ice was beginning to form, he hid his trail. Then he crawled into the heart of a dense thicket and waited. The time passed by, and he slept intermittently for hours. Then he was aroused by Grey Beaver's voice calling him by name. There were other voices. White Fang could hear Grey Beaver's squaw taking part in the search, and Mit-sah, who was Grey Beaver's son.

White Fang trembled with fear, and though the impulse came to crawl out of his hiding-place, he resisted it. After a time the voices died away, and some time after that he crept out to enjoy the success of his undertaking. Darkness was coming on, and for a while he played about among the trees, pleasuring in his freedom. Then, and quite suddenly, he became aware of loneliness. He sat down to consider, listening to the silence of the forest and perturbed by it. That nothing moved nor sounded seemed ominous. He felt the lurking of danger, unseen and unguessed. He was suspicious of the looming bulks of the trees and of the dark shadows that might conceal all manner of perilous things.

Then it was cold. Here was no warm side of a tepee against which to snuggle. The frost was in his feet, and he kept lifting first one forefoot and then the other. He curved his bushy tail around to cover them, and at the same time he saw a vision. There was nothing strange about it. Upon his inward sight was impressed a succession of memory-pictures. He saw the camp again, the tepees, and the blaze of the fires. He heard the shrill voices of the women, the gruff basses of the men, and the snarling of the dogs. He was hungry, and he remembered pieces of meat and fish that had been thrown him. Here was no meat – nothing but a threatening and inedible silence.

His bondage had softened him. Irresponsibility had weakened him. He had forgotten how to shift for himself. The night yawned about him. His senses, accustomed to the hum and bustle of the camp, used to the continuous impact of sights and sounds, were now left idle. There was nothing to do, nothing to see nor hear. They strained to catch some interruption of the silence and immobility of nature. They were appalled by inaction and by the feel of something terrible impending.

He gave a great start of fright. A colossal and formless something was rushing across the field of his vision. It was a tree-shadow flung by the moon, from whose face the clouds had been brushed away. Reassured, he whimpered softly; then he suppressed the whimper for fear that it might attract the attention of the lurking dangers.

A tree, contracting in the cool of the night, made a loud noise. It was directly above him. He yelped in his fright. A panic seized him, and he ran madly toward the village. He knew an overpowering desire for the protection and companionship of man. In his nostrils was the smell of the camp-smoke. In his ears the camp sounds and cries were ringing loud. He passed out of the forest and into the moonlit open where were no shadows nor darknesses. But no village greeted his eyes. He had forgotten. The village had gone away.

His wild flight ceased abruptly. There was no place to which to flee. He slunk forlornly through the deserted camp, smelling the rubbish-heaps and the discarded rags and tags of the gods. He would have been glad for the rattle of stones about him, flung by an angry squaw; glad for the hand of Grey Beaver descending upon him in wrath; while he would have welcomed with delight Lip-lip and the whole snarling, cowardly pack.

He came to where Grey Beaver's tepee had stood. In the centre of the space it had occupied he sat down. He pointed his nose at the moon. His throat was afflicted by rigid spasms, his mouth opened, and in a heart-broken cry bubbled up his loneliness and fear, his grief for Kiche, all his past sorrows and miseries as well as his apprehension of sufferings and dangers to come. It was the long wolf-howl, full-throated and mournful – the first howl he had ever uttered.

The coming of daylight dispelled his fears, but increased his loneliness. The naked earth, which so shortly before had been so populous, thrust his loneliness more forcibly upon him. It did not take him long to make up his mind. He plunged into the forest and followed the river bank down the stream. All day he ran. He did not rest. He seemed made to run on for ever. His iron-like body ignored fatigue. And even after fatigue came, his heritage of endurance braced him to endless endeavour, and enabled him to drive his complaining body onward.

Where the river swung in against precipitous bluffs, he climbed the high mountains behind. Rivers and streams that entered the main river he forded or swam. Often he took to the rim-ice that was beginning to form, and more than once he crashed through and struggled for life in the icy current. Always he was on the look-out for the trail of the gods, where it might leave the river and proceed inland.

White Fang was intelligent beyond the average of his kind; yet his mental vision was not wide enough to embrace the other bank of the Mackenzie. What if the trail of the gods led out on that side? It never entered his head. Later on, when he had travelled more and grown older and wiser and come to know more of trails and rivers, it might be that he could grasp and apprehend such a possibility. But that mental power was yet in the future. Just now he ran blindly, his own bank of the Mackenzie alone entering into his calculations.

All night he ran, blundering in the darkness into mishaps and obstacles that delayed but did not daunt. By the middle of the second day he had been running continuously for thirty hours, and the iron of his flesh was giving out. It was the endurance of his mind that kept him going. He had not eaten in forty hours, and he was weak with hunger. The repeated drenchings in the icy water had likewise had their effect on him. His handsome coat was draggled. The broad pads of his feet were bruised and bleeding. He had begun to limp, and this limp increased with the hours. To make it worse, the light of the sky was obscured, and snow began to fall – a raw, moist, melting, clinging snow, slippery under foot, that hid from him the landscape he traversed, and that covered over the inequalities of the ground, so that the way of his feet was more difficult and painful.

Grey Beaver had intended camping that night on the far bank of the Mackenzie, for it was in that direction that the hunting lay. But on the near bank, shortly before dark, a moose coming down to drink had been espied by Kloo-kooch, who was Grey Beaver's squaw. Now, had not the moose come down to drink, had not Mit-sah been steering out of the course because of the snow, had not Kloo-kooch sighted the moose, and had not Grey Beaver killed it with a lucky shot from his rifle, all subsequent things would have happened differently. Grey Beaver would not have camped on the near side of the Mackenzie, and White Fang would have passed by and gone on, either to die or to find his way to his wild brothers and become one of them – a wolf to the end of his days.

Night had fallen. The snow was flying more thickly, and White Fang, whimpering softly to himself as he stumbled and limped along, came upon a fresh trail in the snow. So fresh was it that he knew it immediately for what it was.

Whining with eagerness, he followed back from the river bank and in among the trees. The camp sounds came to his ears. He saw the blaze of the fire, Kloo-kooch cooking, and Grey Beaver squatting on his hams and mumbling a chunk of raw tallow. There was fresh meat in camp!

White Fang expected a beating. He crouched and bristled a little at the thought of it. Then he went forward again. He feared and disliked the beating he knew to be waiting for him. But he knew, further, that the comfort of the fire would be his, the protection of the gods, the companionship of the dogs – the last, a companionship of enmity, but none the less a companionship and satisfying to his gregarious needs.

He came cringing and crawling into the firelight. Grey Beaver saw him, and stopped munching the tallow. White Fang crawled slowly, cringing and grovelling in the abjectness of his abasement and submission. He crawled straight toward Grey Beaver, every inch of his progress becoming slower and more painful. At last he lay at the master's feet, into whose possession he now surrendered himself, voluntarily, body and soul. Of his own choice, he came in to sit by man's fire and to be ruled by him. White Fang trembled, waiting for the punishment to fall upon him. There was a movement of the hand above him. He cringed involuntarily under the expected blow. It did not fall. He stole a glance upward. Grey Beaver was breaking the lump of tallow in half. Grey Beaver was offering him one piece of the tallow! Very gently and somewhat suspiciously he first smelled the tallow and then proceeded to eat it. Grey Beaver ordered meat to be brought to him, and guarded him from the other dogs while he ate. After that, grateful and content, White Fang lay at Grey Beaver's feet, gazing at the fire that warmed him, blinking and dozing, secure in the knowledge that the morrow would find him, not wandering forlorn through bleak forest-stretches, but in the camp of the man-animals, with the gods to whom he had given himself and upon whom he was now dependent.

CHAPTER

5

THE COVENANT

When December was well along, Grey Beaver went on a journey up the Mackenzie. Mit-sah and Kloo-kooch went with him. One sled he drove himself, drawn by dogs he had traded for or borrowed. A second and smaller sled was driven by Mit-sah, and to this was harnessed a team of puppies. It was more of a toy affair than anything else, yet it was the delight of Mit-sah, who felt that he was beginning to do a man's work in the world. Also, he was learning to drive dogs and to train dogs; while the puppies themselves were being broken in to the harness. Furthermore, the sled was of some service, for it carried nearly two hundred pounds of outfit and food.

White Fang had seen the camp-dogs toiling in the harness, so that he did not resent overmuch the first placing of the harness upon himself. About his neck was put a moss-stuffed collar, which was connected by two pulling-traces to a strap that passed around his chest and over his back. It was to this that was fastened the long rope by which he pulled at the sled.

There were seven puppies in the team. The others had been born earlier in the year, and were nine and ten months old, while White Fang was only eight months old. Each dog was fastened to the sled by a single rope. No two ropes were of the same length, while the difference in length between any two ropes was at least that of a dog's body. Every rope was brought to a ring at the front end of the sled. The sled itself was without runners, being a birch-bark toboggan, with upturned forward end to keep it from ploughing under the snow. This construction enabled the weight of the sled and load to be distributed over the largest snow-surface; for the snow was crystal-powder and very soft. Observing the same principle of widest distribution of weight, the dogs at the ends of their ropes radiated fan-fashion from the nose of the sled, so that no dog trod in another's footsteps.

There was, furthermore, another virtue in the fan formation. The ropes of varying length prevented the dogs attacking from the rear those that ran in front of them. For a dog to attack another, it would have to turn upon one at a shorter rope. In which case it would find itself face to face with the dog attacked, and also it would find itself facing the whip of the driver. But the most peculiar virtue of all lay in the fact that the dog that strove to attack one in front of him must pull the sled faster, and that the faster the sled travelled, the faster could the dog attacked run away. Thus, the dog behind could never catch up with the one in front. The faster he ran, the faster ran the one he was after, and the faster ran all the dogs. Incidentally, the sled went faster; and thus, by cunning indirection, did man increase his mastery over the beasts.

Mit-sah resembled his father, much of whose grey wisdom he possessed. In the past he had observed

Lip-lip's persecution of White Fang; but at that time Lip-lip was another man's dog, and Mit-sah had never dared more than to shy an occasional stone at him. But now Lip-lip was his dog, and he proceeded to wreak his vengeance on him by putting him at the end of the longest rope. This made Lip-lip the leader, and was apparently an honour; but in reality it took away from him all honour, and instead of being bully and master of the pack, he now found himself hated and persecuted by the pack.

Because he ran at the end of the longest rope, the dogs had always the view of him running away before them. All that they saw of him was his bushy tail and fleeing hind-legs – a view far less ferocious and intimidating than his bristling mane and gleaming fangs. Also, dogs being so constituted in their mental ways, the sight of him running away gave desire to run after him and a feeling that he ran away from them.

The moment the sled started, the team took after Lip-lip in a chase that extended throughout the day. At first he had been prone to turn upon his pursuers, jealous of his dignity and wrathful; but at such times Mit-sah would throw the stinging lash of the thirty-foot cariboo-gut whip into his face, and compel him to turn tail and run on. Lip-lip might face the pack, but he could not face that whip, and all that was left him to do was to keep his long rope taut and his flanks ahead of the teeth of his mates.

But a still greater cunning lurked in the recesses of the Indian mind. To give point to unending pursuit of the leader, Mit-sah favoured him over the other dogs. These favours aroused in them jealousy and hatred. In their presence Mit-sah would give him meat, and would give it to him only. This was maddening to them. They would rage around just outside the throwing distance of the whip, while Lip-lip devoured the meat, and Mit-sah protected him. And when there was no meat to give, Mit-sah would keep the team at a distance and make believe to give meat to Lip-lip.

White Fang took kindly to the work. He had travelled a greater distance than the other dogs in the yielding of himself to the rule of the gods, and he had learned more thoroughly the futility of opposing their will. In addition, the persecution he had suffered from the pack had made the pack less to him in the scheme of things, and man more. He had not learned to be dependent on his kind for companionship. Besides, Kiche was well-nigh forgotten; and the chief outlet of expression that remained to him was in the allegiance he tendered the gods he had accepted as masters. So he worked hard, learned discipline, and was obedient. Faithfulness and willingness characterized his toil. These are essential traits of the wolf and the wild dog when they have become domesticated, and these traits White Fang possessed in unusual measure.

A companionship did exist between White Fang and the other dogs, but it was one of warfare and enmity. He had never learned to play with them. He knew only how to fight, and fight with them he did, returning to them a hundredfold the snaps and slashes they had given him in the days when Lip-lip was leader of the pack. But Lip-lip was no longer leader – except when he fled away before his mates at the end of his rope, the sled bounding along behind. In camp he kept close to Mit-sah or Grey Beaver or Kloo-kooch. He did not dare venture away from the gods, for now the fangs of all dogs were against him, and he tasted to the dregs the persecution that had been White Fang's.

With the overthrow of Lip-lip, White Fang could have become leader of the pack. But he was too morose and solitary for that. He merely thrashed his team-mates. Otherwise he ignored them. They got out of his way when he came along; nor did the boldest of them ever dare to rob him of his meat. On the contrary, they devoured their own meat hurriedly, for fear that he would take it away from them. White Fang knew the law well – *to oppress the weak and obey the strong*. He ate his share of meat as rapidly as he could. And then woe the dog that had not yet finished! A snarl and a flash of fangs, and that dog would wail his indignation to the uncomforting stars while White Fang finished his portion for him.

Every little while, however, one dog or another would flame up in revolt and be promptly subdued. Thus White Fang was kept in training. He was jealous of the isolation in which he kept himself in the midst of the pack, and he fought often to maintain it. But such fights were of brief duration. He was too quick for the others. They were slashed open and bleeding before they knew what had happened, were whipped almost before they had begun to fight.

As rigid as the sled discipline of the gods was the discipline maintained by White Fang amongst his fellows. He never allowed them any latitude. He compelled them to an unremitting respect for him. They might do as they pleased amongst themselves. That was no concern of his. But it *was* his concern that they leave him alone in his isolation, get out of his way when he elected to walk among them, and at all times acknowledge his mastery over them. A hint of stiff-leggedness on their part, a lifted lip or a bristle of hair, and he would be upon them, merciless and cruel, swiftly convincing them of the error of their way.

He was a monstrous tyrant. His mastery was rigid as steel. He oppressed the weak with a vengeance. Not for nothing had he been exposed to the pitiless struggle for life in the days of his cubhood, when his mother and he, alone and unaided, held their own and survived in the ferocious environment of the Wild. And not for nothing had he learned to walk softly when superior strength went by. He oppressed the weak, but he respected the strong. And in the course of the long journey with Grey Beaver he walked softly indeed amongst the full-grown dogs in the camps of the strange man-animals they encountered.

The months passed by. Still continued the journey of Grey Beaver. White Fang's strength was developed by the long hours on trail and the steady toil at the sled; and it would have seemed that his mental development was well-nigh complete. He had come to know quite thoroughly the world in which he lived. His outlook was bleak and materialistic. The world as he saw it was a fierce and brutal world, a world without warmth, a world in which caresses and affection and the bright sweetnesses of the spirit did not exist.

He had no affection for Grey Beaver. True, he was a god, but a most savage god. White Fang was glad to acknowledge his lordship, but it was a lordship based upon superior intelligence and brute strength. There was something in the fibre of White Fang's being that made this lordship a thing to be desired, else he would not have come back from the Wild when he did to tender his allegiance. There were deeps in his nature which had never been sounded. A kind word, a caressing touch of the hand on the part of Grey Beaver might have sounded these deeps; but Grey Beaver did not caress nor speak kind words. It was not his way. His primacy was savage, and savagely he ruled, administering justice with a club, punishing transgression with the pain of a blow, and rewarding merit, not by kindness, but by withholding a blow.

So White Fang knew nothing of the heaven a man's hand might contain for him. Besides, he did not like the hands of the man-animals. He was suspicious of them. It was true that they sometimes gave meat, but more often they gave hurt. Hands were things to keep away from. They hurled stones, wielded sticks and clubs and whips, administered slaps and clouts, and, when they touched him, were cunning to hurt with pinch and twist and wrench. In strange villages he had encountered the hands of the children, and learned that they were cruel to hurt. Also, he had once nearly had an eye poked out by a toddling papoose. From these experiences he became suspicious of all children. He could not tolerate them. When they came near with their ominous hands he got up.

It was in a village at the Great Slave Lake that, in the course of resenting the evil of the hands of the man-animals, he came to modify the law that he had learned from Grey Beaver – namely, that the unpardonable crime was to bite one of the gods. In this village, after the custom of all dogs in all villages, White Fang went foraging for food. A boy was chopping frozen moose-meat with an axe, and the chips were flying in the snow. White Fang, sliding by in quest of meat, stopped and began to eat the chips. He observed the boy lay down the axe and take up a stout club. White Fang sprang clear, just in time to escape a descending blow. The boy pursued him, and he, a stranger in the village, fled between two tepees to find himself cornered against a high earth bank.

There was no escape for White Fang. The only way out was between the two tepees, and this the boy guarded. Holding his club prepared to strike, he drew in on his cornered quarry. White Fang was furious. He faced the boy, bristling and snarling, his sense of justice outraged. He knew the law of forage. All the wastage of meat, such as the frozen chips, belonged to the dog that found it. He had done no wrong, broken no law, yet here was this boy preparing to give him a beating. White Fang scarcely knew what happened. He did it in a surge of rage. And he did it so quickly that the boy did not know either. All the boy knew was that he had in some unaccountable way been overturned into the snow, and that his club-hand had been ripped wide open by White Fang's teeth.

But White Fang knew that he had broken the law of the gods. He had driven his teeth into the sacred flesh of one of them, and could expect nothing but a most terrible punishment. He fled away to Grey Beaver, behind whose protecting legs he crouched when the bitten boy and the boy's family came demanding vengeance. But they went away with vengeance unsatisfied. Grey Beaver defended White Fang. So did Mit-sah and Kloo-kooch. White Fang, listening to the wordy war and watching the angry gestures, knew that his act was justified. And so it came that he learned there were gods and gods. There were his gods, and there were other gods, and between them there was a difference. Justice or injustice, it was all the same: he must take all things from the hands of his own gods. But he was not compelled to take injustice from the other gods. It was his privilege to resent it with his teeth. And this also was a law of the gods.

Before the day was out, White Fang was to learn more about this law. Mit-sah, alone, gathering firewood in the forest, encountered the boy that had been bitten. With him were other boys. Hot words passed. Then all the boys attacked Mit-sah. It was going hard with him. Blows were raining upon him from all sides. White Fang looked on at first. This was an affair of the gods, and no concern of his. Then he realized that this was Mit-sah, one of his own particular gods, who was being maltreated. It was no reasoned impulse that made White Fang do what he then did. A mad rush of anger sent him leaping in amongst the combatants. Five minutes later the landscape was covered with fleeing boys, many of whom dripped blood upon the snow in token that White Fang's teeth had not been idle. When Mit-sah told his story in camp, Grey Beaver ordered meat to be given to White Fang. He ordered much meat to be given; and White Fang, gorged and sleepy by the fire, knew that the law had received its verification.

It was in line with these experiences that White Fang came to learn the law of property and the duty of the defence of property. From the protection of his god's body to the protection of his god's possessions was a step, and this step he made. What was his god's was to be defended against all the world – even to the extent of biting other gods. Not only was such an act sacrilegious in its nature, but it was fraught with peril. The gods were all-powerful, and a dog was no match against them; yet White Fang learned to face them, fiercely belligerent and unafraid. Duty rose above fear, and thieving gods learned to leave Grey Beaver's property alone.

One thing in this connection White Fang quickly learned, and that was that a thieving god was usually a cowardly god, and prone to run away at the sounding of the alarm. Also, he learned that but brief time elapsed between his sounding of the alarm and Grey Beaver coming to his aid. He came to know that it was not fear of him that drove the thief away, but fear of Grey Beaver. White Fang did not give the alarm by barking. He never barked. His method was to drive straight at the intruder, and to sink his teeth in if he could. Because he was morose and solitary, having nothing to do with the other dogs, he was unusually fitted to guard his master's property; and in this he was encouraged and trained by Grey Beaver. One result of this was to make White Fang more ferocious and indomitable, and more solitary.

The months went by, binding stronger and stronger the covenant between dog and man. This was the ancient covenant that the first wolf that came in from the Wild entered into with man. And, like all succeeding wolves and wild dogs that had done likewise, White Fang worked the covenant out for himself. The terms were simple. For the possession of a flesh-and-blood god he exchanged his own liberty. Food and fire, protection and companionship, were some of the things he received from the god. In return he guarded the god's property, defended his body, worked for him, and obeyed him.

The possession of a god implies service. White Fang's was a service of duty and awe, but not of love. He did not know what love was. He had no experience of love.

Kiche was a remote memory. Besides, not only had he abandoned the Wild and his kind when he gave himself up to man, but the terms of the covenant were such that if he ever met Kiche again he would not desert his god to go with her. His allegiance to man seemed somehow a law of his being greater than the love of liberty, of kind and kin.

CHAPTER

6

THE FAMINE

The spring of the year was at hand when Grey Beaver finished his long journey. It was April, and White Fang was a year old when he pulled into the home village and was loosed from the harness by Mit-sah. Though a long way from his full growth, White Fang, next to Lip-lip, was the largest yearling in the village. Both from his father, the wolf, and from Kiche, he had inherited stature and strength, and already he was measuring up alongside the full-grown dogs. But he had not yet grown compact. His body was slender and rangy, and his strength more stringy than massive. His coat was the true wolf-grey, and to all appearances he was true wolf himself. The quarter-strain of dog he had inherited from Kiche had left no mark on him physically, though it played its part in his mental make-up.

He wandered through the village, recognizing with staid satisfaction the various gods he had known before the long journey. Then there were the dogs, puppies growing up like himself, and grown dogs that did not look so large and formidable as the memory-pictures he retained of them. Also, he stood less in fear of them than formerly, stalking among them with a certain careless ease that was as new to him as it was enjoyable.

There was Baseek, a grizzled old fellow that in his younger days had but to uncover his fangs to send White Fang cringing and crouching to the right about. From him White Fang had learned much of his own insignificance; and from him he was now to learn much of the change and development that had taken place in himself. While Baseek had been growing weaker with age, White Fang had been growing stronger with youth.

It was at the cutting up of a moose, fresh-killed, that White Fang learned of the changed relations in which he stood to the dog-world. He had got for himself a hoof and part of the shin-bone, to which quite a bit of meat was attached. Withdrawn from the immediate scramble of the other dogs – in fact, out of sight behind a thicket – he was devouring his prize, when Baseek rushed in upon him. Before he knew what he was doing, he had slashed the intruder twice and sprung clear. Baseek was surprised by the other's temerity and swiftness of attack. He stood, gazing stupidly across at White Fang, the raw, red shin-bone between them.

Baseek was old, and already he had come to know the increasing valour of the dogs it had been his wont to bully. Bitter experiences these, which, perforce, he swallowed, calling upon all his wisdom to cope with them. In the old days, he would have sprung upon White Fang in a fury of righteous wrath. But now his waning powers would not permit such a course. He bristled fiercely and looked ominously across the shin-bone at White Fang. And White Fang, resurrecting quite a deal of the old awe, seemed to wilt and to shrink in upon himself and grow small, as he cast about in his mind for a way to beat a retreat not too inglorious.

And right here Baseek erred. Had he contented himself with looking fierce and ominous, all would have been well. White Fang, on the verge of retreat, would have retreated, leaving the meat to him. But Baseek did not wait. He considered the victory already his, and stepped forward to the meat. As he bent his head carelessly to smell it, White Fang bristled slightly. Even then it was not too late for Baseek to retrieve the situation. Had he merely stood over the meat, head up and glowering, White Fang would ultimately have slunk away. But the fresh meat was strong in Baseek's nostrils, and greed urged him to take a bite of it.

This was too much for White Fang. Fresh upon his months of mastery over his own team-mates, it was beyond his self-control to stand idly by while another devoured the meat that belonged to him. He struck, after his custom, without warning. With the first slash, Baseek's right ear was ripped into ribbons. He was astounded at the suddenness of it. But more things, and most grievous ones, were happening with equal suddenness. He was knocked off his feet; his throat was bitten. While he was struggling to his feet the young dog sank teeth twice into his shoulder. The swiftness of it was bewildering. He made a futile rush at White Fang, clipping the empty air with an outraged snap. The next moment his nose was laid open and he was staggering backward away from the meat.

The situation was now reversed. White Fang stood over the shin-bone, bristling and menacing, while Baseek stood a little way off, preparing to retreat. He dared not risk a fight with this young lightning-flash, and again he knew, and more bitterly, the enfeeblement of oncoming age. His attempt to maintain his dignity was heroic. Calmly turning his back upon young dog and shin-bone, as though both were beneath his notice and unworthy of his consideration, he stalked grandly away. Nor, until well out of sight, did he stop to lick his bleeding wounds.

The effect on White Fang was to give him a greater faith in himself and a greater pride. He walked less softly among the grown dogs; his attitude toward them was less compromising. Not that he went out of his way looking for trouble – far from it. But upon his way he demanded consideration. He stood upon his right to go his way unmolested and to give trail to no dog. He had to be taken into account, that was all. He was no longer to be disregarded and ignored, as was the lot of puppies, and as continued to be the lot of the puppies that were his team-mates. They got out of the way, gave trail to the grown dogs, and gave up meat to them under compulsion. But White Fang, uncompanionable, solitary, morose, scarcely looking to right or left, redoubtable, forbidding of aspect, remote, and alien, was accepted as an equal by his puzzled elders. They quickly learned to leave him alone, neither venturing hostile acts nor making overtures of friendliness. If they left him alone, he left them alone – a state of affairs that they found, after a few encounters, to be pre-eminently desirable.

In midsummer White Fang had an experience. Trotting along in his silent way to investigate a new tepee which had been erected on the edge of the village while he was away with the hunters after moose, he came full upon Kiche. He paused and looked at her. He remembered her vaguely, but he *remembered* her, and that was more than could be said for her. She lifted her lip at him in the old snarl of menace, and his memory became clear. His forgotten cubhood, all that was associated with that familiar snarl, rushed back to him. Before he had known the gods, she had been to him the centre-pin of the universe. The old familiar feelings of that time came back upon him, surged up within him. He bounded towards her joyously, and she met him with shrewd fangs that laid his cheek open to the bone. He did not understand; he backed away, bewildered and puzzled.

But it was not Kiche's fault. A wolf-mother was not made to remember her cubs of a year or so before. So she did not remember White Fang. He was a strange animal, an intruder; and her present litter of puppies gave her the right to resent such intrusion.

One of the puppies sprawled up to White Fang. They were half-brothers, only they did not know it. White Fang sniffed the puppy curiously; whereupon Kiche rushed upon him, gashing his face a second time. He backed farther away. All the old memories and associations died down again and passed into the grave from which they had been resurrected. He looked at Kiche licking her puppy and stopping now and then to snarl at him. She was without value to him. He had learned to get along without her. Her meaning was forgotten. There was no place for her in his scheme of things, as there was no place for him in hers.

He was still standing, stupid and bewildered, the memories forgotten, wondering what it was all about, when Kiche attacked him a third time, intent on driving him away altogether from the vicinity. And White Fang allowed himself to be driven away. This was a female of his kind, and it was a law of his kind that the males must not fight the females. He did not know anything about this law, for it was no generalization of the mind, not a something acquired by experience in the world. He knew it as a secret prompting, as an urge of instinct – of the same instinct that made him howl at the moon and stars of nights, and that made him fear death and the unknown.

The months went by. White Fang grew stronger, heavier, and more compact, while his character was developing along the lines laid down by his heredity and his environment. His heredity was a life-stuff that may be likened to clay. It possessed many possibilities, was capable of being moulded into many different forms. Environment served to model the clay, to give it a particular form. Thus, had White Fang never come in to the fires of man, the Wild would have moulded him into a true wolf. But the gods had given him a different environment, and he was moulded into a dog that was rather wolfish, but that was a dog and not a wolf.

And so, according to the clay of his nature and the pressure of his surroundings, his character was being moulded into a certain particular shape. There was no escaping it. He was becoming more morose, more uncompanionable, more solitary, more ferocious; while the dogs were learning more and more that it was better to be at peace with him than at war, and Grey Beaver was coming to prize him more greatly with the passage of each day.

White Fang, seeming to sum up strength in all his qualities, nevertheless suffered from one besetting weakness. He could not stand being laughed at. The laughter of men was a hateful thing. They might laugh among themselves about anything they pleased except himself, and he did not mind. But the moment laughter was turned upon him he would fly into a most terrible rage. Grave, dignified, sombre, a laugh made him frantic to ridiculousness. It so outraged him and upset him that for hours he would behave like a demon. And woe to the dog that at such times ran foul of him. He knew the law too well to take it out on Grey Beaver; behind Grey Beaver were a club and godhead. But behind the dogs there was nothing but space, and into this space they fled when White Fang came on the scene, made mad by laughter.

In the third year of his life there came a great famine to the Mackenzie Indians. In the summer the fish failed. In the winter the caribou forsook their accustomed track. Moose were scarce, the rabbits almost disappeared, hunting and preying animals perished. Denied their usual food-supply, weakened by hunger, they fell upon and devoured one another. Only the strong survived. White Fang's gods were always hunting animals. The old and the weak of them died of hunger. There was wailing in the village, where the women and children went without in order that what little they had might go into the bellies of the lean and hollow-eyed hunters who trod the forest in the vain pursuit of meat.

To such extremity were the gods driven that they ate the soft-tanned leather of their moccasins and mittens, while the dogs ate the harnesses off their backs and the very whiplashes. Also, the dogs ate one another, and also the gods ate the dogs. The weakest and the more worthless were eaten first. The dogs that still lived looked on and understood. A few of the boldest and wisest forsook the fires of the gods, which had now become a shambles, and fled into the forest, where, in the end, they starved to death or were eaten by wolves.

In this time of misery, White Fang, too, stole away into the woods. He was better fitted for the life than the other dogs, for he had the training of his cubhood to guide him. Especially adept did he become in stalking small living things. He would lie concealed for hours, following every movement of a cautious tree-squirrel, waiting, with a patience as huge as the hunger he suffered from, until the squirrel ventured out upon the ground. Even then, White Fang was not premature. He waited until he was sure of striking before the squirrel could gain a tree-refuge. Then, and not until then, would he flash from his hiding-place, a grey projectile, incredibly swift, never failing its mark – the fleeing squirrel that fled not fast enough.

Successful as he was with squirrels, there was one difficulty that prevented him from living and growing fat on them. There were not enough squirrels. So he was driven to hunt still smaller things. So acute did his hunger become at times that he was not above rooting out wood-mice from their burrows in the ground. Nor did he scorn to do battle with a weasel as hungry as himself and many times more ferocious.

In the worst pinches of the famine he stole back to the fires of the gods. But he did not go in to the fires. He lurked in the forest, avoiding discovery and robbing the snares at the rare intervals when game was caught. He even robbed Grey Beaver's snare of a rabbit at a time when Grey Beaver staggered and tottered through the forest, sitting down often to rest, what of weakness and of shortness of breath.

One day White Fang encountered a young wolf, gaunt and scrawny, loose-jointed with famine. Had he not been hungry himself, White Fang might have gone with

him and eventually found his way into the pack amongst
his wild brethren. As it was, he ran the young wolf down
and killed and ate him.

Fortune seemed to favour him. Always, when hardest
pressed for food, he found something to kill. Again,
when he was weak, it was his luck that none of the
larger preying animals chanced upon him. Thus, he was
strong from the two days' eating a lynx had afforded
him when the hungry wolf-pack ran full tilt upon him.
It was a long, cruel chase, but he was better nourished
than they, and in the end outran them. And not only
did he outrun them, but, circling widely back on his
track, he gathered in one of his exhausted pursuers.

After that he left that part of the country and journeyed
over to the valley wherein he had been born. Here, in
the old lair, he encountered Kiche. Up to her old tricks,
she, too, had fled the inhospitable fires of the gods and
gone back to her old refuge to give birth to her young.
Of this litter but one remained alive when White Fang
came upon the scene, and this one was not destined to
live long. Young life had little chance in such a famine.

Kiche's greeting of her grown son was anything but
affectionate. But White Fang did not mind. He had
outgrown his mother. So he turned tail philosophically
and trotted on up the stream. At the forks he took the
turning to the left, where he found the lair of the lynx
with whom his mother and he had fought long before.
Here, in the abandoned lair, he settled down and rested
for a day.

During the early summer, in the last days of the
famine, he·met Lip-lip, who had likewise taken to the
woods, where he had eked out a miserable existence.
White Fang came upon him unexpectedly. Trotting in

opposite directions along the base of a high bluff, they rounded a corner of rock and found themselves face to face. They paused with instant alarm, and looked at each other suspiciously.

White Fang was in splendid condition. His hunting had been good, and for a week he had eaten his fill. He was even gorged from his latest kill. But in the moment he looked at Lip-lip his hair rose on end all along his back. It was an involuntary bristling on his part – the physical state that in the past had always accompanied the mental state produced in him by Lip-lip's bullying and persecution. As in the past he had bristled and snarled at sight of Lip-lip, so now, and automatically, he bristled and snarled. He did not waste any time. The thing was done thoroughly and with dispatch. Lip-lip essayed to back away, but White Fang struck him hard, shoulder to shoulder. Lip-lip was overthrown and rolled upon his back. White Fang's teeth drove into the scrawny throat. There was a death-struggle, during which White Fang walked around, stiff-legged and observant. Then he resumed his course and trotted on along the base of the bluff.

One day, not long after, he came to the edge of the forest, where a narrow stretch of open land sloped down to the Mackenzie. He had been over this ground before, when it was bare, but now a village occupied it. Still hidden amongst the trees, he paused to study the situation. Sights and sounds and scents were familiar to him. It was the old village changed to a new place. But sights and sounds and smells were different from those he had last had when he fled away from it. There was no whimpering nor wailing. Contented sounds saluted his ear, and when he heard the angry voice of a woman, he knew it to be the anger that proceeds from a full stomach. And there was a smell in the air of fish. There was food. The famine was gone. He came out boldly from the forest and trotted into camp straight to Grey Beaver's tepee. Grey Beaver was not there, but Klookooch welcomed him with glad cries and the whole of a fresh-caught fish, and he lay down to wait Grey Beaver's coming.

PART IV

CHAPTER
1

THE ENEMY OF HIS KIND

Had there been in White Fang's nature any possibility, no matter how remote, of his ever coming to fraternize with his kind, such possibility was irretrievably destroyed when he was made leader of the sled-team. For now the dogs hated him – hated him for the extra meat bestowed upon him by Mit-sah; hated him for all the real and fancied favours he received; hated him for that he fled always at the head of the team, his waving brush of a tail and his perpetually retreating hind-quarters for ever maddening their eyes.

And White Fang just as bitterly hated them back. Being sled-leader was anything but gratifying to him. To be compelled to run away before the yelling pack, every dog of which, for three years, he had thrashed and mastered, was almost more than he could endure. But endure it he must, or perish, and the life that was in him had no desire to perish out. The moment Mit-sah gave his order for the start, that moment the whole team, with eager, savage cries, sprang forward at White Fang.

There was no defence for him. If he turned upon them, Mit-sah would throw the stinging lash of the whip into his face. It only remained to him to run away. He could not encounter that howling horde with his tail and hind-quarters. These were scarcely fit weapons with which to meet the many merciless fangs. So run away he did, violating his own nature and pride with every leap he made, and leaping all day long.

One cannot violate the promptings of one's nature without having that nature recoil upon itself. Such a recoil is like that of a hair, made to grow out from the body, turning unnaturally upon the direction of its growth and growing into the body – a rankling, festering thing of hurt. And so with White Fang. Every urge of his being impelled him to spring upon the pack that cried at his heels, but it was the will of the gods that this should not be; and behind the will, to enforce it, was the whip of caribou-gut with its biting thirty-foot lash. So White Fang could only eat his heart in bitterness and develop a hatred and malice commensurate with the ferocity and indomitability of his nature.

If ever a creature was the enemy of its kind, White Fang was that creature. He asked no quarter, gave none. He was continually marred and scarred by the teeth of the pack, and as continually he left his own marks upon the pack. Unlike most leaders, who, when camp was made and the dogs were unhitched, huddled near to the gods for protection, White Fang disdained such protection. He walked boldly about the camp, inflicting punishment in the night for what he had suffered in the day. In the time before he was made leader of the team, the pack had learned to get out of his way. But now it was different. Excited by the day-long pursuit of him, swayed subconsciously by the insistent iteration on their brains of the sight of him fleeing away, mastered by the feeling of mastery enjoyed all day, the dogs could not bring themselves to give way to him. When he appeared amongst them there was always a squabble. His progress was marked by snarl and snap and growl. The very atmosphere he breathed was surcharged with hatred and malice, and this but served to increase the hatred and malice within him.

When Mit-sah cried out his command for the team to stop, White Fang obeyed. At first this caused trouble for the other dogs. All of them would spring upon the hated leader, only to find the tables turned. Behind him would be Mit-sah, the great whip singing in his hand. So the dogs came to understand that when the team stopped by order, White Fang was to be let alone. But when White Fang stopped without orders, then it was allowed them to spring upon him and destroy him if they could. After several experiences, White Fang never stopped without orders. He learned quickly. It was in the nature of things that he must learn quickly if he were to survive the unusually severe conditions under which life was vouchsafed him.

But the dogs could never learn the lesson to leave him alone in camp. Each day, pursuing him and crying defiance at him, the lesson of the previous night was erased; and that night would have to be learned over again, to be as immediately forgotten. Besides, there was a greater consistence in their dislike of him. They sensed between themselves and him a difference of kind – cause sufficient in itself for hostility. Like him they were domesticated wolves. But they had been domesticated for generations. Much of the Wild had been lost, so that to them the Wild was the unknown, the terrible, the ever-menacing and ever-warring. But to him, in appearance and action and impulse, still clung the Wild. He symbolized it, was its personification; so that when they showed their teeth to him they were defending themselves against the powers of destruction that lurked in the shadows of the forest and in the dark beyond the camp-fire.

But there was one lesson the dogs did learn, and that was to keep together. White Fang was too terrible for any of them to face single-handed. They met him with the mass formation, otherwise he would have killed them, one by one, in a night. As it was, he never had a chance to kill them. He might roll a dog off its feet, but the pack would be upon him before he could follow up and deliver the deadly throat-stroke. At the first hint of conflict, the whole team drew together and faced him. The dogs had quarrels among themselves, but these were forgotten when trouble was brewing with White Fang.

On the other hand, try as they would, they could not kill White Fang. He was too quick for them, too formidable, too wise. He avoided tight places, and always backed out of it when they bade fair to surround him. While, as for getting him off his feet, there was no dog among them capable of doing the trick. His feet clung to the earth with the same tenacity that he clung to life. For that matter, life and footing were synonymous in this unending warfare with the pack, and none knew it better than White Fang.

So he became the enemy of his kind, domesticated wolves that they were, softened by the fires of man, weakened in the sheltering shadow of man's strength. White Fang was bitter and implacable. The clay of him was so moulded. He declared a vendetta against all dogs. And so terribly did he live this vendetta that Grey Beaver, fierce savage himself, could not but marvel at White Fang's ferocity. Never, he swore, had there been the like of this animal; and the Indians in strange villages swore likewise when they considered the tale of his killings amongst their dogs.

When White Fang was nearly five years old, Grey Beaver took him on another great journey, and long remembered was the havoc he worked amongst the dogs of the many villages along the Mackenzie, across the Rockies, and down the Porcupine to the Yukon. He revelled in the vengeance he wreaked upon his kind. They were ordinary, unsuspecting dogs. They were not prepared for his swiftness and directness, for his attack without warning. They did not know him for what he was, a lightning-flash of slaughter. They bristled up to him, stiff-legged and challenging, while he, wasting no time on elaborate preliminaries, snapping into action like a steel spring, was at their throats and destroying them before they knew what was happening, and while they were yet in the throes of surprise.

He became an adept at fighting. He economized. He never wasted his strength, never tussled. He was in too quickly for that, and if he missed, was out again too quickly. The dislike of the wolf for close quarters was his to an unusual degree. He could not endure a prolonged contact with another body. It smacked of danger. It made him frantic. He must be away, free, on his own legs, touching no living thing. It was the Wild still clinging to him, asserting itself through him. This feeling had been accentuated by the Ishmaelite life he had led from his puppyhood. Danger lurked in contacts. It was the trap, ever the trap, the fear of it lurking deep in the life of him, woven into the fibre of him.

In consequence, the strange dogs he encountered had no chance against him. He eluded their fangs. He got them, or got away, himself untouched in either event. In the natural course of things there were exceptions to this. There were times when several dogs, pitching on to him, punished him before he could get away; and there were times when a single dog scored deeply on him. But these were accidents. In the main, so efficient a fighter had he become, he went his way unscathed.

Another advantage he possessed was that of correctly judging time and distance. Not that he did this consciously, however. He did not calculate such things. It was all automatic. His eyes saw correctly, and the nerves carried the vision correctly to his brain. The parts of him were better adjusted than those of the average dog. They worked together more smoothly and steadily. His was a better, far better, nervous, mental, and muscular co-ordination. When his eyes conveyed to his brain the moving image of an action, his brain, without conscious effort, knew the space that limited that action and the time required for its completion. Thus, he could avoid the leap of another dog or the drive of its fangs, and at the same moment could seize the infinitesimal fraction of time in which to deliver his own attack. Body and brain, his was a more perfected mechanism. Not that he was to be praised for it. Nature had been more generous to him than to the average animal, that was all.

It was in the summer that White Fang arrived at Fort Yukon. Grey Beaver had crossed the great water-shed between the Mackenzie and the Yukon in the late winter, and spent the spring in hunting among the western outlying spurs of the Rockies. Then, after the break-up of the ice on the Porcupine, he had built a canoe and paddled down that stream to where it effected its junction with the Yukon just under the Arctic Circle. Here stood the old Hudson's Bay Company fort; and here were many Indians, much food, and unprecedented excitement. It was the summer of 1898, and thousands of gold-hunters were going up the Yukon to Dawson and the Klondike. Still hundreds of miles from their goal, nevertheless many of them had been on the way for a year; and the least any of them had travelled to get that far was five thousand miles, while some had come from the other side of the world.

Here Grey Beaver stopped. A whisper of the gold rush had reached his ears, and he had come with several bales of furs, and another of gut-sewn mittens and moccasins. He would not have ventured so long a trip had he not expected generous profits. But what he had expected was nothing to what he realized. His wildest dream had not exceeded a hundred per cent profit; he made a thousand per cent. And like a true Indian he settled down to trade carefully and slowly, even if it took all summer and the rest of the winter to dispose of his goods.

It was at Fort Yukon that White Fang saw his first white men. As compared with the Indians he had known, they were to him another race of beings, a race of superior gods. They impressed him as possessing superior power, and it is on power that godhead rests. White Fang did not reason it out, did not in his mind make the sharp generalization that the white gods were more powerful. It was a feeling, nothing more, and yet none the less potent. As in his puppyhood the looming bulks of the tepees, man-reared, had affected him as manifestations of power, so was he affected now by the houses and the huge fort, all of massive logs. Here was power. Those white gods were strong. They possessed greater mastery over matter than the gods he had known, most powerful among which was Grey Beaver. And yet Grey Beaver was as a child-god among these white-skinned ones.

To be sure, White Fang only felt these things. He was not conscious of them. Yet it is upon feeling, more often than thinking, that animals act; and every act White Fang now performed was based upon the feeling that the white men were the superior gods. In the first place he was very suspicious of them. There was no telling what unknown terrors were theirs, what unknown hurts they could administer. He was curious to observe them, fearful of being noticed by them. For the first few hours he was content with slinking around and watching them from a safe distance. Then he saw that no harm befell the dogs that were near to them, and he came in closer.

In turn he was an object of great curiosity to them. His wolfish appearance caught their eyes at once, and they pointed him out to one another. This act of pointing put White Fang on his guard, and when they tried to approach him he showed his teeth and backed away. Not one succeeded in laying a hand on him, and it was well that they did not.

White Fang soon learned that very few of these gods – not more than a dozen – lived at this place. Every two or three days a steamer (another and colossal manifestation of power) came in to the bank and stopped for several hours. The white men came from off these steamers and went away on them again. There seemed untold numbers of these white men. In the first day or so he saw more of them than he had seen Indians in all his life; and as the days went by they continued to come up the river, stop, and then go on up the river and out of sight.

But if the white gods were all-powerful, their dogs did not amount to much. This White Fang quickly discovered by mixing with those that came ashore with their masters. They were of irregular shapes and sizes. Some were short-legged – too short; others were long-legged – too long. They had hair instead of fur, and a few had very little hair at that. And none of them knew how to fight.

As an enemy of his kind, it was in White Fang's province to fight with them. This he did, and he quickly achieved for them a mighty contempt. They were soft and helpless, made much noise, and floundered around clumsily trying to accomplish by main strength what he accomplished by dexterity and cunning. They rushed, bellowing, at him. He sprang to the side. They did not know what had become of him; and in that moment he struck them on the shoulder, rolling them off their feet and delivering his stroke at the throat.

Sometimes this stroke was successful, and a stricken dog rolled in the dirt, to be pounced upon and torn to pieces by the pack of Indian dogs that waited. White Fang was wise. He had long since learned that the gods were made angry when their dogs were killed. The white men were no exception to this. So he was content, when he had overthrown and slashed wide the throat of one of their dogs, to drop back and let the pack go in and do the cruel finishing work. It was then that the white men rushed in, visiting their wrath heavily on the pack, while White Fang went free. He would stand off at a little distance and look on, while stones, clubs, axes, and all sorts of weapons fell upon his fellows. White Fang was very wise.

But his fellows grew wise in their own way; and in this White Fang grew wise with them. They learned that it was when a steamer first tied to the bank that they had their fun. After the first two or three strange dogs had been downed and destroyed, the white men hustled their own animals back on board and wreaked savage vengeance on the offenders. One white man, having seen his dog, a setter, torn to pieces before his eyes, drew a revolver. He fired rapidly six times, and six of the pack lay dead or dying – another manifestation of power that sank deep into White Fang's consciousness.

White Fang enjoyed it all. He did not love his kind, and he was shrewd enough to escape hurt himself. At first the killing of the white men's dogs had been a diversion. After a time it became his occupation. There was no work for him to do. Grey Beaver was busy trading and getting wealthy. So White Fang hung around the landing with the disreputable gang of Indian dogs, waiting for steamers. With the arrival of a steamer the fun began. After a few minutes, by the time the white men had got over their surprise, the gang scattered. The fun was over until the next steamer should arrive.

But it can scarcely be said that White Fang was a member of the gang. He did not mingle with it, but remained aloof, always himself, and was even feared by it. It is true he worked with it. He picked the quarrel with the strange dog, while the gang waited. And when he had overthrown the strange dog the gang went in to finish it. But it is equally true that he then withdrew, leaving the gang to receive the punishment of the outraged gods.

It did not require much exertion to pick these quarrels. All he had to do when the strange dogs came ashore was to show himself. When they saw him they rushed for him. It was their instinct. He was the Wild, the unknown, the terrible, the ever-menacing, the thing that prowled in the darkness around the fire of the primeval world when they, cowering close to the fires, were reshaping their instincts, learning to fear the Wild out of which they had come, and which they had deserted and betrayed. Generation by generation, down all the generations, had this fear of the Wild been stamped into their natures. For centuries the Wild had stood for terror and destruction. And during all this time free licence had been theirs, from their masters, to kill the things of the Wild. In doing this they had protected both themselves and the gods whose companionship they shared.

And so, fresh from the soft southern world, these dogs, trotting down the gang-plank and out upon the Yukon shore, had but to see White Fang to experience the irresistible impulse to rush upon him and destroy him. They might be town-reared dogs, but the instinctive fear of the Wild was theirs just the same. Not alone with their own eyes did they see the wolfish creature in the clear light of day, standing before them. They saw him with the eyes of their ancestors, and by their inherited memory they knew White Fang for the wolf, and they remembered the ancient feud.

All of which served to make White Fang's days enjoyable. If the sight of him drove these strange dogs upon him, so much the better for him, so much the worse for them. They looked upon him as legitimate prey, and as legitimate prey he looked upon them.

Not for nothing had he first seen the light of day in a

lonely lair and fought his first fights with the ptarmigan, the weasel, and the lynx. And not for nothing had his puppyhood been made bitter by the persecution of Lip-lip and the whole puppy pack. It might have been otherwise, and he would then have been otherwise. Had Lip-lip not existed, he would have passed his puppyhood with the other puppies and grown up more dog-like and with more liking for dogs. Had Grey Beaver possessed the plummet of affection and love, he might have sounded the deeps of White Fang's nature and brought up to the surface all manner of kindly qualities. But these things had not been so. The clay of White Fang had been moulded until he became what he was – morose and lonely, unloving and ferocious, the enemy of all his kind.

CHAPTER

2

THE MAD GOD

A small number of white men lived in Fort Yukon. These men had been long in the country. They called themselves Sour-doughs, and took great pride in so classifying themselves. For other men, new in the land, they felt nothing but disdain. The men who came ashore from the steamers were newcomers. They were known as *chechaquos*, and they always wilted at the application of the name. They made their bread with baking-powder. This was the invidious distinction between them and the Sour-doughs, who, forsooth, made their bread from sour-dough because they had no baking-powder.

All of which is neither here nor there. The men in the fort disdained the newcomers and enjoyed seeing them come to grief. Especially did they enjoy the havoc worked amongst the newcomers' dogs by White Fang and his disreputable gang. When a steamer arrived, the men of the fort made it a point always to come down to the bank and see the fun. They looked forward to it with as much anticipation as did the Indian dogs, while they were not slow to appreciate the savage and crafty part played by White Fang.

But there was one man amongst them who particularly enjoyed the sport. He would come running at the first sound of a steamboat's whistle; and when the last fight was over, and White Fang and the pack had scattered, he would return slowly to the fort, his face heavy with regret. Sometimes, when a soft southland dog went down, shrieking its death-cry under the fangs of the pack, this man would be unable to contain himself, and would leap into the air and cry out with delight. And always he had a sharp and covetous eye for White Fang.

This man was called 'Beauty' by the other men of the fort. No one knew his first name, and in general he was known in the country as Beauty Smith. But he was anything save a beauty. To antithesis was due his naming. He was pre-eminently unbeautiful. Nature had been niggardly with him. He was a small man to begin with; and upon his meagre frame was deposited an even more strikingly meagre head. Its apex might be likened to a point. In fact, in his boyhood, before he had been named Beauty by his fellows, he had been called 'Pinhead'.

Backward, from the apex, his head slanted down to his neck; and forward, it slanted uncompromisingly to meet a low and remarkably wide forehead. Beginning here as though regretting her parsimony, Nature had spread his features with a lavish hand. His eyes were large, and between them was the distance of two eyes. His face, in relation to the rest of him, was prodigious. In order to discover the necessary area, Nature had given him an enormous prognathous jaw. It was wide and heavy, and protruded outward and down until it seemed to rest on his chest. Possibly this appearance was due to the weariness of the slender neck, unable properly to support so great a burden.

This jaw gave the impression of ferocious determination. But something lacked. Perhaps it was from excess. Perhaps the jaw was too large. At any rate, it was a lie. Beauty Smith was known far and wide as the weakest of weak-kneed and snivelling cowards. To complete his description, his teeth were large and yellow, while the two eye-teeth, larger than their fellows, showed under his lean lips like fangs. His eyes were yellow and muddy, as though Nature had run short on pigments and squeezed together the dregs of all her tubes. It was the same with his hair, sparse and irregular of growth, muddy-yellow and dirty-yellow, rising on his head and sprouting out of his face in unexpected tufts and bunches, in appearance like clumped and wind-blown grain.

In short, Beauty Smith was a monstrosity, and the blame of it lay elsewhere. He was not responsible. The clay of him had been so moulded in the making. He did the cooking for the other men in the fort, the dish-washing and the drudgery. They did not despise him. Rather did they tolerate him in a broad human way, as one tolerates any creature evilly treated in the making. Also, they feared him. His cowardly rages made them dread a shot in the back or poison in their coffee. But somebody had to do the cooking; and whatever else his shortcomings, Beauty Smith could cook.

This was the man that looked at White Fang, delighted in his ferocious prowess, and desired to possess him. He made overtures to White Fang from the first. White Fang began by ignoring him. Later on, when the overtures became more insistent, White Fang bristled and bared his teeth and backed away. He did not like the man. The feel of him was bad. He sensed the evil in him, and feared the extended hand and the attempts at soft-spoken speech. Because of all this, he hated the man.

With the simpler creatures, good and bad are things simply understood. The good stands for all things that bring easement and satisfaction and surcease from pain. Therefore, the good is liked. The bad stands for all things that are fraught with discomfort, menace, and hurt, and is hated accordingly. White Fang's feel of Beauty Smith was bad. From the man's distorted body and twisted mind, in occult ways, like mists rising from malarial marshes, came emanations of the unhealth within. Not by reasoning, not by the five senses alone, but by other and remoter and uncharted senses, came the feeling to White Fang that the man was ominous with evil, pregnant with hurtfulness, and therefore a thing bad, and wisely to be hated.

White Fang was in Grey Beaver's camp when Beauty Smith first visited it. At the faint sound of his distant feet, before he came in sight, White Fang knew who was coming, and began to bristle. He had been lying down in an abandon of comfort, but he arose quickly, and as the man arrived, slid away in true wolf-fashion to the edge of the camp. He did not know what they said, but he could see the man and Grey Beaver talking together. Once the man pointed at him, and White Fang snarled back as though the hand were just descending upon him, instead of being, as it was, fifty feet away. The man laughed at this; and White Fang slunk away to the sheltering woods, his head turned to observe as he glided softly over the ground.

Grey Beaver refused to sell the dog. He had grown rich with his trading, and stood in need of nothing.

Besides, White Fang was a valuable animal, the strongest sled-dog he had ever owned, and the best leader. Furthermore, there was no dog like him on the Mackenzie nor the Yukon. He could fight. He killed other dogs as easily as men killed mosquitoes. (Beauty Smith's eyes lighted up at this, and he licked his thin lips with an eager tongue.) No, White Fang was not for sale at any price.

But Beauty Smith knew the ways of Indians. He visited Grey Beaver's camp often, and hidden under his coat was always a black bottle or so. One of the potencies of whisky is the breeding of thirst. Grey Beaver got the thirst. His fevered membranes and burnt stomach began to clamour for more and more of the scorching fluid; while his brain, thrust all awry by the unwonted stimulant, permitted him to go any length to obtain it. The money he had received for his furs and mittens and moccasins began to go. It went faster and faster, and the shorter his money-sack grew the shorter grew his temper.

In the end his money and goods and temper were all gone. Nothing remained to him but his thirst – a prodigious possession in itself, that grew more prodigious with every sober breath he drew. Then it was that Beauty Smith had talk with him again about the sale of White Fang; but this time the price offered was in bottles, not dollars, and Grey Beaver's ears were more eager to hear.

'You ketch um dog you take um all right,' was his last word.

The bottles were delivered, but after two days 'You ketch um dog' were Beauty Smith's words to Grey Beaver.

White Fang slunk into camp one evening, and dropped down with a sigh of content. The dreaded white god was not there. For days his manifestations of desire to lay hands on him had been growing more insistent, and during that time White Fang had been compelled to avoid the camp. He did not know what evil was threatened by those insistent hands. He knew only that they did threaten evil of some sort, and that it was best for him to keep out of their reach.

But scarcely had he lain down when Grey Beaver staggered over to him and tied a leather thong around his neck. He sat down beside White Fang, holding the end of the thong in his hand. In the other hand he held a bottle, which, from time to time, was inverted above his head to the accompaniment of gurgling noises.

An hour of this passed, when the vibrations of feet in contact with the ground foreran the one who approached. White Fang heard it first, and he was bristling with recognition, while Grey Beaver still nodded stupidly. White Fang tried to draw the thong softly out of his master's hand; but the relaxed fingers closed tightly, and Grey Beaver roused himself.

Beauty Smith strode into camp and stood over White Fang. He snarled softly up at the thing of fear, watching keenly the deportment of the hands. One hand extended outward and began to descend upon his head. His soft snarl grew tense and harsh. The hand continued slowly to descend, while he crouched beneath it, eyeing it malignantly, his snarl growing shorter and shorter as, with quickening breath, it approached its culmination. Suddenly he snapped, striking with his fangs like a snake. The hand was jerked back, and the teeth came together emptily with a sharp click. Beauty Smith was frightened and angry. Grey Beaver clouted White Fang alongside the head, so that he cowered down close to the earth in respectful obedience.

White Fang's suspicious eyes followed every movement. He saw Beauty Smith go away and return with a stout club. Then the end of the thong was given over to him by Grey Beaver. Beauty Smith started to walk away. The thong grew taut. White Fang resisted it. Grey Beaver clouted him right and left to make him get up and follow. He obeyed, but with a rush, hurling himself upon the stranger who was dragging him away. Beauty Smith did not jump away. He had been waiting for this. He swung the club smartly, stopping the rush midway and smashing White Fang down upon the ground. Grey Beaver laughed and nodded approval. Beauty Smith tightened the thong again, and White Fang crawled limply and dizzily to his feet.

He did not rush a second time. One smash from the club was sufficient to convince him that the white god knew how to handle it, and he was too wise to fight the inevitable. So he followed morosely at Beauty Smith's heels, his tail between his legs, yet snarling softly under his breath. But Beauty Smith kept a wary eye on him, and the club was held always ready to strike.

At the fort Beauty Smith left him securely tied and went in to bed. White Fang waited an hour. Then he applied his teeth to the thong, and in the space of ten seconds was free. He had wasted no time with his teeth. There had been no useless gnawing. The thong was cut across, diagonally, almost as clean as though done by a knife. White Fang looked up at the fort, at the same time bristling and growling. Then he turned and trotted back to Grey Beaver's camp. He owed no allegiance to this strange and terrible god. He had given himself to Grey Beaver, and to Grey Beaver he considered he still belonged.

But what had occurred before was repeated – with a difference. Grey Beaver again made him fast with a thong, and in the morning turned him over to Beauty Smith. And here was where the difference came in. Beauty Smith gave him a beating. Tied securely, White Fang could only rage futilely and endure the punishment. Club and whip were both used upon him, and he experienced the worst beating he had ever received in his life. Even the big beating given him in his puppyhood by Grey Beaver was mild compared with this.

Beauty Smith enjoyed the task. He delighted in it. He gloated over his victim, and his eyes flamed dully as he swung the whip or club and listened to White Fang's cries of pain and to his helpless bellows and snarls. For Beauty Smith was cruel in the way that cowards are cruel. Cringing and snivelling himself before the blows or angry speech of a man, he revenged himself, in turn, upon creatures weaker than he. All life likes power, and Beauty Smith was no exception. Denied the expression of power amongst his own kind, he fell back upon the lesser creatures, and there vindicated the life that was in him. But Beauty Smith had not created himself, and no blame was to be attached to him. He had come into the world with a twisted body and a brute intelligence. This had constituted the clay of him, and it had not been kindly moulded by the world.

White Fang knew why he was being beaten. When Grey Beaver tied the thong around his neck, and passed the end of the thong into Beauty Smith's keeping, White Fang knew that it was his god's will for him to go with

Beauty Smith. And when Beauty Smith left him tied outside the fort, he knew that it was Beauty Smith's will that he should remain there. Therefore, he had disobeyed the will of both the gods, and earned the consequent punishment. He had seen dogs change owners in the past, and he had seen the runaways beaten as he was being beaten. He was wise, and yet in the nature of him there were forces greater than wisdom. One of these was fidelity. He did not love Grey Beaver; yet, even in the face of his will and his anger, he was faithful to him. He could not help it. This faithfulness was a quality of the clay that composed him. It was the quality that was peculiarly the possession of his kind, the quality that set apart his species from all other species, the quality that had enabled the wolf and the wild dog to come in from the open and be the companions of man.

After the beating, White Fang was dragged back to the fort. But this time Beauty Smith left him tied with a stick. One does not give up a god easily, and so with White Fang. Grey Beaver was his own particular god, and, in spite of Grey Beaver's will, White Fang still clung to him and would not give him up. Grey Beaver had betrayed and forsaken him, but that had no effect upon him. Not for nothing had he surrendered himself body and soul to Grey Beaver. There had been no reservation on White Fang's part, and the bond was not to be broken easily.

So, in the night, when the men in the fort were asleep, White Fang applied his teeth to the stick that held him. The wood was seasoned and dry, and it was tied so closely to his neck that he could scarcely get his teeth to it. It was only by the severest muscular exertion and neck-arching that he succeeded in getting the wood between his teeth, and barely between his teeth at that; and it was only by the exercise of an immense patience, extending through many hours, that he succeeded in gnawing through the stick. This was something that dogs were not supposed to do. It was unprecedented. But White Fang did it, trotting away from the fort in the early morning, with the end of the stick hanging to his neck.

He was wise. But had he been merely wise he would not have gone back to Grey Beaver, who had already twice betrayed him. But there was his faithfulness, and he went back to be betrayed yet a third time. Again he yielded to the tying of a thong around his neck by Grey Beaver, and again Beauty Smith came to claim him. And this time he was beaten even more severely than before.

Grey Beaver looked on stolidly while the white man wielded the whip. He gave no protection. It was no longer his dog. When the beating was over White Fang was sick. A soft southland dog would have died under it, but not he. His school of life had been sterner, and he was himself of sterner stuff. He had too great vitality. His clutch on life was too strong. But he was very sick. At first he was unable to drag himself along, and Beauty Smith had to wait half an hour on him. And then, blind and reeling, he followed at Beauty Smith's heels back to the fort.

But now he was tied with a chain that defied his teeth, and he strove in vain, by lunging, to draw the staple from the timber into which it was driven. After a few days, sober and bankrupt, Grey Beaver departed up the Porcupine on his long journey to the Mackenzie. White Fang remained on the Yukon, the property of a man more than half mad and all brute. But what is a dog to know in its consciousness of madness? To White Fang Beauty Smith was a veritable, if terrible, god. He was a mad god at best, but White Fang knew nothing of madness; he knew only that he must submit to the will of this new master, obey his every whim and fancy.

CHAPTER

3

THE REIGN OF HATE

Under the tutelage of the mad god, White Fang became
a fiend. He was kept chained in a pen at the rear of the
fort, and here Beauty Smith teased and irritated and
drove him wild with petty torments. The man early
discovered White Fang's susceptibility to laughter, and
made it a point, after painfully tricking him, to laugh at
him. This laughter was uproarious and scornful, and at
the same time the god pointed his finger derisively at
White Fang. At such times reason fled from White Fang,
and in his transports of rage he was even more mad than
Beauty Smith.

Formerly, White Fang had been merely the enemy of
his kind – withal a ferocious enemy. He now became the
enemy of all things, and more ferocious than ever. To
such an extent was he tormented, that he hated blindly
and without the faintest spark of reason. He hated the
chain that bound him, the men who peered in at him
through the slats of the pen, the dogs that accompanied
the men and that snarled malignantly at him in his
helplessness. He hated the very wood of the pen that
confined him. And first, last, and most of all, he hated
Beauty Smith.

But Beauty Smith had a purpose in all that he did to White Fang. One day a number of men gathered about the pen. Beauty Smith entered, club in hand, and took the chain from off White Fang's neck. When his master had gone out, White Fang turned loose and tore around the pen, trying to get at the men outside. He was magnificently terrible. Fully five feet in length, and standing two and one-half feet at the shoulder, he far outweighed a wolf of corresponding size. From his mother he had inherited the heavier proportions of the dog, so that he weighed, without any fat and without an ounce of superfluous flesh, over ninety pounds. It was all muscle, bone, and sinew – fighting flesh in the finest condition.

The door of the pen was being opened again. White Fang paused. Something unusual was happening. He waited. The door was opened wider. Then a huge dog was thrust inside, and the door was slammed shut behind him. White Fang had never seen such a dog (it was a mastiff); but the size and fierce aspect of the intruder did not deter him. Here was something, not wood nor iron, upon which to wreak his hate. He leaped in with a flash of fangs that ripped down the side of the mastiff's neck. The mastiff shook his head, growled hoarsely, and plunged at White Fang. But White Fang was here, there, and everywhere, always evading and eluding, and always leaping in and slashing with his fangs and leaping out again in time to escape punishment.

The men outside shouted and applauded, while Beauty Smith, in an ecstasy of delight, gloated over the ripping and mangling performed by White Fang. There was no hope for the mastiff from the first. He was too ponderous and slow. In the end, while Beauty Smith beat

White Fang back with a club, the mastiff was dragged out by its owner. Then there was a payment of bets, and money clinked in Beauty Smith's hand.

White Fang came to look forward eagerly to the gathering of the men around his pen. It meant a fight; and this was the only way that was now vouchsafed him of expressing the life that was in him. Tormented, incited to hate, he was kept a prisoner, so that there was no way of satisfying that hate except at the times his master saw fit to put another dog against him. Beauty Smith had estimated his powers well, for he was invariably the victor. One day, three dogs were turned in upon him in succession. Another day, a full-grown wolf, fresh caught from the Wild, was shoved in through the door of the pen. And on still another day two dogs were set against him at the same time. This was his severest fight, and though in the end he killed them both, he was himself half killed in doing it.

In the fall of the year, when the first snows were falling and mush-ice was running in the river, Beauty Smith took passage for himself and White Fang on a steamboat bound up the Yukon to Dawson. White Fang had now achieved a reputation in the land. As 'the Fighting Wolf' he was known far and wide, and the cage in which he was kept on the steamboat's deck was usually surrounded by curious men. He raged and snarled at them, or lay quietly and studied them with cold hatred. Why should he not hate them? He never asked himself the question. He knew only hate, and lost himself in the passion of it. Life had become a hell to him. He had not been made for the close confinement wild beasts endure at the hands of men. And yet it was in precisely this way that he was treated. Men stared at him, poked sticks between the bars to make him snarl, and then laughed at him.

They were his environment these men, and they were moulding the clay of him into a more ferocious thing than had been intended by Nature. Nevertheless, Nature had given him plasticity. Where many another animal would have died or had its spirit broken, he adjusted himself and lived, and at no expense of the spirit. Possibly Beauty Smith, arch-fiend and tormentor, was capable of breaking White Fang's spirit, but as yet there were no signs of his succeeding.

If Beauty Smith had in him a devil, White Fang had another; and the two of them raged against each other unceasingly. In the days before, White Fang had had the wisdom to cower down and submit to a man with a club in his hand; but this wisdom now left him. The mere sight of Beauty Smith was sufficient to send him into transports of fury. And when they came to close quarters, and he had been beaten back by the club, he went on growling and snarling and showing his fangs. The last growl could never be extracted from him. No matter how terribly he was beaten, he had always another growl; and when Beauty Smith gave up and withdrew, the defiant growl followed after him, or White Fang sprang at the bars of the cage bellowing his hatred.

When the steamboat arrived at Dawson, White Fang went ashore. But he still lived a public life, in a cage, surrounded by curious men. He was exhibited as 'the Fighting Wolf', and men paid fifty cents in gold dust to see him. He was given no rest. Did he lie down to sleep, he was stirred up by a sharp stick, so that the audience might get its money's worth. In order to make the exhibition interesting, he was kept in a rage most of the time.

But worse than all this was the atmosphere in which he lived. He was regarded as the most fearful of wild beasts, and this was borne in to him through the bars of the cage. Every word, every cautious action, on the part of the men, impressed upon him his own terrible ferocity. It was so much added fuel to the flame of his fierceness. There could be but one result, and that was that his ferocity fed upon itself and increased. It was another instance of the plasticity of his clay, of his capacity for being moulded by the pressure of environment.

In addition to being exhibited, he was a professional fighting animal. At irregular intervals, whenever a fight could be arranged, he was taken out of his cage and led off into the woods a few miles from town. Usually this occurred at night, so as to avoid interference from the mounted police of the Territory. After a few hours of waiting, when daylight had come, the audience and the dog with which he was to fight arrived. In this manner it came about that he fought all sizes and breeds of dogs. It was a savage land, the men were savage, and the fights were usually to the death.

Since White Fang continued to fight, it is obvious that it was the other dogs that died. He never knew defeat. His early training, when he fought with Lip-lip and the whole puppy-pack, stood him in good stead. There was the tenacity with which he clung to the earth. No dog could make him lose his footing. This was the favourite trick of the wolf breeds – to rush in upon him, either directly or with an unexpected swerve, in the hope of striking his shoulder and overthrowing him. Mackenzie hounds, Eskimo and Labrador dogs, huskies and Malemutes – all tried it on him, and all failed. He was never known to lose his footing. Men told this to one another, and looked each time to see it happen; but White Fang always disappointed them.

Then there was his lightning quickness. It gave him a tremendous advantage over his antagonists. No matter what their fighting experience, they had never encountered a dog that moved so swiftly as he. Also to be reckoned with was the immediateness of his attack. The average dog was accustomed to the preliminaries of snarling and bristling and growling, and the average dog was knocked off his feet and finished before he had begun to fight or recovered from his surprise. So often did this happen, that it became the custom to hold White Fang until the other dog went through its preliminaries, was good and ready, and even made the first attack.

But greatest of all the advantages in White Fang's favour was his experience. He knew more about fighting than did any of the dogs that faced him. He had fought more fights, knew how to meet more tricks and methods, and had more tricks himself, while his own method was scarcely to be improved upon.

As the time went by he had fewer and fewer fights. Men despaired of matching him with an equal, and Beauty Smith was compelled to pit wolves against him. These were trapped by the Indians for the purpose, and a fight between White Fang and a wolf was always sure to draw a crowd. Once, a full-grown female lynx was secured, and this time White Fang fought for his life. Her quickness matched his; her ferocity equalled his; while he fought with his fangs alone, and she fought with her sharp-clawed feet as well.

But after the lynx, all fighting ceased for White Fang. There were no more animals with which to fight – at least, there was none considered worthy of fighting with him. So he remained on exhibition until spring, when one Tim Keenan, a faro-dealer, arrived in the land. With him came the first bull-dog that had ever entered the Klondike. That this dog and White Fang should come together was inevitable, and for a week the anticipated fight was the mainspring of conversation in certain quarters of the town.

CHAPTER

4

THE CLINGING DEATH

Beauty Smith slipped the chain from his neck and stepped back.

For once White Fang did not make an immediate attack. He stood still, ears pricked forward, alert and curious, surveying the strange animal that faced him. He had never seen such a dog before. Tim Keenan shoved the bull-dog forward with a muttered 'Go to it.' The animal waddled toward the centre of the circle, short and squat and ungainly. He came to a stop and blinked across at White Fang.

There were cries from the crowd of 'Go to him, Cherokee! Sick 'm, Cherokee! Eat 'm up!'

But Cherokee did not seem anxious to fight. He turned his head and blinked at the men who shouted, at the same time wagging his stump of a tail good-naturedly. He was not afraid, but merely lazy. Besides, it did not seem to him that it was intended he should fight with the dog he saw before him. He was not used to fighting with that kind of dog, and he was waiting for them to bring on the real dog.

Tim Keenan stepped in and bent over Cherokee, fondling him on both sides of the shoulders with hands that rubbed against the grain of the hair and that made slight, pushing-forward movements. These were so many suggestions. Also, their effect was irritating, for Cherokee began to growl, very softly, deep down in his throat. There was a correspondence in rhythm between the growls and the movements of the man's hands. The growl rose in the throat with the culmination of each forward-pushing movement, and ebbed down to start up afresh with the beginning of the next movement. The end of each movement was the accent of the rhythm, the movement ending abruptly and the growling rising with a jerk.

This was not without its effect on White Fang. The hair began to rise on his neck and across the shoulders. Tim Keenan gave a final shove forward and stepped back again. As the impetus that carried Cherokee forward died down, he continued to go forward of his own volition, in a swift, bow-legged run. Then White Fang struck. A cry of startled admiration went up. He had covered the distance and gone in more like a cat than a dog; and with the same cat-like swiftness he had slashed with his fangs and leaped clear.

The bull-dog was bleeding back of one ear from a rip in his thick neck. He gave no sign, did not even snarl, but turned and followed after White Fang. The display on both sides, the quickness of the one and the steadiness of the other, had excited the partisan spirit of the crowd, and the men were making new bets and increasing original bets. Again and yet again White Fang sprang in, slashed, and got away untouched; and still his strange foe followed after him, without too great haste, not slowly, but deliberately and determinedly, in a businesslike sort of way. There was purpose in his method – something for him to do that he was intent upon doing and from which nothing could distract him.

His whole demeanour, every action, was stamped with this purpose. It puzzled White Fang. Never had he seen such a dog. It had no hair protection. It was soft, and bled easily. There was no thick mat of fur to baffle White Fang's teeth as they were often baffled by dogs of his own breed. Each time that his teeth struck they sank easily into the yielding flesh, while the animal did not seem able to defend itself. Another disconcerting thing was that it made no outcry, such as he had been accustomed to with the other dogs he had fought. Beyond a growl or a grunt, the dog took its punishment silently. And never did it flag in its pursuit of him.

Not that Cherokee was slow. He could turn and whirl swiftly enough, but White Fang was never there. Cherokee was puzzled too. He had never fought before with a dog with which he could not close. The desire to close had always been mutual. But here was a dog that kept at a distance, dancing and dodging here and there and all about. And when it did get its teeth into him, it did not hold on, but let go instantly and darted away again.

But White Fang could not get at the soft underside of the throat. The bull-dog stood too short, while its massive jaws were an added protection. White Fang darted in and out unscathed, while Cherokee's wounds increased. Both sides of his neck and head were ripped and slashed. He bled freely, but showed no signs of being disconcerted. He continued his plodding pursuit, though once, for the moment baffled, he came to a full stop and blinked at the men who looked on, at the same time wagging his stump of a tail as an expression of his willingness to fight.

In that moment White Fang was in upon him and out, in passing ripping his trimmed remnant of an ear. With a slight manifestation of anger, Cherokee took up the pursuit again, running on the inside of the circle White Fang was making, and striving to fasten his deadly grip on White Fang's throat. The bull-dog missed by a hair's-breadth, and cries of praise went up as White Fang doubled suddenly out of danger in the opposite direction.

The time went by. White Fang still danced on, dodging and doubling, leaping in and out, and ever inflicting damage. And still the bull-dog, with grim certitude, toiled after him. Sooner or later he would accomplish his purpose, get the grip that would win the battle. In the meantime he accepted all the punishment the other could deal him. His tufts of ears had become tassels, his neck and shoulders were slashed in a score of places, and his very lips were cut and bleeding – all from those lightning snaps that were beyond his foreseeing and guarding.

Time and again White Fang had attempted to knock Cherokee off his feet; but the difference in their height was too great. Cherokee was too squat, too close to the ground. White Fang tried the trick once too often. The chance came in one of his quick doublings and counter-circlings. He caught Cherokee with head turned away as he whirled more slowly. His shoulder was exposed. White Fang drove in upon it; but his own shoulder was high above, while he struck with such force that his momentum carried him on across over the other's body. For the first time in his fighting history, men saw White

Fang lose his footing. His body turned a half-somersault in the air, and he would have landed on his back had he not twisted, catlike, still in the air, in the effort to bring his feet to the earth. As it was, he struck heavily on his side. The next instant he was on his feet, but in that instant Cherokee's teeth closed on his throat.

It was not a good grip, being too low down toward the chest; but Cherokee held on. White Fang sprang to his feet and tore wildly around, trying to shake off the bull-dog's body. It made him frantic, this clinging, dragging weight. It bound his movements, restricted his freedom. It was like the trap, and all his instinct resented it and revolted against it. It was a mad revolt. For several minutes he was to all intents insane. The basic life that was in him took charge of him. The will to exist of his body surged over him. He was dominated by this mere flesh-love of life. All intelligence was gone. It was as though he had no brain. His reason was unseated by the blind yearning of the flesh to exist and move, at all hazards to move, to continue to move, for movement was the expression of its existence.

Round and round he went, whirling and turning and reversing, trying to shake off the fifty-pound weight that dragged at his throat. The bull-dog did little but keep his grip. Sometimes, and rarely, he managed to get his feet to the earth and for a moment to brace himself against White Fang. But the next moment his footing would be lost, and he would be dragging around in the whirl of one of White Fang's mad gyrations. Cherokee identified himself with his instinct. He knew that he was doing the right thing by holding on, and there came to him certain blissful thrills of satisfaction. At such moments he even closed his eyes and allowed his body to be hurled hither and thither, willy-nilly, careless of any hurt that might thereby come to it. That did not count. The grip was the thing, and the grip he kept.

White Fang ceased only when he had tired himself out. He could do nothing, and he could not understand. Never, in all his fighting, had this thing happened. The dogs he had fought with did not fight that way. With them it was snap and slash and get away, snap and slash and get away. He lay partly on his side, panting for breath. Cherokee, still holding his grip, urged against him, trying to get him over entirely on his side. White Fang resisted, and he could feel the jaws shifting their grip, slightly relaxing and coming together again in a chewing movement. Each shift brought the grip closer in to his throat. The bull-dog's method was to hold what he had, and when opportunity favoured to work in for more. Opportunity favoured when White Fang remained quiet. When White Fang struggled, Cherokee was content merely to hold on.

The bulging back of Cherokee's neck was the only portion of his body that White Fang's teeth could reach. He got hold toward the base, where the neck comes out from the shoulders; but he did not know the chewing method of fighting, nor were his jaws adapted to it. He spasmodically ripped and tore with his fangs for a space. Then a change in their position diverted him. The bull-dog had managed to roll him over on his back, and still hanging on to his throat, was on top of him. Like a cat, White Fang bowed his hind-quarters in, and, with the feet digging into his enemy's abdomen above him, he began to claw with long tearing strokes. Cherokee might well have been disembowelled had he not quickly pivoted on his grip and got his body off of White Fang's and at right angles to it.

There was no escaping that grip. It was like Fate itself, and as inexorable. Slowly it shifted up along the jugular. All that saved White Fang from death was the loose skin of his neck and the thick fur that covered it. This served to form a large roll in Cherokee's mouth, the fur of which well-nigh defied his teeth. But bit by bit, whenever the chance offered, he was getting more of the loose skin and fur in his mouth. The result was that he was slowly throttling White Fang. The latter's breath was drawn with greater and greater difficulty as the moments went by.

It began to look as though the battle were over. The backers of Cherokee waxed jubilant and offered ridiculous odds. White Fang's backers were correspondingly depressed, and refused bets of ten to one and twenty to one, though one man was rash enough to close a wager of fifty to one. This man was Beauty Smith. He took a step into the ring and pointed his finger at White Fang. Then he began to laugh derisively and scornfully. This produced the desired effect. White Fang went wild with rage. He called up his reserves of strength and gained his feet. As he struggled around the ring, the fifty pounds of his foe ever dragging on his throat, his anger passed on into panic. The basic life of him dominated him again, and his intelligence fled before the will of his flesh to live. Round and round and back again, stumbling and falling and rising, even uprearing at times on his hind-legs and lifting his foe clear of the earth, he struggled vainly to shake off the clinging death.

At last he fell, toppling backward, exhausted; and the bull-dog promptly shifted his grip, getting in closer, mangling more and more of the fur-folded flesh, throttling White Fang more severely than ever. Shouts of applause went up for the victor, and there were many cries of 'Cherokee!' 'Cherokee!' To this Cherokee responded by vigorous wagging of the stump of his tail. But the clamour of approval did not distract him. There was no sympathetic relation between his tail and his massive jaws. The one might wag, but the others held their terrible grip on White Fang's throat.

It was at this time that a diversion came to the spectators. There was a jingle of bells. Dog-mushers' cries were heard. Everybody, save Beauty Smith, looked apprehensively, the fear of the police strong upon them. But they saw, up the trail and not down, two men running with sled and dogs. They were evidently coming down the creek from some prospecting trip. At sight of the crowd they stopped their dogs and came over and joined it, curious to see the cause of the excitement. The dog-musher wore a moustache, but the other, a taller and younger man, was smooth-shaven, his skin rosy from the pounding of his blood and the running in the frosty air.

White Fang had practically ceased struggling. Now and again he resisted spasmodically and to no purpose. He could get little air, and that little grew less and less under the merciless grip that ever tightened. In spite of his armour of fur, the great vein of his throat would have long since been torn open, had not the first grip of the bull-dog been so low down as to be practically on the chest. It had taken Cherokee a long time to shift that grip upward, and this had also tended further to clog his jaws with fur and skin-fold.

In the meantime, the abysmal brute in Beauty Smith

had been rising up into his brain and mastering the small bit of sanity that he possessed at best. When he saw White Fang's eyes beginning to glaze, he knew beyond doubt that the fight was lost. Then he broke loose. He sprang upon White Fang and began savagely to kick him. There were hisses from the crowd and cries of protest, but that was all. While this went on, and Beauty Smith continued to kick White Fang, there was a commotion in the crowd. The tall young newcomer was forcing his way through, shouldering men right and left without ceremony or gentleness. When he broke through into the ring, Beauty Smith was just in the act of delivering another kick. All his weight was on one foot, and he was in a state of unstable equilibrium. At that moment the newcomer's fist landed a smashing blow full in his face. Beauty Smith's remaining leg left the ground, and his whole body seemed to lift into the air as he turned over backward and struck the snow. The newcomer turned upon the crowd.

'You cowards!' he cried. 'You beasts!'

He was in a rage himself – a sane rage. His grey eyes seemed metallic and steel-like as they flashed upon the crowd. Beauty Smith regained his feet and came toward him, sniffing and cowardly. The newcomer did not understand. He did not know how abject a coward the other was, and thought he was coming back intent on fighting. So, with a 'You beast!' he smashed Beauty Smith over backward with a second blow in the face. Beauty Smith decided that the snow was the safest place for him, and lay where he had fallen, making no effort to get up.

'Come on, Matt; lend a hand,' the newcomer called to the dog-musher, who had followed him into the ring.

Both men bent over the dogs. Matt took hold of White Fang, ready to pull when Cherokee's jaws should be loosened. This the younger man endeavoured to accomplish by clutching the bull-dog's jaws in his hands and trying to spread them. It was a vain undertaking. As he pulled and tugged and wrenched, he kept exclaiming with every expulsion of breath, 'Beasts!'

The crowd began to grow unruly, and some of the men were protesting against the spoiling of the sport; but they were silenced when the newcomer lifted his head from his work for a moment and glared at them.

'You damn beasts!' he finally exploded, and went back to his task.

'It's no use, Mr Scott; you can't break 'm apart that way,' Matt said at last.

The pair paused and surveyed the locked dogs.

'Ain't bleedin' much,' Matt announced. 'Ain't got all the way in yet.'

'But he's liable to any moment,' Scott answered. 'There! did you see that? He shifted his grip in a bit.'

The younger man's excitement and apprehension for White Fang was growing. He struck Cherokee about the head savagely again and again. But that did not loosen the jaws. Cherokee wagged the stump of his tail in advertisement that he understood the meaning of the blows, but that he knew he was himself in the right and only doing his duty by keeping his grip.

'Won't some of you help?' Scott cried desperately at the crowd.

But no help was offered. Instead, the crowd began sarcastically to cheer him on and showered him with facetious advice.

'You'll have to get a pry,' Matt counselled.

The other reached into the holster at his hip, drew his revolver, and tried to thrust its muzzle between the bull-dog's jaws. He shoved, and shoved hard, till the grating of the steel against the locked teeth could be distinctly heard. Both men were on their knees, bending over the dogs. Tim Keenan strode into the ring. He paused beside Scott and touched him on the shoulder, saying ominously:

'Don't break them teeth, stranger.'

'Then I'll break his neck,' Scott retorted, continuing his shoving and wedging with the revolver muzzle.

'I said don't break them teeth,' the faro-dealer repeated more ominously than before.

But if it was bluff he intended, it did not work. Scott never desisted from his efforts, though he looked up coolly and asked:

'Your dog?'

The faro-dealer grunted.

'Then get in here and break this grip.'

'Well, stranger,' the other drawled irritatingly, 'I don't mind telling you that's something I ain't worked out for myself. I don't know how to turn the trick.'

'Then get out of the way,' was the reply, 'and don't bother me. I'm busy.'

Tim Keenan continued standing over him, but Scott took no further notice of his presence. He had managed to get the muzzle in between the jaws on one side, and was trying to get it out between the jaws on the other side. This accomplished, he pried gently and carefully, loosening the jaws a bit at a time; while Matt, a bit at a time, extricated White Fang's mangled neck.

'Stand by to receive your dog,' was Scott's peremptory order to Cherokee's owner.

The faro-dealer stooped down obediently and got a firm hold on Cherokee.

'Now!' Scott warned, giving the final pry.

The dogs were drawn apart, the bull-dog struggling vigorously.

'Take him away,' Scott commanded; and Tim Keenan dragged Cherokee back into the crowd.

White Fang made several ineffectual efforts to get up. Once he gained his feet, but his legs were too weak to sustain him, and he slowly wilted and sank back into the snow. His eyes were half closed, and the surface of them was glassy. His jaws were apart, and through them the tongue protruded, draggled and limp. To all appearances he looked like a dog that had been strangled to death. Matt examined him.

'Just about all in,' he announced; 'but he's breathin' all right.'

Beauty Smith had regained his feet and come over to look at White Fang.

'Matt, how much is a good sled-dog worth?' Scott asked.

The dog-musher, still on his knees and stooped over White Fang, calculated for a moment.

'Three hundred dollars,' he answered.

'And how much for one that's all chewed up like this one?' Scott asked, nudging White Fang with his foot.

'Half of that,' was the dog-musher's judgment.

Scott turned upon Beauty Smith.

'Did you hear, Mr Beast? I'm going to take your dog from you, and I'm going to give you a hundred and fifty for him.'

He opened his pocket-book and counted out the bills.

Beauty Smith put his hands behind his back, refusing to touch the proffered money.

'I ain't a-sellin',' he said.

'Oh yes, you are,' the other assured him. 'Because I'm buying. Here's your money. The dog's mine.'

Beauty Smith, his hands still behind him, began to back away.

Scott sprang toward him, drawing his fist back to strike. Beauty Smith cowered down in anticipation of the blow.

'I've got my rights,' he whimpered.

'You've forfeited your rights to own that dog,' was the rejoinder. 'Are you going to take the money, or do I have to hit you again?'

'All right,' Beauty Smith spoke up with the alacrity of fear. 'But I take the money under protest,' he added. 'The dog's a mint. I ain't a-goin' to be robbed. A man's got his rights.'

'Correct,' Scott answered, passing the money over to him. 'A man's got his rights. But you're not a man. You're a beast.'

'Wait till I get back to Dawson,' Beauty Smith threatened. 'I'll have the law on you.'

'If you open your mouth when you get back to Dawson, I'll have you run out of town. Understand?'

Beauty Smith replied with a grunt.

'Understand?' the other thundered, with abrupt fierceness.

'Yes,' Beauty Smith grunted, shrinking away.

'Yes what?'

'Yes, sir,' Beauty Smith snarled.

'Look out! He'll bite!' someone shouted, and a guffaw of laughter went up.

Scott turned his back on him, and returned to help the dog-musher, who was working over White Fang.

Some of the men were already departing; others stood in groups looking on and talking. Tim Keenan joined one of the groups.

'Who's that mug?' he asked.

'Weedon Scott,' someone answered.

'And who in hell is Weedon Scott?' the faro-dealer demanded.

'Oh, one of them crack-a-jack minin' experts. He's in with all the big bugs. If you want to keep out of trouble, you'll steer clear of him; that's my talk. He's all hunky with the officials. The Gold Commissioner's a special pal of his.'

'I thought he must be somebody,' was the faro-dealer's comment. 'That's why I kept my hands offen him at the start.'

CHAPTER
5

THE INDOMITABLE

'It's hopeless,' Weedon Scott confessed.

He sat on the step of his cabin and stared at the dog-musher, who responded with a shrug that was equally hopeless.

Together they looked at White Fang at the end of his stretched chain, bristling, snarling, ferocious, straining to get at the sled-dogs. Having received sundry lessons from Matt, said lessons being imparted by means of a club, the sled-dogs had learned to leave White Fang alone; and even then they were lying down at a distance, apparently oblivious of his existence.

'It's a wolf, and there's no taming it,' Weedon Scott announced.

'Oh, I don't know about that,' Matt objected. 'Might be a lot of dog in 'm, for all you can tell. But there's one thing I know sure, an' that there's no gettin' away from.'

The dog-musher paused and nodded his head confidentially at Moosehide Mountain.

'Well, don't be a miser with what you know,' Scott said sharply, after waiting a suitable length of time. 'Spit it out. What is it?'

The dog-musher indicated White Fang with a backward thrust of his thumb.

'Wolf or dog, it's all the same; he's ben tamed a'ready.'

'No!'

'I tell you yes, an' broke to harness. Look close there. D'ye see them marks across the chest?'

'You're right, Matt. He was a sled-dog before Beauty Smith got hold of him.'

'And there's not much reason against his bein' a sled-dog again.'

'What d' ye think?' Scott queried eagerly. Then the hope died down as he added, shaking his head, 'We've had him two weeks now, and if anything he's wilder than ever at the present moment.'

'Give 'm a chance,' Matt counselled. 'Turn 'm loose for a spell.'

The other looked at him incredulously.

'Yes,' Matt went on; 'I know you've tried to, but you didn't take a club.'

'You try it then.'

The dog-musher secured a club and went over to the chained animal. White Fang watched the club after the manner of a caged lion watching the whip of its trainer.

'See 'm keep his eye on that club,' Matt said. 'That's a good sign. He's no fool. Don't dast tackle me so long as I got that club handy. He's not clean crazy, sure.'

As the man's hand approached his neck, White Fang bristled and snarled and crouched down. But while he eyed the approaching hand, he at the same time contrived to keep track of the club in the other hand, suspended threateningly above him. Matt unsnapped the chain from the collar and stepped back.

White Fang could scarcely realize that he was free.

Many months had gone by since he passed into the possession of Beauty Smith, and in all that period he had never known a moment of freedom except at the times he had been loosed to fight with other dogs. Immediately after such fights he had always been imprisoned again.

He did not know what to make of it. Perhaps some new devilry of the gods was about to be perpetrated on him. He walked slowly and cautiously, prepared to be assailed at any moment. He did not know what to do, it was all so unprecedented. He took the precaution to sheer off from the two watching gods, and walked carefully to the corner of the cabin. Nothing happened. He was plainly perplexed, and he came back again, pausing a dozen feet away and regarding the two men intently.

'Won't he run away?' his new owner asked.

Matt shrugged his shoulders. 'Got to take a gamble. Only way to find out is to find out.'

'Poor devil,' Scott murmured pityingly. 'What he needs is some show of human kindness,' he added, turning and going into the cabin.

He came out with a piece of meat, which he tossed to White Fang. He sprang away from it, and from a distance studied it suspiciously.

'Hi-yu, Major!' Matt shouted warningly, but too late.

Major had made a spring for the meat. At the instant his jaws closed on it, White Fang struck him. He was overthrown. Matt rushed in, but quicker than he was White Fang. Major staggered to his feet, but the blood spouting from his throat reddened the snow in a widening path.

'It's too bad, but it served him right,' Scott said hastily.

But Matt's foot had already started on its way to kick White Fang. There was a leap, a flash of teeth, a sharp exclamation. White Fang, snarling fiercely, scrambled backward for several yards, while Matt stooped and investigated his leg.

'He got me all right,' he announced, pointing to the torn trousers and underclothes, and the growing stain of red.

'I told you it was hopeless, Matt,' Scott said in a discouraged voice. 'I've thought about it off and on, while not wanting to think of it. But we've come to it now. It's the only thing to do.'

As he talked, with reluctant movements he drew his revolver, threw open the cylinder, and assured himself of its contents.

'Look here, Mr Scott,' Matt objected; 'that dog's ben through hell. You can't expect 'm to come out a white an' shinin' angel. Give 'm time.'

'Look at Major,' the other rejoined.

The dog-musher surveyed the stricken dog. He had sunk down on the snow in the circle of his blood, and was plainly in the last gasp.

'Served 'm right. You said so yourself, Mr Scott. He tried to take White Fang's meat, an' he's dead-O. That was to be expected. I wouldn't give two whoops in hell for a dog that wouldn't fight for his own meat.'

'But look at yourself, Matt. It's all right about the dogs, but we must draw the line somewhere.'

'Served me right,' Matt argued stubbornly. 'What'd I want to kick 'm for? You said yourself that he'd done right. Then I had no right to kick 'm.'

'It would be a mercy to kill him,' Scott insisted. 'He's untamable.'

'Now look here, Mr Scott; give the poor devil a fightin' chance. He ain't had no chance yet. He's just come through hell, an' this is the first time he's ben loose. Give 'm a fair chance, an' if he don't deliver the goods, I'll kill 'm myself. There!'

'God knows I don't want to kill him or have him killed,' Scott answered, putting away the revolver. 'We'll let him run loose and see what kindness can do for him. And here's a try at it.'

He walked over to White Fang and began talking to him gently and soothingly.

'Better have a club handy,' Matt warned.

Scott shook his head and went on trying to win White Fang's confidence.

White Fang was suspicious. Something was impending. He had killed this god's dog, bitten his companion god, and what else was to be expected than some terrible punishment? But in the face of it he was indomitable. He bristled and showed his teeth, his eyes vigilant, his whole body wary and prepared for anything. The god had no club, so he suffered him to approach quite near. The god's hand had come out and was descending upon his head. White Fang shrank together and grew tense as he crouched under it. Here was danger – some treachery or something. He knew the hands of the gods, their proved mastery, their cunning to hurt. Besides, there was his old antipathy to being touched. He snarled more menacingly, crouched still lower, and still the hand descended. He did not want to bite the hand, and he endured the peril of it until his instinct surged up in him, mastering him with its insatiable yearning for life.

Weedon Scott had believed that he was quick enough to avoid any snap or slash. But he had yet to learn the remarkable quickness of White Fang, who struck with the certainty and swiftness of a coiled snake.

Scott cried out sharply with surprise, catching his torn hand and holding it tightly in his other hand. Matt uttered a great oath and sprang to his side. White Fang crouched down and backed away, bristling, showing his fangs, his eyes malignant with menace. Now he could expect a beating as fearful as any he had received from Beauty Smith.

'Here! What are you doing?' Scott cried suddenly.

Matt had dashed into the cabin and come out with a rifle.

'Nothin',' he said slowly, with a careless calmness that was assumed; 'only goin' to keep that promise I made. I reckon it's up to me to kill 'm as I said I'd do.'

'No you don't!'

'Yes I do. Watch me.'

As Matt had pleaded for White Fang when he had been bitten, it was now Weedon Scott's turn to plead.

'You said to give him a chance. Well, give it to him. We've only just started, and we can't quit at the beginning. It served me right, this time. And – look at him!'

White Fang, near the corner of the cabin and forty feet away, was snarling with blood-curdling viciousness, not at Scott, but at the dog-musher.

'Well, I'll be everlastin'ly gosh-swoggled!' was the dog-musher's expression of astonishment.

'Look at the intelligence of him!' Scott went on hastily. 'He knows the meaning of firearms as well as you do. He's got intelligence, and we've got to give that intelligence a chance. Put up the gun.'

'All right; I'm willin',' Matt agreed, leaning the rifle against the wood-pile.

'But will you look at that!' he exclaimed the next moment.

White Fang had quieted down and ceased snarling. 'This is worth investigatin'. Watch!'

Matt reached for the rifle, and at the same moment White Fang snarled. He stepped away from the rifle, and White Fang's lifted lips descended, covering his teeth.

'Now, just for fun.'

Matt took the rifle and began slowly to raise it to his shoulder. White Fang's snarling began with the movement, and increased as the movement approached its culmination. But the moment before the rifle came to a level on him, he leaped sidewise behind the corner of the cabin. Matt stood staring along the sights at the empty space of snow which had been occupied by White Fang.

The dog-musher put the rifle down solemnly, then turned and looked at his employer.

'I agree with you, Mr Scott. That dog's too intelligent to kill.'

THE LOVE-MASTER

As White Fang watched Weedon Scott approach, he
bristled and snarled to advertise that he would not submit to punishment. Twenty-four hours had passed since
he had slashed open the hand that was now bandaged
and held up by a sling to keep the blood out of it. In the
past White Fang had experienced delayed punishments,
and he apprehended that such a one was about to befall
him. How could it be otherwise? He had committed
what was to him sacrilege – sunk his fangs into the holy
flesh of a god, and of a white-skinned superior god at
that. In the nature of things, and of intercourse with
gods, something terrible awaited him.

The god sat down several feet away. White Fang could
see nothing dangerous in that. When the gods administered punishment they stood on their legs. Besides, this
god had no club, no whip, no firearm. And furthermore,
he himself was free. No chain nor stick bound him. He
could escape into safety while the god was scrambling to
his feet. In the meantime he would wait and see.

The god remained quiet, made no movement; and
White Fang's snarl slowly dwindled to a growl that
ebbed down in his throat and ceased. Then the god

spoke, and at the first sound of his voice the hair rose on White Fang's neck and the growl rushed up in his throat. But the god made no hostile movement, and went on calmly talking. For a time White Fang growled in unison with him, a correspondence of rhythm being established between growl and voice. But the god talked on interminably. He talked to White Fang as White Fang had never been talked to before. He talked softly and soothingly, with a gentleness that somehow, some- where, touched White Fang. In spite of himself and all the pricking warnings of his instinct, White Fang began to have confidence in this god. He had a feeling of security that was belied by all his experience with men.

After a long time the god got up and went into the cabin. White Fang scanned him apprehensively when he came out. He had neither whip nor club nor weapon. Nor was his uninjured hand behind his back hiding something. He sat down as before, in the same spot, several feet away. He held out a small piece of meat. White Fang pricked his ears and investigated it sus- piciously, managing to look at the same time both at the meat and the god, alert for any overt act, his body tense and ready to spring away at the first sign of hostility.

Still the punishment delayed. The god merely held near to his nose a piece of meat. And about the meat there seemed nothing wrong. Still White Fang suspected; and though the meat was proffered to him with short inviting thrusts of the hand, he refused to touch it. The gods were all-wise, and there was no telling what masterful treachery lurked behind that apparently harmless piece of meat. In past experience, especially in dealing with squaws, meat and punishment had often been disas- trously related.

In the end, the god tossed the meat on the snow at White Fang's feet. He smelled the meat carefully, but he did not look at it. While he smelled it he kept his eyes on the god. Nothing happened. He took the meat into his mouth and swallowed it. Still nothing happened. The god was actually offering him another piece of meat. Again he refused to take it from the hand, and again it was tossed to him. This was repeated a number of times. But there came a time when the god refused to toss it. He kept it in his hand and steadfastly proffered it.

The meat was good meat, and White Fang was hungry. Bit by bit, infinitely cautious, he approached the hand. At last the time came that he decided to eat the meat from the hand. He never took his eyes from the god, thrusting his head forward with ears flattened back and hair involuntarily rising and cresting on his neck. Also a low growl rumbled in his throat as warning that he was not to be trifled with. He ate the meat, and nothing happened. Piece by piece he ate all the meat, and nothing happened. Still the punishment delayed.

He licked his chops and waited. The god went on talking. In his voice was kindness – something of which White Fang had no experience whatever. And within him it aroused feelings which he had likewise never experienced before. He was aware of a certain strange satisfaction, as though some need were being gratified, as though some void in his being were being filled. Then again came the prod of his instinct and the warning of past experience. The gods were ever crafty, and they had unguessed ways of attaining their ends.

Ah, he had thought so! There it came now, the god's hand, cunning to hurt, thrusting out at him, descending upon his head. But the god went on talking. His voice was soft and soothing. In spite of the menacing hand the voice inspired confidence. And in spite of the assuring voice the hand inspired distrust. White Fang was torn by conflicting feelings, impulses. It seemed he would fly to pieces, so terrible was the control he was exerting, holding together by an unwonted indecision the counter-forces that struggled within him for mastery.

He compromised. He snarled and bristled and flattened his ears. But he neither snapped nor sprang away. The hand descended. Nearer and nearer it came. It touched the ends of his upstanding hair. He shrank down under it. It followed down after him, pressing more closely against him. Shrinking, almost shivering, he still managed to hold himself together. It was a torment, this hand that touched him and violated his instinct. He could not forget in a day all the evil that had been wrought him at the hands of men. But it was the will of the god, and he strove to submit.

The hand lifted and descended again in a patting, caressing movement. This continued, but every time the hand lifted the hair lifted under it. And every time the hand descended the ears flattened down and a cavernous growl surged in his throat. White Fang growled and growled with insistent warning. By this means he announced that he was prepared to retaliate for any hurt he might receive. There was no telling when the god's ulterior motive might be disclosed. At any moment that soft, confidence-inspiring voice might break forth in a roar of wrath, that gentle and caressing hand transform itself into a vice-like grip to hold him helpless and administer punishment.

But the god talked on softly, and ever the hand rose

and fell with non-hostile pats. White Fang experienced dual feelings. It was distasteful to his instinct. It restrained him, opposed the will of him toward personal liberty. And yet it was not physically painful. On the contrary, it was even pleasant, in a physical way. The patting movement slowly and carefully changed to a rubbing of the ears about their bases, and the physical pleasure even increased a little. Yet he continued to fear, and he stood on guard, expectant of unguessed evil, alternately suffering and enjoying as one feeling or the other came uppermost and swayed him.

'Well, I'll be gosh-swoggled!'

So spoke Matt, coming out of the cabin, his sleeves rolled up, a pan of dirty dish-water in his hands, arrested in the act of emptying the pan by the sight of Weedon Scott patting White Fang.

At the instant his voice broke the silence White Fang leaped back, snarling savagely at him.

Matt regarded his employer with grieved disapproval.

'If you don't mind my expressin' my feelin's, Mr Scott, I'll make free to say you're seventeen kinds of a damn fool, an' all of 'em different, an' then some.'

Weedon Scott smiled with a superior air, gained his feet, and walked over to White Fang. He talked soothingly to him, but not for long, then slowly put out his hand, rested it on White Fang's head, and resumed the interrupted patting. White Fang endured it, keeping his eyes fixed suspiciously, not upon the man that petted him, but upon the man that stood in the doorway.

'You may be a number one tip-top minin' expert, all right, all right,' the dog-musher delivered himself oracularly, 'but you missed the chance of your life when you was a boy an' didn't run off an' join a circus.'

White Fang snarled at the sound of his voice, but this time did not leap away from under the hand that was caressing his head and the back of his neck with long, soothing strokes.

It was the beginning of the end for White Fang – the ending of the old life and the reign of hate. A new and incomprehensively fairer life was dawning. It required much thinking and endless patience on the part of Weedon Scott to accomplish this. And on the part of White Fang it required nothing less than a revolution. He had to ignore the urges and promptings of instinct and reason, defy experience, give the lie to life itself.

Life, as he had known it, not only had had no place in it for much that he now did, but all the currents had gone counter to those to which he now abandoned himself. In short, when all things were considered, he had to achieve an orientation far vaster than the one he had achieved at the time he came voluntarily in from the Wild and accepted Grey Beaver as his lord. At that time he was a mere puppy, soft from the making, without form, ready for the thumb of circumstance to begin its work upon him. But now it was different. The thumb of circumstance had done its work only too well. By it he had been formed and hardened into the Fighting Wolf, fierce and implacable, unloving and unlovable. To accomplish the change was like a reflux of being, and this when the plasticity of youth was no longer his; when the fibre of him had become tough and knotty; when the warp and the woof of him had made of him an adamantine texture, harsh and unyielding; when the face of his spirit had become iron and all his instincts and axioms had crystallized into set rules, cautions, dislikes, and desires.

Yet again, in this new orientation, it was the thumb of circumstance that pressed and prodded him, softening that which had become hard and remoulding it into fairer form. Weedon Scott was in truth this thumb. He had gone to the roots of White Fang's nature, and with kindness touched to life potencies that had languished and well-nigh perished. One such potency was *love*. It took the place of *like*, which latter had been the highest feeling that thrilled him in his intercourse with the gods.

But this love did not come in a day. It began with *like*, and out of it slowly developed. White Fang did not run away, though he was allowed to remain loose, because he liked this new god. This was certainly better than the life he had lived in the cage of Beauty Smith, and it was necessary that he should have some god. The lordship of man was a need of his nature. The seal of his dependence on man had been set upon him in that early day when he turned his back on the Wild and crawled to Grey Beaver's feet to receive the expected beating. This seal had been stamped upon him again, and ineradicably, on his second return from the Wild, when the long famine was over and there was fish once more in the village of Grey Beaver.

And so, because he needed a god and because he preferred Weedon Scott to Beauty Smith, White Fang remained. In acknowledgment of fealty, he proceeded to take upon himself the guardianship of his master's property. He prowled about the cabin while the sled-dogs slept, and the first night-visitor to the cabin fought him off with a club until Weedon Scott came to the rescue. But White Fang soon learned to differentiate between thieves and honest men, to appraise the true value of step and carriage. The man who travelled, loud-stepping, the direct line to the cabin door, he let alone, though he watched him vigilantly until the door opened and he received the endorsement of the master. But the man who went softly, by circuitous ways, peering with caution, seeking after secrecy – that was the man who received no suspension of judgment from White Fang, and who went away abruptly, hurriedly, and without dignity.

Weedon Scott had set himself the task of redeeming White Fang – or rather, of redeeming mankind from the wrong it had done White Fang. It was a matter of principle and conscience. He felt that the ill done White Fang was a debt incurred by man, and that it must be paid. So he went out of his way to be especially kind to the Fighting Wolf. Each day he made it a point to caress and pet White Fang, and to do it at length.

At first suspicious and hostile, White Fang grew to like this petting. But there was one thing that he never outgrew – his growling. Growl he would, from the moment the petting began till it ended. But it was a growl with a new note in it. A stranger could not hear this note, and to such a stranger the growling of White Fang was an exhibition of primordial savagery, nerve-racking and blood-curdling. But White Fang's throat had become harsh-fibred from the making of ferocious sounds through the many years since his first little rasp of anger in the lair of his cubhood, and he could not soften the sounds of that throat now to express the gentleness he felt. Nevertheless, Weedon Scott's ear and sympathy were fine enough to catch the new note all but drowned in the fierceness – the note that was the faintest hint of a croon of content and that none but he could hear.

As the days went by, the evolution of *like* into *love* was accelerated. White Fang himself began to grow aware of it, though in his consciousness he knew not what love was. It manifested itself to him as a void in his being – a hungry, aching, yearning void that clamoured to be filled. It was a pain and an unrest, and it received easement only by the touch of the new god's presence. At such times love was a joy to him – a wild, keen-thrilling satisfaction. But when away from his god the pain and the unrest returned; the void in him sprang up and pressed against him with its emptiness, and the hunger gnawed and gnawed unceasingly.

White Fang was in the process of finding himself. In spite of the maturity of his years and of the savage rigidity of the mould that had formed him, his nature was undergoing an expansion. There was a burgeoning within him of strange feelings and unwonted impulses. His old code of conduct was changing. In the past he had liked comfort and surcease from pain, disliked discomfort and pain, and he had adjusted his actions accordingly. But now it was different.

Because of this new feeling within him he ofttimes elected discomfort and pain for the sake of his god. Thus, in the early morning, instead of roaming and foraging or lying in a sheltered nook, he would wait for hours on the cheerless cabin-stoop for a sight of the god's face. At night, when the god returned home, White Fang would leave the warm sleeping-place he had burrowed in the snow in order to receive the friendly snap of fingers and the word of greeting. Meat, even meat itself, he would forgo to be with his god, to receive a caress from him, or to accompanying him down into the town.

Like had been replaced by *love*. And love was the plummet dropped down into the deeps of him where like had never gone. And responsive out of his deeps had come the new thing – love. That which was given unto him did he return. This was a god indeed, a love-god, a warm and radiant god, in whose light White Fang's nature expanded as a flower expands under the sun.

But White Fang was not demonstrative. He was too old, too firmly moulded, to become adept at expressing himself in new ways. He was too self-possessed, too strongly poised in his own isolation. Too long had he cultivated reticence, aloofness, and moroseness. He had never barked in his life, and he could not now learn to bark a welcome when his god approached. He was never in the way, never extravagant nor foolish in the expression of his love. He never ran to meet his god. He waited at a distance; but he always waited, was always there. His love partook of the nature of worship – dumb, inarticulate, a silent adoration. Only by the steady regard of his eyes did he express his love, and by the unceasing following with his eyes of his god's every movement. Also, at times, when his god looked at him and spoke to him, he betrayed an awkward self-consciousness, caused by the struggle of his love to express itself and his physical inability to express it.

He learned to adjust himself in many ways to his new mode of life. It was borne in upon him that he must let his master's dogs alone. Yet his dominant nature asserted itself, and he had first to thrash them into an acknowledgment of his superiority and leadership. This accomplished, he had little trouble with them. They gave trail to him when he came and went or walked among them, and when he asserted his will they obeyed.

In the same way, he came to tolerate Matt – as a possession of his master. His master rarely fed him. Matt did that – it was his business; yet White Fang divined that it was his master's food he ate, and that it was his master who thus fed him vicariously. Matt it was who tried to put him into the harness and make him haul sled with the other dogs. But Matt failed. It was not until Weedon Scott put the harness on White Fang and worked him that he understood. He took it as his master's will that Matt should drive him and work him, just as he drove and worked his master's other dogs.

Different from the Mackenzie toboggans were the Klondike sleds with runners under them. And different was the method of driving the dogs. There was no fan formation of the team. The dogs worked in single file, one behind another, hauling on double traces. And here, in the Klondike, the leader was indeed the leader. The wisest as well as strongest dog was the leader, and the team obeyed him and feared him. That White Fang should quickly gain this post was inevitable. He could not be satisfied with less, as Matt learned after much inconvenience and trouble. White Fang picked out the post for himself, and Matt backed his judgment with strong language after the experiment had been tried. But though he worked in the sled in the day, White Fang did not forego the guarding of his master's property in the night. Thus he was on duty all the time, ever vigilant and faithful, the most valuable of all the dogs.

'Makin' free to spit out what's in me,' Matt said one day, 'I beg to state that you was a wise guy all right when you paid the price you did for that dog. You clean swindled Beauty Smith on top of pushin' his face in with your fist.'

A recrudescence of anger glinted in Weedon Scott's grey eyes, and he muttered savagely: 'The beast!'

In the late spring a great trouble came to White Fang. Without warning, the love-master disappeared. There had been warning, but White Fang was unversed in such things, and did not understand the packing of a grip. He remembered afterwards that this packing had preceded the master's disappearance; but at the time he suspected nothing. That night he waited for the master to return. At midnight the chill wind that blew drove him to shelter at the rear of the cabin. There he drowsed, only half asleep, his ears keyed for the first sound of the familiar step. But, at two in the morning, his anxiety drove him out to the cold front stoop, where he crouched and waited.

But no master came. In the morning the door opened and Matt stepped outside. White Fang gazed at him wistfully. There was no common speech by which he might learn what he wanted to know. The days came and went, but never the master. White Fang, who had never known sickness in his life, became sick. He became very sick – so sick that Matt was finally compelled to bring him inside the cabin. Also, in writing to his employer, Matt devoted a postscript to White Fang.

Weedon Scott, reading the letter down in Circle City, came upon the following:

'That damn wolf won't work. Won't eat. Ain't got no spunk left. All the dogs is licking him. Wants to know what has become of you, and I don't know how to tell him. Mebbe he is going to die.'

It was as Matt had said. White Fang had ceased eating, lost heart, and allowed every dog of the team to thrash him. In the cabin he lay on the floor near the stove, without interest in food, in Matt, nor in life. Matt might talk gently to him or swear at him, it was all the same; he never did more than turn his dull eyes upon the man, then drop his head back to its customary position on his fore-paws.

And then, one night, Matt, reading to himself with moving lips and mumbled sounds, was startled by a low whine from White Fang. He had got upon his feet, his ears cocked toward the door, and he was listening intently. A moment later Matt heard a footstep. The door opened, and Weedon Scott stepped in. The two men shook hands. Then Scott looked around the room.

'Where's the wolf?' he asked.

Then he discovered him, standing where he had been lying, near to the stove. He had not rushed forward after the manner of other dogs. He stood, watching and waiting.

'Holy smoke!' Matt exclaimed. 'Look at 'm wag his tail!'

Weedon Scott strode half across the room toward him, at the same time calling him. White Fang came to him, not with a great bound, yet quickly. He was awkward from self-consciousness, but as he drew near his eyes took on a strange expression. Something, an incommunicable vastness of feeling, rose up into his eyes as a light and shone forth.

'He never looked at me that way all the time you was gone,' Matt commented.

Weedon Scott did not hear. He was squatting down on his heels, face to face with White Fang, and petting him – rubbing at the roots of the ears, making long caressing strokes down the neck to the shoulders, tapping the spine gently with the balls of his fingers. And

White Fang was growling responsively, the crooning note of the growl more pronounced than ever.

But that was not all. What of his joy, the great love in him, ever surging and struggling to express itself, succeeding in finding a new mode of expression? He suddenly thrust his head forward and nudged his way in between the master's arm and body. And here, confined, hidden from view all except his ears, no longer growling, he continued to nudge and snuggle.

The two men looked at each other. Scott's eyes were shining.

'Gosh!' said Matt in an awe-stricken voice.

A moment later, when he had recovered himself, he said: 'I always insisted that wolf was a dog. Look at 'm!'

With the return of the love-master, White Fang's recovery was rapid. Two nights and a day he spent in the cabin. Then he sallied forth. The sled-dogs had forgotten his prowess. They remembered only the latest, which was his weakness and sickness. At the sight of him as he came out of the cabin, they sprang upon him.

'Talk about your rough-houses,' Matt murmured gleefully, standing in the doorway and looking on. 'Give'm hell, you wolf! Give 'm hell! – an' then some!'

White Fang did not need the encouragement. The return of the love-master was enough. Life was flowing through him again, splendid and indomitable. He fought from sheer joy, finding in it an expression of much that he felt and that otherwise was without speech. There could be but one ending. The team dispersed in ignominious defeat, and it was not until after dark that the dogs came sneaking back, one by one, by meekness and humility signifying their fealty to White Fang.

Having learned to snuggle, White Fang was guilty of

it often. It was the final word. He could not go beyond it. The one thing of which he had always been particularly jealous was his head. He had always disliked to have it touched. It was the Wild in him, the fear of hurt and of the trap, that had given rise to the panicky impulses to avoid contacts. It was the mandate of his instinct that that head must be free. And now, with the love-master, his snuggling was the deliberate act of putting himself into a position of hopeless helplessness. It was an expression of perfect confidence, of absolute self-surrender, as though he said, 'I put myself into thy hands. Work thou thy will with me.'

One night, not long after the return, Scott and Matt sat at a game of cribbage preliminary to going to bed. 'Fifteen-two, fifteen-four an' a pair makes six,' Matt was pegging up, when there was an outcry and sound of snarling without. They looked at each other as they started to rise to their feet.

'The wolf's nailed somebody,' Matt said.

A wild scream of fear and anguish hastened them.

'Bring a light!' Scott shouted, as he sprang outside.

Matt followed with the lamp, and by its light they saw a man lying on his back in the snow. His arms were folded, one above the other, across his face and throat. Thus he was trying to shield himself from White Fang's teeth. And there was need for it. White Fang was in a rage, wickedly making his attack on the most vulnerable spot. From shoulder to wrist of the crossed arms, the coat sleeve, blue flannel shirt, and undershirt were ripped in rags, while the arms themselves were terribly slashed and streaming blood.

All this the two men saw in the first instant. The next instant Weedon Scott had White Fang by the throat and was dragging him clear. White Fang struggled and snarled, but made no attempt to bite, while he quickly quieted down at a sharp word from the master.

Matt helped the man to his feet. As he arose he lowered his crossed arms, exposing the bestial face of Beauty Smith. The dog-musher let go of him precipitately, with action similar to that of a man who has picked up live fire. Beauty Smith blinked in the lamp-light and looked about him. He caught sight of White Fang, and terror rushed into his face.

At the same moment Matt noticed two objects lying in the snow. He held the lamp close to them, indicating them with his toe for his employer's benefit – a steel dog-chain and a stout club.

Weedon Scott saw and nodded. Not a word was spoken. The dog-musher laid his hand on Beauty Smith's shoulder, and faced him to the right about. No word needed to be spoken. Beauty Smith started.

In the meantime the love-master was patting White Fang and talking to him.

'Tried to steal you, eh? And you wouldn't have it! Well, well, he made a mistake, didn't he?'

'Must 'a' thought he had hold of seventeen devils,' the dog-musher sniggered.

White Fang, still wrought up and bristling, growled and growled, the hair slowly lying down, the crooning note remote and dim, but growing in his throat.

PART V

CHAPTER

1

THE LONG TRAIL

It was in the air. White Fang sensed the coming calamity, even before there was tangible evidence of it. In vague ways it was borne in upon him that a change was impending. He knew not how nor why, yet he got his feel of the oncoming event from the gods themselves. In ways subtler than they knew, they betrayed their intentions to the wolf-dog that haunted the cabin-stoop, and that, though he never came inside the cabin, knew what went on inside their brains.

'Listen to that, will you!' the dog-musher exclaimed at supper one night.

Weedon Scott listened. Through the door came a low, anxious whine, like a sobbing under the breath that has just grown audible. Then came the long sniff, as White Fang reassured himself that his god was still inside, and had not yet taken himself off in mysterious and solitary flight.

'I do believe that wolf's on to you,' the dog-musher said.

Weedon Scott looked across at his companion with eyes that almost pleaded, though this was given the lie by his words.

'What the devil can I do with a wolf in California?' he demanded.

'That's what I say,' Matt answered. 'What the devil can you do with a wolf in California?'

But this did not satisfy Weedon Scott. The other seemed to be judging him in a non-committal sort of way.

'White-man's dogs would have no show against him,' Scott went on. 'He'd kill them on sight. If he didn't bankrupt me with damage suits, the authorities would take him away from me and electrocute him.'

'He's a downright murderer, I know,' was the dog-musher's comment.

Weedon Scott looked at him suspiciously.

'It would never do,' he said decisively.

'It would never do,' Matt concurred. 'Why, you'd have to hire a man 'specially to take care of 'm.'

The other's suspicion was allayed. He nodded cheerfully. In the silence that followed, the low, half-sobbing whine was heard at the door, and then the long, questing sniff.

'There's no denyin' he thinks a hell of a lot of you,' Matt said.

The other glared at him in sudden wrath. 'Damn it all, man! I know my own mind and what's best!'

'I'm agreein' with you, only . . .'

'Only what?' Scott snapped out.

'Only . . .' the dog-musher began softly, then changed his mind, and betrayed a rising anger of his own. 'Well, you needn't get so all-fired het up about it. Judgin' by your actions one'd think you didn't know your own mind.'

Weedon Scott debated with himself for a while, and

then said more gently, 'You are right, Matt. I don't know my own mind, and that's what's the trouble.'

'Why, it would be rank ridiculousness for me to take that dog along,' he broke out after another pause.

'I'm agreein' with you,' was Matt's answer; and again his employer was not quite satisfied with him.

'But how in the name of the great Sardanapolis he knows you're goin' is what gets me,' the dog-musher continued innocently.

'It's beyond me, Matt,' Scott answered with a mournful shake of the head.

Then came the day when, through the open cabin door, White Fang saw the fatal grip on the floor and the love-master packing things into it. Also, there were comings and goings, and the erstwhile placid atmosphere of the cabin was vexed with strange perturbations and unrest. Here was indubitable evidence. White Fang had already sensed it. He now reasoned it. His god was preparing for another flight. And since he had not taken him with him before, so now he could look to be left behind.

That night he lifted the long wolf-howl. As he had howled, in his puppy days, when he fled back from the Wild to the village to find it vanished and naught but a rubbish-heap to mark the site of Grey Beaver's tepee, so now he pointed his muzzle to the cold stars and told to them his woe.

Inside the cabin the two men had just gone to bed.

'He's gone off his food again,' Matt remarked from his bunk.

There was a grunt from Weedon Scott's bunk, and a stir of blankets.

'From the way he cut up the other time you went

away, I wouldn't wonder this time but what he died.'

The blankets in the other bunk stirred irritably.

'Oh, shut up!' Scott cried out through the darkness.
'You nag worse than a woman.'

'I'm agreein' with you,' the dog-musher answered,
and Weedon Scott was not quite sure whether or not the
other had snickered.

The next day White Fang's anxiety and restlessness
were even more pronounced. He dogged his master's
heels whenever he left the cabin, and haunted the front
stoop when he remained inside. Through the open door
he could catch glimpses of the luggage on the floor. The
grip had been joined by two large canvas bags and a
box. Matt was rolling the master's blankets and fur
robe inside a small tarpaulin. White Fang whined as he
watched the operation.

Later on two Indians arrived. He watched them closely
as they shouldered the luggage and were led off down
the hill by Matt, who carried the bedding and the grip.
But White Fang did not follow them. The master was
still in the cabin. After a time Matt returned. The master
came to the door and called White Fang inside.

'You poor devil,' he said gently, rubbing White Fang's
ears and tapping his spine. 'I'm hitting the long trail, old
man, where you cannot follow. Now give me a growl –
the last, good, goodbye growl.'

But White Fang refused to growl. Instead, and after a
wistful, searching look, he snuggled in, burrowing his
head out of sight between the master's arm and body.

'There she blows!' Matt cried. From the Yukon arose
the hoarse bellowing of a river steamboat. 'You've got
to cut it short. Be sure and lock the front door. I'll go out
the back. Get a move on!'

The two doors slammed at the same moment, and Weedon Scott waited for Matt to come around to the front. From inside the door came a low whining and sobbing. Then there were long, deep-drawn sniffs.

'You must take good care of him, Matt,' Scott said as they started down the hill. 'Write and let me know how he gets along.'

'Sure,' the dog-musher answered. 'But listen to that, will you!'

Both men stopped. White Fang was howling as dogs howl when their masters lie dead. He was voicing an utter woe, his cry bursting upward in great heart-breaking rushes, dying down into quavering misery, and bursting upward again with rush upon rush of grief.

The *Aurora* was the first steamboat of the year for the Outside, and her decks were jammed with prosperous adventurers and broken gold-seekers, all equally as mad to get to the Outside as they had been originally to get to the Inside. Near the gang-plank, Scott was shaking hands with Matt, who was preparing to go ashore. But Matt's hand went limp in the other's grasp as his gaze shot past and remained fixed on something behind him. Scott turned to see. Sitting on the deck several feet away and watching wistfully was White Fang.

The dog-musher swore softly in awe-stricken accents. Scott could only look in wonder.

'Did you lock the front door?' Matt demanded.

The other nodded, and asked: 'How about the back?'

'You just bet I did,' was the fervent reply.

White Fang flattened his ears ingratiatingly, but remained where he was, making no attempt to approach.

'I'll have to take 'm shore with me.'

Matt made a couple of steps toward White Fang, but the latter slid away from him. The dog-musher made a rush of it, and White Fang dodged between the legs of a group of men. Ducking, turning, doubling, he slid about the deck, eluding the other's efforts to capture him.

But when the love-master spoke, White Fang came to him with prompt obedience.

'Won't come to the hand that's fed 'm all these months,' the dog-musher muttered resentfully. 'And you – you ain't never fed 'm after them first days of gettin' acquainted. I'm blamed if I can see how he works it out that you're the boss.'

Scott, who had been patting White Fang, suddenly bent closer and pointed out fresh-made cuts on his muzzle and a gash between the eyes.

Matt bent over and passed his hand along White Fang's belly.

'We plump forgot the window. He's all cut an' gouged underneath. Must 'a' butted clean through it, b'gosh!'

But Weedon Scott was not listening. He was thinking rapidly. The *Aurora*'s whistle hooted a final announcement of departure. Men were scurrying down the gangplank to the shore. Matt loosened the bandana from his own neck and started to put it around White Fang's. Scott grasped the dog-musher's hand.

'Goodbye, Matt, old man. About the wolf – you needn't write. You see, I've . . .'

'What!' the dog-musher exploded. 'You don't mean to say . . . ?'

'The very thing I mean. Here's your bandana. *I'll* write to *you* about him.'

Matt paused halfway down the gang-plank.

'He'll never stand the climate!' he shouted back. 'Unless you clip 'm in warm weather!'

The gang-plank was hauled in, and the *Aurora* swung out from the bank. Weedon Scott waved a last goodbye. Then he turned and bent over White Fang, standing by his side.

'Now growl, damn you, growl,' he said, as he patted the responsive head and rubbed the flattening ears.

CHAPTER

2

THE SOUTHLAND

White Fang landed from the steamer in San Francisco. He was appalled. Deep in him, below any reasoning process or act of consciousness, he had associated power with godhead. And never had the white men seemed such marvellous gods as now, when he trod the slimy pavement of San Francisco. The log cabins he had known were replaced by towering buildings. The streets were crowded with perils – wagons, carts, automobiles; great, straining horses pulling huge trucks; and monstrous cable and electric cars hooting and clanging through the midst, screeching their insistent menace after the manner of the lynxes he had known in the northern woods.

All this was the manifestation of power. Through it all, behind it all, was man, governing and controlling, expressing himself, as of old, by his mastery over matter. It was colossal, stunning. White Fang was awed. Fear sat upon him. As in his cubhood he had been made to feel his smallness and puniness on the day he first came in from the Wild to the village of Grey Beaver, so now, in his full-grown stature and pride of strength, he was made to feel small and puny. And there were so many gods! He was made dizzy by the swarming of them. The thunder of the streets smote upon his ears. He was bewildered by the tremendous and endless rush and movement of things. As never before, he felt his dependence on the love-master, close at whose heels he followed, no matter what happened, never losing sight of him.

But White Fang was to have no more than a nightmare vision of the city – an experience that was like a bad dream, unreal and terrible, that haunted him for long after in his dreams. He was put into a baggage-car by the master, chained in a corner in the midst of heaped trunks and valises. Here a squat and brawny god held sway, with much noise, hurling trunks and boxes about, dragging them in through the door and tossing them into the piles, or flinging them out of the door, smashing and crashing, to other gods who awaited them.

And here, in this inferno of luggage, was White Fang deserted by the master – or at least White Fang thought he was deserted, until he smelled out the master's canvas clothes-bags alongside of him, and proceeded to mount guard over them.

''Bout time you come,' growled the god of the car, an hour later, when Weedon Scott appeared at the door. 'That dog of yourn won't let me lay a finger on your stuff.'

White Fang emerged from the car. He was astonished. The nightmare city was gone. The car had been to him no more than a room in a house, and when he had entered it the city had been all around him. In the interval the city had disappeared. The roar of it no longer dinned upon his ears. Before him was smiling country, streaming with sunshine, lazy with quietude. But he had little time to marvel at the transformation. He accepted it as he accepted all the unaccountable doings and manifestations of the gods. It was their way.

There was a carriage waiting. A man and a woman approached the master. The woman's arms went out and clutched the master around the neck – a hostile act! The next moment Weedon Scott had torn loose from the embrace and closed with White Fang, who had become a snarling, raging demon.

'It's all right, mother,' Scott was saying as he kept tight hold of White Fang and placated him. 'He thought you were going to injure me, and he wouldn't stand for it. It's all right – it's all right. He'll learn soon enough.'

'And in the meantime I may be permitted to love my son when his dog is not around,' she laughed, though she was pale and weak from the fright.

She looked at White Fang, who snarled and bristled and glared malevolently.

'He'll have to learn, and he shall, without postponement,' Scott said.

He spoke softly to White Fang until he had quieted him, then his voice became firm.

'Down, sir! Down with you!'

This had been one of the things taught him by the master, and White Fang obeyed, though he lay down reluctantly and sullenly.

'Now, mother.'

Scott opened his arms to her, but kept his eyes on White Fang.

'Down!' he warned. 'Down!'

White Fang, bristling silently, half crouching as he rose, sank back and watched the hostile act repeated. But no harm came of it, nor of the embrace from the strange man-god that followed. Then the clothes-bags were taken into the carriage, the strange gods and the love-master followed, and White Fang pursued, now running vigilantly behind, now bristling up to the running horses and warning them that he was there to see that no harm befell the god they dragged so swiftly across the earth.

At the end of fifteen minutes the carriage swung in through a stone gateway and on between a double row of arched and interlacing walnut trees. On either side stretched lawns, their broad sweep broken here and there by great, sturdy-limbed oaks. In the near distance, in contrast with the young green of the tended grass, sunburnt hayfields showed tan and gold; while beyond were the tawny hills and upland pastures. From the head of the lawn, on the first soft swell from the valley level, looked down the deep-porched, many-windowed house.

Little opportunity was given White Fang to see all this. Hardly had the carriage entered the grounds, when he was set upon by a sheep-dog, bright-eyed, sharp-muzzled, righteously indignant and angry. It was between him and the master, cutting him off. White Fang snarled no warning, but his hair bristled as he made his silent and deadly rush. This rush was never completed. He halted with awkward abruptness, with stiff fore-legs bracing himself against his momentum, almost sitting down on his haunches, so desirous was he of avoiding contact with the dog he was in the act of attacking. It was a female, and the law of his kind thrust a barrier between. For him to attack her would require nothing less than a violation of his instinct.

But with the sheep-dog it was otherwise. Being a

female, she possessed no such instinct. On the other hand, being a sheep-dog, her instinctive fear of the Wild, and especially of the wolf, was unusually keen. White Fang was to her a wolf, the hereditary marauder who had preyed upon her flocks from the time sheep were first herded and guarded by some dim ancestor of hers. And so, as he abandoned his rush at her and braced himself to avoid the contact, she sprang upon him. He snarled involuntarily as he felt her teeth in his shoulder, but beyond this made no offer to hurt her. He backed away, stiff-legged with self-consciousness, and tried to go around her. He dodged this way and that, and curved and turned, but to no purpose. She remained always between him and the way he wanted to go.

'Here, Collie!' called the strange man in the carriage.

Weedon Scott laughed.

'Never mind, father. It is good discipline. White Fang will have to learn many things, and it's just as well that he begins now. He'll adjust himself all right.'

The carriage drove on, and still Collie blocked White Fang's way. He tried to outrun her by leaving the drive and circling across the lawn; but she ran on the inner and smaller circle, and was always there, facing him with her two rows of gleaming teeth. Back he circled, across the drive to the other lawn, and again she headed him off.

The carriage was bearing the master away. White Fang caught glimpses of it disappearing amongst the trees. The situation was desperate. He essayed another circle. She followed, running swiftly. And then suddenly he turned upon her. It was his old fighting trick. Shoulder to shoulder, he struck her squarely. Not only was she overthrown: so fast had she been running that she rolled along, now on her back, now on her side, as she struggled to stop, clawing gravel with her feet, and crying shrilly her hurt pride and indignation.

White Fang did not wait. The way was clear, and that was all he had wanted. She took after him, never ceasing her outcry. It was the straight away now, and when it came to real running, White Fang could teach her things. She ran frantically, hysterically, straining to the utmost, advertising the effort she was making with every leap; and all the time White Fang slid smoothly away from her, silently, without effort, gliding like a ghost over the ground.

As he rounded the house to the *porte-cochère*, he came upon the carriage. It had stopped, and the master was alighting. At this moment, still running at top speed, White Fang became suddenly aware of an attack from the side. It was a deerhound rushing upon him. White Fang tried to race it. But he was going too fast, and the hound was too close. It struck him on the side; and such was his forward momentum and the unexpectedness of it, White Fang was hurled to the ground and rolled clear over. He came out of the tangle a spectacle of malignancy – ears flattened back, lips writhing, nose wrinkling, his teeth clipping together as the fangs barely missed the hound's soft throat.

The master was running up, but was too far away; and it was Collie that saved the hound's life. Before White Fang could spring in and deliver the fatal stroke, and just as he was in the act of springing in, Collie arrived. She had been out-manoeuvred and outrun, to say nothing of her having been unceremoniously tumbled in the gravel, and her arrival was like that of a tornado – made up of offended dignity, justifiable wrath,

and instinctive hatred for this marauder from the Wild.
She struck White Fang at right angles in the midst of his
spring, and again he was knocked off his feet and rolled
over.

The next moment the master arrived, and with one
hand held White Fang, while the father called off the
dogs.

'I say, this is a pretty warm reception for a poor lone
wolf from the Arctic,' the master said, while White Fang
calmed down under his caressing hand. 'In all his life
he's only been known once to go off his feet, and here
he's been rolled twice in thirty seconds.'

The carriage had driven away, and other strange gods
had appeared from out the house. Some of these stood
respectfully at a distance; but two of them, women,
perpetrated the hostile act of clutching the master around
the neck. White Fang, however, was beginning to tolerate this act. No harm seemed to come of it, while the
noises the gods made were certainly not threatening.
These gods also made overtures to White Fang, but he
warned them off with a snarl, and the master did likewise
with word of mouth. At such times White Fang leaned
in close against the master's legs, and received reassuring pats on the head.

The hound, under the command: 'Dick! Lie down,
sir!' had gone up the steps and lain down to one side on
the porch, still growling and keeping a sullen watch on
the intruder. Collie had been taken in charge by one of
the woman-gods, who held arms around her neck and
petted and caressed her; but Collie was very much perplexed and worried, whining and restless, outraged by
the permitted presence of this wolf, and confident that
the gods were making a mistake.

All the gods started up the steps to enter the house. White Fang followed closely at the master's heels. Dick, on the porch, growled; and White Fang, on the steps, bristled and growled back.

'Take Collie inside and leave the two of them to fight it out,' suggested Scott's father. 'After that they'll be friends.'

'Then White Fang, to show his friendship, will have to be chief mourner at the funeral,' laughed the master.

The elder Scott looked incredulously, first at White Fang, then at Dick, and finally at his son.

'You mean that . . . ?'

Weedon nodded his head. 'I mean just that. You'd have a dead Dick inside one minute – two minutes at the furthest.'

He turned to White Fang. 'Come on, you wolf. It's you that'll have to come inside.'

White Fang walked stiff-legged up the steps and across the porch, with tail rigidly erect, keeping his eyes on Dick to guard against a flank attack, and at the same time prepared for whatever fierce manifestation of the unknown that might pounce out upon him from the interior of the house. But no thing of fear pounced out; and when he had gained the inside he scouted carefully around, looking for it and finding it not. Then he lay down with a contented grunt at the master's feet, observing all that went on, ever ready to spring to his feet and fight for life with the terrors he felt must lurk under the trap-roof of the dwelling.

CHAPTER
3

THE GOD'S DOMAIN

Not only was White Fang adaptable by nature, but he had travelled much, and knew the meaning and necessity of adjustment. Here, in Sierra Vista, which was the name of Judge Scott's place, White Fang quickly began to make himself at home. He had no further serious trouble with the dogs. They knew more about the ways of the Southland gods than did he, and in their eyes he had qualified when he accompanied the gods inside the house. Wolf that he was, and unprecedented as it was, the gods had sanctioned his presence; and they, the dogs of the gods, could only recognize this sanction.

Dick, perforce, had to go through a few stiff formalities at first, after which he calmly accepted White Fang as an addition to the premises. Had Dick had his way, they would have been good friends; but White Fang was averse to friendship. All he asked of other dogs was to be let alone. His whole life he had kept aloof from his kind, and he still desired to keep aloof. Dick's overtures bothered him, so he snarled Dick away. In the north he had learned the lesson that he must let the master's dogs alone, and he did not forget that lesson now. But he insisted on his own privacy and self-seclusion, and so thoroughly ignored Dick that that good-natured creature finally gave him up, and scarcely took as much interest in him as in the hitching-post near the stable.

Not so with Collie. While she accepted him because it was the mandate of the gods, that was no reason that she should leave him in peace. Woven into her being was the memory of countless crimes he and his had perpetrated against her ancestry. Not in a day nor a generation were the ravaged sheepfolds to be forgotten. All this was a spur to her, pricking her to retaliation. She could not fly in the face of the gods who permitted him, but that did not prevent her from making life miserable for him in petty ways. A feud ages old was between them, and she, for one, would see to it that he was reminded.

So Collie took advantage of her sex to pick upon White Fang and maltreat him. His instinct would not permit him to attack her, while her persistence would not permit him to ignore her. When she rushed at him he turned his fur-protected shoulder to her sharp teeth, and walked away stiff-legged and stately. When she forced him too hard, he was compelled to go about in a circle, his shoulder presented to her, his head turned from her, and on his face and in his eyes a patient and bored expression. Sometimes, however, a nip on his hind-quarters hastened his retreat, and made it anything but stately. But as a rule he managed to maintain a dignity that was almost solemnity. He ignored her existence whenever it was possible, and made it a point to keep out of her way. When he saw or heard her coming, he got up and walked off.

There was much in other matters for White Fang to learn. Life in the Northland was simplicity itself when

compared with the complicated affairs of Sierra Vista.
First of all, he had to learn the family of the master. In
a way he was prepared to do this. As Mit-sah and
Kloo-kooch had belonged to Grey Beaver, sharing his
food, his fire, and his blankets, so now, at Sierra Vista,
belonged to the love-master all the denizens of the
house.

But in this matter there was a difference, and many
differences. Sierra Vista was a far vaster affair than the
tepee of Grey Beaver. There were many persons to be
considered. There was Judge Scott, and there was his
wife. There were the master's two sisters, Beth and
Mary. There was his wife, Alice; and then there were
his children, Weedon and Maud, toddlers of four and
six. There was no way for anybody to tell him about all
these people, and of blood ties and relationship he knew
nothing whatever, and never would be capable of knowing. Yet he quickly worked it out that all of them belonged to the master. Then, by observation, whenever
opportunity offered, by study of action, speech, and the
very intonations of the voice, he slowly learned the
intimacy and the degree of favour they enjoyed with the
master. And by this ascertained standard White Fang
treated them accordingly. What was of value to the
master he valued; what was dear to the master was to
be cherished by White Fang and guarded carefully.

Thus it was with the two children. All his life he had
disliked children. He hated and feared their hands. The
lessons were not tender that he had learned of their
tyranny and cruelty in the days of the Indian villages.
When Weedon and Maud had first approached him, he
growled warningly and looked malignant. A cuff from
the master and a sharp word had then compelled him

to permit their caresses, though he growled and growled under their tiny hands, and in the growl there was no crooning note. Later, he observed that the boy and girl were of great value in the master's eyes. Then it was that no cuff nor sharp word was necessary before they could pat him.

Yet White Fang was never effusively affectionate. He yielded to the master's children with an ill but honest grace, and endured their fooling as one would endure a painful operation. When he could no longer endure, he would get up and stalk determinedly away from them. But after a time, he grew even to like the children. Still he was not demonstrative. He would not go up to them. On the other hand, instead of walking away at sight of them, he waited for them to come to him. And still later, it was noticed that a pleading light came into his eyes when he saw them approaching, and that he looked after them with an appearance of curious regret when they left him for other amusements.

All this was a matter of development, and took time. Next in his regard, after the children, was Judge Scott. There were two reasons, possibly, for this. First, he was evidently a valuable possession of the master's, and next, he was undemonstrative. White Fang liked to lie at his feet on the wide porch when he read the newspaper, from time to time favouring White Fang with a look or a word – untroublesome tokens that he recognized White Fang's presence and existence. But this was only when the master was not around. When the master appeared, all other beings ceased to exist so far as White Fang was concerned.

White Fang allowed all the members of the family to pet him and make much of him; but he never gave to them what he gave to the master. No caress of theirs could put the love-croon into his throat, and, try as they would, they could never persuade him into snuggling against them. This expression of abandon and surrender, of absolute trust, he reserved for the master alone. In fact, he never regarded the members of the family in any other light than possessions of the love-master.

Also White Fang had early come to differentiate between the family and the servants of the household. The latter were afraid of him, while he merely refrained from attacking them – this because he considered that they were likewise possessions of the master. Between White Fang and them existed a neutrality and no more. They cooked for the master and washed the dishes and did other things just as Matt had done up in the Klondike. They were, in short, appurtenances of the household.

Outside the household there was even more for White Fang to learn. The master's domain was wide and complex, yet it had its metes and bounds. The land itself ceased at the county road. Outside was the common domain of all gods – the road and streets. Then inside other fences were the particular domains of other gods. A myriad laws governed all these things and determined conduct: yet he did not know the speech of the gods, nor was there any way for him to learn save by experience. He obeyed his natural impulses until they ran him counter to some law. When this had been done a few times, he learned the law, and after that observed it.

But most potent in his education was the cuff of the master's hand, the censure of the master's voice. Because of White Fang's very great love, a cuff from the master hurt him far more than any beating Grey Beaver or Beauty Smith had ever given him. They had hurt only the flesh of him; beneath the flesh the spirit had still raged, splendid and invincible. But with the master the cuff was always too light to hurt the flesh. Yet it went deeper. It was an expression of the master's disapproval, and White Fang's spirit wilted under it.

In point of fact, the cuff was rarely administered. The master's voice was sufficient. By it White Fang knew whether he did right or not. By it he trimmed his conduct and adjusted his actions. It was the compass by which he steered and learned to chart the manners of a new land and life.

In the Northland, the only domesticated animal was the dog. All other animals lived in the Wild, and were, when not too formidable, lawful spoil for any dog. All his days White Fang had foraged among the live things for food. It did not enter his head that in the Southland it was otherwise. But this he was to learn early in his residence in Santa Clara Valley. Sauntering around the corner of the house in the early morning, he came upon a chicken that had escaped from the chicken-yard. White Fang's natural impulse was to eat it. A couple of bounds, a flash of teeth, and a frightened squawk, and he had scooped in the adventurous fowl. It was farm-bred and fat and tender; and White Fang licked his chops and decided that such fare was good.

Later in the day he chanced upon another stray chicken near the stables. One of the grooms ran to the rescue. He did not know White Fang's breed, so for weapon he took a light buggy-whip. At the first cut of the whip, White Fang left the chicken for the man. A club might have stopped White Fang, but not a whip. Silently, without flinching, he took a second cut in his forward rush, and as he leaped for the throat the groom cried out, 'My God!' and staggered backward. He dropped the whip and shielded his throat with his arms. In consequence, his forearm was ripped open to the bone.

The man was badly frightened. It was not so much White Fang's ferocity as it was his silence that unnerved the groom. Still protecting his throat and face with his torn and bleeding arm, he tried to retreat to the barn. And it would have gone hard with him had not Collie appeared on the scene. As she had saved Dick's life, she now saved the groom's. She rushed upon White Fang in frenzied wrath. She had been right. She had known better than the blundering gods. All her suspicions were justified. Here was the ancient marauder up to his old tricks again.

The groom escaped into the stables, and White Fang backed away before Collie's wicked teeth, or presented his shoulder to them and circled round and round. But Collie did not give over, as was her wont, after a decent interval of chastisement. On the contrary, she grew more excited and angry every moment, until, in the end, White Fang flung dignity to the winds, and frankly fled away from her across the fields.

'He'll learn to leave chickens alone,' the master said. 'But I can't give him the lesson until I catch him in the act.'

Two nights later came the act, but on a more generous scale than the master had anticipated. White Fang had observed closely the chicken-yards and the habits of the chickens. In the night time, after they had gone to roost, he climbed to the top of a pile of newly hauled lumber. From there he gained the roof of a chicken-house, passed over the ridgepole, and dropped to the ground inside. A moment later he was inside the house, and the slaughter began.

In the morning, when the master came out on to the porch, fifty white Leghorn hens, laid out in a row by the groom, greeted his eyes. He whistled to himself softly, first in surprise, and then, at the end, with admiration. His eyes were likewise greeted by White Fang, but about the latter there were no signs of shame nor guilt. He carried himself with pride, as though, forsooth, he had achieved a deed praiseworthy and meritorious. There was about him no consciousness of sin. The master's lips tightened as he faced the disagreeable task. Then he talked harshly to the unwitting culprit, and in his voice there was nothing but godlike wrath. Also, he held White Fang's nose down to the slain hens, and at the same time cuffed him soundly.

White Fang never raided a chicken-roost again. It was against the law, and he had learned it. Then the master took him into the chicken-yards. White Fang's natural impulse, when he saw the live food fluttering about him and under his very nose, was to spring upon it. He obeyed the impulse, but was checked by the master's voice. They continued in the yards for half an hour. Time and again the impulse surged over White Fang, and each time, as he yielded to it, he was checked by the master's voice. Thus it was he learned the law, and ere he left the domain of the chickens he had learned to ignore their existence.

'You can never cure a chicken-killer.' Judge Scott shook his head sadly at luncheon-table, when his son narrated the lesson he had given White Fang. 'Once they've got the habit and the taste of blood . . .' Again he shook his head sadly.

But Weedon Scott did not agree with his father.

'I'll tell you what I'll do,' he challenged finally. 'I'll lock White Fang in with the chickens all afternoon.'

'But think of the chickens,' objected the Judge.

'And furthermore,' the son went on, 'for every chicken he kills, I'll pay you one dollar gold coin of the realm.'

'But you should penalize father too,' interposed Beth.

Her sister seconded her, and a chorus of approval arose from around the table. Judge Scott nodded his head in agreement.

'All right.' Weedon Scott pondered for a moment. 'And if, at the end of the afternoon, White Fang hasn't harmed a chicken, for every ten minutes of the time he has spent in the yard you will have to say to him, gravely and with deliberation, just as if you were sitting on the bench and solemnly passing judgment, "White Fang, you are smarter than I thought."'

From hidden points of vantage the family watched the performance. But it was a fizzle. Locked in the yard and there deserted by the master, White Fang lay down and went to sleep. Once he got up and walked over to the trough for a drink of water. The chickens he calmly ignored. So far as he was concerned they did not exist. At four o'clock he executed a running jump, gained the roof of the chicken-house, and leaped to the ground outside, whence he sauntered gravely to the house. He had learned the law. And on the porch, before the delighted family, Judge Scott, face to face with White Fang, said slowly and solemnly, sixteen times, 'White Fang, you are smarter than I thought.'

But it was the multiplicity of laws that befuddled White Fang, and often brought him into disgrace. He had to learn that he must not touch the chickens that belonged to other gods. Then there were cats and rabbits and turkeys; all these he must let alone. In fact, when he had but partly learned the law, his impression was that he must leave all live things alone. Out in the back-pasture, a quail could flutter up under his nose unharmed. All tense and trembling with eagerness and desire, he mastered his instinct and stood still. He was obeying the will of the gods.

And then, one day, again out in the back-pasture, he saw Dick start a jackrabbit and run it. The master himself was looking on and did not interfere. Nay, he encouraged White Fang to join in the chase. And thus he learned that there was no taboo on jackrabbits. In the end he worked out the complete law. Between him and all domestic animals there must be no hostilities. If not amity, at least neutrality must obtain. But the other animals – the squirrels, and quail, and cottontails – were creatures of the Wild who had never yielded allegiance to man. They were the lawful prey of any dog. It was only the tame that the gods protected, and between the tame deadly strife was not permitted. The gods held the power of life and death over their subjects, and the gods were jealous of their power.

Life was complex in the Santa Clara Valley after the simplicities of the Northland. And the chief thing demanded by these intricacies of civilization was control, restraint – a poise of self that was as delicate as the fluttering of gossamer wings and at the same time as rigid as steel. Life had a thousand faces, and White Fang found he must meet them all. Thus, when he went to town, in to San Jose, running behind the carriage or loafing about the streets when the carriage stopped, life flowed past him, deep and wide and varied, continually impinging upon his senses, demanding of him instant and endless adjustments and correspondences, and compelling him, almost always, to suppress his natural impulses.

There were butcher-shops where meat hung within reach. This meat he must not touch. There were cats at the houses the master visited that must be let alone. And there were dogs everywhere that snarled at him and that he must not attack. And then, on the crowded sidewalks there were persons innumerable whose attention he attracted. They would stop and look at him, point him out to one another, examine him, talk to him, and, worst of all, pat him. And these perilous contacts from all these strange hands he must endure. Yet this endurance he achieved. Furthermore, he got over being awkward and self-conscious. In a lofty way he received the attentions of the multitudes of strange gods. With condescension he accepted their condescension. On the other hand, there was something about him that prevented great familiarity. They patted him on the head and passed on, contented and pleased with their own daring.

But it was not all easy for White Fang. Running behind the carriage in the outskirts of San Jose, he encountered certain small boys who made a practice of flinging stones at him. Yet he knew that it was not permitted him to pursue and drag them down. Here he was compelled to violate his instinct of self-preservation; and violate it he did, for he was becoming tame and qualifying himself for civilization.

Nevertheless, White Fang was not quite satisfied with the arrangement. He had no abstract ideas about justice and fair play. But there is a certain sense of equity that resides in life, and it was this sense in him that resented the unfairness of his being permitted no defence against the stone-throwers. He forgot that in the covenant entered into between him and the gods they were pledged to care for him and defend him. But one day the master sprang from the carriage, whip in hand, and gave the stone-throwers a thrashing. After that they threw stones no more, and White Fang understood and was satisfied.

One other experience of similar nature was his. On the way to town, hanging around the saloon at the crossroads, were three dogs that made a practice of rushing out upon him when he went by. Knowing his deadly method of fighting, the master had never ceased impressing upon White Fang the law that he must not fight. As a result, having learned the lesson well, White Fang was hard put whenever he passed the crossroads saloon. After the first rush, each time his snarl kept the three dogs at a distance; but they trailed along behind, yelping and bickering and insulting him. This endured for some time. The men at the saloon even urged the dogs on to attack White Fang. One day they openly sicked the dogs on him. The master stopped the carriage.

'Go to it,' he said to White Fang.

But White Fang could not believe. He looked at the master, and he looked at the dogs. Then he looked back eagerly and questioningly at the master.

The master nodded his head. 'Go to them, old fellow. Eat them up.'

White Fang no longer hesitated. He turned and leaped silently among his enemies. All three faced him. There was a great snarling and growling, a clashing of teeth and a flurry of bodies. The dust of the road arose in a cloud and screened the battle. But at the end of several minutes two dogs were struggling in the dirt, and the third was in full flight. He leaped a ditch, went through a rail fence, and fled across a field. White Fang followed, sliding over the ground in wolf fashion and with wolf speed, swiftly and without noise, and in the centre of the field he dragged down and slew the dog.

With this triple killing his main troubles with dogs ceased. The word went up and down the valley, and men saw to it that their dogs did not molest the Fighting Wolf.

CHAPTER

4

THE CALL OF KIND

The months came and went. There was plenty of food and no work in the Southland, and White Fang lived fat and prosperous and happy. Not alone was he in the geographical Southland, for he was in the Southland of life. Human kindness was like a sun shining upon him, and he flourished like a flower planted in good soil.

And yet he remained somehow different from other dogs. He knew the law even better than did the dogs that had known no other life, and he observed the law more punctiliously; but still there was about him a suggestion of lurking ferocity, as though the Wild still lingered in him and the wolf in him merely slept.

He never chummed with other dogs. Lonely he had lived, so far as his kind was concerned, and lonely he would continue to live. In his puppyhood, under the persecution of Lip-lip and the puppy-pack, and in his fighting days with Beauty Smith, he had acquired a fixed aversion for dogs. The natural course of his life had been diverted, and, recoiling from his kind, he had clung to the human.

Besides, all Southland dogs looked upon him with suspicion. He aroused in them their instinctive fear of the Wild, and they greeted him always with snarl and growl and belligerent hatred. He, on the other hand, learned that it was not necessary to use his teeth upon them. His naked fangs and writhing lips were uniformly efficacious, rarely failing to send a bellowing, on-rushing dog back on its haunches.

But there was one trial in White Fang's life – Collie. She never gave him a moment's peace. She was not so amenable to the law as he. She defied all efforts of the master to make her become friends with White Fang. Ever in his ears was sounding her sharp and nervous snarl. She had never forgiven him the chicken-killing episode, and persistently held to the belief that his intentions were bad. She found him guilty before the act, and treated him accordingly. She became a pest to him, like a policeman following him around the stable and the grounds, and, if he even so much as glanced curiously at a pigeon or chicken, bursting into an outcry of indignation and wrath. His favourite way of ignoring her was to lie down, with his head on his fore-paws, and pretend sleep. This always dumbfounded and silenced her.

With the exception of Collie, all things went well with White Fang. He had learned control and poise, and he knew the law. He achieved a staidness, and calmness, and philosophic tolerance. He no longer lived in a hostile environment. Danger and hurt and death did not lurk everywhere about him. In time, the unknown, as a thing of terror and menace ever impending, faded away. Life was soft and easy. It flowed along smoothly, and neither fear nor foe lurked by the way.

He missed the snow without being aware of it. 'An unduly long summer,' would have been his thought, had he thought about it; as it was, he merely missed the snow in a vague, subconscious way. In the same fashion, especially in the heat of summer when he suffered from the sun, he experienced faint longings for the Northland. Their only effect upon him, however, was to make him uneasy and restless without his knowing what was the matter.

White Fang had never been very demonstrative. Beyond his snuggling and the throwing of a crooning note into his love-growl, he had no way of expressing his love. Yet it was given him to discover a third way. He had always been susceptible to the laughter of the gods. Laughter had affected him with madness, made him frantic with rage. But he did not have it in him to be angry with the love-master, and when that god elected to laugh at him in a good-natured, bantering way, he was nonplussed. He could feel the pricking and stinging of the old anger as it strove to rise up in him, but it strove against love. He could not be angry; yet he had to do something. At first he was dignified, and the master laughed the harder. Then he tried to be more dignified, and the master laughed harder than before. In the end, the master laughed him out of his dignity. His jaws slightly parted, his lips lifted a little, and a quizzical expression that was more love than humour came into his eyes. He had learned to laugh.

Likewise he learned to romp with the master, to be tumbled down and rolled over, and be the victim of innumerable rough tricks. In return he feigned anger, bristling and growling ferociously, and clipping his teeth together in snaps that had all the seeming of deadly intention. But he never forgot himself. Those snaps were always delivered on the empty air. At the end of such a romp, when blow and cuff and snap and snarl were fast and furious, they would break off suddenly and stand several feet apart, glaring at each other. And then, just as suddenly, like the sun rising on a stormy sea, they would begin to laugh. This would always culminate with the master's arms going around White Fang's neck and shoulders, while the latter crooned and growled his love-song.

But nobody else ever romped with White Fang. He did not permit it. He stood on his dignity, and when they attempted it, his warning snarl and bristling mane were anything but playful. That he allowed the master these liberties was no reason that he should be a common dog, loving here and loving there, everybody's property for a romp and good time. He loved with single heart, and refused to cheapen himself or his love.

The master went out on horseback a great deal, and to accompany him was one of White Fang's chief duties in life. In the Northland he had evidenced his fealty by toiling in the harness; but there were no sleds in the Southland, nor did dogs pack burdens on their backs. So he rendered fealty in the new way by running with the master's horse. The longest day never played White Fang out. His was the gait of the wolf, smooth, tireless, and effortless, and at the end of fifty miles he would come in jauntily ahead of the horse.

It was in connection with the riding that White Fang achieved one other mode of expression – remarkable in that he did it but twice in all his life. The first time occurred when the master was trying to teach a spirited thoroughbred the method of opening and closing gates without the rider's dismounting. Time and again and many times he ranged the horse up to the gate in the effort to close it, and each time the horse became frightened, and backed and plunged away. It grew more nervous and excited every moment. When it reared, the master put the spurs to it and made it drop its fore-legs back to earth, whereupon it would begin kicking with its hind-legs. White Fang watched the performance with increasing anxiety until he could contain himself no longer, when he sprang in front of the horse and barked savagely and warningly.

Though he often tried to bark thereafter, and the master encouraged him, he succeeded only once, and then it was not in the master's presence. A scamper across the pasture, a jackrabbit rising suddenly under the horse's feet, a violent sheer, a stumble, a fall to earth, and a broken leg for the master, was the cause of it. White Fang sprang in a rage at the throat of the offending horse, but was checked by the master's voice.

'Home! Go home!' the master commanded when he had ascertained his injury.

White Fang was disinclined to desert him. The master thought of writing a note, but searched his pockets vainly for pencil and paper. Again he commanded White Fang to go home.

The latter regarded him wistfully, started away, then returned and whined softly. The master talked to him gently but seriously, and he cocked his ears, and listened with painful intentness.

'That's all right, old fellow; you just run along home,' ran the talk. 'Go on home and tell them what's happened to me. Home with you, you wolf. Get along home!'

White Fang knew the meaning of 'home', and though he did not understand the remainder of the master's language, he knew it was his will that he should go home. He turned and trotted reluctantly away. Then he stopped, undecided, and looked back over his shoulder.

'Go home!' came the sharp command, and this time he obeyed.

The family was on the porch, taking the cool of the afternoon, when White Fang arrived. He came in among them, panting, covered with dust.

'Weedon's back,' Weedon's mother announced.

The children welcomed White Fang with glad cries and ran to meet him. He avoided them and passed down the porch, but they cornered him against a rocking-chair and the railing. He growled and tried to push by them. Their mother looked apprehensively in their direction.

'I confess, he makes me nervous around the children,' she said. 'I have a dread that he will turn upon them unexpectedly some day.'

Growling savagely, White Fang sprang out of the corner, overturning the boy and the girl. The mother called them to her and comforted them, telling them not to bother White Fang.

'A wolf is a wolf,' commented Judge Scott. 'There is no trusting one.'

'But he is not all wolf,' interposed Beth, standing for her brother in his absence.

'You have only Weedon's opinion for that,' rejoined the Judge. 'He merely surmises that there is some strain of dog in White Fang; but as he will tell you himself, he knows nothing about it. As for his appearance – '

He did not finish the sentence. White Fang stood before him, growling fiercely.

'Go away! Lie down, sir!' Judge Scott commanded.

White Fang turned to the love-master's wife. She screamed with fright as he seized her dress in his teeth and dragged on it till the frail fabric tore away. By this time he had become the centre of interest. He had ceased from his growling, and stood, head up, looking into their faces. His throat worked spasmodically, but made no sound, while he struggled with all his body, convulsed with the effort to rid himself of the incommunicable something that strained for utterance.

'I hope he is not going mad,' said Weedon's mother. 'I told Weedon that I was afraid the warm climate would not agree with an Arctic animal.'

'He's trying to speak, I do believe,' Beth announced.

At this moment speech came to White Fang, rushing up in a great burst of barking.

'Something has happened to Weedon,' his wife said decisively.

They were all on their feet now, and White Fang ran down the steps, looking back for them to follow. For the second and last time in his life he had barked and made himself understood.

After this event he found a warmer place in the hearts of the Sierra Vista people, and even the groom whose arm he had slashed admitted that he was a wise dog, even if he was a wolf. Judge Scott still held to the same opinion, and proved it to everybody's dissatisfaction by measurements and descriptions taken from the encyclopaedia and various works on natural history.

The days came and went, streaming their unbroken sunshine over the Santa Clara Valley. But as they grew shorter, and White Fang's second winter in the Southland came on, he made a strange discovery. Collie's teeth were no longer sharp. There was a playfulness about her nips and a gentleness that prevented them from really hurting him. He forgot that she had made life a burden to him, and when she disported herself around him he responded solemnly, striving to be playful, and becoming no more than ridiculous.

One day she led him off on a long chase through the back-pasture and into the woods. It was the afternoon that the master was to ride, and White Fang knew it. The horse stood saddled and waiting at the door. White Fang hesitated. But there was that in him deeper than all the law he had learned, than the customs that had moulded him, than his love for the master, than the very will to live of himself; and when, in the moment of his indecision, Collie nipped him and scampered off, he turned and followed after. The master rode alone that day; and in the woods, side by side, White Fang ran with Collie, as his mother Kiche and old One Eye had run long years before in the silent Northland forest.

CHAPTER

5

THE SLEEPING WOLF

It was about this time that the newspapers were full of the daring escape of a convict from San Quentin prison. He was a ferocious man. He had been ill-made in the making. He had not been born right, and he had not been helped any by the moulding he had received at the hands of society. The hands of society are harsh, and this man was a striking sample of its handiwork. He was a beast – a human beast, it is true, but nevertheless so terrible a beast that he can best be characterized as carnivorous.

In San Quentin prison he had proved incorrigible. Punishment failed to break his spirit. He could die dumb-mad and fighting to the last, but he could not live and be beaten. The more fiercely he fought, the more harshly society handled him, and the only effect of harshness was to make him fiercer. Strait-jackets, starvation, and beatings and clubbings were the wrong treatment for Jim Hall; but it was the treatment he received. It was the treatment he had received from the time he was a little pulpy boy in a San Francisco slum – soft clay in the hands of society, and ready to be formed into something.

It was during Jim Hall's third term in prison that he encountered a guard that was almost as great a beast as he. The guard treated him unfairly, lied about him to the warden, lost him his credits, persecuted him. The difference between them was that the guard carried a bunch of keys and a revolver. Jim Hall had only his naked hands and his teeth. But he sprang upon the guard one day and used his teeth on the other's throat just like any jungle animal.

After this, Jim Hall went to live in the incorrigible cell. He lived there three years. The cell was of iron, the floor, the walls, the roof. He never left this cell. He never saw the sky nor the sunshine. Day was a twilight, and night was a black silence. He was in an iron tomb, buried alive. He saw no human face, spoke to no human thing. When his food was shoved into him, he growled like a wild animal. He hated all things. For days and nights he bellowed his rage at the universe. For weeks and months he never made a sound, in the black silence eating his very soul. He was a man and a monstrosity, as fearful a thing of fear as ever gibbered in the visions of a maddened brain.

And then, one night, he escaped. The warden said it was impossible, but nevertheless the cell was empty, and half in half out of it lay the body of a dead guard. Two other dead guards marked his trail through the prison to the outer walls, and he had killed with his hands to avoid noise.

He was armed with the weapons of the slain guards – a live arsenal that fled through the hills pursued by the organized might of society. A heavy price of gold was upon his head. Avaricious farmers hunted him with shotguns. His blood might pay off a mortgage or send a son to college. Public-spirited citizens took down their rifles and went out after him. A pack of bloodhounds followed the way of his bleeding feet. And the sleuth-hounds of the law, the paid fighting animals of society, with telephone and telegraph and special train, clung to his trail night and day.

Sometimes they came upon him, and men faced him like heroes, or stampeded through barbed-wire fences to the delight of the commonwealth reading the account at the breakfast-table. It was after such encounters that the dead and wounded were carted back to the towns, and their places filled by men eager for the man-hunt.

And then Jim Hall disappeared. The bloodhounds vainly quested on the lost trail. Inoffensive ranchers in remote valleys were held up by armed men and com-pelled to identify themselves. While the remains of Jim Hall were discovered on a dozen mountain-sides by greedy claimants for blood-money.

In the meantime the newspapers were read at Sierra Vista, not so much with interest as with anxiety. The women were afraid. Judge Scott pooh-poohed and laughed, but not with reason, for it was in his last days on the bench that Jim Hall had stood before him and received sentence. And in open courtroom, before all men, Jim Hall had proclaimed that the day would come when he would wreak vengeance on the judge that sentenced him.

For once Jim Hall was right. He was innocent of the crime for which he was sentenced. It was a case, in the parlance of thieves and police, of 'railroading'. Jim Hall was being 'railroaded' to prison for a crime he had not committed. Because of the two prior convictions against him, Judge Scott imposed upon him a sentence of fifty years.

Judge Scott did not know all things, and he did not know that he was party to a police conspiracy, that the evidence was hatched and perjured, that Jim Hall was guiltless of the crime charged. And Jim Hall, on the other hand, did not know that Judge Scott was merely ignorant. Jim Hall believed that the Judge knew all about it, and was hand in glove with the police in the perpetration of the monstrous injustice. So it was, when the doom of fifty years of living death was uttered by Judge Scott, that Jim Hall, hating all things in the society that misused him, rose up and raged in the courtroom until dragged down by half a dozen of his blue-coated enemies. To him Judge Scott was the keystone in the arch of injustice, and upon Judge Scott he emptied the vials of his wrath and hurled the threats of his revenge yet to come. Then Jim Hall went to his living death . . . and escaped.

Of all this White Fang knew nothing. But between him and Alice, the master's wife, there existed a secret. Each night, after Sierra Vista had gone to bed, she rose and let in White Fang to sleep in the big hall. Now White Fang was not a house-dog, nor was he permitted to sleep in the house; so each morning, early, she slipped down and let him out before the family was awake.

On one such night, while all the house slept, White Fang awoke and lay very quietly. And very quietly he smelled the air and read the message it bore of a strange god's presence. And to his ears came sounds of the strange god's movements. White Fang burst into no furious outcry. It was not his way. The strange god walked softly, but more softly walked White Fang, for he had no clothes to rub against the flesh of his body. He followed silently. In the Wild he had hunted live meat that was infinitely timid, and he knew the advantage of surprise.

The strange god paused at the foot of the great staircase and listened, and White Fang was as dead, so without movement was he as he watched and waited. Up that staircase the way led to the love-master and to the love-master's dearest possessions. White Fang bristled, but waited. The strange god's foot lifted. He was beginning the ascent.

Then it was that White Fang struck. He gave no warning, with no snarl anticipated his own action. Into the air he lifted his body in the spring that landed him on the strange god's back. White Fang clung with his fore-paws to the man's shoulders, at the same time burying his fangs into the back of the man's neck. He clung on for a moment, long enough to drag the god over backward. Together they crashed to the floor. White Fang leaped clear, and, as the man struggled to rise, was in again with the slashing fangs.

Sierra Vista awoke in alarm. The noise from downstairs was as that of a score of battling fiends. There were revolver shots. A man's voice screamed once in horror and anguish. There was a great snarling and growling, and over all arose a smashing and crashing of furniture and glass.

But almost as quickly as it had arisen, the commotion died away. The struggle had not lasted more than three minutes. The frightened household clustered at the top of the stairway. From below, as from out an abyss of blackness, came up a gurgling sound, as of air bubbling through water. Sometimes this gurgle became sibilant, almost a whistle. But this, too, quickly died down and ceased. Then naught came up out of the blackness save a heavy panting of some creature struggling sorely for air.

Weedon Scott pressed a button, and the staircase and downstairs hall were flooded with light. Then he and Judge Scott, revolvers in hand, cautiously descended. There was no need for this caution. White Fang had done his work. In the midst of the wreckage of overthrown and smashed furniture, partly on his side, his face hidden by an arm, lay a man. Weedon Scott bent over, removed the arm, and turned the man's face upward. A gaping throat explained the manner of his death.

'Jim Hall,' said Judge Scott, and father and son looked significantly at each other.

Then they turned to White Fang. He, too, was lying on his side. His eyes were closed, but the lids slightly lifted in an effort to look at them as they bent over him, and the tail was perceptibly agitated in a vain effort to wag. Weedon Scott patted him, and his throat rumbled an acknowledging growl. But it was a weak growl at best, and it quickly ceased. His eyelids drooped and went shut, and his whole body seemed to relax and flatten out upon the floor.

'He's all in, poor devil,' muttered the master.

'We'll see about that,' asserted the Judge, as he started for the telephone.

'Frankly, he has one chance in a thousand,' announced the surgeon, after he had worked an hour and a half on White Fang.

Dawn was breaking through the windows and dimming the electric lights. With the exception of the children, the whole family was gathered about the surgeon to hear his verdict.

'One broken hind-leg,' he went on. 'Three broken ribs, one at least of which has pierced the lungs. He has lost nearly all the blood in his body. There is a large likelihood of internal injuries. He must have been jumped upon. To say nothing of three bullet-holes clear through him. One chance in a thousand is really optimistic. He hasn't a chance in ten thousand.'

'But he mustn't lose any chance that might be of help to him,' Judge Scott exclaimed. 'Never mind expense. Put him under the X-ray – anything. – Weedon, telegraph at once to San Francisco for Doctor Nichols. – No reflection on you, doctor, you understand; but he must have the advantage of every chance.'

The surgeon smiled indulgently. 'Of course I understand. He deserves all that can be done for him. He must be nursed as you would nurse a human being, a sick child. And don't forget what I told you about temperature. I'll be back at ten o'clock again.'

White Fang received the nursing. Judge Scott's suggestion of a trained nurse was indignantly clamoured down by the girls, who themselves undertook the task. And White Fang won out on the one chance in ten thousand denied him by the surgeon.

The latter was not to be censured for his misjudgment. All his life he had tended and operated on the soft humans of civilization, who lived sheltered lives and had descended out of many sheltered generations. Compared with White Fang, they were frail and flabby, and clutched life without any strength in their grip. White Fang had come straight from the Wild, where the weak perish early and shelter is vouchsafed to none. In neither his father nor his mother was there any weakness, nor in the generations before them. A constitution of iron and the vitality of the Wild were White Fang's inheritance, and he clung to life, the whole of him and every part of him, in spirit and in flesh, with the tenacity that of old belonged to all creatures.

Bound down a prisoner, denied even movement by the plaster casts and bandages, White Fang lingered out the weeks. He slept long hours and dreamed much, and through his mind passed an unending pageant of Northland visions. All the ghosts of the past arose and were with him. Once again he lived in the lair with Kiche, crept trembling to the knees of Grey Beaver to tender his allegiance, ran for his life before Lip-lip and all the howling bedlam of the puppy-pack.

He ran again through the silence, hunting his living food through the months of famine; and again he ran at the head of the team, the gut-whips of Mit-sah and Grey Beaver snapping behind, their voices crying 'Raa! Raa!' when they came to a narrow passage and the team closed together like a fan to go through. He lived again all his days with Beauty Smith and the fights he had fought. At such times he whimpered and snarled in his sleep, and they that looked on said that his dreams were bad.

But there was one particular nightmare from which he suffered – the clanking, clanging monsters of electric cars that were to him colossal screaming lynxes. He would lie in a screen of bushes, watching for a squirrel to venture far enough out on the ground from its tree-refuge. Then, when he sprang out upon it, it would transform itself into an electric car, menacing and terrible, towering over him like a mountain, screaming and clanging and spitting fire at him. It was the same when he challenged the hawk down out of the sky. Down out of the blue it would rush, as it dropped upon him changing itself into the ubiquitous electric car. Or again, he would be in the pen of Beauty Smith. Outside the pen, men would be gathering, and he knew that a fight was on. He watched the door for his antagonist to enter. The door would open, and thrust in upon him would come the awful electric car. A thousand times this occurred, and each time the terror it inspired was as vivid and great as ever.

Then came the day when the last bandage and the last plaster cast were taken off. It was a gala day. All Sierra Vista was gathered around. The master rubbed his ears, and he crooned his love-growl. The master's wife called him the 'Blessed Wolf', which name was taken up with acclaim, and all the women called him the Blessed Wolf.

He tried to rise to his feet, and after several attempts fell down from weakness. He had lain so long that his muscles had lost their cunning, and all the strength had gone out of them. He felt a little shame because of his weakness, as though, forsooth, he were failing the gods in the service he owed them. Because of this he made heroic efforts to arise; and at last he stood on his four legs, tottering and swaying back and forth.

'The Blessed Wolf!' chorused the women.

Judge Scott surveyed them triumphantly.

'Out of your own mouths be it,' he said. 'Just as I contended right along. No mere dog could have done what he did. He's a wolf.'

'A Blessed Wolf,' amended the Judge's wife.

'Yes, Blessed Wolf,' agreed the Judge. 'And henceforth that shall be my name for him.'

'He'll have to learn to walk again,' said the surgeon; 'so he might as well start in right now. It won't hurt him. Take him outside.'

And outside he went, like a king, with all Sierra Vista about him and tending on him. He was very weak, and when he reached the lawn he lay down and rested for a while.

Then the procession started on, little spurts of strength coming into White Fang's muscles as he used them and the blood began to surge through them. The stables were reached, and there in the doorway lay Collie, a half-dozen pudgy puppies playing about her in the sun.

White Fang looked on with a wondering eye. Collie snarled warningly at him, and he was careful to keep his distance. The master with his toe helped one sprawling puppy toward him. He bristled suspiciously, but the master warned him that all was well. Collie, clasped in the arms of one of the women, watched him jealously, and with a snarl warned him that all was not well.

The puppy sprawled in front of him. He cocked his ears and watched it curiously. Then their noses touched, and he felt the warm little tongue of the puppy on his jowl. White Fang's tongue went out, he knew not why, and he licked the puppy's face.

Hand-clapping and pleased cries from the gods greeted the performance. He was surprised, and looked at them in a puzzled way. Then his weakness asserted itself, and he lay down, his ears cocked, his head on one side, as he watched the puppy. The other puppies came sprawling toward him, to Collie's great disgust; and he gravely permitted them to clamber and tumble over him. At first, amid the applause of the gods, he betrayed a trifle of his old self-consciousness and awkwardness. This passed away as the puppies' antics and mauling continued, and he lay with half-shut patient eyes, drowsing in the sun.

KU-762-083

FALSE WITNESS

Karin Slaughter is one of the world's most popular storytellers. Published in 120 countries with more than 40 million copies sold across the globe, her novels have all been *Sunday Times* bestsellers. Slaughter lives in Atlanta, Georgia, and is the founder of the Save the Libraries project—a nonprofit organization established to support libraries and library programming. Her standalone novel *Pieces of Her* is now a Netflix series, and the Grant County and Will Trent series are in development for television.

For more information visit KarinSlaughter.com
🅵 /AuthorKarinSlaughter
🆃 @SlaughterKarin

Also by Karin Slaughter

Blindsighted
Kisscut
A Faint Cold Fear
Indelible
Faithless
Triptych
Skin Privilege
Fractured
Genesis
Broken
Fallen
Criminal
Unseen
Cop Town
Pretty Girls
The Kept Woman
The Good Daughter
Pieces of Her
The Last Widow
The Silent Wife

EBOOK ORIGINALS
Snatched
Cold, Cold Heart
Busted
Blonde Hair, Blue Eyes
Last Breath
Cleaning the Gold (with Lee Child)

NOVELLAS AND STORIES
Like a Charm (Editor)
Martin Misunderstood

FALSE
WITNESS

KARIN
Slaughter

HarperCollins*Publishers*

HarperCollins*Publishers* Ltd
1 London Bridge Street,
London SE1 9GF

www.harpercollins.co.uk

HarperCollins*Publishers*
1st Floor, Watermarque Building, Ringsend Road
Dublin 4, Ireland

This paperback edition 2021
2

First published in Great Britain in 2021 by HarperCollins*Publishers*

Copyright © Karin Slaughter 2021

Lyrics from "The Music Man" (written by Meredith Willson)

Karin Slaughter asserts the moral right to
be identified as the author of this work

A catalogue record for this book is available from the British Library

ISBN: 978-0-00-830354-9 (PB b-format)
ISBN: 978-0-00-830355-6 (PB a-format)

This book is a work of fiction. References to real people, events, establishments,
organizations, or locales are intended only to provide a sense of authenticity, and
are used fictitiously. All other characters, and all incidents and dialogue, are drawn
from the author's imagination and are not to be construed as real.

Typeset in Sabon by Palimpsest Book Production Ltd, Falkirk, Stirlingshire

Printed and bound in the UK using 100% Renewable Electricity at CPI Group (UK) Ltd

All rights reserved. No part of this publication may be
reproduced, stored in a retrieval system, or transmitted,
in any form or by any means, electronic, mechanical,
photocopying, recording or otherwise, without the prior
permission of the publishers.

MIX
Paper | Supporting
responsible forestry
FSC™ C007454

This book is produced from independently certified FSC™ paper
to ensure responsible forest management.

For more information visit: www.harpercollins.co.uk/green

For my readers

The past is never where you think you left it.
—Katherine Anne Porter

SUMMER 1998

From the kitchen, Callie heard Trevor tapping his fingers on the aquarium. Her grip tightened around the spatula she was using to mix cookie dough. He was only ten years old. She thought he was being bullied at school. His father was an asshole. He was allergic to cats and terrified of dogs. Any shrink would tell you the kid was terrorizing the poor fish in a desperate bid for attention, but Callie was barely holding on by her fingernails.

Tap-tap-tap.

She rubbed her temples, trying to ward off a headache. "Trev, are you tapping on the aquarium like I told you not to?"

The tapping stopped. "No, ma'am."

"Are you sure?"

Silence.

Callie plopped dough onto the cookie sheet. The tapping resumed like a metronome. She plopped out more rows on the three count.

Tap-tap-plop. Tap-tap-plop.

Callie was closing the oven door when Trevor suddenly appeared behind her like a serial killer. He threw his arms around her, saying, "I love you."

She held on to him as tightly as he held on to her. The fist of tension loosened its grip on her skull. She kissed the top of Trevor's head. He tasted salty from the festering heat. He was standing completely still, but his nervous energy reminded her of a coiled spring. "Do you want to lick the bowl?"

The question was answered before she could finish asking it.

1

He dragged a kitchen chair to the counter and made like Pooh Bear sticking his head into a honeypot.

Callie wiped the sweat from her forehead. The sun had gone down an hour ago, but the house was still broiling. The air conditioning was barely functioning. The oven had turned the kitchen into a sauna. Everything felt sticky and wet, herself and Trevor included.

She turned on the faucet. The cold water was irresistible. She splashed her face, then, to Trevor's delight, sprinkled some on the back of his neck.

Once the giggling died down, Callie adjusted the water to clean the spatula. She placed it in the drying rack beside the remnants from dinner. Two plates. Two glasses. Two forks. One knife to cut Trevor's hot dog into pieces. One teaspoon for a dollop of Worcestershire sauce mixed in with the ketchup.

Trevor handed her the bowl to wash. His lips curved up to the left when he smiled, the same way his father's did. He stood beside her at the sink, his hip pressing against her.

She asked, "Were you tapping the glass on the aquarium?"

He looked up. She caught the flash of scheming in his eyes. Exactly like his father. "You said they were starter fish. That they probably wouldn't live."

She felt a nasty response worthy of her mother press against the back of her clenched teeth—*Your grandfather's going to die, too. Should we go down to the nursing home and stick needles under his fingernails?*

Callie hadn't said the words out loud, but the spring inside of Trevor coiled even tighter. She was always unsettled by how tuned in he was to her emotions.

"Okay." She dried her hands on her shorts, nodding toward the aquarium. "We should find out their names."

He looked guarded, always afraid of being the last one to get the joke. "Fish don't have names."

"Of course they do, silly. They don't just meet each other on the first day of school and say, 'Hello, my name is Fish.'" She gently nudged him into the living room. The two bicolored blennies were swimming a nervous loop around the aquarium. She had lost Trevor's interest several times during the arduous process

2

of setting up the saltwater tank. The arrival of the fish had sharpened his focus to the head of a pin.

Callie's knee popped as she knelt down in front of the aquarium. The throbbing pain was more tolerable than the sight of Trevor's grimy fingerprints clouding the glass. "What about the little guy?" She pointed to the smaller of the two. "What's his name?"

Trevor's lips curved up at the left as he fought a smile. "Bait."

"Bait?"

"For when the sharks come and eat him!" Trevor burst into too-loud laughter, rolling on the floor at the hilarity.

Callie tried to rub the throb out of her knee. She glanced around the room with her usual sinking depression. The stained shag carpet had been flattened sometime in the late eighties. Streetlight lasered around the puckered edges of the orange and brown drapes. One corner of the room was taken up by a fully stocked bar with a smoky mirror behind it. Glasses hung down from a ceiling rack and four leather bar stools crowded around the L-shape of the sticky wooden top. The entire room was centered around a giant television that weighed more than Callie. The orange couch had two depressing his-and-her indentations on opposite ends. The tan club chairs had sweat stains at the backs. The arms had been burned by smoldering cigarettes.

Trevor's hand slipped inside of hers. He had picked up on her mood again.

He tried, "What about the other fish?"

She smiled as she rested her head against his. "How about . . ." She cast around for something good—Anne Chovey, Genghis Karp, Brine Austin Green. "Mr. Dar-Sea?"

Trevor wrinkled his nose. Not an Austen fan. "What time is Dad getting home?"

Buddy Waleski got home whenever he damn well got home. "Soon."

"Are the cookies ready yet?"

Callie winced her way to standing so she could follow him back into the kitchen. They watched the cookies through the oven door. "Not quite, but when you're out of your bath—"

Trevor bolted down the hallway. The bathroom door slammed.

She heard the faucet squeak. Water splattered into the tub. He started humming.

An amateur would claim victory, but Callie was no amateur. She waited a few minutes, then cracked open the bathroom door to make sure he was actually in the tub. She caught him just as he dipped his head under the water.

Still not a win—there was no soap in sight—but she was exhausted and her back ached and her knee was pinching when she walked up the hallway so all she could do was grit through the pain until she reached the bar and filled a martini glass with equal parts Sprite and Captain Morgan.

Callie limited herself to two swigs before she leaned down and checked for blinking lights under the bar. She had discovered the digital camera by accident a few months ago. The power had gone out. She'd been looking for the emergency candles when she noticed a flash out of the corner of her eye.

Callie's first thought had been—*sprained back, trick knee, and now her retina was detaching*—but the light was red, not white, and it was flashing like Rudolph's nose between two of the heavy leather stools under the bar. She had pulled them away. Watched the red light flash off the brass foot rail that stringed along the bottom.

It was a good hiding place. The front of the bar was done up in a multi-colored mosaic. Shards of mirror punctuated broken pieces of blue, green, and orange tile, all of which obscured the one-inch hole cut through to the shelves in the back. She'd found the Canon digital camcorder behind a cardboard box filled with wine corks. Buddy had taped the power cord up inside the shelf to hide it, but the power had been off for hours. The battery was dying. Callie had no idea whether or not the camera had been recording. It was pointed directly at the couch.

This is what Callie had told herself: Buddy had friends over almost every weekend. They watched basketball or football or baseball and they talked bullshit and business and women, and they probably said things that gave Buddy leverage, the kind of leverage that he could later use to close a deal, and probably that's what the camera was for.

Probably.

4

She left out the Sprite on her second drink. The spiced rum burned up her throat and into her nose. Callie sneezed, catching most of it with the back of her arm. She was too tired to get a paper towel from the kitchen. She used one of the bar towels to wipe off the snot. The monogrammed crest scratched her skin. Callie looked at the logo, which summed up Buddy in a nutshell. Not the Atlanta Falcons. Not the Georgia Bulldogs. Not even Georgia Tech. Buddy Waleski had chosen to be a booster for the division two Bellwood Eagles, a high school team that went zero-to-ten last season.

Big fish/small pond.

Callie was downing the rest of the rum when Trevor came back into the living room. He wrapped his skinny arms around her again. She kissed the top of his head. He still tasted sweaty, but she had fought enough battles for the day. All she wanted now was for him to go to sleep so that she could drink away the aches and pains in her body.

They sat on the floor in front of the aquarium as they waited for the cookies to cool down. Callie told him about her first aquarium. The mistakes she had made. The responsibility and care it took to keep the fish thriving. Trevor had turned docile. She told herself it was because of the warm bath and not because of the way the light went out of his eyes every time he saw her standing behind the bar pouring herself another drink.

Callie's guilt started to dissipate as they got closer to Trevor's bedtime. She could feel him start to wind himself up as they sat at the kitchen table. The routine was familiar: An argument about how many cookies he could eat. Spilled milk. Another cookie argument. A discussion about which bed he would sleep in. A struggle to get him into his pajamas. A negotiation over how many pages she would read from his book. A kiss goodnight. Another kiss goodnight. A request for a glass of water. Not that glass, this glass. Not this water, that water. Screaming. Crying. More battling. More negotiating. Promises for tomorrow—games, the zoo, a visit to the water park. And so on and so on until she eventually, finally, found herself standing alone behind the bar again.

She stopped herself from rushing to open the bottle like a

desperate drunk. Her hands were shaking. She watched them tremor in the silence of the dingy room. More than anything else, she associated the room with Buddy. The air was stifling. Smoke from thousands of cigarettes and cigarillos had stained the low ceiling. Even the spiderwebs in the corners were orangey-brown. She never took her shoes off inside the house because the feel of the sticky carpet cupping her feet made her stomach turn.

Callie slowly twisted the cap off the bottle of rum. The spices tickled at her nose again. Her mouth started to water from anticipation. She could feel the numbing effects just from thinking about the third drink, not the last drink, the drink that would help her shoulders relax, her back stop spasming, her knee stop throbbing.

The kitchen door popped open. Buddy coughed, the phlegm tight in his throat. He threw his briefcase onto the counter. Kicked Trevor's chair back under the table. Snatched up a handful of cookies. Held his cigarillo in one hand as he chewed with his mouth open. Callie could practically hear the crumbs pinging off the table, bouncing against his scuffed shoes, scattering across the linoleum, tiny cymbals clanging together, because everywhere Buddy went, there was *noise, noise, noise.*

He finally noticed her. She had that early feeling of being glad to see him, of expecting him to envelop her in his arms and make her feel special again. Then more crumbs dropped from his mouth. "Pour me one, baby doll."

She filled a glass with Scotch and soda. The stink of his cigarillo wafted across the room. Black & Mild. She had never seen him without a box sticking out of his shirt pocket.

Buddy was finishing the last two cookies as he pounded his way toward the bar. Heavy footsteps creaking the floors. Crumbs on the carpet. Crumbs on his wrinkled, sweat-stained work shirt. Trapped in the stubble of his five o'clock shadow.

Buddy was six-three when he stood up straight, which was never. His skin was perpetually red. He had more hair than most men his age, a little bit of it starting to gray. He worked out, but only with weights, so he looked more gorilla than man—short-waisted, with arms so muscled that they wouldn't go flat to his sides. Callie seldom saw his hands when they weren't fisted.

Everything about him screamed *ruthless motherfucker*. People turned in the opposite direction when they saw him in the street.

If Trevor was a coiled spring, Buddy was a sledgehammer.

He dropped the cigarillo into the ashtray, slurped down the Scotch, then banged the glass down on the counter. "You have a good day, dolly?"

"Sure." She stepped aside so he could get a refill.

"I had a great one. You know that new strip mall over on Stewart? Guess who's gonna be doing the framing?"

"You," Callie said, though Buddy hadn't waited for her to answer.

"Got the down payment today. They're pouring the foundation tomorrow. Nothing better than having cash in your pocket, right?" He belched, pounding his chest to get it out. "Fetch me some ice, will ya?"

She started to go, but his hand grabbed her ass like he was turning a doorknob.

"Lookit that tiny little thing."

There had been a time early on when Callie had thought it was funny how obsessed he was with her petite size. He would lift her up with one arm, or marvel at his hand stretched across her back, the thumb and fingers almost touching the edges of her hip bones. He called her *little bit* and *baby girl* and *doll* and now . . .

It was just one more thing about him that annoyed her.

Callie hugged the ice bucket to her stomach as she headed toward the kitchen. She glanced at the aquarium. The blennies had calmed down. They were swimming through the bubbles from the filter. She filled the bucket with ice that smelled like Arm & Hammer baking soda and freezer-burned meat.

Buddy swiveled around in his bar stool as she made her way back toward him. He had pinched off the tip of his cigarillo and was shoving it back into the box. "God damn, little girl, I love watching your hips move. Do a spin for me."

She felt her eyes roll again—not at him, but at herself, because a tiny, stupid, lonely part of Callie still bought into his flirting. He was honest-to-God the first person in her life who had ever made her feel truly loved. She had never before felt special, chosen, like she was all that mattered to another human being. Buddy had made her feel safe and cared for.

But lately, all he wanted to do was fuck her.

Buddy pocketed the Black & Milds. He jammed his paw into the ice bucket. She saw dirt crescents under his fingernails.

He asked, "How's the kid?"

"Sleeping."

His hand was cupped between her legs before she caught the glint in his eye. Her knees bowed awkwardly. It was like sitting on the flat end of a shovel.

"Buddy—"

His other hand clamped around her ass, trapping her between his bulging arms. "Look at how tiny you are. I could stick you in my pocket and nobody'd ever know you were there."

She could taste cookies and Scotch and tobacco when his tongue slid into her mouth. Callie returned the kiss because pushing him away, bruising his ego, would take up so much time and end up with her back at the exact same damn place.

For all his sound and fury, Buddy was a pussy when it came to his feelings. He could beat a grown man to a pulp without blinking an eye, but with Callie, he was so raw sometimes that it made her skin crawl. She had spent hours reassuring him, coddling him, propping him up, listening to his insecurities roll in like an ocean wave scratching at the sand.

Why was she with him? She should find someone else. She was out of his league. Too pretty. Too young. Too smart. Too classy. Why did she give a stupid brute like him the time of day? What did she see in him—no, tell him in detail, right now, what exactly was it that she liked about him? Be specific.

He constantly told her she was beautiful. He took her to nice restaurants, upscale hotels. He bought her jewelry and expensive clothes and gave her mother cash when she was short. He would beat down any man who even thought about looking at her the wrong way. The outside world would probably think that Callie had landed like a pig in shit, but, inside, she wondered if she'd be better off if he was as cruel to her as he was to everyone else. At least then she'd have a reason to hate him. Something real that she could point to instead of his pathetic

8

tears soaking her shirt or the sight of him on his knees begging for her forgiveness.

"Daddy?"

Callie shuddered at the sound of Trevor's voice. He stood in the hallway clutching his blanket.

Buddy's hands kept Callie locked in place. "Go back to bed, son."

"I want Mommy."

Callie closed her eyes so she wouldn't have to see Trevor's face.

"Do as I say," Buddy warned. "Now."

She held her breath, only letting it go when she heard the slow pad of Trevor's feet back down the hall. His bedroom door creaked on its hinges. She heard the latch click.

Callie pulled away. She walked behind the bar, started turning the labels on the bottles, wiping down the counter, pretending like she wasn't trying to put an obstacle between them.

Buddy huffed a laugh, rubbing his arms like it wasn't sweltering in this wretched house. "Why's it so cold all a sudden?"

Callie said, "I should go check on him."

"Nah." Buddy came around the bar, blocking her exit. "Check on me first."

Buddy guided her palm to the bulge in his pants. He moved her hand up and down, once, and she was reminded of watching him jerk the rope on the lawnmower to start the motor.

"Like that." He repeated the motion.

Callie relented. She always relented.

"That's good."

Callie closed her eyes. She could smell the pinched-off tip of his cigarillo still smoldering in the ashtray. The aquarium gurgled from across the room. She tried to think of some good fish names for Trevor tomorrow.

James Pond. Darth Baiter. Tank Sinatra.

"Jesus, your hands are so small." Buddy unzipped his pants. Pressed down on her shoulder. The carpet behind the bar felt wet. Her knees sucked into the shag. "You're my little ballerina."

Callie put her mouth on him.

"Christ." Buddy's grip was firm on her shoulder. "That's good. Like that."

Callie squeezed her eyes closed.

Tuna Turner. Leonardo DeCarpio. Mary Kate and Ashley Ocean.

Buddy patted her shoulder. "Come on, baby. Let's finish on the couch."

Callie didn't want to go to the couch. She wanted to finish now. To go away. To be by herself. To take a breath and fill her lungs with anything but him.

"God dammit!"

Callie cringed.

He wasn't yelling at her.

She could tell from the shift in the air that Trevor was back in the hallway. She tried to imagine what he'd seen. One of Buddy's meaty hands gripping the counter, his hips thrusting at something underneath the bar.

"Daddy?" he asked. "Where did—"

"What did I tell you?" Buddy bellowed.

"I'm not sleepy."

"Then go drink your medicine. Go."

Callie looked up at Buddy. He was jamming one of his fat fingers toward the kitchen.

She heard Trevor's chair screech across the linoleum. The back banging against the counter. The cabinet creaking open. A *tick-tick-tick* as Trevor turned the childproof cap on the NyQuil. Buddy called it his sleepy medicine. The antihistamines would knock him out for the rest of the night.

"Drink it," Buddy ordered.

Callie thought of the delicate ripples in Trevor's throat when he threw his head back and gulped down his milk.

"Leave it on the counter," Buddy said. "Go back to your room."

"But I—"

"Go back to your damn room and stay there before I beat the skin off your ass."

Again, Callie held her breath until she heard the *click* of Trevor's bedroom door latching closed.

"Fucking kid."

"Buddy, maybe I should—"

She stood up just as Buddy swung back around. His elbow

10

accidentally caught her square in the nose. The sudden crack of breaking bones split her like a bolt of lightning. She was too stunned to even blink.

Buddy looked horrified. "Doll? Are you okay? I'm sorry, I—"

Callie's senses toggled back on one by one. Sound rushing into her ears. Pain flooding her nerves. Vision swimming. Mouth filling with blood.

She gasped for air. Blood sucked down her throat. The room started spinning. She was going to pass out. Her knees buckled. She frantically grabbed at anything to keep from falling. The cardboard box toppled from the shelf. The back of her head popped against the floor. Wine corks hit her chest and face like fat drops of rain. She blinked up at the ceiling. She saw the bicolored fish swimming furiously in front of her eyes. She blinked again. The fish darted away. Breath swirled inside of her lungs. Her head started pounding along with her heartbeat. She wiped something off her chest. The box of Black & Mild had fallen out of Buddy's shirt pocket, scattering the slim cigarillos across her body. She craned her neck to find him.

Callie had expected Buddy to have that apologetic puppy-dog look on his face, but he barely noticed her. He was holding the video camera in his hands. She'd accidentally pulled it off the shelf along with the box. A chunk of plastic had chipped off the corner.

He let out a low, sharp, "Shit."

Finally, he looked at her. His eyes went shifty, the same way Trevor's did. Caught red-handed. Desperate for a way out.

Callie's head fell back against the carpet. She was still so disoriented. Everything she looked at pulsed along with the throb inside her skull. The glasses hanging down from the rack. The brown water stains on the ceiling. She coughed into her hand. Blood speckled her palm. She could hear Buddy moving around.

She looked up at him again. "Buddy, I already—"

Without warning, he wrenched her up by the arm. Callie's legs struggled to stand. His elbow had smacked her harder than she'd first thought. The world had started to stutter, a record needle caught in the same rut. Callie coughed again, stumbling forward. Her entire face felt smashed open. A thick stream of blood ran

11

down the back of her throat. The room was swirling like a globe. Was this a concussion? It felt like a concussion.

"Buddy, I think I—"

"Shut it." His hand clamped down hard on the back of her neck. He muscled her through the living room and into the kitchen like a misbehaving dog. Callie was too startled to fight back. His fury had always been like a flash fire, sudden and all-encompassing. Usually, she knew where it was coming from.

"Buddy, I—"

He threw her against the table. "Will you fucking shut up and listen to me?"

Callie reached back to steady herself. The entire kitchen turned sideways. She was going to throw up. She needed to get to the sink.

Buddy banged his fist on the counter. "Stop playing around, dammit!"

Callie's hands covered her ears. His face was scarlet. He was so angry. Why was he so angry?

"I'm dead fucking serious." Buddy's tone had softened, but the register had a deep, ominous growl. "You need to listen to me."

"Okay, okay. Just give me a minute." Callie's legs were still shaky. She lurched toward the sink. Twisted on the faucet. Waited for the water to run clear. She stuck her head under the cold stream. Her nose burned. She winced, and the pain shot straight through her face.

Buddy's hand wrapped around the edge of the sink. He was waiting.

Callie lifted her head. The dizziness nearly sent her reeling again. She found a towel in the drawer. The rough material scratched her cheeks. She stuck it under her nose, tried to staunch the bleeding. "What is it?"

He was bouncing on the balls of his feet. "You can't tell anybody about the camera, okay?"

The towel had already soaked through. The blood would not stop pouring from her nose, into her mouth, down her throat. Callie had never wanted so desperately to lie down in bed and close her eyes. Buddy used to know when she needed that. He used to sweep her up in his arms and carry her down the hall

12

and tuck her into bed and stroke her hair until she fell asleep.

"Callie, promise me. Look me in the eye and promise you won't tell."

Buddy's hand was on her shoulder again, but more gently this time. The rage inside of him had started to burn itself out. He lifted her chin with his thick fingers. She felt like a Barbie he was trying to pose.

"Shit, baby. Look at your nose. Are you okay?" He grabbed a fresh towel. "I'm sorry, all right? Jesus, your beautiful little face. Are you okay?"

Callie turned back to the sink. She spat blood into the drain. Her nose felt like it was cranked between two gears. This had to be a concussion. She saw two of everything. Two globs of blood. Two faucets. Two drying racks on the counter.

"Look." His hands gripped her arms, spinning her around and pinning her against the cabinets. "You're gonna be okay, all right? I'll make sure of that. But you can't tell nobody about the camera, okay?"

"Okay," she said, because it was always easier to agree with him.

"I'm serious, doll. Look me in the eye and promise me." She couldn't tell if he was worried or angry until he shook her like a rag doll. "Look at me."

Callie could only offer him a slow blink. There was a cloud between her and everything else. "I know it was an accident."

"Not your nose. I'm talking about the camera." He licked his lips, his tongue darting out like a lizard's. "You can't make a stink about the camera, dolly. I could go to prison."

"Prison?" The word came from nowhere, had no meaning. He might as well have said unicorn. "Why would—"

"Baby doll, please. Don't be stupid."

She blinked, and, like a lens twisting into focus, she could see him clearly now.

Buddy wasn't concerned or angry or eaten up with guilt. He was terrified.

Of what?

Callie had known about the camera for months, but she had never let herself figure out the purpose. She thought about his

13

weekend parties. The cooler overflowing with beer. The air filled with smoke. The TV blaring. Drunken men chuckling and slapping each other on the back as Callie tried to get Trevor ready so they could go to a movie or the park or anything that got them both out of the house.

"I gotta—" She blew her nose into the towel. Strings of blood spiderwebbed across the white. Her mind was clearing but she could still hear ringing in her ears. He had accidentally knocked the shit out of her. Why had he been so careless?

"Look." His fingers dug into her arms. "Listen to me, doll."

"Stop telling me to listen. I *am* listening. I'm hearing every damn thing you say." She coughed so hard that she had to bend over to clear it. She wiped her mouth. She looked up at him. "Are you recording your friends? Is that what the camera is for?"

"Forget the camera." Buddy reeked of paranoia. "You got conked in the head, doll. You don't know what you're talking about."

What was she missing?

He said he was a contractor, but he didn't have an office. He drove around all day working out of his Corvette. She knew he was a sports bookie. He was also an enforcer, muscle for hire. He always had a lot of cash on him. He always knew a guy who knew a guy. Was he recording his friends asking for favors? Were they paying him to break some knees, burn down some buildings, find some leverage that would close a deal or punish an enemy?

Callie tried to hold on to the pieces of a puzzle she couldn't quite snap together in her head. "What're you doing, Buddy? Are you blackmailing them?"

Buddy held his tongue between his teeth. He paused a beat too long before saying, "Yeah. That's exactly what I do, baby. I blackmail them. That's where the cash comes from. You can't let on that you know. Blackmail's a big crime. I could be sent away for the rest of my life."

She stared into the living room, imagined it filled with his friends—the same friends every time. Some of them Callie didn't know, but others were a part of her life and she felt guilty that she was a partial beneficiary of Buddy's illegal scheming. Dr. Patterson, the school principal. Coach Holt from the Bellwood

14

Eagles. Mr. Humphrey, who sold used cars. Mr. Ganza, who manned the deli counter at the supermarket. Mr. Emmett, who worked at her dentist's office.

What had they done that was so bad? What horrible things had a coach, a car salesman, a handsy geriatric asshole for the love of Christ, done that they were stupid enough to confess to Buddy Waleski?

And why did these idiots keep coming back every weekend for football, for basketball, for baseball, for soccer, when Buddy was blackmailing them?

Why were they smoking his cigars? Swilling his beer? Burning holes in his furniture? Screaming at his TV?

Let's finish on the couch.

Callie's eyes followed the triangle from the one-inch hole drilled into the front of the bar, to the couch directly across from it, to the giant TV that weighed more than she did.

There was a glass shelf underneath the set.

Cable box. Cable splitter. VCR.

She had grown used to seeing the three-pronged RCA cable that hung down from the jacks on the front of the VCR. Red for the right audio channel. White for the left audio. Yellow for video. The cable threaded into one long wire that lay coiled on the carpet below the television. Not once, ever, had Callie wondered what the other end of that cable plugged into.

Let's finish on the couch.

"Baby girl." Buddy's desperation was sweating out of his body. "Maybe you should go home, all right? Lemme give you some money. I told you I got paid for that job tomorrow. Good to spread it around, right?"

Callie was looking at him now.

She was really looking at him.

Buddy reached into his pocket and pulled out a wad of cash. He counted off the bills like he was counting off all the ways he controlled her. "Buy yourself a new shirt, all right? Get some matching pants and shoes or whatever. Maybe a necklace? You like that necklace I gave you, right? Get another one. Or four. Be like Mr. T."

"Do you film us?" The question was out before she could

15

consider the kind of hell that the answer could rain down. They never made love in the bed anymore. It was always on the couch. And all those times he'd carried her back to tuck her in? It was right after they had finished on the couch. "Is that what you do, Buddy? You film yourself fucking me and you show it to your friends?"

"Don't be stupid." His tone was the same as Trevor's when he promised he wasn't tapping the glass on the aquarium. "I wouldn't do that, would I? I love you."

"You're a goddam pervert."

"Watch your nasty mouth." He wasn't screwing around with his warning. She could see exactly what was going on now—what had been going on for at least six months.

Dr. Patterson waving at her from the bleachers during pep rallies.

Coach Holt winking at her from the sidelines during football games.

Mr. Ganza smiling at Callie as he passed her mother some sliced cheese over the deli counter.

"You—" Callie's throat clenched. They had all seen her with her clothes off. The things she had done to Buddy on the couch. The things that Buddy had done to her. "I can't—"

"Callie, calm down. You're getting hysterical."

"I *am* fucking hysterical!" she screamed. "They've *seen* me, Buddy. They've *watched* me. They all know what I—what we—"

"Doll, come on."

She dropped her head into her hands, humiliated.

Dr. Patterson. Coach Holt. Mr. Ganza. They weren't mentors or fatherly figures or sweet old men. They were perverts who got off on watching Callie get screwed.

"Come on, baby," Buddy said. "You're blowing this out of proportion."

Tears streamed down her face. She could barely speak. She had loved him. She had done *everything* for him. "How could you do this to me?"

"Do what?" Buddy sounded flip. His eyes darted down to the wad of cash. "You got what you wanted."

She shook her head. She had never wanted this. She had wanted

16

to feel safe. To feel protected. To have someone interested in her life, her thoughts, her dreams.

"Come on, baby girl. You got your uniforms paid for, and your cheerleading camp, and your—"

"I'll tell my mother," she threatened. "I'll tell her exactly what you did."

"You think she gives a shit?" His laugh was genuine, because they both knew it was true. "As long as the cash keeps coming, your mama don't care."

Callie swallowed the glass that had filled her throat. "What about Linda?"

His mouth fished open like a trout's.

"What's your wife gonna think about you fucking her son's fourteen-year-old babysitter for the last two years?"

She heard the hiss of air sucking past his teeth.

In all of the time Callie had been with him, Buddy had talked constantly about Callie's *small hands*, her *tiny waist*, her *little mouth*, but he had never, ever talked about the fact that there was more than thirty years between them.

That he was a *criminal*.

"Linda's still at the hospital, right?" Callie walked over to the phone hanging by the side door. Her fingers traced the emergency numbers that were taped onto the wall. Even as she went through the motions, Callie wondered if she could go through with the call. Linda was always so kind. The news would devastate her. There was no way Buddy would let it get that far.

Still, Callie picked up the receiver, expecting him to wail and plead and beg for her forgiveness and reaffirm his love and devotion.

He did none of this. His mouth kept trouting. He stood like a frozen gorilla, his arms bulging out at his sides.

Callie turned her back to him. She rested the receiver against her shoulder. Stretched the springy cord out of her way. Touched the number eight on the keypad.

The entire world slowed down before her brain could register what was happening.

The punch to her kidney was like a speeding car sideswiping her from behind. The phone slipped from her shoulder. Callie's arms flew up. Her feet left the ground. She felt a breeze on her skin as she launched into the air.

Her chest slammed into the wall. Her nose crushed flat. Her teeth dug into the Sheetrock.

"Stupid bitch." Buddy palmed the back of her head and banged her face into the wall again. Then again. He reared back a third time.

Callie forced her knees to bend. She felt her hair rip from her scalp as she folded her body into a ball on the floor. She had been beaten before. She knew how to take a hit. But that was with someone whose size and strength were relatively close to her own. Someone who didn't thrash people for a living. Someone who had never killed before.

"You gonna fuckin' threaten me!" Buddy's foot swung into her stomach like a wrecking ball.

Callie's body lifted off the floor. She huffed all of the air out of her lungs. A sharp stabbing pain told her that one of her ribs had fractured.

Buddy was on his knees. She looked up at him. His eyes were crazed. Spit speckled the corners of his mouth. He wrapped one hand around her neck. Callie tried to scramble away but ended up on her back. He straddled her. The weight of him was unbearable. His grip tightened. Her windpipe flexed into her spine. He was pinching off her air. She swung at him, trying to aim her fist between his legs. Once. Twice. A sideswipe was enough to loosen his grip. She rolled out from under him, tried to find a way to stand, to run, to flee.

The air cracked with a sound she couldn't quite name.

Fire burned across Callie's back. She felt her skin being flayed. He was using the telephone cord to whip her. Blood bubbled up like acid across her spine. She raised her hand and watched the skin on her arm snake open as the phone cord wrapped around her wrist.

Instinctively, she jerked back her arm. The cord slipped from his grasp. She saw the surprise in his face and scrambled to get her back against the wall. She lashed out at him, punching, kicking, recklessly swinging the cord, screaming, "Fuck you, motherfucker! I'll fucking kill you!"

Her voice echoed in the kitchen.

Suddenly, somehow, everything had come to a standstill.

Callie had at some point managed to spring to her feet. Her hand was raised behind her head, waiting to whip the cord around. Both of them stood their ground, no more than spitting distance between them.

Buddy's startled laugh turned into an appreciative chuckle. "Damn, girl."

She had opened a gash along his cheek. He wiped the blood onto his fingers. He put his fingers in his mouth. He made a loud sucking noise.

Callie felt her stomach twist into a tight knot.

She knew the taste of violence brought out a darkness in him.

"Come on, tiger." He raised his fists like a boxer ready for a knock-out round. "Come at me again."

"Buddy, please." Callie silently willed her muscles to stay primed, her joints to keep loose, to be ready to fight back as hard as they could because the only reason he was acting calm right now was because he had made up his mind that he was going to enjoy killing her. "It doesn't have to be like this."

"Sugar doll, it was always going to be like this."

She let that knowledge settle into her brain. Callie knew that he was right. She had been such a fool. "I won't say anything. I promise."

"It's too far gone, dolly. I think you know that." His fists still hung loose in front of his face. He waved her forward. "Come on, baby girl. Don't go down without a fight."

He had nearly two feet and at least one hundred fifty pounds on her. The heft of an entire second human being existed inside of his hulking body.

Scratch him? Bite him? Pull out his hair? Die with his blood in her mouth?

"Whatcha gonna do, little bit?" He kept his fists at the ready. "I'm giving you a chance here. You gonna come at me or are you gonna fold?"

The hallway?

She couldn't risk leading him to Trevor.

The front door?

19

Too far away.

The kitchen door?

Callie could see the gold doorknob out of the corner of her eye.

Gleaming. Waiting. Unlocked.

She walked herself through the motions—turn, left-foot-right-foot, grab the knob, twist, run through the carport, out into the street, scream her head off the whole way.

Who was she kidding?

All she had to do was turn and Buddy would be on her. He wasn't fast, but he didn't need to be. In one long stride, his hand would be around her neck again.

Callie stared all of her hatred into him.

He shrugged, because it didn't matter.

"Why did you do it?" she asked. "Why did you show them our private stuff?"

"Money." He sounded disappointed that she was so stupid. "Why the hell else?"

Callie couldn't let herself think about all those grown men watching her do stuff she did not want to do with a man who had promised he would always, no matter what, protect her.

"Bring it." Buddy punched a lazy right hook into the air, then a slow-motion uppercut. "Come on, Rocky. Gimme whatcha got."

She let her gaze ping-pong around the kitchen.

Fridge. Oven. Cabinets. Drawers. Cookie plate. NyQuil. Drying rack.

Buddy smirked. "You gonna hit me with a frying pan, Daffy Duck?"

Callie sprinted straight toward him, full out, like a bullet exploding from the muzzle of a gun. Buddy's hands were up near his face. She tucked her body down low so that when he finally managed to drop his fists, she was already out of his reach.

She crashed into the kitchen sink.

Grabbed the knife out of the drying rack.

Spun around with the blade slicing out in front of her.

Buddy grinned at the steak knife, which looked like something Linda had bought at the grocery store in a six-piece set made in Taiwan. Cracked wooden handle. Serrated blade so thin that it bent three different ways before straightening out at the end. Callie had used it to cut Trevor's hot dog into pieces because otherwise he would try to shove the whole thing in his mouth and start to choke.

Callie could see she'd missed some ketchup.

A thin streak of red ran along the serrated teeth.

"Oh." Buddy sounded surprised. "Oh, Jesus."

They both looked down at the same time.

The knife had slashed open the leg of his pants. Left upper thigh, a few inches down from his crotch.

She watched the khaki material slowly turn crimson.

Callie had been involved in competitive gymnastics from the age of five. She had an intimate understanding of all the ways that you could hurt yourself. An awkward twist could tear the ligaments in your back. A sloppy dismount could wreck the tendons in your knee. A piece of metal—even a cheap piece of metal—that cut across your inner thigh could open your femoral artery, the major pipeline that supplied blood to the lower part of your body.

"Cal." Buddy's hand clamped down on his leg. Blood seeped through his clenched fingers. "Get a—Christ, Callie. Get a towel or—"

He started to fall, broad shoulders banging into the cabinets, head cracking off the edge of the countertop. The room shook from his weight as he dropped down.

"Cal?" Buddy's throat worked. Sweat dripped down his face. "Callie?"

Her body was still tensed. Her hand was still gripping the knife. She felt enveloped by a cold darkness, like she'd somehow stepped back into her own shadow.

"Callie. Baby, you gotta—" His lips had lost their color. His teeth began to chatter as if her coldness was seeping into him, too. "C-call an ambulance, baby. Call an—"

Callie slowly turned her head. She looked at the phone on the wall. The receiver was off the hook. Slivers of multi-colored wires stuck out where Buddy had ripped away the springy cord. She found the other end, following it like a clue, and located the receiver underneath the kitchen table.

21

"Callie, leave that—leave that there, honey. I need you to—"

She got down on her knees. Reached under the table. Picked up the receiver. Placed it to her ear. She was still holding the knife. Why was she still holding the knife?

"That one's b-broken," Buddy told her. "Go to the bedroom, baby. C-call an ambulance."

She pressed the plastic tight to her ear. From memory, she summoned a phantom noise, the bleating siren sound that a phone made when it was off the hook too long.

Wah-wah-wah-wah-wah-wah-wah . . .

"The bedroom, baby. G-go to the—"

Wah-wah-wah-wah-wah-wah-wah . . .

"Callie."

That's what she'd hear if she picked up the phone in the bedroom. The unrelenting bleating and, looped over that, the operator's mechanical voice—

If you'd like to make a call . . .

"Callie, baby, I wasn't going to hurt you. I would never h-hurt—"

Please hang up and try again.

"Baby, please, I need—"

If this is an emergency . . .

"I need your help, baby. P-please go down the hall and—"

Hang up and dial 9-1-1.

"Callie?"

She laid the knife on the floor. She sat back on her heels. Her knee didn't throb. Her back didn't ache. The skin around her neck didn't pulse where he had choked her. Her rib didn't stab from his kicks.

If you'd like to make a call . . .

"You fucking bitch," Buddy rasped. "You f-fucking, heartless bitch."

Please hang up and try again.

SPRING 2021

Sunday

1

Leigh Collier bit her lip as a seventh-grade girl belted out "Ya Got Trouble" to a captive audience. A gaggle of tweens skipped across the stage as Professor Hill warned the townsfolk about out-of-town jaspers luring their sons into horse-race gambling.

Not a wholesome trottin' race, no! But a race where they set right down on the horse!

She doubted a generation that had grown up with WAP, murder hornets, Covid, cataclysmic social unrest, and being forcibly home-schooled by a bunch of depressed day drinkers really understood the threat of pool halls, but Leigh had to hand it to the drama teacher for putting on a gender-neutral production of *The Music Man*, one of the least offensive and most tedious musicals ever staged by a middle school.

Leigh's daughter had just turned sixteen years old. She'd thought her days of watching nose-pickers, mamas' boys, and stage hogs break into song were blissfully over, but then Maddy had taken an interest in teaching choreography so here they were, trapped in this hellhole of *trouble with a capital T and that rhymes with P and that stands for pool.*

She looked for Walter. He was two rows down, closer to the aisle. His head was tilted at a weird angle, sort of looking at the stage, sort of looking at the back of the empty seat in front of him. Leigh didn't have to see what was in his hands to know that he was playing fantasy football on his phone.

She slipped her phone out of her purse and texted—*Maddy is going to ask you questions about the performance.*

Walter kept his head down, but she could tell from the ellipses that he was responding—*I can do two things at once.*

Leigh typed—*If that was true, we would still be together.*

He turned to find her. The crinkles at the corners of his eyes told her he was grinning behind his mask.

Leigh felt an unwelcome lurch in her heart. Their marriage had ended when Maddy was twelve, but during last year's lockdown, they had all ended up living at Walter's house and then Leigh had ended up in his bed and then she'd realized why it hadn't worked out in the first place. Walter was an amazing father, but Leigh had finally accepted that she was the bad type of woman who couldn't stay with a good man.

On stage, the set had changed. A spotlight swung onto a Dutch exchange student filling the role of Marian Paroo. He was telling his mother that a man with a suitcase had followed him home, a scenario that today would've ended in a SWAT standoff.

Leigh let her gaze wander around the audience. Tonight was the closing night after five consecutive Sunday performances. This was the only way to make sure all the parents got to see their kids whether they wanted to or not. The auditorium was one-quarter full, taped-off empty seats keeping everyone at a distance. Masks were mandatory. Hand sanitizer flowed like peach schnapps at a prom. Nobody wanted another Night of the Long Nasal Swabs.

Walter had his fantasy football. Leigh had her fantasy apocalypse fight club. She gave herself ten slots to fill out her team. Obviously, Janey Pringle was her first choice. The woman had sold enough toilet paper, Clorox wipes, and hand sanitizer on the black market to buy her son a brand new MacBook Pro. Gillian Nolan knew how to make schedules. Lisa Regan was frighteningly outdoorsy, so she could do things like build fires. Denene Millner had punched a pit bull in the face when it charged her kid. Ronnie Copeland always had tampons in her purse. Ginger Vishnoo had made the AP physics teacher cry. Tommi Adams would blow anything with a pulse.

Leigh's eyes slid to the right, locating the broad, muscular shoulders of Darryl Washington. He'd quit his job to take care of the kids while his wife worked a high-paying corporate gig. Which was sweet but Leigh wasn't going to survive the apocalypse only to end up fucking a meatier version of Walter.

The men were the problem with this game. You could have one guy, possibly two on your team, but three or more and all the women would probably end up chained to beds in an underground bunker.

The house lights came up. The blue and gold curtains swished closed. Leigh wasn't sure whether she had dozed off or gone into a fugue state, but she was extraordinarily happy that the intermission had finally arrived.

No one stood up at first. There was some uncomfortable shifting in seats as people debated whether or not to go to the restroom. This wasn't like the old days when everybody busted down the doors, eager to gossip in the lobby while they ate cupcakes and drank punch in tiny paper cups. There had been a sign at the entrance instructing them to pick up a plastic bag before entering the auditorium. Inside each was a playbill, a small bottle of water, a paper mask, and a note reminding everyone to wash their hands and follow the CDC guidelines. The rogue—or, as the school called them, *non-compliant*—parents were given a Zoom password so they could watch the performance in the maskless comfort of their own living rooms.

Leigh took out her phone. She dashed off a quick text to Maddy— *The dancing was amazing! How cute was that little librarian? I'm so proud of you!*

Maddy buzzed back immediately— *Mom I am working*

No punctuation. No emojis or stickers. But for social media, Leigh would have no idea that her daughter was still capable of smiling.

This was what a thousand cuts felt like.

She looked for Walter again. His seat was empty. She spotted him near the exit doors, talking to another broad-shouldered father. The man's back was to Leigh, but she could tell by the way Walter was waving his arms that they were discussing football.

Leigh let her gaze travel around the room. Most of the parents were either too young and healthy to jump ahead in the vaccine line, or smart and wealthy enough to know they should lie about buying early access. They were all standing in mismatched pairs talking in low murmurs across the required distance. After a nasty brawl had broken out during last year's Non-Denominational Holiday Celebration That Happened Around Christmas, no one talked about politics. Instead, Leigh caught snippets of more sports talk, the mourning of past bake sales, who was in whose bubble, whose parents were Covidiots or maskholes, and how men who wore their masks below their noses were the same jerks who acted like wearing a condom was a human rights violation.

She turned her focus toward the closed stage curtains, straining her ears to pick up the scraping and pounding and furious whispers as the kids changed out the set. Leigh felt the familiar lurch in her heart—not for Walter this time, but because she ached for her daughter. She wanted to come home to a mess in the kitchen. To yell about homework and screen time. To reach into her closet for a dress that had been "borrowed" or search for a pair of shoes that had been carelessly kicked under the bed. She wanted to hold her squirming, protesting daughter. To lie on the couch and watch a silly movie together. To catch Maddy giggling over something funny on her phone. To endure the withering glare when she asked her what was so funny.

All they did lately was argue, mostly via text in the morning and on the phone at six sharp every night. If Leigh had an ounce of intelligence she would back off, but backing off felt too much like letting go. She couldn't stand not knowing if Maddy had a boyfriend or a girlfriend or had left a string of broken hearts in her wake or had decided to give up love for the pursuit of art and mindfulness. The only thing Leigh knew for sure was that every nasty fucking thing she had ever done or said to her own mother kept slamming into her like a never-ending tidal wave.

Except Leigh's mother deserved it.

She reminded herself that their distance kept Maddy safe. Leigh stayed in the downtown condo they used to share. Maddy had moved to the suburbs with Walter. This was a decision they had all reached together.

Walter was legal counsel for the Atlanta Fire Fighters' Union, so his job entailed Microsoft Teams and phone calls made from the safety of his home office. Leigh was a defense attorney. Some of her work was online, but she still had to go into the office and meet with clients. She still had to enter the courthouse and sit through jury selection and conduct trials. Leigh had already caught the virus during the first wave last year. For nine agonizing days, she'd felt like a mule was kicking her in the chest. As far as anyone knew, the risk for kids seemed to be minimal—the school touted its under-one-percent infection rate on its website—but there was no way she was going to be responsible for bringing the plague home to her daughter.

"Leigh Collier, is that you?"

Ruby Heyer pulled her mask down below her nose, then yanked it quickly back up, like it was safe if you did it fast.

"Ruby. Hi." Leigh was grateful for the six feet between them. Ruby was a mom-friend, a necessary companion back when their kids were toddlers and it was either set up a play date or blow out your brains on the coffee table. "How's Keely?"

"She's fine, but long time, huh?" Ruby's red-rimmed glasses bumped up on her smiling cheeks. She was a horrible poker player. "Funny seeing Maddy enrolled here. Didn't you say you wanted your daughter to have an *in-town education*?"

Leigh felt her mask suck to her mouth as she went from mild annoyance to full-on burn-the-motherfucker-down.

"Hey, ladies. Aren't the kids doing a terrific job?" Walter was standing in the aisle, hands tucked into his pants pockets. "Ruby, nice to see you."

Ruby straddled her broomstick as she prepared to fly away. "Always a pleasure, *Walter*."

Leigh caught the insinuation that she wasn't part of the pleasure, but Walter was shooting her his *don't be a bitch* look. She shot back her *go fuck yourself* look.

Their entire marriage in two looks.

Walter said, "I'm glad we never had that three-way with her."

Leigh laughed. If only Walter had suggested a three-way. "This would be a great school if it was an orphanage."

"Is it necessary to poke every bear with a sharp stick?"

She shook her head, looking up at the gold leaf ceiling and professional sound and lighting rigs. "It's like a Broadway theater in here."

"It is."

"Maddy's old school—"

"Had a cardboard box for a stage and Maglite for a spot and a Mr. Microphone for sound and Maddy thought it was the best thing ever."

Leigh ran her hand along the blue velvet seatback in front of her. The Hollis Academy logo was stitched in gold thread along the top, probably courtesy of a wealthy parent with too much money and not enough taste. Both she and Walter had been godless, public school-supporting, bleeding heart liberals until the virus hit. Now they were scraping together every last cent they could find to send Maddy to an insufferably snooty private school where every other car was a BMW and every other kid was an entitled cocksucker.

The classes were smaller. The students rotated in pods of ten. Extra staff kept the classrooms sanitized. PPE was mandated. Everyone followed the protocols. There were hardly ever any rolling lockdowns in the suburbs. Most of the parents had the luxury of working from home.

"Sweetheart." Walter's patient tone was grating. "Every parent would send their kid here if they could."

"Every parent shouldn't have to."

Her work phone buzzed in her purse. Leigh felt her shoulders tense up. One year ago, she had been an overworked, under-compensated self-employed defense attorney helping sex workers, drug addicts, and petty thieves navigate the legal system. Today, she was a cog in a giant corporate machine representing bankers and small business owners who committed the same crimes as her previous clients, but had the money to get away with it.

Walter said, "They can't expect you to work on a Sunday night."

Leigh snorted at his naiveté. She was competing against dozens of twenty-something-year-olds with so much student loan debt that they slept at the office. She dug around in her purse, saying, "I asked Liz not to bother me unless it was life or death."

"Maybe some rich dude just murdered his wife."

She gave him the *go fuck yourself* look before unlocking her phone. "Octavia Bacca just texted me."

"Everything okay?"

"Yes, but . . ." She hadn't heard from Octavia in weeks. They'd made casual plans to meet for a walk at the Botanical Garden, but Leigh had never heard back, so she'd assumed that Octavia had gotten busy.

Leigh could see the text she'd sent at the end of last month—
Are we still on to walk?

Octavia had texted her back just now—*So shitty. Don't hate me.*

Below the text, a link popped up to a news story. The photo showed a clean-cut guy in his early thirties who looked like every clean-cut guy in his early thirties.

ACCUSED RAPIST INVOKES RIGHT TO SPEEDY TRIAL.

Walter asked, "But?"

"I guess Octavia is tied up on this case." Leigh scrolled through the story, pulling out the details. "Stranger assault, not date rape, which isn't the norm. The client is up on some serious charges. He claims he's innocent—ha, ha. He's demanding a jury trial."

"That'll make the judge happy."

"And the jury." No one wanted to risk exposure to the virus in order to hear a rapist say he didn't do it. And even in the likely event that he *did* do it, rape was a fairly easy charge to plead down. Most prosecutors were hesitant to take on the fight because the cases tended to involve people who knew each other, and those pre-existing relationships further muddled the issue of consent. As a defense attorney, you negotiated for unlawful restraint or a lesser charge that would keep your client off the sex offender registry and out of jail and then you went home and took the longest, hottest shower you could tolerate to blast off the stink.

Walter asked, "Did he get bail?"

"'Rona rules." Given the coronavirus, judges were loath to

hold over defendants pending trial. Instead, they mandated ankle monitors and dared them to break the rules. Prisons and jails were worse than nursing homes. Leigh should know. Her own exposure had come courtesy of Atlanta's City Detention Center.

Walter asked, "Prosecutor didn't offer a deal?"

"I'd be shocked if they didn't, but it doesn't matter if the client won't take it. No wonder Octavia's been offline." She looked up from her phone. "Hey, if the rain holds off, do you think I can bribe Maddy into sitting with me on your back porch?"

"I've got umbrellas, sweetheart, but you know she's got an afterparty with her pod."

Tears welled into Leigh's eyes. She hated being on the outside looking in. A year had passed and she still went into Maddy's empty bedroom at least once a month to cry. "Was it this hard for you when she was living with me?"

"It's a lot easier to delight a twelve-year-old than it is to compete for a sixteen-year-old's attention." His eyes crinkled again. "She loves you so much, sweetheart. You're the best mother she could ever have."

Now her tears started to fall. "You're a good man, Walter."

"To a fault."

He wasn't joking.

The lights flickered. Intermission was over. Leigh was about to sit down, but her phone buzzed again. "Work."

"Lucky," Walter whispered.

She sneaked up the aisle toward the exit. A few of the parents glared at her over their masks. Whether it was for the current disruption or for Leigh's part in last year's Christmas-adjacent nasty brawl, she had no idea. She ignored them, feigning interest in her phone. The caller ID flashed BRADLEY, which was odd, because usually when her assistant called, it scrolled BRADLEY, CANFIELD & MARKS.

She stood in the middle of the ridiculously plush lobby, ignoring the gold sconces that had probably been plundered from an actual tomb. Walter claimed she had a chip on her shoulder about ostentatious displays of wealth, but Walter hadn't lived out of his car his first year in law school because he couldn't afford rent.

She answered the phone, "Liz?"

"No, Ms. Collier. This is Cole Bradley. I hope I'm not interrupting."

She nearly swallowed her tongue. There were twenty floors and probably twice as many millions of dollars separating Leigh Collier and the man who had started the firm. She had only laid eyes on him once. Leigh was waiting her turn in the elevator lobby when Cole Bradley had used a key to summon the private car that went straight to the top floor. He looked like a taller, leaner version of Anthony Hopkins, if Anthony Hopkins had put a plastic surgeon on retainer shortly after graduating from the University of Georgia Law School.

"Ms. Collier?"

"Yes—I'm—" She tried to get her shit together. "I'm sorry. I'm at my daughter's school play."

He didn't bother with small talk. "I've got a delicate matter that requires your immediate attention."

She felt her mouth open. Leigh was not setting the world on fire at Bradley, Canfield & Marks. She was doing exactly enough to keep a roof over her head and her daughter in private school. Cole Bradley employed at least one hundred baby lawyers who would stab her in the face to get this phone call.

"Ms. Collier?"

"I'm sorry," Leigh said. "I'm just—honestly, Mr. Bradley, I'll do whatever you want but I'm not sure I'm the right person."

"Frankly, Ms. Collier, I had no idea you even existed until this evening, but the client asked for you specifically. He's waiting in my office as we speak."

Now she was really confused. Leigh's highest-profile client was the owner of a pet supply warehouse who'd been charged with breaking into his ex-wife's house and urinating in her underwear drawer. The case had been joked about in one of Atlanta's alternative papers, but she doubted Cole Bradley read *Atlanta INtown*.

"His name is Andrew Tenant," Bradley said. "I trust you've heard of him."

"Yes, sir. I have." Leigh only knew the name because she'd just read it in the story Octavia Bacca had texted her.

So shitty. Don't hate me.

Octavia lived with her elderly parents and a husband with

31

severe asthma. There were only two reasons Leigh could think of that her friend would refer out a case. She was either skipping out on a jury trial because of the virus risk or she was creeped out by her presumed rapist client. Not that Octavia's motivations mattered right now, because Leigh didn't have a choice.

She told Bradley, "I'll be there in half an hour."

Most passengers flying into Atlanta airport looked out the window and assumed that Buckhead was downtown, but the cluster of skyscrapers at the uptown end of Peachtree Street had not been built for convention-goers, government services or staid, financial institutions. The floors were filled with high-dollar litigators, day traders, and private money managers who catered to the surrounding client base living in one of the wealthiest ZIP codes in the southeast.

The headquarters for Bradley, Canfield & Marks loomed over the Buckhead commercial district, a glass-fronted behemoth that crested at the top like a breaking wave. Leigh found herself in the belly of the beast, trudging up the parking deck stairs. The gate was closed for visitor parking. The first available space she could find was three stories underground. The concrete stairwell felt like murder territory, but the elevators were locked and she hadn't been able to find a security guard. She took advantage of the time by going over in her head what Octavia Bacca had relayed over the phone during the drive over.

Or what she hadn't been able to tell her.

Andrew Tenant had fired Octavia two days ago. No, he hadn't given her an explanation why. Yes, Octavia had thought until that point that Andrew was satisfied with her counsel. No, she couldn't guess why Tenant had made the change, but, two hours ago, Octavia had been instructed to transfer all of his case files to BC&M care of Leigh Collier. The *so shitty* text was meant as an apology for dumping a jury trial into her lap eight days before it was scheduled to begin. Leigh had no idea why a client would drop one of the best defense attorneys in the city when his life was on the line, but she had to assume the man was an idiot.

The bigger mystery to solve was how the hell Andrew Tenant even knew Leigh's name. She had texted Walter, who was just as clueless, and that was the sum total of Leigh's ability to mine information from her past because Walter was the only person currently in her life who had known her before she had graduated from law school.

Leigh stopped at the top of the stairs, sweat dripping down her back. She did a quick inventory of her appearance. She hadn't exactly dressed up for her night at the theater. She had thrown her hair into an old-lady bun and chosen two-day-old jeans and a faded Aerosmith Bad Boys from Boston T-shirt, if only to stand in contrast to the Birkin-bagged bitches in the audience. She would have to swing by her office on the way to the top floor. Like everyone else, Leigh kept a courtroom outfit at work. Her make-up bag was in her desk drawer. The thought of having to put on her face for an accused rapist on a Sunday night that she should've been spending with her family ramped up her level of annoyance. She hated this building. She hated this job. She hated her life.

She loved her daughter.

Leigh looked for a mask in her purse, which Walter called her feedbag because she used it as a briefcase and, in the last year, a mini-pandemic supply store. Hand sanitizers. Clorox wipes. Masks. Nitrile gloves just in case. The firm tested them twice a week, and Leigh had already suffered through the virus, but, with the variants going around, it was better to be safe than sorry.

She checked the time as she looped the mask over her ears. She could steal a few seconds for her daughter. Leigh juggled her two phones, looking for the distinctive blue and gold Hollis Academy case on her personal device. The wallpaper photo was of Tim Tam, the family dog, because the chocolate Lab had shown Leigh a hell of a lot more love lately than her own daughter.

Leigh sighed at the screen. Maddy hadn't texted back to Leigh's profuse apology for her early departure. A quick perusal of Instagram showed her daughter dancing with friends at a small party in what looked like Keely Heyer's basement, Tim Tam sleeping on a beanbag chair in the corner. So much for unquestioning devotion.

Leigh's fingers slid across the screen, typing yet another text to Maddy—*I'm sorry I had to leave, baby. I love you so much.*

She stupidly waited for a response before opening the door.

The overly air-conditioned lobby enveloped her in cold steel and marble. Leigh nodded to the security guard in his Plexiglas booth. Lorenzo was hunkered down over a cup of soup, shoulders up to his ears, bowl close to his mouth. Leigh was reminded of a succulent plant her mother used to keep in the kitchen window.

"Ms. Collier."

Leigh silently panicked at the sight of Cole Bradley standing in the elevator lobby. Her hand flew up to the back of her hair. She could feel tendrils shooting out like a flattened octopus. The BAD BOYS logo across her ratty T-shirt was an affront to his bespoke Italian suit.

"You caught me in the act." He tucked a pack of cigarettes into his breast pocket. "I went outside for a smoke."

Leigh felt her eyebrows rise up. Bradley practically owned the building. No one was going to stop him from doing anything.

He smiled. Or at least she thought he did. He was north of eighty years old but his skin was so tight that only the tips of his ears twitched.

He said, "Given the political climate, it's good to be seen playing by the rules."

The bell rang for the partners' private elevator. The noise was so tinkly that it sounded like Lady Hoopskirts summoning the butler for afternoon tea.

Bradley retrieved a mask from his breast pocket. She assumed this, too, was for appearances. His age alone would've put him in the first group for the vaccine. Then again, the vaccine wouldn't be a get-out-of-jail-free card until almost everyone was inoculated.

"Ms. Collier?" Bradley was waiting at the open elevator doors.

Leigh hesitated, because she doubted underlings were allowed in the private car. "I was going to swing by my office to change into something more professional."

"Unnecessary. They know the circumstances of the late hour." He indicated that she should go in ahead of him.

Even with his permission, Leigh felt like a trespasser as she stepped into the fancy elevator. She pressed her calves against the narrow, red bench along the back wall. She had only glanced inside the private car once but, up close, she realized the black

34

walls were paneled in ostrich skin. The floor was one giant slab of black marble. The ceiling and all of the floor buttons were trimmed in red and black because if you'd graduated from the University of Georgia, pretty much the biggest thing that had ever happened to you in your life was that you had graduated from the University of Georgia.

The mirrored doors slid closed. Bradley's posture was ramrod straight. His mask was black with red piping. A pin on his lapel showed Uga, the Georgia Bulldog mascot. He touched the UP button on the panel, sending them to the penthouse level.

Leigh stared straight ahead, still unsure of the etiquette. There were signs on the plebeian elevator warning people to keep their distance and avoid conversation. No such signs existed here, not even the inspection notice. Her nose tickled with the smell of Bradley's aftershave mixed with cigarette smoke. Leigh hated men who smoked. She opened her mouth to breathe behind her mask.

Bradley cleared his throat. "I wonder, Ms. Collier, how many of your fellow students at Lake Point High School ended up graduating with honors from Northwestern?"

He'd done his homework while she was breaking the sound barrier to get here. He knew she'd grown up on the bad side of town. He knew she'd ended up at a top-tier law school.

Leigh said, "UGA waitlisted me."

She imagined he would've raised one of his eyebrows if the Botox would've let him. Cole Bradley wasn't used to his subordinates having personalities.

He said, "You interned at a poverty law firm based out of Cabrini Green. After Northwestern, you returned to Atlanta and joined the Legal Aid Society. Five years later, you started your own practice specializing in criminal defense. You were doing quite well until the pandemic closed down the courts. The end of this month will mark your first-year anniversary with BC&M."

She waited for a question.

"Your choices strike me as somewhat iconoclastic." He paused, giving her ample opportunity to chime in. "I assume you had the luxury of scholarships, so finances didn't dictate your career options."

She kept waiting.

"And yet here you are at my firm." Another pause. Another

ignored opportunity. "Would it be impolite to note that you're closer to forty than most of our first-year hires?"

She let her gaze find his. "It would be accurate."

He openly studied her. "How do you know Andrew Tenant?"

"I don't, and I have no idea how he knows me."

Bradley took a deep breath before saying, "Andrew is the scion of Gregory Tenant, one of my very first clients. We met so long ago that Jesus Christ himself introduced us. He was waitlisted at UGA, too."

"Jesus or Gregory?"

His ears twitched up slightly, which she understood was his way of smiling.

Bradley said, "Tenant Automotive Group started out with a single Ford dealership back in the seventies. You'll be too young to remember the commercials, but they had a very memorable jingle. Gregory Tenant, Sr., was a fraternity brother of mine. When he died, Greg Jr. inherited the business and turned it into a network of thirty-eight dealerships across the southeast. Greg passed away from a particularly aggressive form of cancer last year. His sister took over the day-to-day operations. Andrew is her son."

Leigh was still marveling at anyone using the word *scion*.

The elevator bell tinkled. The doors slid open. They had reached the top floor. She could feel cold air fighting against the umbrella of heat outside. The space was as cavernous as an aircraft hangar. The overhead fixtures were off. The only lights came from the lamps on the steel and glass desks standing sentry outside closed office doors.

Bradley walked to the middle of the room and stopped. "It never fails to take my breath away."

Leigh knew he meant the view. They were in the trough of the giant wave at the top of the building. Massive pieces of glass reached at least forty feet to the crest. The floor was high enough above the light pollution for them to see tiny pinpoints of stars punching through the night sky. Far below, the cars traveling along Peachtree Street paved a red and white trail toward the glowing mass of downtown.

"It looks like a snow globe," she said.

Bradley turned to face her. He had taken off his mask. "How do you feel about rape?"

"Definitely against it."

His expression told Leigh that the time for her to have a personality was over.

She said, "I've handled dozens of assault cases over the years. The nature of the charge is irrelevant. The majority of my clients are factually guilty. The prosecutor has to prove those facts beyond a reasonable doubt. You pay me a hell of a lot of money to find that doubt."

He nodded, approving of her response. "You've got jury selection on Thursday, with the trial commencing one week from tomorrow. No judge will grant you a continuance based on substituting counsel. I can offer you two full-time associates. Will the truncated timeline be a problem?"

"It's a challenge," Leigh said. "But not a problem."

"Andrew was offered a reduced charge in exchange for one year of monitored probation."

Leigh pulled down her mask. "No sex offender registry?"

"No. And the charges roll off if Andrew stays out of trouble for three years."

Even this far into the game, Leigh was always surprised by how fantastic it was to be a white, wealthy man. "That's a sweetheart deal. What are you not telling me?"

The skin around Bradley's cheeks rippled in a wince. "The previous firm had a private investigator do some digging around. Apparently, a guilty admission on this particular reduced charge could lead to further exposure."

Octavia hadn't mentioned that detail. Maybe she hadn't been updated before she was fired, or maybe she had seen the potential ratfuck and was glad to be out of it. If the PI was right, the prosecutor was trying to lure Andrew Tenant into pleading guilty to one rape so they could show a pattern of behavior that linked him to other assaults.

Leigh asked, "How much exposure?"

"Two, possibly three."

Women, she thought. Two or three more *women* who had been raped.

"No DNA on any of the possible cases," Bradley said. "I've gathered there's some circumstantial evidence, but nothing insurmountable."

"Alibi?"

"His fiancée, but—" Bradley shrugged it off the same as a jury would. "Thoughts?"

Leigh had two: either Tenant was a serial rapist or the district attorney was trying to get him to self-incriminate into being labeled one. Leigh had seen this kind of prosecutorial fuckery when she worked on her own, but Andrew Tenant wasn't a busboy who copped a guilty plea because he didn't have the money to fight it.

She knew in her gut that Bradley was holding something else back. She chose her words carefully. "Andrew is the scion of a wealthy family. The district attorney knows you don't take a shot at the king if you think you'll miss."

Bradley didn't respond, but his demeanor became more guarded. Leigh heard Walter's earlier question zinging around her head. Had she poked the wrong bear with the wrong stick? Cole Bradley had asked her how she felt about rape cases. He hadn't asked her how she felt about innocent clients. By his own admission, he had known the Tenant family since he was in short pants. For all she knew, he could be Andrew Tenant's godparent.

Bradley clearly wasn't going to share his thinking. He extended his arm, indicating the last closed door on the right. "Andrew is in my conference room with his mother as well as his fiancée."

Leigh pulled up her mask as she walked past her boss. She recalibrated herself away from being Walter's wife and Maddy's mother and the plucky gal who'd joked with a human skeleton inside a private elevator. Andrew Tenant had asked for Leigh specifically, probably because she was still coasting on her pre-BC&M reputation, which fell somewhere between a hummingbird and a hyena. Leigh had to be that person now or she'd not only lose the client, but possibly her job.

Bradley reached ahead of her to open the door.

The downstairs conference rooms were smaller than a Holiday Inn toilet and operated on a first-come, first-serve basis. Leigh had been expecting a slightly larger version of the same, but Cole Bradley's personal meeting space was more like a suite at the

Waldorf, down to the fireplace and a wet bar. There was a heavy glass vase of flowers on a pedestal. Photographs of various Uga bulldogs across the years lined the back wall. A painting of Vince Dooley hung above the fireplace. Stacks of legal pads and pens were on the black marble credenza. Trophies for various legal prizes crowded out rows of water bottles. The conference table, which was approximately twelve feet long and six feet wide, was made from redwood. The chairs were black leather.

Three people sat at the far end of the table, faces uncovered. She recognized Andrew Tenant from his photo in the news story, though he was better looking in person. The woman clutching his right arm was late-twenties with a tattoo sleeve and an *eat shit* snarl that any mother would want for her son.

The mother in question sat stiff in her chair, arms crossed low on her chest. Her short blonde hair was streaked with white. A slim gold choker ringed her tanned neck. She was wearing a pale yellow, honest-to-God, down to the little alligator, Izod shirt. The popped collar gave the impression of someone who'd just come off the golf course to sip a Bloody Mary by the pool.

In other words, the type of woman Leigh only knew about from binging *Gossip Girl* reruns with her daughter.

"I'm sorry we kept you waiting." Bradley moved a thick stack of files to the far side of the table, indicating where Leigh should sit. "This is Sidney Winslow, Andrew's fiancée."

"Sid," the girl said.

Leigh had known she'd be called something like Sid or Punkie or Katniss the moment she'd laid eyes on the multiple piercings, clumpy mascara, and jet-black shag cut.

Still, Leigh made nice with her client's other half. "I'm sorry to be meeting you under these circumstances."

"This entire ordeal has been a nightmare." Sidney's voice was as husky as expected. She pushed back her hair, flashing dark blue fingernail polish and a leather bracelet that had pointy-looking metal studs. "Andy nearly got murdered in jail, and he was only there two nights. He's totally innocent. Obviously. No one is safe anymore. Some crazy bitch can just point a finger and—"

"Sidney, let the woman get her bearings." The tightly controlled rage in the mother's tone reminded Leigh of the voice she used when she was reprimanding Maddy in the presence of other people. "Leigh, please take your time."

Leigh held the older woman's smile for a few seconds before she put her game face on.

"I'll just need a moment." She opened the file, hoping a detail would jog her memory as to who the hell these people were. The top page showed the intake form from Andrew Tenant's arrest. Thirty-three years old. Car salesman. High-dollar address. Charged with kidnap and sexual assault March 13, 2020, just as the first wave of the pandemic was taking off.

Leigh didn't read deeply into the details because it was hard to unring a bell. She needed to hear Andrew's version of events first. All that she knew for certain was that Andrew Trevor Tenant had picked a bad time to ask for his day in court. Because of the virus, prospective jurors over sixty-five were generally excused. Only someone under the age of sixty-five would accept that this clean-cut, nice-looking young man could be a serial rapist.

She looked up from the file. She silently debated how to proceed. The mother and son clearly thought that Leigh knew them. Leigh clearly did not. If Andrew Tenant wanted her to be his lawyer, lying to his face the first time they met was the very definition of operating in bad faith.

She took a breath, preparing to confess, but then Bradley cut her off.

"Remind me, Linda, how do you know Ms. Collier?"

Linda.

Something about the name itched at Leigh's memory. She actually reached up to her scalp as if she could scratch it out. But it wasn't the mother who was triggering her recollection. Leigh's eyes skipped across the older woman and went to her son.

Andrew Tenant smiled at her. His lips curved up to the left. "It's been a long time, hasn't it?"

"Decades," Linda told Bradley. "Andrew knows the girls better than I do. I was still in nursing back then. I worked nights. Leigh and her sister were the only babysitters I trusted."

Leigh's stomach turned into a clenched fist that started slowly punching up into her throat.

Andrew asked her, "How's Callie doing? What's she up to?"

40

Callie.

"Leigh?" Andrew's tone implied that she was not acting normal. "Where's your sister these days?"

"She—" Leigh had broken out in a cold sweat. Her hands were shaking. She clutched them together under the table. "She's living on a farm in Iowa. With kids. Her husband's a cow farm—a dairy farmer."

"That sounds about right," Andrew said. "Callie loved animals. She got me interested in aquariums."

He told this last part to Sidney, going into detail about his first saltwater tank.

"Right," Sidney said. "She was the cheerleader."

All Leigh could do was pretend to listen, her teeth clenched tight so that she didn't start screaming. This couldn't be right. None of this was right.

She looked down at the label on the file.

TENANT, ANDREW TREVOR.

The clenched fist kept moving up her throat, every horrific detail she had suppressed over the last twenty-three years threatening to choke her.

Callie's terrifying phone call. Leigh's frantic drive to reach her. The horrific scene in the kitchen. The familiar smell of the dank house, the cigars and Scotch and blood—so much blood.

Leigh had to know for sure. She needed to hear it said out loud. Her teenage voice came out of her mouth when she asked, "Trevor?"

The way Andrew's lips curved up to the left was so chillingly familiar. Leigh felt a tingle of goose bumps prickle her skin. She had been his babysitter, and then, when she was old enough to find real work, she had passed the job on to her baby sister.

"I go by Andrew now," he told her. "Tenant is Mom's maiden name. We both thought it would be good to change things up after what happened with Dad."

After what happened with Dad.

Buddy Waleski had disappeared. He'd abandoned his wife and son. No note. No apologies. That's what Leigh and Callie had made it look like. That's what they had told the police. Buddy had done a lot of bad things. He was in debt to a lot of bad people. It made sense. At the time, all of it had made sense.

41

Andrew seemed to feed off her dawning recognition. His smile softened, the upward curve of his lips slowly smoothing out.

He said, "It's been a long time, Harleigh."

Harleigh.

Only one person in her life still called her by that name.

Andrew said, "I thought you'd forgotten all about me."

Leigh shook her head. She would never forget him. Trevor Waleski had been a sweet kid. A little awkward. A lot clingy. The last time Leigh had seen him, he was drugged into oblivion. She had watched her sister gently kiss the top of his head.

Then the two of them had gone back into the kitchen to finish murdering his father.

Monday

2

Leigh parked her Audi A4 outside the offices of Reginald Paltz and Associates, the private investigation firm handling Andrew Tenant's case. The two-story building had been built for small offices, but made to look like a single colonial house. It had that too-new/too-old feel of the eighties. Gold fixtures. Plastic-trimmed windows. Thin brick fascia. Crumbling concrete stairs up to a set of glass doors. The vaulted lobby had a crooked gold chandelier hanging above a set of winding stairs.

The outdoor temperature was already climbing, expected to hit the mid seventies by the afternoon. She let the car idle so she could keep the air conditioning running. Leigh had gotten here early, allotting herself twenty minutes to get her shit together in the privacy of her car. The thing that had made her a good student, then a good lawyer, was that she could always tune out the bullshit and laser-focus on what was directly in front of her. You didn't help chop up a two-hundred-fifty-pound man and still graduate at the top of your class without learning how to compartmentalize.

What she had to do right now was turn that laser-focus not onto Andrew Tenant, but onto Andrew Tenant's case. Leigh was a very high-priced lawyer. Andrew's trial was scheduled to start in one week. Her boss had requested a full-on strategy session by end of day tomorrow. She had a client looking at serious charges and a prosecutor who was playing more than the usual prosecutor games. Leigh's job was to find a way to poke enough holes in the case for at least one juror to drive a bus through.

She sighed out a stream of anxiety to help clear her thoughts. She scooped up Andrew's file from the passenger seat. She flipped through the pages, found the summary paragraph.

Tammy Karlsen. Comma Chameleon. Fingerprints. CCTV.

Leigh read the entire summation without comprehension. The individual words made sense, but putting them into a coherent sentence was impossible. She tried to go back to the beginning. The lines of text began to swirl around until her stomach started swirling with them. She closed the file. Her hand found the door handle but didn't pull. She gulped in air. Then again. Then again. And again, until she swallowed down the acid that was trying to hurl up her throat.

Leigh's daughter was the only living being who had ever been able to break her focus. If Maddy was sick or upset or justifiably angry, Leigh was miserable until things were set right. That uneasiness was nothing compared to how she felt now. Every nerve ending inside of her body felt like it was being pounded by the rattling chains of Buddy Waleski's ghost.

She tossed the file onto the seat. Squeezed her eyes closed. Pressed her head back. Her stomach wouldn't stop churning. She had been on the edge of vomiting most of the night. She hadn't been able to sleep. She hadn't even bothered getting into bed. She'd sat on the couch for hours in the dark trying to think her way out of representing Andrew.

Trevor.

The night that Buddy had died, the NyQuil had effectively put Trevor into a coma. But they'd had to make sure. Leigh had called his name several times, her voice growing increasingly louder. Callie had snapped her fingers near his ear, then clapped together her hands close to his face. She'd even shaken him a little, before shifting him back and forth like a rolling pin across a piece of dough.

The police had never found Buddy's body. By the time his Corvette was located in an even shittier part of town, the car had been stripped for parts. Buddy did not have an office, so there was no paper trail. The Canon digital camcorder hidden inside the bar had been broken into pieces with a hammer, the parts scattered around the city. They had searched for other mini-cassettes and found none. They had looked for compromising photographs and found none. They had turned over the couch and upended mattresses and rifled drawers and closets and unscrewed grates from the vents and rummaged through pockets and bookshelves and inside Buddy's Corvette and then they had carefully cleaned up after themselves and put everything back in place and left before Linda had gotten home.

Harleigh, what are we going to do?

You're going to stick to the damn story so we both don't end up in prison.

There was so much awful bullshit Leigh had done in her life that still weighed on her conscience, but the murder of Buddy Waleski carried the mass of a feather. He had deserved to die. Her only regret was that it hadn't happened years before he got his hooks into Callie. There was no such thing as a perfect crime, but Leigh was certain they had gotten away with murder.

Until last night.

Her hands started to ache. She looked down. Her fingers were wrapped around the bottom of the steering wheel. The knuckles were bright white teeth biting into the leather. She checked the clock. Her angst had eaten up ten full minutes.

"Focus," she chided herself.

Andrew Trevor Tenant.

His file was still on the passenger seat. Leigh closed her eyes for another moment, summoning the sweet, goofy Trevor who'd loved to run around the yard and occasionally eat paste. That was why Linda and Andrew wanted Leigh to defend him. They had no idea that Leigh was involved in Buddy's sudden disappearance. What they wanted was a defender who would still see Andrew as that harmless child from twenty-three years ago. They didn't want her to associate him with the monstrous acts he was accused of.

Leigh retrieved the file. It was time for her to read about those monstrous acts.

She took another breath to reset herself. Leigh wasn't one of those believers in bad blood or apples not falling far from the tree. Otherwise, she would be an abusive alcoholic with a felony assault conviction. People could transcend their circumstances. It was possible to break the cycle.

Had Andrew Tenant broken the cycle?

Leigh opened the file. She read the charge sheet in depth for the first time.

Kidnap. Rape. Aggravated assault. Aggravated sodomy. Aggravated sexual battery.

You didn't need much more than Wikipedia to understand the accepted definitions of kidnap, rape, sodomy, and battery. The legal definitions were more complicated. Most states used the blanket term *sexual assault* for related sex crimes, so the charge of sexual assault could indicate anything from unwanted ass-grabbing to violent rape.

Some states used degrees to rank the severity of the crime. *First degree* was the most serious, then the others fell into lesser degrees, usually distinguished by the nature of the act—from penetration to coercion to involuntary touching. If a weapon was used, if the victim was a child or law enforcement officer, or had diminished capacity, then felony charges came into play.

Florida used the term *sexual battery*, and no matter how heinous or not-so-heinous the act, unless you were a wealthy, politically connected pedophile, the crime was always charged as a serious felony and could carry a life sentence. In California, *misdemeanor sexual battery* could land you in county jail for six months. Sentencing for *felony sexual battery* ranged anywhere from one year in county lock-up to four years in big-boy prison.

The state of Georgia fell in line with most states so far as *sexual assault* encompassing anything from non-consensual touching to full-on necrophilia. The term *aggravated* was used to indicate the most serious charges. Aggravated sodomy meant force was used against the victim's will. Aggravated assault meant a gun or other life-threatening weapon was involved. A person who committed aggravated sexual battery intentionally penetrated the sexual organ or anus of another person with a foreign object without that person's consent. The sentence for that offense alone could be life, or twenty-five years followed by probation for life. Either way, there was a mandatory lifetime registration on the sex offender registry. If you weren't a hardened criminal when you went into the system, you would be by the time you got out.

Leigh found the booking photo for Andrew Tenant.

Trevor.

It was the shape of his face that reminded her of the boy he used to be. Leigh had spent countless nights with his head in her lap while she read to him. She would keep glancing down, silently begging him to fall asleep so that she could study for school.

Leigh had seen her share of mugshots. Sometimes defendants stuck out their chins or glared at the camera or did other stupid things that they thought made them look tough but played out exactly as you would expect with a jury. In Andrew's photo, he was clearly trying not to show that he was scared, which was understandable. Scions didn't often find themselves arrested and dragged down to the police station. He looked like he was chewing the inside of his bottom lip. His nostrils were flared. The harsh flash from the camera gave his eyes an artificial glimmer.

Was this man a violent rapist? Was that little boy Leigh had read to, colored with, chased around the dirt-packed backyard while he giggled so hard he snorted, capable of growing into the same disgusting type of predator as his father?

"Harleigh?"

Leigh startled, papers flying into the air, a scream bleating out of her mouth.

"I'm so sorry." Andrew's voice was muffled by the closed window. "Did I scare you?"

"Hell yes you scared me!" Leigh grabbed at the loose pages. Her heart had banged into the back of her throat. She had forgotten how Trevor used to sneak up on her when he was a kid.

Andrew tried again, "I'm really sorry."

She shot him a look that she usually reserved for family. And then she reminded herself that he was her client. "It's fine."

His face was red from embarrassment. The mask hanging around his chin came up. It was blue with a white Mercedes logo across the front. The change was not an improvement. He looked like an animal who'd been muzzled. Still, he stepped back so that she could open the car door.

The tremor was back in Leigh's hands when she turned off the engine and pulled together the file. She had never been so grateful for the time it took to find a mask and cover her face. Her legs felt weak as she got out of the car. She kept thinking about the last time she had seen Trevor. He was lying in bed, eyes closed, completely clueless to what was happening in the kitchen.

Andrew tried again, offering, "Good morning."

Leigh swung her purse over her shoulder. She shoved the file deep into her bag. In heels, she was at Andrew's eye level. His blonde hair was combed back. His chest and arms were gym-toned but he had his father's tapered waist and height. Leigh frowned at the suit, which was exactly the kind you'd expect a Mercedes salesman to be wearing—too blue, too fitted, too sharp. A mechanic or plumber on the jury would see that suit and hate him.

"Uh . . ." Andrew indicated the large Dunkin' Donuts cup he'd placed on the roof of her car. "I brought you some coffee, but that seems like a bad idea now that it's happening."

"Thank you," she said, as if they weren't in the middle of a deadly pandemic.

"I'm so sorry I frightened you Har—Leigh. I should call you Leigh. Just like you should call me Andrew. We're both different people now."

"We are." Leigh had to get control over her uneasiness. She tried to put herself on familiar ground. "Last night, I filed an emergency motion with the court to establish myself as counsel. Octavia already withdrew herself as attorney of record, so approval should be pro forma. Judges don't like this last-minute finagling. There's no way we'll get a continuance. Considering Covid, we need to be ready to go at any time. If the jail locks down because of an outbreak or there's another staffing shortage, we have to be ready to go. Otherwise, we could lose our slot and get bumped into next week or next month."

"Thank you." He nodded once, as if he had only been waiting for his turn to speak. "Mom sends her apologies. There's a company-wide meeting every Monday morning. Sidney's already inside. I thought I could talk to you alone for a minute if that's okay?"

"Of course." Leigh's anxiety jacked back up. He was going to ask about his father. She took the coffee off the roof of her car to give herself a reason to turn away. She could feel the heat through the paper cup. The thought of drinking it made her queasiness intensify.

"Have you seen—" Andrew indicated the file she'd stashed in her purse. "Have you read it yet?"

Leigh nodded, not trusting herself to speak.

"I couldn't get through to the end. It's really bad what happened to Tammy. I thought we hit it off. I'm not sure why she's doing this to me. She seemed nice. You don't talk to someone for ninety-eight minutes if you think they're a monster."

The specificity was strange, but he had given Leigh some much-needed prompts. She resurrected the stray words from the summary statement in his file—*Tammy Karlsen. Comma Chameleon. Fingerprints. CCTV.*

Tammy Karlsen was the victim. Prior to the pandemic, Comma Chameleon had been a hot singles bar in Buckhead. The police had found Andrew's fingerprints where they shouldn't be. They had CCTV of Andrew's movements.

Leigh's memory added a stray detail that Cole Bradley had relayed last night. "Sidney is your alibi for the time of the assault?"

"We weren't exclusive then, but I got home from the bar and she was waiting for me on my doorstep." He held up his hands as if to stop her. "I know that sounds totally coincidental, right? Sid shows up at my place on the very night I need an alibi? But it's the truth."

Leigh knew that both the best and the worst alibis could sound wildly coincidental. Still, she wasn't here to believe in Andrew Tenant. She was here to get him to a not guilty. "When did you get engaged?"

"April tenth of last year. We've been off and on for two years,

49

but with the arrest and the pandemic, it all brought us closer together."

"Sounds romantic." Leigh struggled to sound like a lawyer who hadn't survived the first months of the virus by filing dozens of no-fault Covid divorces. "Have you set the date?"

"Wednesday, before jury selection begins on Thursday. Unless you think you can get the case dismissed?"

The hopeful tone in his voice took her straight back to the Waleskis' kitchen when Trevor asked if his mother would be home soon. Leigh hadn't lied to him then and she absolutely couldn't lie to him now. "No, this won't go away. They're coming after you. All we can do is be ready to fight back."

He nodded, scratching at his mask. "I guess it's stupid for me to believe I'm going to wake up one day and this nightmare will be over."

Leigh glanced around the parking lot, making sure they were alone. "Andrew, we couldn't get into the weeds in front of Sidney and Linda last night, but Mr. Bradley explained to you that there are other cases the district attorney will probably open if you plead guilty."

"He did."

"And he told you that if you lose your case at trial, those other cases could still—"

"Cole also said you're ruthless in the courtroom." Andrew shrugged as if that was all it took. "He told Mom that he hired you because you were one of the best defense attorneys in the city."

Cole Bradley was full of shit. He didn't even know which floor Leigh worked on. "I'm also brutally honest. If the trial goes sideways, you are looking at serious time."

"You haven't changed a bit, Harleigh. You always put all your cards on the table. That's why I wanted to work with you." Andrew wasn't finished. "You know, the sad part is, the MeToo movement really woke me up. I try hard to be an ally. We should believe women, but this—it's unconscionable. False allegations only hurt other women."

Leigh nodded, though she didn't find his words persuasive one way or another. The problem with rape was that a guilty man

50

generally knew enough about the prevailing culture to say the same things an innocent man would. Soon Andrew would start talking about *due process* without realizing that what he was going through right now was exactly that.

She said, "Let's go inside."

Andrew stepped back so she could walk ahead of him toward the building. Leigh tried to get her head on straight in the interim. She had to stop acting like the worst kind of criminal. As a defense attorney, she knew that her clients didn't get caught because the cops were brilliant detectives. The client's own stupidity or guilty conscience usually landed them in legal peril. They either bragged to the wrong person or confessed to the wrong person or, most of the time, stepped on their own dicks, and then they needed a lawyer.

Leigh wasn't worried about guilty feelings, but she would have to be careful that her fear of getting caught didn't somehow give her away.

She transferred the coffee cup to her other hand. She steeled herself as she climbed up the crumbling concrete steps to the entrance.

Andrew said, "I've looked for Callie over the years. What part of Iowa is she in?"

Leigh felt the hairs on the back of her neck rise up. The biggest mistake a liar could make was to offer too many specifics. "Northwest corner, close to Nebraska."

"I'd love the address."

Shit.

Andrew reached ahead of her to open the lobby door. The carpet was worn in front of the stairs. The walls were scuffed. The inside of the building felt more dreary and sad than it had from the outside.

Leigh turned around. Andrew had gone down on one knee to untuck the leg of his pants from his ankle monitor. The device was geo-targeted, limiting him to home, work, and meetings with his attorneys. Anything else and an alarm would go off at the monitoring station. Technically. Like every other resource in the pandemic-wracked city, the probation office was stretched thin.

Andrew looked up at her, asking, "Why Iowa?"

This, at least, Leigh was prepared for. "She fell in love with a man. Got pregnant. Got married. Got pregnant again."

Leigh checked the sign. REGINALD PALTZ & ASSOC was upstairs.

Again, Andrew let her go first. "I bet Callie's a terrific mom. She was always so kind to me. It felt more like she was my sister."

Leigh gritted her teeth as she rounded the landing. She couldn't figure out if Andrew's questions were appropriate or intrusive. He had been so transparent as a child—immature for his age, gullible, easy to pin down. Now, all of Leigh's finely honed gut instinct was falling to the wayside.

He said, "Northwest corner. Is that where the derecho hit?"

She squeezed the coffee cup so hard that the top almost popped off. Had he read everything he could find about Iowa last night? "They got some flooding, but they're fine."

"Did she stick with cheerleading?"

Leigh turned around at the top of the stairs. She had to redirect this before he put more words in her mouth. "I forgot you guys moved away after Buddy disappeared."

He had stopped on the landing. He blinked up at her, silent.

Something about his expression felt off, though it was hard to tell because all she could really see were his eyes. She silently ran back through the conversation, trying to find out where it could've gone wrong. Was he acting strange? Was she?

Leigh asked, "Where did you move to?"

He adjusted his mask, pinching it around the bridge of his nose. "Tuxedo Park. We stayed with my uncle Greg."

Tuxedo Park was one of Atlanta's oldest, monied neighborhoods. "You were a real Fresh Prince."

"No kidding." His laugh sounded forced.

Actually, everything about him felt forced. Leigh had worked with enough criminals to develop an internal warning siren. She felt it flashing bright red as she watched Andrew readjust his mask again. He was completely unreadable. She had never seen someone with such a flat, vacant look in their eyes.

He said, "Maybe you don't know the story, but Mom was really young when she met Dad. Her parents gave her an

52

ultimatum: we'll sign off on the legal stuff so you can get married, but we'll disown you if you go through with it."

Leigh clenched her jaw so that it wouldn't drop open. The legal age for marriage with parental consent was sixteen. As a teenager, Leigh had thought all adults were old, but now she realized that Buddy had been at least twice Linda's age.

"The bastards followed through on their threat. They abandoned Mom. They abandoned us," Andrew said. "Grandpa only had one dealership then, but they had plenty of money. Enough to make our lives easier. Nobody lifted a finger. Not until Dad was gone, then Uncle Greg came swooping in talking about forgiveness and all this religious crap. He's the one who made us change our last names. Did you know that?"

Leigh shook her head. Last night, he'd made it sound like a choice.

"It ruined our lives when Dad disappeared. I wish whoever made him go away understood what that felt like."

Leigh swallowed down a wave of paranoia.

"Anyway, it all worked out, right?" Andrew gave a self-deprecating laugh. "Until now."

He fell back into silence as he climbed the stairs. There had been an inflection of anger in his voice, but he'd quickly gotten it under control. It occurred to Leigh that her own guilt might not be at play here. Andrew could be uncomfortable around her for his own reasons. He probably felt like she was testing him, trying to weigh his guilt or innocence. He wanted her to believe he was a good man so that she would fight harder for him.

He was wasting his time. Leigh rarely considered guilt or innocence. Most of her clients were guilty as hell. Some of them were nice. Some were assholes. None of it mattered because justice was blind except when it came to the color green. Andrew Tenant would have all of the resources his family's money could buy—private investigators, specialists, forensic experts, and anyone else who could be monetarily induced to persuade a jury of his blamelessness. One lesson that working at BC&M had taught Leigh was that it was better to be guilty and rich than innocent and poor.

Andrew indicated the closed door at the end of the hall. "He's down—"

The unmistakable husky laugh of Sidney Winslow echoed from the distance.

"Sorry. She can be loud." Andrew's cheeks turned a slight red above his mask, but he told Leigh, "After you."

Leigh didn't move. She had to remind herself yet again that Andrew was clueless about her role in what had really happened to his father. Only a stupid mistake on her part could make him start asking questions. Whatever sirens Andrew was setting off probably came courtesy of the fact that he could very well be a rapist.

And Leigh was his lawyer.

She launched into the spiel she should've given Andrew in the parking lot. "You understand that Octavia Bacca's firm hired Mr. Paltz to do the investigation. And now Bradley, Canfield & Marks hired him to stay on the case, correct?"

"Well, I brought Reggie into this, but yes."

Leigh would deal with the *Reggie* part later. Right now, she needed to make sure Andrew's ass was covered. "So you understand that the reason the law firm hires an investigator rather than a client hiring him directly is because any discussions we have about strategy or any advice given falls under my work product, which is privileged information. Which means the prosecutor can't compel the investigator to testify about what we've discussed."

Andrew was nodding before she finished. "Yes, I understand."

Leigh tried to be careful about this next part, which she happened to be something of an expert in. "Sidney doesn't have that privilege."

"Right, but we'll be married before the trial, so she'll have it."

Leigh knew from experience that a lot could happen between now and the trial. "But you're not married at the moment, so anything you say to her *now* isn't protected."

She couldn't tell if Andrew's shocked look above his mask came from fear or genuine surprise.

"Even after you're married, it's tricky." Leigh explained, "In Georgia criminal proceedings, spouses have the adverse testimony privilege—that's the one where she can't be compelled to testify— and they also have the confidential communication privilege, which means you can prevent your spouse from testifying about anything you said to her as part of your spousal communication."

He nodded, but she could tell he didn't fully understand.

"So if you and Sidney are married, and you're alone in your kitchen one night, and you say, 'Hey, I feel like I shouldn't keep secrets from you, so you should know that I'm a serial killer.' You could invoke confidential communication and she would not be allowed to testify."

Andrew was paying close attention now. "Where does it get tricky?"

"If Sidney tells a friend, 'This is crazy, but Andrew told me he's a serial killer,' then that friend can be called to testify as a hearsay witness."

The bottom part of his mask moved. He was chewing the inside of his lip.

Leigh dropped the bomb that she'd heard ticking the moment she'd spotted Sidney's leather accessories and various piercings. "Or let's say Sidney told a friend you did something kinky in bed. And that kinky thing is something similar to what was done to the victim. Then that friend could testify about that kink, and the prosecutor could claim that it showed a pattern of behavior."

Andrew's throat worked. His concern was almost palpable. "So I should tell Sid—"

"As your lawyer, I can't tell you what to say. I can only explain the law so that you understand the implications." She asked, "Do you understand the implications?"

"Yes, I understand."

"Hey!" Sidney was clomping toward them in chunky combat boots. Her mask was black with chrome studs. She was slightly less goth today, but still radiated an unpredictable energy. Leigh could've been looking at herself at that age, which was both galling and depressing.

Andrew said, "We were—"

"Talking about Callie?" Sidney turned to Leigh. "I swear he's obsessed with your sister. Did he tell you he had an enormous crush on her? She's his one hall pass. Did he tell you?"

Leigh shook her head, not to say *no*, but because she needed to wake up her stupid brain. Of course Andrew still had a crush on Callie. That's why he kept bringing her up.

She tried to steer the topic away from her sister, asking Andrew, "How do you know Reggie Paltz?"

"We've been friends for . . ." He shrugged, because he wasn't really paying attention to Leigh now. He was thinking about what she had told him about spousal privilege.

Sidney picked up on the tension, asking Andrew, "What's going on, baby? Did something else happen?"

Leigh didn't need or want to be here for the coming conversation. "I'll get started with the investigator while you two talk."

Sidney raised one overly arched eyebrow. Leigh realized her tone had sounded chillier than she'd intended. She tried to project neutrality as she passed the young woman in the hallway, fighting the urge to itemize every single part of her that she found annoying. There was no doubt in her mind that Sidney talked to her friends about Andrew. When you were that young and stupid, sex was all that you had going for you.

"Andy, come on." Sidney dropped into blowjob voice. "What's wrong baby boy, why do you look so upset?"

Leigh closed the door behind her.

She found herself in a cramped outer office with a metal desk, no secretary, no chair. There was a kitchenette along the side wall. She dumped the coffee in the sink then tossed the cup into the trashcan. The usual was on offer: coffeemaker, teakettle, hand sanitizer, a stack of disposable masks. There was an open door leading down a short hallway, but Leigh wanted to form an impression before she met Reggie Paltz.

White walls. Dark blue wall-to-wall carpet. Popcorn ceiling. The artwork wasn't professional enough to be anything but vacation photos: a tropical beach sunrise, dogs sledding across the tundra, snowcapped mountain peaks, the Great Steps of Machu Picchu. A battered lacrosse stick hung on the wall over a black leather loveseat. Old copies of *Fortune* magazine were scattered across the glass coffee table. A tie-dyed blue rug straight out of an Office Depot catalogue sat like a postage stamp under the glass.

Younger than she'd guessed. Well-educated; you didn't learn

to play lacrosse in the projects. Definitely not a cop. Probably divorced. No kids, otherwise child support would've ruled out the exotic vacations. A college athlete who didn't want to give up the glory. Probably an unfinished MBA on his college transcripts. Used to having money in his pocket.

Leigh availed herself of the hand sanitizer before going through to the back.

Reggie Paltz was sitting behind a desk that had taken its cues from the *Resolute*. His office was sparsely furnished, with another leather couch shoved against a wall and two mismatched chairs in front of the desk. He had the requisite leather blotter and masculine accessories of every man who'd ever had an office, down to a colored glass paperweight, a personalized business card holder, and the exact same sterling silver Tiffany letter opener that Leigh had bought for Walter a few Christmases ago.

She said, "Mr. Paltz?"

He stood up from his desk. No mask, so she could see a once-sharp jawline sliding into softness. Leigh's snap judgment hadn't been far off. He was mid-thirties with a tightly trimmed goatee and a flippy early-Hugh Grant wave in his thinning dark hair. He was dressed in khakis and a light gray button-down shirt. A thin gold necklace was around his thick neck. His eyes gave her the once-over, an expert face-to-breast-to-leg evaluation that Leigh had been getting since puberty. He came off as a good-looking asshole, but not Leigh's type of good-looking asshole.

"Mrs. Collier." In normal times, they would've shaken hands. Now, he kept his hands in his pockets. "Call me Reggie. Nice to finally meet you."

Leigh felt every single muscle in her body stiffen as she clocked the *Mrs.* and the *finally*. This entire time, she had been in such a hurry to figure out how to extricate herself from this fucking case that she hadn't given one damn thought to how she had gotten into it in the first place.

Mrs.

Leigh had taken Walter's last name when they had married in college. She hadn't bothered to change it back to her maiden name because she hadn't bothered to divorce him. She had legally changed her first name from Harleigh to Leigh three years before they'd met.

So how did Andrew know to ask for Leigh Collier? As far as he knew, she was still going by Harleigh, still using her mother's last name. Leigh had been very careful over the years to make sure that connecting her past and her present took jumping through several hoops.

That led to the bigger question of how Andrew had found out that Leigh was a lawyer. Sure, the Tenant family knew Cole Bradley, but Cole Bradley hadn't heard about Leigh until twelve hours ago.

Finally.

Andrew must have hired Paltz to look for her. He was glad to *finally* meet her after doing a deep dive, jumping through the hoops, landing in the middle of Leigh's life. And if he knew how Harleigh had become Leigh, then he would know about Walter and Maddy and—

Callie.

"Guys, I'm sorry." Andrew shook his head as he walked into the office. He slumped into the low couch. "Sid's down in the car. That did not go well."

Reggie pulled a face. "Dude, does it ever?"

Leigh's knees felt weak. She sank into the chair closest to the door. Sweat rolled down her back. She watched Andrew slip down his mask around his chin. He was texting on his phone. "She's already asking how long."

Reggie's chair squeaked as he sat back down. "Tell her to shut the fuck up."

"Thanks for the advice. I'm sure that will calm her down." Andrew's thumbs started moving across the screen. An emotion had finally punched through his unreadable veneer. He was visibly worried. "Shit. She's furious."

"Dude, stop replying." Reggie tapped his laptop awake. "We're burning through your mama's cash big time."

Leigh unhooked her mask. The *Mrs.* and the *finally* kept knocking around inside her skull. She had to clear her throat before she could speak. "How did you two meet?"

Reggie volunteered, "Andrew sold me my first Mercedes. What was that, dude, three, four years ago?"

Leigh cleared her throat again, waiting, but Andrew was still distracted by his phone.

She finally asked, "Is that so?"

"Yeah, dude used to be a fucking stallion until Sid neutered him with that engagement ring." He caught a sharp look from Andrew and abruptly shifted back into business, telling Leigh, "I got your firm's server encryption key from your assistant this morning. I'll have everything uploaded for you by this afternoon."

Leigh forced herself to nod. She mentally tried to unwind her paranoia. The *Mrs.* was because he had done his homework. It wasn't unusual for high-income clients to make sure they knew who they were dealing with. The *finally* meant—what? The simplest explanation was the same as the one for the *Mrs.* Andrew had hired Reggie Paltz to investigate her, to delve into her life and family, and he was *finally* meeting Leigh after reading so much about her.

"Y'all, I'm sorry." Andrew stood up, eyes still on his phone. "I should check on her."

"Ask for your balls back." Reggie shook his head for Leigh's benefit. "Dude's back in high school with this chick."

Leigh felt the unwelcome tremor return to her hands as Reggie hunched over his laptop. The simplest explanation still did not answer the most important question. How had Andrew found Leigh in the first place? He was an accused rapist staring down a jury trial that started in one week. It didn't make sense that he would stop in the middle of it to find his babysitter from two decades ago.

Which was why her internal warning siren was still flashing bright red.

"Mrs. Collier?" Reggie's head was turned in her direction. "You all right?"

Leigh had to stop her emotions from rollercoastering. Walter's one abiding complaint about her was the very quality that made Leigh a survivor. Her personality changed depending on who was in front of her. She was sweetheart or Mom or Collier or Counselor or baby or you fucking bitch or, very occasionally, Harleigh. Everyone got a different piece of her, but nobody got the whole.

Reggie Paltz ran hot, so Leigh needed to run ice cold.

She reached into her purse to retrieve her notepad and Andrew's case file. She clicked her pen. "I'm on limited time, Mr. Paltz. My boss wants a full rundown tomorrow afternoon. Take me through it quickly."

"Call me Reggie." He angled his laptop so they could both see the image on the screen: a nightclub entrance, a neon sign with a large comma followed by the word CHAMELEON. "CCTV clocked Andrew doing everything but taking a crap. I spliced it together. Took six freaking hours, but it's Linda's cash."

Leigh pressed her pen to the notepaper. "I'm ready."

He started the video. The date stamp read February 2, 2020, almost a month before the pandemic closed everything down. "The cameras are 4K, so you can see every speck of dirt on the floor. This is Andrew early on. He talked to a couple of foxes, one on the roof deck, another at the lower bar. The roof babe gave Andy her number. I tracked her down, but you don't want her on the stand. The minute she figured out why I was talking to her, she got all up in that hashtag shit and turned into a raging bitch."

Leigh looked down at her notepad. She had gone into autopilot as she recorded the details. She started to turn the page. Her hand stopped.

Mrs.

Her wedding ring. She had never taken it off, even after four years of separation from Walter. She let her lips part, slowly exhaled some of her stress.

"Here." Reggie pointed to the screen, "This is when Andrew first meets Tammy Karlsen. She's got a nice body. Face, not so much."

Leigh ignored the casual misogyny and trained her gaze on the video. She saw Andrew sitting on a low, cushioned bench with a petite-looking woman whose back was to the camera. Her brown hair was shoulder-length. She was wearing a fitted black dress with three-quarter sleeves. She turned her head as she reached for her drink on the coffee table, laughing at something Andrew had said. In profile, Tammy Karlsen was attractive. Button nose, high cheekbones.

"Body language says it all." Reggie tapped a key to double-time the video. "Karlsen scooches closer as the night rolls on.

Around the ten-minute mark, she starts touching his hand to make a point or laugh at one of his jokes." Reggie looked up at Leigh, saying, "I'm guessing that's when she figured out that the Tenant stood for Tenant Automotive. Damn straight I'd be scooching close to a dude with that kind of cash."

Leigh waited for him to continue.

Reggie tripled the speed, rushing through the video. "Eventually, Andrew's got his arm along the back of the bench, and he starts stroking her shoulder. You can see him looking down at her tits, so it's pretty clear he's sending out messages and she's receiving them one hundred percent. Around forty minutes in, she starts rubbing his thigh like a freaking stripper doing a lap dance. They went on like that for ninety-eight minutes."

Ninety-eight minutes.

Leigh remembered Andrew using the exact same number in the parking lot. She asked, "Are you certain about the time?"

"As certain as anybody can be. All this shit can be faked down to the metadata if you know what you're doing, but I got the raw footage from the bar, not through the prosecutor."

"Has Andrew seen the video?"

"My guess is no way. I sent Linda a copy, but Andy's going down that river called De Nile. Thinks this is gonna be over and he's gonna get his life back." Reggie fast-forwarded until he got to the spot he wanted to show her next. "So look, it's just after midnight. Andrew walks Karlsen downstairs to the valet. He's got his hand on her back as they go down the stairs. Then she's holding on to his arm until they get to the valet. While they're waiting, she leans in and he gets the hint."

Leigh watched Andrew kiss Tammy Karlsen on the mouth. The woman's hands wrapped around his shoulders. The space between their bodies disappeared. Leigh should've noted the number of seconds they held the kiss, but what had caught her attention was the look on Andrew's face before their mouths had met.

Entitlement? Derision?

His eyes had been their familiar blank and unreadable, but his lips had twitched, the left corner tugging into a smirk the same way Leigh had seen when Andrew was a boy promising her that he hadn't eaten the last cookie, he had no idea where her history assignment was, he hadn't drawn a dinosaur in her Algebra II textbook.

She wrote down the time stamp so she could go back to it later.

Reggie called out the obvious. "Valets come with their cars. Andrew tips the guys for both of them. You can see here where Karlsen gives Andy her business card, then another kiss on the cheek. She gets into her Beemer. He gets in his Merc. They both turn in the same direction, north on Wesley. Not the best way for him to get home but it's *a* way to get home."

Leigh tuned out Reggie's road-by-road call-out of each twist and turn the cars took. She thought about the *finally*, as in nice to *finally* meet you. Leigh had come on to the case last night, but Andrew had fired Octavia two days ago. That left at least forty-eight hours for Reggie Paltz to dig into Leigh's life. Where else had that *finally* led him? Had he located Callie, too?

"Then it's south on Vaughn, then we got no more CCTV or traffic cams," Reggie continued, seemingly clueless to her internal conflict. "You can see from this last shot that Andrew's Merc has dealer plates."

Leigh knew he was expecting her input. "Why is that relevant?"

"Andrew took a loaner off the lot that night. His personal car was in the shop. Classic cars are finicky. It happens sometimes, but not a lot of times."

Leigh drew a box around the word *car*. When she looked up, Reggie was studying her again. She didn't have to think back through the conversation to know why. They were getting to the part where Andrew's actions would be harder to explain away. Reggie had been testing Leigh with his crass language, trying to see if his *bitches* and *tits* and *lap dance* would draw a rebuke that would indicate she wasn't on Andrew's side.

She kept her tone icy cold, asking him, "Did Karlsen tell Andrew to follow her back to her place?"

"No." He paused after the word, making it crystal clear that he was on alert. "Karlsen says in her statement she told him to call her if he was interested. Her memory's shaky after she got her car from the valet. Next thing she's sure about, she's waking up and it's morning."

"The police are saying Andrew spiked her drink?"

"That's the theory, though if he slipped her a roofie, it doesn't show on the videos or in her tox screen. Between you and me, I pray to the good Lord that she was drugged. You'll see what I'm talking about when we get to the crime scene photos. You're gonna wanna do everything you can to get them suppressed. I didn't even download the files to my laptop. Everything's encrypted under Triple DES. Nothing goes to a cloud because a cloud can be hacked. Both the primary and the backup server are locked in that closet over there."

Leigh turned, seeing a serious-looking padlock on the steel door.

"I'm very careful when I work these high-profile cases. You don't want this shit getting out, especially when the client is wealthy. People come out of the woodwork looking for money." Reggie had turned the laptop back in his direction. He typed two-fingered. "Idiots don't realize it is a hell of a lot more lucrative to work on the inside than it is to have your nose pressed against the glass."

Leigh asked, "How do you know me?"

He paused again. "What's that?"

"You said nice to *finally* meet you. That implies that you'd heard about me, or you were looking forward to—"

"Ah, gotcha. Hold on." More pecking on his damn laptop. He swiveled it back around to show her the screen. The *Atlanta INtown* masthead filled the top of the page. A photo showed Leigh walking out of the courthouse. She was smiling. The headline explained why.

LAWYER: THERE'S NO DATE STAMP ON URINE.

Reggie gave her a shit-eating grin. "That's some jujitsu lawyering, Collier. You got their own expert witness to admit he couldn't say whether the guy pissed in his wife's panty drawer before or after the divorce."

Leigh felt her stomach start to unfurl.

"You got some balls telling a judge that water sports fall under spousal privilege." Reggie barked out another laugh. "I showed that shit to everybody I know."

Leigh had to hear him say the words. "You showed the story to Andrew?"

"You're damn right I did. No offense to Octavia Bacca, but when I heard the cops were trying to jam up Andrew on these three other cases, I knew he needed a goddam cheetah with a razor blade." He rocked back in his chair. "It's crazy he recognized your face, right?"

Leigh desperately wanted to believe him. Both the best and the worst alibis could sound wildly coincidental. "When did you show it to him?"

"Two days ago."

Right when Andrew had fired Octavia Bacca. "He had you look into me?"

Reggie let another one of his dramatic pauses fill the void. "You've got a lot of questions."

"I'm the one signing off on your invoices."

He looked nervous, which gave the entire game away. Reggie Paltz wasn't on some kind of secret mission. The reason he was bragging about his encrypted server and the need for discretion was because he wanted Leigh to give him more business.

She adjusted her evaluation, kicking herself because she should've recognized the type: a poor kid who had managed to scholarship his way into the rarefied air of the filthy rich. That explained the lacrosse stick and the exotic trips and the shitty office and the expensive Mercedes and the way he kept constantly referring to money. Cash was like sex. You didn't talk about it unless you weren't getting enough of it.

She tested him, saying, "I work with a lot of investigators on a lot of cases."

Reggie smiled, one shark to another. He was smart enough to not take the first bite. "Why'd you change your name? Harleigh's killer."

"Doesn't fit with corporate law."

"You didn't go over to the Dark Side until the pandemic hit." Reggie leaned forward, lowered his voice. "If you're worried about what I think you're worried about, he hasn't asked me to. Yet."

There were so many different things he could be referring to that Leigh could only feign ignorance.

"Really?" Reggie asked. "Dude has a massive hard-on for your sister."

Leigh felt her stomach start to seize again. "He wants you to find her?"

"He's talked about her off and on for years, but now that you're right in front of him, reminding him every day?" Reggie shrugged. "He'll ask eventually."

Leigh felt like hornets were under her skin. "You're Andrew's friend. He's going to trial in less than a week. Do you think he needs that kind of distraction right now?"

"I think if Sid finds out he's chasing his first wet dream, dude's gonna end up with a knife in his chest and we'll both be out of jobs."

Leigh glanced down the short hallway to the outer office, making sure they were alone. "Callie had some problems after high school, but she lives in northern Iowa now. She has two kids. She's married to a farmer. She wants to keep her past in her past."

Reggie drew out the moment way too long before finally saying, "If Andrew asks, I could tell him I'm too busy working other cases."

Leigh dangled some more bait. "I've got a client with a cheating husband who likes to travel."

"Sounds like my kind of assignment."

Leigh nodded once, and she hoped to God this meant they had an understanding.

Still, Reggie Paltz was only part of the problem. Leigh was mere days away from what looked like a very compelling case against her client. She said, "Tell me about these other victims the prosecutor has in his pocket."

"There's three of 'em, and they're a guillotine hanging over Andy's neck. They come down on him, his life is over."

"How did you hear about them?"

"Trade secret," he said, which was how any investigator answered when they didn't want to give up a cop informant. "You can take it to the bank, though. If you can't get Andrew out of the Karlsen charge, he's gonna spend the rest of his life trying not to drop the soap in the shower."

Leigh had too many clients behind bars to think prison rape jokes were funny. "How does Tammy Karlsen's attack tie into the others?"

"Similar MOs, similar bruising, similar wounds, similar morning after." Reggie shrugged again, as if these were hypothetical injuries rather than real harms against real women. "The big thing is, Andrew's credit card pinged at or near various businesses where they were last seen."

"At or near?" Leigh asked. "Does Andrew live in the area? Are these businesses he would normally frequent?"

"This is why I told Andy to hire you," Reggie pointed his finger at his temple, making it clear he was the smart one. "The three attacks stretched out over 2019, all in DeKalb County, which is where Andrew lives. The first victim was at the CinéBistro, spitting distance from his house. Credit card shows him at the *Men in Black* matinee on June twenty-second. The victim was there three hours later for *Toy Story 4*."

Leigh started taking notes in earnest. "There are cameras in the lobby?"

"Yes. Shows him arriving, ordering popcorn and a Coke, then leaving when the credits rolled. No overlap between him and the first victim, but he walked home. No cell phone records. He said he forgot to bring it."

Leigh underlined the date on her notepad. She would need to check for rainfall because the prosecutor sure as hell would. Even without that, June in Atlanta saw average temperatures in the high eighties and the kind of rancid humidity that warranted an official health warning. "What time was the matinee?"

"Twelve fifteen, right around lunchtime."

Leigh shook her head. The hottest time of day. Another mark against Andrew.

Reggie said, "For what it's worth, every single one of the businesses where the victims were last seen—Andrew frequented them a lot."

That wasn't necessarily a point in his favor. The prosecutor could argue he was staking out the scenes. "Second victim?"

"She was eating out late with her friends at a strip mall that has a Mexican place."

"Was Andrew there that night?"

"It's one of his regular spots. Goes there at least twice a month. He got take-out half an hour before the second victim showed up. And like always, he paid with his credit card. No car again. No phone. Dude took another walk in the heat." Reggie's shrug had a hint of defensiveness. He knew this didn't look good. "Like I said, it's a guillotine."

Leigh's pen stopped. It wasn't a guillotine. It was a very well-constructed case.

Ninety percent of Atlanta fell inside Fulton County while the remaining ten percent was in DeKalb. The city had its own police force, but DeKalb investigations were handled by the DeKalb Police Department. Fulton had by far the largest number of violent crimes but, between MeToo and the pandemic, the last two years had seen a spike in rape reporting across the board.

Leigh thought about a detective at an over-burdened DeKalb precinct spending hours cross-referencing hundreds of credit card payments at a movie theater and a Mexican restaurant against reported assaults. They hadn't picked Andrew's name from thin air. They had been waiting for him to make a mistake.

She said, "Tell me about the third victim."

"She was at a bar called Maplecroft, and Andrew was on the prowl back then. You can see it in his credit card statements. Dude charges a pack of gum. Never carries cash on him. No Ubers or Lyfts. Seldom has his phone. But he was buying a lot of women a lot of drinks all over town."

Leigh needed him to make the connection. "Andrew's credit card statements put him at Maplecroft on the night of the attack?"

"Two hours before the third victim disappeared. But Andrew had been there at least five times before." Reggie added, "No CCTV on this one. The bar burned down at the beginning of the pandemic. Very convenient for them, but good for Andy because the server melted down and they didn't back up to the cloud."

Leigh looked for a pattern across the three cases, the same way a police detective would. A movie theater. A restaurant. A bar. All establishments where you'd drink from an open container. "The cops think Andrew roofied all three?"

"Just like with Tammy Karlsen," he said. "None of them can remember jack shit about the assaults."

Leigh tapped her pen on the notepad. Rohypnol cleared the

blood in twenty-four hours and urine in seventy-two. The well-documented side effect of selective amnesia could last forever. "Did the victims drive themselves to these places?"

"All of them. The first two, their cars never left the parking lots. Cops found them the next morning. Victim number three, the one from Maplecroft, was involved in a single car accident. Hit a telephone pole two miles from her house. No traffic cams or CCTV. Car was found abandoned with the door unlocked. Tammy Karlsen's BMW was on a side street about a mile from Little Nancy Creek Park. Purse still inside the car. Same as with the others, no CCTV or traffic cams caught any of this, so the guy's either an evil genius or damn lucky."

Or he'd been smart enough to stake out the places well ahead of time. "Where were the victims found the day after?"

"All in City of Atlanta parks located inside DeKalb County."

He should've led with that, which was what was called a *modus operandi* by people who knew how to do their jobs. "Were all of the parks within walking distance of Andrew's house?"

"All but one," Reggie hedged. "But there's tons of people who live within walking distance of those places. Atlanta's full of parks. Three hundred thirty-eight, to be exact. City parks and rec maintains two hundred forty-eight. The rest are taken care of by volunteer organizations."

She didn't need his Wikipedia recitation. "What about cell phone records?"

"Nothing." Reggie looked circumspect. "But I told you, Andrew never has his phone on him."

Leigh felt her eyes narrow. "Does he have a separate work phone and personal phone?"

"Just the one. Dude's that guy who says he doesn't want to be connected all the time, but then he's always borrowing my phone when we're out."

"Andrew was driving a Mercedes that he took from the lot on the night he met Karlsen," Leigh said. "I remember reading about a Big Brother lawsuit in the UK over tracking devices?"

"They have it here, too. It's called Mercedes me, but you've got to set up an account and agree to the terms before it's activated. At least that's what the Germans will tell you."

Leigh was seven days from trial. She didn't have time to knock on that door. She could only hope that the prosecutor felt the same. One positive for Andrew was that December's astronomical Covid deaths and January's attempted political coup had put trans-Atlantic goodwill on hold.

She asked, "What else do you have?"

Reggie closed the traffic cam video and started typing and clicking. Leigh saw five folders: LNC_MAP, CRIME SCENE PHOTOS, VICTIM PHOTOS, CHARGING SHEET, SUPPORTING DOCS.

He opened VICTIM PHOTOS.

"Here's Karlsen. She woke up under a picnic table. Like I said, no memory of what happened but she knew shit got real the night before."

Leigh flinched when the photo loaded. The woman's face was barely recognizable. She had been beaten to a pulp. Her left cheekbone was out of place. Her nose was broken. Bruises ringed her neck. Red and black splotches peppered her chest and arms.

Aggravated assault.

Reggie clicked open the folder labeled LNC_MAP. "Here's a sketch of Little Nancy Creek Park. Closed eleven p.m. to six a.m. No lights. No cameras. You can see the pavilion here. That's where Karlsen was found by a dog walker the next morning."

Leigh concentrated on the map. A one-and-a-half-mile jogging trail. Wood and steel bridge. Community garden. Playground. Open-air pavilion.

Reggie opened CRIME SCENE PHOTOS and clicked on a series of JPEGs. Numbered yellow markers indicated evidence. Blood splotches trailing down the stairs. Shoe print in the mud. A Coke bottle resting in a patch of grass.

Leigh moved to the edge of her seat. "That's a glass Coke bottle."

Reggie said, "They still make them here, but this one comes from Mexico. They use real cane sugar down there, not high-fructose corn syrup. You can really taste the difference. First time I ever had one was when I was getting my Merc serviced at Tenant. They stock it behind the bar in the service center. Apparently, Andrew insists on it."

Leigh looked him in the eye for the first time since she'd entered the office. "How far does Andrew live from the park?"

"One-point-nine miles by car, less if you cut through the country club."

Leigh directed her attention back to the map. She would need to walk the terrain herself. "Has Andrew been to the park before?"

"Guy's a nature lover, apparently. Likes to look at butterflies." Reggie smiled, but she could tell he knew this was bad. "Fingerprints are like urine, right? There's no time or date stamp. You can't prove when the Coke bottle was left in the park, or when Andrew touched it. The real perp could've been wearing gloves."

Leigh ignored the tip. "What about the shoe print in the mud?"

"What about it?" he asked. "They say there's a possible match to a pair of Nikes they found in Andrew's closet, but possible ain't enough to pull them over the finish line."

Leigh was tired of Reggie controlling the pace of the story. She reached for the laptop and clicked through the photos herself. The prosecutor's case came into sharp relief. She gave Reggie a lesson on getting to the point.

"Andrew's right index print was found on the bottle along with Tammy Karlsen's DNA. *Aggravated sexual battery.* That looks like fecal matter. *Aggravated sodomy.* Bruising on her thighs consistent with penetration. *Rape.* She was taken to a secluded place. *Kidnap.* They can't prove she was drugged or the charge would be there. What about weapons?"

"A knife," Andrew said.

Leigh turned around.

Andrew was leaning against the doorjamb. His suit jacket was off. His shirtsleeves were rolled up. The discussion with Sidney clearly had not gone well. He looked utterly exhausted.

Still, his eyes had not lost their unsettling emptiness.

Leigh could reflect on that later. Now, she skimmed through the rest of the photos. No other physical evidence was documented. Just the video at the bar, the tangentially connected Nike shoe-print, and the fingerprint on the glass Coke bottle. She assumed that Andrew's prints had not been in the state database. In Georgia, only a felony arrest would garner that dubious honor.

She asked, "Do you know how you were identified?"

"Tammy told the police that she recognized my voice from the bar, but that's not—I mean, she'd just met me, so she doesn't really know my voice, does she?"

Leigh pressed together her lips. You could just as easily say it was fresh in the victim's mind, especially after hearing him talk for ninety-eight minutes. The biggest point in Andrew's favor so far was the Rohypnol. Leigh had an expert witness who could argue the amnesia caused by the drug made Karlsen's identification unreliable.

She asked Andrew, "When did the cops get your fingerprints?"

He said, "They came to my work and threatened to drag me down to the police station if I didn't voluntarily go with them."

Reggie said, "You should've called a lawyer right on the spot."

Andrew shook his head in visible regret. "I thought I could clear it up."

"Yeah, my dude, the cops don't want you to clear shit up. They want to arrest you."

Leigh turned back around in her chair. She paged through the case file. She found a warrant for the prints signed by a judge who would sign off on waterboarding if it got him onto the golf course faster. Still, the fact that they'd gotten a warrant rather than snagged his prints off a water bottle in the interrogation room told Leigh that the prosecutor had not been playing around.

Andrew said, "I used to think if you're innocent, you've got nothing to hide. See where that got me? My entire life has gone to hell because one person pointed her finger at me."

"Dude, that's why we're here," Reggie said. "Collier can take down that crazy bitch with one hand tied behind her back."

"She shouldn't have to," Andrew said. "Tammy and I had a good time. I would've called her the next day if Sid hadn't shown up on my doorstep."

Reggie's chair squeaked as he leaned back. "Look, dude, this is war. You're fighting for your life. You gotta play dirty because the other side sure as hell is. Don't be sitting your ass in prison going all *I wish*. Tell him, Collier. This ain't no time to be a gentleman about it."

Leigh wasn't going to put herself between them. She pulled the laptop closer and returned to the VICTIM PHOTOS file. Her finger pressed the arrow key as she paged through to the rape-kit documentation. Each close-up was more devastating than the previous. God knew that Leigh had witnessed her share of brutality, but she felt a sudden vulnerability sitting in a small room with two loud men who were arguing about bitches while the horrific evidence of a savage sexual assault flashed across the screen.

The skin along Tammy Karlsen's back had been clawed out. Bite marks riddled her breasts and shoulders. Handprint-shaped bruises wrapped around her arms, stretched across her ass and the back of her legs. The Coke bottle had ripped her open. Contusions and lacerations scraped up her thighs into the groin. Fissures sliced her anus. Her clitoris had been ripped, only a tiny piece of tissue keeping it connected. The wounds had bled so profusely that the impression of her buttocks was sealed in blood against the concrete of the pavilion floor.

"Jesus," Andrew said.

Leigh suppressed a shiver. Andrew was standing right behind her. The photo on the laptop showed Tammy Karlsen's mutilated breast. Bite marks dug into the soft flesh around the nipple.

He said, "How could anyone think I would do that? And how stupid would I be to follow her from the bar with all of those cameras?"

Leigh felt relieved when he walked over to the couch.

"It doesn't make sense, Harleigh." Andrew's tone went soft as he took his place on the couch. "I always assume I'm on camera. Not just at a bar. At an ATM. On the streets. At the dealership. People have cameras in their driveways, on their doorbells. They're everywhere. Always watching. Always recording everything you're doing. It defies logic that you could hurt someone—anyone—without a camera catching you in the act."

Leigh had picked the wrong time to look him in the eye. Andrew held her directly in his sights. His expression changed right in front of her, the left corner of his mouth twitching into a smirk. In seconds he transformed himself from hapless innocent to the suave psychopath who had kissed Tammy Karlsen, then followed her car, waiting for her to pass out so that he could kidnap and rape her.

"Harleigh," he said, his voice almost a whisper. "Think about what they're saying I did."

Kidnap. Rape. Aggravated assault. Aggravated sodomy. Aggravated sexual battery.

"You've known me longer than anybody but Mom," Andrew said. "Could I do that?"

Leigh didn't need to look at the laptop to see the rape-kit photos flashing in front of her eyes. Open wounds, gouges, bites, scratches, all caused by the animal who was now staring at her like fresh prey.

"Think about how clever I would have to be," Andrew said. "Avoid the cameras. Avoid witnesses. Avoid leaving any clues."

She felt her throat catch as she tried to swallow.

"I wonder, Harleigh, if you were going to commit a terrible crime, a crime that would destroy another person's life, would you know how to get away with it?" He had moved to the edge of the couch. His body was tensed. His hands clenched. "It's not like when we were kids. You could get away with cold-blooded murder back then. Couldn't you, Harleigh?"

Leigh felt herself slipping back in time. She was eighteen, packing for college even though it was a month away. She was picking up the phone in her mother's kitchen. She was listening to Callie say that Buddy was dead. She was in her car. She was in Trevor's room. She was in the kitchen. She was telling Callie what to do, how to clean up the blood, where to drop the pieces of broken video camera, how to dispose of the body, what to do with the money, what to say to the cops, how they were going to get away with this because she had thought of everything.

Almost everything.

Slowly, she turned toward Reggie. He was clueless, absently typing on his phone.

"Did—" The word caught in her throat. "The attacker used a knife on Karlsen. Did the police find the knife?"

"That's a negative." Reggie kept typing. "But from the wound size and depth, they think the blade was serrated, maybe five inches long. Probably a cheap kitchen knife."

Cracked wooden handle. Bent blade. Sharp, serrated teeth.

Reggie finished typing. "You'll see it in the files when I put them on your server. Cops say the same knife was used on the three other victims. They all had the same wound in the same place."

"Wound?" Leigh heard her own voice echo in her ears. "What wound?"

"Left thigh, a few inches south of the groin." Reggie shrugged. "They got lucky. Any deeper, and he would've cut open the femoral artery."

3

Leigh barely made it more than a mile from Reggie's office before her stomach turned inside out. Horns blared as she swerved her car over to the side of the road. She lunged across the passenger seat. The door flew open. Torrents of bile shot out of her mouth. Even when there was nothing left, she couldn't stop gagging. Daggers stabbed into her abdomen. She hung her head so low that her face almost touched the ground. The smell made her gag again. She started to dry-heave. Tears poured from her eyes. Sweat beaded across her face.

They think the blade was serrated.

She hacked so hard that stars burst against her eyelids. She gripped the door to keep from falling. Her body was wracked by a series of agonizing spasms. Slowly, painfully, the heaving subsided. Still, she waited, hanging out of the car, eyes squeezed closed, begging her body to stop shaking.

Maybe five inches long.

Leigh opened her eyes. A thin line of saliva fell from her mouth, pooled into the flattened grass. She gulped down a breath. She let her eyes close again. She kept waiting for more, but nothing came.

Probably a cheap kitchen knife.

She tested herself, gently moving into an upright position. She wiped her mouth. She closed the door. She stared at the steering wheel. Her ribs ached where she'd stretched across the console between the two seats. The car shook as a truck whizzed past.

Leigh hadn't panicked inside Reggie Paltz's office. She had gone into a sort of fugue state—still physically there but somehow not there, her soul hovering above the room, seeing everything but not feeling anything.

Below, she had watched the other Leigh look at her watch, register surprise at the time. She had made an excuse about having a meeting downtown. Andrew and Reggie had both stood when she did. Other Leigh had lifted her purse onto her shoulder. Reggie had returned his attention to his laptop. Andrew had watched her every move. Like a fluorescent tube flickering back on, he'd turned all cow-eyed and innocent again. His words had come rushing at her like a fire hose. *I'm sorry you have to leave I thought we were just getting into things should I give you a call or will I see you at the meeting with Cole tomorrow afternoon?*

Floating against the ceiling, Leigh had watched her other self make promises or excuses, she wasn't sure which because she couldn't hear her own voice. Then her fingers had looped her mask around her ears. Then she was waving goodbye. Then she was walking through to the outer office.

Her other self continued to project an outward calm. She had stopped to get some hand sanitizer. She had looked at the empty Dunkin' Donuts coffee cup that had been taken out of the trash and placed prominently on the counter. Then she was walking down the hall. Then she was going down the stairs. She had opened the glass door. She had walked out onto the concrete stoop. Navigated her way down the crumbling stairs. Looked out at the parking lot.

Sidney Winslow was smoking a cigarette. Her mouth had twisted in disgust when she'd seen Leigh. She had thumbed off some ash, leaned back against a low sports car.

Andrew's car.

Leigh had staggered forward, reeling from the impact of her soul slamming back into her body. She was herself again, one person, one woman who had just heard a sadistic rapist all but confess that he not only knew that Leigh had been involved in Buddy's murder, but that he was also refining the same technique on his own victims.

Any deeper, and he would've cut open the femoral artery.

"Hey, bitch." Sidney had aggressively pushed herself away from

76

the car. "I don't appreciate you making it out like my own damn fiancé can't trust me."

Leigh had said nothing, just stared at the stupid girl. Her heart was jackrabbiting. Her flesh was hot and cold at the same time. Her stomach had filled with razor blades. It was Andrew's car that was setting her off.

He drove a yellow Corvette.

The same color, the same body style, as the one that Buddy had driven.

Suddenly, Leigh heard a loud horn. The Audi shook violently as a truck swerved by. She looked in the side mirror. Her back tire was on the line. Instead of moving, she watched the traffic coming toward her, silently daring someone—anyone—to hit her. More horns. Another truck another sedan another SUV but no flash of yellow from Buddy's Corvette.

Andrew.

He would never be Trevor to her again. The thirty-three-year-old man was not the creepy five-year-old who used to jump out from behind the couch to scare her. Leigh could still remember the invisible tears the little boy had wiped away when she'd screamed at him to stop. Andrew clearly knew some details about his father's death, but how? What had they done to give themselves away? What stupid mistake had Leigh made that night that somehow, eventually, had allowed Andrew to put together the pieces?

If you were going to commit a terrible crime, a crime that would destroy another person's life, would you know how to get away with it?

Leigh sniffed, and a chunk of something thick and putrid slid down her throat. She looked for a tissue in her purse. Couldn't find one. Dumped her purse onto the passenger seat. Everything scattered. She saw the pack of tissue obscuring a distinctive orange pill bottle.

Valium.

Everyone had needed something to get through the last year. Leigh didn't drink. She hated feeling out of control, but she hated not sleeping even more. During the drawn-out election insanity, she had gotten a script for Valium. The doctor had called them Pandemic Pleasers.

Sleepy medicine.

That's what Buddy had called Andrew's NyQuil. Every time Buddy got home and Andrew was still awake, he would tell Leigh, *Hey doll I can't put up with his shit tonight, do me a favor before you go and give the kid his sleepy medicine.*

Leigh could hear Buddy's distinctive baritone as if he were sitting in the back seat of her car. Unbidden, she conjured the feel of his fumbling hands rubbing her shoulders. Leigh's own hands started trembling so badly that she had to use her teeth to open the cap on the Valium. Three orange tablets scattered onto her palm. She tossed them all back, dry-swallowing them like candy.

She gripped her hands together to stop the shake. She waited for the release. Four more tablets were left in the bottle. She would take them all if it came to that. She couldn't be like this right now. Wallowing in fear was a luxury she could not afford.

Andrew and Linda Tenant were not trashy poor Waleskis anymore. They had Tenant Auto Group fuck-you money. Reggie Paltz could probably be bought off with the promise of more work from Leigh's firm, but he wasn't the only private investigator in town. Andrew could hire an entire team of investigators who could start asking questions no one had bothered to ask twenty-three years ago, like—

If Callie was worried about Buddy, why hadn't she called Linda? The woman's number was taped to the wall by the kitchen phone.

If Andrew had in fact accidentally ripped the phone cord out of the wall, why couldn't he remember doing it? And why was he so groggy the next day?

Why had Callie called Leigh to drive her home that night? She'd made the ten-minute walk hundreds of times before.

Why did the next-door neighbors say they'd heard Buddy's Corvette stalling several times in the driveway? He knew how to drive a manual transmission.

What happened to the machete in the shed?

Why was the can of gasoline missing?

What about Callie's broken nose and cuts and bruises?

And why did Leigh leave for college a month early when she had nowhere to stay and no money to waste?

$86,940.

The night that Buddy died, he had just been paid for a big job. His briefcase had been packed with fifty grand. They had found the rest hidden around the house.

Not for the first time, Callie and Leigh had argued about what to do with the money. Callie had insisted they leave something for Linda. Leigh had been equally insistent that leaving a dime would give them away. If Buddy Waleski was really skipping town, he would take all of the cash he could lay his hands on because he didn't give a shit about anybody but himself.

Leigh could remember the exact words that had finally persuaded Callie: *It's not blood money if you pay for it with your own blood.*

Another car horn beeped. Leigh startled again. The sweat had dried to a chill on her skin. She dialed back the air conditioner. She felt weepy, which helped nothing. She needed to summon her focus. In the courtroom, she had to be ten steps ahead of everybody else, but now she had to use all of her energy to figure out which first step would take her in the best direction.

She called up Andrew's exact words, the taunting sneer on his lips.

It's not like when we were kids. You could get away with cold-blooded murder back then.

What had Leigh and Callie missed? They hadn't exactly been teenage gangsters, but they'd both spent time in juvie and they had both grown up in the 'hood. They intuitively knew how to cover their tracks. Their bloody clothes and shoes had gone into a burn barrel. The video camera was broken into pieces. The house was thoroughly cleaned. Buddy's car was stripped and burned. His briefcase was destroyed. They'd even packed a suitcase full of his clothes and tossed in a pair of his shoes.

The knife was the only thing left.

Leigh had wanted to get rid of it but Callie had told her that Linda would notice it was missing from the set. In the end, Callie had washed off the thin line of blood in the sink. Then they had soaked the wooden handle in bleach. Callie had even used a toothpick to clean around the tang, a word Leigh only knew because she had marked every year since it happened by going

79

over all the details of a possible case that could be built against them.

She did a quick review in her head, knocking down the long list of questions, which relied either on the memories of children or on a pair of elderly neighbors who had both died eighteen years ago.

There was no physical evidence. No body found. No murder weapon. No unexplained hair, teeth, blood, fingerprints, DNA. No child porn. The only men who knew that Buddy Waleski had been raping Callie were the same men who were incentivized to keep their disgusting pedophile mouths shut.

Dr. Patterson. Coach Holt. Mr. Humphrey. Mr. Ganza. Mr. Emmett.

Maddy. Walter. Callie.

Leigh had to keep her priorities front and center. The time for wallowing in fear was over. She checked the side-view mirror. She waited for the lane to clear, then pulled out onto the road.

As she drove, the Valium stretched into her bloodstream. She felt some of the edges smoothing out. Her shoulders relaxed against the seat. The yellow line on the road turned into the belt on a treadmill. Buildings and trees and signs and billboards blurred by—Colonnade Restaurant, Uptown Novelty, *Mitigate! Vaccinate! Keep Atlanta Open for Business!*

"Shit," she hissed, her foot going down to the floor. The car in front of her had braked suddenly. Leigh turned the a/c back up. The cold air slapped her face. She passed the stopped car. Drove so carefully that she felt like an old lady. Ahead, the green light started to turn, but she didn't rush it. She rolled to a stop. Pushed up the turn signal. The digital sign outside the bank gave the time and temperature.

Eleven fifty-eight a.m. Seventy-two degrees.

Leigh turned off the air conditioning. She rolled down the window. She let the heat envelop her. It felt only fitting that she should be sweating. By the end of the stifling August night that Buddy Waleski had died, Leigh and Callie's clothes were soaked through with blood and sweat.

Buddy was a contractor, or at least that's what he'd told people. The tiny trunk of his Corvette had held a toolbox with pliers and a hammer. Inside the shed in the backyard were tarps and tape and plastic and a giant machete that hung from a hook on the back of the door.

First, they had rolled Buddy onto the plastic. Then they had gotten on their hands and knees to clean up all the blood underneath him. Next, they had used the kitchen table and chairs to create an impromptu bathtub around the body.

Every second of what happened next was seared into Leigh's memory. Slicing off chunks of skin with the sharpest knives. Hacking joints with the machete. Breaking teeth with the hammer. Prying up fingernails with pliers in case Callie's skin was underneath. Scoring fingers with a razor blade to obscure prints. Splashing bleach onto everything to wash away any trace of DNA.

They had taken turns because the work was not just mentally grueling. Cutting up the massive body and shoving the pieces into black lawn bags had taken every last ounce of their physical strength. Leigh had gritted her teeth the whole time. Callie had kept chanting the same maddening lines over and over again— *If you'd like to make a call, please hang up and try again . . . If this is an emergency . . .*

Silently, Leigh had added her own chant—*This-is-my-fault-this-is-all-my-fault-this-is-my-fault . . .*

Leigh was thirteen and Trevor was five when she'd started babysitting for the Waleskis. She'd gotten the referral by word of mouth. That first night, Linda had delivered a long-winded lecture about the importance of being trustworthy, then made Leigh read aloud from the list of emergency numbers by the kitchen telephone. Poison Control. Fire department. Police department. Pediatrician. Linda's number at the hospital.

There had been a quick tour of the depressing house as Trevor had clung to Linda's waist like a desperate monkey. Lights were turned on and off. The fridge and kitchen cabinets were opened and closed. Here was what they could eat for dinner. There were the snacks. This was his bedtime. Those were the books to read. Buddy would be home by midnight at the latest, but Linda needed Leigh to promise on her life that she would not leave until Buddy was there. And if he didn't come home, or if he showed up drunk—knee-walking drunk, not just a little drunk—Leigh was to call Linda immediately so she could leave work.

The lecture had seemed like overkill. Leigh had grown up in Lake Point, where the last wealthy white residents had drained the lake on their way out of town so that no black people could swim in it. The small, abandoned houses had been turned into crack dens. Gunshots could be heard at all hours. Leigh walked to school past a park where there were more broken syringes than children. During her previous two years of babysitting, no one had ever questioned her street smarts.

Linda must've picked up on her bristling. She had quickly turned down the threat level. Apparently, the Waleskis had been plagued by irresponsible flakes. One sitter had abandoned Trevor, not even locking the door behind her. Another had stopped showing up. Another refused to answer her phone. Linda was mystified. So was Leigh.

And then three hours after Linda had left for work, Buddy had come home.

He'd looked at Leigh in a way that she had never been looked at before. Top to bottom. Appraising her. Sizing her up. Lingering on the shape of her lips, the two tiny bumps pressing against the front of her faded Def Leppard T-shirt.

Buddy was so big, so looming, that his footsteps shook the house as he walked toward the bar. He had poured himself a drink. He had wiped his sloppy mouth with the back of his hand. When he spoke, his words fell all over each other, a cataclysm of sly questions buried in inappropriate compliments—*How old are you dolly you can't be more than thirteen right but damn you look like you're already a full-grown woman I bet your daddy has to beat the boys off with a stick what's that you don't know your daddy that's a shame baby girl a little thing like you needs a big tough guy to protect her.*

Initially, Leigh had thought he was giving her the third degree the same way Linda had but, looking back, she understood that he'd been testing the waters. In law enforcement circles, this was called grooming, and pedophiles followed the same relentlessly predictable playbook.

Buddy had quizzed her on her interests, the subjects she enjoyed in school, joked with her about her seriousness, implied she was smarter than him, more interesting, led a more fascinating life. He wanted to hear all about her. He wanted her to know that he wasn't like those old farts she had met before. Sure, he was an old fart, too, but he understood what kids were going through. He offered her some weed. She passed. He offered her a drink. She sipped something that tasted like cough syrup and silently pleaded with him to please, please mister, please just let her go home so she could study.

Finally, Buddy had made a big deal about looking at the giant gold watch on his thick wrist. His mouth had dropped open dramatically—*wow dolly, where did the time go I could talk to you all night but your mother must be waiting up for you right I bet she's a real bitch about that always keeping track of you even though you're practically an adult and you should get to make your own decisions right?*

Unthinking, Leigh had rolled her eyes because the only reason her mother would be up was to make sure Leigh handed over the cash she'd made for watching Trevor.

Had Buddy picked up on the eye-roll? All Leigh knew was that everything had changed in that moment. Maybe he was putting together the information he'd gathered. No father. Useless mother. Not many friends at school. Not likely to tell.

He'd started talking about how dark it was outside. How bad the neighborhood was. That maybe it was going to rain. Sure, Leigh lived a ten-minute walk away, but she was too beautiful to be out on her own at night. *Tiny little thing like you some bad dude could scoop you up and hide you in his pocket and what about that a fucking tragedy because then Buddy would never be able to see her beautiful little face ever again did she want that to happen he would be heartbroken could she really do such an awful thing to him?*

Leigh had felt sick and guilty and shamed and, worst of all, trapped. She'd dreaded the possibility that he was going to insist she stay the night. But then Buddy had told her he would drive her home. She had been so relieved that she hadn't argued, just grabbed up all her homework and shoved it into her backpack.

The light changed, but Leigh was so lost in thought that it

took a moment for her to register the green. Yet another car horn urged her on. She took the turn. Her movements felt robotic as she drove down a shady side street. There was no wind to rustle the trees, but she could hear the rush of air through her open window as she sped down the road.

The Waleskis had a carport on the side of their house. The windows were already rolled down in Buddy's yellow Corvette when they left by the kitchen door. The car was an older model. Rust rimmed the hood. The paint was faded. A permanent oil stain marked his space on the concrete. The interior had smelled like sweat and cigars and sawdust. He had made a big deal about opening the door for Leigh, flexing his biceps to show her how strong he was. *Prince Charming at your service little madam just snap your fingers anytime and your ol' pal Buddy will be there.*

Then he'd walked around to the driver's side, and her first thought was that he was like a clown jamming himself into a toy car. Buddy was groaning and huffing as he wedged his hulking body behind the wheel. Shoulders hunched. Seat raked back. Leigh could remember watching his enormous hand wrap around the stick shift. The entire gear box had disappeared. He kept his bear paw there, tapping along to the song on the radio.

Callie was haunted by the phantom bleating tone of the operator on the broken kitchen telephone. Leigh was haunted by Buddy's creaky falsetto as he sang along with Hall & Oates' "Kiss on My List."

They were two minutes into the trip when, in the dim orange light of the radio, Buddy's hand wandered in her direction. He kept his eyes straight ahead, but his fingers tapped on her knee the same as they had on the shifter.

I like this song do you like this song dolly I bet you do but I wonder have you ever kissed a boy do you know what that feels like?

Leigh was paralyzed, trapped in the bucket seat, sweat melding her skin into the cracked leather. Buddy's hand didn't leave her knee as he slowed the car and pulled to the side of the road. She recognized the Deguils' house. She had babysat for their daughter, Heidi, a few times last summer. Their front porch light was on.

That's okay little girl don't be scared your ol' pal Buddy would never hurt you okay but Jesus your skin is so soft I can feel the peach fuzz you're almost like a baby.

He still hadn't looked at her. His eyes stayed focused straight ahead. Tongue darting out between his lips. His sausage fingers tickled along her knee, dragging her skirt along with them. The weight of his hand on her leg was an anvil.

Leigh gasped for breath. Her head swam as she felt herself spinning back into the present. Her heart was beating so hard in her throat that she pressed her hand to her chest to make sure it hadn't dislodged itself. Her skin was clammy. She could still hear Buddy's last words as she got out of the car —

Let's keep this between you and me how about that here's some extra cash for tonight but promise me you won't tell I don't want your mama getting mad at you and punishing you so I can't ever see you again.

Leigh had told her mother about Buddy's tickling fingers on her knee the second she'd walked through the door.

Jesus Christ Harleigh you're not a helpless baby just slap away his hand and tell him to fuck off when he tries it again.

Of course Buddy had tried it again. But her mother had been right. Leigh had slapped away his hand and screamed at him to fuck off and that was the end of it. *Damn dolly okay okay I get it no big deal but watch it tiger you're gonna give some poor fella a run for his money someday.*

Afterward, Leigh had forgotten about the incident the way you forget about things that are too awful to remember, like the male teacher who kept talking about how Leigh's breasts were developing so fast or the old man at the grocery store who told her she was turning into a *real woman*. Three years later, when Leigh had saved up enough to buy a car so she could drive to a better job at the mall, she had passed on the babysitting gig to a grateful Callie.

The light turned green. Leigh's foot moved to the accelerator. Tears were streaming down her face. She started to wipe them away, but fucking Covid stopped her. She pulled a tissue from the pack and carefully dabbed underneath her eyes. Another sharp breath filled her lungs. She held on to the air until it hurt, then *shushed* it out between her teeth.

Leigh had never told Callie about what had happened to her in the Corvette. She had never warned her baby sister to slap Buddy's hand away. She had never told Buddy to leave Callie the fuck alone. She hadn't warned Linda or anyone else because Leigh had pushed the awful memory so far down that by the time Buddy's murder bubbled it all up, all she could do was drown in her own guilt.

Her mouth opened for another breath. She felt disoriented again. Leigh looked around, trying to get her bearings. The Audi knew where it was going before she did. Left turn, coast a few yards, right turn into the strip-mall parking lot.

Sergeant Nick Wexler's squad car was backed into its usual lunchtime spot between a frame shop and a Jewish deli. The lot was only half-full. A distanced line led to the deli's front door for take-out.

Leigh took her time before getting out of the car. She freshened her make-up. Chewed a couple of breath mints. She put on her Fuck Me Red lipstick. Her notebook and a pen were retrieved from the pile. She turned past the notes on Andrew's case and found a clean page. She wrote along the bottom of the paper. The Valium was doing the trick. Her hands had stopped shaking. She could no longer feel her own heartbeat.

She tore off the bottom part of the page, folded it into a tight square, then tucked it into her bra strap.

Nick was already watching her when she got out of the Audi. Leigh exaggerated the sway of her hips. Flexed her calves with every step. The walk bought her time to carousel through her personalities. Not vulnerable like she was with Walter. Not icy cold the way she'd been with Reggie Paltz. With Nick Wexler, Leigh was the kind of woman who could flirt with an Atlanta police sergeant while he was writing her up for speeding and end up fucking his face off three hours later.

Nick wiped his mouth with his fingers as she got closer. Leigh smiled, but the corners of her lips curled up too much. That was the Valium. It made her a grinning idiot. She felt Nick's eyes track her as she walked around the front of his squad car.

The windows were down.

Nick said, "Damn, Counselor. Where you been hiding yourself?"

She waved at the detritus he kept on the passenger seat. "Move your shit out of my way."

Nick flipped up the dash-mounted laptop and used his arm to sweep everything else onto the floor. Leigh's hand missed the door handle on the first try. Her vision clouded. She blinked the fog away, smiling at Nick as she pulled open the door. His navy Atlanta Police Department uniform was wrinkled from the heat. As sweaty as he smelled, Nick was an unabashedly sexy man. Bright white teeth. Thick, black hair. Deep blue eyes. Ropey strong arms.

Leigh climbed into the squad car. Her heel slipped on his lunch bag. She hadn't bothered with a mask. The Valium had made her loose, but her judgment wasn't completely shot. Frontline workers had been eligible for the vaccine back in February. Leigh figured she was more likely to get syphilis from Nick Wexler than Covid.

He said, "I hope you're here to badger my witness."

Leigh stared out the dirty windshield. The line to the deli was inching forward. The grin tightened the muscles in her face. Her anxiety was simmering in an unreachable part of her brain. Andrew receded into the darkness along with it.

"Hey." Nick snapped his fingers. "You wanna share some of that shit you're on?"

"Valium."

"Rain check," he said. "I'd settle for a handjob."

"Rain check," she said. "Since when do you settle?"

He chuckled with appreciation. "What brings you to my ride after all this time, Counselor? You up to something?"

Conspiracy to commit murder. Improper disposal of a body. Lying to a law enforcement officer. Signing a false statement. Fleeing prosecution across state lines.

She told him, "I need a favor."

He raised his eyebrows. They didn't do favors. They were occasional fuckbuddies who would both be drummed out of their respective occupations if their dalliances got out. Cops and defense attorneys got along about as well as Churchill and Hitler.

She said, "It's not about a case."

He was clearly skeptical. "Oh-kay."

"Deadbeat client. I need to track her down so I can get paid."

"Are the Shylocks getting antsy at Buttfuck, Cunt & Motherfucker?"

The silly grin picked at her mouth. "Something like that."

He was still dubious. "They make you chase down your own receivables?"

"I'll try somebody else." Leigh reached for the door.

"Hey-hey. Hold up, Counselor. Stay with me." He was talking to her like a cop, but his hand gently rested on her shoulder. His thumb stroked her neck. "What's the matter?"

She shook off his hand. They didn't soothe each other. Only Walter got that version of Leigh.

Nick tried again, asking, "What's wrong?"

She hated his *let me fix this* tone, which was one of the reasons she hadn't seen him in a while. "Do I look like something's wrong with me?"

He laughed. "Counselor, ninety-nine percent of the time I got no idea what the hell is going on in that gorgeous head of yours."

"You make up for it with the one percent." She hadn't meant to put the suggestive lilt in her tone. Or maybe she had. There was a certain amount of self-harm that came with what they were doing. Leigh fully appreciated that the risk was what kept bringing her back.

Nick had never cared about her motivations. He let his eyes travel down her body to her legs. He was a man who knew how to look at a woman. Not the sleazy way that Buddy had sized up a thirteen-year-old. Not the casually sexist fuckable/not fuckable appraisal Reggie Paltz had given her in his office. The kind of look that said *I know exactly where to touch you and for how long*.

Leigh bit her bottom lip.

"Shit," Nick said. "All right, what's the client's name?"

She knew better than to show her eagerness. "Left bra strap."

His eyebrow shot back up. He checked to make sure no one was watching. His finger slipped inside her blouse. Her skin was sweaty from the heat. His finger traced along her collarbone, down to her breast. She could feel her breathing change as he found the piece of paper. He slowly slid it out between two fingers.

He said, "It's wet."

She smiled again.

"Jesus Christ." He pushed down his laptop. He peeled open the paper and laid it flat on his leg. He laughed when he read the name. "Let's see what kind of trouble homegirl got herself into."

"Racial profile much?"

He side-eyed her. "If I want someone to break my balls and not fuck me, I can go home to my wife."

"If I want to fuck somebody whose balls are breakable, I would go home to my husband."

He chuckled, typing into the keyboard with one finger.

Leigh took a deep breath and slowly let it out. She shouldn't have said that about Walter. This was the nasty side that Nick brought out in her. Or maybe Walter was the only man on earth who could bring out that tiny little bit of Leigh that was good.

"Oh, damn." Nick squinted at the screen. "Theft. Possession of a controlled substance. Trespassing. Vandalism. Controlled substance. Controlled substance. Jesus Christ, how is this bitch not in jail?"

"She's got a damn good lawyer."

Nick shook his head as he paged down the screen. "We work our asses off to make these cases and it goes to hell the second you cocksuckers show up."

"Yeah, but at least you get your cock sucked."

He gave her the look again. They both knew why she kept bringing this back to sex.

Nick said, "I could get fired for looking this up for you."

"Tell me when a cop ever got fired for anything."

He grinned. "Do you know how miserable desk duty is?"

"Beats being shot in the back." She could tell by his sharp look that she had pushed him too far. So she pushed him farther. "Are you worried at all that white people are starting to distrust the cops, too?"

The sharp look got sharper, but he said, "Counselor, you better be glad your legs look so damn good today."

She watched him turn back to his computer. His finger slid across the track pad. "Here we go. Previous addresses—Lake Point, Riverdale, Jonesboro."

Not the northern corner of Iowa. Not on a farm. Not married. Not raising two kids.

"Lady prefers your finer establishments." Nick took the pen and spiral notebook from his breast pocket. "Two weeks ago, she was given a citation for jaywalking. She gave an address at a no-tell motel. She in the game?"

Leigh shrugged.

"The name doesn't exactly set her up for success." He laughed. "Calliope DeWinter."

"Callie-ope," Leigh corrected, because their mother was too stupid to know how to pronounce it. "She goes by Callie."

"So she's capable of making at least one good choice."

"It's not about making good choices. It's about *having* good choices."

"Sure." Nick ripped the page out of his spiral notebook. He folded the address in half and held it between his two fingers. He didn't try to slip it underneath her bra strap because he was a cop and he wasn't stupid. "What do you make, Counselor, ten grand an hour?"

"Something like that."

"And a low-level junkie prostitute pays for that how?"

Leigh forced herself not to snatch the address out of his hand. "She's a trust-fund baby."

"Is that the story you wanna tell me?"

Only one emotion could cut through the Valium: anger. "Jesus fuck, Nick. What's with the third degree? Either give me the information or—"

He tossed the address onto her lap. "Get outta my ride, Counselor. Go find your junkie."

Leigh didn't get out. She unfolded the paper.

ALAMEDA MOTEL 9921 STEWART AVENUE.

Back when Leigh worked Legal Aid, she'd had a lot of clients living in the long-term motel. They charged $120 a week to poor people who could find a hell of a lot better place to live if they could save up the deposit money to rent a place that charged $480 a month.

Nick said, "I got work to do. Either start talking or start walking."

Her mouth opened. She was going to tell him the truth.

She's my sister. I haven't seen her in over a year. She lives like a junkie prostitute while I live in a gated condo building and send my daughter to a twenty-eight-grand-a-year school because I pushed my baby sister into the arms of a sexual predator and was too ashamed to tell her that he'd come after me, too.

"Fine." Leigh couldn't tell Nick the whole truth, but she could tell him part of it. "I should've been up front with you from the beginning. She's one of my previous clients. Back when I worked for myself."

Nick clearly expected more.

"She was a gymnast in elementary school. Then she got into competitive cheerleading." Leigh narrowed her eyes to ward off a crass cheerleader joke. "She was a flyer. Do you know what that is?"

He shook his head.

"There's a couple of guys, sometimes as many as four, who are spotters. They do things like raise up the flyer on the palms of their hands while she holds a pose. Or sometimes they just throw her up into the air as high as they can. We're talking fifteen, sometimes twenty feet off the ground. The flyer spins around, does a couple of flips, then she comes down, and the spotters interlock their arms to form a basket for her to land in. But if they don't catch her, or they catch her wrong, then she can mess up her knee, break an ankle, sprain her back." Leigh had to stop to swallow. "Callie landed wrong on an X-Out basket toss and ended up fracturing two vertebrae in her neck."

"Jesus."

"She was so strong that the muscles held it in place. She kept performing. But then her legs went numb and she was rushed to the ER and she had spinal fusion surgery and she had to wear a halo to keep her head from turning and she started taking Oxy for the pain and—"

"Heroin." Nick was on the streets. He'd seen the progression in real time. "That's quite a sob story, Counselor. The judge must'a bought it since her ass isn't behind bars where it belongs."

The judge had bought a confession from the innocent junkie Leigh had bribed to take the fall.

Nick asked, "She on the needle or smoking it?"

"Needle. It's been off and on for almost twenty years." Leigh's heart had started pounding again. The crushing guilt of her sister's tortured life had broken through the veil of Valium. "Some years are better than others."

"Christ, that's a hard road to walk."

"It is." Leigh had watched it play out like a never-ending horror novel. "I wanted to check on her because I feel guilty."

His eyebrows arched back up. "Since when does a defense lawyer ever feel guilty?"

"She almost died last year." Leigh couldn't look at him anymore. She stared out the window instead. "I gave her Covid."

SUMMER 1998

The night was pitch black. Harleigh's eyes sharpened on every detail picked out by her car's headlights. Mailbox numbers. Stop signs. Taillights on parked cars. A cat's eyes as it scrambled across the road.

Harleigh, I think I killed Buddy.

Callie's hoarse whisper had been barely perceptible on the other end of the telephone. There was a scary flatness to her voice. She had shown more emotion this morning when she couldn't find her socks for cheerleading practice.

I think I killed him with a knife.

Harleigh hadn't asked questions or demanded a reason why. She had known exactly why, because in that moment, her mind had taken her back to that sweaty yellow Corvette, the song on the radio, Buddy's enormous hand covering her knee.

Callie, listen to me. Don't move until I get there.

Callie had not moved. Harleigh had found her sitting on the floor of the Waleskis' bedroom. She still had the phone to her ear. The operator's staticky voice was talking over the screeching *wah-wah-wah* sound that the phone made when you left it off the hook too long.

Callie's hair was out of its usual ponytail, shrouding her face. Her voice sounded raspy as she spoke the words along with the recording. "If you'd like to make a call . . ."

"Cal!" Harleigh dropped to her knees. She tried to pry the phone out of her sister's hands, but Callie wouldn't let go. "Callie, please."

Callie looked up.

Harleigh fell back in horror.

The whites in her sister's eyes had turned black. Her nose had been broken. Blood dripped from her mouth. Finger-shaped red slashes ringed Callie's neck where Buddy had tried to choke the life out of her.

Harleigh was responsible for this. She had protected herself from Buddy, but then she had put Callie directly in his path.

"Cal, I'm sorry. I'm so sorry."

"What—" Callie coughed, and blood misted out from her lips. "What are we going to do?"

Harleigh gripped Callie's hands like she could keep them both from sinking farther down. So much ran through her mind—*you're going to be okay. I'll fix this. We'll get through it together*—but she saw no way to fix this, no path out of hell. Harleigh had entered the house through the kitchen. Her eyes had flickered across Buddy the same guilty way you'd pretend to not see a homeless person freezing in a doorway.

But he wasn't homeless.

Buddy Waleski was connected. He had friends all over the place, including inside the police force. Callie wasn't some coddled suburban white kid with two parents who would lay down their lives to protect her. She was a trashy teenager from the bad side of town who'd already spent time in juvie for stealing a pink cat collar from the dollar store.

"Maybe—" Tears welled into Callie's eyes. Her throat was so swollen that she had trouble speaking. "Maybe he's okay?"

Harleigh didn't understand. "What?"

"Will you see if he's okay?" Callie's black eyes caught the reflection from the table lamp. She was looking at Harleigh, but she was somewhere else, a place where everything was going to work out all right. "Buddy was mad, but maybe he's not mad anymore if he's okay? We can—we can get him help. Linda won't be home until—"

"Cal—" Harleigh's sob strangled around the word. "Was it—did Buddy try something? Did it happen before or . . ."

Callie's face gave her the awful answer. "He loved me, Har. He said he was going to take care of me always."

Harleigh was literally bowled over by the pain. She touched

94

her forehead to the filthy carpet. Tears seeped from her eyes. Her mouth opened as a moan escaped from deep inside of her body.

This was her fault. This was all her fault.

"It's okay." Callie rubbed Harleigh's back, trying to comfort her. "He loves me, Harleigh. He'll forgive me."

Harleigh shook her head. The stiff carpet scratched against her face. What was she going to do? How was she going to fix this? Buddy was dead. He was too heavy for them to carry. There was no way he would fit in Harleigh's tiny car. They couldn't dig a hole deep enough for him to rot in. They couldn't leave because Callie's fingerprints were on everything.

Callie said, "He'll take care of me, Har. Just tell him I'm s-sorry."

This was her fault. This was all her fault.

"Please—" Callie's broken nose whistled with every breath. "Please will you check?"

Harleigh kept shaking her head. Her chest felt like claws were digging into her ribcage, pulling her back into the stinking shithole that was her life. She was supposed to leave for college in four weeks and one day. She was supposed to get away, but she couldn't abandon Callie like this. The police wouldn't see the cuts and bruises as evidence that her sister had fought for her life. They would see the tight clothes, the make-up, the way she wore her hair, and say she was a conniving, murdering Lolita.

And if Harleigh came to her defense? If she said that Buddy had tried it with her, too, but she'd been so busy getting on with her life that she hadn't warned her sister?

It's your fault. It's all your fault.

"Please check on him," Callie said. "He looked cold, Harleigh. Buddy hates being cold."

Harleigh saw her future circling down the drain. All the things she'd planned for—the brand-new life she'd pictured in Chicago with her own apartment, her own things, maybe a cat and a dog and a boyfriend who didn't already have a criminal record—were gone. All the extra classes in school, all the nights she'd spent studying in between working two, sometimes three different jobs, putting up with handsy bosses and harassing comments, sleeping in her car between shifts, hiding money from her mother, all to end up exactly where every other miserable, hopeless kid in this ghetto ended up.

"He—" Callie coughed. "He was m-mad because I f-found the camera. I knew about it but not—he taped us doing—Har, people watched. They know w-what we did."

Harleigh silently replayed her sister's words. The apartment in Chicago. The cat and dog. The boyfriend. All of it melted into the ether.

She forced herself to sit back up. Every part of her brain was telling her not to ask, but she had to know. "Who watched you?"

"A-all of them." Callie's teeth had started chattering. Her skin was pale. Her lips had turned the blue of a jay's crest. "Dr. Patterson. C-coach Holt. Mr. Humphrey. Mr. G-ganza. Mr. Emmett."

Harleigh's hand went to her stomach. The names were as familiar to her as the last eighteen years of her life. Dr. Patterson, who'd warned Harleigh to dress more modestly because she was distracting the boys. Coach Holt, who kept telling her his house was right up the street if she ever needed to talk. Mr. Humphrey, who'd made Harleigh sit in his lap before he'd let her test drive a car. Mr. Ganza, who'd wolf-whistled at her last week at the supermarket. Mr. Emmett, who would always rub his arm across her breasts when she was in the dentist's chair.

She asked Callie, "They touched you? Dr. Patterson and Coach—"

"N-no. Buddy made . . ." The chattering cut her off. "M-movies. Buddy made m-movies and they w-watched us."

Harleigh's vision started to sharpen again, the same as it had during the drive over. Only this time, everything was red. Everywhere she looked—the scuffed walls, the damp carpet, the stained bedspread, Callie's swollen, battered face—she saw red.

This was her fault. This was all her fault.

She used her fingers to gently wipe away Callie's tears. She watched her own hand move, but it was like watching someone else's hand. The knowledge of what these grown men had done to her baby sister had split Harleigh in two. One side of her wanted to bite down on the pain the same way that she always did. The other side wanted to cause as much pain as possible.

96

Dr. Patterson. Coach Holt. Mr. Humphrey. Mr. Ganza. Mr. Emmett.

She would destroy them. If it was the last thing she did, Harleigh would end their lives.

She asked her sister, "What time does Linda get home in the morning?"

"Nine."

Harleigh looked at the bedside clock. She had less than thirteen hours to fix this.

She asked, "Where is the camera?"

"I—" Callie put her hand to her strangled throat like she needed help pushing out the answer. "The bar."

Harleigh's fists were clenched as she walked down the hallway. Past the guest room, the bathroom. Past Trevor's bedroom.

She stopped, turned around. She cracked open Trevor's door. His night light spun pinprick stars against the ceiling. His face was tucked down into his pillow. He was fast asleep. She knew without asking that Buddy had made him take his sleepy medicine.

"Harleigh?" Callie stood in the doorway. Her skin was so pale that she looked like a ghost hovering in the darkness. "I don't know w-what to do."

Harleigh pulled Trevor's door closed behind her.

She walked up the hallway, past the aquarium, the couch, the ugly leather club chairs with their cigarette-burned arms. The camera was on a pile of wine corks behind the bar. Canon Optura, top of the line, which Harleigh knew because she had sold electronics over the Christmas rush. The plastic case was broken, a chunk missing from the corner. Harleigh ripped the camera away from the power cable. She used her thumbnail to drag the tiny slider to eject the mini-cassette.

Empty.

Harleigh searched the floor, the shelves behind the bar, trying to find the cassette.

Nothing.

She stood up. She saw the couch with its depressing, solo imprints on opposite sides. The grungy orange drapes. The giant television with the cables hanging down.

Cables that went into the camera she was holding in her hands.

The device had no internal storage. The mini-cassette, which was slightly larger than a business card, held the recordings. You could plug in the camera to a TV or VCR, but no cassette meant no movie.

Harleigh had to find that cassette to show it to the cops so that they could see—*what?*

She had never been inside of a courtroom, but she had grown up watching woman after woman get knocked down by men. Crazy bitches. Hysterical girls. Stupid cunts. Men controlled the system. They controlled the police, the courtrooms, the probation agencies, welfare services, juvenile hall and the jails, school boards, car dealerships, supermarkets, dentists' offices.

Dr. Patterson. Coach Holt. Mr. Humphrey. Mr. Ganza. Mr. Emmett.

There was no way to prove they had watched the video, and unless it showed Callie screaming *No* the entire time, the cops, the lawyers, the judges, would all say that she had wanted it because, no matter what happened to women, men always, always covered each other's asses.

"Harleigh." Callie's arms were hugged around her slim waist. She was trembling. Her lips had turned white. It was like watching her baby sister disappear in stages.

This was her fault. This was all her fault.

"Please," Callie said. "He—he could still be alive. Please."

Harleigh looked at her sister. Mascara ran down her face. Blood and lipstick smeared her mouth into a clown's grimace. Like Harleigh, she had been desperate to grow up. Not because she wanted to distract the boys or call attention to herself, but because adults got to make their own decisions.

Harleigh slammed the camera down on the bar top.

She had finally seen their way out of this.

Buddy Waleski was sitting on the kitchen floor, his back against the cabinets under the sink. His head had dropped forward. His arms were at his sides. His legs were splayed out. The cut was in his left leg, a tiny spring of blood bubbling out like sewage from a broken pipe.

"Please ch-check." Callie stood behind her, black eyes unblinking as she stared at Buddy. "P-please, Har. He c-can't be dead. He can't."

Harleigh went to the body, but not to help. She stuck her hand into Buddy's pants pockets, searching for the small cassette. She found a wad of cash on the left side along with a half-roll of Tums and some lint. A remote control for the camera was in the right pocket. She threw it across the floor so hard that the battery cover broke open. She checked the back pockets and found Buddy's cracked leather wallet and a stained handkerchief.

No cassette.

"Harleigh?" Callie said.

Mentally, Harleigh pushed her sister to the side. She needed to keep her focus on the story they would tell the cops—

Buddy had been alive when they'd left the Waleski house. The only reason Callie had called Harleigh to pick her up was because Buddy was acting strange. He'd told Harleigh some guy had threatened to kill him. He'd told Harleigh to get Callie the hell out of here. They had both gone home and then, obviously, the man who had threatened Buddy had murdered him.

Harleigh punched at the story, looking for weak points. Callie's fingerprints and DNA were everywhere, but Callie was here more than Buddy. Trevor was dead asleep, so he wouldn't know anything. Buddy's blood was confined to the area around his leg, so there were no bloody fingerprints or footprints that could be traced back to Callie. Everything had an explanation. Maybe some of it was weak, but it was believable.

"Har?" Callie's arms were still wrapped tight around her narrow waist. She was swaying back and forth.

Harleigh took her in. Black eyes. Strangled neck. Broken nose.

She told Callie, "Mom did this to you."

Callie looked confused.

"If anyone asks, tell them you talked back and Mom gave you a beat-down. Okay?"

"I don't—"

Harleigh held up her hand to stop Callie from talking. She needed to think it all through forward and back again. Buddy came home. He was scared. Someone had threatened his life. He hadn't said who, just that the sisters should go. Harleigh drove Callie home. Buddy was fine when they left. Callie had gotten the shit beaten out of her the same as she had dozens of times before. Social services would be called again, but a couple of months in foster care beat the hell out of the rest of your life in prison.

Unless the police found the mini-cassette, because the cassette gave Callie a motive.

Harleigh asked, "Where would Buddy hide something small, something smaller than his hand?"

Callie shook her head. She didn't know.

Harleigh let her gaze bounce around the kitchen, desperate to find the cassette. She opened cabinets and drawers, looked under pots and pans. Nothing seemed out of place, and Harleigh would know. Before Callie took over, she had practically lived at the Waleskis' five nights a week over three long years. Studying on the couch, cooking Trevor's meals in the kitchen, playing games with him at the table.

Buddy's briefcase was on the table.

Locked.

Harleigh looked for a knife in the drawer. She jammed it under the clasp, ordering Callie, "Tell me what happened. Exactly. Don't leave anything out."

Callie shook her head again. "I don't—I don't remember."

The lock popped open. Harleigh was only momentarily frozen by the sight of so much cash. The spell broke quickly. She unpacked the money, checked the liner, the inside pockets, the folders, asking Callie, "Where did the fight start? Where were you in the house?"

Callie's lips moved without sound.

"Calliope." Harleigh cringed at her mother's tone coming out of her own mouth. "Tell me now, God dammit. Where did it start?"

"We . . ." Callie turned back toward the living room. "Behind the bar."

"What happened?" Harleigh kept her voice hard. "Be exact. Don't leave anything out."

Callie's voice was so weak that Harleigh had to strain to hear the details. She looked over her sister's shoulder, playing out the movements as if the fight were unfolding in real time. Callie's nose taking the pointy end of Buddy's elbow behind the bar. The box of wine corks tumbling. The camera falling off the shelf. Callie being disoriented, lying flat on her back. Walking into the kitchen. Head under the faucet. Threatening Buddy that she was going to tell Linda. The attack. The phone cord being ripped from the wall. The strangling, the kicking and punching and then—the knife.

Harleigh looked up. She saw that Callie had put the receiver back on the hook. The list of emergency numbers was still taped to the wall beside the phone. The only clue that something bad had happened here was the broken cord. "Trevor ripped the cord."

"What?" Callie said.

"Tell them Trevor ripped the phone cord. When he says he didn't, everyone will think he's lying so he doesn't get into trouble."

Harleigh didn't wait for Callie to agree. She repacked Buddy's briefcase and slammed the lid shut. She gave the kitchen another once-over, looking for somewhere Buddy could stash the cassette. Her eyes finally settled on his hulking body. He was still slouched to the side. The cut in his leg continued to sputter.

She felt her own blood stop cold.

You didn't bleed unless your heart was still pumping.

"Calliope." Harleigh swallowed so hard that her throat clicked. "Go check on Trevor. Now."

Callie didn't argue. She disappeared down the hallway.

Harleigh knelt down in front of Buddy. She grabbed a fistful of his hair and lifted up his giant head. His eyelids slitted open. She saw the whites of his eyes as they rolled back.

"Wake up." She slapped his face. "Wake up, you stupid cock-sucker."

The whites flashed again.

She pressed open his eyelids. "Look at me, asshole."

Buddy's lips parted. She could smell his cheap whiskey and cigars. The stench was so familiar that Harleigh was instantly back in his Corvette.

Terrified. Helpless. Longing for escape.

Harleigh slapped him so hard that saliva flew from his mouth. "Look at me."

Buddy's eyes rolled up but, slowly, they came around to center.

She saw the glimmer of recognition, the stupid belief that he was looking at someone who was on his side.

Buddy stared at what was left of the phone, then looked back at Harleigh. He was asking her to call for help. He knew he didn't have long.

She said, "Where's the cassette from the camera?"

He looked at the phone again, then back at her.

She got in his face. "I'll kill you right now if you don't tell me."

Buddy Waleski was not afraid. He viewed Harleigh as a prude, a rule-follower, the girl who knew the difference between right and wrong. The twitch that pulled up the left side of his lips told her he was happy to bring down Miss Goody Two Shoes and her baby sister right alongside him.

"You fucking asshole." Harleigh slapped him harder than the first time. Then she punched him. His head banged into the cabinet. She grabbed his shirt, reared back to punch him again.

Buddy heard the sound before she did. A distinctive *click* coming from his shirt. She watched his confident expression slip into uncertainty. His eyes moved back and forth, trying to get a read on whether or not she understood.

Harleigh was frozen, right fist still raised, left fist still gripping the front of his shirt. She rolled through her senses, trying to force herself back into that exact moment—the copper-penny smell of blood, the rasp of Buddy's faint breathing, the bitter taste of lost freedom souring her mouth, the feel of his dirty work shirt wadded into her tight fist.

She twisted the material tighter, bunching up the thick cotton.

The *click* drew her eyes to his chest.

Harleigh had only checked his pants pockets. Buddy was wearing a Dickies short-sleeved work shirt. The seams were reinforced. Two flapped breast pockets were on either side. The flap of the left pocket was up, worn with two fang-like impressions from the ever-present box of Black & Milds.

Except this time, he'd put the box in backward. The cellophane window on the front faced his heaving chest.

Harleigh slid out the long, skinny box. She stuck her fingers inside.

The mini-cassette.

She held it to his face so that he could see that she had won. Buddy wheezed out a long sigh. He only looked faintly disappointed. His life had been filled with violence and chaos, mostly brought about by his own hand. Compared to that, his death would be easy.

Harleigh looked down at the small, black plastic cassette with its faded white label.

A piece of electrical tape covered the protection tab so that the tape could be recorded over again and again.

Harleigh had watched her sister change over the last three years, but she'd chalked it up to hormones or brattiness or just growing into another person. Callie's heavy make-up, the arrests for shoplifting, the suspensions from school, the late-night whispered calls that went on for hours. Harleigh had ignored them because she'd been too focused on her own life. Pushing herself to work more, to save more money, to do well in school so she could get the hell out of Lake Point.

Now, she was literally holding Callie's life in her hands. Her youth. Her innocence. Her trust that no matter how high she flew into the air, the world would catch her.

It was all Harleigh's fault.

Her hand squeezed into a fist. The sharp edges of the plastic mini-cassette dug into her palm. The world went red again, blood soaking everything she saw. Buddy's fat face. His meaty hands. His balding head. She wanted to punch him again, to beat him into oblivion, to plunge the steak knife into his chest over and over until the bones cracked and the life spewed from his disgusting body.

Instead, she opened the drawer by the stove. She pulled out the roll of cling film.

Buddy's eyes went wide. His mouth finally opened, but he had lost his chance to speak.

Harleigh wrapped the cling film around his head six times before it tore off from the roll.

The plastic sucked into his open mouth. Buddy's hands reached up to his face, trying to claw open a hole to breathe. Harleigh grabbed onto his wrists. The big strong man, the giant, was too

103

weak to stop her. She looked into his eyes, relishing the fear and helplessness, the panic as Buddy Waleski realized that Harleigh was stealing his easy death.

He started to shake. His chest thrust into the air. His legs kicked out. A high whine came from his throat. Harleigh held on to his wrists, pressing them back against the cabinet. She was straddling him the way he had straddled Callie when he'd choked her. She was pressing her weight into him the same way he had pressed Harleigh back into the seat of his Corvette. She was watching him the same way Dr. Patterson, Coach Holt, Mr. Humphrey, Mr. Ganza, Mr. Emmett had all watched her sister. She was finally doing to a man the same fucking thing that men had been doing to Harleigh and Callie for their entire fucking lives.

It was over too soon.

All at once, Buddy's muscles released. The fight had left him. His hands flopped down to the floor. Urine seeped into his pants. If he had a soul, she imagined the Devil grabbing onto it by his filthy shirt collar, jerking him down, down, down into hell.

Harleigh wiped sweat from her forehead. Blood was on her hands, her arms, arced into the crotch of her jeans where she had sat on top of him.

"If you'd like to make a call . . ."

She turned around. Callie was sitting on the floor. She'd pulled her knees to her chest. She was rocking, her body slowly moving back and forth like a wrecking ball.

"Please hang up and dial again."

SPRING 2021

4

"Let's see what's going on with Mr. Pete." Dr. Jerry started examining the cat, tenderly palpating a swollen joint. At fifteen years old, Mr. Pete was roughly the same age in human years as Dr. Jerry. "Maybe some underlying arthritis? Poor fella."

Callie looked down at the chart in her hands. "He was taking a supplement, but developed constipation."

"Oh, the injustices of old age." Dr. Jerry hooked his stethoscope into his ears, which were almost as hairy as Mr. Pete's. "Could you—"

Callie leaned down and blew air in Mr. Pete's face, trying to stop his purring. The cat looked annoyed, and Callie could not blame him. He'd gotten his paw hooked in the frame of the bed when he was trying to jump down for breakfast. It could happen to anybody.

"That's a good boy." Dr. Jerry stroked Mr. Pete's scruff. He told Callie, "Maine Coons are magnificent animals, but they tend to be the linebackers of the feline world."

Callie flipped back through the chart to start taking notes.

"Mr. Pete is a neutered male of portly stature who presented with right forelimb lameness, having fallen from the bed. Physical exam revealed mild swelling but no crepitus or joint instability. Bloodwork was normal. Radiographs showed no obvious fracture. Start on buprenorphine and gabapentin for pain management. Recheck in one week."

She asked, "Bupe is point-oh-two m-g/k-g q8h for how many days?"

"Let's start with six days. Give him one for the road. No one likes car trips."

Callie carefully wrote his instructions into the chart as Dr. Jerry placed Mr. Pete back into his carrier. They were still on Covid protocols. Mr. Pete's mother was currently sitting in her car outside in the parking lot.

Dr. Jerry asked, "Anything else from the medicine cabinet?"

Callie went through the stack of charts on the counter. "Aroo Feldman's parents report an increase in pain."

"Let's send home some more Tramadol." He signed off on a new script. "Bless their hearts. Corgis are such assholes."

"Agree to disagree." She passed another chart. "Sploot McGhee, greyhound meets motor vehicle. Cracked ribs."

"I remember this lanky young man." Dr. Jerry's hands shook as he adjusted his glasses. She saw his eyes barely move as he pretended to read the chart. "Methadone if they bring him in. If he's not up to the visit, send home a fentanyl patch."

They went through the rest of the big dogs—Deux Claude, a Great Pyrenees with patellar displacement. Scout, a German Shepherd who'd nearly impaled himself on a fence. O'Barky, an Irish wolfhound with hip dysplasia. Ronaldo, an arthritic Labrador who weighed as much as a twelve-year-old child.

Dr. Jerry was yawning by the time Callie got to the cats. "Just do the usual, my friend. You know these animals as well as I do, though be careful with that last one. Never turn your back on a calico."

She smiled at his playful wink.

"I'll give Mr. Pete's human a call, then take my executive time." He winked again, because they both knew he was going to take a nap. "Thank you, angel."

Callie kept up her smile until he turned away. She looked down, pretending to read the charts. She didn't want to watch him shuffle down the hallway like an old man.

Dr. Jerry was a Lake Point institution, the only vet in the area who took EBT cards in exchange for services. Callie's first real job had been at this clinic. She was seventeen. Dr. Jerry's wife had just passed away. He had a son somewhere in Oregon who only called on Father's Day and Christmas. Callie was all he had left. Or maybe Dr. Jerry was all that *she* had left. He was like a father figure, or at least like what she'd heard father figures were supposed to be. He knew Callie had her demons but he never punished her for them. It was only after her first felony drug conviction that he'd stopped pushing her to go to vet school. The Drug Enforcement Agency had a crazy rule against giving prescription pads to heroin addicts.

She waited for his office door to close before starting down the hallway. Her knee made a loud pop as she extended her leg. At thirty-seven, Callie was not that much better off than Mr. Pete. She pressed her ear to the office door. She heard Dr. Jerry talking to Mr. Pete's owner. Callie waited a few more minutes until she heard the creaks from the old leather couch as he laid down for his nap.

She let out a breath that she'd been holding. She took out her phone and set the timer for one hour.

Over the years, Callie had used the clinic as a junkie vacation, cleaning herself up just enough so that she could work. Dr. Jerry always took her back, never asked her where she'd been or why she'd left so abruptly the last time. Her longest stretch of sobriety had been too many years ago to count. She'd lasted eight full months before she'd fallen back into her addiction.

This time wouldn't be any different.

Callie had given up on hope ages ago. She was a junkie, and she would always be a junkie. Not like people in AA who quit drinking but still said they were alcoholics. Like somebody who was always, always going to return to the needle. She wasn't sure when she had come into this acceptance. Was it her third or fourth time in rehab? Was it the eight months of sobriety she'd broken because it was Tuesday? Was it because it was easier to have these maintenance spells when she knew they were only temporary?

Currently, only a sense of usefulness was keeping her on the somewhat straight and narrow. Because of a series of mini-strokes in the past year, Dr. Jerry had shortened the clinic hours down to four days a week. Some days were better for him than others.

His balance was off. His short-term memory was unreliable. He often told Callie that without her, he wasn't sure he'd be able to work one day, let alone four.

She should feel guilty for using him, but she was a junkie. She felt guilty about every second of her life.

Callie pulled out the two keys to open the drug cabinet. Technically, Dr. Jerry was supposed to keep the second key, but he trusted her to accurately log in the controlled substances. If she didn't, then the DEA could start snooping around, matching invoices to dosages to charts, and Dr. Jerry could lose his license and Callie could go to jail.

Generally, addicts made the Drug Enforcement Agency's job easier because they were desperately stupid for their next fix. They OD'd in the waiting room or had a heart attack on the toilet or snatched as many vials as they could shove into their pockets and started running for the door. Fortunately, Callie had figured out through big trials and little errors how to steal a steady supply of maintenance drugs that kept her from getting dope sick.

Every day, she needed a total of either 60 milligrams of methadone or 16 milligrams of buprenorphine to ward off the vomiting, headaches, insomnia, explosive diarrhea, and crippling bone pain that came from heroin withdrawal. The only rule Callie had ever been able to stick to was that she never took anything an animal needed. If her cravings got bad, she dropped her keys back through the mail slot in the door and stopped showing up. Callie would rather die than see an animal suffer. Even a corgi, because Dr. Jerry was right. They could be real assholes.

Callie let herself stare longingly at the stockpiles in the cabinet before she started taking down vials and pill bottles. She opened the drug logbook next to the stack of charts. She clicked her pen.

Dr. Jerry's clinic was a small operation. Some vets had machines where you had to use your fingerprint to open the drug cabinet, and your fingerprint had to match the chart and the chart had to match the dosage and that was tricky, but Callie had been working for Dr. Jerry on and off for nearly two decades. She could beat any system in her sleep.

This was how she did it: Aroo Feldman's parents had not asked for more Tramadol, but she'd logged the request into the chart anyway. Sploot McGhee would get the fentanyl patch because cracked ribs were awful and even a haughty greyhound deserved peace. Likewise, Scout, the idiotic German Shepherd who'd chased a squirrel over a wrought iron fence, would get all the medication he needed.

O'Barky, Ronaldo, and Deux Claude were imaginary animals whose owners had transient addresses and non-working phone numbers. Callie had spent hours giving them backstories: teeth cleanings, heartworm meds, swallowed squeaky toys, unexplained vomiting, general malaise. There were more fake patients—a bull mastiff, a Great Dane, an Alaskan Malamute, and a smattering of sheepdogs. Pain meds were dosed based on weight, and Callie made sure to pick breeds that could go north of one hundred pounds.

Freakishly large Borzois weren't the only way to game the system. Spoilage was a reliable fallback. The DEA understood that animals were wriggly and a lot of times half an injection could end up squirted into your face or onto the floor. You recorded that as spoiled in the book and you went about your day. In a pinch, Callie could drop a vial of sterile saline in front of Dr. Jerry and get him to cancel it out in the log as methadone or buprenorphine. Or sometimes, he would forget what he was doing and make the change himself.

Then there were the easier options. When the visiting orthopedic surgeon came every other Tuesday, Callie prepared bags of fluids with fentanyl, a synthetic opioid that was so strong it was generally only prescribed for advanced cancer pain, and ketamine, a dissociative anesthetic. The trick was to siphon off enough of each drug so that the patient was still comfortable for surgery. Then there was pentobarbital, or Euthasol, which was used to euthanize sickly animals. Most doctors pulled three to four times what was actually needed because no one wanted it to not work. The taste was bitter, but some recreational users liked to cut it with rum and zonk out for the night.

Because there weren't enough St. Bernards and Newfoundlands in Lake Point to justify Callie's maintenance doses, she sold or traded what she could in order to buy methadone. The pandemic had been amazing for drug sales. The cost of your average high had gone through the roof. She considered herself the Robin Hood of drug dealers, because most of the money was returned to the clinic so that Dr. Jerry could keep the doors open. He paid her cash every Friday. He was always astonished by the large number of crumpled, small bills in the lockbox.

Callie opened Mr. Pete's chart. She changed the six to an eight, then drew up the buprenorphine syringes for oral use. She didn't tend to steal from cats because they were relatively small and didn't give a big bang for the buck like a beefy rottweiler. Knowing cats, they probably kept their weight down for that very reason.

She stuck the syringes in a plastic bag, then printed out the label. The rest of the booty went into her backpack in the breakroom. Callie's sister had told her a long time ago that she spent more brainpower doing the wrong thing than she would have to expend doing things right, but fuck her sister; she was one of those bitches who could go on a coke binge to study for the LSAT and never think about coke ever again.

Callie could look at a beautiful green tablet of Oxy and dream about it for the next month.

She wiped her mouth, because now she was dreaming about Oxy.

Callie found Mr. Pete in his carrier. She squirted a syringe of pain meds into his mouth. He sneezed twice, then gave her a very nasty look as she put on a mask and gown so she could take him out to the car.

She left on the mask while she cleaned the clinic. The floors were concave from years of Dr. Jerry's Birkenstocks padding from exam room to exam room, then back to his office. The low ceiling was water-stained. The walls were covered in buckled paneling. There were faded photographs of animals plastered everywhere.

Callie used a duster to knock off the grime. She got on her hands and knees to clean the two exam rooms, then moved on to surgery, then the kennel. They didn't usually board animals, but there was a kitten named Meowma Cass that Dr. Jerry was taking home to bottle-feed and a calico who'd come in yesterday with a string hanging out of his butt. The emergency surgery had been too costly for the owners, but Dr. Jerry had spent an hour removing the string from the cat's intestines anyway.

Callie's alarm went off on her phone. She checked her Facebook, then scrolled through Twitter. The majority of her follows were animal-specific, like a New Zealand zoo keeper who was obsessed with Tasmanian devils and an eel historian who'd detailed the American government's disastrous attempt to transfer East Coast eels to California during the nineteenth century.

The scrolling burned through another fifteen minutes. Callie checked Dr. Jerry's schedule. He had four more patients this afternoon. She went to the kitchen and made him a sandwich, sprinkling a generous supply of animal crackers on the side.

Callie knocked on Dr. Jerry's door before entering. He was laid out on the couch, mouth hanging open. His glasses were askew. A book was flattened on his chest. *The Complete Sonnets of William Shakespeare.* A gift from his late wife.

"Dr. Jerry?" She squeezed his foot.

As always, he was a bit startled and disoriented to find Callie hovering over him. It was like Groundhog Day, except everybody knew that groundhogs were vicious murderers.

He adjusted his glasses so he could see his watch. "That went by fast."

"I made you lunch."

"Wonderful."

He groaned as he got off the couch. Callie gave him a little help when he started to fall back.

She asked, "How was your executive time?"

"Very good, but I had a strange dream about anglerfish. Have you ever met one?"

"Not to my recollection."

"I'm glad to hear that. They live in the darkest, loneliest places, which is a very good thing because they are not the most attractive specimens." He cupped his hand to his mouth as if to convey a confidence. "Especially the ladies."

Callie sat on the edge of his desk. "Tell me."

"The male spends all his life sniffing out a female. As I said, it's very dark where they live, so nature gave him olfactory cells that are attracted to the female's pheromones." He held up his hand to stop the story. "Did I mention she has a long, illuminated filament on her head that sticks out like a flashlight finger?"

"No."

"Bioluminescence." Dr. Jerry looked delighted by the word. "So, once our Romeo finds his Juliet, he bites onto her just below the tail."

Callie watched as he illustrated with his hands, fingers clomping down on his fist.

"Then, the male releases enzymes that dissolve both his mouth and her skin, which effectively fuses them together. Then—this is the miraculous part—his eyes and internal organs dissolve until he's just a reproductive sac melded onto her for the rest of his miserable existence."

Callie laughed. "Damn, Dr. Jerry. That sounds exactly like my first boyfriend."

He laughed, too. "I don't know why I thought about that. Funny how the noggin' works."

Callie could've spent the rest of her life worrying that Dr. Jerry was using the anglerfish as a metaphor for how she treated him, but Dr. Jerry wasn't a metaphor guy. He just really loved talking about fish.

She helped him slip into his lab coat.

He asked, "Did I ever tell you about the time I got a house call on a baby bull shark in a twenty-gallon aquarium?"

"Oh, no."

"They're called pups, by the way, though that doesn't have the same joie de vivre as baby shark. Naturally, the owner was a dentist. Poor simpleton had no idea what he was dealing with."

Callie followed him down the hall, listening to him explain the meaning of *viviparous*. She steered him into the kitchen where she made sure he cleaned his plate. Cracker crumbs speckled the table as he told her another story about another fish, then moved on to marmosets. Callie had realized long ago that Dr. Jerry was using her more as paid companionship. Considering what other men had paid Callie for, she was grateful for the change in scenery.

The four remaining appointments made the rest of the day go by fast. Dr. Jerry loved annual check-ups because there was seldom anything seriously wrong. Callie scheduled follow-up visits, teeth cleanings, and, because Dr. Jerry thought it impolite to bring up a lady's weight, lectured a rotund dachshund's owners about food restrictions. At the end of the day, Dr. Jerry tried to pay her, but Callie reminded him that she didn't get paid again until the end of next week.

She had looked up signs of dementia on her phone. If that was what Dr. Jerry was staring down, then she figured he was still okay to work. He might not know what day it was, but he could calculate fluids with electrolytes and additives like potassium or magnesium without writing down the numbers, which was better than most people could claim.

Callie scrolled through Twitter as she walked to the MARTA bus stop. The eel historian had gone silent and the Kiwi zoo keeper was asleep tomorrow, so she went to Facebook.

Drug-seeking canines were not Callie's only creation. Since 2008, she'd been lurking on the assholes she'd gone to high school with. Her profile photo showed a blue Siamese fighting fish who went by the name Swim Shady.

Her eyes glazed over as she read the latest shitposting from Lake Point's illustrious class of 2002. Complaints about schools closing, wild deep-state conspiracies, disbelief in the virus, belief in the virus, pro-vaccine rants, anti-vaccine rants, and the usual racism, sexism and anti-Semitism that plagued social media. Callie would never understand how Bill Gates had been shortsighted enough to give everybody easy access to the internet so that some day, these jackasses could reveal all of his dastardly plans.

She dropped her phone back into her pocket as she sat on the bench at the bus stop. The dirty Plexiglas enclosure was striped with graffiti. Trash rounded off the corners. Dr. Jerry's clinic was in an okay area, but that was a subjective observation. His strip-mall neighbors were a porn shop that was forced to close during the pandemic and a barbershop Callie was pretty sure had only stayed open because it served as a gambling front. Every time she saw a wild-eyed loser stumbling out the back door, she said a small prayer of thanks that gambling was not one of her addictions.

A garbage truck sputtered black exhaust and rot as it slowly rocked past the bus stop. One of the guys hanging off the back gave Callie a wave. She waved back because it was the polite thing to do. Then his buddy started waving and she turned her head away.

Her neck rewarded her for the too-quick turn, tightening the muscles like a clamp. Callie reached up, fingers finding the long scar that zippered down from the base of her skull. C1 and C2 were the cervical vertebrae that allowed for one-half of the head's forward, back, and rotational movements. Callie had two two-inch titanium rods, four screws and a pin that formed a cage around the area. Technically, the surgery was called a cervical laminectomy, but more commonly it was known as a fusion, because that was the end result: the vertebrae fused together into one bony clump.

Even though two decades had passed since the fusion, the nerve pain could be sudden and debilitating. Her left arm and hand could go completely numb without warning. She had lost nearly half the mobility in her neck. Nodding and shaking her head were do-able, but limited. When she tied her shoes, she had to bring her foot to her hands rather than the other way around. She hadn't been able to look over her shoulder since the surgery, a devastating loss because Callie could never be the heroine pictured on the cover of a Victorian mystery.

She tilted back against the Plexiglas so she could look up at the sky. The waning sun warmed her face. The air was cool and crisp. Cars rolled by. Children were laughing on a nearby playground. The steady beat of her own heart gently pulsed in her ears.

The women she'd gone to high school with were currently driving their kids to football practice or piano lessons. They were watching their sons do homework, holding their breath while their daughters practiced cheerleading routines in the backyard. They were leading meetings, paying bills, going to work and living normal lives where they didn't steal drugs from a kindly old man. They weren't shaking inside of their bones because their body was crying out for a drug that they knew would eventually kill them.

At least a lot of them had gotten fat.

Callie heard the hiss of air brakes. She turned to look for the bus. She did it correctly this time, angling her shoulders along with her head. Despite the accommodation, pain shot fire up her arm and into her neck.

"Shit."

Not her bus, but she'd paid the price for looking. Her breath stuttered. She pushed back against the Plexiglas, hissed air between clenched teeth. Her left arm and hand were numb, but her neck pulsed like a pus-filled sac. She concentrated on the daggers flaying her muscles and nerves. Pain could be its own addiction. Callie had lived with it for so long that when she thought of her life before, she only saw tiny bursts of light, stars barely penetrating the darkness.

She knew that there had been a time long ago when all she'd craved was the rush of endorphins that came from running hard or riding her bike too fast or flipping herself diagonally across the gym floor. In cheerleading, she had flown—soared—into the air, doing a hip-over-head rotation, or a back tuck, a front flip, a leg kick, arabesque, the needle, the scorpion, the heel stretch, the bow-and-arrow, a landing spin that was so dizzying all she could do was wait for four sets of strong arms to basket her fall.

Until they didn't.

A lump came into her throat. Her hand reached up again, this time finding one of the four bony bumps that circled her head like points on a compass. The surgeon had drilled pins into her skull to hold the halo ring in place while her neck healed. Callie had worried the spot above her ear so much it felt callused.

She wiped tears from the corners of her eyes. She dropped her hand into her lap. She massaged the fingers, trying to press some feeling back into the tips.

Seldom did she let herself think about what she'd lost. As her mother said, the tragedy of Callie's existence was that she was smart enough to know how stupid she'd been. This weighty knowledge wasn't limited to Callie. In her experience, most junkies understood addiction as well as, if not better than, a lot of doctors.

For instance, Callie knew that her brain, like every other brain, had something called mu opioid receptors. The receptors were also scattered along her spine and other places, but, for the most part, they hung out in the brain. The easiest way to describe a mu receptor's job was to say that they controlled feelings of pain and reward.

The first sixteen years of her life, Callie's receptors had functioned at a reasonable level. She'd sprain her back or twist her ankle and an endorphin rush would spread through her blood and latch onto the mu receptors, which in turn would dampen the pain. But only temporarily and not by nearly enough. In elementary school, she'd used NSAIDs like Advil or Motrin to replace the endorphins. Which had worked. Until they didn't.

Thanks to Buddy, she'd been introduced to alcohol, but the thing about alcohol was, even in Lake Point, not many stores would sell a handle of tequila to a child, and Buddy had for obvious reasons been unable to supply her past the age of fourteen. And then Callie had broken her neck at sixteen and, before she knew it, she was on her way to a lifelong love affair with opioids.

Narcotics could blow an endorphin rush out of the water, and they were laughably better than NSAIDs and alcohol, except once they latched onto the mu receptors, they didn't like to let go. Your body responded by making more mu receptors, but then your brain remembered how great it was to have full mu receptors and told you to fill them back up again. You could watch TV or read a book or try to contemplate the meaning of life, but your mus would always be there tapping their tiny mu feet, waiting for you to feed them. This was called craving.

Unless you were wired like a magical fairy or had Houdini-level self-control, you would eventually feed that craving. And eventually, you would need stronger and stronger narcotics just to keep all those new mus happy, which was incidentally the science behind tolerance. More narcotics. More mus. More narcotics. And so on.

The worst part was when you stopped feeding the mus, because they gave you around twelve hours before they took your body hostage. Their ransom demand was conveyed through the only language they understood, which was debilitating pain. This was called withdrawal, and there were autopsy photos that were more pleasant to look at than a junkie going through opioid withdrawal.

So, Callie's mother was absolutely right in that Callie knew exactly when she'd taken her first step down the road to a lifetime of stupidity. It wasn't when she'd slammed headfirst onto the gymnasium floor, cracking two vertebrae in her neck. It was the first time her script for Oxy had run out and she'd asked a stoner in English class if he knew how she could get more.

A tragedy in one act.

Callie's MARTA bus harrumphed to the stop, beaching itself on the curb.

She groaned worse than Dr. Jerry when she stood up. Bad knee. Bad back. Bad neck. Bad girl. The bus was half-full, some people wearing masks, some figuring their lives were shitty enough so why postpone the inevitable. Callie found a seat in the front with all the other creaky old women. They were housecleaners and waitresses with grandchildren to support, and they gave Callie the same wary look they'd give a family member who had stolen their checkbook one too many times. To save them all the embarrassment, she stared out the window as gas stations and auto parts stores gave way to strip clubs and check-cashing joints.

When the scenery got too bleak, her phone came out. She started doomscrolling Facebook again. There was no logic to her quest to keep up with these nearly middle-aged twits. Most of them had stayed in the Lake Point area. A few had done well, but well for Lake Point, not well for a normal human being. None of them had been Callie's friends in school. She had been the least popular cheerleader in the history of cheerleaders. Even the weirdos at the freak table hadn't welcomed her into the fold. If any of them remembered her at all, it was as the girl who'd shit herself in front of an entire school assembly. Callie could still remember the sensation of numbness spreading down her arms and legs, the disgusting stench of her bowels releasing as she collapsed onto the hard wooden floor of the gymnasium.

All for a sport that had about as much prestige as an egg-rolling contest.

The bus shivered like a whippet as it neared her stop. Callie's knee locked out when she tried to stand. She had to hit it with her fist to get going. As she limped down the stairs, she considered all the drugs in her backpack. Tramadol, methadone, ketamine, buprenorphine. Mix them all into a pint of tequila and she could get a front-row seat to Kurt Cobain and Amy Winehouse talking about what a douche Jim Morrison could be.

"Hey Cal!" Crackhead Sammy waved frantically from his perch in a broken lawn chair. "Cal! Cal! Come here!"

Callie walked across a vacant lot to Sammy's nesting area—the chair, a leaky tent and a bunch of cardboard that didn't seem to serve a purpose. "What's going on?"

"So, your cat, all right?"

Callie nodded.

"There was a pigeon, and he just—" Sammy did a crazy swooping gesture with his arms. "He caught that damn rat-bird in the air and ate it right in front of me. It was fucked up, man. He sat there chewing on pigeon head for half an hour."

Callie grinned proudly as she dug around in her backpack. "Did he share?"

"Hell no, he just looked at me. He looked at me, Callie. And he had this look, like, like I don't know. Like he wanted to tell me something." Sammy guffawed. "Ha! Like, 'Don't smoke crack.'"

"I'm sorry. Cats can be very judgmental." She found the sandwich she'd made for her dinner. "Eat this before you hit it tonight."

"Right, right." Sammy tucked the sandwich under a strip of cardboard. "Listen, though, do you think he was trying to tell me something?"

"I'm not sure," Callie said. "As you know, cats choose not to talk because they're afraid we'll make them pay taxes."

"Ha!" Sammy jabbed a finger at her. "Snitches get stitches! Oh-oh-hey Cal, wait up a sec, okay? I think Trap is looking for you so—"

"Eat your sandwich." Callie walked away, because Sammy could rattle on for the rest of the night. And that was without the crack.

Callie rounded the corner, taking a labored breath. Trap looking for her was not a good development. He was a fifteen-year-old meth freak who'd graduated early with a degree in dipshittery. Fortunately, he was terrified of his mother. As long as Wilma got her patronage, her idiot son stayed on a tight leash.

Still, Callie swung her backpack around to the front of her

118

chest as she got closer to the motel. The walk was not completely unpleasant because it was familiar. She passed by empty lots and abandoned houses. Graffiti scarred a crumbling brick retaining wall. Used syringes were scattered across the sidewalk. By habit, her eye searched for usable needles. She had her dope kit in her backpack, a plastic Snoopy watch case with her tie-off, a bent spoon, an empty syringe, some cotton, and a Zippo lighter.

What she enjoyed most about shooting heroin was the pageantry of the act. The flick of the lighter. The vinegar smell as it cooked on the spoon. Drawing up the dirty brown liquid into the syringe.

Callie shook her head. Dangerous thoughts.

She followed the dirt-packed strip that traced around the back-yards of a residential street. The energy abruptly changed. Families lived here. Windows were thrown open. Music played loudly. Women yelled at their boyfriends. Boyfriends yelled at their women. Children ran around a sputtering sprinkler. It was just like the rich parts of Atlanta, but louder and more cramped and less pale.

Through the trees, Callie spotted two squad cars parked at the far end of the road. They weren't scooping up people. They were waiting for the sun to go down and the calls to come in—Narcan for this junkie, the emergency room for another, a long wait on the coroner's van, child services, probation officers, and Veterans Affairs—and that was just for a Monday night. A lot of people had turned to illicit comforts during the pandemic. Jobs were lost. Food was scarce. Kids were starving. The number of over-doses and suicides had gone through the roof. All the politicians who had expressed deep concern about mental health during the lockdowns had shockingly been unwilling to spend money on helping the people who were losing their minds.

Callie watched a squirrel skitter around a telephone pole. She angled her route toward the back of the motel. The two-story concrete block building was behind a row of scraggly bushes. She pushed aside the limbs and stepped onto the cracked asphalt. The Dumpster gave off a pungent welcome. She scanned the area, making sure Trap didn't sneak up on her.

Her mind wandered back to the lethal cornucopia of drugs in her backpack. Meeting Kurt Cobain would be amazing, but her desire for self-harm had passed. Or at least had simmered down to her usual quest for self-harm, the kind that didn't end in certain death, only possible death, and then maybe she could be brought back so why not bump it up a little more, right? The police would come in time, right?

What Callie wanted tonight was to take a long shower and curl up in bed with her pigeon-snacking cat. She had enough methadone to get her through the night and out of bed in the morning. She could sell on the way to work. Dr. Jerry would have a heart attack if she showed up before noon anyway.

Callie was smiling when she turned the corner because she seldom had an actual plan.

"'Sup girl?" Trap was leaning against the wall smoking a joint. He gave her the once-over, and she reminded herself that he was a teenager with the brain of a five-year-old and a grown man's potential for violence. "Got somebody looking for you."

Callie felt the hairs go up on her neck. She had spent the majority of her adult life making sure that no one ever looked for her. "Who?"

"White dude. Nice car." He shrugged, like that was enough of a description. "Whatchu got in that backpack?"

"None of your fucking business." Callie tried to walk past him, but he grabbed her arm.

"Come on," Trap said. "Mama told me to collect."

Callie laughed. His mother would kick his balls into his throat if he took a cut off her piece. "Let's go find Wilma right now and make sure that's true."

Trap's eyes got shifty. At least that's what she thought. Too late, Callie realized he was signaling someone behind her. She started to turn her body because she could not turn her head.

A man's muscular arm looped around her neck. The pain was instantaneous, like lightning striking down from the sky. Callie's hips jutted forward. She fell back against the man's chest, her body levering like the hinge on a door.

His breath was hot in her ear. "Don't move."

She recognized Diego's shrill voice. He was Trap's fellow meth freak. They'd smoked so much crystal that their teeth were already falling out. Either one of them alone was a nuisance. Together, they were a breaking news rape-and-murder story waiting to happen.

"Whatchu got, bitch?" Diego yanked harder on her neck. His free hand slipped under the backpack and found her breast. "You got these little titties for me, girl?"

Callie's left arm had gone completely numb. She felt like her skull was going to break off at the root. Her eyes closed. If she was going to die, let it be before her spine snapped.

"Let's see what we got." Trap was close enough for her to smell the rotten teeth in his mouth. He unzipped the backpack. "Damn, bitch, you been holdin' out on—"

They all heard the distinctive *click-clack* of a slide being pulled on a nine-millimeter handgun.

Callie couldn't open her eyes. She could only wait for the bullet.

Trap said, "Who the fuck are you?"

"I'm the motherfucker who's gonna put another hole in your head if you assholes don't step the fuck off right now."

Callie opened her eyes. "Hey, Harleigh."

5

"Christ, Callie."

She watched Leigh angrily dump the backpack onto the bed. Syringes, tablets, vials, tampons, jellybeans, pens, notebook, two library books on owls, Callie's dope kit. Instead of railing against the stash, her sister's gaze bounced around the dingy motel room as if she expected to find secret stashes of opium inside the painted concrete block walls.

Leigh asked, "What if I'd been a cop? You know you can't carry this much weight."

Callie leaned against the wall. She was used to seeing different versions of Leigh—her sister had more aliases than a cat—but the side of Leigh that could pull a gun on a couple of junkie teenagers hadn't reared its head in twenty-three years.

Trap and Diego had better thank their fucking stars that she was carrying a Glock instead of a roll of cling film.

Leigh warned, "Trafficking would put you in prison for the rest of your life."

Callie stared longingly at her dope kit. "I hear it's easier for bottoms inside."

Leigh swung around, hands on her hips. She was wearing high heels and one of her expensive ladybitch suits, which made her presence in this shithole motel somewhat comical. And that included the loaded gun sticking out of the waistband of her skirt.

Callie asked, "Where's your purse?"

"Locked in the trunk of my car."

Callie was going to tell her that was a stupid rich white lady thing to do, but her skull was still throbbing from when Diego

122

had nearly cracked the remaining vertebrae in her neck. "It's good to see you, Har."

Leigh stepped closer, looking into Callie's eyes to check her pupils. "How stoned are you?"

Not enough was Callie's first thought, but she didn't want to run Leigh off so soon. The last time she'd seen her sister, Callie was coming off spending two weeks on a ventilator in Grady Hospital's ICU.

Leigh said, "I need you straight right now."

"Then you'd better hurry."

Leigh crossed her arms over her chest. She clearly had something to say, but she just as clearly wasn't ready yet. She asked, "Have you been eating? You're too thin."

"A woman can never be—"

"Cal." Leigh's concern cut like a shovel through bullshit. "Are you okay?"

"How's your anglerfish?" Callie enjoyed the confusion on her sister's face. There was a reason the weirdos hadn't wanted the least popular cheerleader at the freak table. "Walter. How's he doing?"

"He's okay." The hardness left Leigh's expression. Her hands dropped down to her sides. There were only three people alive who ever got to see her guard down. Leigh brought up the third without prompting. "Maddy's still living with him so she can go to school."

Callie tried to rub the feeling back into her arm. "I know that's hard for you."

"Well, yeah, everything's hard for everybody." Leigh started pacing around the room. It was like watching a cymbal-clanging monkey wind itself up. "The school just sent out an email that some stupid mother threw a superspreader party last weekend. Six kids have tested positive so far. The entire class is on virtual learning for two weeks."

Callie laughed, but not over the stupid mother. The world Leigh lived in was like Mars compared to her own.

Leigh nodded at the window. "Is that for you?"

Callie smiled at the muscular black cat on the ledge. Binx stretched his back as he waited for entry. "He caught a pigeon today."

Leigh clearly didn't give a shit about the pigeon, but she tried, "What's his name?"

"Fucking Bitch." Callie grinned at her sister's startled reaction. "I call him Fitch for short."

"Isn't that a girl's name?"

"He's gender fluid."

Leigh pressed together her lips. This wasn't a social visit. When Harleigh socialized, she went to fancy dinner parties with other lawyers and doctors and the Dormouse fast asleep between the Hatter and March Hare.

She only sought out Callie when something really bad had happened. A pending warrant. A visit at the county jail. A looming court case. A Covid diagnosis where the only expendable person who could nurse her back to health was her baby sister.

Callie ran through her most recent transgressions. Maybe that stupid jaywalking ticket had put her in the shit. Or maybe Leigh had gotten a tip-off from one of her connections that Dr. Jerry was being looked at by the DEA. Or, more likely, one of the morons Callie was selling to had flipped to keep his own sorry ass out of jail.

Fucking junkies.

She asked, "Who's after me?"

Leigh circled her finger in the air. The walls were thin. Anyone could be listening.

Callie hugged Binx close. They had both known that one day, Callie would get herself into the kind of trouble that her big sister wouldn't be able to get her out of.

"Come on," Leigh said. "Let's go."

She didn't mean take a stroll around the block. She meant pack up your shit, stick that cat in something, and get in the car.

Callie looked for clothes while Leigh repacked the backpack. She would miss her bedspread and her flowery blanket, but this wasn't the first time she'd abandoned a place. Normally sheriff's deputies were standing outside with an eviction notice. She needed underwear, lots of socks, two clean T-shirts, and a pair of jeans. She had one pair of shoes and they were on her feet. More T-shirts could be found at the thrift store. Blankets would be handed out at the shelter, but she couldn't stay there because they didn't allow pets.

Callie stripped off a pillowcase to hold her meager stash, then loaded in Binx's food, his pink mouse toy, and a cheap plastic Hawaiian lei the cat liked to drag around when he was having feelings.

"Ready?" Leigh had the backpack over her shoulder. She was a lawyer, so Callie didn't explain what a gun and a shit ton of drugs could mean because her sister had earned herself a slot in that rarefied world where the rules were negotiable.

"Just a minute." Callie used her foot to kick Binx's carrier out from under the bed. The cat stiffened, but didn't fight when Callie placed him inside. This wasn't his first eviction, either.

She told her sister, "Ready."

Leigh let Callie go first out the door. Binx started hissing when he was put into the back seat of the car. Callie buckled the seatbelt around his carrier, then got into the front seat and did the same for herself. She watched her sister carefully. Leigh was always in control, but even the way she turned the key in the ignition was done with a strangely precise flick of her wrist. Everything about her was freaked out, which was worrying, because Leigh never freaked out.

Trafficking.

Junkies were by necessity part-time lawyers. Georgia had mandatory sentencing based on weight. Twenty-eight or more grams of cocaine: ten years. Twenty-eight or more grams of opiates: twenty-five years. Anything over four hundred grams of methamphetamines: twenty-five years.

Callie tried to do the math, to divide her list of customers who had probably flipped by the ounces or total grams she had sold in the last few months, but, no matter how she toggled it around, the numerator kept bringing her back to *fucked*.

Leigh turned right out of the motel parking lot. Nothing was said as they pulled onto the main road. They passed the two cop cars at the end of the residential street. The cops barely gave the Audi a glance. They likely assumed the two women were looking for a stoned kid or slumming around trying to score for themselves.

They both kept silent as Leigh pulled out onto the outer loop, past Callie's bus stop. The fancy car smoothly navigated the bumpy asphalt. Callie was used to the jerks and bounces of public transportation. She tried to remember the last time she'd ridden in a car. Probably when Leigh had driven her home from Grady Hospital. Callie was supposed to convalesce at Leigh's zillion-dollar condo, but Callie had been on the street with a needle in her arm before the sun had come up.

She massaged her tingling fingers. Some of the feeling was coming back, which was good but also like needles scraping into her nerves. She studied her sister's sharp profile. There was something to be said for having enough money to age well. A gym in her building. A doctor on call. A retirement account. Nice vacations. Weekends off. As far as Callie was concerned, her sister deserved every luxury she could give herself. Leigh hadn't just fallen into this life. She had clawed her way up the ladder, studying harder, working harder, making sacrifice after sacrifice to give herself and Maddy the best life possible.

If Callie's tragedy was self-knowledge, Leigh's was that she would never, ever let herself accept that her good life wasn't somehow linked to the unmitigated misery of Callie's.

"Are you hungry?" Leigh asked. "You need to eat."

There wasn't even a polite pause for Callie's response. They were in big sister/little sister mode. Leigh pulled into a McDonald's. She didn't consult Callie as she ordered at the drive-thru, though Callie assumed the Filet-O-Fish was for Binx. Nothing was said as the car inched toward the window. Leigh found a mask in the console between the seats. She exchanged cash for bags of food and drinks, then passed it all to Callie. She took off her mask. She kept driving.

Callie didn't know what to do but get everything ready. She wrapped a Big Mac in a napkin and handed it to her sister. She picked at a double cheeseburger for herself. Binx had to settle for two French fries. He would've loved the fish sandwich, but Callie wasn't sure she could clean cat diarrhea out of the contrast stitching in her sister's fancy leather seats.

She asked Leigh, "Fries?"

Leigh shook her head. "You have them. You're too skinny, Cal. You need to back off the dope for a while."

Callie took a moment to appreciate the fact that Leigh had

stopped telling her she needed to quit altogether. It had only taken tens of thousands of dollars of Leigh's money wasted on rehab and countless angst-filled conversations, but both of their lives had become a hell of a lot easier since Leigh had entered into acceptance.

"Eat," Leigh ordered.

Callie looked down at the hamburger in her lap. Her stomach turned. There wasn't a way to tell Leigh that it wasn't the dope that was making her lose weight. She had never gotten her appetite back after Covid. Most days, she had to force herself to eat. Telling that to Leigh would only end up burdening her sister with more guilt that she did not deserve to carry.

"Callie?" Leigh shot her an annoyed look. "Are you going to eat or do I have to force-feed you?"

Callie choked down the rest of the fries. She made herself finish exactly half of the hamburger. She was downing the Coke when the car finally rolled to a stop.

She looked around. Instantly, her stomach started searching for all sorts of ways to get rid of the food. They were smack in the residential part of Lake Point, the same place Leigh used to bring them in her car when they needed to get away from their mother. Callie had avoided this hellhole for two decades. She took the long bus from Dr. Jerry's just so she didn't have to see the depressing, squat houses with their narrow carports and sad front yards.

Leigh left the car running so the air could stay on. She turned toward Callie, leaning her back against the door. "Trevor and Linda Waleski came to my office last night."

Callie shivered. She kept what Leigh had told her at a distance, but there was a faint darkness on the horizon, an angry gorilla pacing back and forth across her memories—short-waisted, hands always fisted, arms so muscled that they wouldn't go flat to his sides. Everything about the creature screamed ruthless motherfucker. People turned in the opposite direction when they saw him in the street.

Get on the couch, little dolly. I'm so hot for you I can't stand it.

Callie asked, "How's Linda?"

"Rich as shit."

Callie looked out the window. Her vision blurred. She could see the gorilla turning, glaring at her. "I guess they didn't need Buddy's money after all."

"Callie." Leigh's tone was filled with urgency. "I'm sorry, but I need you to listen."

"I'm listening."

Leigh had good reason not to believe her, but she said, "Trevor goes by Andrew now. They changed their last name to Tenant after Buddy—after he disappeared."

Callie watched the gorilla start running toward her. Spit sprayed from his mouth. His nostrils flared. His thick arms rose up. He lunged at her, teeth bared. She smelled cheap cigars and whiskey and her own sex.

"Callie." Leigh grabbed her hand, holding so tight that the bones shifted. "Callie, you're okay."

Callie closed her eyes. The gorilla stalked back to its place on the horizon. She smacked her lips. She had never wanted heroin so much as she did in this moment.

"Hey." Leigh squeezed her hand even tighter. "He can't hurt you."

Callie nodded. Her throat felt sore, and she tried to remember how many weeks, maybe as long as a few months, it had taken before she could swallow without pain after Buddy had tried to choke the life out of her.

You worthless piece of shit, her mother had said the day after. *I didn't raise you to let some stupid punk bitch kick your ass on the playground.*

"Here." Leigh let go of her hand. She reached into the back seat to open the carrier. She scooped up Binx and placed him in Callie's lap. "Do you want me to stop talking?"

Callie held Binx close. He purred, pushing his head against the base of her chin. The weight of the animal brought her comfort. She wanted Leigh to stop, but she knew that hiding from the truth would only shift all of the burden onto her sister.

She asked, "Does Trevor look like him?"

"He looks like Linda." Leigh went silent, waiting for another question. This wasn't a legal tactic she'd learned in the courtroom. Leigh had always been a trickle-truther, slowly feeding out information so that Callie didn't freak out and OD in a back alley.

Callie pressed her lips to the top of Binx's head, the same way she used to do with Trevor. "How did they find you?"

"Remember that article in the paper?"

"The urinator," Callie said. She had been so proud to see her big sister profiled. "Why does he need a lawyer?"

"Because he's been accused of raping a woman. Several women."

The information was not as surprising as it should've been. Callie had spent so much time watching Trevor test the waters, seeing how far he could push things, exactly the way his father always had. "So, he's like Buddy after all."

"I think he knows what we did, Cal."

The news hit her like a hammer. She felt her mouth open, but there were no words. Binx grew irritated by the sudden lack of attention. He jumped onto the dashboard and looked out the windshield.

Leigh said it again, "Andrew knows what we did to his father."

Callie felt the cold air from the vents seep into her lungs. There was no hiding from this conversation. She couldn't turn her head, so she turned her body, pressing her back against the door the same way that Leigh had. "Trevor was asleep. We both checked."

"I know."

"Huh," Callie said, which was what she said when she didn't know what else to say.

"Cal, you don't have to be here," Leigh said. "I can take you to—"

"No." Callie hated being placated, though she knew that she needed it. "Please, Harleigh. Tell me what happened. Don't leave anything out. I have to know."

Leigh was still visibly reluctant. The fact that she didn't protest again, that she didn't tell Callie to forget about it, that Leigh was going to handle everything like she always did, was terrifying.

She started at the beginning, which was around this time last night. The meeting at her boss's office. The revelation that Andrew and Linda Tenant were ghosts from her past. Leigh went into detail about Trevor's girlfriend, Reggie Paltz the private detective who was a little too close, the lies about Callie's life in Iowa. She explained the rape charges against Andrew, the possible other victims. When she got to the detail about the knife slicing just above the femoral artery, Callie felt her lips part.

"Hold on," she said. "Back up. What did Trevor say exactly?"

"Andrew," Leigh corrected. "He's not Trevor anymore, Callie. And it's not what he said, it's how he said it. He knows that his father was murdered. He knows that we got away with it."

"But—" Callie tried to wrap her brain around what Leigh was saying. "Trev—Andrew is using a knife to hurt his victims the same way I killed Buddy?"

"You didn't kill him."

"Fuck, Leigh, sure." They weren't going to have that stupid argument again. "You killed him after I killed him. It's not a contest. We both murdered him. We both chopped him up."

Leigh fell back into silence. She was giving Callie space, but Callie didn't need space.

"Harleigh," she said. "If the body was found, it's too late to know how he died. Everything would be gone by now. They'd just find bones. And not even all of them. Just scattered pieces."

Leigh nodded. She had already thought about this.

Callie went through the other options. "We looked for more cameras and cassettes and—everything. We cleaned the knife and put it back in the drawer. I babysat Trevor for another whole damn month before they finally left town. I used that steak knife every time I could. There's no way anybody could link it back to what we did."

"I can't tell you how Andrew knows about the knife, or the cut to Buddy's leg. All I can say is that he knows."

Callie forced her mind to go back to that night, though by necessity she had worked to forget most of it. She flipped through the events quickly, not pausing on any one page. Everybody thought that history was like a book with a beginning, a middle, and an end. That's not how it worked. Real life was all middle.

She told Leigh, "We turned that house upside down."

"I know."

"How does he . . ." Callie flipped back through it again, this time more slowly. "You waited six days before you left for

Chicago. Did we talk about it in front of him? Did we say something?"

Leigh shook her head. "I don't think we did, but . . ."

Callie didn't need her to say the words. They had both been in shock. They had both been teenagers. Neither of them was a criminal genius. Their mother had figured out that something bad had happened, but all she'd told them was *Don't put me in the middle of whatever shit you're tangled up in because I will throw both of your sorry asses under the first bus that swings by.*

Leigh said, "I don't know what mistake we made but, obviously, we made a mistake."

Callie could tell by looking at her sister that whatever this mistake was, Leigh was piling it onto the other pile of guilt that already weighed her down. "What did Andrew say exactly?"

Leigh shook her head, but her recall had always been excellent. "He asked me if I would know how to commit a crime that would destroy somebody's life. He asked if I'd know how to get away with cold-blooded murder."

Callie bit her bottom lip.

"And then he said today isn't like when we were kids. Because of cameras."

"Cameras?" Callie echoed. "He said cameras specifically?"

"He said it half a dozen times—that cameras are everywhere, on doorbells, houses, traffic cameras. You can't go anywhere without being recorded."

"We didn't search Andrew's room," Callie said. That was the only place they hadn't considered. Buddy barely spoke to his son. He wanted nothing to do with him. "Andrew was always stealing things. Maybe there was another cassette?"

Leigh nodded. She had already considered the possibility.

Callie felt her cheeks burn bright red. Andrew was ten when it happened. Had he found a cassette? Had he watched his father screwing Callie every which way he could think of? Was that why he was still obsessed with her?

Was that why he was raping women?

"Harleigh, logic that out. If Andrew has a video, then all it shows is that his father was a pedophile. He wouldn't want that

131

out in the open." Callie fought off a shudder. She didn't want that out in the open either. "Do you think Linda knows?"

"No." Leigh shook her head, but there was no way she could be sure.

Callie put her hands to her burning cheeks. If Linda knew, then that would be the end of her. She had always loved the woman, almost worshipped her for her steadiness and honesty. As a kid, it had never occurred to Callie that she was cheating with Linda's husband. In her screwed-up head, she had seen them both as surrogate parents.

She asked her sister, "Before he started talking about cameras, did Andrew ask you about anything from that night, or around Buddy's disappearance?"

"No," Leigh answered. "And like you said, even if Andrew had a cassette, it wouldn't show how Buddy died. How does he know about the knife? The leg wound?"

Callie watched Binx grooming his paw. She was absolutely clueless.

Until she wasn't.

She told Leigh, "I looked into—I looked up stuff in one of Linda's anatomy textbooks after it happened. I wanted to know how it worked. Andrew could've seen that."

Leigh seemed skeptical, but she said, "It's possible."

Callie pressed her fingers to her eyes. Her neck pulsed with pain. Her hand was still tingling. The gorilla was restless in the distance.

Leigh asked, "How often did you look it up?"

Callie saw a projection on the back of her eyelids: the textbook open on the Waleskis' kitchen table. The diagram of a human body. Callie had traced her finger along the femoral artery so many times that the red line had faded into pink. Had Andrew noticed? Had he seen Callie's obsessive behavior and put it all together?

Or was there a heated conversation between Callie and Leigh that he'd overheard? They had argued constantly about what to do after Buddy—whether their plan was working, what stories they had told to cops and social workers, what to do with the money. Andrew could've been hiding, listening, taking notes. He

132

had always been a sneaky little shit, jumping out from behind things to scare Callie, stealing her pens and books, terrorizing the fish in the aquarium.

Any of these scenarios was possible. Any one would elicit the same response from Leigh: *It's my fault. It's all my fault.*

"Cal?"

She opened her eyes. She only had one question. "Why is this getting to you, Leigh? Andrew doesn't have any proof or he'd be at a police station."

"He's a sadistic rapist. He's playing a game."

"So fucking what? Jesus, Leigh. Sac up." Callie opened her arms in a shrug. This was how it worked. Only one of them could fall apart at a time. "You can't play a game with somebody if they're not willing to suit up. Why are you letting that little freak get into your head? He doesn't have jack shit."

Leigh didn't answer, but she was obviously still rattled. Tears had filled her eyes. Her color was off. Callie noticed a speck of dried vomit on the neck of her shirt. Leigh had never had a strong stomach. That was the problem with having a good life. You didn't want to lose it.

Callie said, "Lookit, what do you always tell me? Stick to the damn story. Buddy came home. He was freaked out about a death threat. He didn't say who had made it. I called you. You picked me up. He was alive when we left. Mom pounded the hell out of me. That's it."

"D-FaCS," Leigh said, using the abbreviation for the Department of Family and Children's Services. "When the social worker came to the house, did she take any photos?"

"She barely took a report." Callie honestly couldn't remember, but she knew how the system worked and so did her sister. "Harleigh, use your brain. We weren't living in Beverly Hills, 90210. I was just another kid whose drunk mother kicked the shit out of her."

"The social worker's report could be somewhere, though. The government never throws anything away."

"I doubt the bitch even filed it," Callie said. "All of the social workers were terrified of Mom. When the cops questioned me about Buddy disappearing, they didn't say a damn thing about how I looked. They didn't ask you about it, either. Linda gave me antibiotics and set my nose, but she never asked one single question. Nobody pushed it with social services. Nobody at school said a damn thing."

"Yeah, well, that asshole Dr. Patterson wasn't exactly a child advocate."

The humiliation flooded back like a tidal wave pounding Callie down onto the shore. No matter how much time had passed, she could not move past not knowing how many men had seen the things she'd done with Buddy.

Leigh said, "I'm sorry, Cal. I shouldn't have said that."

Callie watched Leigh search for a tissue in her purse. She could remember a time when her big sister had concocted murderous plots and grand conspiracies against the men who had watched Callie being defiled. Leigh had been willing to throw her life away in order to get revenge. The only thing that had pulled her back from the brink was the fear of losing Maddy.

Callie told Leigh what she always told Leigh, "It's not your fault."

"I should've never left for Chicago. I could've—"

"Gotten trapped in Lake Point and drop-kicked into the gutter with the rest of us?" Callie didn't let her respond, because they both knew Leigh would've ended up managing a Taco Bell, selling Tupperware, and running a bookkeeping business on the side. "If you'd stayed here, you wouldn't've gone to college. You wouldn't have a law degree. You wouldn't have Walter. And you sure as hell wouldn't have—"

"Maddy." Leigh's tears started to fall. She had always been an easy crier. "Callie, I'm so—"

Callie waved her away. They couldn't get entangled in another *it's all my fault/no it's not your fault*. "Let's say social services has a report, or the cops put it in their notes that I was in bad shape. Then what? Where's the paperwork now?"

Leigh pressed together her lips. She was clearly still struggling, but said, "The cops are probably retired or up the ranks by now. If they didn't document abuse in their incident reports, then it would be in their personal notes, and their personal notes would be in a box somewhere, probably in an attic."

"Okay, so I'm Reggie, the private detective that Andrew hired, and I'm looking into a possible murder that happened twenty-three years ago, and I want to see the police reports and anything the social workers have on the kids who were in the house," Callie said. "What happens next?"

Leigh sighed. She was still not focused. "For D-FaCS, you'd file a FOIA request."

The Freedom of Information Act made all government records publicly available. "And then?"

"The *Kenny A. v. Sonny Perdue Consent Decree* was settled in 2005." Leigh's legal brain started to take over. "It's complicated but, basically, Fulton and DeKalb County were forced to stop screwing over children in the system. It took three years to hash out an agreement. A lot of incriminating paperwork and files conveniently went missing before the settlement."

Callie had to assume any reports on her beat-down were part of the cover-up. "What about the cops?"

"You'd file a FOIA for their official documents and a subpoena for their notebooks," Leigh said. "Even if Reggie tried to go the other way and knocked on their door, they'd be worried about being sued if they documented abuse but never followed up on it. Especially if it's tied into a murder case."

"So, the cops would conveniently be unable to locate anything, too." Callie thought about the two officers who had interviewed her. Another case where men would keep their mouths shut to cover for other men. "But what you're saying is, neither of those are a problem we need to worry about, right?"

Leigh hedged. "Maybe."

"Tell me what you need me to do."

"Nothing," Leigh said, but she always had a plan. "I'll take you out of state. You can stay in—I don't know. Tennessee. Iowa. I don't care. Wherever you want to go."

"Fucking Iowa?" Callie tried to lighten her up. "You couldn't think of a better job for me than milking cows?"

"You love cows."

She wasn't wrong. Cows were adorable. There was an alternate Callie who would've loved being a farmer. A veterinarian. A trash collector. Anything but a stupid, thieving junkie.

Leigh took a deep breath. "I'm sorry I'm so shaky. This really isn't your problem."

"Fuck you," Callie said. "Come on, Leigh. We're both ride or die. You got us out of this before. Get us out of it again."

"I don't know," she said. "Andrew's not a kid anymore. He's a psychopath. And he does this thing where one minute he looks normal, and the next minute you feel your body going into this primal fight-or-flight mode. It freaked me the fuck out. The hairs on the back of my neck stood up. I knew something was wrong the second I saw him, but I couldn't figure it out until he showed me."

Callie took one of Leigh's tissues. She blew her nose. For all of her sister's intelligence, she had been in too many soft places for far too long. She was thinking of the legal ramifications of Andrew trying to open up an investigation. A possible trial, evidence presented, witnesses cross-examined, a judge's verdict, prison.

Leigh had lost her ability to think like a criminal, but Callie could do it for both of them. Andrew was a violent rapist. He wasn't *not* going to the police for lack of a smoking gun. He was torturing Leigh because he wanted to take care of this problem with his own hands.

She told her sister, "I know you've got a worst-case scenario."

Leigh was visibly reluctant, but Callie could tell she was also relieved. "I need you to taper yourself off the dope. You don't have to quit altogether, but if someone comes around asking questions, you need to be straight enough to give them the right answers."

Callie felt cornered, even though she was already doing exactly what her sister had asked. It was different when she had a choice. Leigh's request made Callie want to dump her backpack on the floor and tie off right then and there.

"Cal?" Leigh looked so damn disappointed. "It's not forever. I wouldn't ask if—"

"Okay." Callie swallowed all of the saliva that had flooded into her mouth. "How long?"

"I don't know," Leigh admitted. "I need to figure out what Andrew is going to do."

Callie choked back her panicked questions—*A few days? A week? A month?* She bit her lip so that she didn't start crying.

Leigh seemed to read her thoughts. "We'll take it a couple of days at a time. But if you need to leave town, or—"

"I'll be okay," Callie said, because they both needed it to be true. "But come on, Harleigh, you already know what Andrew is doing."

Leigh shook her head, still lost.

"He's in more trouble than you are." If Callie was going to ride this out, she needed her sister's lizard brain to kick in, the fight instinct to take over flight, so that it didn't drag out too long. "He fired his attorney. He hired you a week before he goes to trial. The rest of his life is literally on the line and he's throwing around these hints about cameras and getting away with murder. People don't make threats unless they want something. What does Andrew want?"

Realization flashed in Leigh's eyes. "He wants me to do something illegal for him."

"Right."

"Shit." Leigh ran through a list. "Suborn a witness. Commit perjury. Aid in the committal of a crime. Obstruct justice."

She had done that and more for Callie.

"You know how to get away with every single one of those things."

Leigh shook her head. "It's different with Andrew. He wants to hurt me."

"So what?" Callie snapped her fingers like she could wake her up. "Where's my bad-ass big sister? You just pointed a Glock at two meth freaks with a bunch of cops one street over. Stop spinning around like a playground bitch who just got her first broken bone."

Slowly, Leigh started nodding, psyching herself up. "You're right."

"Damn straight I'm right. You've got a fancy law degree and a fancy job and a clean record and what does Andrew have?" Callie didn't let her answer. "He's accused of raping that woman. There are more women who can point their fingers at him. If this fucktard rapist starts whining about how you murdered his daddy twenty years ago, who do you think people are going to believe?"

Leigh kept nodding, but Callie knew what was really bothering her sister. Leigh hated a lot of things, but feeling vulnerable could terrify her to the point of paralysis.

Callie said, "He's got no power over you, Harleigh. He didn't even know how to find you until that douchebag private eye showed him your picture."

"What about you?" Leigh asked. "You stopped using Mom's last name years ago. Are there other ways he can find you?"

Callie mentally ran through all the disreputable avenues of locating a person who did not want to be found. Trap could be bought off, but, as was her habit, she'd checked into the motel under an alias. Swim Shady was an internet ghost. She had never paid taxes. She had never had an active lease or a cell phone account or a driver's license or health insurance. Obviously, she had a social security number, but Callie had no idea what it was and her mother had probably burned it out long ago. Her juvenile record was sealed. Her first adult arrest listed her as Calliope DeWinter because the cop who'd asked for her last name had never read Daphne du Maurier and Callie, stoned out of her mind, had found this so hilarious that she'd pissed herself in the back of his squad car, thus halting all further interrogation. Add to that the weird pronunciation of her first name and the aliases piled onto aliases. Even when Callie was in the Grady ICU wasting away from Covid, her patient chart had listed her as Cal E. O. P. DeWinter.

She told Leigh, "He can't find me."

Leigh nodded, visibly relieved. "Okay, so keep laying low. Try to stay sharp."

Callie thought about something Trap had said before he'd tried to rob her.

White dude. Nice car.

Reggie Paltz. Mercedes Benz.

"I promise it won't be long," Leigh said. "Andrew's trial should last two or three days. Whatever he's planning, he'll have to move fast."

Callie took a shallow breath as she studied Leigh's face. Her sister had not really considered what kind of havoc Andrew could cause in Callie's life, mostly because Leigh knew very little about how Callie lived. She had probably tracked down Callie through a lawyer friend. She had no idea Dr. Jerry was still working, let alone that Callie was helping him out.

Setting aside that Reggie Paltz was already asking questions, he clearly had his contacts inside of the police force. He could put Callie's name on their radar. She was already trafficking drugs. If the right cop asked the wrong questions, Dr. Jerry could be looking at the DEA banging down his front door and Callie could be going through a hard detox at the downtown City Detention Center.

Callie watched Binx flop down onto his side, taking advantage of the sunlight hitting the dashboard. She did not know if she was more worried about Dr. Jerry or herself. They didn't offer medically assisted detox in jail. They locked you in a cell by yourself and, three days later, you either walked out on your own power or you were rolled out in a body bag.

She told Leigh, "Maybe it would be better if we made it easy for Andrew to find me."

Leigh looked incredulous. "How the fuck would that be a good thing, Callie? Andrew's a sadistic rapist. He kept asking about you today. His own best friend says he's going to start looking for you eventually."

Callie ignored those facts because they would only scare her into backing down. "Andrew's on bail, right? So he has an ankle monitor with an alarm that will go off if he—"

"Do you know how long it takes for a probation officer to respond to an alarm? The city can barely make payroll. Half of the old-timers took early retirement when Covid hit and the rest are covering fifty percent more cases." Leigh's incredulous look had turned into open bewilderment. "Which means after Andrew murders you, the cops can look up the GPS records and find out what time he did it."

Callie felt her mouth go dry. "Andrew wouldn't look for me himself. He would send his investigator, right?"

"I'm going to get rid of Reggie Paltz."

"Then he gets another Reggie Paltz." Callie needed Leigh to

stop reeling around and think this through. "Look, if Andrew's investigator locates me, then that's something Andrew thinks he has on us, right? The guy will ask me some questions. I'll feed him what we want him to know, which is nothing. Then he'll report all of that back to Andrew. And then when Andrew springs it on you, you'll already know."

"It's too dangerous," Leigh said. "You're basically offering yourself up as bait."

Callie fought off a shudder. So much for trickling the truth. Leigh couldn't know that Callie was already dangling from a hook or she would never let her stay in the city. "I'll put myself in an obvious place so that the investigator can find me, all right? It's easier to deal with someone when you know they're coming."

"Hell no." Leigh was already shaking her head. She knew what the *obvious place* was. "That's insanity. He'll find you in a heartbeat. If you could see the photos of what Andrew did to—"

"Stop." Callie did not have to be told what Buddy Waleski's son was capable of. "I want to do this. I am going to do this. It's not a matter of asking for your permission."

Leigh pressed together her lips again. "I've got cash. I can get more. I'll set you up wherever you like."

Callie was not, could not, leave the only place she had known as her home. But she knew about another option, one that would make sense to anybody who had ever met her. She could leave Binx in the care of Dr. Jerry. She could take all the drugs in the locked cabinet and Kurt Cobain would be giving her a solo performance of "Come As You Are" before the sun went down.

"Cal?" Leigh said.

Her brain was too caught up in the Cobain loop to answer.

"I need—" Leigh grabbed her hand again, pulling her out of the fantasy. "I need you, Calliope. I can't fight off Andrew unless I know you're okay."

Callie looked down at their intertwined hands. Leigh was the only connection she had left to anything that resembled a normal life. They only saw each other in desperate times, but the knowledge that her sister would always be there had gotten Callie out of countless dark, seemingly hopeless situations.

No one ever talked about how lonely addiction could be. You

were vulnerable when you needed a fix. You were completely unguarded when you were high. You always, no matter what, woke up alone. Then there was the absence of other people. You were isolated from your family because they didn't trust you. Old friends fell away in horror. New friends stole your shit or were afraid you would steal theirs. The only people you could talk to about your loneliness were other junkies, and the nature of addiction was such that no matter how sweet or generous or kind you were in your heart, you were always going to choose your next fix over any friendship.

Callie couldn't be strong for herself, but she could be strong for her sister. "You know I can take care of myself. Give me some cash so I can get this over with."

"Cal, I—"

"The three Fs," Callie said, because they both knew the *obvious place* had an entrance fee. "Hurry up before I lose my nerve."

Leigh reached into her purse. She retrieved a thick envelope. She had always been good with money—scrimping, saving, hustling, only investing in the things that would bring back more money. To Callie's expert eye, she was looking at five grand.

Instead of handing it all over, Leigh peeled away ten twenty-dollar bills. "We'll start with this?"

Callie nodded, because they both knew if she had all the money at once it would end up in her veins. Callie turned in the seat, facing forward again. She slipped off her sneaker. She counted out $60, then asked Leigh, "Give me a hand?"

Leigh reached down and tucked three twenties inside Callie's shoe, then helped her slide it back on. "Are you sure about this?"

"No." Callie waited for Leigh to wrangle Binx back into the carrier before she got out of the car. She unzipped her pants. She tucked the rest of the cash like a pad into the crotch of her underwear. "I'll call you so you have my phone number."

Leigh unpacked the car. She put the carrier down on the ground. She hugged the lumpy pillowcase to her chest. Guilt flooded her face, permeated her breath, overwhelmed her emotions. This was why they only saw each other when shit got bad. The guilt was too much for either of them to bear.

"Hold on," Leigh said. "This is a bad idea. Let me take you—"

"Harleigh." Callie reached for the pillowcase. The muscles in her neck screamed in protest, but she worked to keep it off her face. "I'll check in with you, okay?"

"Please," Leigh said. "I can't let you do this, Cal. It's too hard."

"'Everything's hard for everybody.'"

Leigh clearly didn't like having her own words quoted back to her. "Callie, I'm serious. Let's get you out of here. Buy me some time to think about . . ."

Callie listened to her voice trail off. Leigh *had* thought about it. The thinking was what had brought them both here. Andrew was letting Leigh believe that he'd bought her Iowa dairy farm story. If Trap was telling the truth, Andrew had already sent out his investigator to locate Callie. When that happened, Callie would be ready for him. And when Andrew sprung it on Leigh, she wouldn't spin off into a paranoid freakshow.

There was something to be said for being even one tiny step ahead of a psychopath.

Still, Callie felt her resolve start to falter. Like any junkie, she always thought of herself as water finding the easiest path down. She had to fight that instinct for her sister's sake. Leigh was somebody's mother. She was somebody's wife. She was somebody's friend. She was everything that Callie would never be because life was oftentimes cruel but it was usually fair.

"Harleigh," Callie said. "Let me do this. It's the only way we can take away some of his leverage."

Her sister was so easy to read. The guilt washed back and forth across her face as Leigh spun through all the scenarios that she had likely spun through before showing up at the motel with a Glock in her hand. Eventually, thankfully, her lizard brain kicked in. She finally reconciled herself to the inevitable. Her back pressed against the car. Her arms folded across her chest. She waited for what needed to come next.

Callie picked up Binx. The cat squawked in dismay. Pain blazed through Callie's neck and arm, but she gritted her teeth and started walking down the familiar street. As she put distance between herself and her sister, Callie was glad that she couldn't look over her shoulder. She knew Leigh was watching her. She knew that

Leigh would stay by her car, guilt-ridden, hurting, terrified, until Callie turned the corner at the end of the road.

Even then, a few more minutes passed before Callie heard a car door close, the Audi's engine start up.

"That was my big sister," she told Binx, who was stiff and angry in his confinement. "She's got a nice car, right?"

Binx chortled. He preferred an SUV.

"I know you liked the motel, but there are really fat birds here, too." Callie tilted up her head so she could see the sparse trees. Most cats had to be slowly acclimated to new surroundings. Because of their many unplanned relocations, Binx was adept at scoping out new territory and finding his way back home. Still, everyone needed inducements. She assured him, "There's chipmunks. Squirrels. Rats the size of bunnies. Bunnies the size of rats."

The cat offered no response. He did not want to jeopardize his tax situation.

"Woodpeckers. Pigeons. Blue birds. Cardinals. You love cardinals. I've seen your recipes."

Music echoed into her ears as she turned left, going deeper into the neighborhood. Two men were sitting in a carport drinking beer. An open cooler was between them. The next house had another man washing his car in the driveway. The music was coming from his jacked-up audio system. His kids were giggling as they kicked a basketball around the yard.

Callie couldn't ever remember feeling that kind of child-like freedom. She had loved gymnastics, but her mother had seen the potential to make money, so what had been fun had been turned into a job. Then Callie had been cut from the team and she'd taken up cheerleading. Another opportunity for money. Then Buddy had taken an interest in her and there was even more money.

She had loved him.

That was the real tragedy of Callie's life. That was the gorilla she couldn't get off her back. The only person she had ever truly loved was a heinous pedophile.

A long-ago shrink during a long-failed rehab stint had told her that it wasn't really love. Buddy had inserted himself as a substitute father so that Callie would let her guard down. He had given her a feeling of security in exchange for doing something that she had hated.

Only, Callie hadn't hated all of it. In the beginning, when he was gentle, some of it had felt good. What did that say about Callie? What kind of sickness festered inside of her that she could actually end up liking that?

She exhaled slowly as she turned onto the next street. Her breathing was becoming labored from the walk. She shifted the carrier to her other hand, stuck the lumpy pillowcase under her arm. The pull in her neck was like a red-hot glob of molten steel but she wanted to feel the pain.

She stopped in front of a one-story red cottage with a sway-backed roof. Patchy wood siding striped the front of the house. Burglar bars brought a prison-like feel to the open windows and doors. A scruffy mutt with a bit too much Scottish terrier for her liking stood sentry at the screen door.

Callie's knee gristled as she climbed the three wonky stairs. She set Binx down on the front porch. She dropped the pillowcase. She knocked hard on the frame of the metal door. The dog started barking.

"Roger!" a smoke-stained voice bellowed from the back of the house. "Shut your damn snout!"

Callie rubbed her arms as she looked back into the street. Lights were on inside the bungalow across the way, but the house next door was boarded up, the grass in the yard so tall it looked like a desiccated corn field. A pile of shit was on the sidewalk. Callie lifted up on her toes for a better angle. Human.

She heard footsteps behind her. She thought about what she'd told Leigh—*I'll put myself in an obvious place.*

If Andrew Tenant sent someone to look for Callie, there was one obvious place to find her.

"Well fuck me in the face."

Callie turned back around.

Phil stood on the other side of the screen door. She hadn't changed since Callie was in diapers. Thin and rangy like an alley cat. Eyes rimmed dark like a startled raccoon's. Teeth sharp and fanged like a porcupine. Nose as red and distended as a menstruating baboon's ass. A baseball bat was propped against her shoulder. A cigarette dangled from her mouth. Her rheumy eyes went from Callie down to the carrier. "What's the cat called?"

"Stupid Cunt." Callie forced a smile. "Stunt for short."

Phil leveled her with a look. "You know the rule, smart ass. You can't stay at my house unless you're funding me, feeding me, or fucking me."

The three Fs. They had been raised on the rule. Callie kicked off her sneaker. The folded twenties waved like an invitation.

The bat was returned to its spot. The screen door opened. Phil grabbed the sixty bucks. She asked, "You got more in your cooch?"

"Stick your hand down there if you want."

Phil squinted as smoke curled into her eye. "I don't want none of your lesbian shit while you're staying here."

"Yes, Mother."

Tuesday

6

To her great disappointment, Callie was not afforded a moment of disorientation when she woke up in her old bedroom inside of her mother's house. Everything was instantly familiar: the caustic bite of salt in the air, the gurgle of aquarium filters, the chirping of many birds, a dog snuffling outside her locked bedroom door. She knew exactly where she was and why she was there.

The question was, how long would it take Andrew's detective to figure out the same?

From Leigh's description of Reggie Paltz, the guy would stick out in the 'hood as bad as an undercover cop. If Reggie was stupid enough to knock on her mother's front door, Phil could be relied upon to show him the thick end of her baseball bat. But Callie was fairly certain it would not go down that way. Reggie would be under strict orders to stay in the shadows. Andrew Tenant had come at Leigh straight on, but Leigh wasn't his main target. Buddy's son was not paying homage to his father's murder by wrapping cling film around his victim's heads. He was using a cheap kitchen knife, the same type of knife Callie had used to mortally wound his father.

Which meant that whatever game Andrew was playing, Callie was more than likely the prize.

She blinked up at the ceiling. Her old poster of the Spice Girls stared back, the ceiling fan protruding from between Geri

Halliwell's legs. Callie let a few lines of "Wannabe" run through her head. The great thing about being an addict was that it taught you how to compartmentalize. There was heroin, and then there was everything else in the world that didn't matter because it was not heroin.

Callie clicked her tongue in case Binx was awaiting an invitation on the other side of the cat door. When the animal did not appear, she levered herself up in the bed, feet going down to the floor as her shoulders went upright. The sudden change in orientation dropped her blood pressure. She felt dizzy and nauseous and, suddenly, her bones were itching to the marrow. She sat there, investigating the early symptoms of withdrawal. Cold sweat. Aching bowels. Pounding head. Untamed thoughts nagging her skull like a beaver gnawing on a tree.

The backpack was leaning against the wall. Callie was on her knees, on the floor, without a second thought. She made quick work of finding the syringe in her dope kit, locating the nearly full vial of methadone. The entire time she set up the shot, her heart begged with every beat *needle-needle-needle*.

Callie didn't bother to search for a vein in her arms. There was nothing left to use. She slid across the floor, sitting in front of the full-length mirror on the back of her closet door. She used her reflection to locate her femoral vein. Everything was backward, but Callie easily adapted. She watched her reflection as the needle slipped into her leg. The plunger pressed down.

The world got softer—the air, the gurgling sounds, the hard edges of the boxes scattered around the room. Callie let out a long breath as she closed her eyes. The darkness inside her eyelids turned into a plush landscape. Banana trees and dense forest peppering a mountain range. On the horizon, she saw the gorilla waiting for the methadone wave to break.

That was the problem with a maintenance dose. Callie could still feel everything, see everything, remember everything. She shook her head, and like a View-Master, she clicked to another memory.

The anatomy drawing in Linda Waleski's textbook. The common femoral vein was a blue line running alongside the red femoral artery. Veins took blood to the heart. Arteries took it away. That was why Buddy hadn't died immediately. The knife had nicked the vein. If she'd opened the artery, Buddy would've been dead long before Leigh killed him.

Callie shook a fresh image into her head.

Meowma Cass, the bottle-fed kitten Dr. Jerry was taking home with him at night. Callie had named her after Cass Elliot, who had died of a heart attack in her sleep. The opposite of a Cobain, who'd put a shotgun under his chin and pulled the trigger. His suicide note had ended with a beautiful tribute to his daughter—

For her life which will be so much happier without me. I LOVE YOU. I LOVE YOU!

Callie heard a scraping noise.

Her eyelids slowly peeled open. Binx was outside the window, clearly indignant to find it closed. Callie pushed herself up from the floor. Her body ached with every step. She scratched at the glass, letting Binx know she was going as fast as she could. He gamboled about the metal security bars like a dressage horse, if dressage horses were not homicidal adrenaline junkies. There was a pin lock on the window, a long bolt that kept the sash from opening. Callie had to edge it out with her fingernails while Binx stared at her like she was a moron.

"Forgive me, sir." Callie gave his silky back some long pets. He pressed his head up under her chin because cats were social groomers. "Did the wicked witch let you outside?"

Binx told no tales, but Callie knew that Phil had probably fed, watered, and brushed him before offering him the choice of either the couch, a fluffy chair, or the door. The scrawny old bitch would throw her body in front of a bus to save a chipmunk, but her children were on their own.

Not that Phil was that ancient. She'd been fifteen years old when Leigh was born, then nineteen when Callie came along. There had been a constant rotation of boyfriends and husbands, but Phil had told the girls that their father had died during a military training exercise.

Nick Bradshaw had been a radio intercept officer who'd flown with his best friend, a Navy fighter pilot named Pete Mitchell. One day, they had gotten on the wrong side of a Russian MiG during a training exercise. Bradshaw was killed after a flame-out sent their jet into a flat spin. Which was horrifying to think about, but also hilarious if you knew that Pete Mitchell was called Maverick and Bradshaw was Goose and that was basically the first half of *Top Gun*.

Still, Callie found it preferable to the truth, which probably involved Phil passing out after drinking too much. Both Callie and Leigh took it on faith that they would never learn the true story. Their mother was a master of subterfuge. Phil wasn't even her real name. Her birth certificate and her criminal record officially listed her as Sandra Jean Santiago, a convicted felon who collected rent for slumlords around Lake Point. The felony meant Phil wasn't legally allowed to carry a gun, so she carried a baseball bat—she said for protection, but it was clearly for enforcement. The Louisville Slugger was signed by Phil Rizzuto. That's where her nickname had come from. Nobody wanted to get on the bad side of Phil.

Binx shook off Callie's hand as he jumped down. She started to close the window, but a flash of light caught her eye. She felt a flicker of panic burn at the methadone. She looked across the street. The pile of shit was still festering on the sidewalk, but the light had flashed from the direction of the boarded-up house.

Or had it?

Callie rubbed her eyes as if she could manually adjust the focus. There were cars lining the road, trucks and old sedans with the mufflers attached by clothes hangers alongside the BMWs and Mercedes favored by the drug dealers. Maybe the sunlight had hit a mirror or a piece of metal. There could be broken crack pipes or pieces of foil in the yard. Callie squinted at the tall grass, trying to figure out what she'd seen. Probably an animal. Maybe a camera lens.

White dude. Nice car.

Binx arched against her leg. Callie put her hand to her chest. Her heart was beating hard enough to feel the thump. She studied each boarded-up window and door to the house until her eyes watered. Was the methadone fucking her up more than usual? Was she being paranoid?

Did it matter?

Callie closed the window. The pin went back into the sash. She found her jeans, slid on her sneakers. She shoved her ill-gotten gains into her backpack. Her dope kit and the methadone went under the mattress. She would have to hit Stewart Avenue before lunchtime. She needed to sell the rest of this shit so she wasn't carrying if the police stopped her. She turned to leave, but couldn't stop herself from looking out the window again.

Her eyes squinted. She tried to recreate the memory of the flash of light. Her imagination filled in the details. A private eye with a long, telescoping lens on his professional-looking camera. The click of the shutter as he captured Callie in her private moments. Reggie Paltz would develop the photos, take them back to Andrew. Would they both look at her images the way Buddy had? Would the two men use them somehow, some way, that Callie didn't want to know about?

A loud bang sent her heart into her throat. Binx had knocked over one of the boxes that Phil had stacked around the room. Newspapers spilled out, magazine articles, crazy shit that Phil had printed from the internet. Her mother was a rabid conspiracy theorist. And Callie said that as someone who understood that rabies was a virtually fatal virus that caused anxiety, confusion, hyperactivity, hallucinations, insomnia, paranoia, and a fear of drinking fluids.

With the exception of alcohol.

Callie went to the door, which was padlocked from the inside. She dug the key out of her pocket. A handful of coins came with it. Leigh's change from McDonald's last night. Callie stared at the two dimes and three quarters, but her attention was elsewhere. She had to fight the urge to stand at the window again. Instead, she closed her eyes, pressed her head against the door, and tried to convince herself that she was on a bad trip.

Reality edged its way back in.

If Andrew's private eye was watching her from the boarded-up house, wasn't that exactly what Callie wanted? Reggie wouldn't need to go to the motel and bribe Trap or interrogate Crackhead Sammy. He would not find out that she was working at Dr. Jerry's. He would not talk to her customers on Stewart Avenue. He would not tap his friends in the police force to maybe look into her and maybe find out what she'd been up to. His investigation would stop right at Phil's doorstep.

Callie opened her eyes. The coins went back into her pocket. She jammed the key into the lock and twisted it open. Binx scooted up the hallway en route to a pressing appointment. Callie closed the door, put the padlock on the outside. She clicked it shut, then pulled on the hasp to double check that her mother couldn't break into her room.

It was like being a kid again.

The gurgle of saltwater aquarium filters got louder as she made her way up the hall. Leigh's bedroom had been turned into Sea World. Dark blue walls. Light blue ceiling. A beanbag chair with Phil's stringy outline was in the center of the room, offering a panoramic view of tangs, clownfish, firefish, damselfish, coral beauties, swimming through hidden treasures and sunken pirate ships. The smell of pot draped down from the ceiling. Phil liked to get stoned in the dark, wet room, lolled across the beanbag chair like a tongue.

Callie checked to make sure her mother wasn't nearby before going into the room. She peeled back a corner of blue foil covering the window. She knelt down so she could peer out at the boarded-up house. The angle was better from Leigh's room, less conspicuous. Callie could see a piece of plywood had been pulled away from one of the front windows, revealing an opening large enough for a man to crawl through.

"Well," Callie said to herself. She couldn't recall if the plywood had been in that position the night before. Asking Phil would probably send her mother into a delusional rage.

She slid her phone out of her back pocket and took a photo of the house. Callie used her fingers to zoom in on the front window. The plywood had splintered when it was pulled back. There was no way of telling when it had happened short of getting a degree in forensic wood splintering.

Should she call Leigh?

Callie played out the possible conversation, the might-have-beens and could've-beens and all the other half-baked theories that would wind up Leigh's cymbal-clanging inner monkey. Her sister was meeting with Andrew this afternoon. Leigh's boss would be there. She would have to walk a razor's edge. Calling her now, passing on what could be a methadone delusion, seemed like a really bad idea.

The phone returned to her pocket. She pressed the edge of the foil back down over the window. She walked into the living room, where the menagerie continued. Roger stuck his head up from the couch and barked. There was a new dog beside him, another terrier mix, who gave exactly zero fucks when Callie patted his scruffy head. She smelled bird shit, though Phil was religious about cleaning out the three large cages that gave a dozen budgies pride of place in the dining room. Callie gathered by the burn of cigarette smoke that Phil had taken up her position in the kitchen. No matter how well her mother tended to her beloved animals, every single creature living in this goddam house was going to die from secondhand smoke.

"Tell your cat to leave my birds alone," Phil hollered from the kitchen. "He'll end up with his skinny ass sleeping outside if he even thinks about touching one."

"Stupid Cunt . . ." Callie let the words hang for a few seconds ". . . is afraid of birds. They're more likely to hurt him than the other way around."

"Stupid Cunt sounds like a girl's name."

"Well, you tell him that. I can't get through to him." Callie plastered on a smile as she walked into the kitchen. "Good morning, Mother."

Phil snorted. She was sitting at the kitchen table with a plate of bacon and eggs in front of her, a cigarette in her mouth, and her eyes glued to the giant iMac computer that took up half the table. Her mother looked the same as she always did in the morning hours. Last night's make-up was sloppy on her face, mascara clumped, eyeliner smeared, blush and foundation scratched by her pillow. How this bitch wasn't a walking case of pink eye was anyone's guess.

Phil said, "I guess you're laying off the dope. You're getting fat again."

Callie sat down. She wasn't hungry, but she reached for the plate.

Phil slapped her hand away. "You paid for rent, not food."

Callie took the coins out of her pocket and slapped them onto the table.

Phil eyed them suspiciously. She knew where Callie kept her money. "That come out of your pussy?"

"Put it in your mouth and find out."

Callie didn't see the punch coming until Phil's fist was a few inches from her head.

She pivoted too late, getting clipped above the ear as she toppled out of the chair at an almost comically slow pace. The comedy stopped when her head cracked against the floor. The pain was breathtaking. She was too winded to do anything but watch Phil stand over her.

"What the hell, I barely tapped you." Her mother shook her head. "Fucking junkie."

"Crazy drunk bitch."

"At least I can keep a roof over my head."

Callie relented. "Fair."

Phil stepped over her as she left the room.

Callie stared up at the ceiling, her eyes fixed like an owl's. Her ears became alert to the sounds of the house. Gurgling, tweeting, barking. The bathroom door slammed shut. Phil would be in there for at least half an hour. She would shower, slather on her make-up, dress herself up, then sit back down at the table and read her conspiracy bullshit until the Jewish cabal turned everyone infertile and the world ceased to exist.

Pushing herself up from the floor took more strength than Callie had anticipated. Her arms were shaking. The shock was still working its way through her body. She coughed from the remnants of smoke curling around the room.

Phil had stubbed out her cigarette in the eggs.

Callie sat in her mother's chair and started on the bacon. She clicked through the tabs on the computer. Deep state. Hugo Chavez. Child slavery. Child neglect. Rich people drinking the blood of infants. Infants being sold for food. For a woman whose own daughter was literally molested by a pedophile, Phil had come late to the anti-pedophile movement.

Roger's snout pushed at her bare ankle. Callie picked around Phil's crushed cigarette, finding pieces of egg to drop on the floor. Roger hoovered them up. New Dog hot-stepped into the kitchen.

He gave her the kind of persnickety look you would expect from a half terrier.

She told him, "Our safe word is onomatopoeia."

New Dog was more interested in the eggs.

Callie looked at the time. She couldn't put this off any longer. She strained her ears, making sure Phil was still in the bathroom. When Callie was satisfied she wasn't going to get caught, she turned to her mother's computer, selected *incognito* on a new browser window, and typed in TENANT AUTOMOTIVE.

The search returned 704,000 results, which only made sense when you scrolled down and saw that sites like Yelp, DealerRate, CarMax, Facebook, and the Better Business Bureau had all paid for placement.

She selected the main site for Tenant Automotive Group. Thirty-eight locations. BMW, Mercedes, Range Rover, Honda, Mini. They did a little bit of everything, but mostly stuck to high-end vehicles. Callie read through the brief history of the dealership's growth—*From One Small Ford Dealership on Peachtree to Branches All Over the Southeast!* There was a line drawing of a tree showing the short succession: Gregory Sr. to Greg Jr. to Linda Tenant.

The mouse found its way to Linda's name. Callie clicked. A slick-looking photo popped up. Linda's hair was short and frosted, probably courtesy of dropping a godzillion bucks at a tony hair salon. She sat at a Darth Vader-looking desk with a shiny red Ferrari behind her. Papers were stacked neatly to her left and right to impart the message that she was a lady who did business. Her hands were clasped together in front of her. No wedding ring because she was married to the job. The collar of her white Izod polo was popped. A choker of pearls lay like gerbil orthodontia around her suntanned neck. Callie imagined Linda was wearing acid-washed jeans and white Reebok high-tops because who wouldn't fully embrace their Brooke Shields with that kind of money?

The best part was Linda's Miss America Pageant bio. Nothing about living in the 'hood with her rapist pedophile husband. Callie smiled at the selective editing—

Linda Tenant graduated from the Georgia Baptist College of

154

*ursing with a Bachelor of Science in nursing. She worked for
*veral years at Southern Regional Medical Center before joining
*e family business. She volunteers with the American Red Cross
*d continues to lend her medical/managerial expertise to the
ity of Atlanta's Covid-19 advisory panel.

Callie studied the photograph. Linda's face hadn't changed
*uch, except the way that everyone's face had changed in the
*st twenty-three years, which was to say that the important stuff
*d slid a bit lower. The most overriding emotion Callie felt when
*e looked at Linda was love. She had worshipped the woman.
*nda was kind and caring and she had always made it clear that
*er number one priority was her son. Not for the first or last
*me, Callie wondered how different her life would've been if
*nda Waleski had been her mother.

Roger snorted underneath the table. Callie dropped a tiny piece
*f bacon on the floor. Then another piece because New Dog
*norted, too.

She found a map on the site, then navigated to the Mercedes
*ealership in Buckhead. She clicked on *Meet Our Sales Team!*

Callie sat back in the chair. There were eight photos in two
*ws of four, all but one a man. At first, she didn't read the
*ames. She studied each man's headshot, looking for signs of
*nda or Buddy. Her eyes went back and forth, row by row,
*awing a blank. Finally, she relented and identified Andrew
*enant in the second photo from the top. His Miss America
*geant bio was even better than Linda's.

*Andrew loves animals and hiking in the great outdoors. He
*lunteers most of his weekends at DeKalb's no-kill shelter. An
*id reader, Andrew enjoys the fantasy novels of Ursula K. Le
uin and the feminist essays of Mary Wollstonecraft.

Callie gave him little credit for the thick layer of bullshit. He
*ould've mentioned *Hamlet*, because shethinks the rapist doth
*otest too much.

If there was none of Linda or Buddy in Andrew's face, she saw
*bsolutely no sign of Trevor, either. In fact, Andrew was wholly
*nremarkable compared to his fellow frat-boy-attractive car
*ealers. Strong jawline, neatly combed hair, closely shaved face.
*is dark blue suit was the only thing that gave him away. Callie

could tell by the stitching around the lapels that an actual human being had sewn it. His shirt looked equally expensive—light blue with stripes just a shade darker. The tie set it off, a vivid royal blue that brought out the color of his eyes.

His sandy hair was the only attribute he shared with his father. Andrew had the same thinning at the temples, half-scoops taken out of his hairline. Callie could remember how embarrassed Buddy had been about losing his hair. *I'm just an old man little doll why do you want anything to do with me what do you see in me come on tell me I really wanna know.*

Safety.

Buddy had never sucker-punched her at the kitchen table. At least not until the end.

So.

They had argued a lot, mostly about Callie wanting to spend more time with him. Which was crazy because, almost from the beginning, she had hated spending time with him. And yet there she was, telling him she was going to quit school and he was going to leave Linda and happily-ever-after blah-blah-blah. Buddy would laugh and give her money and then eventually, sometimes he would take her to hotels. Nice ones at first, before everything turned seedy. They ordered room service, which was Callie's favorite part. Then, he would get down on his knees and take his time pleasing her. Buddy was so much bigger than Callie that everything else he did hurt.

And toward the end, the everything else was all that he had wanted to do, and he always wanted to do it on the couch. *Stop crying I'm almost there Jesus Christ you feel so good I can't stop baby girl please don't make me stop.*

The bathroom door banged open. Phil hacked out a wet hair ball of a cough. Her Doc Martens clomped up the hallway. Callie closed Andrew's bio page. She was back in her chair when Phil returned to the kitchen.

"What've you been up to?" Phil demanded. She'd plastered on her war paint, a goth version of Mrs. Danvers if Mrs. Danvers favored spiked dog collars and had a nose piercing and instead of loving Rebecca had scuttled the uppity bitch's boat during an alcohol-fueled bender.

Callie asked, "What is anybody ever up to?"

"Jesus, you're so fucking squirrelly."

Callie wondered if her mother's Sid Vicious T-shirt was meant to be a celebration of a suicidal heroin addict or if she just liked the anarchy symbol in the background. "Awesome shirt, Mom."

Phil ignored the compliment as she jerked open the fridge. She took out a pitcher of micheladas, which was an ungodly mixture of salt, powdered chicken bouillon, a dash of Worcestershire, a shot of lemon juice, a bottle of Clamato, and two ice-cold bottles of Dos Equis beer.

Callie watched her pour the concoction into a Thermos. "Is it collection day?"

"One of us has to work." Phil took a generous sip straight from the pitcher. "What about you?"

Callie had $140 of Leigh's money in her backpack. She could save it or she could use it to fund her methadone habit instead of stealing from Dr. Jerry or she could just stick it in his cash box and let him think that everybody in the neighborhood had stocked up on heartworm medication this week because the other option—sticking it into her veins—was on the back burner for now.

She told Phil, "I thought I'd do a little of this, then, if I still have time, a little of that."

Phil scowled, screwing the top onto the Thermos. "You hear from your sister lately?"

"Nope."

"She's got all that money. Do you think I ever see any of it?" Phil took another swig from the pitcher before putting it back in the fridge. "What're you doing for cash?"

"The police would call it trafficking."

"You get caught with that shit in my house, I'll flip on you so fast your head will spin."

"I know."

"It's for your own good, asshole. Harleigh needs to stop bailing you out. Make you pay the consequences of your actions."

"I think you mean 'suffer,'" Callie said. "You suffer the consequences of your own actions."

"Whatever." Phil grabbed a bag of dog kibble out of the pantry.

"She has a daughter, you know. Kid has to be twenty by now and I've never even met her. Have you?"

Callie said, "I heard they're handing out disability for Covid survivors. Maybe I'll try to sign up."

"Bunch of bullshit." Phil ripped open the bag with her teeth. "I ain't never met nobody who died from that."

"I've never met anyone who died of lung cancer." Callie shrugged. "Maybe it doesn't exist, either."

"Maybe." Phil started mumbling to herself as she measured out food into two bowls. The dogs were getting antsy for breakfast. New Dog's collar jingled as he pranced alongside Roger. "Dammit, Brock, what did I tell you about manners?"

Callie had to admit Brock was a good name for the half terrier. He looked like a banker.

"Poor little thing gets constipated." Phil mixed a teaspoon of olive oil into the dry food. "Do you remember how backed up Harleigh used to get? Had to take her to the hospital. Two Benjamins for some genius doctor to tell me she had a retarded colon."

"That's really funny, Mom." Who didn't find it hilarious that an eight-year-old messed up her colon because she was too terrified to go to the bathroom in her own house? "Tell me another story."

"I'll tell you a fucking story."

Callie listened to the needle scratch along the same old record. *I did the best I could with you two. You don't know how hard it is to be a single mother. It wasn't all miserable you ungrateful bitch. Remember that time when I—and then we—and then I—*

That was how it was with abusive parents. They only remembered the good times and you only remembered the bad.

Phil skipped on to another track. Callie stared at the back of the iMac. She should've looked up the private detective instead of strolling down memory lane, but seeing Reggie Paltz online would somehow make him real in her life, and the boarded-up house and the flash of light would be real, too.

"How about that?" Phil stabbed her finger into the counter. "Who took two different buses to pick up your sister from juvie?"

"You did," Callie answered, but only to break Phil's momentum

158

Hey, is someone living in that abandoned house across the street?"

Phil's head cocked to the side. "Did you see someone in there?"

"I don't know," Callie said, because the best way to scratch Phil's crazy was to show indecision. "It's probably my imagination. I saw one of the boards was pulled back. But there was a flash of light or something?"

"Fucking crackheads." Phil banged the bowls onto the floor before she shot out of the kitchen. Callie followed her to the front of the house. The bat by the door swung up onto Phil's shoulder as she kicked open the metal screen.

Callie stood at the window watching her mother storm toward the boarded-up house.

"Cocksucker!" Phil bellowed, bolting up the front walk. "Did you shit on my sidewalk?"

"Damn," Callie mumbled as Phil pounded the thin plywood covering the door. She hoped like hell nobody was stupid enough to call the police.

"Come out!" Phil turned the Louisville Slugger into a battering ram. "You fucking shitter!"

Callie cringed at the *crack* of wood against wood. This was the problem with weaponizing Phil. You couldn't control the explosion.

"Get the fuck out of there!" Phil rammed the bat again. This time, the plywood splintered. She yanked back the bat, and the rotted wood came off with it. "Gotcha!"

Callie didn't know exactly what Phil had caught. The flash of light could've been just that—a flash of light. Maybe the methadone had hit Callie the wrong way. Maybe she'd shot up too much or too little. Maybe she should stop Phil from attacking some poor houseless man whose only crime was seeking shelter.

Too late. She saw her mother disappear into the house.

Callie's hand went to her mouth. There was another flash. Not light this time, but motion. It came from the side of the house. A piece of plywood bent up from one of the windows like a mouth opening. A man was disgorged into the tall grass. Seconds later, he was on his feet, shoulders hunched as he made his way across the yard. He climbed over a rusted chain-link fence. He was gripping a professional-looking camera around the telescoping lens like he was strangling it by the neck.

"Motherfucker!" Phil bellowed from inside.

Callie's eyes followed the camera until it disappeared into another yard. What would be on the memory card? How close had the man gotten to her window? Had he taken photographs of her sleeping in bed? Had he managed to capture Callie sitting in front of the mirror sticking a needle into her leg?

Her hand cupped her neck. Beneath her fingers and thumb, the blood pulsed in her jugulars. She could feel the gorilla's claw digging into her skin. The rake of the telephone cord gouging her back. His hot breath in her ear. The pressure of him fingering up her spine. Callie closed her eyes, thought about falling back into the gorilla, surrendering to the inevitable.

Instead, she found her backpack and left her mother's house through the kitchen door.

7

eigh hadn't fallen asleep until two this morning, then her alarm
ad gone off at four. She was punch-drunk from yesterday's
alium spree and the enormous stress that had caused her to
reak down and take it. Several cups of coffee had ramped up
er jitters and done nothing for her clarity. It was almost noon
nd her brain felt like a Jell-O mold packed with buckshot.

Somehow, through it all, she had managed to come up with a
orking Andrew Hypothesis:

He knew about Buddy's camera behind the bar because, even
s a kid, he'd been a nosey shit who sneaked through your things.
le knew about the femoral artery because he'd seen Callie worrying
ver the anatomical drawing in the textbook. Like Leigh, her sister
aned toward the obsessive compulsive. She could easily imagine
allie sitting at the kitchen table tracing the artery until her finger
abbed a blister. Andrew would've been sitting beside her because
ndrew was always where you didn't want him to be. He'd stored
oth facts into his sick, twisted brain and then somehow, years
ter, he'd put it all together.

That was the only explanation that made sense. If Andrew
ally knew what had happened that night, he would know that
e knife hadn't actually killed his father.

Leigh had.

What she needed to do right now was find a way to throw
ndrew Tenant's case while Cole Bradley was looking over her
oulder. Leigh had barely made a dent in the volumes of paper-
ork attached to the looming trial. Andrew's files were splayed
cross her desk, overflowing from boxes couriered over by Octavia

161

Bacca. Two associates were in the process of compiling an index cross-referencing Octavia's work with the mountains of horseshit that the prosecutor had provided during discovery. Liz, Leigh's assistant, had taken over a conference room to spread out everything on the floor so she could develop a timeline that backed up the footage that Reggie Paltz had spliced together on his laptop.

And still, there was always more work to be done. Even though Cole Bradley had cleared the decks so Leigh could focus on Andrew's case, that didn't mean her calendar was completely open. She had to finish filing motions and compose interrogatories, review documents for discovery, call clients, schedule depositions, push back Zoom and court appearances, research case law and on top of everything else, she had to worry about her sister dangling herself as bait in front of a psychopath with a well documented history of violently assaulting women.

Callie had been right about one thing last night. Leigh had to stop flailing around like a helpless bitch. It was about time she flexed her hard-earned right to play by rich people rules. She had graduated summa cum laude from Northwestern. She worked at a white-shoe firm and had clocked in nearly two thousand hours of billing in the last year. She was married to one of the most admired men in his field. She had a beautiful daughter. Her reputation was spotless.

Andrew Tenant was credibly accused of kidnapping, raping, beating, and sodomizing a woman.

Who were they going to believe?

Leigh looked at the time. Three more hours before she was expected in Cole Bradley's office. Andrew would be waiting for her. Leigh would have to come fully armed, ready for whatever game he was going to play.

She rubbed her temples as she looked down at the first responding officer's statement.

Female victim was handcuffed to picnic table in center of open-air pavilion located in . . .

Leigh's vision doubled on the rest of the paragraph. She tried to refocus her eyes by looking out the glass wall that separated her rarefied kind from the first-year associates. There was no breathtaking view of the downtown skyline, just a windowless cubicle farm that spread like prison bars across the entire floor. Plexiglas barriers kept the occupants from breathing on each other, but masks were still required. Janitors came through once an hour to sanitize the surfaces. All of the baby lawyers worked off hot desks, which meant they took whichever desk was available when they arrived. And since they were baby lawyers, most of them arrived at six in the morning and worked in the dark until the overhead lights came on at seven. If they had been surprised to see Leigh had beaten them into the office, they were too weary to show it.

She checked her personal phone, though she knew Callie hadn't texted because Callie wasn't going to text until Leigh was so tense that her head was about to explode.

As expected, there was nothing from her sister, but Leigh's heart did a funny little flip when she saw a notification on the screen. Maddy had posted a video. Leigh watched her daughter lip-synching around Walter's kitchen as Tim Tam, their chocolate Lab, played unwitting backup.

Leigh strained to follow the lyrics, desperate for cues on how to post a response that didn't get an eye-roll or, worse, completely ignored. At least she was able to recognize Ariana Grande. She scrolled to the description, but 34+35 made absolutely no sense. She had watched the video two more times before her mind performed the simple addition and she realized what the song was really about.

"Oh for the love of—" She snatched up her desk phone. She started to punch in Walter's number, but there was no way to talk to Walter without telling him that she had seen Callie.

The phone dropped back into the cradle. Walter knew everything about Leigh except for the one thing that mattered the most. She had told him Callie had been molested, but the details had stopped there. Leigh wasn't going to give Walter a name to look up on the internet or a stray comment that would make him start wondering what had really happened all those years ago. She had held back the information not because she didn't trust Walter, or because she was worried it would make him love her less. She did not want to burden her gentle husband, her precious daughter's father, with the weight of her guilt.

Liz knocked on the glass door. She was wearing a fuchsia mask that matched the flowers on her jumpsuit. Leigh put on her mask before waving her in.

There was never any preamble with Liz. She said, "I've moved the Johnson depo by two weeks. The judge on the Bryant case wants your response to the motion by six on Friday. I've put Dr. Unger on the sixteenth; it's updated in your Outlook. You're due in Bradley's office in three hours. I'll bring you lunch, just let me know if you want a salad or a sandwich. You'll need your heels for Bradley. They're in the closet."

"Sandwich." Leigh had written the details on her notepad as Liz rattled them off. "Did you read the incident reports about Andrew's ankle monitor?"

Liz shook her head. "What's up?"

"He's had four separate issues in the last two months. Anything from the GPS going off-line to the fiber optic cable in the strap shorting out. Each time the alarm went off, he called the probation office, but you know how bad things are right now. Anywhere between three and five hours passed before an officer was dispatched to reset the system."

"Was there any evidence of tampering?"

"Not that the officer reported."

"Three to five hours." Liz seemed to understand the problem. An argument could be made that Andrew was testing the response time. Not to mention that, for three to five hours, his whereabouts were likely unknown.

Liz said, "I'll see what I can find out."

Leigh wasn't finished. "Did you speak to Reggie Paltz yesterday?"

"I gave him the encryption key to upload his files onto our server," she said. "Should I log in for you on your desktop?"

"I've got it, thanks." Leigh appreciated the way she had worded the offer, leaving out *you ancient dinosaur.* "Did Paltz ask any questions about me?"

"Lots, but he was mostly confirming," Liz said. "Where you went to school, how long you worked at Legal Aid, how long you were on your own. When you started working here. I told him to go to the website if he wanted your CV."

Leigh had never once considered that she was on the company website. "What did you think about him?"

"Work-wise, he's pretty damn good," Liz said. "I read his background profile on Tenant. Very thorough, doesn't look like there are any skeletons, but I can backstop it with one of our usual investigators if you want?"

"I'll ask the client." Leigh was perfectly fine with letting the prosecutor surprise her with a dark detail from Andrew's past during the trial. "But what about in general terms? How did Paltz come across to you?"

"Kind of a dick, but okay-looking." Liz smiled. "He's got a website, too."

Another technological blindspot on Leigh's part. "I want you to put him on the Stoudt case. He's willing to travel, but keep him on a tight leash. I don't want him padding the bill."

"He's already doing it, judging by the invoices Octavia sent over." Liz tapped one of the boxes with her hip. "I went through these last night. Paltz doesn't take a dump without charging a quarter for the extra flush. His timeline is an illustration of five-star Yelp reviews."

"Let him know we're watching."

Liz was already out the door by the time Leigh took off her mask and woke up her computer. Bradley, Canfield & Marks had exactly the sort of boring website you'd expect. The thick borders were red and black in honor of UGA. Times Roman font. The only embellishment was the curly ampersand.

Appropriately, Leigh found her name under LAWYERS. The photo was the same as the one on her employee badge, which was mildly embarrassing. She was listed as *of counsel*, a polite way of saying she was not a partner but also not an associate.

Leigh scrolled past the first paragraph, reading that she had appeared before State and Superior Courts and specialized in litigating DUI, theft, fraud, high-net-worth divorce, and white-collar defense. The *Atlanta INtown* article was hyperlinked for anyone seeking a urine law specialist. The next paragraph listed her awards, pro bono work, various speaking engagements, and articles she had written in the early days of her career when that kind of thing had really mattered. She slipped down to the last line—*Mrs. Collier enjoys spending time with her husband and their daughter.*

Leigh tapped her finger on the mouse. She was going to have to give the private investigator's story the benefit of the doubt. It seemed plausible that Reggie had shown Andrew the *INtown* article featuring Leigh's photo and that Andrew had recognized Leigh's face. It also seemed likely that Andrew would have had Reggie do a background check on Leigh before hiring her. Actually, Reggie was probably more dangerous at this point, because he struck Leigh as the type of investigator who was good at digging up skeletons.

Which was why she was going to get Reggie out of the state. Jasper Stoudt, her divorce client's cheating husband, was about to take his mistress on a ten-day fly-fishing trip to Montana. Leigh imagined Reggie would be too busy ordering catfish tacos off of the room service menu to worry about Andrew Tenant.

For her part, Leigh was doing enough worrying about Andrew for both of them. She bolstered herself by mentally bulletpointing Callie's speech last night.

- If Andrew had proof of the murder, then he would've shown it to the police.
- If Andrew had one of Buddy's videos, all it would show was that his father was a pedophile.
- If Andrew had put together the clues because Callie couldn't stop tracing a damn artery on a diagram of a leg, then so what? Even Nancy Drew had to show some actual evidence.
- No one had ever found Buddy Waleski's body—or the pieces of his body. There was no blood evidence on the steak knife. There was no forensic evidence taken from the Waleski house. There was no forensic evidence found in Buddy's burned-out Corvette.
- There were more than likely no official documents regarding Callie's beating, and certainly nothing that tied it to Buddy's disappearance.
- No one had ever asked Leigh about the $82,000 she had used to help pay her way through law school. Before 9/11, nobody was asking questions about piles of cash. Even with

166

Buddy's ill-gotten gains, Leigh had worked as a waitress and a bartender and a delivery driver and a hotel room cleaner and even lived out of her car to save money. It wasn't until Walter had found her nesting in the stacks of the Gary Library and invited her to sleep on his couch that Leigh had ever had a sense of permanency.

Maddy. Walter. Callie.

She had to keep her eye on what was important. Without them, Leigh would've already taken the Glock and ended Andrew's miserable life. Despite evidence to the contrary, she had never thought of herself as a murderer, but she was damn sure capable of pre-emptive self-defense.

There was a quick knock before the door opened. Jacob Gaddy, one of the associates, was balancing a sandwich and a can of ginger ale on two file boxes. He set them down on the floor, telling Leigh, "I confirmed the tox screen was negative. You'll find the indexes on top of the boxes. The search of the house turned up some really high-end, artistic S&M photos framed in one of the back hallways, but nothing in the bedroom."

Leigh wasn't worried about the photos. *Fifty Shades* had taken the shock away from millions of housewives around the world. She waited for Jacob to put her lunch down on the edge of her desk. She knew why he had volunteered to play waiter. She would need a second chair at the defense table, and the associates would go into a cage match if it came to that.

She decided to put him out of his misery. "You'll be my second. Make sure you know the case backward and forward. No mistakes."

"Yes ma—" He caught himself. "Thank you."

Leigh banished the almost *ma'am* from her mind. She couldn't suspend her review of Andrew's files any longer. She took a sip of ginger ale. She finished the sandwich as she flipped through the pages of notes she'd made so far. With any case, she always searched for weak spots that the prosecutor could exploit, but now she was looking to see how she could use those weak spots to build a shadow case that would send Andrew away for the rest of his life.

All while keeping herself and Callie free.

167

She had argued against the prosecutor before. Dante Carmichael approached his job with a front-runner's sense of entitlement. He liked to brag about his win/loss record, but it was easy to brag about your wins when you only ever tried cases you were ninety-nine percent certain would go your way. This was the sole reason that so many rape cases were not prosecuted. In matters of he said/she said, jurors were inclined to believe a man was telling the truth and a woman was looking for attention. Dante's plea deals were more like extortion to keep his record untarnished. Everyone who worked at the courthouse had a nickname, and Deal 'Em Down Dante had come by his honestly.

Leigh paged back through the official correspondences. Dante had proffered an incredibly generous deal in April of last year, a month after Andrew's arrest. She was loath to agree with Reggie Paltz, but her gut was telling her that Dante Carmichael had laid a trap. Once Andrew took a plea on the Karlsen assault, he'd be linked by MO to the three others. If Leigh was careful, if she was clever, if she was lucky, she would find an alternate way to push Andrew into that trap.

By habit, she picked up her pen. Then she put it back down. Strategizing her potential crimes on paper was never a good idea. Leigh mentally ran through her options, trying to find different ways to screw up while holding herself blameless.

Andrew wasn't her only obstacle. Cole Bradley had forgotten more about the law than Leigh had ever learned. If he thought she was throwing the case, firing would be the least of her worries. The timing was also an issue. Normally, Leigh had months if not a full year to prepare for a criminal trial. And that was when she was honestly defending her client. Now, she had six days to become intimately familiar with the crime scene photos, forensic reports, timelines, witness statements, police incident reports, medical reports, rape-kit analysis, and the heartbreaking victim's statement, which had also been recorded on camera.

The video was the reason Leigh kept letting herself get distracted. She could run dozens of strategies on her shadow case against Andrew Tenant, but every single option would require her to aggressively question his victim. As a defense attorney, it wasn't just expected of her, it was required. Tammy Karlsen had been violently attacked and raped, but those physical scars would pale in comparison to the emotional destruction she would undergo at Leigh's hands.

In Georgia, as in the majority of states, criminal cases did not allow for depositions except under extenuating circumstances. The first time that Leigh would speak to Tammy Karlsen would be during the victim's cross-examination. At that moment, Tammy would represent the top piece of a very stable pyramid that Dante Carmichael would construct to support her testimony. The base would consist of a substantial cast of credible witnesses: police officers, medics, nurses, doctors, various experts, and the dog walker who had found Tammy handcuffed to the picnic table in the park. They would all give the jury a rock-solid reason to believe every word that came out of Tammy's mouth.

Then Leigh would be expected to take a sledgehammer and knock the pyramid down.

BC&M spent a great deal of money finding out what motivated the average juror. They hired specialists and even brought in consultants on some of the higher-profile cases. Leigh had been privy to their work product. She knew that in rape trials, juror comments could run from insulting to demoralizing. If a victim was high or drunk at the time of the assault, then what did she think would happen? If she was angry or defiant on the stand, they didn't like her attitude. If she cried too much or cried too little, they wondered if she was making it up. If the victim was overweight, then maybe she had been desperate and led the man on. If she was too beautiful, then maybe she was stuck-up and deserved what she had gotten.

Whether or not Tammy Karlsen would be able to thread the needle was unknowable. Everything Leigh knew about the victim had come from crime scene photos and statements. Tammy was thirty-one years old. She was a regional manager at a telecom company. She'd never been married, had no children, and lived in a condo she owned in Brookhaven, an area that abutted downtown Buckhead.

On February 2, 2020, she had been violently raped and left handcuffed to a picnic table inside an open pavilion located in a City of Atlanta public park.

Leigh stood up from her desk. She closed the blinds on the windows and door. She sat back down. She turned to a fresh page in her legal pad. She tapped open the recording from Tammy Karlsen's official interview and pressed play.

The woman had been found nude so, in the video, she was wearing hospital scrubs. She sat in a police interview room that was clearly meant for children. The couches were low and colorful, with beanbag chairs and a play table filled with puzzles and toys. This was what passed for a non-threatening environment for a rape victim: stick her in a room for children to constantly remind her that not only had she been raped, she could also be pregnant.

Tammy was seated on a red couch with her hands clasped between her knees. Leigh knew from the notes that Tammy was still bleeding at the time of the interview. She had been given a pad at the hospital, but, eventually, a surgeon had been called in to repair the internal injuries from the Coke bottle.

The video captured the woman rocking back and forth, trying to soothe herself. A female police officer stood with her back to the wall on the opposite side of the room. Protocol required that the victim not be left alone. This wasn't to make her feel safe. The officer was on suicide watch.

A few seconds passed before the door opened and a man walked in. He was tall and imposing, with gray hair and a neatly trimmed beard. Probably mid-fifties, with a Glock on the thick leather belt that reined in his big belly.

His appearance gave Leigh pause. Women tended to do these interviews because they made more empathetic witnesses on the stand. Leigh could still remember cross-examining a male detective who had confidently stated that he always knew a woman was lying about an assault if she didn't want him in the room. He had never considered that a woman who had been raped by a man would not want to be alone with another man.

It was 2020. Why had they sent in this bear of a detective?

Leigh stopped the video. She clicked back through the incident reports to find the first detective on scene. Her memory was that the primary investigator was a woman. She checked the list, then the incident statements, to verify that Detective Barbara Klieg was the officer in charge. Leigh searched the other reports for a possible ID on the man in the video, then rolled her eyes because all she had to do was press play.

He said, "Ms. Karlsen, I'm Detective Sean Burke. I work with the Atlanta Police Department."

Leigh wrote down the name and underlined it. The *with* made her think that he was a consultant, not an employee. She would need to know what cases Burke had worked on, how many successful prosecutions he'd been a part of, how many citations or warnings were in his file, how many lawsuits settled, how he behaved on the witness stand, what weak points had been opened up by other defense attorneys.

Burke asked, "Is it okay with you if I sit down over here?"

Tammy nodded, her eyes on the floor.

Leigh watched Burke move to a straight-backed wooden chair across from Tammy. He was not slow, but he was deliberate. He wasn't taking up all the oxygen in the room. He gave an almost imperceptible nod to the female officer against the wall before he took his seat. He leaned back, kept his legs from doing the usual manspreading, and clasped together his hands in his lap, making himself a study in non-intimidation.

One giant mark against Andrew. Detective Burke exuded professional competence. This was why Barbara Klieg had called him in. He would know how to help Tammy lay down the foundation of her story. He would know how to testify in front of a jury. Leigh could parry with him, but she wouldn't be able to break him.

Not just a mark against Andrew, but a possible nail in his coffin.

Burke said, "I know Detective Klieg already explained this to you, but there are two cameras in this room, there and there."

Tammy did not look to where he pointed.

Burke explained, "You can see the green lights mean they're recording both video and audio, but I want to make sure that you're all right with that. I will turn them off if you don't want them on. Do you want them on?"

Instead of answering, Tammy nodded her head.

"I should ask, though, is it okay that we talk in here?" Burke's voice was soothing, almost like a lullaby. "We could go somewhere more formal, like an interview room, or I could take you to my office, or I could take you home."

"No," she said, then quieter, "no, I don't want to go home."

"Would you like me to call a friend or family member?"

Tammy started shaking her head before he finished. She didn't want anyone to know about this. Her shame was so palpable that Leigh pressed her hand to her chest, trying to keep her feelings in check.

"All right, we'll stay here, but you can change your mind at any time. Just tell me you want to stop, or you want to go, and we'll do whatever you say." Burke was clearly in authority, but he was going out of his way to give her a sense of choice. He asked, "What should I call you—Tammy or Ms. Karlsen?"

"Ms.—Ms. Karlsen." Tammy coughed around the words. Her voice was strained. Leigh could see the bruises around the woman's neck were already starting to come up. Her face was obscured by her hair, but the photos taken during the rape-kit collection had been a study in devastation.

"Ms. Karlsen," Burke confirmed. "Detective Klieg told me that you are a district manager for DataTel. I've heard of the company, of course, but I'm not quite sure what they do."

"System logistics and telecom engineering." Tammy cleared her throat again, but the rasp would not go away. "We provide data support for medium to small businesses needing microsystems, optics and photonics, and systems controls. I'm in charge of sixteen divisions across the southeast."

Burke nodded like he understood, but the purpose of this line of questioning was to help remind Tammy Karlsen that she was a credible professional. He was signaling that he believed her story.

Burke said, "That sounds a lot more impressive than my job description. I bet you had to go to school for that."

"Georgia Tech," she said. "I have a master's in electrical and computer engineering."

Leigh hissed out a long sigh. She knew one of Octavia's boxes would contain information from Tammy Karlsen's social media, specifically anything to do with Tech's alumni page. Tammy's classmates were at that age of nostalgia, and there were probably ample posts about wild college years. If Tammy had a reputation as a woman who enjoyed drinking or sex, then Leigh could bring that out at trial, as if every woman didn't have a right to enjoy drinking and sex.

Regardless, Andrew had probably earned a point in his favor.

The video played on as Burke engaged in more small talk. The jury would follow him off a cliff. His easy confidence was better than Valium. His voice never left the lullaby register. He looked directly at Tammy even though she never looked up at him. He was attentive, believing, and, above all, compassionate. Leigh could've run a checklist from the police manual on the proper way to interview a sexual assault victim. That a police officer was actually following it was a stunning revelation.

Burke finally got to the point of the interview. He shifted in the chair, crossing his legs at the knees. "Ms. Karlsen, I can't begin to know how difficult this is for you, but if you feel like you can, would you please tell me what happened last night?"

She said nothing at first, and Burke had the experience not to push her. Leigh stared at the numbers in the upper right-hand corner, watching the time tick by until, forty-eight seconds later, Tammy finally spoke.

"I don't—" She cleared her throat again. Her esophagus wasn't raw just from the strangulation. During the rape exam, a nurse had stuck a long swab down her throat to find traces of semen. "Sorry."

Burke stretched to his left and opened a mini fridge Leigh had not noticed before. He took out a bottle of water, twisted open the top, and placed it on the table in front of Tammy before sitting back.

She hesitated, but finally took the bottle. Leigh winced as she watched the woman struggle to swallow. Water dripped from the corners of Tammy's swollen lips, pooling into the collar of her scrubs, darkening the green.

Burke said, "There's no rule to this, Ms. Karlsen. You start the story where you feel comfortable. Or don't. You can walk out of here at any time."

Tammy's hands shook as she returned the bottle to the table. She looked at the door, and Leigh wondered if she was going to leave.

But she didn't.

Tammy took a few tissues from the box on the table. She wiped her nose, flinching from the pain. She worked the tissues in her hand as she started talking, slowly walking Burke through the beginning of a normal evening that had turned into a nightmare. Getting off work. Deciding to go out for a drink. Leaving her car with the valet. Sitting alone at the bar as she drank a gin martini. She'd been ready to leave when Andrew offered to buy her another drink.

Leigh flipped back in her notepad. She counted off the two and a half gin martinis that the security cameras at Comma Chameleon had recorded Tammy consuming.

As Tammy told the story of moving to the rooftop deck, she was off her alcohol consumption by half, but most people didn't remember how much they drank. It didn't matter. Leigh would look petty in front of the jury if she pushed the woman on actually ordering three martinis instead of two.

She turned her attention back to the video.

Tammy was describing Andrew the same way anyone would describe him—a little hard to read, but nice, professional, an adult at an age when a lot of her generation was not. Tammy was clearly cut from the same cloth. She told Burke that she felt like they had hit it off. No, she didn't know Andrew's last name. He worked at a car dealership, she thought. Maybe a mechanic? He liked to talk about classic cars.

"I let him—I kissed him," Tammy said, the guilt in her tone implying that she thought that made everything that had happened afterward her own fault. "I flirted with him, then at the valet, I kissed him for a while. For too long. And then I gave him my business card because—because I wanted him to call me."

Burke let her sit in silence. He was clearly making the connection that Tammy had spent so much time talking about Andrew for a reason, but he was wise enough not to try to put words in her mouth.

For her part, Tammy was looking down at her hands. She had shredded the tissues. She tried to clean up the mess, gathering the stray fibers on the table. When she reached down to the floor, she groaned, and Leigh was reminded of the damage that the Coke bottle had done.

Burke leaned to his left again, this time to pick up the trashcan. He placed it by the table. He was so big and the room was so small that he did all of this without leaving his chair.

Tammy worked to get every single wisp of torn tissue into the wastebasket. Seconds passed. Then minutes.

Burke patiently watched. Leigh imagined he was processing the story so far, checking his own boxes, making sure that he'd gotten answers: Where did the victim first come into contact with the suspect? How much alcohol was consumed? Were they taking illegal drugs? Was the victim with friends? Who could be a potential witness?

Or maybe Burke was considering the next batch of questions: Did the victim shove, punch or kick her assailant? Did she say "Stop" or "No" at any time? How did the assailant behave prior, during, and after the assault? What was the chronology of the sex acts performed? Was force or threat used? What about a weapon? Did he ejaculate? Where did he ejaculate? How many times?

Tammy had finished cleaning up the tissue. She sat back on the couch. Her head started to shake back and forth, as if she'd heard Burke's silent questions and already knew her response. "I don't remember what happened next. When I got to the valet. I was in the car, I think? Or—I don't know. Maybe I remember some things. I can't be sure. I don't want to—I can't ruin—if I don't remember—I know I need to be sure."

Again, Burke waited. Leigh admired his discipline, which spoke to his intelligence. Twenty years ago, an officer in his position would've grabbed Tammy by the shoulders, shaken her, yelled about how she needed to talk if she wanted to punish the guy who did this, or was she making it all up because she wanted attention?

Instead, Burke told Tammy, "My son fought in Afghanistan. Two rotations."

Tammy's head tilted up, but she still would not look him in the eye.

Burke said, "When he came back, he was different. So much had happened over there that he couldn't bring himself to talk about. Now, I've never served, but I know what post-traumatic stress looks like because I spend a lot of time talking to women who have survived sexual assault."

Leigh could see Tammy's jaw start to clench and unclench. She hadn't put it into those stark terms yet. She was not a regional manager or a Tech grad. She was a victim of sexual assault. The scarlet letter would burn into her chest for the rest of her life.

Burke said, "PTSD is triggered by a traumatic event. Symptoms include nightmares, anxiety, uncontrollable thoughts, flashbacks, and sometimes amnesia."

"Are you—" Tammy's voice caught. "Are you saying that's why I don't remember?"

"No, ma'am. We should know more about that when we get back the toxicology report." Burke was going out on a limb, but he pulled himself back. "What I'm saying is everything you're experiencing—whether you're sad, or angry, or in shock, or wanting revenge, or not wanting revenge, or wanting to punish this guy, or maybe you never want to see him again—all of that is perfectly normal. There is no right way or wrong way to act here. What you're feeling—all of that is right for you."

The revelation broke Tammy Karlsen. She started to sob. There was no guidebook women were given at birth about how to respond to sexual trauma. It was like getting your period, or miscarrying a child, or going through menopause: the kind of thing every woman dreaded but was for unknown reasons taboo to mention.

"Jesus Christ," Leigh mumbled. This gentle giant was going to single-handedly turn the jury away from Andrew. She should send him a fruit basket after the trial.

Leigh checked her heartlessness. This wasn't a game. On the video, Tammy's body was wracked by sobs. She grabbed a fistful of tissues. Burke didn't go to comfort her. He stayed in the chair. He glanced at the female officer to make sure she did not move, either.

"I don't—" Tammy said. "I don't wanna ruin anybody's life."

"Ms. Karlsen, I say this with great respect, but you do not have that kind of power."

She finally looked up at him.

Burke said, "I know that you are an honest woman. But my

elief and your words are not enough for a court of law. Anything ou tell me has to be investigated, and if your memory has failed ou, or you've mixed up events, then our investigation will find at out in quick order."

Leigh sat back in her chair. It was like watching Jimmy Stewart ive a speech on the courthouse steps.

"All right," Tammy said, but still, almost a full minute passed efore she continued. "I was in the park. That's where I woke up.)r came to. I've never been there before, but it—it was a park. nd I—I was handcuffed to the table. That old man, the one with e dog? I don't know his name. He called the police and—"

In the silence, Leigh could hear Tammy's breath on the audio, quick in and out as she tried not to hyperventilate.

Burke told the woman, "Ms. Karlsen, sometimes, our memories ome to us in images. They flash like an old movie across the reen. Is there anything about the attack, any stray detail, that ou can tell me about the man who raped you?"

"He—" her voice caught again. The word *rape* had just cut rough the fog. She had been raped. She was a rape victim.

She said, "He had a ski mask on. And h-handcuffs. He hand- uffed me."

Leigh wrote *premeditated* on her notepad, because the ski mask nd handcuffs had been brought to the scene.

She stared down at the word.

Burke was right about the way memories could flash up. Leigh ought about the vacation photos in Reggie Paltz's office. If she new her grifters, Andrew had probably paid for those trips so at he could set the agenda. There might be a photo of him omewhere in a ski mask.

One more possible mark against Andrew.

"I—" Tammy's throat worked as she tried to swallow. "I asked im to stop. To please stop."

Leigh made another note. She had seen more than one jury ang up on the fact that a woman had been too terrified, or too verwhelmed, to forcefully say the word *no*.

"I don't remember if—" Tammy swallowed a breath. "He took y clothes off. His fingernails were long. They scraped—I felt em scrape my—"

Leigh watched Tammy's hand go to her right breast. She hadn't noticed Andrew's fingernails. If he was still keeping them long at the start of the trial, she certainly wasn't going to tell him to clip them.

"He kept telling me that—" Tammy's voice cut off again. "He told me that he loved me. Over and over. That he loved my—my hair, and my eyes, and that he loved my mouth. He kept saying I was so tiny. He said it, like—your hips are so slender, your hands are so small, your face is perfect like a Barbie doll. And he kept saying that he loved me and—"

Burke didn't rush in to fill the silence, but Leigh saw him clasp together his hands in his lap, as if he needed to keep himself from reaching out to reassure her that everything was going to be okay.

Leigh felt the same need as she watched Tammy Karlsen rocking back and forth, hair falling into her face to hide her expression as she tried to disappear from this cruel world.

Callie had done the same thing the night Buddy had died. She'd rocked back and forth on the floor, sobbing, repeating the line from the operator in a mechanical tone.

If you'd like to make a call . . .

There was a pack of Kleenex in Leigh's desk drawer. She used one to wipe her eyes. She waited through the silence as Tammy Karlsen shook with grief. The woman was clearly blaming herself, trying to think about how she had messed up, what stupid thing she had said or done that had put her in this position. She should be at work right now. She had a job. She had a master's degree. And now she had fleeting memories of a violent attack that had completely devastated her carefully planned life.

Leigh intimately knew that self-blame, because it had almost happened to her in college. She had been sleeping in her car, trying to save money, and woken up with a stranger on top of her.

"I'm sorry," Tammy apologized.

Leigh blew her nose. She sat up in her chair, leaned closer to the monitor.

"I'm sorry," Tammy repeated. She was shaking again. She felt humiliated and stupid and completely out of control. In the course of twelve hours, she had lost everything, and now she had no

lea how to get it back. "I can't—I can't remember anything
se."

Leigh swallowed her own self-loathing and made a tick on her
otepad. That was the fifth time Tammy Karlsen had said that
e couldn't remember anything.

Five points for Andrew.

She looked back at the screen. Burke remained motionless. He
aited a few seconds before prompting, "I know that his face
as covered, but with a ski mask—now, correct me if I'm wrong—
ou can see the eyes, is that right?"

Tammy nodded. "And the mouth."

Burke kept gently pushing her toward the obvious question.
Did you recognize anything about him? Anything at all?"

Tammy swallowed loudly again. "His voice."

Burke waited.

"It was the guy from the bar. Andrew." She cleared her throat.
We talked a long time. I recognized his voice when he was—when
e was doing what he did."

Burke asked, "Did you call him by name?"

"No, I thought—" she stopped herself. "I didn't want to make
im angry."

Leigh knew from her earlier reading that Andrew had been
ompelled to participate in an audio line-up along with five other
en. Their voices had been recorded as each one repeated phrases
om the attack. When the detective had played all of the samples
ack for Tammy, she had immediately picked out Andrew.

Burke asked, "What makes the man's voice distinctive?"

"It's soft. I mean, the tone is soft, but the register is deep,
nd—"

Burke's supernatural composure showed a crack. "And?"

"His mouth." Tammy touched her own lips. "I recognized that,
o. It went up on the side, like he was . . . I don't know. Like
e was playing a game. Like, he was saying he loved me, but he
as enjoying that—that I was terrified."

Leigh knew that smirk. She knew that voice. She knew that
ightening, dispassionate look in Andrew's cold, dead eyes.

She let the video play out. There were no more notes to take,
xcept three more ticks to the running count of Tammy saying

she couldn't remember. Burke tried to tease out more details. Trauma or Rohypnol had ensured that her recollection was shaky. Everything Tammy relayed came from the beginning of the attack. She couldn't remember the knife. Getting cut on her leg. The violation with the Coke bottle. She didn't know what had happened to her purse or her car or her clothes.

Leigh closed the video when Tammy Karlsen was escorted from the room and Burke ended the recording. She searched for a particular crime scene photo. Tammy's purse had been located shoved under the driver's seat of her BMW. Her clothes had been found at the scene. They were neatly folded in the corner of the pavilion.

As an obsessive compulsive, Leigh appreciated the careful symmetry of the staging. Tammy's gray twill skirt had been folded into a tight square. On top of that was the matching suit jacket. The black silk blouse was tucked inside the jacket the way you'd see the set displayed in a store. A black thong was laid across the pile. The matching black lace bra was clasped around the bundle like a bow on a gift. Tammy's black high heels were to the side, upright and carefully aligned to the tight square.

Leigh remembered the way Andrew used to play with his food at snack-time. He would layer cheese and crackers in a Jenga tower, then try to slide one out without toppling the pile. He did the same thing with apple slices, nuts, leftover kernels of popcorn.

The desk phone rang. Leigh wiped her eyes, blew her nose.

"Leigh Collier."

Walter asked, "Is side dick like side boob?"

She took a long moment to realize that he was talking about Maddy's lip-synch video. "I think it's like a dick you fuck on the side."

"Ah," he said. "Well."

She had to give him credit for not saying, *Like mother like daughter*, because when Leigh said she was honest with her husband, she was honest about everything.

Almost everything.

"Sweetheart," he said. "Why are you crying?"

Her tears had stopped, but she felt them threaten to fall again. "I saw Callie last night."

"Would it be stupid to ask if she's in trouble?"

"Nothing I couldn't handle." Leigh would tell him about the unregistered Glock later. Walter had gotten the gun from one of his firemen buddies when she had started working on her own. "She looks bad. Worse than usual."

"You know it goes in cycles."

What Leigh knew was that, eventually, Callie wouldn't be able to pull herself out of a dive. She wasn't even sure that Callie could taper off. Especially with Phil around. There was a reason Callie had turned to heroin instead of her mother. And maybe there was a reason she hadn't turned to Leigh. When Leigh had seen her sister's dope kit in the motel last night, she had wanted to throw it against the wall and scream, *Why do you love this shit more than you love me?*

She told Walter, "She's too thin. I could see the outlines of her bones."

"So, you feed her."

Leigh had tried. Callie had barely managed half a cheeseburger. She'd made a face like Maddy the first time she'd tried broccoli. "Her breathing was wrong. Labored. I could hear her wheezing. I'm not sure what's going on."

"Is she smoking?"

"No." Phil had smoked enough for the entire family. Neither one of them could stand the stench. Which was why it was doubly cruel that Leigh had let Callie go to their mother's last night. What had she been thinking? If Andrew or one of his private detectives didn't terrorize her into overdosing, then Phil would.

It was her fault. It was all her fault.

"Sweetheart," Walter said. "Even if it's Long-Covid, every day you hear about some people finally getting better. Callie's got more lives than a cat. You know that."

Leigh thought about her own battle with Covid. It had started with four hours of uncontrolled coughing that had gotten so bad she'd burst a blood vessel in her eye. The hospital had discharged her with Tylenol and instructions to call an ambulance if she couldn't breathe. Walter had begged Leigh to let him take care of her, but she'd sent him to find Callie instead.

It was her fault. It was all her fault.

181

"Honey," Walter said. "Your sister is an incredibly kind and unique person, but she's got a lot of problems. Some of them you can fix, and some you can't. All you can do is love her."

Leigh dried her eyes again. She'd heard the stutter on Walter's line. "Is someone trying to call you?"

He sighed. "Marci. I can call her back."

Marci was Walter's current side piece. Unfortunately, he hadn't opted to spend the four years since their split pining for Leigh's return.

She felt the need to tell him, "It would take ten minutes to file a no-fault divorce online."

"Sweetheart," Walter said. "I'll be your side dick as long as you'll be my side boob."

Leigh didn't laugh. "You know you're always front and center with me."

He said, "That seems like a good note to end on."

Leigh kept the phone to her ear even after he'd hung up. She let the self-recriminations come to a boil before resting the receiver back in the cradle.

There was a knock on her door. Liz popped in and out quickly, saying, "You've got five minutes to get upstairs."

Leigh went to the closet to find her heels. She freshened up her make-up at the mirror on the inside of the door. BC&M didn't just spend money on jury consultants for defendants. They wanted to know what jurors thought about their lawyers. Leigh was still haunted by a case she'd lost where her client had gone to prison for eighteen years perhaps because, according to one of the male jurors who'd been polled, Leigh's pulled-back hair, J. Crew pant-suit and low heels couldn't hide that she was "obviously a knock-out but needed to make more of an effort to look like a woman."

"Crap," she said. She'd put on lipstick when the mask would cover her mouth. She used a Kleenex to wipe it off. She looped on her mask, then stacked together her legal pads and grabbed her phones.

The low din of the cubicle farm enveloped her in white noise as she walked toward the elevators. Leigh looked at her personal phone. Still no text or call from Callie. She tried not to read too much into the silence. It was coming up on four in the afternoon. Callie could be sleeping or stoned or selling drugs on Stewart Avenue or doing whatever it was she did with her endless amounts of time. An absence of communication didn't necessarily mean that she was in trouble. It just meant she was Callie.

At the elevator, Leigh used her elbow to summon the car. Since her phone was out, she dashed off a text to Maddy—*I am a future employer. I check your TikTok. What do I think?*

Maddy wrote back immediately—*I assume you are a Broadway director and you think, "Wow that woman knows her shit!"*

Leigh smiled. The punctuation was a small victory. Her sixteen-year-old baby calling herself a woman who knows her shit was a triumph.

And then her smile dropped, because Maddy's TikTok was exactly the kind of evidence that Leigh would show a jury if she were trying to impugn her daughter's character.

The elevator doors slid open. There was another person in the car, a baby lawyer she recognized from one of the lower cubicle farms. Leigh stood on one of the four stickers in each corner that were meant to remind people to keep their distance. A sign above the panel advised no speaking or coughing. Another sign advertised some kind of high-tech coating on the buttons that was supposed to stop viral transmission. Leigh kept her back to baby lawyer, though she heard a gasp when she used her elbow to hit the penthouse button.

The doors rolled closed. Leigh started composing a text to Maddy about college admissions, respect from your co-workers, and the importance of a good reputation. She was trying to think of a way to bring the beauty of sex into the mix without mortifying them both when her phone buzzed with another text.

Nick Wexler was asking—*DTF?*

Down to fuck.

Leigh sighed. She regretted circling back into Nick's life again, but she didn't want to come off as a bitch after asking him for a favor.

She kicked it down the road, writing—*raincheck?*

A thumbs up and an eggplant rewarded her response.

Leigh contained the urge to sigh again. She returned to Maddy's text, deciding she would have to climb back onto her high horse at a later date. She replaced the lecture with—*Looking forward to talking tonight!*

The baby lawyer exited on the tenth floor, but he couldn't stop himself from glancing back at Leigh, trying to figure out who she was and how she had gained access to the partners' floor. She waited for the doors to close, then let her mask hang from one ear. She took a deep breath, using the moment alone to recalibrate herself.

This would be Leigh's first meeting with Andrew after he'd shown his real nature. A duplicitous client was nothing new but, no matter how sadistic their alleged crimes, they were generally docile by the time they made it to Leigh's doorstep. Suffering the humiliation of arrest, enduring inhumane confinement, being threatened by hardened cons, knowing they could be sent back to jail or prison if Leigh didn't help them, gave her the upper hand.

That was the warning siren that Leigh had talked herself out of listening to yesterday morning. Andrew Tenant had maintained the upper hand the entire time, and only in retrospect did Leigh realize how it had happened. Defense lawyers always joked that their worst nightmare was an innocent client. Leigh's worst nightmare was a client who wasn't scared.

The bell dinged. PH flashed above the doors. Leigh put her mask back in place. A trim older woman wearing a black pantsuit and red mask stood waiting for her. It was like *The Handmaid's Tale*, UGA version.

The woman said, "Ms. Collier, Mr. Bradley wants to speak with you privately in his office."

Leigh felt a sudden jolt of dread. "Is the client here?"

"Mr. Tenant is in the conference room, but Mr. Bradley wanted a word with you first."

Leigh's gut twisted into a knot, but she had no choice but to follow the woman across the giant, open space. She stared at the closed conference room door. Her mind started racing through tortuous plots. Andrew had gotten Leigh fired. Andrew had gone to the police. Andrew had kidnapped Callie and was holding her hostage.

184

The ridiculousness of the last scenario helped spool her paranoia back inside its box. Andrew was a sadistic rapist, but he was no Svengali. Leigh reminded herself of her Andrew Hypothesis. All that he had were stray childhood memories and guesses about why his father had disappeared. The stupidest thing she could do right now was behave in a way that confirmed his suspicions.

"Through here." Bradley's assistant opened an office door.

Despite her return to logic, Leigh's mouth had gone completely dry by the time she entered the office. No detectives or cops with handcuffs were waiting. Just the predictable red and black décor. Cole Bradley sat behind a giant marble desk. Files and papers were stacked around him. His light gray suit jacket hung on a rack. His shirtsleeves were rolled up. His face was bare.

She asked, "Will Andrew be joining us?"

Instead of answering, he indicated a red leather chair across from his desk. "Take me through it."

Leigh wanted to kick herself for missing the obvious. Bradley wanted her to prep him so that he looked like he knew what he was talking about in front of the client.

She sat down. She took off her mask, opened her notepad, and dove straight in. "The victim's audio ID of Andrew's voice is confident during her initial interview. After his arrest, she chose him out of an audio line-up. She's shaky on some things, but they used a forensic interviewer who took her into the story. His name is Sean Burke."

"Never heard of him," Bradley said.

"Me, either. I'll find out what I can, but he's a home run on the stand. I don't know how Tammy Karlsen, the victim, will play out. She's very sympathetic in the recorded interview. On the night of the attack, she wasn't dressed provocatively. She didn't drink that much. She doesn't have a criminal record. No DUIs. No speeding tickets. Credit record is solid. Student loans are almost paid off. I'll dig into her social media, but she's got a master's in software engineering from Tech. She's probably scrubbed anything that's bad."

"Tech," he said. UGA's long-running rival. "How sympathetic is she?"

"There's no question about lack of consent. She got the absolute

185

hell beaten out of her. She gave a firm *no* during the attack. The pictures alone buy her a massive amount of compassion."

Bradley nodded. "Evidence?"

"There's a muddy shoe print consistent with a Nike size nine found in Andrew's closet. I can argue that *consistent* isn't *exact*. There are several deep bite marks, but there was no DNA found when they swabbed the wounds, and the prosecutor wouldn't dare try to put up an odontologist when he knows I can easily debunk the junk science." Leigh paused to take a breath. "The Coke bottle is more difficult. Andrew's print was found on the bottom of the glass. Right pinky finger, but it's a solid, peer-reviewed match from the Georgia Bureau of Investigation. There's nothing else on the base of the bottle but fecal matter and the victim's DNA. The attacker probably used gloves, and the pinky tore, or it's a bottle that Andrew touched before the assault. He's been to that park before."

Bradley took a moment to process that last piece of information. "Problem areas?"

"On their side, Rohypnol is suspected, so I can argue temporary amnesia. Karlsen suffered a concussion, so traumatic amnesia is a given. I've already put two specialists on standby who are very good with a jury." Leigh paused to look down at her notes. "On our side, the crime scene photos are horrific. I can keep some out, but even the okay ones are bad for Andrew. I can try to shake the audio identification of Andrew's voice, but, like I said, it comes off as very confident both times. I've seen the prosecutor's list of possible witnesses and they've got a forensic audio expert I would've used if they hadn't snagged him first."

"And?"

"Karlsen is hazy on almost everything else. The hazy might cancel out the confident, but if it sounds like I'm at fifty/fifty on a not guilty, that's because I am."

"Ms. Collier," Bradley said. "Get to the problem."

Leigh should've been impressed by his insight, but she was furious because Bradley had seen in five minutes what it had taken her all morning to strategize around. "Sidney Winslow is Andrew's alibi for the night of the attack. The jury will want to hear from her."

Bradley sat back in his chair, steepling together his fingers. "Ms. Winslow will have to waive spousal privilege in order to testify, which means that Dante will be able to take a crack at her. Do you foresee a problem with that?"

Leigh felt her teeth start to grit. She had intended to use Sidney as a Trojan horse, letting her burn down Andrew's life while Leigh held herself blameless. "Dante's no Perry Mason, but it won't take much. Either Sidney's going to get pissed off and say something stupid or she'll try to help Andrew and say something stupid."

"In my day, *saying something stupid* under oath was called perjury."

Leigh wondered if Bradley was encouraging her or warning her. Lawyers were not allowed to put witnesses on the stand if they believed they were going to lie. Suborning perjury was a criminal offense that carried a sentence of one to ten years and a hefty fine.

Bradley was waiting for her response. Her boss had made a legal observation, so Leigh gave him a legal rebuttal. "I'll advise Sidney exactly as I always advise witnesses. Stick to the truth, don't try to be helpful, only answer the questions you're asked, and never embellish."

Bradley's nod indicated that was good enough for him. "Any other issues I should be made aware of?"

"Andrew's ankle monitor has gone off several times. False alarms, but someone could say that he's testing the response times."

"Let's make sure no one says that," Bradley told her, as if Leigh had any control. "Your second on the case—"

"Jacob Gaddy," Leigh provided. "I've tried a few cases with him before. He knows his way around the forensics. He's good with witnesses."

Bradley nodded, because it was accepted strategy to balance out a woman with a man. "Who's the judge?"

"It was Alvarez, but—"

"Covid." Bradley sounded grave. Alvarez had been his contemporary. "When will you know who you're getting?"

"They're still figuring out the new rotations. Everything's upside down at the courthouse. We've got jury selection on Thursday and probably Friday, then the trial starts Monday, but who knows whether they'll move it up or postpone it. It depends on the infection rates, whether or not the jail gets locked down again. No matter what, I'll be ready to go."

"Is he guilty?"

Leigh was taken aback by the question. "I can see a path to a not guilty, sir."

"It's a simple yes or no."

Leigh wasn't going to give him a simple answer. She was in the process of trying to throw a case for her own personal gain. The biggest mistake criminals made was to appear overconfident. She said, "Probably."

"And the other possible cases?"

"There are similarities between the three other victims and the Tammy Karlsen attack." Leigh knew she was circling around the point. She had to keep Bradley convinced that she was doing everything possible to get Andrew to a not guilty. "If you're asking me did he rape the three other women? Probably. Can Dante Carmichael prove it? I'm on the fence, but if they nail Andrew on Tammy Karlsen, my *probably* slides over to an *absolutely*. At that point, it's just a matter of whether his sentencing will be concurrent or consecutive."

Bradley kept his fingers steepled as he took another moment to think. Leigh was expecting a question, but he told her, "I worked the Stocking Strangler case back in the seventies. Well before you were born. I'm sure you've never heard of it."

Leigh knew the case because Gary Carlton had been one of Georgia's most notorious serial killers. He'd been sentenced to death for raping and strangling three elderly women, but it was believed that he'd attacked countless others.

"Carlton didn't start out killing. That's where he ended up, but there were many, many other cases where the victim survived." Bradley paused to make sure she was following. "One of those FBI profilers looked at the case. This happened years later when that kind of thing was in vogue. He said there was a pattern of escalation with most killers. They start off with the fantasy, then the fantasy takes over. Peeping Tom turns into rapist. Rapist turns into murderer."

Leigh didn't tell him he was relaying knowledge that anyone with a Netflix account could access. She had thought the same thing when she'd seen the photos from Tammy Karlsen's rape kit. Andrew's attack had been savage, just short of killing the woman. It wasn't a leap to say that sometime, maybe next time, the knife would cut open the artery and the victim would bleed out in a pool of her own blood.

She told Bradley, "The three other cases. Someone went to a lot of trouble to connect them to Andrew. I wonder if there's more going on behind the scenes."

"Such as?"

"Some officer or a detective who worked one of the earlier attacks. Maybe she wanted to charge Andrew, but the DA or her boss told her to drop it."

"She?" he asked.

"You ever tell a woman to drop something?" Leigh watched Bradley's ears twitch in his version of a smile. "There's no way any boss approved all the man hours it must've taken to tie together these three other cases. The department can barely keep gas in their squad cars right now."

Bradley was listening intently. "Extrapolate."

"Somehow, maybe from credit card receipts or video footage or something we haven't thought of yet, the police already had Andrew's name on their list. They didn't have enough probable cause to bring him in. Considering his financial resources, they knew they would only get one chance to question him."

Bradley leapt to the obvious conclusion. "There might be even more attacks that we have yet to learn of, which means that everything rests on winning the Karlsen case."

Leigh kept up her rah-rah attitude. "I only need to persuade one juror to break the case. Dante has to persuade twelve."

Bradley leaned farther back in his chair. He folded his hands behind his head. "I met Andrew's father once. Gregory Senior tried to pay him off, but of course Waleski reneged. Terrible human being. Linda was little more than a child when she married him. The best thing that ever happened to her was his disappearance."

Leigh could've told him that Buddy Waleski's disappearance had been good for a lot of people.

He asked, "Would you put Andrew on the stand?"

"I could shoot him in the chest and save the jury a verdict." Leigh reminded herself that she was speaking to her boss, and that she needed to provide herself a framework of legitimacy. "I can't stop Andrew if he wants to testify, but I'll tell him he'll lose the case if he does."

"Let me ask you a question," Bradley said, as if he hadn't been doing just that. "Assuming Andrew is guilty of the assaults, how are you going to feel if you get him off scot-free and he does it again? Or he does something even worse the next time?"

Leigh knew the answer he was looking for. It was the answer that made people hate defense attorneys—until they needed one. "If Andrew walks, I'm going to feel like Dante Carmichael didn't do his job. The burden is on the state to prove guilt."

"Good." Bradley nodded. "Reginald Paltz. What do you think about him?"

Leigh hesitated. After the conversation with Liz, she had wiped Reggie from her mind. "He's good. I think his background work on Andrew is excellent. We won't be surprised at trial by anything the prosecution digs up. I'm putting him on one of my divorce cases."

"Delay that," Bradley ordered. "Mr. Paltz is on exclusive retainer for the duration of the trial. He's waiting in the conference room with Andrew. I won't be joining you, but I think you'll find he has some interesting things to say."

8

Leigh braced herself as she walked toward the conference room. Instead of trying to anticipate the *interesting things* that Reggie Paltz had to say, she silently recited her Andrew Hypothesis: when Andrew was a kid, he had found Buddy's camera behind the bar. After his father had disappeared, he'd seen Callie worrying the femoral artery diagram in the textbook. For some unknown reason, at some point, the two memories had collided, and now he was out there copying his own sick interpretation of his father's murder.

A bead of sweat rolled down the back of Leigh's neck. The hypothesis didn't seem as strong with Andrew less than twenty feet away. She was giving him a lot of credit for making the connection. There was no such thing as a criminal mastermind. Leigh was missing a detail, a *B* that connected the *A* and *C*.

Bradley's UGA handmaiden cleared her throat.

Leigh was standing like a statue in front of the closed conference room door. She gave the woman a nod before going inside.

The room looked the same, though the flowers in the heavy glass vase had started to wilt. Andrew was at the fireplace end of the conference table. A thick file folder was closed in front of him. Light blue, not the sort that they used at the firm. Reggie Paltz was two chairs away. The set-up was familiar from their previous meeting. Reggie was working on his laptop. Andrew was frowning at his phone. Neither was masked.

When Leigh closed the door, Andrew was the first to look up. She caught his expression mid-transformation. Irritated one moment, completely soulless the next.

191

"My apologies for being late." Leigh walked stiffly. Her body felt suspended in the same perpetual fight-or-flight mode as before. Her senses were heightened. Her muscles felt tensed. The urge to flee coursed through every molecule.

She bought herself some time as she found a pen in the cup on the credenza. She sat down in the same spot she'd taken two nights ago. Her two phones went flat to the table. She knew the only way to get through the next hour was to stick to business. "Reggie, what do you have for me?"

Andrew answered. "I remembered something Tammy told me at the bar."

Leigh felt a sharp prickle of a warning trace up her spine. "What's that?"

He let the question linger as he picked at the corner of the light blue file folder. The *tick-tick-tick* drew out the silence. Leigh estimated there were around one hundred pages inside. She knew instinctively that she didn't want to know what they contained. And she also knew that Andrew wanted her to ask about them.

She heard Callie's admonishment. *You can't play a game with somebody if they're not willing to suit up.*

Leigh did the opposite of suiting up. She raised an eyebrow, asking, "Andrew, what did Tammy tell you in the bar?"

He let another moment slip by, then said, "She was raped and had an abortion when she was sixteen years old."

Leigh felt her nostrils flare as she worked to keep the shock off of her face.

He said, "It happened over the summer of 2006. The boy was on her debate team. They were at a camp in Hiawassee. She said that there was no way she could keep the baby, because she knew she would never love it."

Leigh pressed together her lips. She had watched every frame of the ninety-eight-minute video. There was no point at which Tammy Karlsen was engaging in anything but light banter and flirting.

"You see the value of this information, I assume?" Andrew was watching her closely. The *tick* kept its steady rhythm. "Tammy Karlsen has falsely accused a man of rape before. She murdered her unborn child. Can the jury really believe a word she says?"

Leigh tried to look at him, but the open menace in his eyes broke her nerve. She didn't know what to do but play along. She asked, "Reggie, what do you have to support this?"

The ticking stopped. Andrew was waiting.

"Yeah, uhm—" Reggie was a study in dishonesty, which told Leigh that he had obtained the information by dishonest means. "So, Andrew told me about—about how he remembered. So, I tracked down some of Karlsen's high school friends. They confirmed the abortion. And that she told everybody she was raped."

"Did the friends go on the record?" Leigh tested. "Are they willing to testify?"

Reggie shook his head, looking somewhere over Leigh's shoulder. "They prefer to remain anonymous."

Leigh nodded as if she accepted the explanation. "That's too bad."

"Well," Reggie glanced at Andrew. "Still, you can legitimately ask Karlsen about it when she testifies. Like, has she ever had an abortion? Has she ever thought that she's been raped before?"

Leigh pushed back on his armchair lawyering. "You have to lay down a foundation for asking the questions. Since none of Tammy's friends will go under oath, I'll need to put you on the stand, Reggie."

Reggie scratched his goatee. He gave Andrew a nervous glance. "You could get it in otherwise. I mean—"

"No, you'll do great," Leigh said. "Walk me through your investigation. How many of Tammy's friends did you speak with? How did you locate them? Did you talk to any counselors from the camp? Did Tammy file a complaint with the director? Was there a police report? What was the boy's name? How far along was she? What clinic did she use? Who took her? Do her parents know?"

Reggie wiped his forehead with the back of his arm. "That's, uh—those are—"

"He'll be ready to go when you need him." Andrew had not looked away from Leigh since she had entered the room, and he didn't break off contact now. "Won't you, Reg?"

The *tick-tick-tick* started up again.

Leigh watched Reggie's throat work from across the room. She gathered from his silence that he was suddenly uncomfortable with his crimes. And *crimes* was the appropriate word. Private detectives were barred from using illegal means to gather information, just like attorneys were barred from using unlawfully obtained information in court. If Reggie went on the stand, he would be opening himself up to a perjury charge. If Leigh called him up knowing he was going to lie, she would be facing the same.

Andrew was trying to fuck them both over in plain sight.

He prodded, "Reg?"

"Yeah." Reggie's throat worked again as he swallowed. "Sure. I'll be ready."

"Good," Andrew said. "What's next?"

Tick-tick-tick.

"Just give me a minute to—" Leigh indicated her blank notepad. The pen clicked. She started writing nonsense words so that Andrew would think she was seriously contemplating losing her law license and being thrown in jail.

At least Cole Bradley's absence from the meeting made sense. The slick bastard didn't want to expose himself to prosecution, but he had no problem letting Leigh take the risk. He'd even tested her back in his office, asking her opinion on whether or not she felt comfortable suborning perjury with Sidney on the stand. Now, she had to work her shadow case against Andrew, plus the actual case, plus put on whatever dog and pony show Cole Bradley was expecting.

"All right." With great difficulty, Leigh made herself look at Andrew. "Let's go over your appearance in court. First, I want to talk to you about your presentation. What you're going to wear, how you're going to behave. You have to remember during voir dire that potential jurors are watching your every move. Do you have any questions about procedure?"

The ticking had stopped again. Something about Andrew's posture held a warning. He took his time asking, "Voir dire?"

Leigh fell back into lawyer mode, launching into her usual speech. "Voir dire is the process by which each side gets to question prospective jurors. Generally, a pool of around fifty people is randomly selected. We'll get an opportunity to question each person. We'll be looking for perceived bias, backgrounds, qualifications, who we think will be sympathetic to our side—or not."

"How do we know?" Andrew had broken her rhythm. She could tell he had done it on purpose. "What if they lie?"

"That's a good question." Leigh had to stop to swallow. His voice was different, softer but still deep in register, the same way that Tammy had described. "All jurors have to fill out a questionnaire, which we'll get access to ahead of time."

"Can we investigate them?" Andrew asked. "Reggie can—"

"No, we don't get enough time and it's counter-productive." One glance at Reggie told Leigh that he was on board with whatever Andrew wanted. She tried to move them away from another scheme to rig the system. "When prospective jurors are on the stand, they are under oath. They have to be honest, and judges will give you a lot of leeway to look for possible conflicts."

Reggie said, "You should really get a jury consultant."

"We've already discussed that." Andrew kept his attention on Leigh. "What kind of questions will you ask?"

Leigh's internal siren sounded an alert, but she listed off some of the possibilities. "The judge will ask some general questions first, like have you or a family member ever been the victim of a violent crime? Do you think you're capable or incapable of being impartial? Then we'll get into education, work experience, clubs or organizations they belong to, religious affiliation, whether there's any relation between themselves and anyone on the case, whether or not they are prepared to hear graphic details about sexual assault, whether they've been sexually assaulted themselves."

"Right," Andrew said. "Will they have to talk about that? If they believe they've been sexually assaulted?"

Leigh shook her head. She didn't know where this was going. "Sometimes."

"And are you saying we do or we do not want those people on the jury?"

"It—" Her throat had gone dry again. "We get challenges, and—"

"I think the best strategy is to try to pull out the details. For instance, how old they were when it happened, whether it was child abuse or—" He paused. "Forgive me, is there a difference between a sex act with, say, a teenager and one with an adult?"

Leigh couldn't speak. She could only look at his mouth. Tammy Karlsen had talked about the derisive curl of his lips behind the ski mask. Now, he was clearly enjoying the fact that he was making Leigh squirm.

He continued, "Because it seems to me that a person who had a sexual experience as a teenager wouldn't necessarily be inclined to believe an adult sexual experience that got a little out of hand is a bad thing."

Leigh bit her lip to keep herself from correcting him. Nothing had gotten *a little out of hand*. Tammy had nearly been destroyed. Andrew had known exactly what he was doing.

"Something to think about." Andrew shrugged, but even the up and down movement of his shoulder was tightly controlled. "You're the expert. I leave the decision to you."

Leigh stood up. She walked over to the credenza. A mini fridge was behind the cabinet door. She took out a bottle of water, asking Andrew, "Thirsty?"

For the first time, light flickered behind his eyes. His excitement was almost palpable, like a predator stalking fresh prey. He was soaking in her discomfort, reveling in her anxiety.

Leigh turned her back to him. Her hands were trembling so badly that she could barely twist the cap on the water bottle. She took a long drink. She sat back down. She returned to the safety of her well-rehearsed speech.

"So, as I was saying, we get a specified number of challenges to dismiss jurors, some for cause, some for people we just don't like. The prosecutor gets the same number. At the end of the process, we'll have twelve jurors and two alternates picked for your trial."

Leigh's breath ran on the last word. She coughed, trying to cover her jitters. "Sorry."

Andrew's dark gaze covered her face like a veil as she took another drink from the bottle.

She continued, "One of our associates, Jacob Gaddy, will be second chairing me. He'll navigate the paperwork and some of the procedural details. I'll use him to interview a few of the witnesses. At the table, I'll sit on your right, Jacob will be on your left. He's your attorney, too, so if you have any questions or comments while I'm performing interviews, then direct them to Jacob."

Andrew said nothing.

She kept going. "During voir dire, all of your potential jurors will be watching you. The case can be won or lost in that moment, so I need you on best behavior. Hair trimmed, nails clean, face shaved. Make sure you have at least four clean suits ready. I expect the trial will last three days, but it's good to be prepared. Wear the same mask every day. The one you had on yesterday from the dealership is fine."

Reggie stirred in his chair.

Leigh willed him to stay silent, telling Andrew, "The judge will probably give you the option of taking off your mask once the trial starts. We can go over the rules if it comes to that. Keep your expression as neutral as possible. You need to show the jury you respect women. So when I talk, you need to listen to me. Pull out my chair. Carry any boxes—"

"Wouldn't that look bad?" Reggie chose this moment to contribute to the defense. "I mean, some jurors might think Andy's putting on an act, right? So, what you're talking about, the sharp suit and the slick haircut? All of that could turn the jury against him."

"It's hard to know." Leigh shrugged, but she found herself wondering about Reggie's motivations. This clearly wasn't a blackmail situation. Otherwise, Reggie would've kept his mouth shut and let Andrew burn in whatever fire Leigh was trying to set. That left money. Reggie had agreed to perjure himself on the stand. He knew that could mean anything from losing his license to losing his freedom. The risk must've had a very high reward.

She told Andrew, "This is your trial. It's up to you. I can only make recommendations."

Reggie tried another pop quiz. "Would you put him on the stand?"

"It's his decision," Leigh said. "But if you want my opinion, no. He's not likely to come across well. Women won't like him."

Reggie guffawed. "Dude can't walk through a bar without every bitch in the room giving him her number."

Leigh turned all of her attention onto Reggie. "Women in bars are looking for a reasonably clean, gainfully employed man who can string two words together without sounding like a jackass. Women on juries have a different agenda."

Reggie's belligerence was out in the open now. "Which is?"

"Compassion."

Reggie didn't have a response.

Neither did Andrew.

He let his silence chew at her nerves. Leigh looked at him, blurring her eyes so she didn't have to see his face. He was sitting back in his chair, spine straight, hand resting on the file, yet every part of him seemed ready to pounce. She watched his fingers gently stroke the corner of the light blue folder, tickling apart the edge. His hands were large like his father's. The gold watch hanging loose from his wrist reminded her of the one Buddy had worn.

"All right," Andrew said. "That's voir dire. What about the trial?"

Leigh looked away from his hand. She struggled to find her place. "The prosecutor will start with establishing a timeline. While he's presenting his case, keep silent, don't shake your head or make any noises of disbelief or disagreement. If you have questions for me, or comments, then write them down on a notepad, but keep it to a minimum."

Andrew nodded once, but she couldn't tell if any of this mattered at all. He was toying with her, playing at Leigh's edges the same way he was playing with the file. "How does the prosecutor establish the timeline?"

Leigh cleared her throat. "He'll take the jury through the night at the bar. He'll call the bartender, the valet, then the dog walker who found the victim in the park. Next up is the first officer on scene, then the paramedics, then the nurses and doctor who performed the rape exam, the detective who—"

"What about Tammy?" Andrew asked. "I've gathered from Reggie that your job will be to annihilate her. Are you ready to annihilate her?"

Something had shifted. Leigh recognized the unsettling sensation from the day before, her *flight* triggering into overdrive. She tried to act as if the subtext was meaningless. "I'm ready to do my job."

"Right." Andrew started clenching and unclenching his fist. "You'll start with showing how Tammy was aggressive with me in the bar. You can point out how, in the video, she keeps touching my leg, my hand. At one point she even touches the side of my face."

Leigh waited, but then she realized that Andrew was expecting a response. She picked up her pen, ready to write. "Go ahead."

"She had three drinks in two hours. Double gin martinis. She was clearly getting sloppy."

Leigh nodded for him to continue, recording every single word. She had wasted hours figuring out a shadow strategy to tank his case. Andrew was clearly willing to do the heavy lifting for her.

She told him, "Keep going."

"Then, at the valet stand, she grabbed me by the neck and kissed me for thirty-two seconds." Andrew paused, as if to give her time. "And of course, she offered me her business card, which I still have. I didn't ask for her number. She gave it to me."

Leigh nodded again. "I'll make sure to bring that out during cross."

"Good," Andrew said, a new edge to his tone. "The jury needs to understand that I had plenty of opportunities for sex that night. Reggie might have framed it crassly, but he's right. Any woman at that bar would've gone home with me."

Leigh couldn't give him too much rope. Reggie was not her compatriot. Cole Bradley would be expecting her to put up a plausible defense. "And if the prosecutor argues that rape isn't about sex, it's about control?"

"Then you'll explain that I have plenty of control in my life," Andrew said. "I can do anything I like. I live in a three-million-dollar house. I have my pick of luxury cars. I have access to our family jet. I don't chase after women. Women chase after me."

Leigh nodded her head to encourage him, because his arrogance was her biggest advantage. Andrew had picked the wrong part of Atlanta to commit his crimes. The jury pool would be drawn from registered voters in DeKalb County, a demographic that was overwhelmingly comprised of politically active people of color. They weren't inclined to give a rich, white asshole like Andrew Tenant the benefit of the doubt. And Leigh wasn't inclined to change their minds.

She asked, "What else?"

Andrew's eyes narrowed. Like any predator, his senses were finely tuned. "I assume you agree that going over Tammy's sordid past is the best course of action?"

Reggie saved her from answering. "It's he said/she said, right? The only way you can fight back is to make sure the jury hates her."

Leigh wasn't going to openly challenge a graduate of the Twitter School of Law. "There's more nuance to it than that."

"Nuance?" Reggie repeated, clearly trying to justify his paycheck. "What does that mean?"

"A subtle difference or distinction." Leigh pulled back on the sarcasm. "It means that, generally, you have to be very careful. Tammy will come across as extremely sympathetic."

"Not when you tell them she nearly ruined a guy's life in high school," Reggie said. "And then killed his baby."

Leigh pushed the pile of shit back in his lap. "Honestly, Reggie, everything will rest on your testimony. You'll have to be flawless on the stand."

Reggie's mouth opened, but Andrew's hand went up to stop him.

He told his lapdog, "I'd like a cup of coffee. Sugar, no cream."

Reggie stood up. He left his laptop and phone on the table. He kept his eyes straight as he passed by Leigh. She heard a *click*, but she wasn't sure if it was from the door closing or from Andrew's finger picking at the corner of the file.

He knew that something was wrong, that somehow, at some point, he had lost the upper hand.

For Leigh's part, all that she could think about was that she had not been alone with Andrew since their brief conversation in the parking lot. She looked at the pen on the table in front of her. She did an inventory of the objects in the room. The trophies on the credenza. The heavy glass vase with its wilting flowers. The hard edge of her phone case. They could all be used as weapons.

Again, she returned to her safe spot, which was the case. "We should go over—"

Andrew banged his fist onto the file.

Leigh jumped before she could tell herself not to. Her arms instinctively flew up. She expected Andrew to explode, to come across the room and attack her.

Instead, his expression maintained its usual icy composure as he shoved the file across the table.

She watched the pages flutter as the folder slid across the polished wood and stopped a few inches away from her notepad. Leigh dropped her defensive posture. She recognized the gold seal of the Georgia Institute of Technology. Black letters designated the file as from Student Mental Health Services. The name on the tab read KARLSEN, TAMMY RENAE.

Leigh's inner siren started trilling so loudly she could barely hear herself think. HIPAA, the healthcare law guaranteeing that all medical data was kept private, fell under the purview of Health and Human Services. Violations were investigated by the Office for Civil Rights, and if they found criminal acts, they referred the case to the Department of Justice for prosecution.

Federal law. Federal prosecutor. Federal prison.

She bought herself time, asking Andrew, "What is this?"

"Intel," he said. "I want you to study those records front to back and, when the time comes, I want you to use every detail inside to shred Tammy Karlsen on the stand."

The siren grew louder. The medical chart looked like the original, which meant Reggie had either broken into a secure location inside Georgia Tech, a state institution that took federal dollars, or he had paid someone working in the office to steal the file for him. The list of crimes behind the theft or the receipt of stolen property were almost impossible to calculate.

And if Leigh used the ill-gotten gains, she could be setting herself up as a co-conspirator.

She straightened the pen against the edge of her notepad. "This is not *A Few Good Men*. The Jack Nicholson moment you and Reggie are looking for could turn the jury completely against me. They'll think I'm a raging bitch."

"And?"

"And," Leigh said. "You need to understand that when I am in the courtroom, I am you. Whatever comes out of my mouth, however I behave, whatever tone I set, helps the jury form their opinion of what kind of man you really are."

"So, you go after Tammy, and I stand up and order you to stop," Andrew said. "That way you tear down her credibility and I look like a hero."

Leigh wanted that to happen more than Andrew realized. The judge would probably declare a mistrial and Leigh could get kicked off the case.

Andrew asked, "Is that a good strategy?"

He was testing her again. He could go back to Cole Bradley and ask him to weigh in, and then Leigh wouldn't just be dealing with an enraged psychopath. She would be looking for a job.

She said, "It's *a* strategy."

Andrew was smiling without the smirk. He was telling Leigh that he knew what she was trying to do, but he didn't care.

She felt her heart skip.

Why didn't he care? Was Andrew holding back something even more horrifying than stealing Tammy Karlsen's most intimate therapy moments? Did he have a strategy that Leigh could not divine? Cole Bradley's Netflix Detective warning came back to her.

Peeping Tom turns into rapist. Rapist turns into murderer.

Andrew's smile had intensified. It was the first time since she'd met him that he truly seemed to be enjoying himself.

Leigh broke contact before her fight or flight sent her running out of the building. She looked down at her notepad. She turned to a fresh page. She had to clear her throat again before she could speak. "We should—"

Reggie chose this moment to return. His footsteps dragged as he placed the steaming cup of coffee in front of Andrew. He sat back heavily in the chair. "What did I miss?"

"Nuance." Andrew took a sip from the cup. He grimaced. "Damn, that's hot."

"It's coffee," Reggie said, absently checking his phone.

"I hate when I burn my mouth like that." Andrew was looking directly at Leigh again, making sure she knew that his words

202

were meant for her. "And then you put on your mask, and it feels like you can't catch your breath."

"Hate that." Reggie wasn't paying attention, but Leigh was.

She felt like she was caught in a tractor beam. Andrew was doing the same thing he had done the day before, luring her into his sights, gently pressing at Leigh's weak points until he found a way to break her.

"I'll tell you what it feels like," Andrew said. "Like—what's that kitchen stuff called? Is it plastic film? Cling film?"

Leigh's breath abruptly stopped.

"Do you ever get that feeling?" Andrew asked. "Like somebody took out a roll of cling film from the kitchen drawer and wrapped it around your face six times?"

Vomit rushed into her mouth. Leigh clamped her jaw tight. She tasted the bitter remnants of lunch. Her hand went to her mouth before she could stop it.

"Dude," Reggie said. "That's a weird way to put it."

"It's horrible," Andrew said, light playing across his dark, callous eyes.

Leigh choked the vomit back down. Her stomach pulsed with her heartbeat. This was too much. She couldn't process it all. She needed to get away, to run, to hide.

"I—" her voice caught. "I think we have enough for today."

Andrew asked, "Are you sure?"

There was the smirk again. There was the soft but deep voice. He was feeding off Leigh's terror the same way he had fed off Tammy Karlsen's.

The room turned sideways. Leigh was lightheaded. She blinked. The out-of-body sensation took over, sending her soul somewhere into the firmament while her other self performed the menial tasks that would extricate her from his talons. Left hand closing her notepad, right thumb clicking the pen, then stacking together her two phones, standing on trembling legs, turning to leave.

"Harleigh," Andrew called.

With effort, Leigh turned back around.

His smirk had turned into a pleased grin. "Don't forget the file."

9

Callie scrolled through *Nat Geo*, reading about the African crested rat, who rubs against the bark of the poison arrow tree to store lethal poison in the porcupine-like hairs on his back. Dr. Jerry had warned her about the creature as they were counting out the cash drawer at the end of the day. If he noticed there were more crumpled twenties than usual, he didn't bring it up. He seemed more concerned that Callie never, ever accept an invitation to one of the prickly rodent's dinner parties.

She let the phone rest in her lap as she looked out the bus window. Her body ached the way it always ached when her brain was telling her that the two maintenance doses of methadone every day were not enough. She tried to ignore the craving, focusing instead on the sun as it flashed through the tops of passing trees. The taste of rain was in the air. Binx would want to cuddle. Dr. Jerry had persuaded Callie to take one of the twenties as a bonus. She could give it to Phil as down payment on next week's rent and possibly something to eat for dinner, or she could get off at the next stop, head back to Stewart Avenue and buy a quantity of heroin that would have Janis Joplin clutching her pearls.

The bus wheezed to a slow stop for a red light. Callie turned in her seat, looking through the back window. Then she looked at the vehicles lined up beside the bus.

Only a handful of *white dudes*, but none driving a *nice car*.

After sneaking out of her mother's house this morning, Callie had taken two different bus routes to Dr. Jerry's. Then she had gotten off early and walked down the long, straight road to the clinic so that she could make sure no one was following her. Even with that, she couldn't shake the sensation that she was going to turn around and see the camera's unblinking eye tracking her every move.

Now, she ran through the mantra that had helped her get through the day: No one was watching her. No one had taken photos of her through the plate-glass windows that fronted the vet clinic. No camera-strangling man from the boarded-up house was waiting for her back at Phil's.

Reggie.

Callie should use the name of Andrew's private detective, at least in her head. She should also tell Leigh about him, maybe turn it into a funny story about Phil streaking across the road with her baseball bat and scaring the shit out of him, but the thought of texting her sister, of giving her a point of return contact, felt burdensome.

As much as Callie enjoyed having Leigh back in her life, there was always the downside of seeing her own miserable existence through her sister's eyes. Was Callie eating enough? Was she doing too much dope? Why was she so thin? Why was she breathing so hard? Was she in trouble again? Did she need money? Was this too much money? Where had she been all day?

Well, after I unleashed Mom on my stalker, I sneaked out through the backyard, caught the bus, then I trafficked narcotics on Stewart Avenue, then I passed the proceeds on to Dr. Jerry, then I went to a tanning salon so I could shoot up in the privacy of a small, windowless space instead of going home to my depressing childhood bedroom where a telephoto lens could capture me jamming a needle into my leg again.

Callie rubbed her thigh. A painful bump pressed back against her fingers. She could feel the heat of an abscess festering inside her femoral vein.

Technically, methadone was designed to pass through the digestive system. The take-home syringes they used at the clinic were needle-less because owners were incapable of helping their pets maintain a healthy weight; very few of them were going to jam a needle into their beloved fluff.

Oral medications took longer to hit the system, which was why the usual burst of euphoria was delayed. Injecting it directly into your veins was shitifyingly stupid. The oral suspension contained glycerin and flavoring and coloring and sorbitol, all of which easily broke down in your stomach. Pushing it into your blood-stream could result in particles traveling straight into your lungs and heart or a clog developing at the site of the injection, which resulted in the very type of nasty abscess Callie could feel growing under her fingertips.

Stupid junkie.

The only thing Callie could do was wait for it to get large enough to drain and steal some antibiotics from the drug locker. Then she could steal some more methadone and inject more methadone and get another abscess that had to be drained because what was her life if not a series of drastically bad choices?

The issue was that most IV drug users weren't only addicted to the drug. They were addicted to the process of shooting the drug. It was called a needle fixation, and Callie was so fixated on the needle that even now, her fingertips pressing at what was likely to become a raging infection, all she could think about was how good it would feel when the needle pierced the abscess on its way into her femoral vein again.

Why this made her think of Leigh again was something for her biographers to decipher. Callie tightened her fingers around the phone in her hand. She should call her sister. She should let her know that she was okay.

But, was she really okay?

Callie had made the mistake of looking at her entire naked self in the mirror inside the tanning salon. In the blue glow of the ultraviolet bulbs, her ribs had stood out like whalebone on a corset. She could see the joint in her elbows where the radius and ulna plugged into the humerus. Her hips looked as if someone had clipped her legs to a clothes hanger meant for trousers. There were red, purple, and blue tracks on her arms, belly, legs. Broken needle tips that had been surgically removed. Old abscesses. The new one starting in her leg. Scars she had made, scars that had been made upon her. A pinkish bump in her neck where the Grady doctors had inserted a central line directly into her jugular in order to deliver the medications to treat her Covid.

Callie reached up and lightly traced her finger along the tiny scar. She had been severely dehydrated when Leigh had brought her to the emergency room. Her kidneys and liver were shutting down. Her veins were blown from almost two decades of abuse. Callie was generally a master at blocking out most of the unpleasant moments of her life, but she could easily recall shivering uncontrollably in the hospital bed, breathing through the tube shoved down her throat, and the spacesuit-clad nurse gasping at the state of Callie's ravaged body when she'd come to change the sheets.

There were all kinds of postings on the Covid message boards about what it felt like to be intubated, alone, isolated in the ICU while the world raged on, mindless to your suffering and in some cases denying that it even existed. Most people talked about ghostly visits from long-dead relatives or getting maddening songs like "Wake Me Up Before You Go-Go" stuck inside their heads, but, for Callie, it was one moment that had stayed with her for almost the entire two weeks—

Tap-tap-tap.

Trevor's grubby little fingers menacing the nervous blennies.

Trev, are you tapping on the aquarium like I told you not to?

No, ma'am.

The bus gave off another low hiss, slithering to another stop. Callie watched passengers getting off and on. She allowed herself a brief moment to think about the man Trevor Waleski had grown into. Callie had met her share of rapists. Hell, she'd fallen in love with one before she was out of middle school. From what Leigh had said, Andrew was not big and obnoxious like his father. You could see that much from his website photo. There was none of the stalking, angry gorilla in Buddy's only child. Andrew sounded more like a stargazer, a fish that buried itself in the sand in order to ambush unsuspecting prey. As Dr. Jerry would say, their spiteful reputations were rightfully earned. They had venomous spines to poison their prey. Some had weird, electrified eyeballs that could shock an unsuspecting invertebrate on the ocean floor.

Leigh had certainly been shocked last night. Andrew had scared the shit out of her during the meeting with Reggie Paltz. Callie knew exactly what her sister meant by the cold, dead look in his eyes. When Andrew was a kid, Callie had seen flashes of his burgeoning psychopathy, but of course Andrew's transgressions had been in the order of snack-stealing and pinching Callie's arm while she was trying to fix dinner, not being accused of sadistically raping a woman and slicing her leg the same way that Callie had sliced Buddy's.

She shivered as the bus revved away from the curb. Callie forced her thoughts away from Andrew's current crimes and put her focus squarely back on Leigh.

It was painful to watch her big sister flounder around, because Callie knew the worst part for Leigh was feeling like she had no control. Everything in her sister's life was kept neatly sectioned off. Maddy and Walter and Callie. Her job. Her clients. Her work friends. Whoever she was screwing on the side. Any time there was an intermingling, Leigh lost her mind. Her burn-the-motherfucker-down instinct was never stronger than when she felt vulnerable. Aside from Callie, the only other person who could talk her off the ledge was Walter.

Poor Walter.

Callie loved Leigh's husband almost as much as her sister did. He was much tougher than he looked. Walter had been the one to end their marriage, not the other way around. There was only a certain number of times you could watch someone set themselves ablaze before you stepped away. Callie assumed that growing up with two drunks for parents had taught Walter to choose his battles. This made him particularly understanding of Callie's situation. It made him even more understanding of Leigh's.

If Callie had a needle fixation, Leigh had a chaos fixation. Her big sister longed for the calm normalcy of life with Walter and Maddy, but every time she reached a certain level of tranquility, she found a way to blow it up.

Over the years, Callie had watched the pattern play out dozens of times. It started back in elementary school when Leigh was in line for a spot at the magnet school and ended up losing her slot because she had gone after a girl who'd teased Callie about her hair.

In high school, Leigh had qualified to take special courses at the college, but she'd gotten caught slashing her sleazy boss's tires and ended up with two months in juvie. Then there was her meltdown with Buddy less than a month before she was due in Chicago, though admittedly Callie had laid the dry powder for that particular explosion.

Why Leigh continued the pattern into her adult life was a puzzle that Callie could not solve. Her big sister would have these bursts of joyful wife- and motherhood where she'd be carpooling Maddy and going to dinner parties with Walter and writing white papers on crazy smart shit and doing speaking engagements at legal conferences and then, eventually, something trivial would happen and Leigh would use it as a reason to self-sabotage her way out. She never did anything bad with Maddy, but she would force an argument with Walter or yell at a room mother or get sanctioned by a judge for mouthing off or, if the usual routes failed her, she would do something incredibly stupid that she knew would send her back to purgatory.

There wasn't a hell of a lot of daylight between what Leigh did with her good life and what Callie did with the needle.

The bus bristled against the curb like an exhausted porcupine. Callie pushed herself up from the seat. Her leg immediately started to throb. Navigating down the stairs took an inordinate amount of concentration. She already had issues with her knee. Now, she had added the burgeoning abscess to her list of maladies. She hefted the backpack onto her shoulders and, suddenly, her neck and back moved up to the number one and two slots. Then the pain radiated down her arm, her hand went numb, and, by the time she turned onto Phil's street, all she could think was that another bump of methadone was the only way she was going to get to sleep tonight.

That was how it always started, that slow decline from tapering off to function and then slowly falling back into not functioning. Junkies were always, always going to find the solution to any problem at the tip of a needle.

Phil would take care of Binx. She wouldn't read books to him, but she would keep him brushed and educate him about birds and maybe even give him some advice on his tax situation since she'd spent a lot of time reading up on sovereign citizenship. Callie reached into her pocket. The bright green goggles she had bought at the tanning salon clicked against her fingers. She had thought the cat would want to see them. He knew nothing of indoor tanning.

Callie wiped tears out of her eyes as she trudged the last few yards toward her mother's house. The pile of shit across the street had been smeared by an unfortunate shoe. Her gaze moved upward to the boarded-up house. There was no flicker of light or motion from the front. She saw that the piece of plywood that had disgorged the camera-strangling man had closed its mouth. The brambles and weeds were trampled where he'd run across the yard, robbing Callie of her fleeting hope that the entire thing had been a product of her methadone-addled imagination.

She turned, then kept going in a complete three-sixty.

No *white dude*. No *nice car*, unless you counted Leigh's Audi cooling in the driveway behind Phil's redneck Chevy truck.

That was definitely not a good sign. Leigh wouldn't panic over Callie's lack of a text or phone call because Callie had long ago burnished her reputation as an unreliable correspondent. Her sister would only panic if something bad had happened, and she would not be inside Phil's house for the first time since she'd left for Chicago unless something really, really horrific had brought her there.

Callie knew that she should go inside but, instead, she tilted her head back, watching the sun wink its way through the leaves on the treetops. Dusk was coming fast. In a few minutes, the streetlights would wake up. The temperature would drop. Eventually, the rain she could taste in the air would start to fall.

There was an alternate Callie who could walk away from this. She had disappeared before. If it weren't for Leigh, Callie would've been riding with Binx on a bus right now—it was foolish to think she could leave him at Phil's—and they would've been discussing the fine selection of cheap motels, deciding which one was seedy enough to have dealers but not so seedy that Callie would get raped and killed.

If she was going to die, it was going to be by her own hands.

Callie knew she could dawdle outside the house sorting through fantasies for only so long. She walked up the creaky stairs to her mother's front porch. She was met at the door by the sight of

Binx dragging around his plastic lei, which meant he was having feelings. She longed for her own crutch, but that could come later. Callie knelt to stroke the cat along his back a few times before she let the invisible wire of tension pull her deeper into the house.

Everything was out of whack. Roger and Brock were alert on the couch rather than rolled up in a dognap. The gurgle of aquariums was muted by the seldom-closed door. Even the birds in the dining room were keeping their chirps on the downlow.

She found Leigh and Phil sitting across from each other at the kitchen table. Phil's goth was showing signs of wear. The heavy black eyeliner had turned full-on Marilyn Manson. Leigh had put on her own armor. She'd changed into jeans, a leather jacket, and biker boots. They were both tensed like scorpions waiting for the opportunity to strike.

Callie said, "Another beautiful family moment."

Phil snorted. "What shit did you drop yourself into now, smart ass?"

Leigh said nothing. She looked up at Callie, eyes kaleidoscoping in agony, regret, fear, anger, trepidation, relief.

Callie looked away. "I've been thinking about the Spice Girls. Why is Ginger the only one named after a spice?"

Phil said, "What the fuck are you talking about?"

"*Posh* isn't a spice," Callie said. "Why aren't they named Saffron, or Cardamon, or even Anise?"

Leigh cleared her throat. She said, "Maybe they ran out of thyme."

They smiled at each other.

"Both of you can go fuck yourselves." Phil understood enough to know that she was being left out. She pushed herself up from the table. "Don't eat any of my fucking food. I know what's in there."

Leigh nodded toward the back door. She had to get out of this house.

Callie's neck was killing her from lugging around the backpack, but she didn't want her mother stealing anything so she carried it with her as she followed Leigh outside.

Her sister nodded again, though not toward her Audi parked in the driveway. She wanted to go for a walk, the same way they had gone for walks as kids when being out in the 'hood was safer than being around Phil.

Side by side, they started up the street. Without being asked, Leigh took the backpack. She looped it over her shoulder. Her purse was probably locked in the trunk, and Phil was probably squinting at the fancy car right now, trying to decide whether to break into it or strip it for parts.

Callie couldn't worry about Leigh's car or her mother or anything else at the moment. She looked at the sky. They were heading west, directly into the sunset. The heaviness of promised rain seemed to be lifting. There was a tinge of warmth fighting against the slight drop in the temperature. Still, Callie shivered. She didn't know if the sudden chill was from the lingering effects of Covid, the fading sun, or fear of what her sister was eventually going to say.

Leigh waited until their mother's house was well behind them. Instead of dropping an atom bomb on their existence, she said, "Phil told me a spotted panther has been shitting on the sidewalk to warn her something bad is about to happen."

Callie tested the waters, saying, "She went across the street with her bat this morning, started banging on the boarded-up house for no reason."

"Jesus," Leigh mumbled.

Callie studied her sister's profile, looking for a reaction that would tell her Phil had mentioned the man with the camera.

Leigh asked, "She hasn't hit you, has she?"

"No," Callie lied. Or maybe it wasn't a lie because Phil hadn't meant to hit her so much as Callie had been unable to duck out of the way. "She's calmer now."

"Good," Leigh said, nodding her head because she wanted to believe it was true.

Callie stuck her hands into her pockets though, weirdly, she wanted to hold on to Leigh's hand the same way they'd done when they were little. She curled her fingers around the goggles. She should tell Leigh about the *white dude/nice car*. She should let her know about the telescoping lens on the camera. She should stop shooting up methadone in tanning salons.

The air turned crisp as they continued their stroll. Callie saw the same scenes as the night before: kids playing in the yard, men

212

drinking beers in their carports, another guy washing another muscle car. If Leigh had thoughts on any of the sights, she kept them to herself. She was doing the same thing Callie had done when she'd seen Leigh's Audi in the driveway. She wanted to draw out this false sense of normalcy as long as possible.

Callie wasn't going to stop her. The man with the camera could wait. Or he could get stored somewhere in the back of her brain with the rest of the terrible no-good things that haunted her. She wanted to enjoy this peaceable walk. Callie was seldom out once dusk started to settle. She felt vulnerable at night. Her darting days were over. She couldn't turn her head to see if the stranger behind her was looking at his phone or running toward her with a gun in his hand.

She wrapped her arms around her waist to ward off the chill. She looked up at the trees again. The leaves were popping out like Skittles. Faltering sunlight seeped through the thick fingers of the limbs. She felt her heartbeat slow, matching the soft slap of their footfalls against the cooling asphalt. If Callie could stay in this quiet moment, big sister by her side, for the rest of her life, then she would be happy.

But that wasn't how life worked.

And even if it did, neither one of them had the stomach for it.

Leigh took another left onto a crappier street. Yards overgrown. More boarded-up houses, more poverty, more hopelessness. Callie tried to take a deep breath. The air whistled through her nose, then churned like butter in her lungs. After the grind of Covid, Callie never walked for very long without being aware that she had lungs in her chest and that those lungs were not the same. The sound of her own labored breathing threatened to push her back into those weeks in the ICU. The fearful looks from the nurses and doctors. The distant echo of Leigh's voice when they held up the telephone to Callie's ear. The constant, unrelenting memory of Trevor standing at the aquarium. Buddy banging open the kitchen door.

Pour me one, baby doll.

She took another breath, holding on to it for a few seconds before letting it go.

And then she realized where Leigh had taken her, and Callie had no air left anywhere in her body.

213

Canyon Road, the street that the Waleskis had lived on.

"It's all right," Leigh said. "Keep walking."

Callie wrapped her arms tighter around her body. Leigh was with her, so this should be okay. This should be easy. One foot in front of the other. No turning around. No running away. The one-story ranch was on the right, the low roof sagging from years of neglect. As far as Callie knew, no one had lived there after Trevor and Linda had moved out. Callie had never seen a for-sale sign in front of the house. Phil had never been tasked with finding desperate tenants to rent the three-bedroom crime scene. Callie guessed that one of the neighborhood's many slumlords had rented it out until there was nothing left but a leaking hull.

As they drew closer, Callie felt goose bumps trill along her skin. Not much had changed since the time of the Waleskis. The yard was more overgrown, but the mustard-colored paint was baked into the vinyl siding. All of the windows and doors were boarded up. Graffiti skirted the lower half. No gang tags, but plenty of schoolyard taunts and slut-shaming along with the normal array of spurting cocks.

Leigh kept her pace consistent, but she told Callie, "Look, it's for sale."

Callie shifted her body so she could see into the yard. The FOR SALE BY OWNER sign was being swallowed up by pokeweed. No graffiti had blocked out the letters yet.

Leigh had noticed the same thing. "It must be recent."

Callie asked, "Do you recognize the number?"

"No, but I can do a search on the deed to see who owns the property."

"Let me do that," Callie offered. "I can use Phil's computer."

Leigh hesitated, but said, "Don't let her catch you."

Callie shifted forward again. The house was out of her line of vision, but she could feel it staring her down as they walked past the broken mailbox. She assumed they were going to make the long loop back to Phil's, trapping Callie in an endless *Inferno* circle of her past. She rubbed her neck. Her arm had gone numb up to the shoulder. Her fingertips felt like they were being stabbed by thousands of African crested rats.

The problem with a cervical fusion was that the neck was

214

designed to flex. If you fused one section, then the section below took all of the stress and, over time, the disc wore down and the ligaments gave up and the unfused vertebrae slipped forward and touched the adjacent vertebrae, usually at an angle, usually compressing a nerve, which in turn caused incapacitating pain. This process was called degenerative spondylolisthesis, and the best way to fix it was to fuse the joint together. Then time passed and it happened again so you fused the next joint. Then the next.

Callie wasn't going to go through another cervical fusion. For once, the heroin wasn't the issue. She could be medically detoxed, the same as they'd done when Covid put her in the ICU. The problem was any neurologist would take one listen to the glassy crinkle inside her lungs and tell her she wouldn't survive the anesthesia.

"This way," Leigh said.

Instead of turning right to make the journey back to Phil's, Leigh went straight. Callie didn't ask questions. She just kept walking by her sister's side. They returned to their companionable silence all the way to the playground. This, too, had not changed that much during the ensuing years. Most of the rides were broken, but the swings were in good shape. Leigh shifted the backpack onto both shoulders so she could sit down in one of the cracked leather seats.

Callie walked around the swing set so she was facing the opposite direction from Leigh. She winced at the pinch in her leg when she sat down. Her hand went to her thigh. The heat was still pulsing through her jeans. She pressed her knuckle into the bump until the pain swelled like helium stretching a balloon.

Leigh was watching her, but she didn't ask what was going on. She held tight to the chains, took two steps back, then lifted her feet into the air. She disappeared for a few seconds, then swung back into Callie's line of sight. She wasn't smiling. Her face had a grim set to it.

Callie started her swing. The balance was surprisingly harder when you couldn't use the full range of motion in your head. She finally got the hang of it, pulling on the chains, leaning back into the upswing. Leigh zoomed by, going faster each time. They could be two trunks on a couple of drunken elephants, if elephants weren't notorious teetotalers.

The silence continued as they both swung back and forth—nothing crazy, they were women of a certain age now, but they kept up a steady, graceful sway that helped dissipate some of the anxious energy between them.

Leigh said, "I used to take Maddy to the park when she was little."

Callie blurred her eyes at the darkening sky. The sun had slipped away. Streetlights started flickering on.

"I would watch her on the swings and think about how you used to try to go high enough to flip around the bar." Leigh swung by, legs pushing out. "You almost did a few times."

"I almost fell flat on my ass."

"Maddy's so beautiful, Cal." Leigh went silent as she disappeared, then picked back up when she was facing Callie. "I don't know why I got something so perfect in my life, but I'm grateful every single day. So grateful."

Callie closed her eyes, feeling the cold rush of wind in her face, listening to the *swish* every time Leigh soared past.

"She loves sports," Leigh said. "Tennis, volleyball, soccer, the usual stuff kids do."

Callie marveled at the idea that this was usual. The playground they were swinging in had been her only outlet for fun. At ten, she'd been pushed into finding an after-school job. By the time she'd turned fourteen, she was either obsessing about how to keep Buddy in her life or obsessing about how to handle his death. She would've killed to run up and down a field kicking around a ball.

Leigh said, "She's not passionate about competing. Not like you were. It's just fun for her. This generation—they are all incredibly, boringly, sportsmanlike."

Callie opened her eyes. She couldn't dive any deeper into this conversation. "I guess there's something to be said for Phil's style of parenting. Neither one of us has ever been sportsmanlike."

Leigh slowed her swing, turning to watch Callie. She wasn't going to drop the subject. "Walter hates soccer, but he's at every practice and every game."

That sounded like a very Walter kind of thing to do.

"Maddy hates hiking," Leigh said. "But the last weekend of

every month, they hike up Kennesaw Mountain because she loves spending time with him."

Callie leaned back in the leather seat, pushing herself to go higher. She liked the idea of Walter in a comically tall red and brown ball cap with matching pantsuit, but she understood he probably did not go on hikes dressed like Elmer Fudd hunting wabbits.

"She loves to read," Leigh said. "She reminds me of you when you were a kid. Phil used to get furious when you had your nose in a book. She didn't understand what the stories meant to you."

Callie swung past, her sneakers turning into white fangs biting into the dark sky. She wanted to stay suspended in the air like that forever, to never drop down into reality.

"She loves animals. Rabbits, gerbils, cats, dogs."

Callie swung back, passing Leigh one more time before she let her feet drag the ground. The swing came to a slow standstill. She twisted the chains to face her sister.

She asked, "What happened, Leigh? Why are you here?"

"To—" Leigh laughed, because she seemed to realize that what she was about to say was stupid, but she said it anyway. "To see my sister."

Callie wanted to keep twisting the chains the way she used to, spinning up in one direction, then down in another, until she got so dizzy that she had to stagger to the seesaw to find her bearings. She asked Leigh, "Do you think the word seesaw is because you *see* someone when they're up, and then you *saw* them when—"

"Cal," Leigh said. "Andrew knows how I killed Buddy."

Callie gripped the cold chains tight in her hands.

"We were in the conference room going over his case," Leigh said. "He told me that his mask made it hard to breathe. He said it was like someone wrapped cling film around his head six times."

Callie felt shock freeze its way through her body. "Is that how many—"

"Yes."

"But—" Callie ran back through the tiny snippets she could remember from the night Buddy had died. "Andrew was asleep, Harleigh. We kept going back into his room. He was drugged out of his mind."

"I missed something," Leigh said, always eager to take the blame. "I don't know how he knows, or what else he knows, but it gives him power over every single part of my life. I control nothing right now. He can do what he likes, force me to do whatever he wants."

Callie saw the point of her misery. "What does he want you to do?"

Leigh looked down at the ground. Callie was used to seeing her sister angry or annoyed, but never ashamed.

"Harleigh?"

"Tammy Karlsen, the victim. Reggie stole her patient chart from Tech's student mental health services. She attended one session a week for almost two years. There's all kinds of personal details in it. Stuff that she wouldn't want anyone to know." Leigh let out a long, pained breath. "Andrew wants me to use the personal information to break her on the stand."

Callie thought about her own medical charts scattered across so many different rehab centers and psych units. Had Reggie looked for those, too? She had never said anything about the murder, but there were things in those notes that she wouldn't want anyone reading.

Especially her sister.

Leigh said, "He's looking for a moment, like in a movie, where Tammy breaks down and—I don't know—gives up? It's like he wants to watch her being assaulted again."

Callie didn't ask Leigh whether or not she was capable of making this moment happen. She could tell by her sister's demeanor that her legal brain had already developed a blueprint. "What's in her medical chart?"

Leigh pressed together her lips. "Tammy was raped in high school. She got pregnant, got an abortion. She never told anybody but, after, she became isolated. She lost her friends. She started cutting herself. Then drinking to excess. Then she developed an eating disorder."

"Did no one tell her about heroin?"

Leigh shook her head. She wasn't in the mood for dark humor. "A professor noticed some of the warning signs. He sent Tammy to student mental health. She got therapy, and it really turned her life around. You can see it in the chart. She was a total mess, but then, slowly, she started to get better. She took control of her life. She graduated with honors. She has—had—a good life. She made that for herself. She crawled out of that pit and made it."

Callie wondered if Leigh was asking why Callie hadn't been able to pull herself out of a similar tailspin. There were too many *if onlys* behind that question—*If only* the social workers had taken them away from Phil. *If only* Linda had been their mother. *If only* Leigh had known that Buddy was a pedophile. *If only* Callie hadn't broken her neck and ended up a stupid fucking junkie.

"I—" Leigh looked up at the sky. She had started crying. "My clients are never good people, but I usually like them. Even the assholes. Especially the assholes. I understand how you can make bad choices. How you can get angry and do bad things. Terrible things."

Callie didn't need clarification on the terrible things.

"Andrew's not afraid of being convicted," Leigh said. "He's never been scared, not since the moment I met him. Which means he's got a way out of this."

Callie knew the best way out for Tammy. She had considered the option for herself often enough.

Leigh said, "It was one thing when I felt like it was just me who could get in trouble. I did a bad thing. I should've gone to prison. That's fair. But Tammy is innocent."

Callie watched her kick at the dirt. This defeated woman was not the sister she had grown up with. Leigh never gave up on anything. If you came at her with a knife, she came back at you with a bazooka. "So what's next?"

"What's next is this is getting too dangerous. I want you to get your things, pack up your cat, and I'll drive you somewhere safe." Leigh caught her eye. "Andrew already has me under his thumb. It's just a matter of time before he comes after you."

This would've been a really good time to tell Leigh about the man in the boarded-up house, but Callie needed her sister to focus, not spin off into a paranoid vortex.

She said, "If you want to measure the height of a mountain, the hardest part isn't finding the peak, it's figuring out where the bottom starts."

Leigh gave her a confused look. "Did you get that off a fortune cookie?"

Callie was fairly certain she had stolen it from an eel historian. "What's the rock-bottom question about Andrew that we can't answer?"

"Oh," Leigh seemed to understand. "I thought of it as the Andrew Hypothesis, but I couldn't figure out the *B* that connects the *A* and the *C*."

"I think we should spend the next two hours pinning down the correct terminology."

Leigh groaned, but she clearly needed this. "It's a two-part question. First part: *what* does Andrew know? Second part: *how* does he know it?"

"So, to find the *what* and the *how*, begin at the beginning." Callie rubbed her numb hand, pressing blood into the fingers. She had worked so hard to forget everything about Buddy's murder, but now she didn't have a choice but to confront it head-on. "Did I check on Andrew after the fight with Buddy? I mean, before I called you?"

"Yes," Leigh said. "That was the first thing I asked you about when I got there, because I was worried there was a witness. You told me that you left Buddy in the kitchen, you went into Andrew's room and kissed his head, then you called me from the master bedroom. You told me he was completely out of it."

Callie mentally walked herself through the Waleskis' filthy house. She could see herself kissing Andrew on the head, making certain he was really asleep, then heading down the hall to the master bedroom and picking up the pink princess phone by Linda's side of the bed.

She told Leigh, "The cord was ripped off the phone in the kitchen. How could I call you from the bedroom?"

"You hung the receiver back up. I saw it on the wall phone when I got there."

That made sense, so Callie believed her. "Was anyone else there? Like, a neighbor who could've seen?"

"When it was happening?" Leigh shook her head. "We would've heard about it before now. Especially when Linda came into all

220

of that family money. Someone would've approached her about buying the information."

She had that right. There was not one person in the entire 'hood who would've let the opportunity for a cash payday slip by. "Was there a time when we were both out of the house?"

"Not until the end when we were loading the trash bags into my car," Leigh said. "And before that, we backtracked the fight. It took us four hours, and we kept making sure Andrew was asleep every twenty minutes at least."

Callie nodded, because she could vividly recall that she had been the one to go into the room each time. Andrew always slept on his side, his tiny body curled into a ball, a clicking sound coming out of his open mouth.

"We're back where we started," Leigh said. "We still don't know how much Andrew knows or how he knows it."

Callie didn't need the reminder. "Tell me the list you've been going over for the last two days."

"We searched for more cameras. We searched for more video cassettes," Leigh counted off the items on her fingers. "We checked every book on the shelves, turned over the furniture and mattresses, shook the jars and vases, the potted plants. We took everything out of the kitchen cabinets. We unscrewed the grills from all the air vents. You even put your hand inside the aquarium."

Leigh had run out of fingers.

Callie asked, "Maybe Andrew was pretending to be asleep? He could've heard me in the hallway outside his door. The boards creaked."

"He was ten years old," Leigh said. "Kids that age are ridiculously transparent."

"We were kids, too."

Leigh was already shaking her head. "Think about how complicated the cover-up would have to be. Andrew would have to pretend he hadn't seen his father murdered. Then keep pretending when Linda got home from work the next morning. Then lie to the cops. Then lie to whoever asked him about the last time he'd seen his father. Then keep the secret from you for a month while you were still babysitting him. Then keep the secret for all these years."

"He's a psychopath."

"Sure, but he was still a baby," Leigh said. "Cognitively, even smart ten-year-olds are a mess. They try to act like adults, but they still make kid mistakes. They lose stuff all the time—jackets, shoes, books. They can barely be trusted to bathe themselves. They tell stupid lies you can see straight through. There's no way even a ten-year-old psychopath could pull off that level of deceit."

If anyone knew how bad a liar Andrew had been at ten, it was Callie at fourteen. "What about Andrew's girlfriend?"

"Sidney Winslow," Leigh provided. "Yesterday at Reggie's office, I gave Andrew my little speech on the exceptions to spousal privilege. He looked like he was going to shit himself. He made Sidney wait in the parking lot. She pitched a fit. He knows he can't trust her."

"Which means he probably hasn't shared anything about how his father really died." Callie asked, "Do you think we could use her to get to him?"

"She's definitely a weak link," Leigh said. "If you take it on faith that Andrew was planning to screw with me during that first meeting with Reggie Paltz, the thing that sidetracked him was Sidney."

"What do you know about her?"

"Not a damn thing," Leigh said. "I found a credit check that the previous lawyer had Reggie do last fall. No outstanding debt. Nothing suspicious or damning, but the report is very superficial. Normally, when I want a deep dive on a witness, I assign an investigator to ask questions and follow them around, check all social media, look into where they work, but my boss made Reggie the exclusive investigator on the case. If I hire another one, Andrew or Linda or my boss will see the charges on my billing and ask for an explanation."

"Can't you pay somebody out of your own pocket?"

"I'd have to use my credit card or checking account, both of which would leave a trail. And all the investigators I know are already working for the firm, so that would get out almost immediately. And then I'd have to explain why I was doing it privately instead of through the firm, and then that gets me back to Andrew finding out." Leigh anticipated the alternative. "You can't use

Phil's computer for something like this. It's not looking up a deed."

"The cameras at the downtown library have been broken for the last year. I'll use one of the public computers." Callie shrugged. "Just me and the other junkies wasting time in the air conditioning."

Leigh cleared her throat. She hated Callie calling herself a junkie almost as much as she hated the fact that Callie was a junkie. "Make sure the cameras are still broken. I don't want you to take any risks."

Callie watched Leigh wipe away her tears.

Leigh said, "We still haven't found the *B*."

"You mean the rock-bottom." Callie watched her sister's eyes roll. She repeated the two questions. "What does Andrew know? How does he know?"

"And what's he going to do with the information?" Leigh added. "He's not going to stop with Tammy. That's for damn sure. He's like a shark that keeps moving forward."

"You're giving him too much power," Callie said. "You're always telling me that nobody is a criminal mastermind. They get lucky. They don't get caught with their hand in the cookie jar. They don't brag about stealing cookies. It's not like Andrew had a secret army of drones in the sky when he was ten years old. Obviously, he—"

Leigh stood up. Her mouth opened, then closed. She looked out in the street. She turned back to Callie. "Let's go."

Callie didn't ask where. She could tell by the look on her sister's face that Leigh had thought of something. All Callie could do was try to keep up as she followed her sister out of the park.

Her lungs were not prepared for the brisk pace. Callie was breathless by the time they reached the road that looped back to Phil's. Except Leigh didn't take the left. She kept going straight, which would lead them past the Waleskis' mustard-colored house again. The route added no more than three minutes. Callie knew because she had walked both many times before. There had been no streetlights back then, just the dark silence and the understanding that she had to wash off what had just happened before she could go to bed in her mother's house.

"Keep up," Leigh said.

Callie struggled to match Leigh's purposeful stride. Her heart started to thump against her ribs. Callie imagined it was like two pieces of flint striking against each other until the spark ignited and her heart was on fire because they weren't just going to walk past the Waleskis' house. Leigh turned left, heading up their driveway.

Callie followed her until her feet refused to take another step. She stood at the edge of the faded oil stain where Buddy used to park his rusted-out yellow Corvette.

"Calliope." Leigh had turned around, hands on her hips, already annoyed. "We're doing this, so suck it up and stick close to me."

Her sister's bossy tone was the exact same as the one she had used the night they had chopped up Buddy Waleski. *Get his toolbox out of the car. Go to the shed and find the machete. Bring the gas can. Where's the bleach? How many rags can we use without Linda noticing they're gone?*

Leigh turned and disappeared into the black hole of the carport.

Callie reluctantly followed, blinking her eyes to help them adjust. She could see shadows, an outline of her sister standing at the door that led into the kitchen.

Leigh reached up, using her bare hands to pry back the slab of plywood nailed over the opening. The wood was so old it splintered. Leigh didn't stop. She grabbed at the jagged edge and pulled until there was a wide enough space for her to reach the doorknob.

The kitchen door swung open.

Callie was expecting the familiar damp, musty odor but the stench of meth filled the air.

"Christ." Leigh covered her nose to fight the ammonia smell. "Cats must've gotten into the house."

Callie didn't correct her. She hugged her arms to her waist. Somewhere in her head, she knew why Leigh wanted to be here, but she imagined that revelation being folded into a triangle, and then into the shape of a kite, and eventually transforming into an origami swan gliding toward the inaccessible currents deep within her memories.

"Let's go." Leigh stepped over the plywood hurdle and, like

224

that, she was inside the Waleskis' kitchen for the first time in twenty-three years.

If it bothered her, Leigh didn't say. She held out her hand to Callie, waiting.

Callie didn't take her hand. Her knees wanted to buckle. Tears wept from her eyes. She couldn't see into the dark room but she heard the loud *pop* of Buddy opening the kitchen door. The *hack* of a wet cough. The *slap* of his briefcase on the counter. The *bang* of a chair being kicked under the table. The *ping* of cookie crumbs dropping from his mouth, because everywhere Buddy went there was *noise, noise, noise.*

Callie blinked again. Leigh was snapping her fingers in front of her face.

"Cal," Leigh said. "You were able to stay with Andrew in this house and pretend for an entire month that nothing happened. You can pretend for another ten minutes."

Callie had only been able to pretend because she'd siphoned off alcohol from the bottles behind the bar.

Leigh said, "Calliope, sac the hell up."

Her voice was hard, but Callie could hear that she was starting to crack. The house was getting to Leigh. This was the first time her sister had returned to the scene of their crimes. She wasn't ordering Callie so much as begging her to please, for the love of God, help her get through this.

That was how it worked. Only one of them could fall apart at a time.

Callie grabbed onto Leigh's hand. She started to raise her leg but, the second she was clear of the splintered plywood, Leigh yanked hard enough to pull her inside.

Callie stumbled into her sister. She felt her neck crack. She tasted blood where she'd bitten down on her tongue.

Leigh asked, "Are you okay?"

"Yes," Callie said, because anything that hurt her now could be chased away by the needle later. "Tell me what to do."

Leigh took out two phones, one from each of her back pockets. She turned on the flashlight apps. The beams caught the tired linoleum. Four deep indentations showed where the legs of the Waleskis' kitchen table had been. Callie stared at the divots until

225

she felt her face pressing into the table while Buddy stood behind her.

Doll you gotta stop squirming I need you to stop so I can—

"Cal?" Leigh was holding out one of the phones.

Callie took it, shining the light around the kitchen. No table and chairs, no blender and toaster. The cabinet doors were hanging off. Pipes were missing under the sink. The outlets were stripped out where someone had stolen the electrical wiring for the copper.

Leigh pointed her light up at the popcorn ceiling. Callie recognized some of the old water stains, but the gouges where the wire had been ripped out of the Sheetrock were new. The light scanned the tops of the cabinets. A soffit ran around the perimeter of the room. The air-conditioner grills had been pulled off. The holes were black, empty mouths that flashed when the light hit the metal duct in the back of the throats.

Callie felt the origami swan raising her head. The pointy beak opened as if to share a secret, but then just as suddenly as the creature had appeared, she folded back down her head and disappeared into the well of Callie's untapped memories.

"Let's look in here." Leigh left the kitchen. She walked into the living room.

Callie slowly traced her sister's footsteps, stopping in the middle of the room. No tired orange couch, no leather club chairs with cigarette-burned arms, no giant TV forming the apex of a triangle, cables hanging down like a coiled snake.

The bar was still hulking in the corner.

The mosaic was busted off, chips of ceramic littering the floor. The smoked mirrors had been splintered. Callie heard heavy footsteps behind her. She saw Buddy striding across the room, bragging about the money for a new job, slapping cookie crumbs off his shirt.

Pour me one, baby doll.

Callie blinked, and the scene was replaced with shattered crack pipes, pieces of burned foil, used syringes, and four stained mattresses laid out on shag carpet that was so old it crunched under her shoes. The realization that they were in a shooting gallery made every pore in Callie's skin pucker, desperate for a needle to drown the origami swan in wave after wave of bright white heroin.

"Callie," Leigh called. "Help me."

Reluctantly, Callie left the sanctuary. Leigh was standing at the end of the hall. The bathroom door was gone. Callie saw the sink was broken, more pipes stolen. Leigh had her light trained up at the ceiling.

Callie heard the floorboards creak as she passed Andrew's bedroom. She couldn't look up. "What is it?"

"The access panel to the attic," Leigh said. "I never noticed it before. We didn't search it."

Callie stepped back, tilting to look up at the world's tiniest tray ceiling. The panel was less than two feet square. Because her entire knowledge of attics came from horror movies and *Jane Eyre*, she asked, "Shouldn't there be stairs?"

"No, you idiot. Give me a boost so I can get up there."

Callie moved without thinking, crouching down, lacing together her hands.

Leigh put her foot in the basket. The sole of her boot was scratchy against Callie's palms. Leigh's hand went to Callie's shoulder. She tested her weight.

Fire roiled through Callie's neck and shoulders. Her teeth clamped down. She had started to shake even before Leigh had shifted her full weight into Callie's hands.

Leigh said, "You can't lift me, can you?"

"I can do it."

"No, you can't." Leigh returned her foot to the floor. "I know your arm is numb because you keep rubbing it. You can barely turn your head. Help me slide over those mattresses. We can make a pile and—"

"Get hepatitis?" Callie finished. "Leigh, you can't touch those mattresses. They're covered in cum and—"

"What else am I going to do?"

Callie knew what had to come next. "I'll go up."

"I won't let you—"

"Just fucking lift me, okay?"

Leigh didn't hesitate nearly long enough for Callie's liking. She had forgotten how cut-throat the old Leigh could get. Her sister bent her knees, offered her hands as a step. This was how Leigh got when she was determined to do something. Not even guilt could stop her from making one more horrible mistake.

And Callie knew instinctively that whatever she found in that attic would be a horrible mistake.

She knelt to place the phone flat on the floor. The flashlight was a spot on the ceiling. She didn't let herself think about how many times she had stepped her foot into a fifteen-year-old boy's hands, then been raised up into the air like a ballerina on a music box. The trust it took to perform the maneuver was part training, part lunacy.

It was also twenty years ago. Now, just lifting her foot meant Callie had to maintain her balance by holding on to the wall and grabbing Leigh's shoulder. The lift was far from graceful. Callie kicked out her free leg, bracing her sneaker against the wall so she didn't topple over. The effect was to make her look like a fly caught in a web.

Callie could not tilt back far enough to see what was right above her. She raised her hands over her head and located the panel by feel. She pressed her palms into the center, but the damn thing was either painted shut or so old that it had melded into the trim. Callie banged her fist into the wood hard enough that it gonged down into each and every millimeter of her spine. She squeezed her eyes shut against the sharp cramps of misfiring nerves and pounded until the wood cracked down the center.

Dirt and grime and chunks of insulation rained down on her face. She used her fingers to wipe grit out of her eyes and nose. The beam of light from the phone had opened like an umbrella into the attic.

Leigh lifted her higher. Callie saw that the panel hadn't been painted shut. Nails jutted into the air. They were shiny in the rays of the flashlight. She told her sister, "These look new."

"Come down," Leigh said. She wasn't even winded from the effort of holding Callie's full weight. "I can pull myself up and—"

Callie stepped onto her shoulder. She poked her head into the attic like a meerkat. The smell was rancid, but not from meth. Squirrels or rats or both had set up nests in the narrow attic space. Callie couldn't tell if any of them were still in residence.

What she did know was that the ceiling was too low for her to stand. Callie guessed there was about three feet of space between the rafters that held up the roof and the joists that the ceiling was nailed to. The slope of the roof narrowed down to less than a foot at the outside walls of the house.

"Stay on the joists," Leigh said. "Otherwise you'll fall through the ceiling."

As if Callie hadn't watched Tom Hanks in *The Money Pit* dozens of times.

She folded back the broken access panel, forcing the nails to flatten down with it. Leigh helped from below, but Callie's arms shook as she raised herself up high enough to bend at the waist. She managed to cram the rest of her body into the attic by cater-pillaring on her belly as Leigh pistoned her hands around Callie's legs.

"Hold on," Leigh said, as if Callie had a choice.

Light flashed into the attic. Then again. Then again. Leigh was jumping, by the sound of it, either trying to see into the space or providing a strobing ambience to the ghosts-in-the-attic atmosphere.

Callie asked, "What are you doing?"

"You left the phone on the floor," Leigh said. "I'm trying to see where to throw it."

Again, Callie had no choice but to lay on her belly and wait. She'd lucked up, because there was something underneath her hips that bridged the joists. Plastic, by the flex of it. Rough against her bare belly, because her Care Bears T-shirt had ripped on a nail. Another outfit ruined.

"Here it comes," Leigh said. There were some loud thumps before she tossed the phone in Callie's direction. "Can you reach it?"

Callie blindly felt behind her. The toss had been good. She told Leigh, "Got it."

"Can you see anything?"

"Not yet." Light didn't exactly solve the problem. There was no way for Callie to look ahead from this angle. Her nose was almost touching the back of the Sheetrock that covered the ceiling. Insulation was sucking into her lungs. She had to shove the phone into her back pocket to test whether or not she could raise herself up on her hands and knees. Right hand and knee on one joist. Left hand and knee on the other. Ceiling down below waiting for her to fall through and crack another vertebra into pieces.

The last part didn't happen, but her muscles howled from straddling the sixteen-inch gap in the joists. There had been a time when Callie could skip along a balance beam, throw herself around the uneven bars, flip head over heels across the gym floor. There was no muscle in her body that held on to that memory. She despised herself for her perpetual fragility.

"Cal?" Leigh called up, her anxiety like the squiggly lines on a cartoon sun. "Are you okay?"

"Yes." Callie reached out her left hand, dragged along her left knee, then did the same on the right side, testing her ability to inch forward along the joists before responding, "I don't see anything yet. I'm going to poke around."

Leigh didn't answer. She was probably holding her breath or pacing or finding some way to absorb all the guilt that had been trapped inside this house for over two decades.

Callie used the phone to shine a path. What she saw gave her a moment of hesitation. "Someone's been up here recently. The insulation has been pulled back."

Leigh already knew this. It's why she had wanted to go into the attic. They needed to answer the rock-bottom questions, which was the terminology that people who actually crawled through the attic got to use instead of something stupid like the *B* that linked the *A* and the *C*.

What did Andrew know? How did he know it?

Callie ignored the rock-bottom, visualizing the origami swan gracefully pushing back against the current that wanted to drag it down. She had purposefully built her life around the luxury of never having to think ahead. Now, she went against that lifetime of training and crawled forward on her hands and knees, keeping to the path of insulation that had been parted like the Red Sea. A skinny gray cable lay on the seabed. Rats had munched it into pieces, which was the plight of being a rat. Their teeth were constantly growing and they teethed on wires like babies with pacifiers, if a bite from a baby could give you hantavirus.

"Cal?" Leigh called.

"I'm good," she lied. "Stop asking."

Callie paused her forward progress, trying to settle her mind, catch her breath, focus her thoughts on the task at hand. None of that worked, but she resumed crawling, carefully picking her way over a thick beam. The roughly hewn rafters scraped at her back as the pitch of the roof narrowed the space. She knew that she had just crossed over into the kitchen. Every muscle in her body knew it, too. She tried to lift her hand, but it wouldn't leave the joist. She tried to move her leg. Same problem.

Sweat rolled off her nose and splattered onto the back of the Sheetrock. The heat in the attic had sneaked up on her, slowly tightening its fingers around her neck. Another drop of sweat puddled into the other. Her eyes closed. She visualized the kitchen below. Lights on. Faucet running. Chairs tucked under the table. Buddy's briefcase on the counter. His body on the floor.

Callie felt a snort of hot breath on the back of her neck.

The gorilla was behind her. Gripping her by the shoulders. Breathing into her ear. His mouth moved closer. She smelled cheap whiskey and cigars and *Stay still, little dolly, I can't stop I'm sorry baby girl I'm so sorry just relax into it come on just breathe.*

She opened her eyes. Gasped in a mouthful of warm air. Callie's arms were shaking so hard she was afraid they wouldn't support her much longer. She rolled to her side, lining up her body along the narrow joist like a cat balancing on the back of a couch. She looked at the underside of the roof. Nails spiked through the wood where the shingles had been pounded in. Water stains spread like dark thought bubbles above her head.

The beautiful origami swan was gone, devoured by the malicious gorilla, but Callie could not suppress the truth any longer.

She turned the light not straight ahead, but to the side. She pushed up on her elbow, making herself look over the beam, back toward the access panel. A plastic cutting board spanned two joists. Callie's hand went to her stomach. She could still feel where the gouged plastic had scratched across her belly when she'd first crawled into the attic.

She remembered the large cutting board from Linda Waleski's kitchen. It had been on the counter one day then gone the next, and Callie had assumed that Linda had decided it was easier to throw it away than to clean it.

But now she understood that Buddy had stolen the board for his attic project.

Callie used the light to follow the rat-chewed cable that trailed back to the board. Without any other information, she knew that a VCR had been placed on the plastic. She knew that the gray, three-pronged RCA cable had hung down from the jacks on the front of the machine. Red for the right audio channel. White for the left audio. Yellow for video. The cable threaded into one long wire that now stretched in pieces back in Callie's direction, then took a turn to the left.

She followed the cable, inching on her elbows until her body lay across the joists instead of alongside them. The space narrowed even more. She used the light to examine the back of the Sheetrock. There wasn't enough room to get anything but a harsh reflection off the shiny brown paper. She tucked the phone into her pocket, sending the attic into darkness.

Even with that, Callie still closed her eyes. She ran her fingers along the flat surface. Almost immediately, she found a shallow indentation. Over time, something had left an impression in the soft pulp of the Sheetrock. Something two inches round, the same size as the focus ring on a camera. The same kind of camera that plugged into the end of the chewed cable that wound back to the missing VCR.

She heard movement below. Leigh was in the kitchen. Callie listened to her sister's footsteps crunching against the grit on the floor. Leigh was standing where the table and chairs had been. A few steps forward and she'd be at the sink. A few steps back and she'd be by the wall where the kitchen phone used to be.

"Callie?" Leigh turned her phone upward. A beam of light shone through the hole in the ceiling. "What did you find?"

Callie did not respond.

What she had found was the answer to both of their rock-bottom questions.

Andrew knew everything because he had seen everything.

Wednesday

10

Leigh looked at the clock. It was exactly eight in the morning and rush-hour traffic was already tangling up the roads. She was back behind the wheel of her Audi but, for the first time in days, she no longer felt like she was drowning on dry land. Leigh's sense of relief ran counter to what Callie had found in the Waleskis' attic last night, but Andrew had already made it clear that he knew the intimate details of his father's murder. What Leigh had not known, what had pushed her to the brink of insanity, was *how* he knew. Now that Leigh had the *how*, Andrew was robbed of some of the power he held over her.

That Callie had been the one to give Leigh the leverage made it even sweeter. Her sister's observation that Andrew didn't have *a secret army of drones in the sky* had clicked something in Leigh's head. At eighteen, she had been woefully unfamiliar with the basics of house construction. There were walls and floors and ceilings and somehow the water got to the faucet and the electricity got to the lights. She had not yet been forced to navigate a crawlspace looking for the water shut-off valve because her husband had chosen that weekend to visit his mother. She had never hidden Christmas presents in the attic to keep them secreted away from a very curious and clever little girl.

From the moment Andrew had reappeared in her life, Leigh had been going through that horrible night of the attack over and over again trying to see what they had missed. Until that moment on the swings, it had never occurred to her that they had looked everywhere but *up*.

After that, there were no surprises. Every Christmas during high school, Leigh had worked at the audio/visual department at Circuit City. They got paid on commission, so Leigh had worn a tight shirt and blown out her hair to attract the hapless men who'd wander in at the last minute looking for something expensive to buy their wives that they could actually use for themselves. She had sold dozens of Canon Optura camcorders. Then she had sold storage cases, tripods, cables, extra batteries, and VHS tapes because the mini-cassettes only held around ninety minutes of video, so you either had to erase the content or back it up.

Callie had taken several photos of Buddy's attic set-up, but Leigh knew exactly what it looked like before her sister had even come down. The RCA cable connected to the camera on one end and the VCR on the other. You pressed a button on the camera, then you pressed record on the VCR and everything backed up. What Callie's photos had done was trigger a long-lost memory of Leigh finding the remote control in Buddy's pants pocket. She had flung it across the floor so hard that the battery compartment had cracked open.

Buddy had not walked around all day with the remote in his pocket. He had deliberately put it in there, the same way he had deliberately hidden the mini-cassette from the bar camera in the box of Black & Milds. The fact that he had pressed record on the camera hidden over the kitchen table before the fight broke out with Callie was what the legal world called premeditation. The only reason Buddy Waleski had started the camera was because he had known when he followed Callie into the kitchen that he was going to hurt her.

And now his son had it all on tape.

Leigh mentally reviewed the many things that Andrew Tenant had *not* done with the recording: He had not gone to the police. He had not shown it to Cole Bradley. He had not confronted Leigh with the evidence. He had not told anyone who could do anything about it.

What he *had* done was use the information to force Leigh into doing something she did not want to do. She had taken Tammy Karlsen's medical chart off the conference room table. She had read the therapy notes. She had formed, at least in her head, a way to use the information to bring Tammy to her knees.

For now, Leigh's only crime was receiving stolen property. The charge was mitigated by the fact that she was Andrew's lawyer and hadn't advised him to steal it, or done anything criminal with it herself, and for that matter, how did she know it was stolen? Anyone with a printer could make a file folder look official. Anyone with a chunk of free time could generate the roughly 138 pages front-and-back that constituted summaries from over sixty alleged therapy sessions.

Leigh glanced over at her purse as she waited for the light to change. The folder was sticking out of the top. There was a shape to the notes inside, almost like a novel. The crushing pain of Tammy's early sessions, the gradual opening up where she confessed the horror and shame of what had happened to her in high school. The stumbles on the way to getting her drinking, her cutting, her bulimia, all under control. The failed attempts at reconciliation. The slow understanding that she could not change her past, but she could try to shape her future.

What the chart mostly revealed was that Tammy Karlsen was smart and insightful and funny and driven—but all Leigh could think while she read through to the last pages was, *why couldn't her sister do this?*

The intellectual part of Leigh understood the science of addiction. She also knew that two-thirds of Oxy abusers were stupid kids experimenting with drugs, not pain patients who got hooked. But even within that group of pain patients, fewer than ten percent became addicted. Roughly four to six percent transitioned to heroin. More than sixty percent matured out of their addiction or went through what was called natural recovery, where they got tired of being addicts and found a way to quit—one-third of them without treatment. As for treatment, in-patient rehab was a statistical failure, and Nar-Anon was more miss than hit. Methadone and Suboxone were the best-studied maintenance medications, but doctors who prescribed medication-assisted treatment were so heavily regulated that they couldn't help more than one hundred patients in their first year and no more than 275 thereafter.

Meanwhile, around 130 Americans died of an overdose every single day.

Callie knew these facts better than anybody, but nothing about them had ever compelled her to quit. At least not for a meaningful amount of time. Over the past twenty years, she had created her own fantasy world to live in, where everything unpleasant or troubling was blurred out by opioids or willful denial. It was like her emotional maturation had stopped the second she'd swallowed that first Oxycontin. Callie had surrounded herself with animals who would not hurt her, books set in the past so that she knew everything turned out okay, and people who would never really know her. Callie did not Netflix and chill. She had left no digital footprint. She had purposefully kept herself a stranger to the modern world. Walter once said if you only understood pop cultural references from before 2003, then you understood Callie.

The car's GPS told Leigh to take a left at the next light. She swerved into the turning lane. She waved her hand over her shoulder at the driver who'd wanted to get there first. Then she ignored him as he flipped her off and started screaming.

Leigh tapped her finger on the steering wheel as she waited for the light to change. After last night, she could only pray that her sister wasn't lying dead somewhere with a needle sticking out of her arm. Callie had been a wreck when she'd dropped out of the attic. Her teeth were chattering. She couldn't stop rubbing her arms. Even when they'd finally reached Phil's house, Callie had been so intent on getting inside that she'd put up no resistance when Leigh had asked for her phone number.

Leigh hadn't called to check on her. She hadn't texted. The not knowing was almost worse than the knowing. Since Callie's very first overdose, Leigh had grappled with the same dark premonition playing out in her head: a phone ringing in the middle of the night, a heavy knock on the door, a police officer with his hat in his hand telling Leigh that she needed to go to the morgue to identify her baby sister's body.

It was her fault. It was all her fault.

Leigh's personal phone rang, pulling her out of her downward

236

spiral. She clicked the button on the steering wheel as she took the left-hand turn.

"Mom!" Maddy rushed out the word.

Leigh felt her heart do that funny lurch. Then panic set in, because Maddy never made an actual voice call unless something was wrong. "Is Dad okay?"

"Yes," Maddy said, instantly irritated Leigh had put the thought in her mind. "Why would you even ask that?"

Leigh pulled over to the side of the residential street. She knew that explaining herself would only give Maddy a platform for martyrdom, so she waited for her daughter to flitter to the next topic.

"Mom," Maddy said. "Necia Adams is having a thing at her house this weekend, and there are only going to be five people, and we're going to do it outside so it's really safe and—"

"What did Dad say when you asked him?"

Maddy hesitated. She would never be a litigator.

"Dad told you to ask me?" Leigh guessed. "I'll talk to him about it tonight."

"It's only—" Maddy hesitated again. "Keely's mom left."

Leigh felt her eyebrows furrow. She had just seen Ruby, Keely's mother, last weekend. "She left?"

"Yes, that's what I'm trying to tell you." Maddy clearly thought Leigh should know this already, but thankfully she filled in the blanks. "Like, in the middle of the night, Ms. Heyer got into some kind of huge screaming fight with Mr. Heyer, but Keely ignored it because, duh. But then, Keely came down for breakfast this morning and her dad was all like 'Your mom needs some time to herself, but she'll call you later, and we love you very much,' and then he said he had Zooms all day, and Keely's upset because—obviously—so we thought we'd get together this weekend to support her."

Leigh felt a nasty grin on her face. She remembered Ruby's bitchy little quip at *The Music Man*. The woman would soon learn the value of an *in-town education* when it came time to pay her part of Keely's private school fees.

None of which Leigh could say to her daughter. "I'm sorry, baby. Sometimes things don't work out."

Maddy was silent. She had gotten used to the strange arrangement between Leigh and Walter because they had done the only thing that parents can do in strange times, which was to keep everything as normal as possible.

At least Leigh hoped that she had gotten used to it.

"Mom, you don't understand. We wanted to cheer Keely up, because what Ms. Heyer is doing is bullshit." Maddy never sounded so strident as when she was fighting an injustice. "Like, she hasn't called Keely or anything. She just sent a peace-out-do-your-homework-TTYL text, and Keely is so upset. All she does is cry."

Leigh shook her head, because that was a shitty thing to do to your kid. Then she wondered if Maddy was trying to tell her something. "Sweetheart, I'm sure Ms. Heyer will call Keely soon. Dad and I already left each other and you can't get rid of either of us."

"Yes, that has been made abundantly clear." Maddy sounded so much like Callie that Leigh felt tears fill her eyes. "Mom, I gotta go. My Zoom is about to start. You promise you'll talk to Dad about the party?"

"I'll try to get in touch with him before I call you tonight." Leigh didn't press her on the fact that the emotional support group had turned into a party. "I love—"

Maddy hung up.

Leigh brushed her fingers underneath her eyes, trying not to ruin her eyeliner. The distance between herself and her daughter still brought a physical ache. She could not imagine her own mother ever feeling such longing. There were spiders who took better care of their young. If Maddy had ever told Leigh that a grown man had put his hand on her leg, Leigh would not have told her daughter to slap away his hand the next time. She would've taken a shotgun and blown the man's head into bloody chunks.

The GPS was flashing. Leigh zoomed out on the screen. She saw the grounds of the Capital City Country Club, which belonged to one of the oldest private social clubs in the south. The neighborhood was dripping with money. Hip-hop stars and basketball players lived alongside old-school Biffs and Muffys, which Leigh only knew because a few years ago Maddy had talked her into trying to find Justin Bieber's house when he'd lived in the area.

She turned off the guidance. She pulled back onto the road. The mansions that rolled by were breathtaking—not in their beauty, but in their audacity. Leigh could never live in a house where it took more than thirty seconds to lay eyes on her child.

The golf course rolled along on her left as she wound her way along East Brookhaven Drive. She knew the road turned into West Brookhaven on the other side of the course. If she'd been on foot, Leigh could've cut through the greens, skirted around the lake, walked past the tennis courts and club house and found herself within a few blocks of Little Nancy Creek Park.

Andrew's $3.1 million house was on Mabry Road. The deed was held by the Tenant Family Trust, the same trust that held the Canyon Road dump the Waleskis had lived in. Leigh hadn't been willing to wait for Callie to get around to finding the information, then to get around to passing it along. She had run the search herself before leaving her condo this morning. If it left a trail that came up later, she could say she was looking into Andrew's real estate holdings in case it came up at trial. No one could fault her for being too thorough.

Leigh slowed so she could read the numbers on the mailboxes, which were almost as stately as the houses. Andrew's was a combination of white-painted brick, steel, and cedar. The numbers were lighted neon because it made sense to spend more on mailbox construction than most people spent on their actual houses. Leigh pulled her Audi through the open gates. The driveway whipped around to the back, but she parked in front of the house. She wanted Andrew to see her coming.

Predictably, the house was one of those ultra-modern glass and steel structures that looked like the murder mansion in a Swedish thriller. Leigh's heel left a black scuff on the pristine white driveway when she got out of the car. She put a grinding twist into her step, hoping that Andrew would be out here with a toothbrush when she pulled away.

Square shrubs served as the only landscaping. Tombstone-like white marble slabs led to the front door, sprigs of dwarf mondo filling the breaks. The green was too bright against the high white of everything else. If there had been a way for Leigh to get the jury here OJ-style, she would've jumped at the chance.

She walked up the three low steps to the glass front door. She could see straight into the back of the house. White walls. Polished concrete floor. Stainless steel kitchen. Swimming pool. Cabana. Outdoor kitchen.

There was a doorbell, but Leigh used the palm of her hand to slap the glass by way of knocking. She turned around to look back at the street. A camera was mounted in the corner of the overhang. Leigh remembered from the search warrant that the police had been authorized to take any recordings from surveillance devices out of the house. Andrew's system had conveniently been offline for the entire week.

She heard the faint clack of chunky heels across the polished concrete floor.

Leigh turned around. She had the full effect of Sidney Winslow doing an Elle Macpherson down the walkway toward the front door. The goth had been toned down for the day. Sidney's make-up was light, almost natural. She was dressed in a tight gray skirt and a navy silk blouse. Her shoes matched the color of the shirt exactly. Without all of the leather and attitude, she was an attractive young woman.

The door opened. Leigh could feel the chill of air conditioning mixing into the morning heat.

Sidney said, "Andrew's getting dressed. Is something wrong?"

"No, I just need to go over some things with him. Is it okay if I come in?" Leigh was already inside by the time she finished asking permission. "Wow, what a spread."

"It's crazy, right?" Sidney turned to close the door.

Leigh made sure she was halfway down the hall by the time the latch clicked. There was nothing more unsettling than someone pushing their way into your private space.

But this wasn't Sidney's private space. At least not yet. According to Reggie's cursory background check, Sidney kept a condo in Druid Hills, where she was a graduate student at Emory University. That the girl was studying psychiatry was something Leigh would find time to laugh about later.

Leigh walked down the hallway, which was at least twenty feet long. The expected artwork hung on the walls—photos of half-naked women, a painting by an Atlanta artist known for painting veiny, sweaty horses for bachelor pads. The dining room was stark white. The study, the front parlor, the living room were all so blindingly monochromatic it was like glancing behind the closed doors of a 1930s insane asylum.

By the time they reached the back of the house, Leigh's eyes were burning from a sudden burst of color. An entire wall had been devoted to an aquarium. Large tropical fish swam behind a thick slab of glass that stretched from floor to ceiling. A white leather couch sat across from it, a kind of viewing station for the show. Leigh's brain flashed up the memory of Callie sticking her hand into the ten-gallon tank she'd set up in the Waleskis' living room. Callie's fingers had been caked with blood. She'd insisted on washing her hands at the sink first so that the fish didn't get sick.

"They're cool, right?" Sidney was typing on her phone, but she nodded toward the aquarium. "So, it was the same guy who did something at the Atlanta Aquarium. Andrew can tell you about it. He's really into fish. I just texted him that you're here."

Leigh turned around. She realized this was the first time she'd had a private conversation with Andrew's fiancée. Unless she counted Sidney calling her a bitch across the parking lot.

"Look," Sidney said, as if she'd read Leigh's mind. "Sorry about the other day. This is all so very upsetting. Andy's such a lost little puppy sometimes. I feel very protective."

Leigh nodded. "Understood."

"I feel like—" She held up her hands in an open shrug. "What is going on with this bullshit? Why do the cops have it out for him? Is it because he's got money or he drives nice cars or is it some kind of vendetta because Linda worked on that Covid task force?"

Leigh was constantly amazed when rich white people assumed the system always worked until they found themselves wrapped up in it. Then, it had to be some kind of goddam conspiracy.

She told Sidney, "I had a client who got arrested for stealing a lawnmower. He died of Covid in jail because he couldn't afford the five-hundred-dollar cash bail."

"Was he guilty?"

Leigh knew a lost cause when she saw one. "I'm doing everything I can to help Andrew."

"I fucking hope so. He's paying you enough." Sidney was back on her phone before Leigh could formulate a response.

Since she was being ignored, Leigh took the opportunity to walk to the wall of windows along the back of the house. The same square shrubs lined the tombstone path toward the pool. The decking was more white marble. All of the outdoor furniture was white. Four lounge chairs. Four chairs around a glass table. None of it looked inviting. None of it looked used. Even the grass looked artificial. The only variation in color came from the steel and cedar fence marking the property line in the distance.

If she had the gift of poetry, she'd come up with a verse about the house being the frigid embodiment of Andrew's soul.

"Harleigh."

Leigh slowly turned around. Andrew had sneaked up on her again, but, this time, she hadn't startled. She gave him a cool look of appraisal. In contrast to the house, he was dressed in all black, from his T-shirt to his sweatpants to the matching slippers on his feet.

She told him, "We should talk."

"Sid?" His raised voice bounced against the hard surfaces. "Sid, are you here?"

Andrew walked into the hall, looking for his fiancée. Leigh could see that the back of his hair was still damp. He'd probably just gotten out of the shower.

"I bet she went to pick up the cake for the wedding," Andrew said. "We've got a small ceremony planned for tonight. Just Mom and some people from the dealerships. Unless you'd like to come?"

Leigh said nothing. She wanted to see if she could make him uncomfortable.

His bland expression didn't change, but he finally asked, "Are you going to tell me why you're here?"

Leigh shook her head. She had already been caught on one camera. She wasn't going to get caught on another one. "Outside."

Andrew raised his eyebrows, but she could tell he was enjoying the intrigue. He unlocked the door. The entire set of windows accordioned back. "After you."

Leigh stepped carefully across the threshold. The marble was textured, but her high heels couldn't find even purchase. She slipped them off and left them by the door. She said nothing to Andrew as she headed toward the pool. Leigh didn't stop at the edge of the marble decking. She stepped down the stairs that lined the disappearing edge. The artificial turf was stiff under her bare feet, still wet from the morning dew. She could hear Andrew's heavier footsteps hitting the ground behind her. Leigh wondered if this was the sound Tammy Karlsen had heard as he'd followed her into the park. Or was she already handcuffed by then? Was she gagged so that she couldn't scream? Was she too drugged to know that she needed to?

Only Andrew would ever know the truth.

The backyard was roughly half a football field. Leigh stopped in the middle, equidistant to the pool and the back fence. The sun was already beating down. The turf was getting hot under her feet. She told Andrew, "Hold up your hands."

He kept smiling, but he did as he was told.

Leigh patted his pockets the same way she had patted Buddy's in the kitchen. She found a tube of ChapStick, but no wallet, keys or phone.

Andrew explained, "I was getting dressed for work."

"You didn't take the week off to prepare for your trial?"

"My lawyer's got that all in hand." His smile was unsettling, as fake as the grass under their feet. "Did you read Tammy's medical records?"

Leigh knew what he was looking for. "She has a history of alcohol abuse. She drank two and a half martinis the night that she was with you."

"Yes." His tone of voice had turned intimate. "And she said she was raped before. Don't forget that. I imagine a jury of my peers won't take too kindly to her abortion, either."

"It's funny that you think you'll be judged by your peers." Leigh didn't give him time to respond. "How old were you when I started babysitting you?"

"I—" The question had obviously thrown him. He laughed

to cover his discomfort. "Six? Seven? You would know better than I."

"You were five and I was thirteen," Leigh said. "I remember because I'd just gotten out of juvie. Do you know why I was in juvie that time?"

Andrew looked back at the house. He seemed to realize that Leigh had set the terms of this conversation and he had blindly followed along. "Enlighten me."

"A girl was teasing Callie about her haircut," Leigh said, though *haircut* was a nice way to say that Phil had gotten drunk and cut off most of Callie's hair. "So I found a piece of broken glass, and I followed the girl out to recess, and I held her down and hacked off her hair until her scalp was bleeding."

He looked fascinated. "And?"

"I did that to a stranger who pissed me off. What do you think I'm going to do to you?"

Andrew paused a moment, then laughed. "You're not going to do anything to me, Harleigh. You think you have some agency here, but you really don't."

"Buddy made you put a camera in the attic."

His face registered surprise.

She said, "There's no way he could've wedged his fat ass up into that small space. So he made you do it for him."

Andrew said nothing, but she could tell that she had finally gotten to him.

Leigh kept punching. "Linda listed the house for sale with Re/Max in May of 2019, one month before you found your first rape victim at the CinéBistro."

His jaw worked as he clenched it.

"I'm guessing that's when you remembered putting the camera in the attic for Buddy." Leigh raised one shoulder in a shrug. "You wanted to relive that father/son bonding experience. And now you're a rapist just like he was."

Andrew loosened his jaw. He looked back at the house. When he turned to Leigh, the darkness had returned to his eyes. "You and I both know that Callie understood exactly what she was doing."

"Callie was twelve years old when it started," Leigh said. "Buddy was almost fifty. She had no idea what—"

244

"She loved it," Andrew said. "Did she tell you that part, Harleigh? She loved what Dad did to her. And I know because, every night, I would lie in bed and listen to her moaning his name."

Leigh struggled to keep her emotions in check. With very little effort, her memory summoned Callie's raspy whisper begging Leigh to check on Buddy, to make sure he was okay, that he wouldn't be mad if they got him help.

He loves me, Harleigh. He'll forgive me.

Andrew said, "You're right about the attic. Dad had me go up there a few weeks before you murdered him."

Leigh felt sweat break out on her skin. This was why she had brought him back here away from cameras and recorders and prying eyes. She was sick of dancing around the subject, performing a show for Reggie's clueless benefit. "Did he tell you why?"

"There were some break-ins in the neighborhood." Andrew let out a sharp laugh, as if he regretted his childhood innocence. "Dad said it was for security in case someone broke in. Pretty stupid that I believed him, I suppose."

Leigh said, "You were never very clever."

He blinked, and she saw a hint of the vulnerable little boy who always cried when he thought that Leigh was mad at him.

Then he blinked again, and it was gone.

She asked, "What does Sidney know?"

"She knows that I love her." Andrew shrugged, as if to acknowledge the lie. "As much as I can love anyone."

"And Reggie?"

"Reggie is as loyal as my pockets are deep."

Leigh tensed when Andrew moved, but he was only kneeling down to smooth a mark out of the artificial grass.

He looked up at her, saying, "Callie loved him, Harleigh. Didn't she tell you? She was in love with him. He was in love with her. They could've been happy together. But you took that away from them."

Leigh couldn't listen to this bullshit anymore. "What do you want, Andrew?"

He took his time standing back up. He smoothed an invisible crease out of his pants. "I want to be normal. I want to fall in love, to get married, to have kids, to live the kind of life I would've had if you hadn't taken my father away from me."

She laughed, because the fantasy was ludicrous. "Buddy couldn't stand to—"

"Don't ever laugh at me." The change had happened again, but this time he did nothing to temper the threat. "Do you know what happens to women who laugh at me?"

His tone stopped any more sound from leaving her throat. Leigh looked back at the house. She looked over the fence. She had thought having this conversation in isolation would protect her, but now she could see that she'd given him an opportunity, too.

"I know what you're planning to do, Harleigh." He had somehow gotten closer to her. She could smell mint on his breath. "You think you're going to use your legal maneuvering to make it look like you're defending me, but all the while you're going to be doing everything you can to make sure I get sent to prison."

She looked up at him, too late realizing her mistake. Leigh became transfixed by his gaze. She had never seen anything so malevolent. Her soul threatened to leave her body again. Like any predator, Andrew exploited the weakness. Leigh could do nothing as his hand reached toward her chest. He pressed his palm flat to her heart. She felt it pounding into his palm, a rubber ball bouncing endlessly against a brutally hard surface.

"This is what I want, Harleigh." He smiled as her lips started to tremble. "I want you to be terrified that any day, any moment, I can send that tape to the police and everything you have—your perfect, fake mommy life with your PTA meetings and school plays and your stupid husband—will disappear the same way my life disappeared when you murdered my father."

Leigh stepped back. Her throat felt as if his hands were wrapped around it. Sweat rolled down the side of her face. She gritted together her teeth to keep them from chattering.

Andrew studied her like he was taking in a performance. His hand stayed exactly where she had left it, hanging in the air as if it was still pressed to her heart. While she watched, he moved his palm to his face. He closed his eyes. He inhaled, as if he could smell her scent.

She said, "You can't mail a tape from prison."

"You were supposed to be the smart one, Harleigh." His eyes had opened. His hand went into his pocket. "Don't you know I've got a backup plan?"

Leigh hadn't really been that stupid. She wanted him to admit he had a fail-safe. "Why did you save the knife?"

"You can thank Callie for that. She kept holding on to it, walking around the house with it in her hand, keeping it with her while we watched cartoons. And then she'd sit at the kitchen table for hours looking at that damn anatomy drawing." Andrew shook his head. "Poor, sweet Callie. She's always been the delicate one, hasn't she? The guilt of what you made her do was too much for her to handle."

Leigh felt her throat strain to swallow. She wanted to cut her sister's name out of his disgusting mouth.

"I kept the knife so I had something to remember her by." His lips tugged up at the side. The smirk was making its first appearance. "And then I saw how she used it on Dad, and it finally made sense."

Leigh had to get herself back under control, but, more importantly, she had to move him off of Callie. She asked, "Andrew, has it ever occurred to you what that tape will really show?"

He raised his eyebrows. "Enlighten me."

"Let's game this out, all right?" She waited for him to nod. "You show the cops the tape. The cops arrest me. I go through booking and all of that. You remember the procedure from the first time you were arrested, right?"

He nodded, clearly bemused.

"So, what I'll do then is I will ask for a meeting with the prosecutor. And the prosecutor and I will watch the tape together so I can explain that the way your father's femoral vein was nicked shows the same pattern of behavior that you used with all of the women you raped."

Andrew looked as startled as Leigh had seconds before. He'd never considered the possibility.

"It's called a modus operandi, Andrew, and it will send you to prison for the rest of your life." Leigh put a finer point on it. "Mutually assured destruction."

He took only a moment to recalibrate. He made a point of slowing it down, shaking his head theatrically, even tsking his teeth. "Silly girl, do you think that's the only tape I can show people?"

Leigh felt her bones shaking beneath her skin. He sounded so much like his father that she was back in the yellow Corvette again, her legs clenched together, her heart racing, her stomach turning inside out.

Andrew said, "I've got hours of your poor, fragile little sister being fucked in every hole she's got."

Leigh felt as if each word was a punch to her face.

"I found them in my VHS collection when I went to college. I thought I'd get some nostalgia in by watching Disney, but then I realized Dad threw out the tapes and put his private collection in."

Leigh's eyes filled with tears. They had never searched his room. Why hadn't they searched his room?

"Hour after hour of the best porn I've ever seen in my life." Andrew studied her face, taking in her pain like a drug. "Is Callie still small the same way she was back then, Harleigh? Is she still like a little baby doll with her thin waist and her wide eyes and her tiny little pussy?"

Leigh pressed her chin to her chest to deprive him of the pleasure of her agony.

He said, "The second anything bad happens to me, every man, woman, and child with access to the internet will be able to watch your sister getting shredded."

Leigh squeezed her eyes closed to keep the tears from falling. She knew Callie was haunted by that very scenario. Her sister couldn't walk down the street without worrying that someone would recognize her from Buddy's movies. Dr. Patterson. Coach Holt. Mr. Humphrey. Mr. Ganza. Mr. Emmett. Their violation had hurt Callie almost as much as Buddy had. Andrew letting countless other disgusting men watch the vile acts would splinter Callie into so many pieces that no amount of heroin would be able to pull her back together.

She used her fist to wipe her eyes. She asked the same damn question that she kept asking. "What do you want, Andrew?"

"Mutually assured destruction only works until someone loses their nerve," he said. "Convince the jury that I'm innocent. Tear apart Tammy Karlsen on the stand. Then, we'll see what else you can do for me."

Leigh looked up. "How long, Andrew? How long is this going to last?"

"You know the answer to that, Harleigh." Andrew gently wiped away her tears. "For as long as I want it to."

11

"Mrs. Takahashi?"

Callie swung her legs to the side of the chair so that she could look up at the librarian. The woman's mask said READ MORE BOOKS! She was holding a copy of *A Compendium of North American Snails and Their Habitats.* "I found this for you in the return bin."

"Wonderful, thank you." Callie took the thick paperback. "*Arigatou.*"

The librarian either bowed or did a kindly brontosaurus as she took her leave, both of which could be construed as cultural appropriation.

Callie turned back around. She placed the book beside the computer keyboard. She assumed that she was the only junkie who had ever committed identity theft for a library card. Himari Takahashi had been a war bride. She'd sailed across the Pacific to marry her dashing soldier lover. They'd both enjoyed reading and taking long walks. He'd passed away before her, but she had contented herself with gardening and spending time with her grandchildren.

At least that was the story Callie had told herself. In truth, she had never spoken to Mrs. Takahashi. The woman had been zipped inside a black body bag the first and last time they had met. Back in January, when Covid was wiping out nearly four thousand people a day, Callie had taken a cash-paying job with one of the local nursing home chains. She had worked alongside the ranks of other citizens who were desperate enough to risk their own health by loading Covid-positive bodies into refrigerated trailers that the National Guard had trucked in.

Someone in the computer room coughed and everyone winced, then immediately turned accusatory, eyes darting around as if they wanted to burn the culprit at the stake.

Callie made sure her mask was in place. Junkies always ended up on the wrong end of the pointing finger. She used her left hand to reach for the mouse. For a change, her right hand had decided to go completely numb this morning. Her entire body was sore from her long crawl through the attic space. She was so disgustingly weak. The most strenuous thing Callie had done in the last few months was arm-wrestle Dr. Jerry for animal crackers. The competition usually ended in a draw. Neither of them wanted the other to lose.

She pulled the keyboard close. She highlighted the search bar, but she didn't type anything in. Her eyes scanned the monitor. The Fulton County Tax Assessor's office revealed that the Tenants still owned the Canyon Road house.

Callie should tell Leigh. She should text her the information. She should call.

She tapped her finger on the mouse. She glanced around. There was a camera in the corner, its black eye silently watching. The DeKalb County system was more on top of its security than the City of Atlanta. Callie had promised Leigh that she would go to the downtown library, but Leigh had promised Callie twenty-three years ago that they would never have to think about Buddy Waleski ever again.

She opened Facebook on the computer. She typed in *Sidney Winslow Atlanta*.

Only one page came back, which was surprising because girls these days seemed to all be named variations of the same. It wasn't like when Callie was growing up and people teased her about not being able to correctly pronounce her own name.

Sidney's banner photo showed the outside of what used to be called Grady High School. The most recent post was from 2012, a picture of eight teenage girls crammed together at a concert inside the Georgia Dome. Judging by their conservative attire and the number of crosses in the background, Callie assumed Passion 2012 was not her kind of scene.

Just as Facebook would no longer be Sidney Winslow's scene. Andrew's fiancée did not fall into the Facebook demographic, where a twenty-something might run into an embarrassing photo their parents had posted back in the mid-aughts.

Callie went to TikTok and hit the Sidney Winslow jackpot. She felt her eyebrows arch at the volume of videos. She supposed this was what it was like to be a youngster these days. Sidney's social media was practically a part-time job. Her profile photo showed a close-up of a pierced lip that had been generously smeared with purple lipstick, a clear indicator that the religious fervor had been a passing phase.

There were thousands of videos listed, though Callie couldn't play them because the library didn't allow you to use sound without headphones. From the descriptions under the stills, she quickly sussed out that Sidney Winslow was a twenty-five-year-old student seeking an incredibly practical doctorate of psychiatry at Emory University.

"Well," Callie said, because she finally understood why Leigh's tone dropped to a register of disgust every time she said Sidney Winslow's name.

When Sidney was on campus or waxing poetic behind the wheel of her car, she kept her hair pulled back, make-up just so, a colorful hat on her head or jaunty scarf around her neck. Nights out called for a very different look. The girl basically transformed into an updated version of Phil's geriatric goth. Her tight shirts and leather pants were offset by an impressive number of piercings. Heavy make-up. Pouty lips. Shirt collar low enough to offer an enticing glimpse of her breasts.

Callie had to admit that her breasts were fantastic.

But she also had to wonder why Andrew Tenant was not part of Sidney's well-documented life. She kept scrolling through the stills, finding not even a passing mention of Andrew, which was strange considering they were about to be married. She checked who was following Sidney and found many Sidney-like clonegirls along with a smattering of young men who seemed to prefer to be photographed shirtless. And fair enough, because they looked damn good shirtless.

She clicked to see who Sidney was following. Dua Lipa, Janelle

Monáe, Halsey, Bruno Mars, countless #bromiesexuals, but no Andrew.

Callie switched to Instagram and, after clicking enough times to put a cramp in her finger, finally found a photo of them both together. Two years ago. Backyard barbecue. Sidney was beaming at the camera. Andrew looked reluctant, his head down, his lips pressed into a thin, white, *I am humoring you but hurry* line. Callie had to think if you were a rapist and murderer, you wanted to avoid social media.

He'd picked the wrong girl for the task. There were thousands of posts across the platforms, almost always accompanied by a generously poured container of alcohol. Drinking wine at parties. Drinking beer at bars. Drinking martinis on a deck. Drinking mojitos at the beach. Drinking slim cans of rock and rye in a car. Callie shook her head, because the young woman's life was a train wreck. And Callie said this as someone whose life was a train wreck inside of a crashing airplane inside of the mushroom cloud of an atomic bomb.

Sidney's Twitter account revealed the consequences of #YOLO. The party girl had gotten a DUI one month ago. Sidney had documented the process, tweeting out pithy thoughts about the criminal justice system, describing the mind-numbing uselessness of attending the DUI school on Cheshire Bridge Road, photographing her court-mandated log-in sheet to prove that she was attending the required number of AA meetings.

Callie squinted at the log, which was familiar from her own travails through the court system. Sidney had been given the standard thirty meetings in thirty days, then two a week thereafter. Callie recognized the church where the early morning meetings were held. They had delicious coffee, but the cookies at the Baptist across the street were better.

She looked at the time.

Two thirty-eight p.m.

Callie logged out of the computer. She looked for her backpack, but then remembered she had left it locked in her room along with her stash. Callie had shoved everything into the pockets of the yellow satin jacket she'd found inside of her closet. The collar was frayed, but a glorious rainbow decal was sewn onto the back.

It was the first item of clothing she had ever bought for herself with Buddy's money.

She used the automated system to check out *A Compendium of North American Snails and Their Habitats*. The paperback fit snugly into the jacket pocket, the edges sticking not unpleasantly into her ribs. Callie groaned as she walked toward the exit. Her back would not straighten out. She had to shuffle like an old woman, though she took it on faith that even at eighty-six years old, Himari Takahashi had maintained excellent posture.

The sun blinded Callie as soon as she pushed open the door. She reached into her jacket pocket and found the green tanning bed goggles. The sun dialed down several notches when she put them on. Callie could feel the heat beating against her back and neck as she trudged toward the bus stop. Eventually, she was able to force herself upright. The vertebrae clicked like chattering teeth. The numbness in her fingers flowed back up into her arm.

At the bus stop, a fellow traveler was already sitting on the bench. Houseless, mumbling to himself, counting off numbers on his fingers. Two overflowing paper sacks were at his feet. They were filled with clothes. She recognized the anxious look in his eyes, the way he kept scratching his arms.

He glanced at her, then took a closer look. "Cool shades."

Callie removed the goggles and offered them to the man.

He snatched them away like a gerbil taking a treat.

Her eyes started to water again. She felt a pang of regret as the man put on the goggles, because they were really amazing. Even so, she fished Leigh's last twenty-dollar bill out of her back pocket and handed it to the man. That left Callie with only fifteen bucks, because she'd spent $105 on a package from the tanning salon the day before. In retrospect the impulse buy seemed like a bad idea, but that was junkie budgeting for you. Why not spend the money today when you weren't sure whether or not you'd be getting a free concert from Kurt Cobain tomorrow?

The man said, "The vaccine put microchips in my brain."

Callie confided, "I'm worried my cat is saving up to buy a motorcycle."

They both sat in companionable silence for the next ten minutes, when the bus flopped in front of the curb like a tubby echidna.

Callie climbed aboard and took a seat in the front. Her stop was only two away, and it was a kindness to make sure the driver could see her because the look he'd given Callie when she got onto the bus clearly said that the man thought she was going to be trouble.

She kept her hands on the rail to let him know she was not going to do something crazy. Though it did seem crazy to touch a rail with your bare hands in the middle of a pandemic.

She stared absently out the front window, letting the air conditioning freeze the sweat on her body. Her fingers went to her face. She had forgotten that she was wearing a mask. A quick look at the other riders showed masks in various stages of coverage: pulled down below the nose, ringing the chin, and, in one case, pulled up over a man's eyes.

She pulled her own mask up to cover her eyebrows. She blinked at the filtered light. Her eyelashes brushed against the material. She quashed the desire to giggle. It wasn't this morning's maintenance dose that was making her feel high. She had shot up again before heading to the library. Then swallowed an Oxy on the long bus ride to Gwinnett. There was more Oxy in her back pocket. She would eventually take it, and then she would shoot up more methadone and, eventually, she would be back on heroin.

This was how it always happened. Callie was good until the goodness broke down.

She pulled the mask back into place over her mouth and nose. She stood up as the bus belched its way to her stop. Her knee started to ache as soon as she walked down the stairs. On the sidewalk, she patterned her breath after her steps, letting three *pops* of her knee go by before she inhaled, then slowly letting air hiss between her teeth during the next three.

The chain-link fence on her right ringed around a massive outdoor stadium. Callie let her fingers trail along the metal diamonds until they abruptly stopped at a tall pole. She found herself in a wide, open concrete space at the mouth of a soccer stadium. There was a sign outside with a bumble bee buzzing out BEE HAPPY — BEE SAFE — BEE WELL — WE ARE ALL IN THIS TOGETHER.

Callie doubted that last part was meant to be taken literally. When she was a teenager, she had seen stadiums like this when her cheerleading team had competed against private schools. The Lake Point girls were muscled stallions with thick waists and bulging arms and thighs. By comparison, the Hollis Academy girls had been pale grasshoppers and stick-bugs.

Callie passed the closed concession stand on her way into the stadium. Thirty yards away, a security guard in a parked golf cart was tracking her progress. She didn't want trouble. She entered through the first tunnel she could find. Then she put her back to the wall and waited in the cool shade for the sound of the battery whirring as the rent-a-cop came to eject her from the premises.

There was no whir, but paranoia soon flooded her brain. Had the security guard made a phone call? Was there someone inside the stadium waiting for her? Had she been followed from the bus stop? Had she been followed from home?

Back at the library, Callie had perused the website for Reginald Paltz and Associates. Reggie looked every inch the rapey-gone-to-seed fratboy that Leigh had described, but Callie couldn't honestly say that he had been the same camera-strangling man who'd been disgorged from the boarded-up house. Nor could she say that all of the faces she kept scanning, all of the people in the cars on the road or inside the library, hadn't been in league with him.

Callie pressed her hand to her chest as if she could knead away the anxiety. Her heart flicked against her ribs like a hungry lizard's tongue. She hadn't seen the glimmer or flash of a stalker in the last two days but, everywhere she went, she could not shake the feeling that she was being recorded. Even now, hidden in this damp, dark place, she felt like a lens was capturing her every move.

You can't make a stink about the camera, dolly. I could go to prison.

She pushed away from the wall. She was halfway through the tunnel when she heard yelling and clapping from the stands. Again, the light blinded Callie as she walked out into the sun. She cupped her hands to her eyes and scanned the crowd. Parents were seated in clumps across the rows, mangy cheering sections for the girls on the field. Callie turned again, and she watched the team run practice drills. The high schoolers looked like gazelles, if gazelles wore soccer uniforms and didn't bounce up and down like lunatics when they felt threatened.

Another turn, another look at the stands. Callie spotted Walter easily enough. He was one of two fathers watching soccer practice, even though she had it on good authority that Walter did not, in fact, enjoy soccer.

He clearly recognized Callie as she made the arduous climb up the stadium stairs. His eyes were unreadable, but she could guess what was going on in his mind. Still, he kept his own counsel as she made her way down his row. Callie gathered the school was adhering to Footloose Rules: no dancing, no singing, no hollering, no fun. She left three seats between her and Walter when she sat down.

He said, "Welcome, friend."

Callie peeled off her mask so she could catch her breath. "It's good to see you, Walter."

His eyes were still guarded, which was fair. The last time Callie and Walter had been in the same room together was not their finest hour. They were outside Leigh's condo in the little utility closet that contained the trash chute. For ten days, Walter had come by twice a day to inject heroin between Callie's toes because the only way that she could take care of Leigh was if she had enough dope to keep herself from getting sick.

Her sister's husband was tougher than he looked.

Walter said, "I like your jacket."

"It's from high school." Callie turned around in her seat so he could see the rainbow on the back. "I can't believe it still fits."

"Nice," he said, though she could tell he had bigger issues on his mind. "Your sister seems to be crying a lot lately."

"She's always been a big baby," Callie said, though people often misunderstood Leigh's tears. She cried when she was frightened or hurt, but she also cried when she took a piece of broken glass and hacked chunks of hair out of your scalp.

Walter said, "She thinks that Maddy doesn't need her anymore."

"Is that true?"

"You were sixteen once. Didn't you need your mother?"

Callie thought about it. At sixteen, she had needed everything.

"I'm worried about my wife," Walter said, and his tone implied he had been waiting a very long time to share this thought with someone. "I want to help her, but I know she won't ask me to."

Callie felt the weight of his confession. Men seldom got to share their feelings and, when they did, despondency wasn't on the acceptable list.

She tried to cheer him up. "Don't be worried, Walter. Harleigh's expendable caretaker is back on the job."

"No, Callie. You're wrong about that." Walter turned to look at her, and she gathered this next part had weighed on him, too. "When Leigh got sick, we had a plan of care already in place. My mother was going to drive up to take care of Maddy. Leigh was going to quarantine in the master bedroom. I was going to leave food outside her door and call an ambulance if she needed it. She lasted one night and then she broke down and started crying that she wanted her sister. So I went out and found her sister."

Callie had never heard the story before, but she knew that Walter would not lie about something so consequential. He would do anything for Leigh. Even score heroin for her junkie sister.

She asked, "Haven't you been to enough Al-Anon meetings to know you can't save somebody who doesn't want to be saved?"

"I don't want to save her. I want to love her." He turned back in his seat, eyes tracking the girls on the field. "Besides, Leigh can save herself."

Callie debated whether or not this point was worth discussing. She studied Walter's profile as he watched his amazing daughter sprint after a ball. Callie wanted to tell him consequential things, too. Like that Leigh loved him. That she was only fucked up because Callie had made her do terrible things. That she blamed herself for not somehow knowing that Buddy Waleski was a bad man. That she was crying because she was terrified that Andrew Tenant would bring them both back to that same dark place that his father had.

Should Callie tell Walter the truth? Should she throw open the doors to Leigh's cage? There was a sense of inevitability to the disaster her sister had made of her life. It was as if, instead of leaving for Chicago, Leigh had stayed in stasis for twenty-three years, then woke up to the life Phil had raised her to live: broken family, broken marriage, broken heart.

The only thing holding her sister together right now was Maddy.

Callie turned away from Walter. She allowed herself the pleasure of watching the teenagers on the field. They were so nimble, so fleet. Their arms and legs moved in tandem as they kicked the ball. Their necks were long and graceful like origami swans who'd never been close to swampy spirals or steep waterfalls.

Walter asked, "Can you spot our beautiful girl?"

Callie had already found Leigh and Walter's daughter the moment she'd walked into the stadium. Maddy Collier was one of the smallest girls, but she was also the fastest. Her ponytail barely had time to brush her shoulders as she ran after the defensive midfielder. The girl was playing attack, which Callie only knew because she had looked up soccer positions at the library.

This was after she had googled the soccer practice schedule for Hollis Academy's girls' team. Callie had not found herself here after a Scooby Doo level of deciphering. The school crest was on the back of Leigh's phone. Established in 1964, around the time white parents across the south spontaneously decided to enroll their children in private schools.

"Crap," Walter muttered.

Maddy had accidentally tripped the midfielder. The ball spun loose but, instead of chasing after it, Maddy stopped to help the other girl stand up. Leigh was right. Phil would've beaten the shit out of either of them for doing something so sportsmanlike. If you can't go big, then don't bother to go home.

Walter cleared his throat, the same way Leigh did when she was about to say something difficult. "Practice will be over soon. I would love for you to meet her."

Callie pressed together her lips, the same way Leigh did when she was nervous. "Hello, I must be going."

"Phil Collins," Walter said. "Classic."

The drummer/superstar had taken the line from Groucho Marx, but Callie had more important things on her mind. "When you tell Leigh about seeing me, don't tell her I was high."

Walter had an uncomfortable set to his mouth. "If she asks, I'll have to tell her the truth."

259

He was way too good for this family. "I commend you for your honesty."

Callie stood up. She was wobbly around the knees. The methadone was lingering. Or the long-release coating on the Oxy was doing its job. This was the reward for tapering off. The more slowly you eased yourself back in, the longer the euphoria could linger.

Until the lingering wasn't enough.

Callie gave him a tight salute. "Adios, friend."

Her knee gave out when she started to turn. Walter stood to help, but Callie stopped him with a wave of her hand. She didn't want Maddy to see her father struggling with a worthless junkie in the stands.

She picked her way down the row, but the stairs nearly did her in. There was no railing to hold on to. She stepped carefully down, down, down. Callie tucked her hands deep into her jacket pockets as she walked along the field. The snail paperback crowded out her fist. The sun was so intense that her eyes were wet with tears. Her nose was running. She should not have given away the goggles. She still had nine tanning sessions left on her membership card; $9.99 for new goggles was a lot of money to burn when you only had fifteen bucks to your name.

She used the back of her sleeve to wipe her nose. Stupid sunlight. Even in the shade of the tunnel, her eyes kept watering. She could feel heat coming off her face. She hoped like hell she didn't run into the security guard on his golf cart. Her mind kept playing back the pity in Walter's eyes when he had watched her walk away. Callie's hair was knotted in the back because she hadn't been able to lift her arms high enough to use the comb this morning. Her fingers had not been able to squeeze the tube of toothpaste to brush her teeth. Her jacket was stained and wrinkled. Her clothes were the same ones she'd slept in. The abscess in her leg was throbbing because she was so fucking pathetic that she couldn't stop injecting poison into her veins.

"Hello, Callie."

Without warning, the gorilla snorted his foul, hot breath onto the back of her neck.

260

Callie spun around expecting to see the flash of white fangs as he lunged at her throat.

There was only a man. Tall and slim with sandy blonde hair. His hands were tucked into the pockets of his navy trousers. The sleeves of his blue shirt were rolled up just below the elbows. An ankle monitor bulged above his left loafer. A giant gold watch was on his left wrist.

Buddy's watch.

Before they had chopped off his arms, Callie had unstrapped the watch and placed it on the bar. She had wanted Trevor to have something to remember his father by.

And now, she saw that he did.

"Hey, Callie." Andrew's voice was soft, but it had a familiar deepness that brought Callie right back to the first time she had met Buddy. "I'm sorry it's been such a long time."

Sand filled her lungs. He was acting so normal, like this was nothing, but her skin felt like it was being flayed off her bones.

"You look—" He chuckled. "Well, you don't look great, but I'm glad that I found you."

She glanced back at the stadium, then toward the exit. They were completely alone. She had nowhere to go.

"You're still so . . ." His eyes flickered across her body as he seemed to look for the word. "Tiny."

You're so fucking tiny but I'm almost there just try to relax okay just relax.

"Callie-ope." Andrew sang her name like a tune. "You came a long way to watch a bunch of girls play soccer."

Callie had to open her mouth to breathe. Her heart was jumping. Was he here for Walter? For Maddy? How had he known about the school? Was he following Callie? Had she missed something on the bus?

Andrew asked, "Are they really that good?"

Her eyes found his hands tucked deep into his pockets. The hair on the back of his arms was slightly darker than the hair on his head. Just like Buddy's.

Andrew craned his neck, looking into the field. "Which one is Harleigh's?"

Callie heard the small crowd cheering from the stands. Clapping.

Shouting. Whistling. Then the cheering died down and what she heard, what she knew was inside the tunnel with them, was the gorilla.

"Callie." Andrew stepped forward, close but not closing in. "I want you to listen to me very carefully. Can you do that?"

Her lips were still parted. She could feel the air sucking in, drying the back of her throat.

"You loved my father," Andrew said. "I heard you telling him that so many times."

Callie couldn't move her feet. He was here for her. That was why he was standing so close. That was why he seemed so calm, so in control. She blindly reached behind her. She could hear the gorilla approaching, then his breath was in her ear, then warming her neck, then the taste of his sweaty musk was curling into her mouth.

"How did it feel when you chopped him up?" Andrew asked. "I couldn't see your face in the video. You never looked up. You just did what Harleigh told you to do."

It was almost a relief to feel the gorilla's hand wrap around her neck, his arm loop around her waist. She was locked in place, trapped, the way that he always wanted her.

"You don't have to let her keep bossing you around," Andrew said. "I can help you get away from her."

The gorilla pressed into her back, fingering up her spine. She heard his grunts. Felt his excitement. He was so big. So overpowering.

"Just tell me you want to get away." Andrew took another step. "Say the word and I can take you somewhere. Anywhere you want to go."

The scent of Andrew's breath mints swirled into Buddy's cheap whiskey and cigars and sweat and cum and blood—so much blood.

Andrew said, "Walter David Collier, aged forty-one, legal counsel for the Atlanta Fire Fighters' Union."

Callie's heart shook inside of her chest. He was threatening Walter. She had to warn him. She clawed at the gorilla's arm, trying to loosen his hold.

Andrew said, "Madeline Félicette Collier, aged sixteen."

Pain dug into her arm. Not the tingling numbness or the misfiring nerves but the agony of her skin being ripped open.

"Maddy's a gorgeous little girl, Callie." Andrew's smile pulled at the corners of his mouth. "Such a tiny little thing."

Callie looked at her arm. She was shocked by the sight of blood dripping from four deep gashes. She looked at her other hand. Her own blood and skin were furled underneath the fingernails.

"It's funny, Callie, how Harleigh's daughter looks so much like you." Andrew winked at her. "Like a *little dolly*."

Callie shuddered, but not because Andrew sounded like his father. The gorilla had stepped into her body, melted into her bones. His strong legs were her strong legs. His fists were her fists. His mouth was her mouth.

She lunged at Andrew, fists flying, teeth bared.

"Jesus!" Andrew yelled, holding up his arms, trying to fend her off. "Crazy fucking—"

Callie went into a blind frenzy. No sound came from her mouth, no breath from her lungs, because all of her energy was directed toward killing him. She pounded him with her fists, scratched with her fingernails, tried to rip off his ears, gouge out his eyes. Her teeth bit deep into the flesh of his neck. She wrenched back her head, trying to rip out his jugular, but her neck stiffly caught on the frozen pivot at the top of her spine.

And then she was lifted into the air.

"Stop!" the security guard ordered, his arms bear-hugging her waist. "Hold the fuck still."

Callie kicked out, trying to break the bonds. Andrew was on the ground. His ear was bleeding. Skin hung from his jaw. Red welts surrounding the bite in his neck. She was going to kill him. She had to kill him.

"I said stop!" The security guard slammed Callie face down onto the ground. His knee jammed into her back. Her nose banged into the cold concrete. She was breathless but still tensed, ready to strike again even as she heard the click of handcuffs.

"No, officer. It's okay." Andrew's voice sounded raspy as he tried to catch his breath. "Please, just escort her away from the school."

"You cocksucker," Callie hissed. "You fucking rapist."

263

"Are you serious, man?" The guard kept his knee pressed to her back. "Look at her arms. Bitch is a needle junkie. You need to call the cops, get her tested."

"No." Andrew was standing up. Out of the corner of her eye, Callie could see the flashing red light on his ankle monitor. He told the guard, "None of this will look good for the school, will it? And it won't look good for you because you're the one who let her get past the gate."

This seemed to sway the guard, but he still asked, "Are you sure, man?"

"Yes." Andrew knelt down so he could look at Callie's face. "She doesn't want you calling the police, either. Do you, miss?"

Callie was still tensed, but her reason was starting to return. She was inside the stadium where Maddy went to school. Walter was in the bleachers. Maddy was on the field. Neither Callie nor Andrew could afford for the police to come.

"Help her stand." Andrew stood. "She's not going to cause any more trouble."

"You're crazy, man." Still, the guard tested Callie, releasing some of the pressure on her back. She felt the fight leave her body and agony flood back in. Her legs wouldn't work. The guard had to lift her up and physically put her back on her feet.

Andrew stood close, daring her to come at him again.

Callie wiped the blood from her nose. She could taste blood in her mouth. Andrew's blood. She didn't just want more of it. She wanted all of it. "This isn't over."

"Officer, make sure she gets on the bus." Andrew held out his hand to the guard, passing some folded twenties. "A woman like her can't be trusted around children."

SUMMER 2005

Chicago

Leigh scrubbed at the lasagna pan even as her own sweat dropped into the water. Fucking northerners. They had no idea how to use air conditioning.

Walter said, "I can do that."

"I've got it." Leigh tried not to sound like she wanted to beat his brains out with the pan. He had been trying to do something sweet for her. He'd even called his mother to get her lasagna recipe. And then he had baked it so long in the oven that Leigh's skin was going to rub off her fingers before the burned sauce came out of the non-stick bottom.

Walter said, "You know that pan only cost five bucks."

She shook her head. "If you saw five bucks on the ground, would you leave it?"

"How dirty is the five bucks?" He was behind her, arms wrapped around her waist.

Leigh leaned back into him. He kissed her neck, and she wondered how in the hell she had turned into the stupid kind of woman who felt her stomach flip when a man touched her.

"Here." Walter reached under her arms, grabbing the sponge and pan. She watched him awkwardly scrub for almost a full minute before realizing the futility of the task.

Still, Leigh couldn't give up entirely. "I'll let it soak a little longer."

"What'll we do to pass the time?" Walter's teeth nipped at her ear.

Leigh shuddered, holding on to him tightly. Then she let go, because she couldn't show him how desperate she was to be near him. "Don't you have a paper to write on organizational behaviors?"

Walter groaned. His arms dropped away as he walked to the fridge and took out a can of ginger ale. "What point is an MBA? The unions up here, their succession plan is ten-deep. My name won't come up until I'm drawing social security."

Leigh knew where this was going, but she tried to steer him in a different direction. "You like Legal Aid."

"I like being able to pay my share of the rent." He drank from the can as he walked back into the living room. He flopped down onto the couch. He stared at his laptop. "I've written twenty-six pages of jargon that even I can't understand. There is no practical, real-world application for any of this."

"All that matters is the degree on your resumé."

"That can't be all that matters." He leaned his head back, watched her wipe her hands on a kitchen towel. "I need to feel useful."

"You're useful to me." Leigh shrugged, because there was no use talking around the obvious. "We can move, Walter. Just not to Atlanta."

"That job with the fire department is—"

"In Atlanta," she said, the one place she had told him she would never go back to.

"Perfect," he said. "That's the word I was going to use—perfect. Georgia is a right-to-work state. No one is going to let their cousin's uncle's grandkid skip the line. The job in Atlanta is perfect."

Leigh sat beside him on the couch. She clasped together her hands so that she didn't start wringing them together. "I told you that I will follow you anywhere."

"Except there." Walter gulped down the rest of the ginger ale. The can went to the coffee table, where it would leave a ring. He tugged at her arm. "Are you crying?"

"No," she said, though tears had welled into her eyes. "I'm thinking about the lasagna pan."

"Come here." He tugged at her arm again. "Sit in my lap."

"Sweetheart," she said. "Do I look like the kind of woman who would sit in a man's lap?"

He laughed. "I love how you southern women say *sweetheart* like a Yankee woman would say *dumbass*."

Leigh rolled her eyes.

"Sweetheart." He held her hand. "You can't annex an entire city from your life just because you're afraid you'll run into your sister."

Leigh looked down at their hands. She had never in her life wanted to hold on to someone else so tightly. She trusted him. No one had ever made her feel safe.

She said, "We wasted fifteen grand on her, Walter. Fifteen thousand dollars in cash and credit card debt, and she lasted one day."

"It wasn't a waste," he said, which was generous considering five grand of the money had been his. "Rehab usually doesn't work the first time. Or the second or third time."

"I don't—" she struggled to articulate how she felt. "I don't understand why she can't quit. What is it about that life that she enjoys?"

"She doesn't enjoy it," Walter said. "Nobody enjoys that."

"Well she's getting something out of it."

"She's an addict," Walter said. "She wakes up, she needs a fix. The fix wears off and she has to hustle to get the next one, the next one, the next one, to stop from getting dope sick. All of her friends, her community, that's the world they're trapped in, constantly hustling so they don't get sick. Her addiction isn't just mental. It's physical. Why would somebody do that to themselves if they didn't have to?"

Leigh would never be able to answer that question. "I liked coke in college, but I wasn't going to throw my life away for it."

"You're really lucky you were able to make that choice," Walter said. "With some people, their demons are too big. They can't overcome them."

Leigh pressed together her lips. She had told Walter that her sister had been molested, but that was where the story had ended.

He said, "You can't control what Callie does. All you can

control is how you respond to her. I just want you to make peace with it."

She knew that he was thinking of his father. "It's easier to make peace with the dead."

He gave a rueful smile. "Trust me, baby, it's much easier to make peace with the living."

"I'm sorry." Leigh stroked the side of his face. The sight of the thin gold ring on her finger momentarily threw her. They had been engaged for less than a month and she still could not get used to seeing the ring.

He kissed her hand. "I should finish this worthless paper."

"I need to review some case law."

They kissed before retreating to opposite sides of the couch. This was what she loved most of all about their lives, the way they silently worked together, separated by one couch cushion between them. Walter leaned over his laptop on the coffee table. Leigh surrounded herself with pillows, but she extended her leg across the cushion, pressing her foot against his thigh. Walter absently rubbed her calf as he read his pointless paper.

Her fiancé.

Her future husband.

They hadn't talked about children yet. She assumed that Walter hadn't brought it up because children were a foregone conclusion. He probably had no qualms about possibly passing on the addictions that had nearly destroyed his side of the family. It was easier for men. No one blamed a father when a child ended up on the streets.

Leigh instantly chastised herself for being so cold. Walter would be a magnificent father. He didn't need a role model. He had his own goodness to guide him. Leigh should be more concerned about her mother's mental illness. They had called it manic depression when Leigh was a child. Now they called it bipolar disorder, and the change had made not one bit of difference because Phil was never going to get any kind of help that didn't come out of a pitcher of micheladas.

"Fuh-fuh-fuh . . ." Walter mumbled, searching for a word as his fingers rested on the keyboard. He nodded to himself, and the typing resumed.

She asked, "Are you backing that up?"

"Of course I am. And all my supporting data." He stuck in the USB drive. The light flashed as the files backed up. "I'm a man, baby. I know all about computering."

"So impressive." She pushed him with her foot. He leaned over and kissed her knee before returning to his paper.

Leigh knew she should get back to work, but she took a moment to look at his handsome face. Rugged, but not hardened. He knew how to work with his hands, but he knew how to use his brain so he could pay someone else to do the job.

Walter was by no means soft, but he had grown up with a mother who adored him. Even when she was deep in the bottle, Celia Collier had been a pleasant kind of drunk, given to spontaneous hugs and kisses. Dinner was always on the table at six o'clock. There were snacks in his backpack to take to school. He'd never been forced to wear dirty underwear or beg strangers for money to buy food. He'd never hidden under his bed at night because he was afraid his mother would get drunk and knock the shit out of him.

Leigh loved countless things about Walter Collier. He was kind. He was brilliant. He was deeply caring. But most of all, she adored him for his relentless normalcy.

"Sweetheart," he said. "I thought we were working."

Leigh smiled. "That's not how you say it, sweetheart."

Walter chuckled as he typed.

Leigh opened her book. She had told Walter she needed to familiarize herself with the updated guidelines to the Americans with Disabilities Act in regards to disabled tenants but, secretly, Leigh was looking into the limits of spousal privilege. As soon as she and Walter returned from their honeymoon, she was going to sit him down and tell him everything about Buddy Waleski.

Maybe.

She leaned her head back on the couch, staring up at the ceiling. There was not much about Leigh's life that Walter did not know. She had told him about her two stints in juvenile detention and exactly why she'd landed there. She'd described her terrifying night in county lock-up for slashing her sleazy boss's tires. She had even told him about the first time she had realized she could fight back when her mother attacked her.

Each time she unburdened herself, each time Walter absorbed the details without flinching, Leigh had to fight the urge not to tell him the rest.

But the rest was too much. The rest was such a burden that her sister would rather shoot herself up with poison than live with the memories. Walter had never touched a drop of alcohol, but what would happen if he learned exactly what his wife was capable of? It was one thing to hear about Leigh's distant, violent past, but Buddy Waleski had been chopped up in his own kitchen less than seven years ago.

She tried to walk herself through that conversation. If she told Walter one thing, she would have to tell him everything, which would start back at the beginning when Buddy had rested his fat fingers on her knee. How could someone even as understanding as Walter believe that Leigh had let herself forget about that night? And how could he forgive her if she could never, ever forgive herself?

Leigh wiped her eyes with the back of her hand. Even with spousal privilege, was it fair to make the only man she would ever love a conspirator to her crimes? Would Walter look at her differently? Would he stop loving her? Would he decide that Leigh could never be the mother of his child?

The last thought opened the floodgates. She had to stand up to find a tissue so that he didn't see her fall apart.

"Baby?" Walter asked.

She shook her head, letting him think she was upset about Callie. She wasn't afraid of Walter turning her in to the police. She knew that he would never do that. She was afraid that his legal mind would understand the difference between self-defense and cold-blooded murder.

Leigh herself had known the weight of her sins when she had put Atlanta in her rearview mirror. The law twisted itself into knots over the question of intent. What a defendant was thinking when they committed a criminal act could be the deciding factor behind anything from fraud to manslaughter.

She knew exactly what she had been thinking when she had wrapped the cling film around Buddy Waleski's head six times: *you are going to die by my hand and I am going to enjoy watching it happen.*

"Sweetheart?" Walter asked.

She smiled. "That's going to get old pretty fast."

"Is it?"

Leigh walked back to the couch. Against her better judgment, she sat in his lap. Walter wrapped his arms around her. She pressed her head to his chest and tried to tell herself that she didn't cherish every second of being held by him.

He asked, "Do you know how much I love you?"

"No."

"I love you so much that I'll stop talking about my dream job in Atlanta."

She should've felt relieved, but she felt guilty. Walter's life had turned upside down when his father had died. The union had saved his mother, and he wanted to pay back that kindness by fighting for other workers who found their lives thrown into chaos.

Leigh had been drawn in by Walter's need to help other people. She had admired it so much that, against her better judgment, she had gone out on a date with him. In a week, she had gone from sleeping on his couch to curling alongside him in bed. Then they had graduated and gotten jobs and gotten engaged and both of them were ready to start their lives—except for Leigh holding Walter back.

"Hey," he said. "That was meant to be sexy, that sacrifice I made for you there."

She brushed back his curly hair. "Do you know—"

Walter kissed away her tears.

"I would kill for you," Leigh said, with a full understanding of exactly what that would entail. "You mean everything to me."

"But you wouldn't really—"

"No." She cupped his face in her hands. "I would do anything for you, Walter. I mean it. If you want to go to Atlanta, then I'll find a way to live in Atlanta."

"I've gone off the idea, actually." He smiled. "Atlanta can get pretty hot."

"You can't—"

"What about California?" he asked. "Or Oregon? I hear Portland is crazy."

She kissed him to shut him up. His mouth felt so good. She had never met a man who knew how to take his time getting a kiss right. Her hands moved down, unbuttoning his shirt. His skin was sweaty. She tasted salt on his chest.

Then some fucking idiot started banging their fist on the door.

Leigh startled, hand to her heart. "What time is it?"

"It's only eight thirty, Grandmother." Walter slid out from under her. He buttoned his clothes as he walked to the door. Leigh watched him press his eye to the peephole. He glanced back at her.

"Who is it?"

Walter swung open the door.

Callie stood in the hallway. She was dressed in the usual pastel and cartoon offerings from the kids' rack at Goodwill because even the petite adult sizes didn't fit her. Her *Piglet's Big Movie* T-shirt was long-sleeved, even in the heat. Her baggy jeans had tears at both knees. She was carrying a stuffed pillowcase under her arm. Her body listed to the side, balancing out the cardboard cat carrier she gripped by the handles.

Leigh heard a mewing sound through the airholes in the sides.

Callie said, "Good evening, friends."

"Long time," Walter said, with absolutely no indication that the last time he'd seen Callie, she was vomiting down the back of his shirt as he carried her into rehab.

"Callie." Leigh stood up from the couch. She felt stunned, because Callie never left the ten square miles around Phil's house. "What are you doing in Chicago?"

"Everybody deserves a vacation." Callie's body bobbed back and forth as she walked in with the heavy carrier. She gently placed it on the floor by the couch. She dropped her pillowcase beside it. She looked around. "Nice digs."

Leigh still needed an answer. "How did you find my address?"

"You sent me a Christmas card at Phil's house."

Leigh muttered a curse under her breath. Walter was the card-sender. He must've gone through her address book. "Have you been living with Phil?"

"What is life, Harleigh, if not a series of rhetorical questions?"

"Callie," Leigh said. "Tell me why you're here."

"I thought I'd see what the big deal is about the ol' Windy City. I have to say, I do not recommend the bus stops. Junkies are everywhere."

"Callie, please—"

"I got sober," Callie said.

Leigh was speechless. She had longed to hear those words come from her sister's mouth. She let herself look at Callie's face. Her cheeks were full. She had always been small, but Leigh could no longer see the bones under her skin. She actually looked healthy.

Callie said, "Almost eight months. How about that?"

Leigh hated herself for feeling hopeful. "How long will it last?"

"Let history be your guide." Callie turned her back on the prospect of disappointment. She walked around their tiny apartment, a bull in a china shop. "This is a nice spread. How much do you guys pay for rent? I bet it's a million bucks a month. Is it a million bucks?"

Walter took the question. "We pay half of that."

"God damn, Walter. That is a fucking bargain." She leaned down to the cat carrier. "Do you hear that, kitty? This fella knows how to strike a deal."

Walter caught Leigh's eye. He smiled, because he didn't understand that Callie's humor always came at a price.

"This looks fancy." Callie was leaning over his laptop like a bird pecking down. "What's this you've got going here, Walter? The fundamental disposition of blah-dee-blah-dee-blah. That sounds very smarty-pants."

"It's my final paper," Walter said. "Half my grade."

"So much pressure." Callie stood back up. "All it proves is that you can make any words come out of your mouth."

He laughed again. "That's very true."

Leigh tried, "Cal—"

"Walter, I gotta say, I love the whole idea of this." She had moved on to the bookcases Walter had built from cement blocks and slabs of wood. "Very masculine, but it works with the overall style of the room."

Walter bobbed his eyebrows at Leigh, as if Callie didn't know that Leigh despised the bookcase.

"Look at this amazing gewgaw." Callie shook the snow globe

273

they'd bought at a roadside stand on the drive to Petoskey. She couldn't tilt her head down, so she brought it to her eyes to watch the tumult inside. "Is that real snow, Walter?"

He smiled. "I believe it is."

"God damn, you guys—I don't even understand the fancy-ass world you live in. Next you'll tell me you keep all your perishables in a refrigerated box."

Leigh watched her sister tromp around the room, picking up books and souvenirs Walter and Leigh had collected on the scant few vacations they could afford because fifteen thousand dollars was a lot to blow on someone who was going to spend one day in rehab.

"Hello?" Callie called into the mouth of an empty flower vase.

Leigh felt her jaw clench. She hated herself for feeling like the perfect little space that only she and Walter had ever shared was being ruined by her obnoxious, junkie sister.

The wasted fifteen grand wasn't the only money Callie had effectively set on fire. Over the last six years, Leigh had flown back to Atlanta half a dozen times to help her sister. Renting motel rooms for Callie to detox in. Physically sitting on her to keep her from running out the door. Rushing her to the emergency room because a needle had broken off in her arm and the infection had nearly killed her. Multiple doctor's appointments. An HIV scare. A Hep C scare. Mind-numbing mountains of paperwork for bail to be processed, commissary accounts to be funded, calling cards to be activated. Waiting—constantly waiting—for a knock on the door, a cop with his hat in his hands, a trip to the morgue, the sight of her sister's pale, wasted body on a slab because she loved heroin more than she loved herself.

"Sooooo," Callie drew out the word. "I know this is going to come as a shock to both of you, but I'm between places right now, and—"

"Right now?" Leigh exploded. "God dammit, Callie. The last time I saw you, I was bailing you out of jail for crashing a car. Did you skip bail? Did you show up at your hearing? There could be a warrant out for—"

"Whoa there, sister," Callie said. "Let's not crank up the crazy."

Leigh could've slapped her. "Don't you *ever* talk to me the way you talk to Phil."

Callie held up her hands, taking a step back, then another.

Leigh crossed her arms so she didn't strangle her. "How long have you been in Chicago?"

"I got here yesterweek," Callie said. "Or was it lasterday?"

"Callie."

"Walter," Callie turned away from Leigh. "I hope I'm not being rude when I say this, but you seem like an excellent provider."

Walter's eyebrows went up. Technically, Leigh made more than him.

Callie said, "You have provided my sister with an awesome home. And I see by that ring on her finger that you've decided to make her an honest woman. Or as honest as she can be. Nonetheless, and what I'm saying is, I'm very happy for you both, and congratulations."

"Callie." If Leigh had a dollar for every time she'd said her sister's name in the last ten minutes, she could pay herself back for rehab. "We need to talk."

Callie pivoted back around. "What do you want to talk about?"

"Jesus fucking Christ," Leigh said. "Would you stop acting like a goddam ostrich and get your head out of your ass?"

Callie gasped. "Are you comparing me to a murder dinosaur?"

Walter laughed.

"*Walter*." Leigh knew she sounded like a harpy. "Don't laugh at her. It's not funny."

"It's not funny, Walter." Callie turned her body back toward Walter.

Leigh still found the robotic movements jarring. When she thought of her sister, she thought of the athlete, not the girl whose neck had been broken and fused back together. And certainly not the junkie who was standing in front of the man Leigh desperately wanted to create a new, boring, normal life with.

"Come on." Walter smiled at Leigh. "It's a little funny."

"It's libelslander, Walter, and, as a legal brainiac, you should recognize that." Callie put her hands on her hips as she launched into a half-ass Dr. Jerry impersonation. "An ostrich will kill a lion with his foot for absolutely no reason. Except the lion is also a known murderer. I forget my point, but only one of us has to understand what I am saying."

Leigh covered her face with her hands. Callie had said *I got sober*, not that she was currently sober, because she was clearly stoned out of her mind. Leigh couldn't deal with this again. It was the hope that killed her. She had lain awake for too many nights strategizing, planning, laying out a path that took her baby sister away from a terrifying death spiral.

And every single fucking time, Callie jumped back in.

She told her sister, "I can't—"

"Hold on," Walter said. "Callie, do you mind if Leigh and I talk in the back?"

Callie waved her arms, theatrically. "Be my guest."

Leigh had no choice but to trudge back to the bedroom. She hugged her arms to her waist as Walter gently shut the door.

She said, "I can't do this again. She's high as a kite."

"She'll come down," Walter said. "It's just a few nights."

"No." Leigh felt her head start to shake. Callie had been back for fifteen minutes and Leigh was already exhausted. "It's not a few nights, it's my life, Walter. You have no idea how hard I worked to get away from this. The sacrifices I made. The awful things that I—"

"Leigh," he said, sounding so reasonable she wanted to run from the room. "She's your sister."

"You don't understand."

"My dad—"

"I know," she said, but she wasn't talking about Callie's addiction. She was talking about the guilt, about the grief, about the *How old are you dolly you can't be more than thirteen right but damn you look like you're already a full-grown woman.*

Leigh was the one who had pushed Callie into Buddy Waleski's clutches. Leigh was the one who had murdered him. Leigh was the one who had forced Callie to lie so much that the only relief she got was from a drug that was going to eventually kill her.

"Baby?" Walter said. "What's wrong?"

She shook her head, hating the tears in her eyes. She was so frustrated, so sick of hoping that one day, as if by magic, the guilt would disappear. All she wanted in the world was to run away from the first eighteen years of her life and spend the next part building her world around Walter.

He rubbed her arms. "I'll take her to a motel."

"She'll have a party," Leigh said. "She'll invite half the neighborhood and—"

"I can give her money."

"She'll OD," Leigh said. "She's probably stealing the cash out of my purse right now. God, Walter, I can't keep doing this. My heart is broken. I don't know how many more times I can—"

He pulled her into a tight embrace. She finally broke down sobbing, because he would never understand. His father had been a drunk, but Walter had never put a bottle in his hand. The guilt he carried was a child's guilt. In many ways, Leigh carried the guilt of two scarred, broken children inside of her heart every single day.

Leigh could never be a mother. She could never hold Walter's baby in her arms and trust herself to not damage their child as badly as she had damaged her sister.

"Honey," Walter said. "What do you want to do?"

"I want to—"

Tell her to leave. Tell her to lose my number. Tell her I never want to see her again. Tell her I can't live without her. Tell her that Buddy tried it with me, too. Tell her it's my fault for not protecting her. Tell her I want to hold on to her as tight as I can until she understands that I will never be healed until she is.

The words came so easily when Leigh knew they were always going to stay in her head.

She told Walter, "I can't get to know that cat."

He looked down at her, confused.

"Callie is really amazing at picking out cats, and she'll make me love it, and then she'll leave it here and I'll end up taking care of it for the next twenty years." Walter had every right to look at her like she had lost her mind. "We'll never be able to go on vacation because I won't have the heart to leave it alone."

"Right," Walter said. "I hadn't realized it was this serious."

Leigh laughed, because that was all she could do. "We'll give her a week, okay?"

"Callie, you mean." Walter held out his hand so they could shake on it. "One week."

"I'm sorry," she said.

"Sweetheart," he told her. "I knew what I was signing up for when I said you could sleep on my couch."

Leigh smiled, because he'd finally learned the proper way to use *sweetheart*. "We really shouldn't leave her alone. I wasn't kidding about my wallet."

Walter opened the door. Leigh kissed him on the mouth before going back into the living room.

She should not have been surprised at what she found, but Leigh still felt the jolt of shock.

Callie was gone.

Leigh's eyes bounced around the room the same way Callie had. She saw her purse open, the wallet devoid of cash. The snow globe was gone. The flower vase was gone. Walter's laptop was gone.

"Motherfuck!" Walter swung back his foot to kick the coffee table, but stopped at the last minute. His hands balled into fists. "Jesus fucking—"

Leigh saw Walter's empty wallet on the table by the door.

This was her fault. This was all her fault.

"Shit." Walter had stepped on something. He reached down, then held up the USB drive, because of course Callie had left him the copy of his paper before stealing his computer.

Leigh pressed together her lips. "I'm sorry, Walter."

"What is—"

"You can use my—"

"No, the noise. What is that?"

Leigh listened in the silence. She heard what had caught his attention. Callie had taken the pillowcase, but she'd left the cat. The poor thing was mewing inside the box.

"Dammit," Leigh said, because abandoning the cat was almost as bad as robbing them blind. "You're going to have to deal with it. I can't see it."

"Are you kidding me?"

Leigh shook her head. He would never understand how much she detested her mother for passing on an abiding love of animals. "If I see it, I'll want to keep it."

"All right, well this is a fantastic hill for you to die on." Walter walked over to the box. He found the letter Callie had left folded into the flap of the handles. Leigh recognized her sister's curly handwriting with a heart over the *i*.

For Harleigh & Walter because I love you.

Leigh was going to beat the life out of her sister the next time they were in the same room together.

Walter unfolded the note and read, "'Please accept the gift of this beautiful—'"

The cat mewed again, and Leigh felt a lurch in her heart. Walter was taking too long. She knelt in front of the carrier, making a list in her head. Litter box, scoop, kitten food, some kind of toy, but not with catnip because kittens didn't respond to catnip.

"Sweetheart." Walter reached down and squeezed her shoulder.

Leigh opened the handles on the box, silently cursing her sister the entire time. She moved the blanket aside. Her hands slowly rose up to cover her mouth. She looked into two of the most beautiful brown eyes she had ever seen.

"Madeline," Walter said. "Callie says to call her Maddy."

Leigh reached into the box. She felt the warmth of the miraculous little creature spread up her arms and into her broken heart.

Callie had given them her baby.

SPRING 2021

12

Leigh smiled as she listened to Maddy report on the usual teenage girl contretemps at school. Andrew didn't matter. Callie didn't matter. Leigh's legal career, the video tapes, the fail-safe, her freedom, her life—none of it mattered.

All she wanted right now was to sit in the dark and listen to the lovely sound of her daughter's voice.

Her only quibble was that they were having this conversation on the phone. Gossip was the kind of thing you listened to while you cooked dinner and your daughter played on her phone, or, if it was something serious, you heard with your daughter's head on your chest while you stroked back her hair.

"So, Mom, of course I was like, we can't do that, because it's not fair. Right?"

Leigh chimed in, "Right."

"But then she got really mad at me and walked off," Maddy said. "So, about an hour later, I looked at my phone, and she retweeted this video, like, of a dog running after a tennis ball, so I thought I'd be nice and say something about how the dog was a spaniel, and spaniels are super sweet and loving, but then she all-capped me back, 'THAT IS CLEARLY A TERRIER AND YOU OBVIOUSLY KNOW NOTHING ABOUT DOGS SO SHUT UP.'"

"That's ridiculous," Leigh said. "Terriers and spaniels look nothing alike."

"I know!" Maddy launched into the rest of the story, which was more complicated than an evidentiary hearing for a RICO case.

Callie would've loved this conversation. She would've loved it so much.

Leigh leaned her head against the car window. In the privacy of the Audi, she allowed her tears to flow unchecked. She had parked down the street from Walter's house like a stalker. Leigh had wanted to see her daughter's light on in her bedroom, maybe catch Maddy's shadow as she paced by. Walter would've gladly let Leigh sit on the porch, but she couldn't face him yet. She had driven to the suburbs on autopilot, her body yearning for the closeness of her family.

The fact that Celia Collier's RV was parked in the driveway hadn't exactly brought her comfort. The tan and brown monstrosity looked like the meth lab from *Breaking Bad*. Leigh had casually pried it out of Maddy that Walter's mother had decided to come visit on a whim, but Celia didn't do anything on a whim. Leigh knew that she had gotten both doses of the vaccine. She had a sinking feeling Maddy's grandmother was here to babysit while Walter took a weekend away with Marci.

"Mom, are you listening?"

"Of course I am. What did she say next?"

Despite the strident tone in her daughter's voice, Leigh felt her blood pressure drop. The faint sound of crickets came through the car windows. The moon was a sliver low in the sky. She let her mind wander back to that first night she had spent with her daughter. Walter had put pillows all around the bed. They had curled their bodies around Maddy like a protective heart, so in love that neither of them could speak. Walter had cried. Leigh had cried. Her list of cat litter and kitten food had turned into diapers and formula and onesies and plans for Walter to immediately accept the job in Atlanta.

The paperwork that Callie had left in the bottom of the cat carrier had made it impossible for them to stay in Chicago. As with everything else in her sister's life, Callie had spent more brain-power doing the wrong thing than she would've had to expend doing things right.

Without telling anyone, Callie had moved to Chicago eight months prior to Maddy's birth. During her pregnancy, she had used Leigh's name at the women's health clinic on the South Side. Walter was listed as Maddy's father on her birth certificate. All of Callie's prenatal visits and blood pressure checks and her inpatient hospital visits and wellness checks had been covered by the Moms & Babies program of the Illinois Department of Healthcare and Family Services.

Leigh and Walter had been given two choices: They could move to Atlanta with all of the medical records and pretend that Maddy was their baby, or they could tell the truth and send her sister to prison for Medicaid fraud.

And that was assuming the investigators would believe the story. There was a chance that the government would've accused Walter and Leigh of being in on the scam. Maddy could've ended up in foster care, a risk neither one of them was willing to take.

Please accept the gift of this beautiful girl, Callie had written. *I know that no matter what happens, you will both always and forever keep her happy and safe. I only ask that you will call her Maddy. PS: Félicette was the first cat astronaut. You can look it up.*

Once they were safe in Atlanta, once the fear had died down, once they were sure that Callie wouldn't tear back into their lives and try to take Maddy away, they had tried to introduce her sister to their daughter. Callie had always politely refused. She had never asserted ownership. She had never implied in any way that Leigh was not Maddy's mother, or that Walter was not her father. The child's existence had become like everything else in Callie's life—a distant, vague story that she let herself forget.

As for Maddy, she knew that Leigh had a sister, and she knew that the sister suffered from the disease of addiction, but they still had not told her the truth. At first, they had waited for the statute of limitations to run out on the fraud, and then Maddy wasn't old enough to understand, and then she was going through a difficult time at school, and then being a twelve-year-old with parents who were separating was bad enough without having Mom and Dad sit you down to explain that you weren't really their biological child.

Unbidden, Leigh found herself recalling Andrew's words while they stood in his backyard this morning. He had said that Callie loved what Buddy had done to her, that she had moaned his name.

None of that mattered. Callie might have enjoyed the touching, because touching felt good, but children were incapable of making adult choices. They had no comprehension of romantic love. They lacked the maturity to understand the way their bodies reacted to sexual contact. They were physically and emotionally unprepared for intercourse.

Leigh had not really understood that at eighteen, but she clearly understood it now as a mother. When Maddy had turned twelve, Leigh had gotten a front-row seat to the magic of a twelve-year-old little girl's life. She knew how sweet they were, how desperate for attention. She knew you could convince her to do cartwheels with you up and down the driveway. You could watch her break into giddy laughter one moment and burst into inexplicable tears the next. You could tell her that you were the only person she could trust, that no one else would ever love her the way you do, that she was special, that no matter what, she had to keep what was happening a secret because no one else would understand.

It was no coincidence that Leigh had crashed and burned her marriage when Maddy had turned twelve. Callie had been twelve years old when she had first started babysitting for the Waleskis.

The understanding of how profoundly vulnerable her sister had been, what Buddy Waleski had stolen from her, was a cancer that had nearly killed Leigh. There had been days when she could barely look at her own daughter without having to run to the bathroom to break down. Leigh had kept herself so tightly wound around Maddy that she had spun out of control with Walter. He had put up with Leigh's erratic behavior until she had found the one thing that would make him leave. It wasn't an affair. Leigh had never cheated on him. In many ways, what she had done was far worse. She'd started binge drinking after Maddy had gone to bed. Leigh had thought that she was getting away with it until

283

one morning she had woken up still drunk on the bathroom floor. Walter was sitting on the edge of the tub. He had literally held up his hands in surrender and told her that he was done.

"What was I going to do?" Maddy asked. "I mean, for reals, Mom. Tell me."

Leigh was at a loss, but she had been down this road before. "I think what you did was exactly the right thing, baby. She'll either come around or she won't."

"I guess." Maddy sounded unconvinced, but she pivoted. "Did you talk to Dad about the party this weekend?"

Leigh had taken the coward's way out and texted Walter. "You can't sleep over, and you have to promise everyone will keep their masks on."

"I promise," Maddy said, but, short of peering through the basement windows, there was no way of knowing. "Keely said she finally called."

Leigh's daughter was the Where's Waldo of proper nouns, but she usually planted enough clues. "Ms. Heyer?"

"Yeah, she said something about how one day Keely would understand but she met somebody and she still loves her dad because he would always be her dad but she had to move on."

Leigh shook her head, trying to extricate the meaning. "Ms. Heyer is seeing someone? She's cheating on Mr. Heyer?"

"Yeah, Mom, that's what I said." Maddy fell back into her comfort zone, irritation. "And she keeps texting, like, hearts and shit and I mean, why won't she call again to talk about what's going to happen next and how this is gonna work out instead of texting?"

For Maddy's sake, Leigh said, "Sometimes, texting is easier, you know?"

"Yeah, okay, I've gotta go. Love you."

Maddy abruptly ended the call. Leigh assumed someone more interesting had made themselves available. Still, she stared at her phone until the screen went black. Part of Leigh wanted to jump into whatever mom text chain was going around about Ruby Heyer getting her groove back, but that was not why Leigh had driven out to the suburbs at eight in the evening. She had come here to find Walter and blow up her entire life.

284

Andrew clearly considered Tammy Karlsen nothing more than collateral damage in his war of mutually assured destruction. What he really wanted was for Leigh to live in fear. For her to know that at any moment, her *perfect mommy life with its PTA meetings and school plays and her stupid husband* could disappear the same way that Andrew's life had disappeared when she had murdered his father.

The only way to take away Andrew's power was to take away his control.

Before Leigh could lose her nerve, she texted Walter—*are you busy?*

He wrote back immediately—*Love Machine.*

Leigh looked up at Celia's RV. They had started calling it the Love Machine after Walter had accidentally walked in on his mother and the man who ran the Hilton Head RV park.

The front door to Walter's house opened. He waved to Leigh as he walked toward the Love Machine. She glanced around the cul-de-sac. She should not have been surprised that one of the neighbors had ratted her out. Six firemen fanned out around Walter's house. He had gone to bat for each of them on several occasions, negotiating pension settlements, medical bills and, in one case, sending one to rehab rather than jail. They all treated Walter like he was a brother.

Leigh left her phone on the seat as she got out of the car. Walter was folding up the table when she stepped inside the Love Machine. Celia hadn't spent much money on decorating, but everything was neat and functional. A long banquette served as a couch between two partitions. The galley kitchen ran along the back with a closet and bathroom making a small hallway to the bedroom at the rear. Walter had turned on the running lights along the strip of carpeted floor. The soft glow brought out the sharp angle of his jawline. She could see the shadow of a beard growing. He had started shaving every other day since the pandemic. Leigh hadn't realized how much she liked it until those brief months during the first lockdown when she had found herself back in his bed.

"Shit." She put her hand to her bare face. "I forgot my mask."

"It's all right." Walter took a step back, leaving some distance between them. "Callie made an appearance at Maddy's soccer practice today."

Leigh felt the usual mix of emotions—guilt that she still had not called to check on her sister since last night and hope that finally Callie had shown some interest in being part of her family.

"She looks okay." He leaned against the partition. "I mean, she's way too skinny, but she was smiling and joking around. Same old Callie. I swear to God, she looked like she had a tan."

"Did she . . ."

"No, I offered, but she didn't want to meet Maddy. And yes, she was high, but not falling down or making a scene."

Leigh nodded, because that wasn't the worst news. "How's Marci?"

"Getting married," Walter said. "She's back with her old boyfriend."

For the first time in days, Leigh felt the anvil lift a tiny bit of its weight off of her chest. "I thought when I saw the RV—"

"I'm gonna quarantine out here for ten days. I asked Mom to drive up so she can keep an eye on Maddy."

Leigh felt the weight come back. "Were you exposed?"

"No, I was going to call you tomorrow, but then you showed up here and—" He shook his head, like the details didn't matter. "I wanted to be able to do this."

Without warning, he closed the gap between them and pulled Leigh into his arms.

She put up no resistance. She let her body melt into his. A sob came from her mouth. She wanted so desperately to stay with him, to pretend like everything was okay, but there was nothing she could do but try to memorize this moment so that she could think about it for the rest of her life. Why did she always cling to the bad things and let the good things slip away?

"Sweetheart." Walter tilted up her face so that she would look at him. "Tell me what's wrong."

Leigh touched her fingers to his mouth. She felt in her soul that she was on the precipice of doing lasting harm to what was left of their marriage. She could have sex with him. She could fall asleep in his arms. But then tomorrow or the next day she

286

would still have to tell him the truth, and the betrayal would cut that much deeper.

"I need to—" Leigh's voice caught. She took a deep breath. She led Walter to the banquette and sat down beside him. "I have to tell you something."

"This sounds serious," he said, not sounding serious at all. "What is it?"

She looked down at their intertwined fingers. Their wedding rings were both scratched, but neither of them had ever taken them off.

Leigh couldn't keep dragging this out. She made herself pull away. "I need to tell you something out of the confines of our marriage."

He laughed. "Okay."

"I mean, it's not part of our marital privilege. This is just you and me talking."

He finally picked up on her tone. "What's wrong?"

Leigh couldn't be this close to him anymore. She slid across the seat until her back was against the partition. She thought about all those times she'd reached her foot across the couch cushion because she couldn't stand not somehow being connected to him. What she was about to say could sever that tie irrevocably.

There was no more putting it off. She started at the beginning. "Do you remember I told you I started babysitting kids in the neighborhood when I was eleven?"

Walter shook his head, not because he didn't remember, but because he thought it was crazy that anyone had believed it was a good idea for an eleven-year-old child to be left in charge of other children.

"Yes," he said. "Of course I do."

Leigh struggled against her tears. If she broke down now, she would never survive telling him everything. She took a deep breath before continuing.

"When I was thirteen, I got a permanent babysitting gig for a five-year-old boy whose mom was in nursing school, so I was at their house every weekday after school until midnight."

Leigh was talking too fast, her words threatening to trip over each other. She made herself slow down.

"The woman's name was Linda Waleski. She had a husband. His name was—well, I honestly don't know his real name. Everyone called him Buddy."

Walter rested his arm along the back of the banquette. He was giving her his full attention.

"The first night, Buddy drove me home and—" Leigh stopped again. She had never said this part to herself, let alone aloud. "He pulled the car over to the side of the road, and he pushed my legs apart, and he shoved his finger inside of me."

She watched Walter's anger compete with his grief.

"He masturbated himself. And then he drove me home. And he gave me all this money."

Leigh felt heat rush to her face. The money made it worse, like payment for a service. She looked over Walter's shoulder. Her eyes blurred the twinkling lights along the neighbor's driveway.

"I told Phil that all he did was rest his hand on my knee. I didn't tell her about the rest of it. That when I went to the bathroom, there was blood. That for days, every time I peed it stung where his fingernail cut me."

The memories brought back the burning sensation between her legs. She had to stop again to swallow.

"Phil just laughed it off. She told me to slap away his hand the next time he tried it. So that's what I did. I slapped his hand and he never tried anything else."

Walter's breathing was slow and steady but, out of the corner of her eye, Leigh watched his fist clench.

"I forgot about it." She shook her head, because she knew why she had forgotten about it, but she couldn't think of how to explain the reason to Walter. "I—I forgot about it, because I needed the job, and I knew if I made trouble, if I said anything, then no one would hire me again. Or I would get blamed for doing something wrong, or—I don't know. I just knew that I was supposed to keep my mouth shut. That no one would believe me. Or that they would believe me, but it wouldn't matter."

She looked at her husband. He had let her talk uninterrupted this entire time. He was trying so desperately hard to understand.

"I know that sounds crazy, to forget something like that. But when you're a girl, especially if you start to develop early, and you get breasts and hips, and you have all these hormones that you don't know what to do about, grown men will say inappropriate things to you all the time, Walter. All the time."

He nodded, but his fist was still clenched.

"They wolf-whistle or they touch your breasts or they brush their cocks against your back and then pretend it's an accident. Or they talk about how sexy you are. Or they say that you're mature for your age. And it's gross because they're so old. And it makes you feel disgusting. And if you call them on it, they laugh or they say you're uptight or you're a bitch or you can't take a joke." Leigh had to make herself slow down again. "The only way you can get through it, the only way you can breathe, is that you just put it somewhere else so that it doesn't matter."

"But it matters." Walter's voice was hoarse with sorrow. He was thinking of their beautiful girl. "Of course it matters."

Leigh watched tears roll down his face, knowing that what she said next would turn him completely against her. "When I was sixteen, I saved enough money to buy a car. I quit babysitting. And I passed the job at the Waleskis' along to Callie."

Walter had no time to hide his shock.

"Buddy raped her for two and a half years. And he hid cameras around the house to film himself doing it. He showed the movies to his friends. They had these weekend parties. They drank beer and they watched Buddy rape my sister." Leigh stared down at her hands. She twisted her wedding ring around her finger. "I didn't know at the time that it was happening, but then one night Callie called me from the Waleskis' house. She told me that she had gotten into a fight with Buddy. She had found one of his cameras. He was worried that she would tell Linda and he would get arrested. So he attacked her. He beat her. He nearly choked the life out of her. But somehow, she managed to grab a kitchen knife to defend herself. She told me that she had killed him."

Walter said nothing, but Leigh couldn't hide from him any longer. She looked him directly in the eye.

"Buddy was still alive when I got there. Callie had nicked his femoral vein with the knife. He didn't have long, but we could've called an ambulance. He might've been saved. But I didn't try to save him. Callie told me what he'd been doing to her. That's when

I remembered what happened in the car. It was like a light switch turning on. One minute I didn't remember. The next minute, I did." Leigh tried to take another breath, but her lungs would not fill. "And I knew that it was my fault. I pimped out my own sister to a pedophile. Everything that happened to her, everything that brought me there, was my fault. So I told Callie to go into the other room. I found a roll of cling film in the kitchen drawer. And I wrapped it around Buddy's head and I suffocated him."

She watched Walter's lips part, but he still said nothing.

"I murdered him," she said, in case that wasn't vividly clear. "And then I made Callie help me chop up his body. We used a machete from the shed. We buried the pieces in the foundation for a strip mall off Stewart Avenue. They poured the concrete the next day. We cleaned up after ourselves. We let Buddy's wife and kid believe that he had left town. And I stole around eighty-six grand from him. That's how I paid for law school."

Walter's mouth moved, but he still said nothing.

"I'm sorry," she said, because there was more to this confession. If she was going to finally tell him the truth, she was going to tell him the whole truth. "Callie has—"

Walter held up his hand, asking her for a moment. He stood up. He paced to the back of the RV. He turned around. One hand rested on the kitchen counter. The other braced against the wall. He shook his head again, completely without words. It was his expression that killed her. He was looking at a stranger.

She pushed herself to continue.

"Callie has no idea that Buddy tried it with me first," Leigh said. "I never had the balls to tell her. And I guess while I'm at it, I should tell you that I don't regret killing him. She was a child, and he took everything from her, but it was my fault. It was all my fault."

Walter started to slowly shake his head like he was desperate for her to take it back.

"Walter, I need you to understand that I really mean what I just said. Not warning Callie—that's the only part of this that I regret. Buddy deserved to die. He deserved to suffer more than the two minutes that it took for him to suffocate."

Walter turned his head, wiping his mouth on his shirtsleeve.

"I carry that guilt with me every second of the day, with every breath, with every molecule inside of me," Leigh said. "Every time Callie has overdosed, every emergency room visit, every stretch of time when I don't know whether she's alive or dead or in trouble or in jail, the one thing that my mind always goes back to is *why didn't I make that motherfucker suffer more?*"

Walter gripped the countertop. His breathing was erratic. He looked like he wanted to bust apart the cabinets, to pull down the ceiling.

"I'm sorry," she said. "I should've told you before, but I told myself that I didn't want to burden you or I didn't want you to get upset, but the truth is, I was too ashamed. What I did to Callie is unforgivable."

He wouldn't look at her. His head bowed. His shoulders shook. She waited for him to scream, to rail against her, but he only wept.

"I'm sorry," she whispered, her heart breaking at the sound of his grief. If she could've held him for just one moment, if there had been a way for her to ease his pain, she would've done it. "I know you hate me. I'm so sorry."

"Leigh." He looked up at her, tears pouring from his eyes. "Don't you know that you were a child, too?"

Leigh stared at him in disbelief. He wasn't disgusted or angry. He was astonished.

"You were only thirteen years old," Walter said. "He molested you, and nobody did anything. You said you should've protected Callie. Who protected you?"

"I should have—"

"You were a child!" He banged his fist against the counter so hard that the glasses shook in the cabinet. "Why can't you see that, Leigh? You were a child. You should've never been in that position in the first place. You shouldn't have been worried about money or getting a goddam job. You should've been at home in bed thinking about which boy you had a crush on in school."

"But—" He didn't understand. He was thinking about Maddy and her friends. It was different in Lake Point. Everyone grew up faster there. "I killed him, Walter. That's first-degree murder. You know that."

"You were only two years older than Maddy is now! The man had molested you. You'd just found out that your sister—"

"Stop," she said, because there was no point in arguing the facts. "I'm telling you this for a reason."

"Does there have to be a reason?" He couldn't move off his outrage. "Jesus Christ, Leigh. How could you live with this guilt for so long? You were a victim, too."

"I wasn't a fucking victim!"

She had screamed the words so loud she was afraid Maddy would hear them inside of the house. Leigh stood up. She walked over to the little window in the door. She looked up at Maddy's bedroom. The bedside lamp was still on. She pictured her precious girl curled up with her nose in the book, the same way Callie used to do when she was a kid.

"Baby," Walter said. "Look at me. Please."

She turned back around, arms hugging her waist. She could not stand the softness in his voice. She did not deserve his easy forgiveness. Callie was her responsibility. He would never understand that.

She told him, "The client, the rapist I had to meet with Sunday night. Andrew Tenant. That's who I babysat for. He's Buddy and Linda's son."

Walter had gone speechless again.

"Andrew has all of his father's videos. He found the murder tape in 2019, but he's had the rape videos since he went off to college." Leigh wasn't going to let herself think about what Andrew had said about watching the tapes. "There were at least two cameras recording everything. There are hours of Buddy raping Callie. Everything that happened the night of the murder was recorded, too. Callie getting into the fight with Buddy, slicing his leg with the knife, then me coming in and murdering him."

Walter waited, a grim set to his mouth.

"The woman Andrew raped, all the other women he raped, he cut their leg right here." She put her hand to her own thigh. "The femoral vein. Exactly where Callie cut Buddy."

Walter waited for the rest.

"Andrew didn't just rape these women. He drugged them. He kidnapped them. He tortured them. He ripped them apart the same way his father ripped apart Callie." Leigh put a finer point on it. "He's psychotic. He's not going to stop."

"What—" Walter had the same question that Leigh had. "What does he want?"

"To make me suffer," Leigh said. "He's blackmailing me. Voir dire starts tomorrow. Andrew told me he wants me to destroy the victim on the stand. He stole her medical records. I've got the information to do it. And then he's going to make me do something else. Then something else. I can't stop him."

"Wait." Walter's sympathy was finally draining away. "You just said this guy is a violent psychopath. You have to—"

"What?" she asked. "Throw the trial? He told me he has a fail-safe—either a backup to the cloud or maybe he has the tapes in a bank vault or I don't know. He said if anything bad happens to him, then he'll release all of the videos."

"So fucking what?" Walter said. "Let him release them."

It was Leigh's turn to be astonished. "I told you what's on those tapes. I'll end up in prison. Callie's life will be over."

"Callie's life?" Walter repeated. "You're worried about Callie's fucking life?"

"I can't—"

"Leigh!" He banged his fist again. "Our teenage daughter is twenty feet away inside of our house. This man is a violent rapist. Did it never occur to you that he could hurt Maddy?"

Leigh was rendered speechless, because Maddy had nothing to do with this.

"Answer me!"

"No." She started shaking her head, because that would never happen. This was between her and Andrew and Callie. "He wouldn't—"

"He wouldn't rape our sixteen-year-old daughter?"

Leigh felt her mouth move, but she couldn't respond.

"God dammit!" he yelled. "You and your fucking compartments!"

He was falling back into their old argument when this was completely different. "Walter, I never—"

"What? You never thought the violent, sadistic rapist who's been threatening your freedom would spill into your fucking private life because what—because you won't let him? Because you're so goddam good at keeping everything separate?" Walter punched the cabinet door off its hinges. "Jesus fucking Christ! Are you taking your fucking parenting tips from Phil now?"

The wound felt deep and fatal. "I didn't—"

"Think?" he demanded. "You didn't get it through your twisted fucking head after it happened to Callie, after you intentionally and willfully murdered a man, that maybe it's a bad idea to connect another teenage girl with a goddam rapist?"

All of the breath left her body.

She felt her feet start to float away from the floor. Her hands fluttered into the air as if her blood had been replaced with helium. She recognized the sensation from the days before, the lightness that came when her soul couldn't take what was happening, so it abandoned her body to deal with the consequences. She realized now that the first time she had felt it happen was inside Buddy's yellow Corvette. The Deguils' house was outside the window. Hall & Oates was playing softly on the radio. Leigh had floated against the ceiling, her eyes closed but somehow still seeing Buddy's monstrous hand wrenching apart her legs.

Jesus your skin is so soft I can feel the peach fuzz you're almost like a baby.

Now, Leigh watched her own shaking hand reach for the small, silver handle on the door. Then she was stepping down the metal stairs. Then she was walking down the driveway. Then she was getting into her car. Then the engine was rumbling and the gear was shifting and the steering wheel was turning and Leigh drove along the empty road away from her husband and child, alone in the darkness.

Thursday

13

At what felt like the crack of dawn, Callie got off the MARTA bus at Jesus Junction, an intersection at three roads in Buckhead where three different churches competed for clientele. The Catholic cathedral was the most impressive, but Callie had a soft spot for the Baptist steeple, which looked like something out of *Andy Griffith*, if Mayberry had been filled with ultra-wealthy conservatives who thought everybody else was going to hell. They also had better cookies, but she had to admit that the Episcopalians knew how to rock a pot of coffee.

The Cathedral of St. Phillip was at the crest of a hill that Callie had been able to easily climb before Covid. Now, she followed the sidewalk around to the side, taking a slower incline to reach the meeting space. And still, her mask was too much for the journey. She had to let it hang from her ear so she could catch her breath as she walked toward the driveway.

BMWs and Mercedes peppered the parking lot. Smokers in business attire were already congregating around the closed door. There were more women than men, which was not unusual in Callie's experience. The preponderance of DUI arrests fell on men, but women were more likely to get court-ordered AA than their male counterparts, especially in Buckhead where high-dollar lawyers like Leigh helped them walk away from responsibility.

Callie was twenty feet from the entrance when she felt eyes on her, but not in the usual, wary way that people looked at junkies. Probably because she wasn't dressed like a junkie. Gone were the cartoony pastels she normally chose from the kids' rack at Goodwill. A deep raid of her bedroom closet had delivered a long-sleeved black spandex top with a scooped neck and form-fitting jeans that made Callie feel like a slinky panther when she'd modeled them for Binx. She'd tied it all together with a pair of scuffed Doc Martens she'd found thrown under Phil's bed. And then she'd risked pink-eye using her mother's make-up to follow a ten-year-old doing a YouTube smoky eye tutorial.

At the time of her self-Pygmalion, Callie's only concern had been to pass as a non-junkie, but now that she was out in the open, she felt conspicuously female. Men were appraising her. Women were judging her. Gazes lingered around her hips, her breasts, her face. On the streets, her low weight was a sign that something was wrong. In this crowd, her thinness was an attribute, something to be appreciated or coveted.

She was grateful to be able to pull up her mask. A man in a dark suit nodded at her as he held open the door. Callie resisted the urge to shudder at the attention. She had wanted her costume to buy her entry into normal society, but she hadn't realized what that society was like.

The door closed behind her. Callie leaned against the wall. She pulled down her mask. From down the hall, she heard beeping and snorting and giggles from the pre-school of boisterous children gearing up for the day. Callie took another few moments to collect herself. She pulled her mask back on. She went the opposite direction from the toddlers, coming face to face with a giant banner that said GOD IS FRIENDSHIP.

Callie doubted God would approve of the kind of friendship that she had in mind this morning. She walked under the banner toward the meeting rooms, passing photographs of the *reverends* and the *very reverends* and the *reverend canons* from years past. A paper sign taped to the wall pointed toward an open door.

8:30 AA MEETING

Callie loved AA meetings, because it was the only time she could truly let her competitive side out for a stroll.

Fiddled with by an uncle? *Call me when you murder him.*

Gang raped by your brother's friends? *Did you chop them all to pieces?*

Uncontrollable shakes from the DTs? *Lemme know when you shit a pint of blood out of your asshole.*

Callie walked into the room. The set-up was the same as every other AA meeting happening in every other corner of the world right now. Folding chairs in a large circle with big pandemic gaps in between. Serenity prayer in a picture frame on a table beside pamphlets with titles like *How It Works!* and *The Promises* and *The Twelve Traditions.* The line for the coffee urn was ten-deep. Callie stood behind a guy in a black business suit and green surgical mask who looked like he would rather be brainstorming outside of the box or putting a pin in his vision board or anywhere else but here.

"Oh," he said, stepping back so that Callie could go ahead of him, which she supposed was what polite gentlemen did for ladies who didn't look like heroin junkies.

"I'm fine, thank you." Callie turned away, showing great interest in a poster of Jesus holding an astray sheep.

The basement was cool, but sweat still rolled down her neck. The exchange with Business Suit had been as unsettling as the looks in the parking lot. Because of her small stature, because she tended to favor Care Bear T-shirts and rainbow jackets, Callie was often mistaken for a teenager, but she was rarely mistaken for a thirty-seven-year-old woman, which technically—she guessed—was what she was. A quick glance around the room told her that she wasn't being paranoid. Curious eyes looked back. Maybe it was because she was new, but Callie had been new at this very same church before and people had shied away like she might suddenly lunge at them and ask for cash. She had looked like a junkie then. Maybe they would give her the money now.

The coffee line moved up. Callie stuck her hand in her purse. She found the pill bottles she'd tucked into the pocket, a hangman's collection she'd traded for a vial of ketamine. As discreetly as she could, she slipped out two Xanax, then turned so she could tuck her fingers under her mask.

Instead of swallowing the tablets, she left them under her tongue. The medication would enter her system faster that way.

As her mouth filled with saliva, Callie forced herself to melt away with the Xanax.

This was her new identity: She was in Atlanta for a job interview. She was staying at the St. Regis. She had been sober for eleven years. She was at a stressful point in her life and she needed the comfort of fellow travelers.

"Fuck," someone muttered.

Callie heard the woman's voice, but she didn't turn around. There was a mirror above the coffee station. She easily spotted Sidney Winslow sitting in one of the folding chairs that had been placed in a circle around the room. The young woman was leaning over her phone, eyebrows knitted. Soft make-up. Hair gently brushing her shoulders. Callie recognized Sidney's more sedate daytime attire, a black pencil skirt and white blouse with capped sleeves. Most women would look like the hostess at a mid-market steak house in the get-up, but Sidney managed to make it look elegant. Even when she muttered another *fuck* as she got up from the chair.

Every man in the room watched her traverse the space. Sidney had absolutely no qualms about the eyes eagerly taking in her body. She had the bearing of a dancer, her posture exact, every movement fluid and somehow sexually charged.

Business Suit made a low noise of appreciation. He saw Callie catching him in the act and raised his eyebrows over his mask, as if to say, *who can blame me?* Callie raised her eyebrows back in a *certainly not I* response because if there was one thing the group seemed to agree upon, other than that alcohol was delicious, it was that Sidney Winslow was fucking gorgeous.

Too bad she was with a rapist asshole who had threatened Maddy's tranquil, perfect existence, because Callie was going to fuck with her so hard that Andrew would be left with nothing but tattered shreds of the woman Sidney Winslow used to be.

"I can't—" Sidney's husky voice carried from the hallway.

Callie took a tiny step back so that she could peer into the hall. Sidney was leaning against the wall, phone pressed to her ear. She had to be arguing with Andrew. Callie had checked the court docket this morning. Andrew's jury selection was starting in two hours. Callie hoped that he looked bruised and battered from their scuffle in the stadium tunnel yesterday afternoon. She wanted every juror to have it at the front of their mind that something was not right about the defendant.

At the very least, Leigh should thank Callie for making her job easier.

And then Leigh should go fuck herself for making Callie climb into Buddy's attic.

Business Suit had finally reached the coffee urn. Callie waited for him to finish, then poured herself two cups because she knew the meeting would run long. There were no cookies. She guessed that was the pandemic at work, but considering what most of these people were willing to do for booze, there was a low risk that a cookie would be the thing that killed them.

Or maybe not. Statistically, ninety-five percent of them would quit the program within a year.

Callie noticed that Sidney had left her purse under her chair. She found a seat opposite, then one back, which would make it easier for her to keep an eye on her prey. Callie put her purse on the floor beside her extra cup of coffee. She crossed her legs. She looked down at her calf, which still had a nice shape to it under the tight jeans. She let her eyes travel up. The fingernail on her right index finger was ripped down to the nailbed from trying to claw Andrew's face off. She had thought about covering it with a Band-Aid, but Callie wanted a visual reminder of how much she despised Andrew Tenant. All she had to do was think about Maddy's name coming out of the twisted fucker's mouth and the rage threatened to explode again like lava spewing from a volcano.

Seventeen years ago, when Callie had first realized she was pregnant, she had known that she had choices, just like she had known that heroin was always going to win. The appointment with the clinic had already been booked. She had mapped out the bus route, planned her convalescence at one of the southside's finer motels.

Then a Christmas card had arrived from Chicago.

Walter had clearly forged Leigh's signature, but what Callie had found remarkable was that he cared enough about his girl-friend to try to keep her from completely breaking away from her baby sister.

And by that time, Walter was more than familiar with Leigh's junkie pain-in-the-ass baby sister. Callie had gone through detoxes where Walter had forced her to drink Gatorade and she had thrown up on his lap and then down his back and Callie was pretty sure at one point she had punched him in the face.

The one consistent fact that had penetrated her misery was the knowledge that her sister deserved this good, kind man, and that eventually this good, kind man was going to ask Leigh to marry him.

There was no question in Callie's mind that Leigh would say yes. She was profoundly, stupidly in love with Walter, her hands flitting around him like a butterfly because she always wanted to touch him, her head going back as she laughed too hard at his jokes, her voice nearly breaking into song when she said his name. Callie had never seen her sister like that before, but she could predict based on past behavior exactly where it would end. Walter would want a family. And he should, because even then Callie had known he'd be a fantastic father. And she had known that Leigh would be an equally fantastic mother because it wasn't Phil who had raised them.

But Callie also knew that Leigh was never going to let herself be that happy. Even without the well-documented history of self-sabotage, her sister would not trust herself enough to have a child. Either getting pregnant or staying pregnant would've been rife with fear and trepidation. Leigh would've fretted about Phil's mental illness. She would've grown too anxious about Callie's addictions tainting her DNA. She would not have trusted herself to do all of the things for a baby that had never been done for her. She would've talked about the *what ifs* for so long that Walter would've either grown deaf or found someone else who would give him the family that he deserved.

That was why Callie had white-knuckled through sobriety for eight excruciating months. It was why she had moved to a god-awful city that was either too cold or too hot and too noisy and too dirty. It was why she had lived in a shelter and let herself get poked and prodded by doctors.

Callie had fucked up so many things in Leigh's life, including bringing her sister to murder. The least—the very least—Callie could do was move to Chicago and grow her sister a baby.

"One minute." An older woman in a pink tracksuit clapped her hands for attention. She had the demeanor of a drill sergeant, though no one at AA was really supposed to be drill-sergeanty. Tracksuit glanced out the door. She repeated the countdown in a lower voice to Sidney. "One minute."

Callie pressed her thumb into her ripped fingernail. The pain reminded her why she was here. She looked at the masked strangers in the circle around her. Someone coughed. Someone else cleared their throat. Tracksuit started to close the door. In the hall, Sidney's eyes went wide. She whispered something into the phone, then darted inside before the door shut.

"Good morning." Tracksuit trotted through the preamble, then said, "For those of you who wish, let's start with the serenity prayer."

Callie kept her body turned toward Tracksuit, but she watched Sidney getting settled. The young woman was clearly still flustered from the call. She checked her phone before shoving it into her purse. She crossed her legs. She pushed back her hair. She crossed her arms. She pushed back her hair again. Every quick movement said she was pissed off and would've loved nothing more than to run out into the hall and finish her conversation, but when a judge told you thirty meetings in thirty days, and the tracksuited fascist who signed off on your court-ordered log wasn't prone to forgiveness, you stayed for the whole hour.

Tracksuit opened up the room to discussion. The men kicked it off, because men always assumed people were interested in what they had to say. Callie listened with half an ear to business dinners gone wrong, embarrassing DUIs, confrontations with angry bosses. The Westside AA meeting was a lot more fun. Bartenders and strippers were not worried about their bosses. Callie had never heard anyone top the story of a twink who'd woken up in his own vomit, then eaten it for the alcohol content.

She raised her hand during a lull. "I'm Maxine, and I'm an alcoholic."

The group returned, "Hi, Maxine."

She said, "Actually, I'm called Max."

There were some chuckles, then, "Hi, Max."

Callie took a breath before launching in. "I was sober for eleven years. And then I turned twelve."

More chuckles, but the only one that counted was the husky, low laugh of Sidney Winslow.

"I was a professional dancer for eight years," Callie began. She had spent hours prepping the story she would tell at the meeting. She hadn't worried about leaving a digital trail. She had used her phone to dig deeper into Sidney's social media so she would know which points to hit the hardest. Started taking ballet in middle school. Raised in a very religious family. Rebelled after high school. Estranged from her family. Lost all of her friends. Made new ones in college. Track team. Yoga. Pinkberry. Beyhive.

"There's a clock on dancing professionally and, once my time ran out, I fell into despair. No one understood my loss. I stopped going to church. Lost touch with my friends and family. Found solace at the bottom of a bottle." Callie shook her head at the tragedy. "And then I met Phillip. He was rich and handsome and he wanted to take care of me. And in all honesty, I was tired of being on my own. I needed someone else to be the strong one for a change."

If Sidney had been a beagle, her floppy ears would've perked up as she wondered at the parallels between Max's life and her own.

"We had three wonderful years together—traveling, seeing the world, going to great restaurants, talking about art and politics and the world." Callie went in for the kill. "And then one day, I pulled into the garage and Phillip was lying face down on the floor."

Sidney's hand went to her heart.

"I rushed over to him, but his body was cold. He'd been dead for hours."

Sidney's head started to shake.

"The police said he'd overdosed. I knew he'd started taking muscle relaxers to help with his back, but I never . . ." Callie carefully looked around the room, ratcheting up the suspense. "Oxycontin."

There were plenty of nods. Everyone knew the stories.

Sidney murmured, "Fucking Oxy."

"The loss was a desecration to the love we had together." Callie let her shoulders slump from the weight of her imaginary grief. "I remember sitting in the lawyer's office, and he was telling me about all the money and properties, and it meant nothing. You know, I read a story last year about Purdue Pharmaceuticals coming up with a formula. They were going to pay out $14,810 for every overdose that was attributable to Oxycontin."

She heard the expected quacks of outrage.

"That's what Phillip's life was worth." Callie wiped away a tear. "$14,810."

The room went silent, waiting for the rest. Callie was content to let them extrapolate. They were alcoholics. They knew how it ended.

Callie didn't have to look at Sidney to know that the young woman had been sucked in. Sidney's eyes had not left Callie the entire time. It wasn't until Tracksuit led them in a *keep coming back it works if you work it* chant that Sidney managed to pull her attention away. She had her phone in her hand and a scowl on her face as she walked toward the door.

Callie's heart tripped because she had stupidly assumed Sidney would stay for the afterparty. She scooped up her purse and trailed her out the door. Fortunately, Sidney went left instead of right toward the exit. Then she took another right toward the ladies' room. The phone was to her ear. Her voice was a growly mumble. The romantic drama continued.

Old-lady perfume wafted out of the Sunday school rooms as Callie trailed behind Sidney. The odor made Callie long for her early Covid days when she couldn't smell or taste anything. She turned, checking behind her. Everyone else was streaming toward the parking lot, probably on their way to work. Callie took a right then pushed open the door.

Three sinks on a long counter. One giant mirror. Three stalls, only one of them occupied.

"Because I said so, you dumbass," Sidney hissed from the last stall. "Do you think I care about your fucking mother?"

Callie gently closed the door.

"Fine. Whatever you say." Sidney let out a frustrated groan. There were a couple more *fucks*, then she seemed to decide that since she was sitting on a toilet, she might as well pee.

Callie turned on the faucet to make her presence known. She stuck her hands under the cold water. The bare flesh under her torn fingernail started to sting. Callie pressed into the side, bringing out a thin line of blood. Her mouth filled with saliva again. She heard Andrew's voice, so much like Buddy's voice, echoing through the dark stadium tunnel.

Madeline Félicette Collier, aged sixteen.

The toilet flushed. Sidney came out of the stall. Her face was absent a mask. She was even more attractive in person than on her social. She told Callie, "Sorry, fucking boyfriend. Husband. Whatever. He got mugged yesterday afternoon. We're talking just hours before our wedding. But he won't call the cops or tell me what happened."

Callie nodded, pleased that Andrew had come up with a good lie.

"I don't know what his problem is." Sidney twisted on the faucet. "He's being a total dickwad."

"Love is brutal," Callie said. "At least that's what I carved onto my last girlfriend's face."

Sydney's hand went to her mouth as she guffawed. She seemed to realize her face was uncovered. "Fuck, sorry, I'll put on my mask."

"It's cool," Callie said, peeling off her own mask. "I hate these fucking things anyway."

"Preach." Sidney punched the lever on the soap dispenser. "I'm, like, so ready to be over these meetings. What's the point?"

"I always feel better hearing people are worse off than I am." Callie took some soap for herself. She adjusted the water to make it warmer. "Do you know any good places to get breakfast around here? I'm staying at the St. Regis and I can't take another room service meal."

"Oh, right, you're from Chicago." Sidney turned off the faucet, shook out her hands. "So you used to be a dancer?"

"Long time ago." Callie pulled out a paper towel from the dispenser. "I still do my routines, but I miss performing."

"I bet," Sidney said. "I took dance all the way through high school. I loved it, like, crazy I-wanna-do-this-for-the-rest-of-my-life loved it."

"You've still got it," Callie said. "I noticed it when you walked across the room. You don't ever lose that poise."

Sidney preened.

Callie pretended to look for something in her purse. "Why'd you stop?"

"Not good enough."

Callie looked up, skeptical eyebrow raised. "Trust me, there were a lot of girls who weren't good enough who still made it onto stage."

Sidney shrugged, but she looked enormously pleased. "I'm too old now."

"I would say you're never too old, but we both know that's bullshit." Callie kept her hand in her purse, like she was waiting for Sidney to leave. "Hey, it was nice meeting you. I hope things work out with your husband."

Sidney's disappointment was writ large on her face. And then her eyes did exactly what Callie wanted them to do. They traveled down to the purse. "You holding?"

Bingo.

Callie winced with faked regret as she pulled out one of the prescription bottles. Stimulants were generally the last thing that Callie wanted, but she had assumed a woman of Sidney's generation would be all about the Adderall.

"Study Buddies." Sidney smiled at the label. "Mind sharing? I am so fucking hungover."

"My pleasure." Callie shook out four peach-colored tablets onto the sink counter. Then she used the edge of the bottle to start crushing them.

"Shit," Sidney said. "I haven't snorted since high school."

Callie made a face. "Oh, honey, if it's too much—"

"Fuck, why not?" Sidney whipped out a twenty-dollar bill and straightened it back and forth over the edge of the counter. She grinned at Callie. "Still got it."

Callie walked over to the bathroom door. She reached up to turn the lock. Blood was rolling down from her torn fingernail. She clicked the lock, leaving her own bloody print on the metal. Then she returned to the counter and continued crushing the tablets into a fine, peach-colored powder.

Adderall came in two versions, IR for immediate release and XR for extended release. The XR came in capsules with tiny microbeads that were coated in a time-release film. As with Oxy, the film could be crushed off but that was hard to do and the XR burned the shit out of your nose and basically gave you the same rush as the IR, which was incidentally cheaper, and Callie was not one to pass up a bargain.

The important part was that snorting the powder jacked the entire dose immediately and directly into your system. The amphetamine/dextroamphetamine cocktail entered through the blood vessels in the nose, then carried on the party up to the brain. No time for the stomach or liver to filter down the euphoria. The rush could be intense, but it could also be overwhelming. The brain could freak out, causing your blood pressure to skyrocket and, in some cases, could bring on anything from seizures to psychosis.

It would be terribly hard for Andrew to stalk a sixteen-year-old girl while his beautiful young wife was strapped down to a hospital gurney.

Callie expertly wielded the edge of the bottle cap, chopping out four thick lines. She watched Sidney lean down. The woman might not have snorted since high school, but she certainly knew how to put on a show while she did it. Her legs crossed at the ankles. She pushed out what was a very well-defined ass. The tip of the rolled-up twenty went into her nose. She waited for Callie to look at her in the mirror, and then she winked before hoovering up a line.

"F-f-fuck!" Sidney stuttered, which was a bit much. It took about ten minutes to really hit you. "Praise, Jesus!"

Callie supposed the religious fervor was a holdover from her bible school days.

She asked Sidney, "Good?"

"Fuck yes. Go. Your turn." Sidney offered the twenty. Callie didn't take it. She reached up to Sidney's face and used her thumb to wipe away a fine dusting around the woman's nostril. And then she let her thumb travel down to her perfect rosebud mouth. Sidney didn't need encouragement. Her lips parted. Her tongue darted out. She slowly licked the side of Callie's thumb.

Callie smiled as her hand dropped away. She slid the rolled-up twenty from between Sidney's fingers. She leaned down. Out of the corner of her eye, she could see Sidney bouncing on her toes, shaking out her hands like a boxer. Callie cupped her left hand to her face, pretending to press her nostril closed. She switched the twenty to her mouth, blocked the back of her throat with her tongue, and sucked up a line.

Callie coughed. Some of the powder had tickled into her throat, but most of it had plastered to the bottom of her tongue. She coughed again, and spit the wad of paste into her fist.

"Yes!" Sidney grabbed the twenty and swooped down for more.

Then it was Callie's turn again. She performed the same pantomime—the cupping, the sucking, the horking. More powder slipped past her tongue this time, but that was the cost of doing business.

"Sushi!" Sidney was blinking her eyes entirely too fast. "Sushi-sushi-sushi. We should go to lunch together, okay? Is it too early for lunch?"

Callie made a show of looking at her watch. She'd found it in the back of one of Phil's drawers. The battery was dead, but it had to be around ten. "We could do brunch?"

"Mimosas!" Sidney shouted. "I know a place. My treat. I'll drive. Is that good? I need a fucking drink, okay?"

"Sounds like fun," Callie told her. "Let me use the toilet, then I'll meet you outside."

"Yes! Okay. I'll be outside. In my car. Okay? Right." Sidney's hands slipped around the lock until she finally managed to get it open. Her low, husky laughter drained off as the door closed behind her.

Callie turned on the faucet. She scraped the white paste off of her hand. She used a wet paper towel to wipe the rest of the Adderall off the counter. All the while, she did a silent inventory of the other prescription bottles inside of her purse.

Her gaze found her reflection in the mirror. Callie stared back at herself, wanting to feel bad about what she was going to do. The feeling wouldn't come. What she saw instead was Leigh and Walter's beautiful girl running down the field, oblivious to the monster hiding in the tunnel.

Andrew was going to pay for threatening Maddy. He was going to pay with Sidney's life.

14

Leigh stood in line for security outside the DeKalb County court-house, a white marble mausoleum of a building with a toothy, dark-brick main entrance. Faded stickers on the ground designated the proper standing distance. Signs warned that masks were mandated. Large posters were taped to the doors advising visitors that they were not allowed inside per the statewide emergency order from the Chief Justice of the Supreme Court of Georgia.

The courthouse had only recently opened back up for business. Through the pandemic, all of Leigh's cases had been tried via Zoom, but then vaccinations for court employees had made it possible for the government to open up in-person trials again. Never mind the jurors, attorneys, and defendants who were still playing Corona Russian roulette.

Leigh used her foot to push a file box along to the next sticker. She nodded to one of the deputies who came out to check the line and warn stragglers. There were ten divisions to the Superior Court. All but two of the judges were women of color. Of the two outliers, one had come from a prosecutorial background, but was known to be incredibly fair. The other was a man named Richard Turner, a proud graduate of the good ol' boy school of judging who had a reputation for being much more lenient toward defendants who looked like him.

In a life of perpetually falling upward, Andrew had drawn Judge Turner for his trial.

Leigh took no pleasure in accepting this as good news. She had resigned herself to defending Andrew Tenant to the fullest of her abilities, even if that required her to break every moral and legal code. She would not let those videos get out. She would not let Callie's fragile life get shattered. She would not allow herself to think about the implications for Maddy or the argument with Walter last night or the deep and fatal wound he had inflicted on her soul.

Are you taking your fucking parenting tips from Phil now?

She edged up the file box to the next decal as the line shifted forward. Leigh looked down at her hands. The shaking was gone. Her stomach had settled. There were no tears in her eyes.

Walter's one abiding complaint was that Leigh's personality changed depending on who was in front of her. She put everything into separate compartments, never letting one spill over into the other. He saw this as a weakness, but Leigh saw it as a survival skill. The only way she was going to make it through the next few days was to completely partition off her emotions.

The transition had started last night. Leigh was standing in her kitchen pouring an entire bottle of vodka down the sink. Then she was standing over the toilet flushing the rest of her Valium. Then she was prepping for Andrew's case, re-reading motions, re-watching Tammy Karlsen's interview, doing a deeper dive into her therapy notes, devising a working strategy to win the case because, if she didn't win, Andrew's fail-safe would kick in and it would be all for nothing.

By the time the sun came up, the floating feeling had completely evaporated. Walter's fury, his rage, his deep and fatal wound, had somehow forged Leigh into cold, hard steel.

She picked up the box as she went inside. She stood in front of the iPad stand that took her temperature. The green box told her to proceed. At the checkpoint, she took her phones and laptop out of her purse and placed them in bins. The box went on the belt behind them. She walked through the metal detector. There was a giant bottle of hand sanitizer on the other side. Leigh pumped a glob into her hand and instantly regretted it. One of the local distilleries was riding out the pandemic by using their stills to churn out disinfectants. The white rum residue in the tanks made the entire courthouse smell like Panama City Beach during Spring break.

"Counselor," someone said. "Your number's up."

A deputy had pulled her bins off the belt. Adding to the miseries of the day, Leigh had been selected for random screening. At least she knew the deputy. Maurice Grayson's brother was a fireman, which gave him a close connection to Walter.

She easily clicked herself into the role of Walter's wife, smiling behind her mask. "This is blatant racial profiling."

Maurice laughed as he started unpacking her purse. "More like sexual harassment, Counselor. You're looking dope today."

She took the compliment, because she'd paid special attention to everything this morning. Light blue button-down blouse, dark charcoal skirt and blazer, thin white gold necklace, hair down around her shoulders, three-inch black heels—exactly the way the consultants said that Leigh should dress for the jury.

Maurice rolled around the contents of her clear make-up bag, ignoring the tampons. "Tell your husband his Flex is a joke."

Leigh guessed this had to do with fantasy football. Just like she guessed that Walter did not give one shit about the game that had taken every moment of his free time before last night. "I'll pass that along."

Maurice finally cleared her, and Leigh grabbed her things off the belt. Even though she was masked, the smile stayed on her face as she walked into the lobby. She went into lawyer mode, nodding at colleagues, biting her tongue at the idiots who'd let their masks slip below their noses because real men could only get Covid through their mouths.

She didn't want to wait for the elevator. She carried the box up two flights. At the door, she took a moment, trying to reforge herself into steel. Maurice bringing up Walter had led her thoughts toward Maddy, and thinking about Maddy threatened to open a giant, gaping hole in her heart.

Leigh had texted her daughter this morning, the usual cheery rise and shine along with the detail that she would be in court all day. Maddy had sent back an oblivious thumbs up along with a heart. Leigh would have to talk to her daughter eventually, but she was afraid if she heard Maddy's voice, she would lose it. Which made Leigh just as much of a coward as Ruby Heyer.

She heard voices coming up the stairs. Leigh used her hip to open the door. Jacob Gaddy waved to her from the end of the hall. The associate had managed to snag one of the rarely available attorney/client conference rooms.

"Well done on the room." Leigh let him take the box. "I need these catalogued and ready for Monday."

"Got it," Jacob said. "The client's not here yet, but Dante Carmichael was looking for you."

"Did he say what he wanted?"

"I mean—" Jacob shrugged, as if it was obvious. "Deal 'Em Down Dante, right?"

"Let him find me." Leigh walked into the empty room. Four chairs, one table, no windows, flickering overhead lights. "Where's—"

"Liz?" Jacob asked. "She's downstairs trying to snag the jury questionnaires."

"Don't let anyone interrupt me if I'm with the client." Leigh's personal phone started to ring. She reached into her purse.

Jacob said, "I'll keep an eye out for Andrew."

Leigh didn't respond because Jacob had already shut the door. Her mask came off. She looked at her phone. Her stomach threatened to churn, but Leigh willed it to calm. She answered on the fourth ring. "What is it, Walter? I'm about to go into court."

He was silent for a moment, probably because he'd never met Leigh the frigid bitch before. "What are you going to do?"

She chose to be obtuse. "I'm going to try to select a jury that will find my client not guilty."

"And then?"

"And then I'm going to see what he wants me to do next."

Another hesitation. "That's your plan, just let him keep pushing you around?"

She would've laughed if she wasn't terrified that showing one emotion would break open the others. "What else can I do, Walter? I told you he has a fail-safe. If you've got a brilliant alternative then, please, tell me what you want me to do."

There was no response, only the sound of Walter's breathing through the phone. She thought about him in the RV last night, the sudden fury, the deep and mortal wound. Leigh closed her eyes, tried to still her pounding heart. She imagined herself standing alone on a small wooden boat, gliding away from the shore where Walter and Maddy stood waving goodbye as Leigh floated toward the rushing waters of a waterfall.

That was how her life was supposed to end up. Leigh was never meant to move to Chicago, or meet Walter, or accept the gift of Maddy. She was meant to be trapped in Lake Point, drop-kicked into the gutter along with everybody else.

Walter said, "I want you here tomorrow night at six. We're going to talk to Maddy and explain that she's going to go on a trip with Mom. She can do school virtually from the road. I can't have her around while this guy is out there. I can't—I won't—let anything bad happen to her."

Leigh was not as caught out as Walter. She had heard him use his current tone exactly once, four years ago. She'd been lying on the bathroom floor, still drunk from the previous night's binge. He was explaining to Leigh that she had thirty days to get sober or he was going to take Maddy away from her. The only difference between that ultimatum and this one was that the first had been given out of love. Now, he was doing it out of hate.

"Sure." She took a breath before launching into the three sentences she'd rehearsed in the car this morning. "I filed the paperwork this morning. I'll send you the link. You need to e-sign your part and we'll be divorced thirty-one days after it's processed."

He hesitated again, but not for nearly long enough. "What about custody?"

Leigh felt her resolve start to crumble. If she talked to him about Maddy, she would end up on the floor again. "Play that out, Walter. We do a contested divorce. We go to mediation or you put me in front of a judge. I try to get visitation and then what, you file a motion stating that I'm a danger to my child?"

He said nothing, which was a form of confirmation.

"I intentionally and willfully murdered a man," she said, reminding him of his words last night. "You wouldn't want me connecting another teenage girl with a goddam rapist."

If he had a response, Leigh wasn't going to hear it. She ended the call. She placed the phone face down on the table. The Hollis Academy crest glittered on the back. Leigh traced her fingers around the outline. The sight of her bare finger caught her out.

Her wedding ring was in the soap dish she kept by her kitchen sink. Leigh had not taken it off since they'd left Chicago.

Please accept the gift of this beautiful girl. I know that no matter what happens, you will both always and forever keep her happy and safe.

She used the back of her hand to rub the tears out of her eyes. How was she going to tell her sister that she had fucked up everything? Over twenty-four hours had passed since Leigh had walked Callie back to Phil's. They hadn't spoken to each other once they'd left the Waleskis' house. Callie had been shaking uncontrollably. Her teeth were chattering the same way they'd chattered the night that Buddy had died.

Leigh had forgotten what it felt like to walk beside her sister in the street. It was difficult to describe the feeling of no longer being a solitary adult, only responsible for the workings of your own body. The anxiety she felt around Callie—the fear for her safety, for her emotional well-being, for her physical health, for her not to trip over her own damn feet and fall and break something—reminded Leigh of what it felt like when Maddy was a little girl.

The responsibility for her child had brought incomprehensible joy. With Callie, Leigh felt endlessly burdened.

"Leigh?" Liz knocked on the door as she entered. The look on her face said that something was wrong. Leigh didn't have to ask for an explanation.

Andrew Tenant stood behind Liz. His mask hung from one ear. An angry, deep gash was engraved along his jawline. White butterfly strips pinned down a torn part of his earlobe. He had what looked like a giant hickey on his neck. And then he came closer and Leigh could see teeth marks.

Leigh's immediate response wasn't concern or outrage. It was a single, shocked laugh.

Andrew's jaw set. He turned to shut the door, but Liz was already closing it behind her.

He waited until they were alone. He took off his mask. He pulled out a chair. He sat down. He told Leigh, "What did I tell you about laughing at me?"

She waited to feel the same, visceral fear that her body always

313

conjured in response to his presence. But her skin wasn't crawling. The hairs on the back of her neck were not at attention. Her fight or flight had somehow deactivated. If this was the result of Walter's fatal wound, then she was all the better for it.

She asked Andrew, "What happened to you?"

His eyes went back and forth across her face as if she were a book that he could read.

He sat back in his chair. He rested his hand on the table. "I went for a jog after you left my house yesterday morning. Physical exercise is an approved part of my bail conditions. Someone mugged me. I tried to fight back. Unsuccessfully, as it turns out. They stole my wallet."

Leigh didn't comment on the fact that he'd already taken his shower when she'd arrived at his house. "Do you always jog with your wallet?"

His hand went flat to the table. There was no sound, but she was reminded of the power in his body. The fight or flight slowly stirred at the base of her spine.

She asked, "Is there something else I should know?"

"How's Callie doing?"

"She's fine. I talked to her this morning."

"Is that right?" His tone of voice had turned intimate. Something had changed.

Leigh did not attempt to understand how she'd managed to cede some of her power. She could feel it in her body, that familiar visceral reaction that told her a shift had occurred. "Is there anything else?"

Each of his fingers tapped once on the table. "I should tell you that my monitor went off at 3:12 yesterday afternoon. I called my probation officer immediately. She arrived over three hours later to reset it. She interrupted the cocktail party before my wedding ceremony."

Leigh hadn't noticed the ring on his finger, but she saw him noting the lack of a ring on hers. She crossed her arms, asking, "You realize how this looks, right? You show up for jury selection on your rape trial with the kind of defensive wounds a man gets from a woman fighting him off, and then you add to that the documented fact that your ankle monitor was off for over three hours?"

"Is that bad?"

Leigh remembered their conversation yesterday morning. This was all part of his plan. Every step of the way, he made things harder for her. "Andrew, you've got four other documented occasions that your ankle monitor alarm went off. Each time, it took three to four hours for probation to respond. Did it ever occur to you that the prosecutor would argue that you were testing the system to see how long it takes for someone to come out?"

"That sounds very incriminating," Andrew said. "Good thing my lawyer is highly motivated to argue my innocence."

"There's a huge difference between innocent and not guilty."

His mouth twitched in a smile. "Nuance?"

Leigh felt the tingle of fear trace up her spine. He had seamlessly managed to reassert his dominance. He didn't know that Leigh had revealed the truth to Walter, but Walter had never really been a weapon in Andrew's arsenal. The videos were all he needed. Either by whim or through his fail-safe, he could end Leigh and Callie's lives.

She opened her purse and found her make-up bag. "Come here."

Andrew stayed seated. He wanted to remind her who was in charge.

Leigh unzipped her bag. She laid out primer, concealer, foundation, and powder. The asshole had gotten lucky again. All of the damage was on the left side of his face. The jury would be seated to his right.

She asked him, "Do you want this or not?"

He stood up, making his motions slow and deliberate, letting her know that he was still in charge.

Leigh felt the panic start to well inside of her chest as he sat down in front of her. He had the uncanny ability to turn his malevolence off or on. Being close to him, Leigh felt the revulsion roil her stomach. The tremble was back in her hands.

Andrew smiled, because this was what he wanted.

Leigh squeezed primer onto the back of her hand. She found a sponge in her bag. Andrew leaned closer. He smelled of musky cologne and the same mint that had been on his breath the day before. Leigh's fingers felt awkward on the sponge as she dabbed at the bite marks on his neck. The bruises imprinted around the teeth marks were vivid blue, but they would probably turn black over the weekend, just in time for the trial.

Leigh said, "You're going to need to hire a professional to do this Monday morning."

Andrew winced when she moved up to the gash in his jaw. The skin was angry and red. Specks of fresh blood wept into the sponge. Leigh didn't use a delicate hand. She loaded up a brush with concealer and jammed the bristles deep into the wound.

He hissed air between his teeth, but he didn't pull away. "Do you like hurting me, Harleigh?"

She softened her touch, repulsed by the fact that he was right. "Turn your head."

He kept his eyes on her as his chin moved to the right. "Did you learn how to do this when you were little?"

Leigh switched to a larger brush for the foundation. Her skin tone was darker than his. She would need to use more powder.

"I remember you and Callie used to show up with black eyes, cut lips." Andrew gave another low hiss as she used her fingernail to scrape away a trickle of blood from his chin. "Mom would say, 'Those poor girls and their crazy mother. I don't know what to do.'"

Leigh felt a pain in her mouth from clenching her teeth. She had to get this over with. She found the powder, another brush. She caked it onto his wound, using her finger to feather out the edges.

"If only she had called the police, or children's services," Andrew said. "Think about how many lives she could've saved."

"Jacob is my second chair," Leigh said, because talking about work was the only way to keep herself from screaming. "He's my associate. I mentioned him the other day at Bradley's. Jacob will be handling the procedural side, but I'll let him interview some of the prospective jurors if it seems like they'll respond better to a man. You need to cut the bullshit around him. He's young, but he's not stupid. If he picks up on anything—"

"Harleigh." Andrew pushed out her name in a long, low sigh. "You know, you really are quite beautiful."

His hand touched her leg.

Leigh reeled away from him. Her chair scraped across the floor.

She was on her feet, back to the wall, before she let herself process what had just happened.

"Har-leigh," Andrew stood up from the table. The toothy grin was back, the one that said he was enjoying everything about this moment. His footsteps shuffled across the floor. "What's the perfume you're wearing? I really like it."

Leigh started to shake.

He leaned in closer, inhaling her scent. She could feel her hair brushing his face. His hot breath was in her ear. There was nowhere to go. Leigh's shoulder blades were stabbing into the wall. All she had was the make-up brush that she still clenched in her hand.

Andrew looked into her eyes, watching her carefully. His tongue darted out between his lips. She felt the pressure of his knee pushing against her clenched legs.

That's okay little girl don't be scared of your ol' pal Buddy.

A loud boom of laughter came from the other side of the door. The sound echoed through the hallway. She struggled to remind herself that she was not trapped inside of the yellow Corvette. She was in a tiny conference room inside the Superior Court for DeKalb County. Her associate was outside. Her assistant was nearby. Sheriff's deputies. Prosecutors. Colleagues. Detectives. Cops. Social workers.

They would believe her this time.

She asked Andrew, "Does Linda know you're a rapist like your father?"

A subtle change crossed his face. "Does your husband know you're a murderer?"

Leigh stared all of her hate into him. "Get the fuck away from me before I start screaming."

"Harleigh." His toothy grin returned. "Don't you know by now that I love it when a woman screams?"

She had to slide along the wall to get away from him. She felt her legs shaking as she walked to the door. Opened it. Went into the nearly deserted hallway. Two men stood near the elevators. Another pair was entering the men's room. Liz was sitting on a bench against the wall. She had her iPad on her lap, her phone in her hand. Leigh walked toward her, hands clutched into fists because she didn't know what to do with all of the adrenaline in her body.

Liz said, "Jacob's in the courtroom going through the questionnaires. We're ten minutes out."

"Good." Leigh looked down the hall, trying to banish her anxiety. "Anything else?"

"No." Liz didn't return to her electronics. She stood up. "Actually, yes."

Leigh couldn't take one more bad thing. "What's wrong?"

"It just occurred to me that I've never seen you upset. Like, your hair could be on fire and you'd ask me to bring a glass of water when it's convenient." She glanced at the conference room. "Do you need me in there? Or Jacob? Because he creeps me the hell out, too."

Leigh couldn't worry about her emotions being on full display. Her legs could still feel the pressure of Andrew's knee trying to pry them apart. She didn't want to go back into that room again, but the only thing worse than being alone with Andrew was giving him an audience.

She was saved the decision by the sight of Dante Carmichael getting off the elevator. The prosecutor had brought a team. Miranda Mettes, his second chair, was on his right. On his left was Barbara Klieg, the detective in charge of the Tammy Karlsen investigation. Taking up the rear were two uniformed DeKalb County police officers.

"Shit," Leigh whispered. She had only looked at Andrew's mugging story and his failed ankle monitor as individual pieces. Now she saw them as a whole. Another woman had been violently attacked. Andrew had been connected to the case. They were here to arrest him.

"Harleigh?" Andrew was holding up her personal cell phone. "Who's Walter? He's been trying to call you."

Leigh grabbed the phone out of his hand. She warned him, "Keep your fucking mouth shut."

His eyebrow rose up. He thought this was all a joke. "Are you worried about your family, Harleigh?"

"Collier," Dante called. "I need to talk to your client."

Leigh gripped her phone so tightly that she felt the edges press

318

against the bones in her fingers. They were all watching her, waiting. The only thing she could think to do was to show them the bitchy litigator they were expecting. "Go fuck yourself, Dante. You're not going to talk to him."

"Just trying to clear some things up," Dante said, as if he were being entirely reasonable. "What's the harm in a few questions?"

"No," Leigh said. "He's not—"

"Harleigh," Andrew interrupted. "I'd be happy to answer any questions. I've got nothing to hide."

Barbara Klieg had been silently taking photos of Andrew's wounds with her phone. "Looks like you're trying to hide some fairly nasty cuts and bruises there, pal."

"You're right, *pal*." Andrew's smile was chilling. He was completely unafraid. "As I told my lawyer, I was attacked on my morning jog yesterday. It must've been a junkie looking for a quick buck. Isn't that what you said, Harleigh?"

Leigh bit her lip to keep herself from losing it. The stress was going to split her in two. "Andrew, I'm advising you to—"

"Did you file a report?" Klieg asked.

"No, officer," Andrew said. "Given my recent interactions with the police, I didn't feel it would be worth my while to ask for help."

"What about last night?" Klieg said. "Your ankle monitor was off for over three hours."

"A fact I immediately reported to my probation officer." His gaze found Leigh, but not out of desperation. He wanted to watch her squirm. "My lawyer can confirm that she was also informed. Isn't that right?"

Leigh said nothing. She looked down at her phone. Maddy's school crest was on the back. She knew that Andrew had seen it.

Are you worried about your family, Harleigh?

Walter was right. Leigh had been a fool for thinking that she could keep this monster packed inside a separate compartment.

Klieg asked Andrew, "Can you account for your whereabouts between the hours of five and seven thirty last night?"

"Andrew," Leigh warned, silently begging him to stop. "I am advising you to remain silent."

Andrew ignored the advice, telling Klieg, "My wedding ceremony was held at my home yesterday evening. I let the caterers in around five thirty. My mother arrived promptly at six to make sure everything was running smoothly. I'm sure you know my probation officer, Teresa Singer, showed up around six thirty to reset my ankle monitor. Guests were already arriving by then for cocktails and light hors d'oeuvres. Then Sidney and I walked down the aisle around eight. Does that satisfy your inquiry?"

Klieg exchanged a look with Dante. Neither one of them was happy with his answer. There were too many potential witnesses.

Andrew offered, "I can show you the photos I took on my phone. I'm sure the metadata will support my alibi. Everything is time and location stamped."

Leigh remembered Reggie telling her that metadata could be faked if you knew what you were doing. She went from hoping Andrew would shut up to praying he knew what the hell he was doing.

Klieg said, "Let's see the pictures."

"Andrew," Leigh said, but only because it was expected of her. He was already reaching into his inside jacket pocket.

"Here we go." He angled the screen so that everyone could watch him scroll through the photos. Andrew posing with a line of caterers behind him. Standing beside Linda as she held up a flute of champagne. Andrew helping to hang a banner that read CONGRATULATIONS MR. & MRS. ANDREW TENANT!

The photos were compelling, but what was absent told the real story. There were no solitary pictures of cakes and decorations. No guests standing alone at the front door. No Sidney in her wedding dress. Every photo contained Andrew and, at every angle, you could see the scrapes and bruises on his face and neck.

Klieg said, "How about I take your phone and let our experts look at it?"

Leigh gave up. Andrew was going to do whatever he wanted. Trying to warn him wasn't worth the effort it took to open her mouth.

"The password is six ones." He gave a self-deprecating laugh, acknowledging the simplicity. "Anything else, officer?"

Klieg was clearly disappointed, but she made a show of pulling an evidence bag out of her blazer pocket and holding it open so that Andrew could drop in his phone.

Dante spoke to Leigh. "I need a private moment."

The sick feeling welled back up. He was going to offer Andrew another deal and Andrew was going to tell her to pass because he was always three steps ahead of her.

Leigh followed Dante into the conference room. She crossed her arms and leaned back against the wall as he closed the door. He had a folder in his hands. Leigh was sick and tired of men showing her the abhorrent contents of their folders.

Dante said nothing. He was probably expecting her to start this off with another *Go fuck yourself*, but Leigh was out of fucks. She raised her personal phone. There were two missed calls from Walter. He had probably signed the divorce papers. He had probably changed his mind about letting her say goodbye to Maddy. He was probably on his way out of town.

She told Dante, "We're expected in front of the judge in five minutes. What're you offering?"

"Felony murder." He dropped the file on the table.

Leigh could see the edges of glossy, color photographs peering out. If he was trying to shock her, he was too late. Cole Bradley had predicted this forty-eight hours ago—

Peeping Tom turns into rapist. Rapist turns into murderer.

"When?" She knew that determining time of death could be more art than science. "How do you know she was murdered between five and seven thirty last night?"

"She called her family at five. Body was found in Lakehaven Park around seven thirty."

Leigh knew there was a lake at the country club near Andrew's house. She had to assume the body had been left just like the others—at another park that was a fifteen minute walk from where he lived. She pressed together her lips, trying to figure out how Andrew had pulled this off. On the surface, his alibi was solid. The metadata on the photos would place him at his house. Sidney would back up anything he said. Linda was the outlier. Leigh didn't know if Andrew's mother would swear under oath that the champagne flute photo had been taken at the indicated time. And then there were the cuts and bruises on Andrew's face and neck.

Something occurred to her.

She told Dante, "It takes two to three hours for that kind of dark coloring to come up. You saw the pictures on his phone. The marks on Andrew's neck were turning purple by the time the caterers showed up at five thirty. The cut on his jaw had stopped bleeding."

"What about these photos?" Dante opened the file folder. He started slapping down the crime scene photos on the table. The dramatic flourish was unnecessary. Leigh was too jaded to be shockable, and what he was showing her was nothing she had not seen before.

A woman's face beaten so badly that her features were indistinguishable.

Teeth marks surrounding the open wound where a nipple used to be.

A cut to the left thigh just over the femoral artery.

The metal handle of a knife sticking out between her legs.

"Stop." Leigh recognized Andrew's handiwork. She asked the same question she had been asking every man in her life lately. "What do you want from me?"

"That's probably what the victim said when your client was raping and killing her." Dante held the last photo between his hands. "You know he did this, Collier. Don't bullshit a bullshitter. It's just us girls in here. Andrew Tenant is guilty as hell."

Leigh wasn't so sure—at least not this time. The coloring of the bite marks was bothering her. She had worked so many domestic violence cases in private practice that she could probably qualify as an expert witness. "You said the victim had a phone call with her family at five. If you're saying Andrew attacked the victim right after the call, then got home by five thirty to let the caterers in—or at the very latest he was home by six thirty when his parole officer showed up to reset his ankle monitor—explain the dark coloring of the marks on his neck."

"I think you mean teeth marks, but so what?" Dante shrugged. "You get your expert to testify to one thing and I get my expert to testify to another."

"Let's see it." Leigh nodded for him to put the last photo on the table. Dante had been holding it back for a reason.

322

He bypassed the flourish as he placed the photograph in front of her.

Another close-up. The back of the victim's head. Chunks of her straight black hair were missing. The scalp showed deep gouges where something sharp and brutal had been used to cut deep into the roots.

Leigh had seen those kinds of wounds only once before in her life. She was ten years old. She was gripping a piece of broken glass, attacking one of Callie's tormentors on the playground.

I held her down and hacked off her hair until her scalp was bleeding.

Leigh felt sweat roll down her neck. The walls started to close in. Andrew had done this. He had listened to Leigh's story about punishing the mean little girl and he had played it out in a sick, twisted homage.

Suddenly, a moment of panic gripped Leigh's heart. Her eyes darted across the photos, but the woman's arms and legs were not stick-thin. There were no track marks and old scars from needles that had broken off in her veins. Nor did she show the signs of baby fat that Leigh's own beautiful girl needlessly fretted over in front of the mirror.

"The victim," Leigh said. "What's her name?"

"She's not just a victim, Collier. She was a mother, a wife, a Sunday school teacher. She's got a sixteen-year-old daughter, just like you."

"Save the violins for your closing argument," Leigh said. "Tell me her name."

"Ruby Heyer."

15

"Fucking yeah!" Sidney screamed into the air whipping around her convertible BMW. The radio was blaring a song that dropped more n-words than a white nationalist convention. Sidney sang along, her fist pumping toward the sky with every beat. She was drunk as hell from three pitchers of mimosas, stoned out of her mind from the molly Callie had slipped into her last drink, and probably going to lose control of the car if she didn't put her eyes back on the road.

The BMW fishtailed at a stop sign. Sidney racked the heel of her palm into the horn. Her foot slammed down on the gas. "Outta my way, motherfucker!"

"Woot!" Callie yelled, raising a companionable fist in the air. Despite herself, she was having fun. Sidney was hilarious. She was young and stupid and she hadn't completely fucked up her life yet, though clearly, she was working on it.

"Fucker!" Sidney yelled at another driver as she blew through a stop sign. "Fuck you in the face, motherfucker!"

Callie laughed as the elderly driver used both hands to flip them off. Her mind was racing. Her heart was a hummingbird. Colors burst in front of her eyes—neon-green trees, blazing yellow sun, vivid blue sky, bright white trucks and siren-red cars and flashing yellow lines popping up from the jet-black asphalt.

She had forgotten how fantastic it felt to party. Before she'd broken her neck, Callie had tried coke and molly and bennies and meth and addys because she had thought that the answer to her problems was to make the world spin as fast as it could.

The Oxy had changed that. Callie had known the first time

the drug hit her system that what she really needed was to revel in the slow. Like a monkey, her feet had turned into fists. She could hang in one place while the world passed her by. The zen from those early days of opioids had been ludicrously off the chart. And then weeks went by, then months, then years, then her standing-still life had narrowed down solely to the pursuit of more heroin.

She fished out one of the pill bottles from her purse, found another Adderall. She placed it on her tongue. Showed it to Sidney.

Sidney leaned over and sucked the tablet off of Callie's tongue. Her lips melted into Callie's. Her mouth was hot. The sensation was electric. Callie tried to make it last, but Sidney slipped away, turning her attention back to the car. Callie shuddered, her body waking up in a way it hadn't in years.

"God damn!" Sidney yelled, pushing the car to go faster as she slalomed down a residential street. The BMW skidded into a sharp curve. She came to a jarring stop. "Fuck."

Callie was jerked forward as Sidney pushed the gear into reverse. Tires burned against the blacktop. Sidney backed up several yards, hit the gear again, and they were heading up a long driveway to a giant white house.

Andrew's house.

Back at the restaurant, Callie had made noises about taking the party to her pretend hotel room, but she'd dropped in the detail that they'd need to keep quiet and Sidney had said the exact words that Callie had teed up—

Fuck being quiet let's go back to my place.

It shouldn't have been surprising that Andrew lived in what looked like a serial killer's murder mansion. Everything was white but for the sugar-cube-shaped shrubs. The place embodied the dead-inside vibe Andrew had exuded inside the stadium tunnel.

And it was the most likely location that Andrew would store the video tape of Buddy's murder.

Callie pressed down on her torn fingernail, the pain bringing her back to reality. She wasn't here to party. Sidney was young and innocent, but so was Maddy. Only one of them had a rapist psychopath in their lives. Callie was going to keep it that way.

Sidney swung the car around the back of the house. The BMW

screeched to a stop in front of an industrial-looking glass garage door. Sidney pressed a button on the bottom of the rearview mirror. She told Callie, "Don't worry, he's tied up all day."

He was one of the ways she referred to Andrew. She called him *my stupid boyfriend* or *my idiot husband*, but she had never used his name.

The car lurched into the garage, nearly hitting the back wall.

"Fuck!" Sidney yelled, jumping out of the car. "Let's get this party started!"

Callie reached over and pressed the button to turn off the engine. Sidney had left the keys in the cupholder along with her phone and her wallet. Callie looked around the garage, searching for a hiding place for a video tape, but the space was a clean white box. Even the floor was spotless.

"Do you swim?" Sidney was reaching under her shirt to take off her bra. "I've got an extra suit that'll fit you."

Callie had a moment of darkness as she thought about the scars and track marks underneath her long-sleeved shirt and jeans. "It's too hot for me, but I love to watch."

"I bet you do." Sidney slid out her bra through her sleeve. She fumbled with the buttons on her shirt, opening up a V-shaped view of her cleavage. "Fuck it, you're right. Let's just get wasted in the air conditioning."

Callie watched her disappear into the house. Her knee caught as she got out of the car. She tried to register the pain, but her nerves were dulled by the chemicals coursing through her body. She had been careful at the restaurant, making sure she didn't let herself get too out of hand. The problem was that she really, really wanted to let things get out of hand. The receptors in her brain hadn't been on stimulants in such a long time that it felt like every second a new one was popping awake, begging for more.

She found another Xanax in her purse to bring her down a notch.

Andrew's house beckoned her inside. Sidney had left her bra and shoes on the floor. Callie looked at her Doc Martens but the only way the boots would come off was if she got on the floor and pulled. She made her way up a long, white hallway. The temperature dropped like she was walking into a museum. No rugs. Stark white walls and ceiling. White fixtures. Black and white art showing extremely sexy women posed in artistic states of bondage.

Callie was so used to hearing gurgling aquarium filters that she didn't register the sound until she was in the main part of the house. The view was meant to showcase the backyard but Callie ignored it. An entire wall had been dedicated to a magnificent reef aquarium. Soft and hard coral. Anemones. Sea urchins. Starfish. Lionfish. French angelfish. Harlequin tuskfish. Lipstick tangs.

Sidney was close beside her, shoulders touching. "It's beautiful, right?"

All Callie wanted in the world right now was to sit on the couch, take a fistful of Oxy and watch the colorful creatures float around until she either fell asleep or met Kurt Cobain. "Is your husband a dentist?"

Sidney gave one of her husky laughs. "Car salesman."

"Fuck me." Callie forced herself to look around the giant living room, which had an Apple Store meets Soviet Union aesthete. White leather couches. White leather chairs. Steel and glass coffee and side tables. Floor lamps dipping their white metal heads like leprotic cranes. The television was a giant black rectangle on the wall. None of the components were showing.

Callie joked, "Maybe I should start selling cars."

"Fuck, Max, I'd buy anything you were selling."

Callie hadn't gotten used to being called by her fake name. She took a moment to recalibrate. "Why pay when they're giving it away?"

Sidney laughed again, nodding for Callie to follow her into the kitchen.

Callie kept her pace slow, listening for the hum of electronics that would supply the television. There were no bookshelves, no storage bins, no obvious hiding places for a VCR, let alone a video tape. Even the doors were obscured, nothing but a thin black outline indicating they existed. She had no idea how they opened without doorknobs.

"His mom controls the money." Sidney was in the kitchen washing her hands at the bar sink. They had both left their masks back at the restaurant. "She's such a fucking bitch. She controls

327

everything. The house isn't even in his name. She gave him a fucking allowance to furnish it. Even told him which stores he was allowed to go to."

Callie felt her teeth ache at the sight of the ultra-modern kitchen. White marble countertops, high-gloss white cabinets. Even the stove was white. "I guess she's already gone through menopause."

Sidney didn't get the period joke, which was fair. She had a small remote control in her hand. She pressed a button, and music filled the room. Callie had expected more pounding n-words, not Ed Sheeran crooning about being love drunk.

Another button was pressed. The lights were lowered, softening the room. Sidney winked at her, asking, "Scotch, beer, tequila, rum, vodka, absinthe?"

"Tequila." Callie sat down on one of the torturous, low-backed bar stools. The romantic ambience had thrown her, so she pretended it hadn't happened. "You wouldn't be the first wife who didn't get along with her mother-in-law."

"I fucking hate her." Sidney hinged open one of the upper cabinets. The alcohol bottles were all evenly spaced, labels out, in keeping with serial killer fashion. She grabbed a beautiful-looking amber bottle. "The week before the wedding, she offered me a hundred K to back out."

"That's a lot of money."

Sidney waved her arms around the house. "Bitch, please."

Callie laughed. She had to hand it to Sidney for gaming the system. Why take a quick payday when she could milk the Tenant cash cow for as long as she stayed married to Andrew? Especially with the looming prospect of prison in Andrew's future. It wasn't a bad gamble.

"He's such a fucking sycophant around his mother," Sidney confided. "Like, with me, he's all, like, *I hate that fucking cunt I wish she'd die already*. But then she walks into the room and he turns into this idiot mama's boy."

Callie felt a pang of sadness. The one thing she had accepted as gospel when she was babysitting Andrew was that Linda had loved her son unconditionally. The mother's entire existence had been built around keeping him safe and trying to find a way to make their lives better.

"It's smart," Callie said. "I mean, you don't wanna piss her off if she's giving you all of this."

"It's his anyway." Sidney used her teeth to open the plastic seal on the bottle. Don Julio Añejo, a sipping tequila. "Once the old bitch dies, he's going to make some changes. She's doing all this stupid shit like the internet never happened. It was his idea to go virtual when the pandemic hit."

Callie gathered that a lot of people had gotten the brilliant idea to go virtual when the pandemic hit. "Wow."

"Yeah," Sidney said. "You want margaritas or straight?"

Callie grinned. "Both?"

Sidney laughed as she leaned down to find the blender. Her ass went out again. The girl was a walking soft porn photo shoot. "I swear to God, I am so fucking happy I ran into you. I was supposed to go to work today, but fuck that."

"Where do you work?"

"I answer phones at the dealership, but that's just so my parents will stop nagging me about spending the rest of my life in college. That's how I met Andy." If she realized this was the first time she'd actually said his name, Sidney didn't show it. "We work at the same dealership."

"Andy?" Callie said. "Sounds like a mama's boy."

"Right?" Sidney pushed one of the cabinet fronts. The door popped open. She scooped up shot and margarita glasses with the expertise of a bartender. Callie watched her move. She really was extraordinary. She had to wonder what the woman saw in Andrew. It had to be more than money.

Sidney plopped the glasses down on the counter. "I know you're here for an interview, but what are you doing for work?"

Callie shrugged. "Nothing, really. My husband left me with enough money, but I know what happens when I have too much free time."

"Speaking of which." Sidney filled two shot glasses to the rim.

Callie held hers up in a toast, then took a sip while Sidney knocked hers back, which was something you could do when your neck wasn't frozen at the base of your skull. She watched Sidney fill another shot. She was going for a third when Callie put her glass down for a refill.

"Oh fuck." Sidney seemed to remember something. She pushed open another cabinet and found a round wooden container. She placed it on the counter, knocking off the lid. Then she licked her finger and stuck it inside to pull up tiny crystals of black salt. She wagged her eyebrows as she sucked it off the tip of her finger.

Their eyes met, and Callie forced herself to pull away. "I can't remember the last time I saw a salt cellar."

"Is that what it's called?" Sidney went back to work. She pressed her hand against another cabinet front, but this time a long handle popped out. She opened the fridge door. "It was a wedding gift from one of Linda's rich bitch friends. I looked it up online. Hand-carved Kenyan wood, whatever that is. Fucking thing cost three hundred dollars."

Callie weighed the cellar in her palm. The salt was obsidian black and smelled faintly of charcoal. "What is this?"

"I dunno, some expensive shit from Hawaii. Costs more by weight than coke." She turned, holding six limes between her hands. "Shit, I'd kill for some coke."

Callie wasn't going to disappoint. She reached into her purse and flashed two eight-balls.

"Fuck me." Sidney snatched one of the baggies away. She held it up to the light. She was looking for the sparkly flakes that indicated purity, which put her up there with the professional coke users. "Damn, this looks lethal."

Callie wondered if that would be the case. Sidney was already buzzing on enough stims to take down a wildebeest. You didn't get that kind of tolerance from recreational use.

As if to prove the point, Sidney opened a drawer and took out a small mirror with a razor blade on top and a four-inch gold-plated straw that was either intended to aid particularly wealthy toddlers in the consumption of juice or for spoiled rich assholes to snort coke.

Callie tested the waters. "You ever inject it?"

For the first time, Sidney looked guarded. "Shit man, that's a whole 'nother level."

"Forget I asked." Callie opened the plastic bag and shook the pure white powder onto the mirror. "How long did you two know each other before you got married?"

"Uh . . . I think it was two years ago?" Sidney was watching the coke with a hungry eye. Maybe her life was already on the downslope after all. "He's got this jag-off friend, Reggie. He'd come into the dealership like he owned the place. He was always hitting on me but come on."

Callie knew what she meant. Sidney wasn't going to waste her beauty and youth on a man who couldn't afford it.

"And then Andrew came up to me one day and we started talking, and I was like, *what a surprise this guy's not a total douche.* Which, considering Reggie, was like a fucking miracle."

Callie made a show of chopping the blade through the white powder. She listened as Sidney droned on about Reggie—how he was always leering at her, how he was basically Andrew's lapdog, but her eyes stayed on the razor blade the same hungry way Sidney's were.

If a scientist had been tasked with developing a drug that would make people waste all of their money, cocaine was what they would've come up with. The high lasted about fifteen to twenty minutes, and you could spend the rest of your miserable life chasing that first rush because it was never going to be better than the first big, beautiful hit. The joke was that two people could do a trailer load of coke between them and, when they were done, they'd both agree that all it would take was one more trailer load to get them high.

Which was why Callie had laced the coke with fentanyl.

She cut out four lines, asking Sidney, "So, how'd he ask you out?"

"He caught me reading one of my psych books for school, and we started talking, and, unlike ninety-nine percent of the fucking mansplainers who try to educate me about what I've been studying for, like, six years, he actually knew what he was talking about." The woman's gaze had not left Callie's hand, but now, she pulled herself away. More cabinets were opened. A small marble cutting board came out. She found a ceramic bowl for the limes. "Then he started flirting with me, keeping me from answering the phones, and I was, like, *Dude, you're going to get me fired.* And he was like, *Dude, I'm going to fire you if you don't go out with me.*"

Callie gathered that was the official definition of workplace harassment, but she said, "I like a man who knows what he wants."

Sidney opened another drawer. "You like that in a woman, too?"

Callie's mouth opened to answer, but then she saw what Sidney took out of the drawer.

The razor blade slipped through Callie's fingers, screeching across the small mirror.

Cracked wooden handle. Serrated blade bent three different ways. The steak knife looked like something Linda had bought at the grocery store. Callie had used it to cut Andrew's hot dog into pieces. Then she had used it to slice open Buddy's leg.

"Max?" Sidney asked.

Callie searched for her voice. The sound of her own heartbeat was overwhelming, drowning out the soft music, muffling Sidney's deep voice. "That—that's a pretty cheap wedding gift."

Sidney looked at the knife. "Yeah, Andy gets pissed off when I use it, like he couldn't go out and buy fifty more. He stole it from his babysitter or something. I don't know the story. He's so weird about it."

Callie watched the blade cut through one of the limes. Her lungs felt shaky. "He's got a babysitter fetish?"

"Girl," Sidney said. "He's got an everything fetish."

Callie felt a pinch of pain in her thumb. The razor had shaved off a thin layer of skin. Blood trickled down her wrist. She had come here with a plan, but the sight of the knife had taken her back to the Waleskis' kitchen.

Baby, you gotta c-call an ambulance, baby. Call an—

Callie picked up the straw. She leaned down. She snorted up all four lines in quick succession.

She sat back up, eyes watering, heart tripping, ears buzzing, bones shaking.

"Fuck." Sidney wasn't going to be left out. She dumped the second eight-ball onto the mirror. She cut out the lines quickly, so eager to join the fun that she skipped the ass-pushing-out and the wink and hoovered up four lines herself. "Jesus! Fucking! Christ!"

Callie gummed the residue. She could taste the fentanyl like a hidden message to her body.

"Yes!" Sidney yelled, dancing around the kitchen. She disappeared into the living room, screaming, "Fuck yes!"

Callie felt her eyes wanting to roll back in her head. Sidney had left the knife on the counter. Callie saw herself in the Waleskis' kitchen, soaking the handle in bleach, picking around the crevices with a toothpick. Her fingers went to her throat. She could feel her heart pushing its way up toward her mouth. The coke was settling in, the fentanyl chasing its tail. What the fuck had she been thinking? The videos were here. Sidney was here. Andrew was in court but he would get out and then what would he do? What did he have planned for Maddy?

She found the Xanax in her purse and popped three before Sidney came back into the kitchen.

"Maxie, come look at the fish," she said, taking Callie's hand, pulling her into the living room.

The music got louder. The lights got lower. Sidney dropped the remote on the coffee table as she tugged Callie down to the couch.

Callie sank back into the soft cushions. The couch was so deep that her feet would not touch the ground. She curled up her legs, resting her arm on a pile of pillows. How the hell she recognized Michael Bublé on the speakers was a fascinating puzzle until she saw a lionfish scuttle behind a rock, the multiple spikes showing off red and black bands. The venomous fin rays made the fish one of the most dangerous predators in the ocean, but it only used the weapon defensively. The other fish were safe so long as they were too big to fit into the lionfish's gawping tunnel of a mouth.

"Max?" Sidney asked, her voice low and sultry. She played with Callie's hair, her fingernails gently scratching the scalp.

Callie felt a distant trill from the sensation, but she could not break her concentration away from a short-nosed unicorn fish flitting past a startled-looking starfish. Then the tang joined the party. Then the seagrass started to wave its slim fingers in her direction. There was no telling how long Callie sat there watching the colorful parade, but she could tell by the dulling colors that the Xanax was finally taking her down a notch.

"Max?" Sidney repeated. "You want to shoot me up?"

Callie's attention strayed from the aquarium. Sidney was leaning against her, fingers still stroking through Callie's hair. Her pupils were blown wide open. Her lips were lush and wet. She was so fucking ripe.

Callie had syringes in her purse. A tie-off. Lighter. Cotton. This was what she'd planned, to talk Sidney into more, then a little more, until she was sticking a needle into Sidney's arm, giving her a taste of the dragon she would chase into a deep, dark well of despair.

If it didn't kill her first.

"Hey there." Sidney bit her bottom lip. She was so close Callie could taste the tequila on her breath. "Do you know how fucking adorable you are?"

Callie felt her body respond before her mouth could. She ran her fingers through Sidney's thick, silky hair. Her skin was unbelievably soft. The color of her eyes reminded Callie of the expensive salt in the hand-carved cellar.

Sidney kissed her on the mouth. Callie had pulled away the first two times their lips had touched, but now, she let herself give in. Sidney's mouth was perfect. Her tongue was velvet. Tingles ran up Callie's spine. For the first time in twenty years, there was no pain in her body. She laid back on the couch. Sidney was on top, her mouth pressing against Callie's neck, then her breasts, then Callie's jeans were unbuttoned and Sidney's fingers slipped inside of her.

Callie moaned. Tears wept into her eyes. It had been so damn long since she'd had someone inside of her who she really wanted inside of her. She rocked against Sidney's hand. Sucked on her mouth, her tongue. The sensation started to build. Callie felt dizzy as breath flooded into her open lungs. Her eyes closed. Her mouth opened to call Sidney's name—

Breathe into it I'm almost there come on.

Callie's eyes opened. Her heart slammed against her chest. There was no gorilla, just the clear sound of Buddy Waleski's voice.

Buddy, please, it hurts too much please stop please . . .

Her own voice, fourteen years old. Hurting. Terrified.

Buddy, please stop I'm bleeding I can't—

Callie threw Sidney off of her. The sound was coming from the speakers.

Shut the fuck up Callie I said hold the fuck still.

Buddy's voice was everywhere, booming from the speakers, echoing around the sterile, white room. Callie grabbed the remote off the coffee table. She frantically pressed the buttons, trying to stop the sound.

Fucking bitch I told you to stop struggling or I'll—

Silence.

Callie did not want to turn around, but she did.

She did not want to look at the television, but she did.

The stained shag carpet. Streetlight lasering around the puckered edges of the orange and brown drapes. The tan club chairs with sweat-stained backs and cigarette-burned arms. The orange couch with its two depressing indentations at opposite ends.

The sound was muted, but she heard Buddy's voice in her head—

Come on, baby. Let's finish on the couch.

What was happening on the television did not mirror the memories inside of her head. The video twisted them around, turned them into something sleazy and brutal.

Buddy was silently grinding into her fourteen-year-old body, his massive weight pressing so hard that the frame of the couch flexed in the middle. Callie watched her younger self struggle for freedom, scratching out, trying to fight him off. He grabbed both of her hands in one meaty paw. With his other hand, he ripped the belt out of the loops in his pants. Callie was horrified to watch him bind her wrists with the belt, flip her over, and start raping her from behind.

"No . . ." she breathed, because that was not how it had happened. Not once she got used to it. Not once she learned how to finish him with her mouth.

Sidney asked, "Do you still like it rough?"

Callie heard a clatter of sound. She had dropped the remote. It lay on the floor in pieces. Slowly, she turned. All of the beauty had drained out of Sidney's face. She looked as hard and merciless as Andrew.

Callie's voice shook when she asked, "Where is the tape?"

"*Tapes*," Sidney said, her voice hard. "Plural. As in more than one."

"How many?"

"Dozens." Sidney put her fingers in her mouth, making a loud smacking noise as she sucked the taste of Callie off of them. "We can watch more if you want."

Callie punched her in the face.

Sidney stumbled back, stunned by the impact. Blood poured from her broken nose. She blinked like a stupid punk bitch taking her first hit on the playground.

"Where are they?" Callie demanded, but she was already walking around the room, pressing her hand against the walls, trying to find another hidden cabinet. "Tell me where they are."

Sidney collapsed onto the couch. Blood dripped onto the white leather, pooled onto the floor.

Callie kept touching the walls, leaving blood prints from her own wounded hands. A door finally clicked open. She saw a sink and toilet. She pushed another door. Heat poured off a rack of electronic equipment. Her finger traced down the components, but there was no VCR.

Sidney asked, "Did you really think it would be that easy?"

Callie looked at her. She was standing up, hands at her side while blood flowed down her face and neck. Her white shirt was turning crimson. She seemed to be recovered from the sudden punch to the face. Her tongue licked out, tasting the trickle of blood from her lip.

She warned Callie, "It won't be so easy the next time."

Callie wasn't going to have a conversation with the bitch. This wasn't the end of a *Batman* episode. She stalked into the kitchen. Without thinking, her hand found Linda's kitchen knife.

She continued through the house, passing a powder room, then a home gym. No closets. No cabinets. No video tapes. Next room, Andrew's office. The desk drawers were narrow, filled with pens and paper clips. The closet was stacked with paper and notecards and files. Callie used her arm like a shovel and swept everything onto the floor.

Sidney said, "You're not going to find them."

Callie pushed past her, stalking down another long hallway with more bondage photos. She could hear Sidney trailing behind her. Callie knocked the frames off the walls, sending them shattering to the floor. Sidney yelped as she stepped on broken glass. Callie kicked open doors. Guest room. Nothing. Another guest room. Nothing. Master bedroom.

Callie stopped in the open doorway.

Instead of white, everything was black. Walls, ceiling, carpet, silk sheets on the bed. She slapped the wall switch. Light flooded the room. She scuffed her boots across the carpet. She ripped open the bedside drawers. Handcuffs and dildos and butt plugs fell onto the dark floor. No video tapes. The television on the wall was almost as tall as Callie. She looked behind it, pulled at the wires. Nothing. She checked the walls for secret panels. Nothing. She found the walk-in closet. Black cabinets. Black drawers. Black as the rot inside this fucking house.

The safe was out in the open, roughly the size of a dorm fridge. Combination lock. Callie turned around, because she knew that Sidney was there. The woman seemed heedless to the blood on her face, the bloody footprints that led like breadcrumbs to the closet door.

Callie told the bitch, "Open it."

"Calliope." Sidney shook her head the same sad way that Andrew had in the tunnel. "Even if I wanted to, do you think Andy would give me the combination?"

Callie felt her teeth grit. She ran through the inventory in her purse. She could pump enough heroin into this evil cunt to stop her heart. "When did you know it was me?"

"Oh, baby girl, from the moment you walked into the meeting." Sidney was smiling, but there was nothing fun or sexy about her mouth now, because she had been playing Callie like a fiddle the entire time. "I gotta say, *Max*, you clean up really nice."

"Where are the tapes?"

"Andy was right." Sidney was openly looking at her again, appraising her body. "You really are a perfect little fucking doll, aren't you?"

Callie's nostrils flared.

"Why don't you stick around, baby girl?" Sidney's smirk was

sickeningly familiar. "Andy will be home in a couple of hours. I can't think of a better wedding present than letting him watch me fuck you."

Callie looked down at her hand. She was still holding Linda's knife. "Why don't I cut the skin off your face and leave it hanging on the front door?"

Sidney looked startled, as if it had never occurred to her that fucking with a needle junkie who had survived on the streets for twenty years was a bad idea.

Callie didn't give her time to consider the implications.

She lunged at the woman, knife first. Sidney screamed. She fell onto her back. Her head banged against the floor. Callie could smell the huff of tequila as she jumped on top of her. She raised the knife over her head. Sidney scrambled to defend herself, catching Callie's wrist with both of her hands. Her arms shook as she tried to keep the knife from plunging into her face.

Callie let Sidney's focus stay on the knife, because the knife only mattered if you played fair. Callie hadn't played fair since she'd chopped up Buddy Waleski. She rammed her knee straight up between Sidney's legs so hard that she felt her kneecap crack against Sidney's pelvis.

"Fuck!" Sidney screamed, rolling to the side, gripping her hands between her legs. Vomit spewed from her mouth. Her body was shaking. Tears poured from her eyes.

Callie grabbed her by the hair, wrenching back her head. She showed Sidney the knife.

"Please!" Sidney begged. "Please don't!"

Callie pressed the tip of the knife into the soft skin of Sidney's cheek. "What's the combination?"

"I don't know!" Sidney wailed. "Please! He won't tell me!"

Callie pressed the knife harder, watching the skin curve against the blade, then finally give, opening up a line of bright red blood.

"Please . . ." Sidney sobbed, helpless. "Please . . . Callie . . . I'm sorry. Please."

"Where's the tape from before?" Callie gave her a moment to answer, and when she didn't, she started to pull the blade down.

"The rack!" Sidney screamed.

Callie stopped. "I checked the rack."

"No . . ." She was panting, terror filling her eyes with tears. "The player is behind . . . there's a space behind the rack. It's on the . . . there's a shelf."

Callie didn't remove the knife from her face. She could so easily reach down, cut Sidney's leg, and watch the woman's life slowly ebb away. But that wouldn't be good enough. Andrew wouldn't see it happen. He wouldn't suffer the way that Callie needed him to suffer. She wanted him terrified, bleeding, unable to stop the pain the same way she had been every time his father had raped her.

She told Sidney, "Tell Andy if he wants his knife back, he's going to have to come and get it."

16

Leigh had put her emotions into stasis inside the cramped conference room with Dante Carmichael. She had known that the only way she would survive the rest of the day was to divide herself between being an attorney and being everything else in her life. One compartment could not spill into the other or there would not be any pieces left to categorize.

Dante had left the photographs of Ruby Heyer's mutilated body spread across the table, but Leigh had not looked at them again. She had stacked them together. She had returned them to their file folder. She had put the folder inside of her purse and then she had walked out into the hallway and told her client to get ready for jury selection.

Now, she looked at the clock on the courtroom wall as she waited for the cleaner to sanitize the stand for the next prospective juror. They had half an hour left in the schedule. The room felt muggy. Pandemic protocols dictated that only the judge, the bailiff, a deputy, the court reporter, the prosecution, the defense, and the defendant were allowed in the room. Normally, there were dozens of spectators or at least a court monitor in the gallery. Without them, the process felt staged, as if they were all actors doing their parts.

That wasn't going to change anytime soon. Only nine jurors had been seated so far. They needed three more, plus two alternates. The initial questions from the judge had winnowed the pool of forty-eight down to twenty-seven. They had six left to interview, then a fresh batch would be scheduled for tomorrow morning.

Andrew shifted in his chair. Leigh avoided his gaze, which was hard to do when someone was sitting directly beside you. Liz had her head bent down as she scribbled notes at the end of the table. Jacob was on Andrew's left, sifting through the remaining questionnaires, trying to glean a detail that would make him look brilliant and useful.

One of Leigh's professors in law school had insisted that cases were lost or won during jury selection. Leigh had always enjoyed trying to game out the system, picking and choosing the right personalities for deliberations—the leaders, the followers, the questioners, the intransigent true believers. The process today was particularly meaningful because it would likely be the last time Leigh sat in the attorney's chair at the defense table.

Walter had tried to call two more times before Leigh had turned off both her phones. All devices were supposed to be silenced during court, but that wasn't the reason why she wasn't answering. Gossip traveled at the speed of light in the Hollis Academy community. Leigh knew that Walter would be calling about Ruby Heyer's brutal murder. She knew that Walter would be sending Maddy away with his mother. She knew that he would end up at the police station telling the cops everything because that was the only way to guarantee Maddy's safety.

At least that was what Leigh told herself every other hour.

She spent the hours in between telling herself that Walter would never turn her in. He hated her right now, but he was neither rash nor vengeful. Leigh thought that he would talk to her before he went to the cops. And then she thought about how sickened Walter would be by Ruby's murder and how terrified he would be about Maddy's safety and the rollercoaster started back up the hill again.

The cleaner had finished sanitizing the stand from the last prospective juror, a retired English professor who had made it clear she could not be impartial. Normally, the jurors were seated in groups inside the courtroom, but Covid protocols had scattered them down a long hallway and into the deliberation room. They were allowed to bring books and use the courthouse WiFi, but the wait could be mind-numbingly tedious.

The bailiff opened the door, calling, "Twenty-three, you're up."

They all stirred as an older man took his place to be sworn in. Jacob slid the jury questionnaire in front of Leigh. Andrew sat back, but he didn't bother to look down at the page. His interest had evaporated once he'd realized there was no psychological angle to be played. Only questions and answers and gut instinct. The law was never what anyone thought it was or wanted it to be.

Twenty-three's name was Hank Bladel. He was sixty-three years old and had been married for forty years. Leigh studied his craggly face as he sat down. Bladel had a spattering of white in his beard and the ropey arms of a man who kept himself fit. Shaved head. Straight shoulders. Firm voice.

Jacob had drawn two horizontal lines in the corner of Bladel's questionnaire, which meant he was on the fence as to whether or not the man would be good for Andrew. Leigh knew which way she was leaning, but she tried to keep an open mind.

"Good afternoon, Mr. Bladel." Dante had been keeping his examinations brief. It was late in the day. Everybody was tired. Even the judge seemed to be nodding off, his head tilted down toward the papers on his desk, his eyes doing slow blinks as he pretended to listen.

Turner had been true to form so far, bending over backward to give Andrew the white man's golden handshake. Leigh had learned the hard way that she had to speak carefully around the judge. He demanded the kind of formality that you would expect of a supreme court justice. She had lost more than one ruling because he didn't brook mouthy women.

She tuned back into Dante's questioning, which followed the same predictable pattern. Bladel had never been the victim of sexual assault. He had never been the victim of a crime. Neither had any family members that he knew of. His wife was a nurse. Both of his daughters were nurses, too. One was married to an EMT, the other to a warehouse supervisor. Before Covid, Bladel had worked full-time as a driver for an airport limo company, but now he was part-time and volunteering at the Boys and Girls Club of America. All of that lined up beautifully for the defense but for one thing: he had served twenty years in the military.

This was why Leigh was leaning toward striking Bladel from the jury. The defense wanted people who questioned the system. The prosecution wanted people who thought that the law was always fair, that cops never lied and that justice was blind.

Given the last four years, it was becoming harder and harder to find anyone who thought the system worked the same for everybody, but the military could be a reliably conservative group to pull from. Dante had already blown through seven of his nine preemptory challenges, which could be used to strike any juror for any reason except on the basis of race. Thanks to Judge Turner's leniency, Leigh had four challenges remaining, plus another when it came to selecting the two alternates.

She checked her grid of seated jurors. Five women. Three men. Retired teacher. Librarian. Accountant. Bartender. Mailman. Two stay-at-home moms. Hospital orderly. She felt good about the line-up, but then the line-up didn't matter because none of this would make it to trial. The rollercoaster was on its downward spiral where Walter had talked to the police and both Leigh and Andrew would be waiting for their separate arraignments before Monday morning rolled around.

Andrew had a fail-safe tape of Leigh murdering his father.

Leigh had it by her client's own admission that Andrew was sitting on a large stash of child porn featuring her then-fourteen-year-old sister.

"Judge," Dante said. "The prosecution accepts this juror and asks that he be seated."

Turner's head jerked up. He paged through his paperwork as he gave off a howl of a yawn under his mask. "Ms. Collier, you may cross."

Dante slumped back into his chair with a heavy sigh, because he assumed Leigh would use one of her challenges to strike the man.

Leigh stood up. "Mr. Bladel, thank you for being here today. I'm Leigh Collier. I represent the defendant."

He nodded. "Nice to meet you."

"I should thank you for your service, too. Twenty years. That's admirable."

"Thank you." He nodded again.

Leigh took in his body language. Legs wide. Arms at his side. Posture straight. He seemed open rather than closed off. The previous occupant of the chair had looked like Quasimodo in comparison.

She said, "You used to be a limo driver. What was that like?"

"Well," he began. "It was very interesting. I hadn't realized how many international travelers we get into the city. Did you know that Atlanta has the busiest passenger airport in the world?"

"No, I didn't," Leigh answered, though she did. The point of her questions wasn't so much about getting details as it was to figure out what kind of person Hank Bladel was. Could he be impartial? Could he listen to the facts? Could he understand the evidence? Could he persuade others? Could he parse out the true meaning of reasonable doubt?

She said, "You mentioned in your questionnaire that you were stationed overseas for eight years. Do you speak any foreign languages?"

"I never had the ear for it, but I'll tell you, most of my airport rides have a better grasp of the English language than my grandchildren." He chuckled with the judge, sharing an old man's bafflement with the younger generation. "Now, some of them like to talk, but others, you figure out you just need to be quiet, let them make their calls, keep under the speed limit, and get them there on time."

Leigh nodded as she catalogued his answer. Open to new experiences, willing to listen. He'd make an excellent foreman. She just didn't know for which side. "You told my colleague that you volunteer with the Boys and Girls Club. What's that like?"

"I'll be honest. It's become one of the most rewarding parts of my life."

Leigh nodded as he talked about the importance of helping young men and women get on the right track. She liked that he had a firm sense of right and wrong, but she still didn't know whether that would work in Andrew's favor.

She asked, "Are you a member of any other organizations?"

Bladel smiled with pride. "I am a brother with the Yaarab Shriners, which belongs to the Ancient Arabic Order of the Nobles of the Mystic Shrine for North America."

Leigh turned so that she could see Dante's face. He looked like someone had just shot his dog. Shriners were a more liberal offshoot of Freemasons. They staged clown parades, wore funny hats, and raised millions of dollars for children's hospitals to supplement America's deplorably imbalanced healthcare system.

Leigh had never seated a Shriner on a jury who didn't go out of his way to understand the real-life implications of *beyond a reasonable doubt.*

She asked the man, "Can you tell me a little bit about the organization?"

"We are a fraternity based on the masonic principles of brotherly love, relief and truth."

Leigh let him keep talking, enjoying the theater of the courtroom exchange. She paced in front of the stand, thinking about where Bladel would sit on the jury, how she would frame her argument, when she should lean into the forensics, when she should deploy her experts.

Then she turned and saw the bored look on Andrew's face.

He was staring blankly at the court reporter, completely uninterested in the cross-examination. He had only used the notepad she'd given him once, and that was when they'd first been seated. Andrew had wanted to know where Tammy was. He had been expecting to see his victim in the courtroom because he didn't understand how criminal trials worked. The State of Georgia had charged Andrew Tenant with felony crimes. Tammy Karlsen was their witness. The rule of sequestration forbade her from attending any part of the trial until she gave testimony. Even a brief appearance in the gallery would've likely resulted in a mistrial.

"Thank you, sir," Leigh said, taking advantage of Mr. Bladel's pause for breath. "Judge, we accept this witness and ask for him to be seated."

"Very well." Turner let out another loud yawn behind his mask. "Excuse me. We'll finish there for the day and resume at ten tomorrow morning. Ms. Collier, Mr. Carmichael, do you have any business that needs attending?"

To Leigh's surprise, Dante stood up.

He said, "Your honor, as a bit of housekeeping, I'd like to amend my witness list. I've added two—"

"Judge," Leigh interrupted. "It's a bit late to spring two new witnesses."

The judge gave her a strident look. Men who interrupted were passionate about their case. Women who interrupted were shrill.

"Ms. Collier, I recall signing off on your own very late motion for substitution of counsel."

He was giving her a warning. "Thank you, your honor, for approving the substitution. I'm more than ready to proceed, but I would ask for a delay to—"

"Your two propositions sit in tension," Turner said. "Either you are ready or you are not ready."

Leigh knew the battle was already lost. So did Dante. He handed her the filing on his way to give the judge a copy. Leigh saw that he'd added Lynne Wilkerson and Fabienne Godard, two women she'd never heard of. When she put the page in front of Andrew, he barely gave it a glance.

Turner said, "Approved as submitted. Are we finished?"

Dante said, "Your honor, I'd also like to request an emergency hearing to revoke bond."

"Are you fuh—" Leigh caught herself. "Your honor, this is ridiculous. My client has been out on bond for more than a year, and has had ample opportunity for flight. He is here to vigorously participate in his defense."

Dante said, "I've got an affidavit from Mr. Tenant's probation officer documenting five separate instances where Mr. Tenant has interfered with the functioning of his ankle monitor."

Leigh said, "That's a very umbrageous way to describe what is clearly a technical issue that probation has yet to resolve."

Turner waved his hand for the affidavit. "Let me see it."

Again, Leigh was given her own copy to read. She skimmed the details, which took up less than one page and listed the times and dates of the alarms, but with only ephemeral causes—*possible tampering with optical cable*; *possible use of GPS blocking*; *possible breach of set perimeter*.

She started to open her mouth to point out that *possible* wasn't *proof*, but then she stopped herself. Why was she trying to keep Andrew out of jail?

The fail-safe. The tapes. Callie. Maddy.

Leigh felt the rollercoaster slowly clicking its way back up the hill. Why was she so sure that Walter had turned her in? What was that gut feeling based on?

Maybe it's a bad idea to connect another teenage girl with a goddam rapist?

Turner said, "Ms. Collier, I'm waiting."

She jumped back into the defense. "Four of these false alarms date back over the last two months, Judge. Why is the last one different, other than the fact that we are four days from trial in the middle of a pandemic? Is Mr. Carmichael hoping that my client gets infected in detention?"

Turner gave her a sharp look. No one was allowed to talk about the fact that inmates were Corona cannon fodder. "Watch yourself, Ms. Collier."

"Yes, Judge," she demurred. "I would simply restate that my client is not a flight risk."

"Mr. Carmichael," Turner said. "Your response?"

"Flight is not the issue, your honor. We're basing our motion on the fact that Mr. Tenant is suspected of committing related crimes," Dante said. "He tampered with his ankle monitor to evade detection."

Turner looked exasperated by the lack of details. "What are these crimes?"

Dante tried to bluff his way around the question. "I'd rather not get into it, your honor, but suffice to say we could be looking at a capital offense."

Leigh was disheartened to hear him bring up the death penalty. Dante was clearly throwing a Hail Mary. His case on Ruby Heyer's murder was weak. He was either trying to buy himself time to break Andrew's alibi or scare Andrew into confessing.

She said, "Judge, as you know, that's a very serious allegation. I would ask that the prosecutor either put up or shut up."

Turner narrowed his eyes at Leigh. She was pushing too much. "Ms. Collier, would you like to rephrase that?"

"No thank you, your honor. I think my meaning is plain. Mr. Carmichael has no evidence that my client's ankle monitor was tampered with. He has *possible* reasons but nothing concrete. As for the so-called capital crime, are we meant to extrapolate from his—"

Turner held up his hand to stop her. He sat back in his chair.

His fingers rested on the bottom part of his mask. He looked out at the vacant gallery.

Andrew was finally interested now that his freedom was under threat. He lifted his chin for Leigh to come over and explain what was happening. She held up a finger, telling him to wait.

On television, judges who ruled from the bench usually did it quickly, but that was because they had a script that told them what to say. In real life, they took their time thinking through the finer points, weighing the options, trying to anticipate whether or not they would be overturned on appeal. This looked a lot like staring into the void. Turner was known to take longer than usual.

Leigh sat down. She saw Jacob writing on one of the legal pads, explaining the judge's silence to Andrew. Andrew still hadn't reacted to the two new names on Dante's witness list. Lynne Wilkerson and Fabienne Godard. Were they two of the three previous victims that Reggie had been tipped off about? Were they new victims who'd come forward when they'd seen that Andrew was going to trial?

Walter was right about so many things, but never so much as about Leigh's role in Andrew Tenant's crimes. Her silence had allowed him to continue hurting people. Ruby Heyer's blood was on her hands. Worse, Leigh had been willing to go after Tammy Karlsen in order to keep Andrew from releasing the videos. She had never let herself think too hard about the consequences of Andrew's freedom. More women abused. More violence. More lives destroyed.

Their beautiful girl forced to flee her home.

"All right," Turner said.

Leigh and Dante stood up.

Turner looked at Andrew. "Mr. Tenant?"

Leigh indicated Andrew should stand.

Turner said, "I find these reports on your ankle monitor malfunctions to be very troublesome. While the cause of the alarms cannot be pinpointed, I want you to understand that my continued lack of remand depends on nothing further occurring. Do you understand?"

Andrew looked at Leigh.

She shook her head, because of course the judge had ruled in his favor. "He's not revoking your bail. Don't fuck with your monitor again."

She could tell Andrew was grinning. "Yes, your honor. Thank you."

Turner banged his gavel. The bailiff called it a day. The court reporter started to pack up her things.

Jacob told Leigh, "I'll put together profiles and email them to you later tonight. I'm assuming we're working through the weekend?"

"Yes." Leigh powered back on her work phone. "I want you to finish out the examinations tomorrow. I'm going to tell Cole Bradley that I'm moving you to co-counsel."

Jacob looked surprised, but he was too overjoyed to ask her why. "Thank you."

Leigh's throat worked. It felt good to do something right for a change. "You've earned it."

She looked down at her phone as Jacob left. She started the email to Bradley. Her hands were still steady. Dante and Miranda were powering up their phones as they walked out of the courtroom. The rollercoaster was steadily falling toward Walter speaking to the police. Leigh needed to find Callie tonight. Her sister had a right to know the amount of hell that was about to rain down.

"Harleigh."

Leigh had let herself block out Andrew. She looked up.

His mask was off. He was at the witness stand. "Is this where Tammy will sit?"

Leigh sent the email to Bradley and dropped her phone into her purse. "Who are Lynne Wilkerson and Fabienne Godard?"

He rolled his eyes. "Jealous ex-girlfriends. One's an alcoholic, the other's a crazy bitch."

"You're going to need a better story than that," Leigh said. "These women didn't spontaneously decide to come forward today. Dante has been keeping them under wraps. These women are going to get on that stand and do exactly what I warned you Sidney might do."

"Which is?"

"Testify in front of a jury that you're a sadist who gets too rough in bed."

"Can't argue with that," Andrew said. "But history tells me that a cash inducement will persuade them both it's better to sit this one out."

Leigh warned, "That's called bribery and tampering with witnesses."

He shrugged, because he didn't care. "Reggie will meet you at your car. Give him the list of the jurors so far. He's going to start looking into them, see if there are any weak points we can exploit."

"How does Reggie know where my car is?"

He tsked his teeth, shaking his head at her stupidity. "Harleigh, don't you know that any time I want, I can find you or your sister?"

Leigh wasn't going to give him the satisfaction of seeing her rattled. Andrew's eyes tracked her as she walked out of the courtroom. She looked down at her personal phone. Her thumb pressed the power button. She watched the screen, waiting for the signal to pick up.

She was in the stairwell when the notifications came in. Six calls from Walter. Two from Maddy. They had both left voice messages. Leigh clutched the phone to her chest as she walked down the stairs. She would listen to them in the car. She would let herself cry. She would find her sister. Then she would figure out what to do next.

The lobby was full of stragglers. The metal detectors were blocked off. Court was closed for the day. Two deputies stood guard by the exit. She nodded to Walter's friend. He winked at her in response.

Sunlight washed over her face as she walked through the square. She felt her phone buzz again. Not Walter or Maddy this time, but Nick Wexler with another *DTF*? Leigh mentally ran through some polite rejections before she realized that Nick wouldn't care. They had barely been lovers. They had never been friends. And once Leigh's crimes were out in the open, they would likely be enemies.

Her phone went back to her side. She crossed the street at the light. She had parked her Audi in the deck opposite the square. Before Covid, the lot had been filled with customers for the restaurants, bars, and boutique stores that used to line the streets of downtown Decatur. This morning, Leigh had found a prime spot on the first floor.

The overhead lights flickered maniacally as she walked through the garage. Shadows danced around the three cars parked close to the front gate. The rest of the spaces were empty but for Leigh's Audi, which was parked at the base of the ramp. Out of habit, she let her house key stick out between her fingers. Between the dark shadows and low ceiling, this was just the kind of place where women disappeared.

Leigh shuddered. She knew what happened to women who disappeared.

She looked at the time on her phone. Reggie was probably on his way to retrieve the jury list. Leigh had worked enough contentious divorce cases to know how the private investigator would locate her Audi. She ran her hand under the car's rear bumper. She checked the wheel wells. The GPS tracker was in a magnetized box stuck above her right back tire.

Leigh tossed the box onto the ground. She opened her trunk. Out of habit, she punched in the combination on the safe she'd had bolted to the floor. She might've been a suburban mom, but she wasn't a stupid suburban mom. Leigh's Glock was in the safe. Sometimes, she shoved her purse inside when she didn't want to carry it around. Now, she needed a spot to store Ruby Heyer's crime scene photos. Her hand rested on the file. She thought about the knife that had been left inside of the woman. The state of Andrew's dark bruises.

"Leigh?"

She turned around, shocked to find Walter standing there. Then she looked behind him, wondering if he'd brought the police.

Walter turned, too. He said, "What is it?"

Leigh swallowed the saliva that had rushed into her mouth. "Is Maddy safe?"

"Mom has her. They left after we talked this morning." He crossed his arms. His anger hadn't abated, but it had become focused. "Ruby Heyer's dead. Did you know that?"

"Andrew did it," Leigh said.

He didn't look surprised because nothing about it was surprising. Of course Andrew had escalated. Of course he had killed someone in Leigh's orbit. Walter had told her last night that it was going to happen.

He said, "Keely had to be sedated. Maddy is a wreck."

Leigh waited for him to confess his actions, but then she realized that making Walter say the words was cruel. "It's okay. I know you went to the police."

His eyebrows furrowed. His mouth opened, then closed, then opened again. "You think I dimed out my own wife to the cops?"

Leigh didn't know what to say, so she said nothing.

"Fuck, Leigh. Do you really think I'd do that to you? You're the mother of my child."

Guilt washed away her steely resolve. "I'm sorry. You were so angry with me. You're still so angry."

"What I said—" He reached out for her, but then he let his hands fall away. "I said it wrong, Leigh, but you weren't thinking. Or you were thinking too hard, assuming that everything would work out because you're too fucking smart to let it go sideways."

She took a shaky breath.

"You *are* smart, Leigh. God damn, you're smart. But you can't control everything. You have to let people in."

He had stopped to let her respond, but she didn't have the words.

He said, "What you're doing right now, tearing shit down, thinking that you're the only one who knows how to build it back up, that's not working. It has never worked."

She couldn't contradict him. There were thousands of variations on this same argument they'd had over the years, but this was the first time that she accepted he was absolutely right.

She said out loud the mantra she had only ever said to herself. "It's my fault. It's all my fault."

"Some of it is, but so what?" Walter acted like it was that simple. "Let's put our heads together and figure this out."

She closed her eyes. She thought about the sweltering night in Chicago when Callie had brought them their gift. Before that fateful knock on the door, Leigh had finally relented and sat in Walter's lap. Then she had curled into him like a cat, and he had made her feel safer than she had ever felt in her entire life.

She told him now what she had been unable to tell him then. "I can't live without you. I love you. You are the only man that I will ever feel this way about."

He hesitated, and it broke her heart all over again. "I love you, too, but it's not that easy. I don't know if we're going to get past this."

Leigh's throat worked. She had finally touched the bottom of his seemingly bottomless well of forgiveness.

He said, "Let's talk out the problem that's in front of us. How do we save you? How do we save Callie?"

Leigh brushed away her tears. It would be so easy to let Walter help carry the burden, but she had to say, "No, sweetheart. I can't let you get involved in this. Maddy needs one of us to be her parent."

"I'm not negotiating," he said, as if he had a choice. "You told me Andrew has a fail-safe. That means someone else has copies of the videos, right?"

Leigh humored him. "Right."

"So, who would that be?" Walter could sense her intransigence. "Come on, sweetheart. Who would Andrew trust? He can't have that many friends. It's a physical device—a thumb drive or an external hard drive. He makes a call, the fail-safe retrieves the device, releases it on the internet, takes it to the cops. Where would it be kept? Bank vault? Safe? Train station locker?"

Leigh started to shake her head, but then she found herself at the most obvious answer, the one that had been right in front of her from day one.

Both the primary and the backup server are locked in that closet over there.

She told Walter, "Andrew's private detective, Reggie. He has a server. He bragged about the fancy encryption and how he doesn't back up to a cloud. I bet he's got it stored on there."

"Is Reggie in on it?"

She shrugged and shook her head at the same time. "He's never in the room when Andrew pulls his bullshit. All he cares about is money. Andrew's his bank. He would follow through on a fail-safe if Andrew got arrested, no questions asked."

"Okay, so we get the server."

"You mean breaking and entering?" Leigh had to draw a hard line. "No, Walter. I'm not going to let you do that, and it solves nothing. Andrew still has the originals."

"So help me think of another way." He was clearly irritated

by her logic. "Maddy needs her mother. All she did all day was cry and ask me where you were."

The thought of Maddy calling her name, of Leigh not being there, was gut-wrenching.

She told Walter, "I'm sorry I'm such a shitty mother. And wife. And sister. You were right. I try to keep everything separate and all that ends up doing is punishing everyone else."

Walter looked down at the ground. He didn't disagree with her. "We steal the server, all right? And then we need to find the originals. Where would Andrew keep them? They won't be in the same place as the server. Where does he live?"

Leigh pressed together her lips. He wasn't thinking this through. Reggie's office was probably closed at night. He had no visible security. The hasp lock on his closet would be easy to break. All it would take was a screwdriver to back out the screws.

Andrew's house had cameras and a security system and it would more than likely have Andrew, who had already murdered one person and made it clear he was willing to hurt many more.

"Leigh?" Walter said. He was ready to do this. "Tell me about Andrew's house. Where does he live?"

"We're not *Ocean's Eleven*, Walter. We don't have a ninja and a safe-cracker."

"Then we—"

"Blow up his car? Burn down his house?" Leigh could get just as crazy as he could. "Or maybe we could torture him until he tells us. Strip him down, chain him to a chair, rip out his finger-nails, pull out his teeth. Is that what you were thinking?"

Walter rubbed his cheek. He was doing the same thing Leigh had done the first year she had moved to Chicago.

Dr. Patterson. Coach Holt. Mr. Humphrey. Mr. Ganza. Mr. Emmett.

Leigh had come up with thousands of gory fantasies where she ended their disgusting existence—burning them alive, cutting off their dicks, humiliating them, punishing them, destroying them— but then she had realized that her homicidal rage had died in the Waleskis' dreary kitchen on Canyon Road.

"When I killed Buddy," she told Walter. "I was in this—I think it was a fugue state. It was me. I did it. But it wasn't me. It was the girl he'd molested in the car. It was the girl whose sister he'd raped, the one who kept getting pushed around and touched and fondled and laughed at and called a liar and a bitch and a whore. Do you know what I'm saying?"

He nodded, but there was no way he truly got it. Walter had never kept his keys jutting between his fingers as he walked to his car. He had never darkly joked with himself about being raped in a garage because physical vulnerability was not in her husband's range of emotions.

Leigh pressed her palm flat to Walter's chest. His heart was pounding. "Sweetheart, I love you, but you're not a murderer."

"We can find another way."

"There's not—" She stopped, because Reggie Paltz had impeccable timing. He was hopping over the gate instead of walking around to the garage entrance. "He's here. The investigator. Give me a minute to talk to him, okay?"

Walter looked behind him.

Then he looked again.

He asked, "That's the guy? Reggie, the investigator?"

"Yes," Leigh said. "I'm supposed to—"

Without any warning, Walter took off in a dead run.

Reggie was thirty feet away. He didn't have time to respond. His mouth opened in protest, but Walter punched it closed with his fist.

"Walter!" Leigh yelled, running to stop him. "Walter!"

He was straddling Reggie, his fists windmilling. Blood splattered the concrete. She saw a piece of tooth, tendrils of bloody mucus. Bones cracked like kindling. Reggie's nose flattened.

"Walter!" Leigh tried to grab his hand. He was going to kill Reggie if she didn't stop him. "Walter, please!"

One final punch cracked Reggie's mouth open. His jaw twisted sideways. His body went limp. Walter had knocked him out. Still, he raised his fist, ready to strike again.

"No!" She grabbed his hand, holding as tight as she could. His muscles were like cables. She had never seen him like this before. "Walter."

He looked back at her, still furious. Rage distorted his features. His chest heaved with every breath. Blood whipped across his shirt, slashed along his face.

"Walter," she whispered, wiping the blood out of his eyes. He was soaked with sweat. She could feel his muscles tensing as he tried to control the animal inside of him. Leigh looked around the garage. There was no one, but she didn't know how long that would last. "We need to get out of here. Stand up."

"It was him." Walter's head dropped down. He held tight to her hand. She watched the rise and fall of his shoulders as he tried to regain his control. "He was there."

Leigh looked around again. They were yards from a courthouse full of police officers. "Tell me in the car. We have to get out of here."

"The play," Walter said. "Reggie was there. He was sitting in the audience at Maddy's play."

Leigh sank down to the ground. She felt numb again, too overwhelmed to do anything but listen.

"During the intermission." Walter was still breathing hard. "He came up to talk to me. I don't remember the name he gave. He said he was new. He said his daughter went to the school. He said his brother was a cop, and then we were talking about the union and . . ."

Leigh's hand covered her mouth. She remembered intermission—standing up from her seat, searching the auditorium for Walter. He had been talking to a man with short, dark hair who'd kept his back to Leigh the entire time.

"Leigh." Walter was looking at her. "He asked me about Maddy. He asked about you. I thought he was another dad."

"He tricked you." Leigh hated the sound of guilt straining his voice. "It wasn't your fault."

"What else does he know?" Walter asked. "What are they planning?"

Leigh checked the parking garage again. No one was around. The only cameras tracked the cars entering and exiting. Reggie had jumped the fence instead of going around to the front gate.

"Put him in the trunk," she told Walter. "We'll find out."

17

Leigh stood back as Walter opened the trunk. Reggie was still out cold. There had been no need to cut the emergency pull cord or bind his hands with the roll of duct tape that Leigh kept in her emergency roadside kit. Leigh's husband, her sweet, thoughtful husband, had almost killed the man.

Walter turned, checking the perimeter. The parking lot outside of Reggie's office was empty, but the road was twenty yards away, only obscured by a patchy row of Leyland cypress. Walter had parked the Audi by the crumbling concrete steps. The sun had dropped down, but Xenon lights put the parking lot on full display.

She held the Glock in her hand because she was afraid of what Walter would do if he had the opportunity to use it. She had never seen him so feral before. He was clearly standing on the edge of a dark precipice. Leigh couldn't think about her part in his descent, but she knew that she had brought it on with her own stupid belief that she could keep everything under control.

Walter started to reach down for Reggie, but then he looked back at Leigh. "Is there an alarm?"

"I don't know," Leigh said. "I don't remember seeing one, but probably."

Walter shoved his hand into Reggie's front pocket and pulled out a ring loaded with keys. He passed them to Leigh. She had no choice but to leave him at the car so she could open the glass front door. Her eyes traveled around the lobby as she looked for an alarm keypad.

Nothing.

Walter grunted as he started to drag Reggie from the trunk.

She tried several keys before the lock turned. The door opened. She nodded to Walter. She glanced out at the road. She looked around the parking lot. Her heartbeat was so loud in her ears that she couldn't hear what must've been more grunts and groans as her husband lifted Reggie into a fireman's carry over his shoulder. Walter struggled under the weight as he climbed up the stairs and dropped Reggie onto the lobby floor.

Leigh didn't look down. She did not want to see Reggie's damaged face. She locked the glass door. She told Walter, "His office is upstairs."

Walter lifted Reggie again. He went first up the stairs. Leigh stuck the Glock deep into her purse, but she kept her hand wrapped around the weapon. Her finger rested along the trigger guard, the way that Walter had taught her. You didn't put your finger on the trigger unless you were prepared to use it. There was no conventional safety on the gun. When you pressed back on the trigger, the weapon fired. Leigh did not want to find herself facing another murder charge because she had gotten startled and made a horrible mistake.

But it wasn't just herself she had to worry about. Felony murder didn't care who pulled the trigger. The moment Walter had put Reggie into the trunk of the car, they'd both become accessories to each other's crimes.

On the landing, Walter paused to shift Reggie's weight. He was breathing heavily again, more animal than man. He had said very little on the drive over. They had not made a plan because there was nothing to plan. They would find the server. They would destroy the fail-safe. What happened beyond that was nothing that either of them was willing to say out loud.

Leigh rounded the landing. She thought about Andrew standing on this same spot three short days ago. He had been angry when he talked about losing his father. She had ignored the warning siren in her gut. She'd been obsessed with finding out what Andrew really wanted when he had told her straight to her face.

It ruined our lives when Dad disappeared. I wish whoever made him go away understood what that felt like.

This was what Andrew Tenant wanted—what was happening

with Walter right now, their beautiful girl forced into hiding, Callie nowhere to be found. Andrew wanted everything Leigh cared about, everything she had ever loved, to be thrown into chaos the same way his life had been ruined when Buddy died. She had played right into his hands.

Walter had reached the end of the hallway. He leaned down. Reggie's feet went to the ground, his back against the wall. Walter held him up with a fist to his chest. Reggie groaned, his head rolling.

"Hey." Walter slapped his face. "Wake up, asshole."

Reggie's head rolled again. The light from the parking lot cut through the window, spotlighting the damage Walter had caused. The man's left eye was swollen shut. His jaw looked unnatural and loose. The bridge of his nose was nothing more than a pinkish white bone where the skin had been punched away.

Leigh searched for the key to Reggie's office, her hands trembling as she tried each one in the deadbolt.

"Come on," Walter said, slapping Reggie again. "Wake the fuck up."

Reggie coughed.

Blood sprayed onto Walter's face, but Walter didn't blink. "What's the alarm code?"

Reggie's jaw popped. He let out a low wheeze.

"Look at me, asshole." Walter pressed his thumbs into Reggie's eyelids, forcing them open. "Tell me the alarm code or I will beat the life out of you."

Leigh's skin prickled with fear. She looked up from the lock. She knew that Walter wasn't making an empty threat. Reggie did, too. His wheezing spiraled as he tried to push out sound with a jaw that Walter had broken off its hinge.

"Th-three . . ." Reggie started. The number was awkward and muffled when it came out of his mouth. "Nine . . . six . . . three."

Leigh felt the final key on the ring slide into the lock, but she didn't open the door. She told Walter, "It could be a trick. It might make a silent alarm go off."

Walter said, "If that happens, then we'll shoot him in the head and take the server. We'll be gone before the police get here."

Leigh was chilled by the determination in his voice.

She gave Reggie a chance, asking, "You're sure about the code? Three-nine-six-three?"

Reggie huffed out a cough. Pain etched lines into his face.

Walter told Leigh, "Show him the gun."

Reluctantly, she lifted the Glock from her purse. She saw the whites of Reggie's eyes as he stared down at the weapon. In her head, she told herself that Walter was bluffing. He had to be bluffing. They were not going to murder anyone.

Walter wrenched the gun from her hand. He pressed the muzzle into Reggie's forehead. His finger stayed along the trigger guard. He asked again, "What's the code?"

Reggie's body convulsed as he coughed. His mouth wouldn't close. Drool mixed with blood as it slid from his lip onto his shirt.

"Five," Walter said, counting down. "Four. Three."

Leigh watched his finger move to the trigger. He was not bluffing. Her mouth opened to tell him to stop, but Reggie spoke first.

"Backward," he said, the word sloppy from the effort. "Three, six, nine, three."

Walter kept the gun pressed to Reggie's head. He told Leigh, "Try it."

She turned the key in the lock. She opened the door. A beeping sound filled the dark outer office. She followed the noise down the short hallway. The keypad was inside the main office. A red button was flashing. The beeping sped up, counting down the seconds until the alarm went off.

Leigh entered the code. Nothing happened. She leaned down, trying to figure out what to do. The beeping got faster. The alarm was going to go off. The phone was going to ring. Someone was going to ask for a safe word and there was no way that Reggie would give it. If he was still alive by then because Walter had already told them both what would happen.

"Fuck," she whispered, scanning the numbers. The word OFF was written in small print under the *1* button. She pressed in the code again, then added a *1*.

The keypad gave one final, long beep.

The red button turned green.

Leigh put her hand to her heart, but she was still waiting for the phone to ring. Her ears strained in the silence. All she heard was the door closing in the other room, then the turn of the lock, then heavy footsteps as Walter dragged Reggie down the hallway.

The lights came on. Leigh dropped her purse on the couch. She went to the window to close the blinds. The same two questions chased each other around her brain: *What were they going to do? How was this going to end?*

Walter shoved Reggie into one of the chairs. She was shocked when Walter pulled out the roll of duct tape from the back of his pants. He'd brought it from the trunk of her car, which meant that he had thought this through. Worse, he had a plan, and Leigh was the one who'd put it in his mind.

Strip him down, chain him to a chair, rip out his fingernails, pull out his teeth.

"Walter," she said, her voice pleading with him to rethink this.

"Is that where the server is?" Walter pointed to the metal door on the back wall. The hasp lock was held closed by a black padlock that looked like something out of a military catalogue.

Leigh said, "Yes, but—"

"Get it open." Walter wrapped tape around Reggie's chest, binding him to the chair. He checked that the man's wrists were still held together before going down on one knee to tape his ankles to the chair legs.

Leigh had no words. It was like watching her husband fall into madness. There was no way to stop him. All she could do was go along until he found his senses. She pulled on the padlock. The hasp held fast. The screws in the metal door and frame were Phillips head. She had a screwdriver in her emergency roadside kit. She had teased Walter when he'd put it in her trunk but now she wanted to go back in time and leave it in the garage in her building because it would be only a matter of time before he told her to go downstairs and get it.

Leigh knew if she left the two men alone in the room, she would only find one of them alive when she returned.

Walter looped more tape around Reggie's wrists, saying, "You're going to talk to me, motherfucker."

Leigh checked Reggie's key ring. Nothing looked right. The key would be short with chunky teeth. She started to try them anyway.

Walter dragged the other chair across the room. He sat down opposite Reggie. He was so close that their knees touched. The gun was in his lap. His finger rested along the side.

He asked Reggie, "Why were you at my daughter's school?"

Reggie said nothing. He was watching Leigh at the closet.

"Don't look at my wife. Look at me." Walter waited for Reggie to comply before he repeated the question. "Why were you at my daughter's school?"

Reggie still didn't answer.

With one hand, Walter tossed the gun into the air and caught it by the muzzle. He backhanded Reggie with the plastic handle. The blow was so hard that Reggie's chair nearly toppled.

Leigh had clamped her hand over her mouth to keep from screaming. Blood had splattered onto her shoes. She saw bits of teeth in the carpet.

Reggie's shoulders convulsed. He vomited down the front of his shirt. His head rolled around his neck. His face was swollen. His left eye had disappeared. His mouth hung so loose that he couldn't keep his tongue inside.

Kidnapping. Aggravated assault. Torture.

Walter asked Leigh, "Can you get the padlock open?"

She shook her head. "Walter—"

"Hey." Walter slapped Reggie's head with his open palm. "Where is it, asshole? Where's the key?"

Reggie's eyes were rolling again. Leigh could smell the stench of his vomit.

Leigh told Walter, "He's concussed. If you hit him again, he'll pass out. Or worse."

Walter looked at her, and she was shocked to find the same cold deadness that she had seen in Andrew's eyes so many times before.

She begged, "Walter, please. Think about what we're doing. What we've already done."

Walter wouldn't look at her again. He could only see the threat to Maddy. He raised the Glock, pointing it at Reggie's face. "Where's the key, asshole?"

"Walter," Leigh said, her voice shaking. "We can back out the screws, okay? All we have to do is back out the screws. Please, baby. Just put the gun down, okay?"

Slowly, Walter let the gun return to his lap. "Hurry."

Leigh's legs were shaky as she went to the desk. She pulled open drawers, dumping their contents onto the floor, searching for the small key. She silently begged Walter to not remember the screwdriver in her car. She needed to get her husband out of here, to make him see reason. They had to stop this. They needed to take Reggie to the hospital. And then Reggie would go straight to the police and Walter would be arrested and Andrew would show the tapes and—

Leigh felt her thoughts lurch to a halt.

Her brain had been making connections in the background, telling her that something wasn't right. She inventoried the items on Reggie's desk. Laptop. Black leather blotter. Colored glass paperweight. Personalized business card holder.

The Tiffany 1837 Makers letter opener was missing.

Leigh knew that the seven-inch long, sterling silver desk accessory cost $375. She had bought the same one for Walter a few Christmases ago. It had the distinctive, masculine look of a knife.

"Walter," she said. "I need to talk to you in the hall."

He didn't move. "Get the screwdriver out of your car."

Leigh went to the couch. She reached into her purse. Ruby Heyer's crime scene photos were still in the folder. "Walter, I need you to come into the hall with me. Now."

Her curt tone of voice somehow managed to cut through the fog. Walter stood up, telling Reggie, "We'll be right outside that door. Don't try a goddam thing or I will shoot you in the back. Understood?"

Reggie lifted his head. His eyes were closed, but he managed to nod once in agreement.

Leigh didn't move until Walter did. She led him into the hall, but he stopped before they reached the outer office, hovering near the doorway so he could keep his eyes on Reggie.

Walter spoke through gritted teeth. "What is it?"

"Do you remember the letter opener I bought you?" Leigh said. "Do you still have it?"

363

Slowly, Walter turned his head in her direction. "What?"

"The letter opener, the one from Tiffany that I bought you. Do you remember it?"

Walter's expression slowly changed into one of confusion. He almost looked like her husband again.

Leigh thumbed through Ruby Heyer's file, keeping the photos obscured so that Walter wasn't set off again. She found the close-up of the knife sticking out between Ruby's legs. She still didn't show it to him. Most of Walter's legal career had been spent on a phone or behind a desk. He'd never tried a criminal case before, let alone a violent murder.

She said, "I'm going to show you a photo. It's very graphic, but you need to see it."

Walter glanced back at Reggie. "Jesus, Leigh, just get to the point."

She knew he wasn't ready, so she walked him through the details. "Andrew has an alibi for Ruby's murder. Are you listening to me?"

Walter nodded, but he wasn't really.

"Andrew got married last night," Leigh said, trying to keep the information as simple and repetitive as she would for a jury. "When the police confronted him this morning about Ruby's murder, he had an alibi. He showed them photos on his phone. The photos showed Andrew with the caterer, and another one with his mother at the cocktail party, and then with friends waiting for Sidney to walk down the aisle."

Walter's jaw worked. He wasn't going to entertain her for much longer.

"This morning, before court, I saw Andrew. He had bite marks on his neck, and a scratch here." She put her hand to her face and waited for Walter to look. "They were defensive wounds. Andrew had defensive wounds this morning."

"Ruby fought back," Walter said. "So?"

"No, remember the alibi photos from the night before? You can see the bite marks on Andrew's neck, but the bruises are already coming up. The timing doesn't work out. It kept bothering me because I know how long it takes for bruises to get dark like that. Andrew got the bite marks around three, maybe four

364

yesterday afternoon. Ruby talked to her family at five on the telephone. Andrew has photos of himself meeting with the caterers at five thirty. The police think Ruby was murdered around six or seven. Her body was found at seven thirty. Andrew was at home the entire time, surrounded by witnesses."

Walter's impatience was on full display.

Leigh put her palm flat to his chest, the same way she always did when she needed his undivided attention.

He finally looked at her. She could see him silently running back through the details, trying to figure out the important parts. Finally, he said, "Keep going."

"I don't think that Andrew killed Ruby. I think that someone else did it for him. The killer used the same MO that Andrew used on his other victims. And Andrew made sure he had a solid, unbreakable alibi for when it happened."

Walter was giving her his undivided attention.

"When I was in Reggie's office three days ago, he had a letter opener on his desk. The same kind of letter opener I bought you for Christmas." She paused a moment to make sure he was ready. "The letter opener isn't on Reggie's desk anymore. It's not in his drawers."

Walter looked down at the folder. "Show me."

Leigh pulled out the crime scene photo. The blunt, sterling silver handle of the knife-like letter opener showed where a metal punch had imprinted T&CO MAKERS into the metal.

The hardness drained from Walter's expression. He wasn't seeing the letter opener. He wasn't connecting the dots from Leigh's story. He was seeing the woman he'd laughed with over backyard barbecues. The mother of his daughter's friend. The parent he'd joked with at PTA meetings and school events. The person whose brutal, intimate death had been captured in the photograph Leigh held in front of his face.

His hand went to his head. Tears sprang into his eyes.

Leigh couldn't take his anguish. She started crying, too. She hid the photograph from his sight. Of all the horrible violations of their marriage, this one felt the most brutal.

"You're saying . . . you mean that he . . ." The sorrow on Walter's face was unbearable. "Keely has a right to . . ."

"She has a right to know," Leigh finished.

"I don't . . ." Walter turned around. He looked at Reggie. "What are we going to do?"

Leigh reached down. She slipped the gun from his grasp. "You're going to leave. I can't let Maddy lose you, too. This is my responsibility. I'm the reason all of this happened. I want you to take my car and—"

"No." Walter was looking down at his hands. He flexed his fingers. His knuckles were bleeding. Sweat still poured from his body. His DNA was all over the office, the Audi, the parking deck. "We have to think, Leigh."

"There's nothing to think about," she said, because all that mattered was that Walter was as far from this as possible. "Please, baby, get in my car and—"

"We can use this," he said. "It's leverage."

"No, we can't let—" Leigh stopped mid-sentence. There was nothing to add to the *can't* because she knew that he was right. They had kidnapped and tortured Reggie, but Reggie had murdered Ruby Heyer.

Mutually assured destruction.

"Let me talk to him," Leigh said. "Okay?"

Walter hesitated, but he nodded.

Leigh stuck the folder under her arm. She walked back into the office.

Reggie heard her approach. He looked up with his one milky eye. He turned his head, glancing back at Walter standing in the doorway. Then he looked at Leigh again.

"This isn't good cop/bad cop." Leigh showed him the gun. "This is two people who've already kidnapped and beaten you. Do you think that murder is far behind?"

Reggie kept staring up at her, waiting.

"Where were you last night?"

Reggie said nothing.

"Did Andrew invite you to his wedding?" she asked. "Because you're not in any of the photos that he showed the police. He documented everything with his phone. He has an unbreakable alibi."

Reggie blinked again, but she could sense uncertainty. He didn't know where this was going. She could almost see him running

366

the calculations in his head—*how much did they know, what were they going to do, what were the odds he could get out of this, how long would it take for Andrew to make them pay for hurting him?*

Leigh took a page from Dante Carmichael's book. She opened the folder and slapped down the crime scene photos across the desk with a flourish. Instead of holding back the close-up of Ruby's scalp, she held back the one that showed the Tiffany letter opener.

She asked Reggie again, "Where were you last night?"

He looked at the photo array, then looked back at Leigh. His jaw was too loose for his mouth to close, but he grunted, "Who?"

"Who?" she repeated, because she hadn't expected the question. "You don't know the name of the woman that Andrew had you murder?"

Reggie blinked. He looked genuinely confused. "What?"

She showed him the close-up photo of the letter opener. Again, his response was unexpected.

Reggie leaned in, turning his head so that his good eye could get a closer look. He studied the photograph. His gaze went to his desk, as if to search for the letter opener. He finally looked back up at Leigh. His head started shaking.

"No," he said. "No-no-no."

"You were at Maddy's school Sunday night," Leigh told him. "You saw me talking to Ruby Heyer. Did you tell Andrew about her? Is that why he had you kill her?"

"I—" Reggie coughed. The muscles along his jaw were spasming. For the first time, he looked afraid. "No. Not me. Told Andy she left her husband. Fucking her physical therapist. Moved to the hotel. But I didn't—no. I wouldn't. She was fine."

Leigh asked, "You're telling me that you followed Ruby Heyer to the hotel, then you told Andrew where she was, but you didn't do anything else?"

"Right." He kept looking at the photos. "Not me. Never."

Leigh studied what was left of his face. She'd thought from the beginning that he was an easy read. Now, she wasn't so sure. Reggie Paltz was showing Leigh the kind of fear that Andrew Tenant had never shown.

"Leigh." Walter was picking up on it, too. "Are you sure?"

Leigh wasn't sure of anything. Andrew was always three steps ahead. Had he gotten the drop on Reggie, too?

She told Reggie, "Even if what you're saying is true, you're still opening yourself up to a conspiracy to commit murder charge. You told an accused rapist how to locate a vulnerable woman who'd just left her family and was living on her own."

Reggie winced as he tried to swallow down his terror.

She asked, "What about your story about how Andrew located me? You said that you showed him the *Atlanta INtown* article and he recognized my face. Is that true?"

He nodded quickly. "Yes. Promise. Saw the article. Showed it to him. He recognized you."

"And he had you look into me and my family?"

"Yes. Paid me. That's all." Reggie looked at the crime scene photos again. "Not this. I wouldn't. Couldn't."

Leigh felt in her gut that he was being honest. She exchanged a look with Walter. They were both silently asking the same question—*what now?*

"The—" Reggie's cough was wet. His eye turned toward the server closet. "On the ledge."

Walter went to the door. He reached up to the top of the trim. He showed Leigh the padlock key. His eyes mirrored the apprehension that Leigh was feeling.

She didn't need a siren in her gut to tell her this wasn't right. She let herself think back over the last five minutes, then she ran through the last few days. Reggie had been willing to break a few laws for Andrew. Leigh could even believe that he would commit murder for the right sum of money. Where she got caught up was accepting that Reggie would commit *this* kind of murder. The brutality visited upon Ruby Heyer was clearly doled out by someone who enjoyed what they were doing. No sum of money could buy that level of frenzy.

She asked Reggie, "Did Andrew ask you to store some digital files for him?"

Reggie gave a single, painful nod.

"You were told to release them if something happened to him?"

Again, he managed to nod.

Leigh watched Walter twist the key into the padlock. He opened the door.

She had been expecting a large rack with flashing components, something out of a Jason Bourne movie. What she saw instead were two tan metal boxes sitting on top of a filing cabinet. Each was as tall and wide as a gallon of milk. Green and red lights flashed on the fronts. Blue cords snaked out of the backs and plugged into a modem.

She asked Reggie, "Did you look at the files?"

"No." His neck strained as he tried to speak. "Paid me. That's it."

"They're videos of a child being raped."

Reggie's eye went wide. He started shaking. Now his fear was unequivocal.

Leigh couldn't tell if he was disgusted or terrified of the legal ramifications. Almost every pedophile the FBI had ever arrested claimed they had no idea that child porn was on their devices. Then they spent the next chunk of their lives in prison wondering if they should've tried a different excuse.

She asked Reggie, "What are you going to do?"

"There," Reggie said, his head tilting toward the filing cabinet in the closet. "Top drawer. Back."

Walter didn't move. He was clearly exhausted. The adrenaline rush that had brought him to this place had ebbed away, only to be replaced by the horror he felt over his own violent actions.

Leigh couldn't fix that right now. She opened the top drawer of the filing cabinet. She saw rows of tabs with client names. The sight of the last five folders in the back made her heart wilt.

CALLIOPE "CALLIE" DEWINTER

HARLEIGH "LEIGH" COLLIER

WALTER COLLIER

MADELINE "MADDY" COLLIER

SANDRA "PHIL" SANTIAGO

Leigh told Walter, "I want you to wait in the car."

He shook his head. He was too much of a good man to leave her now.

Leigh yanked out the folders. She returned to the desk so that

369

Walter couldn't look over her shoulder. She started with Maddy's file, because that was the one that mattered the most.

In Leigh's legal capacity, she had read hundreds of reports from private investigators. They all had the same predictable uniformity: logs, photographs, receipts. Maddy's was the same, though Reggie's notes were handwritten rather than printed from a spreadsheet.

The records of her daughter's comings and goings had started two days prior to the Sunday performance of *The Music Man* and were as recent as yesterday afternoon.

> 8:12 a.m. – carpools to school with Keely Heyer, Necia Adams, and Bryce Diaz
> 8:22 a.m. – stops at McDonald's, goes through drive-thru, eats in car en route
> 8:49 a.m. — arrives at Hollis Academy
> 3:05 p.m. — sighted in auditorium at play practice
> 3:28 p.m. – on field for soccer practice (father attending)
> 5:15 p.m. – home with father

Leigh thought about Andrew screwing with his ankle monitor, but she wouldn't let her mind go to the possibility that Andrew had ended up sitting in the Hollis auditorium watching Maddy check in with the younger kids or lurking around the stadium where Maddy practiced soccer three times a week, because the loaded Glock was too close at hand.

Instead, she paged to the thick stack of color photographs behind the logs. More of the same. Maddy in the car. Maddy on stage. Maddy stretching on the sidelines.

Leigh didn't show the photos to Walter. She wasn't going to turn him back into the feral animal who had been willing to murder Reggie Paltz.

She selected Callie's folder next. The log had started one day after Maddy's. Callie was selling drugs on Stewart Avenue. She was working at Dr. Jerry's clinic. She was living at the motel, then she was meeting Leigh, then they were in her car, then Callie was walking to Phil's. The photos backed up the log, but there was more: her sister waiting at the bus stop, letting her cat in through the window at Phil's house, walking outside a strip mall that was so familiar to Leigh that her eyes burned at the sight of it.

Callie was pictured standing underneath a covered breezeway. She was in the exact location where they had buried the butchered chunks of Buddy Waleski's body.

Leigh asked Reggie, "Where were you last night?"

"Watch—" He cleared his throat. There was no denying the apprehension on his face. He knew that this was bad. He knew that even if he managed to walk out of here, Andrew or the police would be waiting for him. "Watching your sister."

Leigh examined Callie's log for yesterday. She had visited the library, then gone to Maddy's soccer practice, then she had returned home on the bus. According to Reggie's notes, he had stayed outside Phil's house from five in the evening until midnight last night.

Investigators were paid by the hour. It was generally frowned upon if they wasted time setting up outside a house unless there was the possibility that the subject would leave. Leigh didn't have to look back through the logs to know that Callie never left once she settled in for the night. Her sister was disabled. She was vulnerable because of her addictions. She didn't go out at night unless she had to.

Leigh asked, "Did Andrew know you were watching Callie at five o'clock?"

"Called. Said to stay." Reggie knew what her next question would be. "Burner phone. Made me leave . . . other one here."

Leigh said, "And your logs are handwritten, not backed up onto the computer."

Reggie gave a slight nod to confirm. "No copies."

Leigh looked at Walter, but he was staring down at the broken skin on the back of his hand.

She asked Reggie, "Where were you the night that Tammy Karlsen was raped?"

The stunned look that crossed Reggie's face was quickly replaced with dread. "Andrew hired—I followed Sidney."

"What about the memory cards in the camera? Does Andrew have those, too?"

371

Reggie's head moved in a quick nod.

"And he paid you cash, right? So there are no invoices."

He didn't answer, but he didn't have to.

Leigh knew Reggie hadn't considered the worst of it. She laid out the rest of Andrew's plan. "What about the other nights, the three women who were raped near Andrew's regular haunts. Where were you?"

"Working," Reggie said. "Following exes."

Leigh remembered the names of the two new witnesses on Dante's list. "Lynne Wilkerson and Fabienne Godard?"

Reggie let out a low, distressed sigh.

"Jesus," Leigh said, because everything was lining up. "What about your car's GPS?"

His eye had closed. Blood seeped from the corner. "Turned it off."

Leigh watched him silently making the connections. Reggie did not have an alibi for any of the rapes. He had no alibi for Ruby Heyer's murder. He hadn't logged his notes into his computer. There were no invoices itemizing his activities. There was no phone or camera or memory card that would pinpoint his location while the attacks were occurring. An argument could be made that he'd turned off the tracking in his car to avoid incrimination.

This was why Andrew had never been afraid. He had set up Reggie to take the fall.

"Fucker," Reggie said, because he knew it, too.

"Walter," Leigh said. "Take the servers. I'll get the laptop."

Leigh jammed his laptop into her purse. She waited for Walter to pull all of the wires and plugs out of the metal boxes. Instead of leaving, she returned to the filing cabinet. She found the files for Lynne Wilkerson and Fabienne Godard. She stacked them with the others on the desk so that Reggie could see. "I'm keeping all of these. They're your only alibi, so fuck with me and I'll fuck you into the ground. Do you understand?"

He nodded, but she could tell he wasn't worried about the files. He was worried about Andrew.

Leigh found the scissors where she'd dumped them out of the desk drawer. She told Reggie, "If I were you, I'd get myself to the hospital and then find a damn good lawyer."

Reggie watched her cut through the tape around his wrists.

That was all the help she was going to give him. She left the scissors in his hand.

She gathered up the stolen items, telling Walter, "Let's go."

Leigh waited for him to leave the room first. She still didn't trust Walter to not go after Reggie again. Her husband was quiet as he carried the servers down the stairs. Through the lobby. Out the door. She threw everything into the trunk. Walter did the same with the two servers.

He had driven them here, but Leigh got behind the wheel of her car. She reversed out of the space. Her lights flashed along the front of the building. She saw the shadow of Reggie Paltz standing at his office window.

Walter said, "He'll go to the police."

"He'll get himself cleaned up, and then he'll catch the first flight to Vanuatu, Indonesia, or the Maldives," Leigh said, listing a few of the preferred nations that did not extradite to the United States. "We need to find Callie's videos on his server and destroy them. We have to keep the rest for insurance."

"For what?" Walter asked. "Andrew's still got the originals. We're still trapped. He's got us in the same damn place as before."

"We're not," Leigh said. "He hasn't."

"He paid that cocksucker to follow Maddy. He knows where she was, where she's going. He took photographs. I saw your face when you saw them. You were terrified."

Leigh wasn't going to argue with him because he was right.

"And what he did to Ruby. Jesus Christ, she was mutilated. He didn't just kill her. He tortured her and—" Walter's throat gave out a strangled sound of grief. He put his head in his hands. "What are we going to do? Maddy will never be safe. We'll never get away from him."

Leigh pulled over to the side of the road. She wasn't that far from the same spot she'd pulled over to after the first meeting in Reggie Paltz's office. Then, she had been sick with panic. Now, her steely resolve took over.

She held on to Walter's hands. She waited for him to look at her, but he didn't.

"I understand," he said. "I get why you did it."

Leigh shook her head. "Did what?"

"Callie's always been more like your daughter. She's always been your responsibility." Walter finally looked up at her. He had cried more in the last twenty minutes than she had seen him cry in nearly twenty years. "When you told me that you killed him, I—I don't know. It was too much to take in. I couldn't understand. There's right and wrong and—what you did . . ."

Leigh felt her throat work.

"I couldn't imagine ever being capable of hurting somebody like that," he continued. "But when I recognized Reggie in the parking lot, and then I realized the threat to Maddy—I couldn't see. I was blind with rage. I was going to kill him, Leigh. You knew that I was going to murder him."

Leigh pressed together her lips.

"I don't understand everything you told me about what happened," Walter said. "But I understand that."

Leigh studied her sweet, kind husband. In the light of the dashboard, the streaks of sweat and blood across his face took on a purple hue. She had done this to him. She had put their daughter in danger. She had turned her husband into a raving lunatic. She had to fix this, and she had to do it now.

She told Walter, "I need to find Callie. She has a right to know what's happened. What's going to happen."

Walter asked, "What's going to happen?"

"I'm going to do what I should've done three days ago," Leigh told him. "I'm going to turn myself in."

18

Callie stood in front of the locked drug cabinet in Dr. Jerry's clinic. She had abandoned Sidney's convertible BMW across two parking spaces outside. Driving was harder than the last time she had stolen a car. There had been lots of stops and starts, beginning in Andrew's garage where she'd scraped off the right side of the BMW trying to get out. In the driveway, the back end had clipped his watchtower mailbox. The rims had bitten into several curbs as she'd miscalculated turns.

That the car had survived her stay inside the shooting gallery off Stewart Avenue was a testament to heroin's stupification. She had taken Sidney's wallet and phone inside to trade, but no one had stripped off the car's expensive tires. No one had broken the windows and ripped out the radio. They were either too high to formulate a plan or too desperate to wait for the chop shop to send a runner.

Callie, on the other hand, had been mournfully aware. Her methadone tapering regimen had not been rewarded the same way it had been so many times before. She'd been expecting the rapturous rush of euphoria with her first taste, but her body had cycled through the heroin so fast that she had chased the high along an eternal loop of despair. The sudden seconds of sickness as the liquid pushed in, the five short minutes of bliss, the heaviness that lasted for less than an hour before her brain told her she needed *more more more*.

This was called tolerance, or sensitization, which was defined as the body requiring a higher dose of the drug in order to achieve the same response. Predictably, the mu receptors played a big role in tolerance. Repeated exposure to opiates dampened the analgesic effect, and no matter how many new mus your body created, those mus were going to inherit the memories of the mus that came before.

Tolerance was incidentally why addicts started cross-mixing drugs, adding in fentanyl or Oxy or benzos or, in most cases, shooting themselves up with so much shit that they ended up laughing with Kurt Cobain about how his daughter was now older than he'd been on the day he'd rested that shotgun beneath his chin. Maybe he would softly sing the Neil Young passage he quoted in his suicide note—

It's better to burn out than to fade away.

Callie stared at the drug cabinet, trying to summon her rage. Andrew in the stadium tunnel. Sidney writhing on the closet floor. The disgusting video of Callie and Buddy playing on the television. Maddy running across the bright green field, no cares in the world because she was cherished and loved and she would always feel that way.

The first key slid into the lock. Then the second key. Then the cabinet was open. With an expert's light touch, Callie traced her fingers along the vials. Methadone, ketamine, fentanyl, buprenor-phine. On any other day, she would be shoving as many vials as she could into her pockets. Now, she left them alone and found the lidocaine. She started to close the cabinet, but her mind rushed to stop her. Several vials of pentobarbital were lined up along the bottom shelf. The liquid was blue, like the color of glass cleaner. The containers were larger than the others, almost three times the size. She selected one, then locked the doors.

Instead of going into a treatment room, she went to the front lobby. The plate-glass windows gave an overview past the burglar bars and into the parking lot. The streetlights had been busted out, but Callie could clearly see Sidney's shiny convertible. Nothing else was in the lot except for a stray rat making its way toward the Dumpster. The barbershop was closed. Dr. Jerry was probably at home reading sonnets to Meowma Cass, the bottle-fed kitten. Callie wanted to tell herself that coming here was a good idea, but after a lifetime of rash decisions, she found herself absent her usual disregard for any and all consequences.

Tell Andy if he wants his knife back, he's going to have to come and get it.

Callie wasn't a complete Luddite. She knew cars gave off signals to GPS satellites that told people exactly where they were. She knew Sidney's ridiculously expensive BMW would act as a giant neon sign, pointing Andrew to her location. She also knew several hours had passed since Andrew had been released from his jury selection.

So why hadn't he come for her?

Callie grabbed a surgical pack on her way to the breakroom. Her leg was aching so much that she was limping by the time she reached the table. She gently placed one little and one big vial on the table. She opened up the surgical pack. Her hand went to her thigh as she sat down. The abscess in her leg felt like a robin's egg under her jeans. She pressed into it, because the physical pain was better than the pain she was feeling inside.

She closed her eyes. She stopped her brain's fight against the inevitable and let the video play in her head.

Callie's fourteen-year-old self trapped on the couch.

Buddy, please, it hurts too much please stop please . . .

Buddy's enormous body grinding into her.

Shut the fuck up Callie I said hold the fuck still.

She hadn't remembered it that way. Why hadn't she remembered it that way? What was wrong with her brain? What was wrong with her soul?

At the snap of her fingers, Callie could relay in intricate detail ten thousand horrible things that Phil had done when Callie was little, whether it was beating her unconscious or abandoning her on the side of the road or scaring the shit out of her in the middle of the night because the tinfoil hat men were waiting outside with their probes.

Why was it that Callie had never, ever in the last twenty-three years let herself recall how many times Buddy had threatened her, thrown her across the room, kicked her, forced himself inside of her, tied her up, even strangled her? Why had she blocked the memories of the ten thousand times he'd told Callie that it was her fault because she cried too much or begged too much or couldn't do all of the things that he wanted her to do?

Callie heard the smack of her lips. Her brain had drawn a direct line from Phil to Buddy to the locked drug cabinet.

Methadone. Ketamine. Buprenorphine. Fentanyl.

She had picked up her backpack at Phil's when she'd changed out of the slinky black top and into her torn Care Bears T-shirt and yellow satin rainbow jacket. She'd snapped the front up to her neck because it felt safer that way, almost like a security blanket. Callie's dope kit was inside the backpack. Her tie-off. Her lighter. Her spoon. A used syringe. A fat baggie filled to the top with off-white powder.

Without thinking, she was reaching down. Without a thought, she was opening the kit, her muscle memory laying out the lighter, the tie-off, the fat baggie with its unknowable mysteries.

The dealer who'd sold her the heroin wasn't someone Callie knew. She had no idea what he'd cut it with—baking soda, powdered milk, meth, fenty, strychnine—or even how pure the drug was when he'd started. What had mattered at the time was that she had forty dollars and some prescription pills left over from her debacle with Sidney and he'd had enough heroin to kill an elephant.

Callie swallowed the blood in her mouth. Her lip was bleeding because she could not stop biting it. With effort, she managed to pull her attention away from the dope. She leaned up in the chair so that she could slide down her jeans. In the overhead light, her thigh was the color of Elmer's glue, if you dropped a bright red, pus-filled glob at the top. She gently brushed her fingers along the abscess. Heat pulsed into her fingertips. There were dried specks of blood where she had injected herself through the infection.

All for less than five minutes of a high that she was never, ever going to catch again no matter how many times she chased it.

Fucking junkies.

She drew back a few ccs of lidocaine, not bothering to measure the dose. She watched the needle dip into the abscess. Another trickle of blood rewarded the effort. There was no pinch of pain because everything in her body hurt right now. Her neck, her arms, her back, her kneecap that she'd drilled into Sidney's crotch. The heavy feeling from the heroin that used to lull Callie into a senseless sleep had turned into a weight that was going to eventually smother her.

She closed her eyes as she felt the lidocaine spreading through the abscess. She listened for the gorilla. Strained to feel his hot breath on her neck. The loneliness was stark. She had lived with the threat of him stalking on the horizon since that night in the kitchen, but now, there was nothing. The creature had disappeared inside the stadium tunnel a few moments before she had attacked Andrew. The puzzle of that paradox would not stop nagging at Callie's brain. If she pushed to the edges of the equation, the solution was simple: all of these years, Buddy Waleski had not been the gorilla.

The ferocious, bloodthirsty demon had been Callie all along.

"Hello, friend," Dr. Jerry said.

Callie spun around to face him, her soul igniting with shame. Dr. Jerry was standing in the doorway. His eyes flitted across the table. Her dope kit with the fat baggie of heroin. The surgical pack. The lidocaine syringe. The large bottle of blue pentobarbital.

"Goodness." Dr. Jerry turned his attention to the giant red knot in her leg. "May I help with that?"

Callie's mouth flooded with apologies, but her lips wouldn't let them come out. There were no excuses for this situation. Her guilt was laid out like evidence at a trial.

"Let's see what we have here, young miss." Dr. Jerry sat down. His lab coat was wrinkled. His glasses were askew. His hair had not been combed. She could smell the sour odor of sleep on his breath as his fingers gently pressed around the abscess. He told her, "If you were a calico, I would say that you'd gotten into a very nasty altercation. Which, of course, is not unusual for a calico. They can be quite pugilistic. Unlike pugs, who are notorious recounters. Especially if you get a few drinks into them."

Callie's vision blurred with tears. The shame had spread to every fiber of her being. She couldn't just sit here the same way she always did when he shared one of his stories.

"I see you've already started with the lidocaine." He tested her leg, asking, "Does this feel numb enough, do you think?"

Callie felt her head nod, though she could still feel the sharp burn from the infection. She had to say something, but what could she say? How could she apologize for stealing from him? For jeopardizing his practice? For lying to his face?

Dr. Jerry seemed unconcerned as he took a pair of gloves from the surgical pack. Before he started, he smiled at Callie, giving her the same soothing preamble that he would offer to a frightened whippet. "You'll be fine, young lady. This will be a little uncomfortable for us both, but I'll be as quick as I can, and soon, you will feel much better."

Callie looked at the refrigerator behind him as he sliced open the abscess. She felt his fingers pressing out the infection, wiping it away with the gauze, pressing again until the sac was empty. Cool saline dripped down her leg when he irrigated the opening. She couldn't look down, but she knew that he was being thorough because he always took special care of every wretched animal that showed up at his door.

"There we go, all done." Dr. Jerry took off the gloves. He found the first-aid kit in the drawer and selected a medium-sized Band-Aid. He covered the incision, saying, "We should discuss antibiotics, if you're amenable? I prefer mine hidden inside a piece of cheese."

Callie still couldn't make herself speak. Instead, she lifted up in the chair so she could pull her jeans back on. The waist gapped around her stomach. She would need to find a belt.

Belt.

She looked down at her hands. She saw Buddy jerking the belt out of his pants, wrapping it tight around her wrists. Twenty-three years of forgetting had culminated in a flashing horror show that she couldn't clear from her eyes.

"Callie?"

When she looked up, Dr. Jerry seemed to be patiently waiting for her attention.

He said, "I normally don't bring up weight, but, in your case, I think it would be appropriate for us to discuss the dispensing of treats. You're clearly in need of more nutrition."

She opened her mouth, and the words flooded out. "I'm sorry, Dr. Jerry. I shouldn't be here. I should've never come back. I'm a horrible person. I don't deserve your help. Or your trust. I've been stealing from you and I'm—"

"My friend," he said. "That is what you are. You're my friend, as you have been since you were seventeen years old."

She shook her head. She wasn't his friend. She was a leech.

He asked, "Do you remember that first time you knocked on my door? I'd put out a help wanted sign, but I had secretly hoped that the help would come from someone as special as you."

Callie couldn't take his kindness. She started crying so hard that she had to gulp for breath.

"Callie." He held on to her hand. "Please don't cry. There is nothing here that surprises or dismays me."

She should've felt relieved, but she felt more awful because he had never said anything. He had just played along like she was getting away with it.

He said, "You've been very clever with the charts and covering your tracks, if that's any consolation."

It was no consolation. It was an indictment.

"The unexpected twist is, I might be losing my marbles, but even I would remember an Akita with hip dysplasia." He winked at her, as if theft of controlled substances was nothing. "You know what bitchy little babies Akitas can be."

"I'm sorry, Dr. Jerry." Tears poured down her face. Her nose was running. "I've got a gorilla on my back."

"Ah, then you know that lately, demographic shifts in the gorilla world have led to unusual behavior."

Callie felt her lips tremble into a smile. He didn't want to lecture her. He wanted to tell her an animal story.

She stuttered in a breath, asking, "Tell me."

"Gorillas are generally quite peaceable so long as you give them space. But that space has become limited because of man, and of course sometimes there are downsides to protecting species, mainly that those species begin to repopulate in greater numbers." He asked, "Say, have you ever met a gorilla?"

She shook her head. "Not to my recollection."

"Well, that's good, because it used to be that one lucky fella was in charge of the troop, and he had all the gals to himself, and he was very, very happy." Dr. Jerry paused for dramatic effect. "Now, instead of going off to form their own troops, young males are staying put and, absent the prospect of love, they've taken to attacking weaker, solitary males. Can you believe that?"

Callie wiped her nose with the back of her hand. "That's terrible."

"Indeed it is," Dr. Jerry said. "Young men without a purpose can be quite troublesome. My youngest son, for instance. He was bullied terribly at school. Did I ever tell you that he struggled with addiction?"

Callie shook her head, because she had never heard of a younger son. She only knew about the one in Oregon.

"Zachary was fourteen years old when he started using. It was a lack of friendship, you see. He was very lonely, but he found acceptance within a group of kids who were not the sort of kids we would've liked for him to be around." Dr. Jerry explained, "They were the school stoners, if that's a word that's still used. And membership in the club was contingent upon experimenting with drugs."

Callie had been sucked into a similar group in high school. Now, they were all married with kids and driving nice cars and she was stealing narcotics from the only man who had ever shown her genuine fatherly love.

"Zachary was a week away from his eighteenth birthday when he died." Dr. Jerry walked around the breakroom, opening and closing cabinets until he found the fun-sized box of animal crackers. "I wasn't keeping Zachary from you, my dear. I hope you'll understand that there are some topics that are too difficult to discuss."

Callie nodded, because she understood more than he knew.

"My lovely wife and I desperately tried to help our boy. It's why his brother moved across the country. For nearly four years, the entirety of our focus was on Zachary." Dr. Jerry chewed on a handful of crackers. "But there was nothing we could do, was there? The poor young fella was helplessly caught up in the throes of his addiction."

Callie's junkie brain ran the numbers. A younger son would've come of age in the eighties, which meant crack. If cocaine was addictive, crack was annihilating. Callie had watched Crackhead Sammy scratch the skin off his arm because he was certain that parasites were burrowing underneath.

"During Zachary's short lifetime, the science of addiction was well-documented, but it's different when it's your own child. You assume they know better, or are somehow different, when the fact is that as special as they are, they are just like everyone else." Dr. Jerry confided, "I'm ashamed when I think back on my behavior. Had I the ability to redo those last few months, I would spend those precious hours telling Zachary that I loved him, not screaming at the top of my lungs that he must've had some kind of moral failure, an absence of character, a hatred for his family, that made him choose not to stop."

He shook the box of treats. Callie didn't want any, but she held out her hand, watched him pour out tigers and camels and rhinoceroses.

Dr. Jerry took another handful for himself before sitting back down. "June was diagnosed with breast cancer the day after we buried Zachary."

Callie seldom heard him say his wife's name out loud. She had never met June. The woman was already dead the first time Callie had seen the sign in the clinic window. There was no junkie math needed this time. Callie had been seventeen, the same age that Zachary was when he'd OD'd, when she had knocked on Dr. Jerry's door.

"Oddly, the pandemic reminds me of that time in my life. First Zachary was gone and, before we had time to mourn that loss, June was in the hospital. Then of course June passed very quickly. A blessing, but also a shock." He explained, "How I compare it to now is, at this moment we are all living through, everyone on earth is experiencing a suspension of loss. Over half a million people dead in the United States alone. The number is too over-whelming to accept, so we go on with our lives and we do what we can but, in the end, the staggering loss will be waiting for us. It always catches up to you, doesn't it?"

Callie took more animal crackers when he offered her the box.

He said, "You don't look well, my friend."

She couldn't disagree with him, so she did not try.

He said, "I had the strangest dream a while ago. It was about a heroin addict. Have you ever met one?"

Callie's heart dropped. She didn't belong in one of his funny stories.

"They live in the darkest, loneliest places, which is very sad, because they are universally known to be wonderfully caring creatures." He cupped his hand to his mouth as if to convey a confidence. "Especially the ladies."

Callie held back a sob. She didn't deserve this.

"Did I mention they have a particular affinity for cats? Not as dinner, but rather as dining companions." Dr. Jerry held up his hands. "And oh, but they are notoriously loveable. It's almost impossible to not love them. You would have to have a very hard-hearted individual to resist the compunction."

Callie shook her head. She couldn't let him redeem her.

"Also, they are legendary for their munificence!" Dr. Jerry looked delighted by the word. "They have been known to leave hundreds of dollars in the cash box for the benefit of other, more vulnerable creatures."

Callie's nose was running so badly that she couldn't keep up.

Dr. Jerry took his handkerchief out of his back pocket and offered it to her.

Callie blew her nose. She thought about his hanger-on, dissolving fish dream and the rats who stored toxin in their needly fur story and considered for the first time that maybe Dr. Jerry wasn't a metaphor guy after all.

He said, "The thing about addicts is, once you open your heart to one of these rascals, you will never, ever stop loving them. No matter what."

She shook her head, again because she didn't deserve his love.

He asked, "Pulmonary cachexia?"

Callie blew her nose to give her hands something to do. She had been so damn transparent this entire time. "I didn't know you knew people-doctor things, too."

He sat back in his chair, arms crossed over his chest. "You are using more calories to breathe than you are taking in through food. That's why you're losing so much weight. Cachexia is a wasting disease. But you know that, don't you?"

Callie nodded again, because another doctor had already explained this to her. She had to eat more, but not too much protein because her kidneys were shot, and not too much processed food because her liver was barely functioning. Then there were the crackles he could hear in her lungs and the white ground glass opacity that appeared in her X-rays, and the disintegrating vertebrae in her neck, and the precocious arthritis in her knee, and there was more but by that time she had stopped listening.

Dr. Jerry asked, "It's not much longer, is it? Not if you continue down this path."

Callie chewed her lip until she tasted blood again. She thought about chasing the high in the shooting gallery, the dawning realization that she had plateaued to a point where heroin alone wasn't going to take away the pain.

He said, "My oldest son, my only remaining son, wants me to live with him."

"In Oregon?"

"He's been asking since the mini-strokes. I told him I was worried if I moved to Portland, Antifa would force me to stop eating gluten, but . . ." He let out a long sigh. "May I tell you something in confidence?"

"Of course."

"I've been here since you left yesterday afternoon. Meowma Cass has enjoyed the attention, but . . ." He shrugged. "I forgot my way home."

Callie bit down on her lip. She had left three days ago. "I can write it down for you."

"I looked it up on my phone. Did you know you can do that?"

"No," she said. "That's amazing."

"Indeed. It gives directions and everything, but I find it very troubling that people are so easy to find. I miss anonymity. People have a right to disappear if they want to. It's a personal decision, isn't it? Everyone should have autonomy. We owe it to them as fellow human beings to support their decisions, even if we do not agree with them."

Callie knew they weren't talking about the internet anymore. "Where's your truck?"

"It's parked in the back," he said. "Can you believe that?"

"That's crazy," she said, though Dr. Jerry always parked his truck in the back. "I could go with you to make sure you find your way home."

"That's very generous, but unnecessary." He held on to her hand again. "You're the only reason I've been able to work these last few months. And I do understand the sacrifice on your part. What it takes for you to be able to do this."

He was looking at her dope kit on the table. She told him, "I'm sorry."

"You will never, ever need to apologize to me." He held her hand to his mouth, giving her a quick kiss before letting her go. "Now, what are we trying to achieve here? I'd hate for you to go awry."

Callie looked at the pentobarbital. The label identified it as Euthasol, and they used it for exactly what the name implied. Dr. Jerry thought he understood her motive for taking it out of the cabinet, but he was wrong.

She said, "I've run across a very dangerous Great Dane."

He scratched his chin, considering the implications. "That's unusual. I would say the blame lies squarely with the owner. Danes are normally very friendly and compassionate mates. They are called gentle giants for a reason."

"There's nothing gentle about this one," Callie said. "He's hurting women. Raping them, torturing them. And he's threatening to hurt people I care about. Like my sister. And my—my sister's daughter. Maddy. She's only sixteen. She's got her whole life ahead of her."

Dr. Jerry understood now. He picked up the vial. "How much does this animal weigh?"

"About one hundred seventy-five pounds."

He studied the bottle. "Freddy, the magnificent Great Dane who held the world record for largest dog, came in at one hundred ninety-six pounds."

"That's a big dog."

He went silent. She could tell he was doing the calculation in his head.

He finally decided, "I would say to be certain, you'd need at least twenty ml's."

Callie puffed air between her lips. "That's a big syringe."

"That's a big dog."

Callie considered her next question. They normally ran an IV and sedated an animal before they put it down. "How would you administer it?"

"The jugular would be good." He thought about it some more. "Intracardial would be the quickest route. Directly into the heart. You've done that before, yes?"

She'd done it at the clinic, but before Narcan was so readily available, she'd also done it in the streets.

Callie asked, "What else?"

"The heart sits at an axis inside the body, so the left atrium would be the most posterior, thus easier to access, correct?"

Callie took a moment to visualize the anatomy. "Correct."

"The sedative effect should take hold within seconds, but the entire dose would be required to pass the creature on to the next life. And of course the muscles would tense. You'd hear agonal breathing." He smiled, but there was a sadness in his eyes. "If you don't mind my saying, it seems to me that it would be very dangerous for someone of your petite stature to take on this task."

"Dr. Jerry," Callie said. "Don't you know by now that I live for danger?"

He grinned, but the sadness was still there.

"I'm sorry," she said. "What happened with your son, you need to know that he always loved you. He wanted to stop. Part of him, at least. He wanted a normal life where you could be proud of him."

"I appreciate your words more than I can express," Dr. Jerry said. "As for you, my friend, you have been a delightful presence in my life. There is nothing about our relationship that has ever, ever not brought me joy. You remember that, okay?"

"Promise," she said. "And the same goes for you."

"Ah." He tapped the side of his forehead. "That is something I will never forget."

After that, there was nothing else for him to do but leave.

Callie found Meowma Cass curled up on the couch in Dr. Jerry's office. The cat was too sleepy to protest the insult of being placed inside of a carrier. She even allowed Callie to reach down and kiss her round belly. The bottle-feeding had paid off. Cass was stronger now. She was going to make it.

Dr. Jerry expressed some surprise to find his truck parked behind the building, but Callie admired his ability to adapt to novel situations. She helped him strap the seatbelt around the cat carrier, then around himself. Neither one of them said anything as he turned on the engine. She put her hand to his face. And then she reached down and kissed his scruffy cheek before letting him leave. His truck rolled slowly down the alley. The left-side blinker started flashing.

"Fuck," Callie muttered, waving for his attention. She saw him wave back. The left blinker went off. The right blinker turned on.

Once she disappeared around the corner, she went back inside the building. She double checked the door to make sure the lock had engaged. Fucking junkies would hit the clinic the moment they let their guard down.

The 20-ml syringes were kept in the kennel. They were rarely used. Holding one in her hand, all that Callie could think was that it was much bigger than she'd thought. She took it back with her to the breakroom. She uncapped the needle. She drew out the dose of pentobarbital from the vial. The plunger was almost all of the way out. When she put the cap back, the syringe from end to end was probably as big as a paperback novel.

Callie tucked the loaded syringe in her jacket pocket. It fit snugly into the corners.

She put her hand in her other pocket. Her fingers brushed up against the knife.

Cracked wooden handle. Bent blade. Callie had used it to cut Andrew's hot dog into pieces because, otherwise, he would try to shove the whole thing in his mouth and start to choke.

Where was Andrew now?

Sidney's car was parked outside like a welcome sign at a rest stop. Callie had stolen his favorite knife. She had ensured his wife wouldn't be able to pee straight for the next six weeks. She had found his VCR and his video tape behind the rack in the electronics closet. She had gouged his white leather couches and scraped long, angry lines into his pristine walls.

What was he waiting for?

Callie felt a heaviness in her eyelids. It was almost midnight. She was exhausted from today and tomorrow wasn't going to get any easier. Somehow, telling Dr. Jerry the truth had made her body accept the hard fact that her wicked ways were finally catching up with her. Everything hurt. Everything felt wrong.

She looked at her dope kit. She could shoot up now, try to

388

chase the high again, but she had a feeling that Andrew would show up the moment she started to nod. The giant syringe in her pocket wasn't meant for the medical examiner to find. It was meant to put down Andrew so that Maddy would be safe and Leigh could get on with her life.

The idea wasn't even a plan but, regardless, it was as foolish as it was dangerous. Dr. Jerry was right. Callie was too small and Andrew was too large and there was no way she would surprise him again because, this time, he would be expecting her to go batshit crazy.

She could've spent the next few minutes or hours trying to figure out a better way, a sneakier way, but Callie had never been known to look too far ahead, and the pins and rods in her neck made it impossible for her to look back. All she had on her side was a determination for this to be over. It might not turn out well in the end, but at least it would be the end.

Friday

19

The clock was just passing midnight by the time Leigh found herself squinting through the burglar bars lining the front windows of Dr. Jerry's darkened waiting room. She'd assumed that the old man was dead, but Reggie's surveillance photos of Callie had proved otherwise. The clinic's Facebook page showed recent photos of animals they'd treated. Leigh had recognized Callie's handiwork in the names. Cleocatra. Mewssolini. Meowma Cass. Binx, which was apparently the real name of Fucking Bitch, or Fitch for short.

Leave it to Callie to remember the cat from *Hocus Pocus*, a movie they had watched so many times that even Phil started quoting some of the lines. Leigh would've laughed if she hadn't been so frantic to locate her sister. The fact that Leigh hadn't talked to Callie in two days was usually a relief. Now, only the worst-case scenarios were running through her mind—an altercation with Andrew, a bad dose of dope, a phone call from the emergency room, a cop at the door.

Walter asked, "Are you sure she's here?"

"That was Dr. Jerry we passed down the road. She has to be here." Leigh tapped on the glass with her fingers. She was worried about the silver BMW convertible taking up two spaces in front of the building. They were not only in the 'hood, they were in Fulton County. The tag on the car was from DeKalb, which was where Andrew lived.

"Sweetheart, it's late." Walter pressed his hand to the small of her back. "We're meeting with the lawyer in seven hours. We might not be able to find Callie before then."

Leigh wanted to shake him, because he didn't understand. "We have to find her now, Walter. The minute Andrew can't get in touch with Reggie, he's going to know something's wrong."

"But he won't really know."

"He's a predator. He goes by instinct," Leigh told him. "Think about it. Reggie's gone, then Andrew finds out voir dire is postponed and I'm nowhere to be found. I promise you he'll either post all of the videos online or he'll show the original murder video to the cops, or—whatever he does, I can't let Callie be here for the blowback. We've got to get her out of town as quickly as possible."

"She's not going to leave town," Walter said. "You know that. This is her home."

Leigh wasn't going to give her sister a choice. Callie had to disappear. There was no arguing the point. She tapped harder on the glass.

Walter said, "Leigh."

She ignored him, walking farther down, cupping her hands to her eyes to help her see into the dark waiting room. Her heart was in her throat. Her fight or flight was spinning like a Ferris wheel. Leigh could only take her life in five-minute increments because if she let herself think past those few minutes, then everything would start to snowball and she would be staring down the fact that life as she knew it was about to be over.

She was frantic to protect her sister from the coming avalanche.

"Leigh," Walter tried again, and if she hadn't been so worried about her husband, she would've screamed at him to stop saying her fucking name.

They were both exhausted and shellshocked by what they had done to Reggie. Driving around aimlessly most of the night hadn't diminished their anxiety. They had coasted by Phil's, knocked on doors at Callie's cheap motel, roused clerks at other nearby motels, cruised past shooting galleries, called the booking desk at the police station, talked to nurses at five different emergency rooms. It was just like old times and it was still horrible and still emotionally draining and they still had not found her sister.

391

Leigh wasn't going to give up. She owed it to Callie to warn her about the tapes.

She owed it to Callie to finally tell her the truth.

"There." Walter pointed through the burglar bars just as the lights came on inside the waiting room. Callie was wearing jeans and a satin yellow jacket that Leigh recognized from middle school. Despite the heat, she had snapped it closed all the way up to her neck.

"Cal!" Leigh called through the glass.

Her tone didn't put any urgency in Callie's step as her sister slowly made her through the waiting room. Walter was right about the tan. Callie's skin was almost golden. But the sickliness was still there, the painful thinness, the hollowed-out look to her eyes.

The harsh lights put Callie's deterioration on full display when she finally reached the door. Her movements were labored. Her expression was blank. She was breathing through her mouth. No matter what, Callie always looked pleased to see Leigh, even when it was over a metal table at the county jail. Now, she looked wary. Her eyes darted around the parking lot as she slipped a key into the lock.

The glass door swung back. Another key opened the security gate. Up close, Leigh could see faded make-up on her sister's face. Smeared eyeliner. Splotchy eyeshadow. Callie's lips were stained dark pink. Decades had passed since Leigh had seen her sister with anything more than cat whiskers drawn in straight lines across her cheeks.

Callie spoke to Walter first. "Long time, friend."

Walter said, "Good to see you, friend."

Leigh couldn't stomach their Chip and Dale routine right now. She asked Callie, "Are you okay?"

Callie gave a Callie response. "Is anyone ever really okay?"

Leigh nodded toward the BMW. "Whose car is that?"

"It's been parked there all night," Callie said, which wasn't technically an answer.

Leigh opened her mouth to demand more details, but then she realized there was no point. The car didn't matter. She had come here to talk to her sister. She had rehearsed her speech throughout the long, endless night. All that she needed from

Callie was time, one of the very few resources that Callie always had in abundance.

"I'll leave you to it," Walter said, as if taking a cue. "It's good to see you, Callie."

Callie returned a salute. "Don't be a stranger."

Leigh didn't wait for an invitation. She went inside the building, pulled the gate closed. The lobby hadn't changed in decades. Even the smell was familiar—wet dog with a tinge of bleach because Callie would get on her hands and knees to scrub the floor if it meant Dr. Jerry wouldn't have to.

"Harleigh," Callie said. "What's going on? Why are you here?"

Leigh didn't answer. She turned to check on Walter. His shadow was unmoving in the passenger seat of her Audi. He was looking down at his hands. She had watched him flex his fingers for almost a full hour before she'd made him stop. And then he had picked at the open wounds on his knuckles until blood had roped down his hands and onto the seat. It was like he wanted a permanent reminder of the violence he had visited upon Reggie Paltz. Leigh kept trying to get him to talk about it, but Walter wouldn't talk. For the first time in their marriage, he was unreadable to her. Another life she had destroyed.

Leigh turned away, telling Callie, "Let's go to the back."

Callie didn't ask why they couldn't sit in waiting room chairs. Instead, she led Leigh down the hallway to Dr. Jerry's office. Like the other spaces, nothing had changed. The funny light with a tubby chihuahua as the base. The faded watercolors on the wall showing animals wearing Regency clothing. Even the old green and white tartan couch was the same. The only difference was Callie. She looked haggard. It was as if life had finally caught up with her.

Leigh knew that she was going to make it worse.

"Okay." Callie leaned against the desk. "Tell me."

For once, Leigh didn't censor the thoughts running through her head. "Walter and I kidnapped Andrew's investigator, Reggie Paltz."

"Huh," was all that Callie offered.

"He had the fail-safe," Leigh continued. "But I'm still going to turn myself in, and I felt I owed it to you to tell you first because you're on those tapes, too."

Callie tucked her hands into her jacket pockets. "I have questions."

"It doesn't matter. I've made up my mind. This is what I have to do to keep Maddy safe. To keep other people safe, because I don't know what else he's going to do." Leigh had to stop to swallow down the panic bubbling up her throat. "I should've done this the moment Andrew and Linda showed up in Bradley's office. I should've confessed to all of them, then Ruby would still be alive and Maddy wouldn't be on the lam and—"

"Harleigh, slow your roll," Callie said. "The last time we talked, I was having a panic attack in an attic, and now you're telling me there's a fail-safe and you're turning yourself in and somebody named Ruby is dead and something's wrong with Maddy?"

Leigh realized she was worse than her daughter trying to rush out a story. "I'm sorry. Maddy is fine. She's safe. Walter just talked to her on the phone."

"Why did Walter talk to her? Why didn't you?"

"Because . . ." Leigh struggled to organize her thoughts. The decision to turn herself in had brought a certain level of peace. But now that she was standing in front of her sister, now that the time had finally come to tell Callie everything, Leigh kept finding reasons not to.

She explained, "Ruby Heyer is—was—a mom-friend of mine. She was murdered Wednesday night. I don't know if Andrew killed her himself or if he had someone else do it, but I know without a doubt that he was involved."

Callie didn't react to the information. Instead, she asked, "And the fail-safe?"

"Reggie had two servers in his office. Andrew asked him to store backups of Buddy's video tapes as a fail-safe. If anything happened to Andrew, Reggie was supposed to release them. Walter and I stole the servers. His laptop had the encryption key to get them open. We found fourteen video files, plus the murder video."

All of the color drained from Callie's face. This was her nightmare come to life. "Did you watch them? Did Walter—"

"No," Leigh lied. She had made Walter leave the room because she needed to know what they were dealing with. The brief glimpses of the Callie videos were enough to make her physically ill. "The file names gave us what we needed—your name, then a number, one to fourteen. The murder video had your name and mine. It was easy to figure out. We didn't have to watch them to know."

Callie chewed her lip. She was as unreadable as Walter. "What else?"

"Andrew hired Reggie to watch you," Leigh said. "He followed you on the bus to the library, to Phil's, to here. I saw his logs, his photos. He knew everything that you were doing, and he told Andrew."

Callie didn't seem surprised, but a bead of sweat rolled down the side of her face. The room was too hot for the jacket. She had buttoned it up to her neck.

Leigh asked, "Have you been crying?"

Callie didn't answer. "Are you sure Maddy is safe?"

"Walter's mother took her on a road trip. She's confused, but—"

Leigh's throat worked. She was losing her nerve. Callie clearly wasn't well. This was the wrong time. Leigh should wait, but waiting had only made it worse. The passage of time had turned her secret into a lie and her lie into a betrayal.

She said, "Cal, none of this matters. Andrew still has the original video tapes. But it's not only about the tapes. As long as he's free, you, me, Walter, Maddy—none of us is safe. Andrew knows where we are. And he's going to keep hurting, possibly killing, more women. The only way to stop him is to turn myself in. Once I'm in custody, I'll turn state's evidence and take Andrew down with me."

Callie waited a beat before speaking. "That's your plan, to sacrifice yourself?"

"It's not a sacrifice, Callie. I murdered Buddy. I broke the law."

"*We* murdered Buddy. *We* broke the law."

"There's no *we*, Cal. You defended yourself. I killed him." Leigh had watched the murder video from beginning to end. She had seen Callie strike out at Buddy in fear. She had seen herself deliberately murder the man. "There's something else. Something I never told you. I want you to hear it from me, because it will come out during the trial."

Callie ran her tongue along her teeth. She had always known

395

when Leigh was going to tell her something that she did not want to hear. Normally, she found a way to throw Leigh off, and now was no different. "I stalked Sidney at AA, then I got her stoned, and we went to Andrew's house, and she fucked me, and then there was a fight, but I kneed her really hard between the legs, and I think the original tapes are inside the safe in his closet."

Leigh felt her stomach drop like a stone. "You what?"

"I stole this, too." Callie pulled a knife out of her jacket pocket.

Leigh blinked, disbelieving what was right in front of her, though she could describe the knife from memory—*Cracked wooden handle. Bent blade. Sharp, serrated teeth.*

Callie shoved the knife back into her pocket. "I told Sidney to tell Andrew to find me if he wants his knife back."

Leigh sank down onto the couch before her legs gave out.

"It was in the kitchen drawer," Callie said. "Sidney used it to cut limes for our margaritas."

Leigh felt like she was absorbing the story sideways. "She fucked you, or she fucked *with* you?"

"Technically, both?" Callie shrugged. "Sidney knows about the tapes, is the point I am making. She didn't actually come out and tell me, but she let me know the originals are locked inside the safe in Andrew's closet. And she knows that the knife is important. That I used to use it when Andrew was little."

Leigh shook her head, trying to make sense of what she had heard. Stoned, fucked, fight, kicked, safe. In the end, none of it was worse than what she'd let happen to Reggie Paltz. "Jesus Christ, every day, we're both more and more like Phil."

Callie sat down on the couch. She clearly wasn't finished dropping bombs. "That's Sidney's BMW outside."

Grand theft auto.

Callie said, "I thought you'd be Andrew when you knocked on the door. He hasn't come for me. I don't know why."

Leigh looked up at the ceiling. Her brain couldn't absorb all of this at once. "You incapacitated his girlfriend. I chased off his private investigator. He has to be furious."

Callie asked, "Is Walter okay?"

"No, I don't think so." Leigh turned her head so that she could look at Callie. "I'm going to have to tell Maddy everything."

396

"You can't tell her about me," Callie insisted. "I don't want that, Leigh. I'm the soil. I grew her for you and Walter. She was never mine."

"Maddy will be okay," Leigh said, but she knew in her heart that none of them would come out of this unscathed. "You should've seen her when we first went into lockdown. All of my friends were complaining about their kids, but Maddy was so good, Cal. She had every right to throw a fit or do something stupid or make our lives miserable. I asked her about it, and she said she felt bad for the kids who had it worse."

As usual, Callie found something else to focus on. Her eyes were glued to the Regency paintings on the wall as if they were the most important thing in the room. "Her father was a good guy. I think you would've liked him."

Leigh said nothing. Callie had never mentioned Maddy's biological father before and neither Walter nor Leigh had ever had the courage to ask.

"He took away some of my loneliness. He never yelled or raised his hand to me. He never tried to push me into doing shit so we could score." Callie didn't have to tell Leigh what women usually got pushed into doing. "He was a lot like Walter, if Walter was a heroin addict with one nipple."

Leigh laughed out loud. And then tears sprang into her eyes.

"His name was Larry. I never got his last name, or maybe I did and I forgot it." Callie let out a long, slow breath. "He OD'd in the Dunkin' Donuts off Ponce de Leon. You can probably find the police report if you want his name. We were shooting up together in the bathroom. I was stoned, but I could hear the cops coming, so I just left him there because I didn't want to get arrested."

"He cared about you," Leigh said, because she knew how impossible it was for anyone to *not* care about her sister. "He wouldn't have wanted you to get arrested."

Callie nodded, but she said, "I think he would've wanted me to stick around long enough to give him CPR so he didn't die."

Leigh kept her head turned so she could study her sister's sharp features. Callie had always been pretty. She had none of the guarded, bitchy look that plagued Leigh. All her sister had ever wanted was kindness. That she had found it in such short supply was not Callie's fault.

"Okay," Callie finally said. "Tell me."

Leigh wasn't going to set this up slowly because there was no way to soften the hard truth. "Buddy tried it with me first."

Callie stiffened, but she said nothing.

Leigh said, "The first night I started babysitting Andrew, Buddy drove me home. He *made me* let him drive me home. And then he pulled over in front of the Deguils' house, and he molested me."

Callie still did not respond, but Leigh saw her start to rub her arm the way she always did when she was upset.

"It only happened once," Leigh said. "When he tried it again, I said no, and that was it. He never tried anything else."

Callie closed her eyes. Tears seeped out at the corners. Leigh wanted nothing more than to hold her, to soothe her, to make everything okay, but she was the cause of her sister's pain. She had no right to wound her, then offer solace.

Leigh pushed herself to continue. "Afterward, I forgot about it. I don't know how or why, but it just went out of my mind. And I didn't warn you. I told you to go work for him. I put you right in his path."

Callie sucked in her bottom lip. She was crying now, big mournful tears rolling down her face.

Leigh felt her heart breaking into pieces. "I could tell you I'm sorry, but what does that even mean?"

Callie said nothing.

"How does it even make sense that I forgot, that I let you work for them, that I ignored everything when you started to change? Because I did notice that you'd changed, Callie. I saw it happen and I never put it together." Leigh had to stop for a breath. "I only really remembered the details when I told Walter last night. It all came flooding back. The cigars and cheap whiskey and the song playing on the radio. It was there all along, but I guess I just buried it."

Callie stuttered out a breath. Her head started to shake in a tight, constricted arc on her frozen spine.

Leigh said, "Cal, please. Tell me what you're thinking. If you're mad or you hate me or you never want to—"

"What song was playing?"

Leigh was thrown by the question. She had been expecting recriminations, not trivia.

Callie shifted her body on the couch so that she could look at Leigh. "What song was on the radio?"

"Hall & Oates," Leigh said. "'Kiss on My List.'"

"Huh," Callie said, as if Leigh had made an interesting point.

"I'm sorry," Leigh said, knowing that the apology was meaningless but unable to stop herself. "I'm so sorry I let this happen to you."

"Did you?" Callie asked.

Leigh swallowed. She didn't have an answer.

"I forgot, too." Callie waited a moment, as if she wanted to give the words room to breathe. "I didn't forget all of it, but most of it. The bad parts, at least. I forgot those, too."

Leigh was still without words. All of these years, she'd thought that the heroin was because Callie had remembered everything.

"He was a pedophile." Callie spoke quietly, still testing the weight of her words. "We were kids. We were pliable. That's what he wanted—a child he could exploit. It didn't matter which one of us he got to first. What mattered to him was which one of us he could make come back for more."

Leigh swallowed so hard again that her throat hurt. Her logical mind told her that Callie was right. Her heart still told her that she had failed to protect her baby sister.

"I wonder who else he did it to?" Callie asked. "You know we weren't the only ones."

Leigh was aghast. She had never considered there were other victims, but of course there were other victims. "I don't—I don't know."

"Maybe Minnie what's-her-name?" Callie said. "She babysat for Andrew when you were in juvie. Do you remember that?"

Leigh didn't, but she could clearly recall Linda's exasperation over the number of previous sitters who had abandoned her son for seemingly no reason.

"He convinced you that you were special." Callie wiped her nose on her sleeve. "That's what Buddy did. He made it seem like you were the only one. That he was a normal guy until you came along, and now he was in love with you because you were special."

Leigh pressed together her lips. Buddy had not made her feel special. He had made her feel dirty and ashamed. "I should've warned you."

"No." Callie's tone was as firm as it had ever been. "Listen to me, Harleigh. What happened is what happened. We were both his victims. We both forgot how bad it was because that was the only way we could survive."

"It wasn't—" Leigh stopped herself, because there was no counter-argument. They had both been children. They had both been victims. All she could do was go back to where she started. "I'm sorry."

"You can't be sorry for something that you couldn't control. Don't you get that?"

Leigh shook her head, but part of her desperately wanted to believe what Callie was saying was true.

"I want you to hear me," Callie said. "If this is the guilt you've been carrying around for your entire adult life, then set it the fuck down, because it doesn't belong to you. It belongs to him."

Leigh was so used to crying that she didn't notice her own tears. "I'm so sorry."

"For what?" Callie demanded. "It's not your fault. It was never your fault."

The twist on her familiar mantra broke something inside of Leigh. She put her head in her hands. She started to sob so hard that she couldn't hold herself up.

Callie wrapped her arms around Leigh, taking some of the burden. Her lips pressed into the top of Leigh's head. Callie had never held her before. Usually, it was the other way around. Usually, it was Leigh providing the comfort, because Walter was right. From the beginning, Phil had never been their mother. It was only Leigh and Callie, back then, and it was only Leigh and Callie right now.

"It's okay," Callie said, kissing the top of her head the same way she did with her cat. "We're going to get through this, all right?"

Leigh sat back up. Her nose was running. Her eyes stung with tears.

Callie got up from the couch. She found a tissue pack in Dr. Jerry's desk. She took a few for herself, then passed the rest to Leigh. "What's next?"

Leigh blew her nose. "What do you mean?"

"The plan," Callie said. "You always have a plan."

"It's Walter's plan," Leigh said. "He's taking care of everything."

Callie sat back down. "Walter's always been tougher than he looks."

Leigh wasn't so sure that was a good thing. She found a fresh tissue and wiped under her eyes. "I'm going to FaceTime with Maddy in a few hours. I wanted to do it in person, but we can't risk Andrew somehow following us to Maddy's location."

"Through the satellites, you mean?"

"Yes." Leigh was surprised Callie knew even that much about tracking devices. "Walter already had his mother stop at a gas station. They checked under the RV to make sure there weren't any trackers. I found one on my car, but I got rid of it."

Callie said, "I thought Andrew would use the GPS in Sidney's BMW to find me."

"You wanted him to find you?"

"I told you—I told Sidney to tell Andrew I had the knife if he wants it back."

Leigh didn't press her on the suicide mission. The burn-the-motherfucker-down trait was a dominant gene in their family. "We've scheduled a meeting with my lawyer at seven. He's a friend of Walter's. I've already talked to him a little over the phone. He's aggressive, which is what I need."

"Can he get you out of this?"

"There's no getting me out of this," Leigh said. "We'll meet with the district attorney at noon tomorrow. We'll make a proffer. It's sometimes called 'queen for a day.' I'll be able to tell them the truth, but nothing I say can be used against me. Hopefully, I can provide evidence against Andrew that will put him away."

"Don't you have privilege or something?"

"It doesn't matter. I'm never going to practice law again." Leigh felt the weight of her words threatening to bog her down. She pushed through, saying, "Technically, I can break privilege if I think my client is committing crimes or if he becomes a threat to other people. Andrew definitely meets both criteria."

"What will happen to you?"

"I'll go to prison," Leigh said, because even the aggressive lawyer had agreed that there was no way around serving time. "If I'm lucky, it will be five to seven years, which means four with good behavior."

"That seems harsh."

"It's the video, Cal. Andrew is going to release it. I can't stop that." Leigh wiped her nose. "Once it's out there, once people see what I did, it'll become too political. The DA will be expected to do a full court press."

"But what about what happened?" Callie asked. "What Buddy did to me. What he did to you. Doesn't that matter?"

"Who knows?" Leigh said, but she had been in enough courtrooms to understand that prosecutors and judges cared more about optics than justice. "I'm going to prepare myself for the worst, and if the worst doesn't happen, then I'm luckier than most."

"Will they let you out on parole?"

"I can't answer that, Callie." Leigh needed her to see the bigger picture. "It's not just the murder video that's going to be out there. It's the rest. The fourteen videos that Buddy made of the two of you together."

Callie's response wasn't the one she'd expected. "Do you think Sidney is in on it?"

Leigh felt a giant lightbulb turning on inside of her head, because Sidney being in on it made obvious sense.

Andrew had a well-documented alibi for Ruby Heyer's murder. If Reggie's surveillance logs were to be believed, he'd been parked outside of Phil's house the night of the attack. That left one person who could commit the crime. Andrew had left the clue in plain sight. There were no wedding photos of Sidney on his phone. He'd hinted at the fact that she hadn't arrived until it was time to walk down the aisle. She'd had plenty of time to murder Ruby Heyer, then slip into her wedding gown and be ready for the ceremony at eight.

Leigh told Callie, "Ruby left her husband for another man.

She was staying at a hotel. Reggie admitted to me that he told Andrew her location. Andrew's wedding photos give him a solid alibi, which leaves Sidney."

"Are you sure?"

"I'm sure," Leigh said. "The way that Ruby was killed— Andrew would've had to tell Sidney the details. There's no other way that she would've known what to do. How to do it. And it was clear that Sidney enjoyed it."

"She really enjoyed fucking with me. Both ways, if I'm being honest," Callie said. "Which means we're not just dealing with one psycho. We're dealing with two."

Leigh nodded, but none of this changed what needed to happen right now. "I've got ten thousand dollars in the car. Walter and I want you to leave town. You can't be here for this. I mean it. We'll drive you back to Phil's. You can pack up Binx. We'll take you to the bus stop. I can't do this if I know you're not safe."

Callie asked, "Could Maddy watch him instead?"

"Of course. She would love that." Leigh tried not to read too much into the request. She wanted nothing more than for her sister to know her daughter. "Walter will take him home tonight, okay? He'll be waiting for Maddy when she gets back."

Callie chewed her lip. "You should know he keeps all of his money in Bitcoin."

"Fucking taxes."

Callie smiled.

Leigh smiled back.

She offered, "I could always send you back to rehab."

"I said no, no no."

Leigh laughed at the Amy Winehouse impersonation. She would have to tell Walter that Callie had made a pop-culture reference that took place after 2003.

Callie said, "I guess we should go."

Leigh stood up. She reached for Callie's hand to help her up from the couch. Her sister didn't let go as they left the office. Their shoulders bumped in the narrow hall. Callie still didn't let go when they reached the waiting room. They used to walk to school like this. Even when they were older and it looked strange, Callie had always held on tight to Leigh's hand.

"BMW is still here." Callie sounded disappointed to find the car parked outside.

"Andrew's a control freak," Leigh said. "He's making us wait because he knows it's killing us."

"Then take away his control," Callie said. "Let's drive over to his house right now and get the tapes."

"No," Leigh said. She had already gone down this road with Walter. "We're not criminals. We don't know how to break into houses and threaten people and crack safes."

"Speak for yourself." Callie pushed open the door.

Leigh felt her heart trip.

Walter was not inside the Audi.

She looked left, then right.

Callie was doing the same. She called, "Walter?"

They both listened in the silence.

"Walter?" Callie tried again.

This time, Leigh didn't wait for a response. She took off. Her heels stabbed into the broken concrete as she jogged past the barbershop. She rounded the corner. Picnic table. Empty beer cans. Piles of trash. Behind the building showed more of the same. She took off again, making a full loop around to the front. She didn't stop until she saw Callie leaning past the open door of the Audi.

Callie stood back up. She was holding a torn piece of paper in her hand.

"No . . ." Leigh whispered, her feet moving again, arms pumping, as she ran toward her car. She grabbed the note out of Callie's hand. Her eyes wouldn't focus. Light blue lines. Dark red blood seeping in from the torn corner. One sentence scribbled across the middle.

Andrew's handwriting hadn't changed since he'd doodled in Leigh's textbooks. Back then, he'd drawn dinosaurs and motorcycles with thought bubbles filled with nonsensical things. Now, he had written a threat that mirrored the one Callie had passed on through Sidney.

If you want your husband back, come and get him.

20

Callie stepped back as Leigh's vomit splattered at their feet. Her sister was doubled over, wracked by terror. An almost animal wail came out of her mouth.

Callie looked around the parking lot. The BMW was still there. The road was dark, absent any cars. Andrew had come and gone.

"Oh, God!" Leigh dropped to her knees. Her head was in her hands. "What have I done?"

Andrew's note had fluttered to the ground. Instead of trying to comfort Leigh, Callie leaned down to pick it up. His sloppy handwriting was as familiar to Callie as her own.

"Callie!" Leigh was keening, and then her head was pressing against the asphalt. Another horrible wail came out of her mouth. "What am I going to do?"

Callie felt as removed from Leigh's agony as she'd been the last time her sister had been bowled over by despair. They were in Linda and Buddy Waleski's master bedroom. Leigh had come to save Callie and ended up ruining her life.

Again.

The night they had killed and butchered Buddy Waleski was not the first or last time that Callie had brought her sister to her knees. It went as far back as their early childhood. Callie had come home whining about the girl who'd teased her on the playground. Leigh had ended up in juvie for nearly scalping the child with a broken piece of glass.

Leigh's second stint in juvie was Callie's fault, too. Leigh's sleazy boss had said something about the way Callie's nipples

405

pressed against her T-shirt. That night, Leigh had been arrested for slashing his tires.

There were more examples, both large and small, but they ranged from Leigh risking her career by paying off a junkie to take the fall for Callie's crimes to Leigh losing her husband to a psychopath Callie had openly taunted.

She took another long look at Sidney's BMW. Andrew hadn't taken the car because he had been patiently waiting for better leverage. It was sheer coincidence that Walter had been made available instead of Maddy.

"No!" Leigh sobbed. "I can't lose him. I can't."

Callie wadded up the note into a ball inside of her fist. Her knee cracked as she knelt down beside her sister. She pressed her palm to Leigh's back. She let the agony roll unabated because there was no other choice. After a lifetime of Callie only looking at what was directly in front of her, she had suddenly found herself charmed with the ability to look ahead.

"What are we going to do?" Leigh cried. "Oh, God, Callie. What are we going to do?"

"What we should've done before." Callie pulled at Leigh's shoulders, making her sit up. This was how it worked. Only one of them could fall apart at a time. "Harleigh, get your shit together. You can freak out later when Walter is okay."

Leigh wiped her mouth with the back of her arm. She was trembling. "I can't lose him, Callie. I can't."

"You're not going to lose anyone," Callie said. "We're going to Andrew's house right now and we're going to end this."

"What?" Leigh started shaking her head. "We can't just—"

"Listen to me." Callie tightened her hands around Leigh's shoulders. "We'll go to Andrew's. We'll do what we have to do to get Walter back. We'll find a way to open that safe. We'll get the tapes and we'll leave."

"I . . ." Leigh seemed to regain some of her usual resolve. When lightning struck, she was always going to stand in Callie's way. "I can't take you into that. I won't."

"You don't have a choice." Callie knew how to ramp her panic back up. "Andrew has Walter. How long before he goes after Maddy?"

Leigh looked horrified. "He—I don't—"

"Come on." Callie made her stand. She stepped around the vomit. "We can figure out what we're going to do on the way."

"No." Leigh was clearly struggling to regain her composure. She grabbed Callie's hand, spun her around. "You can't go with me."

"This isn't a discussion."

"You're right," Leigh said. "I have to do this alone, Cal. You know that."

Callie chewed her lip. It was a testament to Leigh's distress that she wasn't seeing through this. "You can't do this on your own. He'll have a gun or—"

"I have a gun." Leigh reached into her car. She found her purse. She took out the Glock she'd brandished at Trap and Diego outside the motel. "I'll shoot him if I have to."

Callie had no doubt that she meant it. "And I'm supposed to wait around here while you're risking your life?"

"Take the money." Leigh reached into her purse, this time to retrieve an envelope thick with cash. "You need to get out of town right now. I can't fix this unless I know you're safe."

"How are you going to fix it?"

Leigh had a crazy look in her eyes. She was going to fix it by throwing more fuel onto the fire. "I need you to be safe."

"I need you to be safe, too," Callie argued. "I'm not leaving you."

"You're right. You're not leaving me. I'm leaving you." Leigh slapped the money into Callie's hand. "This is between me and Andrew. You don't have anything to do with it."

"You're not a criminal," Callie said, reminding her sister of her own words. "You don't know how to break into houses and threaten people and crack safes."

"I'll figure it out." Leigh sounded determined. There was no arguing with her when she got this way. "Promise me you'll be okay so that I can do what I should've done four days ago."

"Turn yourself in?" Callie forced out a laugh. "Leigh, do you really think going to the cops right now will stop Andrew from doing what he's going to do?"

"There's only one way to stop him," Leigh said. "I'm going to kill that twisted motherfucker the same way I killed his father."

407

Callie watched Leigh walk around to the driver's side of the car. In all of their years together, she had never seen her sister so relentlessly driven toward one thing. "Harleigh?"

Leigh turned. Her mouth was set. She was clearly expecting an argument.

Callie said, "What you told me about Buddy. There's nothing to forgive. But if you need to hear it, I forgive you."

Leigh's throat worked. She pulled herself back from the blinding rage for just a second before slipping back in. "I have to go."

"I love you," Callie said. "There has never been a moment in my life when I didn't love you."

Leigh's tears flowed unchecked. She tried to speak but, in the end, she could only nod her head. Callie heard the words anyway.

I love you, too.

The car door closed. The engine grumbled awake. Leigh swerved out of the parking space. Callie watched the taillights brighten as she slowed for the turn. Her eyes stayed on her sister's fancy car until it disappeared into the vacant intersection at the end of the street.

Callie could've stood there all night like a dog waiting for its best friend to come back, but she didn't have time. She thumbed through the fat stack of hundreds in the envelope as she walked back into the clinic. She put the money in Dr. Jerry's lockbox. She thought about what she was going to do next. The giant loaded syringe was still in her right jacket pocket. She packed up her dope kit and shoved it into the left.

She found Sidney's keys in her backpack. Callie would give the BMW one final spin.

Leigh's panic had made her vulnerable, the same way it always had. Callie had used that knowledge to get her sister out of the way. Andrew hadn't taken Walter to his sleek, serial killer murder mansion. There was only one place this would end—the place where it had all started.

The mustard-colored house on Canyon Road.

Callie was sweating inside of the yellow satin rainbow jacket, but she kept it snapped up all the way to her neck as she walked down the street. Phil had already peeled out of the driveway in

Sidney's BMW. This was the second time in her life that Callie had given her mother a stolen car to get rid of.

The first time was when she'd handed off Buddy's Corvette. Callie's feet had barely reached the pedals. She'd had to sit so close to the steering wheel that it stabbed into her ribs. Hall & Oates was playing softly through the car's speakers when she'd careened to a stop in front of Phil's. The *Voices* CD was Buddy's favorite. He loved "You Make My Dreams" and "Everytime You Go Away" and especially "Kiss on My List," which he had sung along to in a funny falsetto.

Buddy had played the song for Callie the first night he'd driven her home from babysitting Andrew. She had wanted to walk, but he'd insisted. She hadn't wanted to drink the rum and Coke he'd put in front of her, but he'd insisted. And then he had pulled over in front of the Deguils' house, halfway between his place and Phil's. And then he had put his hand on her knee, and then on her thigh, and then his fingers were inside of her.

Jesus you're like a baby your skin is so soft I can feel the peach fuzz.

Back in Dr. Jerry's office, Callie's initial response to Leigh's confession had been a blinding jealousy. And then she had felt sad. And then she had felt so incredibly stupid. Buddy hadn't just done the same thing with Leigh. He had done the *exact same thing* with Leigh.

Callie took a deep breath. She held tight to the knife in her pocket as she walked by the Deguils' house. The loaded 20-ml syringe pressed into the back of her hand. She had torn the top part of the pocket to make sure it fit snugly into the lining.

Her eyes traveled upwards. The moon was hanging low in the sky. She had no idea what time it was, but she estimated Leigh was halfway to Andrew's house by now. Callie could only hope that her sister's panic hadn't yet ebbed away. Leigh was impetuous, but she had the same animal cunning as Callie. Her gut would tell her that something was wrong. Eventually, her brain would figure out what.

Callie had given in too easily. She had put the idea of going to Andrew's house in Leigh's head. Leigh had sped away without thinking and, now that she was thinking, she would realize that she needed to turn around.

Waiting for that eventuality was a pointless use of Callie's time. Leigh was going to do what Leigh was going to do. What Callie had to focus on right now was Andrew.

There was always a moment in a crime novel where the detective said something pithy about how the killer wanted to get caught. Andrew Tenant did not want to get caught. He kept making the game more dangerous because he was addicted to the adrenaline rush that came from taking big risks. Callie, Leigh and Walter had done him a favor by going after Sidney and kidnapping Reggie Paltz. Leigh believed that Andrew was panicking because he'd lost control. Callie knew that he was chasing the high the same way she did with heroin. There was no drug that was more addictive than the ones your body could make on its own.

As with opioids, there was an actual science that explained adrenaline junkies. High-risk behaviors rewarded the body by flooding the system with an intense surge of adrenaline. Adrenergic receptors, like their country cousin mus, loved the overly aggressive stimulation, which fell along the same pathways as the fight-or-flight instinct. Most people hated that perilous, exposed sensation, but adrenaline junkies lived for it. It was no coincidence that adrenaline's AKA was epinephrine, a hormone valued by body builders and recreational users alike. An adrenaline rush could make you feel like a god. Your heart raced, your muscles got stronger, your focus sharpened, you felt no pain, and you could out-fuck a rabbit.

Like any addict, Andrew needed more and more of the drug to get high. That was why he had raped a woman who could recognize the sound of his voice. That was why Leigh's mom-friend had been brutally murdered. It was also why Andrew had kidnapped Walter. The bigger the risk, the higher the reward.

Callie let her lips part so that she could take in a deep breath. She could see the mustard-yellow siding from twenty yards away. The overgrown yard still had the FOR SALE BY OWNER sign out front. As she got closer, she saw that the neighborhood graffiti artists had accepted the challenge. A spurting penis covered the phone number, whisker-like hairs jutting from the balls.

A black Mercedes was parked by the mailbox. Dealer tags.

Tenant Automotive Group. Another calculated risk on Andrew's part. The house was still boarded up, so the 'hood would assume a drug dealer was stocking up one of his shooting galleries. Or a police cruiser would drive by and wonder what was going on.

Callie looked inside the car for Walter. The seats were empty. The car was spotless but for a bottle of water in one of the cupholders. She pressed her hand to the hood. The engine was cool. She thought about checking the trunk, but the doors were locked.

She studied the house before steeling herself for the walk up the driveway. Nothing looked amiss, but everything felt wrong. The closer she got to the house, the more the panic threatened to take over. Her legs felt shaky as she stepped around the oil stain where Buddy used to park his Corvette. The carport was dark, shadows overlapping shadows inside. Callie's Doc Martens crunched against the concrete. She looked down. Someone had laid down a ghetto burglar alarm, scattering shards of broken glass along the carport entrance.

"You can stop there," Sidney said.

Callie couldn't see her, but she gathered that Sidney was standing near the kitchen door. She stepped over the glass. Then she took another step.

Click-clack.

Callie recognized the distinctive sound of a slide being pulled back on a nine-millimeter handgun.

She told the woman, "It would be more threatening if I could actually see the gun."

Sidney stepped out of the shadows. She held the weapon like an amateur, her finger clutching the trigger, the gun turned sideways like she was in a gangster movie. "How about now, *Max*?"

Callie had almost forgotten her alias, but she had not forgotten that Sidney had probably murdered Leigh's friend. "I'm surprised you can walk."

Sidney took another step forward to prove that she could. In the light from the street, Callie could see that the professional attire was gone. Leather pants. Tight leather vest. No shirt. Black mascara. Black eyeliner. Blood-red lips. She saw Callie taking in the change. "Like what you see?"

411

"Very much," Callie said. "If you'd looked this good before, I probably would've fucked you back."

Sidney grinned. "I felt bad for not letting you finish."

Callie took another step forward. She was close enough to smell Sidney's musky perfume. "We could always go again."

Sidney kept grinning. Callie recognized a fellow junkie. Sidney was just as addicted to the rush as her sick fuck of a husband.

"Hey," Callie said. "How about a quickie in the trunk of the car?"

The grin intensified. "Andrew called first dibs."

"More like sloppy seconds." Callie felt the muzzle of the gun pressing into her chest. She glanced down. "That's a nice toy."

"I think so," Sidney said. "Andy bought it for me."

"Did he show you where the safety is?"

Sidney turned the gun over, looking for the button.

Callie did what she should've done before.

She pushed the gun out of the way.

She took the knife out of her pocket and she stabbed Sidney in the stomach five times.

"Oh." Sidney's mouth opened in surprise. Her breath smelled like cherries.

Hot blood soaked Callie's hand as she twisted the blade in deeper. The vibration of the serrated teeth scratching against bone went up her arm. Callie's mouth was so close to Sidney's that their lips brushed. She told the woman, "You should've let me finish."

The knife came out with a sucking sound.

Sidney stumbled forward. The gun clattered to the ground. Blood spattered against the smooth concrete. Her feet got caught up at the ankles. She fell in slow motion, body straight, hands holding her guts inside. There was a sickening crunch as her face met the shards of broken glass. Bright red blood poured around her torso like a snow angel's wings.

Callie looked into the empty street. No one was watching. Sidney's body had fallen mostly inside the darkness of the carport. Anyone who got curious would have to walk up the driveway to see her.

The knife went back into Callie's jacket pocket. She scooped up the gun as she walked deeper into the carport. Her thumb

412

toggled off the safety. She located the kitchen door by memory. Her eyes did not adjust until she'd lifted her leg and climbed through the opening Leigh had made two nights ago.

The scent of meth still permeated the air, but there was a smoky undertone she couldn't place. Callie was suddenly glad that Leigh had dragged her into this hellhole before. The memories didn't slap her in the face like they had the first time. She didn't see phantom outlines of the table and chairs, the blender, the toaster. She saw a squalid shooting gallery where souls came to die.

"Sid?" Andrew called.

Callie followed the sound of his voice into the living room.

Andrew was standing behind the bar. A large bottle of tequila and two shot glasses were in front of him. The gun in his hand was identical to the one Callie held in hers. She could see this detail in the otherwise dark and vacant house because candles were everywhere. Small ones, big ones. Lining the bar top, the floor, the ledge of the grimy windows. Light flickered up the walls like demonic tongues. Puffs of smoke cloistered around the ceiling.

"Calliope." He placed the gun down on the bar. The candlelight brought a garish glow to the scratch down the side of his face. Her teeth marks had turned black on his neck. "Nice of you to show up."

She looked around the room. Same soiled mattresses. Same disgusting carpet. Same feeling of hopelessness. "Where's Walter?"

"Where's Harleigh?"

"Probably burning down your ugly McMansion."

Andrew's hands rested flat on the bar. The gun was as close as the bottle of tequila. "Walter's in the hall."

Callie walked sideways, keeping the gun pointed in his direction. Walter was flat on his back. No visible wounds but a busted lip. His eyes were closed. His mouth gaped open. He wasn't tied up, but he wasn't moving, either. Callie pressed her fingers to the side of his neck. She felt a steady pulse.

She asked Andrew, "What did you do to him?"

"He'll live." Andrew picked up the tequila bottle. He twisted off the cap. His knuckles were hairy, but there was no grime under his fingernails. Buddy's heavy gold watch hung loose around his narrow wrist.

413

Pour me one, baby doll.

Callie blinked, because the words were Buddy's, but she had heard them in her own voice.

"Join me?" Andrew filled the two shot glasses.

Callie kept the gun out front as she walked toward the bar.

Instead of the fancy stuff he kept at home, Andrew had brought Jose Cuervo, the Walmart of shitfacing booze. The same brand that Callie had started drinking when Buddy had introduced her to the pleasures of alcohol.

She tasted blood from biting her lip. Buddy hadn't introduced her to any pleasures. He had forced her to drink so that her body would relax and she would stop crying.

Callie glanced back in the hallway. Walter still wasn't moving. Andrew said, "I roofied him. He won't bother us."

Callie had not forgotten that Andrew favored Rohypnol. She told him, "Your father liked it when his victims were passed out and helpless, too."

Andrew's jaw tensed. He slid one of the glasses across the bar. "Let's not delve into revisionist history."

Callie stared at the white liquid. Rohypnol was colorless and tasteless. She grabbed the tequila by the handle and drank straight from the bottle.

Andrew waited for her to finish before he tossed back his drink. He turned the glass over and banged it down on the bar. "I take it from all the blood that Sidney isn't well."

"You could take it that she's dead." Callie watched his face, but no emotion registered in his expression. She imagined that Sidney would've had the same reaction. "Did you have her kill Leigh's friend?"

"I never told her what to do," Andrew countered. "She considered it a wedding gift. Take some of the heat off me. Give her a little taste of the fun."

Callie didn't doubt it. "Was she fucked up before you met her, or did you make her that way?"

Andrew paused before answering. "She was special from the beginning."

Callie felt her resolve start to falter. It was the pause. He was controlling everything, down to the cadence of their conversation.

414

He wasn't worried about the gun. He wasn't worried about her potential for violence. Leigh had said that Andrew was always three steps ahead. He had lured her here. He had something awful planned.

That was the difference between the two sisters. Leigh would be trying to calculate the angles. All Callie could do was stare at the bottle of tequila, longing for another mouthful.

"Excuse me for a moment." Andrew took his phone out of his pocket. The blue light glowed back in his face. He showed Callie the screen. His security cameras had obviously alerted him to movement back at his house. Leigh's fancy car was parked in his driveway. Callie watched her sister walk toward the front door, Glock at her side, before Andrew made the screen go black.

He told Callie, "Harleigh looks distressed."

Callie put Sidney's gun down on the bar. She had to hurry this along. Leigh had made good time. She would drive even faster when she turned back around. "Isn't that what you wanted?"

"I could still smell you on Sid's fingers when I got home." He was watching her closely, hoping for a reaction. "You taste exactly as sweet as I thought you would."

"Let me be the first to congratulate you on your oral herpes." Callie turned the shot glass back over. She poured herself a proper drink. "What do you want out of this, Andrew?"

"You know what I want." Andrew didn't make her guess. "Tell me about my father."

Callie wanted to laugh. "You picked the wrong fucking day to ask me about that asshole."

Andrew said nothing. He was watching her with the same coldness that Leigh had described. Callie realized she was pushing him too much, acting too reckless. Andrew could reach for the gun, there could be a knife under the bar, or he could use his hands because, up close, she realized how big he was, how the muscles rippling under his shirt were not for show. If it came down to physical blows again, Callie did not stand a chance.

She said, "Before yesterday, I would've said Buddy had his demons, but he was an okay guy."

"What happened yesterday?"

He was pretending like Sidney hadn't told him everything. "I saw one of the tapes."

Andrew's curiosity was piqued. "What did you think about it?"

"I think . . ." Callie hadn't let herself process what she thought, other than disgust with her own delusions. "I told myself for so long that he loved me, but then I saw what he did to me. That wasn't really love, was it?"

He shrugged off the question. "It got a little rough, but there were other times you enjoyed it. I saw the look on your face. You can't fake that. Not when you're a kid."

"You're wrong," Callie said, because she had been faking it all of her life.

"Am I?" Andrew asked. "Look at what happened to you without him. You were destroyed the moment he died. You were rendered meaningless without him."

If there was one thing Callie knew, it was that her life had meaning. She had grown Leigh a baby. She had given her sister something that Leigh would've never trusted to give herself. "Why do you care, Andrew? Buddy couldn't stand you. The last thing he said to you was to drink your NyQuil and go the fuck to bed."

Andrew's expression showed that the blow had landed. "We'll never know how Dad felt about me, will we? You and Harleigh robbed us of the chance to get to know each other."

"We did you a favor," Callie said, though she wasn't so sure. "Does your mother know what happened?"

"That bitch doesn't care about anything but work. You were there. She never had time for me then, and she doesn't make time for me now."

"Everything she did was for you," Callie said. "She was the best mother in the neighborhood."

"That's like saying she was the best hyena in the pack." Andrew's jaw clenched, the bone sticking out at a sharp angle. "I'm not talking about my mother with you. That's not why we're here."

Callie turned around. The candles had distracted her. The smoke and mirrors. Walter's unmoving form in the hallway. She hadn't noticed that some of the mattresses had been moved. Three of the larger ones had been stacked on top of each other. They were exactly where the couch used to be.

She felt Andrew's breath on the back of her neck before she realized he was standing behind her. His hands were on her hips. The weight of his touch pressed into her bones.

His hands spread across her belly. His mouth was close to her ear. "Look at how tiny you are."

Callie swallowed down bile. Buddy's words. Andrew's voice.

"Let's see what's under here." He worked the snaps on her satin jacket. "Do you like this?"

Callie felt cool air on her stomach. His fingers slid under her shirt. She bit down on her lip when his hand cupped her breasts. With his other hand, he reached down between her legs. Callie's knees bowed out. It was like sitting on the flat end of a shovel.

"Such a sweet little dolly." He started to pull off her jacket.

"No." Callie tried to move away, but he'd caught her in a vise-like grip between her legs.

"Empty your pockets." His tone had turned dark. "Now."

Fear seeped into every corner of her body. Callie started to shake. Her feet barely touched the ground. She felt like a pendulum on a clock, hinged only by the hand between her legs.

He tightened his grip. "Do it."

She reached into her right pocket. Sidney's blood was sticky on the knife. The loaded syringe brushed against the back of her fingers. Slowly, she pulled out the knife, praying that Andrew didn't go looking for more.

Andrew wrenched the knife from her hand. He tossed it onto the bar top. "What else?"

Callie couldn't stop the trembling as she reached into her left pocket. Her dope kit felt so personal that it was like taking out her own heart.

"What's this?" he asked.

"My-my—" Callie couldn't answer. She had started crying. The fear was too much. Everything was bubbling back up. Her rosy, faint memories of Buddy were colliding against the cold, hard anger of his son. Their hands were the same. Their voices were the same. And both of them had taken pleasure in hurting her.

"Open it," Andrew said.

She tried to pry up the lid with her thumbnail, but the shaking made it impossible. "I can't—"

Andrew snatched the kit away from her. His hand slipped out from between her legs.

Callie felt hollowed out inside. She staggered over to the pile of mattresses. She sat down, pulling her jacket closed.

Andrew stood in front of her. He had opened her kit. "What's this for?"

Callie looked at her tie-off in his hand. The brown leather strap had belonged to Maddy's father. There was a loop on one end. The other end was chewed where Larry, then Callie had grabbed it in their teeth to pull the tourniquet tight enough to make a vein pop out.

"Come on," Andrew said. "What's it for?"

"You—" Callie had to clear her throat. "I don't use it anymore. It's for—I don't have any veins left in my arms that I can use. I shoot up in my leg."

Andrew was silent for a moment. "Where in your leg?"

"The f-femoral vein."

Andrew's mouth opened, but he seemed incapable of speaking. The candles made light flash across his cold eyes. Finally, he said, "Show me how you do it."

"I don't—"

His hand gripped her neck. Callie felt her breath stop. She clawed at his fingers. He slammed her back onto the mattress. The weight of him was unbearable. He pressed what little air she had left out of her body. Callie felt her eyelids start to flutter.

Andrew was above her, scrutinizing her face, feeding off of her terror. He had her pinned down completely with one hand. Callie could do nothing but wait for him to kill her.

But he didn't.

He released his hold on her neck. He ripped open the button on her jeans. He yanked down the zipper. Callie stayed flat on her back, knowing she couldn't stop him as he tugged down her jeans. He brought one of the candles closer so he could see her leg.

He asked, "What's this?"

Callie didn't have to ask him to clarify. He jammed his finger

418

into the Band-Aid Dr. Jerry had used to cover the abscess. The incision split open, sending a sharp pinch through her leg.

"Answer me." He pressed harder.

"It's an abscess," she told him. "From shooting up."

"Does that happen a lot?"

Callie had to swallow before she could speak. "Yes."

"Interesting."

She shivered when his fingers tickled up her leg. Her eyes closed. There was no resolve left inside of her body. She longed for Leigh to break down the door, to shoot Andrew in the face, to rescue Walter, to save her from what was going to happen next.

Callie bit down on her helplessness. She couldn't let any of that happen. She had to do this herself. Leigh would be here eventually. Callie wasn't going to be the reason her sister got more blood on her hands again.

She told Andrew, "Help me sit up."

Andrew grabbed her by the arm. The vertebrae in her neck made a popping sound as he jerked her up. She looked around for her dope kit. He'd left it open on the edge of the mattress.

She told him, "I need water."

He hesitated. "Does it matter if something is in it?"

"No," she lied.

Andrew walked back to the bar.

Callie picked up her spoon. The handle was bent into a ring so she could hold it better. She took the bottle of water from Andrew. She assumed he'd made Walter drink from it. She had no idea what the Rohypnol would do but neither did she care.

"Hold on," Andrew said, bringing the candles closer so he could see what she was doing.

Callie felt her throat work. You didn't do this for porn. You did it in private, or you did it with other junkies because the process was yours and yours alone.

"What's this for?" Andrew pointed at the cotton ball in her kit.

Callie didn't answer him. Her hands had stopped shaking now that she was giving her body what it wanted. She opened the baggie. She tapped the off-white powder onto the bowl of the spoon.

Andrew asked, "Is that enough?"

"Yes," Callie said, though it was actually too much. "Open the bottle for me."

She waited for Andrew to comply. She held a sip of water in her mouth, then squirted it out onto the spoon like a cardinal feeding its baby. Instead of using her Zippo, she picked up one of the candles from the floor. The white vinegar smell was strong as the dope slowly boiled into a liquid. The dealer had fucked her. The stronger the smell, the more shit in the cut.

Her eyes met Andrew's over the smoke rising from the spoon. His tongue had darted out. This was what he'd wanted from the beginning. Buddy had used tequila and Andrew was using heroin but they both wanted the same thing in the end—Callie put into a stupor so that she couldn't fight back.

With her free hand, she tore off a piece of the cotton. She picked up the syringe. Bit the cap off with her teeth. She placed the needle into the cotton and pulled back on the plunger.

"It's a filter," Andrew said, as if a great mystery had been solved.

"Okay." Callie's mouth had filled with saliva the second the smell had hit the back of her throat. "It's ready."

"What do you do?" Andrew's hesitancy gave her the first glimpse of who he'd been as a boy. He was eager, excited to be learning a new, illicit thing. "Can I—can I do it?"

Callie nodded, because her mouth was too full to speak. She twisted her body to bring her feet onto the mattress. Her pale thighs glowed in the candlelight. She saw what everybody else saw. The femurs and bones of her knees so pronounced that she might as well be looking at a skeleton.

Andrew didn't comment. He laid down alongside her legs, propping himself up on his elbow. She thought about all of the times he'd fallen asleep with his head in her lap. He'd loved to be held while she read him stories.

Now, he was looking up at Callie, waiting for instructions on how to shoot her up with heroin.

Callie was sitting at too severe an angle to see the upper part of her thigh. She peeled off the Band-Aid. She found the center of the drained abscess by feel. "Here."

"In the—" Andrew was still hesitant. He had a better view of the drained abscess than she ever would. "That looks infected."

Callie told him both the truth and what he wanted to hear. "The hurt feels good."

Andrew's tongue darted out again. "Okay, what do I do?"

Callie leaned back on her hands. The satin jacket fell open. "Tap the side of the syringe, then gently depress the plunger to get the air out."

Andrew's hands were far from steady. He was as excited as he'd been when she'd shown him the two bicolored blennies she'd bought at the fish store. He made sure Callie was watching, then thumped his finger on the side of the plastic.

Tap-tap-tap.

Trev, are you tapping on the aquarium like I told you not to?

"Good," she said. "Now get rid of the air bubble."

He tested the plunger, holding the syringe up to the candlelight so he could watch the air leave the plastic tube. A trickle of liquid slid down the needle. At any other time, Callie would've licked it off.

She told him, "You want the vein, okay? It's the blue line. Can you see it?"

He leaned down so close that she could feel his breath on her leg. His finger pressed into the abscess. He looked up quickly, making sure it was okay.

"It feels good," she told him. "Press harder."

"Fuck," Andrew whispered, digging in with his fingernail. He practically shivered. Everything about this was exciting to him. "Like this?"

Callie winced, but said, "Yes."

He caught her eye again before tracing the tip of his finger along the vein. She stared at the top of his head. His hair spun out from the crown the same way Buddy's had. Callie remembered running her fingers along his scalp. The embarrassed look from Buddy as he'd covered the thinning patch.

I'm just an old man little dolly why do you want anything to do with me?

"Here?" Andrew asked.

"Yes," she told him. "Put the needle in slowly. Don't press the

421

plunger until I tell you it's in the right place. You want the needle to slide into the vein, not through it."

"What will happen if it goes through?"

"It won't go into the bloodstream," Callie said. "It'll go into the muscle and it won't really do anything."

"Okay," he said, because he had no way of knowing the truth.

She watched him return to his work. He shifted on his elbow to get more comfortable. His hand was steady as the syringe moved toward the center of the abscess.

"Ready?"

He didn't wait for her acquiescence.

The tiny prick of the needle made a sound come out of her mouth. Callie closed her eyes. Her breath was coming as fast as his. She tried to pull herself back from the brink.

"Like that?" Andrew asked.

"Slow," she coaxed, her hand sliding down his back. "Move the needle around inside."

"Fuck," Andrew groaned. She could feel his erection pressing against her leg. He rocked against her, sliding the needle in and out of her vein.

"Keep doing that," she whispered, running her fingers down his spine. She could feel the flex of his ribs as he breathed. "That's good, baby."

Andrew's head fell against her hip. She felt his tongue on her skin. His breath was hot and wet.

She reached into her jacket pocket. She popped the cap off the 20-ml syringe.

"Okay," she told Andrew, her fingers locating the space between his ninth and tenth rib. "Start pushing it in, but do it slow, okay?"

"Okay."

The sickness from the first taste of heroin nagged at her like a virus.

She pulled the syringe out of her pocket. The blue liquid looked dull in the candlelight.

Callie didn't hesitate. She couldn't let him walk out the door. She stabbed down at an angle, puncturing through the muscle and sinew, driving the needle directly into the left ventricle of Andrew's heart.

422

She was already pressing down on the plunger before he realized that something was very wrong.

By then, it was too late for him to do anything about it.

There was no fighting her off. No screaming. No cries for help. The sedative nature of the pentobarbital took away any last words. She heard the agonal breathing Dr. Jerry had warned her about, the brainstem reflex that sounded like a gasp for breath. His right hand was the last part of his body that he had under any control, and Andrew pushed the heroin in so fast that Callie felt her femoral vein turn into fire.

Her teeth clamped together. Sweat poured off of her body. She held tight to the 20-ml syringe, her thumb shaking as she pressed the thick blue liquid through the needle. Adrenaline was the only thing that kept Callie from collapsing. There was still half a dose left. She watched the slow progress of the plunger going down. She had to give him the full dose before the adrenaline burned off. Leigh was going to be here soon. This couldn't be like the last time. Callie wasn't going to make her sister finish the job she had started.

The plunger finally sank to the bottom. Callie watched the last of the drug flood into Andrew's black heart.

Her hand dropped away. She fell back onto the mattress.

The heroin took over, coming for her in waves—not the euphoria, but the slow release of her body finally giving in to the inevitable.

The pungent vinegar smell. The larger than usual portion. The Rohypnol in the water. The fentanyl she had taken from Dr. Jerry's drug locker and chopped into the off-white powder.

Andrew Tenant wasn't the only person who wasn't going to walk out that door.

First her muscles unwrapped themselves from their tight knots. Then her joints stopped aching, her neck stopped hurting, her body let go of the pain it had been holding on to for so many years that Callie had stopped counting. Her breathing was no longer labored. Her lungs no longer needed air. Her heartbeat was like a slow clock counting down the seconds left in her life.

Callie stared up at the ceiling, her eyes fixed like an owl's. She didn't think about the hundreds of times she had stared up at this same ceiling from the couch. She thought about her brilliant sister, and Leigh's wonderful husband, and their beautiful girl running down the soccer field. She thought about Dr. Jerry and Binx and even Phil until finally, inevitably, Callie thought about Kurt Cobain.

He wasn't waiting for her anymore. He was here, talking to Mama Cass and Jimi Hendrix, laughing with Jim Morrison and Amy Winehouse and Janis Joplin and River Phoenix.

They all noticed Callie at the same time. They rushed over, reaching out their hands, helping her stand.

She felt light in her body, suddenly made of feathers. She looked down at the floor and watched it turn into soft clouds. Her head went back and she was looking up at the bright blue sky. Callie looked left and then right and then behind her. There were kindly horses and plump canines and clever cats and then Janis gave her a bottle and Jimi passed her a joint and Kurt offered to read her some of his poetry, and, for the first time in her life, Callie knew that she belonged.

EPILOGUE

Leigh sat in a folding chair beside Walter. The cemetery was quiet but for a few birds chirping in the tree over the grave. They watched Callie's pastel-yellow casket being lowered into the ground. There were no creaks and groans from the pulleys. Her sister had weighed ninety-five pounds by the time she'd arrived at the medical examiner's office. The autopsy report revealed a body that had been ravaged by long-term drug abuse and illness. Callie's liver and kidneys were diseased. Her lungs were only working at half-capacity. She had been dosed with a lethal cocktail of narcotics and poisons.

Heroin, fentanyl, Rohypnol, strychnine, methadone, baking soda, laundry powder.

None of the findings were all that surprising. Neither was the revelation that only Callie's fingerprints were on the spoon, candle, and bag of powder. Andrew's prints joined hers on the syringe in Callie's leg, but Callie's fingerprints alone were on the lethal dose of pentobarbital she had jacked directly into Andrew's heart.

For years, Leigh had convinced herself that she would feel a guilty kind of relieved when Callie finally died, but now what she felt was an overwhelming sadness. Her eternal nightmare that there would be a late-night phone call, a knock at the door, a detective asking her to identify her sister's body, had not come to pass.

There had only been Callie lying on a filthy stack of mattresses in the house that her soul had not left since she was fourteen years old.

At least Leigh had been with her sister at the end. Leigh was standing inside Andrew's empty mansion when she'd realized that Callie had played her. The drive from Brookhaven was a blur. The first thing Leigh could recall was tripping over Sidney's body in the carport. She had completely missed Walter lying in the hallway because her full attention had been directed toward the two bodies on top of a pile of mattresses where the ugly orange couch used to be.

Andrew was lying across Callie. A large, spent syringe was sticking out of his back. Leigh had pushed him off her sister. She had grabbed Callie's hand. Her skin had felt chilled. The heat was already leaving her frail body. Leigh had ignored the needle sticking out of her sister's thigh and listened to the slow, dwindling sounds of Callie's breath.

At first, twenty seconds passed between the rise and fall of her chest. Then thirty seconds. Then forty-five. Then nothing but a long, low sigh, as Callie finally let go.

"Good morning, friends." Dr. Jerry walked to the foot of Callie's grave. His mask had leaping kittens across the front, though Leigh wasn't sure if he had worn it for Callie or if it was just something he had lying around.

He opened a slim book. "I'd like to read a poem by Elizabeth Barrett Browning."

Walter exchanged a look with Leigh. That was a bit on the nose. Dr. Jerry probably had no idea the poet had been a morphine addict most of her life.

"I've chosen the old gal's most popular sonnet, so please feel free to recite along."

Phil snorted from the other side of Callie's grave.

Dr. Jerry cleared his throat politely before beginning, "'How do I love thee? Let me count the ways/I love thee to the depth and breadth and height/My soul can reach . . .'"

Walter's arm wrapped around Leigh's shoulders. He kissed the side of her head through his mask. She was grateful for his warmth. The weather had taken a cold turn. She hadn't been able to find her coat this morning. She'd been distracted by a long phone call with the man who ran the cemetery because he'd kept gently suggesting that a headstone with rabbits and kittens on it was better suited for a child.

Callie was her *child*, Leigh had wanted to scream, but she had passed the phone to Walter so that she didn't reach through the line and rip the man's head off.

Dr. Jerry continued, "'I love thee to the level of every day's/ Most quiet need, by sun and candle-light/I love thee freely, as men strive for right.'"

She looked across the open grave at Phil. Her mother was not wearing a mask, though Georgia's first Covid superspreader event had taken place at a funeral. Phil sat defiantly, legs spread, hands curled into fists. She hadn't dressed any differently for her youngest daughter's funeral than she would've for a day of collecting rent. Dog collar around her neck. Black Sid Vicious T-shirt because heroin was so awesome. Eye make-up straight out of the rabid raccoon collection.

Leigh looked away before she felt the same anger she always felt around her mother. She stared at the camera that was streaming the funeral. Shockingly, Phil's mother was still alive and living in a retirement home in Florida. Even more surprising, Cole Bradley had asked to pay his remote respects. He was technically still Leigh's boss, though she imagined it was only a matter of time before she was called into his office again. The optics were not great, to put it in corporate speak. Leigh's sister had murdered her client and his new wife, and then overdosed herself, all seemingly without explanation.

Leigh had made it clear that she wasn't going to provide that explanation and no one else had stepped forward to fill in the giant blank. Not Reggie Paltz, who as predicted had skipped town. Not a friend or neighbor or lawyer or banker or money manager or paid informant.

But someone out there had to know the truth. Andrew's safe had been wide open the night that Leigh had broken into his house.

It was empty.

She had told herself she was okay with that. The tapes were still in existence. Eventually, someone would go to the police or approach Leigh or—something. However it happened, Leigh would accept the consequences. The only thing she could control was how she lived her life in the meantime.

Dr. Jerry finished, "'I love thee with a love I seemed to lose/ With my lost saints/I love thee with the breath/Smiles, tears, of all my life; and, if God choose/I shall but love thee better after death.'"

Walter let out a long sigh. Leigh felt the same. Maybe Dr. Jerry understood more than they thought.

"Thank you." Dr. Jerry closed the book. He blew Callie a kiss. He walked over to offer Phil his condolences.

Leigh dreaded what her mother would say to the kindly old man.

"You good?" Walter whispered. His eyes were filled with concern. This time last year, she would've been annoyed by his hovering, but now, Leigh was overwhelmed with gratitude. Somehow, it was easier to let herself love Walter completely now that he understood what it felt like to be broken.

"I'm okay," she told him, hoping that saying the words aloud would make it so.

Dr. Jerry was circling back around the grave. "There you are, young lady."

Walter and Leigh stood up to talk with him.

She said, "Thank you for coming."

His mask was wet with tears. "Our Calliope was such a lovely girl."

"Thank you," Leigh repeated, feeling her own mask stick to her face. Every time she thought she'd run out of tears, more showed up. "She really loved you, Dr. Jerry."

"Well." He patted her hand. "Could I tell you a secret that I found out when my dear wife passed away?"

Leigh nodded.

"Your relationship with a person doesn't end when they die. It only gets stronger." He winked at her. "Mostly because they're not there to tell you that you're wrong."

Leigh's throat tightened.

Walter saved her from having to respond. "Dr. Jerry, that Chevy of yours is a classic. Do you mind showing it to me?"

"That would be my pleasure, young man." Dr. Jerry let Walter take his arm. "Tell me, have you ever been punched in the face by an octopus?"

428

"Fuck me." Phil leaned back in her chair. "Old guy's got the dementia. Moving up to Oregon with Antifa or some shit like that."

"Shut up, Mother." Leigh peeled off her mask. She searched her purse for a tissue.

"She was my daughter, you know," Phil shouted at Leigh across Callie's grave. "Who took care of her? Who did she always come home to?"

"Walter will pick up the cat tomorrow."

"Stupid Cunt?"

Leigh was startled, but then she laughed. "Yes, Stupid Cunt will be living at my house. It's what Callie wanted."

"Well, fuck." Phil looked more upset about losing the cat than she'd been when Leigh had told her about Callie. "That's a damn good cat. I hope you know what you're getting."

Leigh blew her nose.

"You know, I'm gonna tell you this." Phil stuck her hands into her hips. "The problem with you and your sister was that Callie couldn't stop looking back and you were always so goddam desperate to keep looking forward."

Leigh hated that she was right. "I think the bigger problem was that we had an incredibly shitty mother."

Phil's mouth opened, but then it snapped closed. Her eyes had gone wide. She was looking past Leigh's shoulder as if a ghost had appeared.

Leigh turned. Worse than a ghost.

Linda Tenant was leaning against a black Jaguar. A cigarette dangled from her mouth. She was wearing the same pearls and popped collar, but her shirt was long-sleeved for the cooler weather. The last time Leigh had seen Andrew's mother, they were sitting around the conference table in Cole Bradley's private office talking about how to defend her son.

"We should—" Leigh stopped, because Phil was hot-stepping in the opposite direction. "Thanks, Mom."

Leigh took a deep breath. She started the long walk toward Andrew's mother. Linda was still leaning against the Jag. Her arms were crossed. She was clearly here to ambush Callie's funeral. Leigh recognized the brazen act as something she would've done herself. The woman's son and daughter-in-law had been murdered. Never mind that Ruby Heyer's family along with Tammy Karlsen and Andrew's three other victims would never see justice. Linda Tenant wanted an explanation.

Leigh still wasn't going to provide one, but she owed Linda the courtesy of giving her someone to scream at.

Linda flicked her cigarette into the grass as Leigh got closer. "How old was she?"

Leigh hadn't been expecting the question, but she guessed they had to start somewhere. "Thirty-seven."

Linda nodded. "So she was eleven when she started working for me."

"Twelve," Leigh said. "One year younger than me when I started."

Linda fished a pack of cigarettes out of her khakis. She shook one out. Her hand was steady on the lighter. She hissed a plume of smoke into the air. There was something so angry about her that Leigh didn't know whether Linda was going to rail at her or run her over with her car.

She did neither of these things. Instead, she told Leigh, "You cleaned up."

Leigh looked down at her black dress, which was a far cry from the jeans and Aerosmith T-shirt she'd worn that first night. She asked rather than said, "Thank you?"

"I'm not talking about your outfit." Linda made a jerky movement as she pulled the cigarette from her lips. "You girls were always tidy, but you never cleaned like that."

Leigh shook her head. She heard the words, but they didn't make sense.

"That kitchen floor was shining when I got home from the hospital." Linda took another angry drag. "And the bleach was so strong that my eyes watered."

Leigh felt her mouth open in surprise. She was talking about the Canyon Road house. After they'd gotten rid of the body, Callie had gotten on her knees to scrub the floors. Leigh had scoured the sinks. They had vacuumed and dusted and wiped down counters and shined doorknobs and baseboards and neither of them had ever once considered that Linda Waleski would come

430

home from work and wonder why they had deep-cleaned her normally damp, dirty house.

"Huh," Leigh said, hearing echoes of Callie when she didn't know what to say.

"I thought you'd killed him for the money," Linda said. "And then I thought something bad had happened. Your sister—the next day—that was awful. There had clearly been a fight or—or something. I wanted to call the police. I wanted to beat up that piece of shit you call a mother. But I couldn't."

"Why?" was all that Leigh could ask.

"Because it didn't matter why you did it. What mattered was that you got rid of him, and you got paid, and that seemed fair." Linda sucked hard on the cigarette. "I never asked questions because I got what I wanted. He was never going to let me leave. I tried once, and he beat the holy hell out of me. Smacked me until I was unconscious, then left me on the floor."

Leigh wondered how Callie would've felt about this information. Probably sad. She had loved Linda so much. "You couldn't go to your family?"

"I made my bed, didn't I?" Linda picked a piece of tobacco off of her tongue. "Even after you got rid of him, I had to prostate myself in front of my prick of a brother. He would've put me out in the streets. I had to beg him to take me in. He made me wait a month, and even then, I wasn't allowed in his house. We had to live in a squalid apartment over the garage like the damn servants."

Leigh held her tongue. There were far worse places to live.

"I did wonder, though. Not all the time, but sometimes, I wondered why you two girls did it. I mean, what'd he get paid for that framing job, fifty grand?"

"Fifty was in his briefcase," Leigh said. "We found thirty-six more hidden around the house."

"Good for you. But it still didn't make sense. You girls weren't like that. Some of the other kids in the neighborhood—sure. They'd cut your throat for ten dollars, do God knows what for 86K. But not you two. Like I said, that part always bothered me." Linda took the keyfob off her belt. Her thumb rested on a button. "And then I found these in my garage, and I finally understood."

The trunk popped open.

Leigh walked around to the back of the Jaguar. A black plastic garbage bag was inside. The top was open. She saw a pile of VHS cassettes. Leigh didn't have to count them to know that there were fifteen in all. Fourteen featuring Callie. One with Callie and Leigh.

"The night Andrew died, he came by my house. I heard him in the garage. I didn't ask him why. Sure, he was acting strange, but he was always strange. Then a few days ago I remembered. I found that garbage bag shoved into the back of one of the storage cabinets. I didn't tell the police, but I'm telling you."

Leigh felt her throat grow tight again. She looked up at Linda.

The woman hadn't moved except to keep smoking. "I was only thirteen when I met his father. He had me but good. It took three years of me running away, being sent to my grandparents, even to boarding school, before they realized I wasn't going to give him up and they finally let us get married. Did you know that?"

Leigh wanted to grab the bag, but Linda was the one with all the power. There could be copies. There could be another server.

"I never thought . . ." Linda's voice trailed off as she took another puff. "Did he try it with you?"

Leigh stepped away from the trunk. "Yes."

"Did he succeed?"

"Once."

Linda shook another cigarette out of the pack. She lit the fresh one off the old one. "I loved that girl. She was a sweetheart. And I always trusted her with Andrew. I never for a moment thought that anything bad would happen. And the fact that it did—that she was hurt so bad that, even after he was gone, he found a way to keep hurting her . . ."

Leigh watched tears slide down the woman's face. She hadn't once said Callie's name.

"Anyway." Linda coughed, smoke coming out of her mouth and nose. "I'm sorry for what he did to you. And I'm real damn sorry for what he did to her."

Leigh said the same thing that Walter had said to her. "You never thought a pedophile who molested you when you were thirteen would molest other thirteen-year-olds?"

432

"I was in love." She gave a bitter laugh. "I suppose I should throw in an apology for your husband. Is he all right?"

Leigh didn't answer. Walter had been knocked out, held at gunpoint, and forced to drink a date-rape drug. He wasn't going to be all right for a really long time.

Linda had sucked the cigarette down to the filter. She did the same as before, shaking out another, lighting the new off the old. She said, "He raped that woman, didn't he? Killed the other one?"

Leigh gathered she was talking about Andrew and Sidney's respective crimes now. She tried to make Linda say Tammy Karlsen and Ruby Heyer's names. "Which women are you talking about?"

Linda shook her head as she blew out more smoke. "It doesn't matter. He was as rotten as his father. And that girl he married — she was just as bad as he was."

Leigh looked down at the tapes. Linda had brought them for a reason. "Do you want to know why Callie killed Andrew and Sidney?"

"No." She tossed the cigarette into the grass. She walked to the back of the car. The garbage bag came out. She dropped it onto the ground. "Those are the only copies I know about. If anything else comes out, I'll say it's a lie. A deepfake. Whatever they call it. I'll have your back the same as before, is what I'm saying. And for what it's worth, I told Cole Bradley what happened wasn't your fault."

"Am I supposed to thank you?"

"No," Linda answered. "I'm thanking you, Harleigh Collier. As far as I'm concerned, you put one animal down for me. Your sister put down the other."

Linda climbed into her car. She gunned the engine as she drove away.

Leigh watched the sleek black Jaguar prowl its way out of the cemetery. She considered Linda's anger, the manic chain-smoking, the total lack of compassion, the laughable thought that, all of these years, Linda Waleski had persuaded herself that her husband had been murdered by two incredibly hygienic teenage hitmen.

Callie would've had questions.

Leigh couldn't begin to answer them. She looked up at the sky.

Rain had been in the forecast, but white clouds were rolling in. She wanted to think her sister was up there reading Chaucer to a kitten who was using digital currency to hide his money from the IRS, but reality kept her from going that far.

She hoped instead that Dr. Jerry was right. Leigh wanted to continue to have a relationship with her sister. She wanted the Callie who wasn't on heroin, who had a job at a vet clinic and fostered baby animals and came by for lunch every weekend and made Maddy laugh at funny jokes about turtles being farty assholes.

For now, Leigh had their last moment together in Dr. Jerry's office. The way that Callie had held her. The way that she had forgiven Leigh for her lie that had turned into a secret that had festered into a betrayal.

If this is the guilt you've been carrying around for your entire adult life, then set it the fuck down.

Leigh hadn't felt the burden lift when Callie had said the words, but with every day that passed, she felt a lightness in her chest, as if slowly, eventually—maybe—the weight would finally, one day, be gone.

There were other more tangible things that Callie had left Leigh to remember her by. Dr. Jerry had found Callie's backpack inside the breakroom. A Boo Radley assortment was inside—a tanning salon membership card for Juliabelle Gatsby, a DeKalb County Library card for Himari Takahashi, a paperback book on snails, a burner phone, twelve dollars, an extra pair of socks, Leigh's Chicago driver's license that Callie had stolen out of her wallet, and a tiny corner of the blanket that had been wrapped around Maddy inside the cat carrier.

The last two items were particularly meaningful. During the past sixteen years, Callie had been to jail, to prison, to various rehabs, and had lived in cheap motels and on the street, but she had managed to hang onto a photo of Leigh, and Maddy's baby blanket.

Her daughter still had the blanket at home. She still did not know the story of the missing piece. Walter and Leigh went back and forth about whether or not it was time to tell her the truth. Every time they decided they had to be honest, that there wasn't a choice—that the secret had already turned into a lie and it wouldn't be too long before it blossomed into a betrayal—Callie talked them out of it.

She had left a note for Leigh inside of her backpack, the words mirroring the note she had left with Maddy sixteen years ago. Callie had obviously written it after their conversation in Dr. Jerry's office, just as Callie had obviously known that she was never going to see Leigh ever again.

Please accept the gift of your beautiful life, Callie had written. *I am so proud of you, my lovely sister. I know that no matter what happens, you and Walter will always and forever keep Maddy happy and safe. I only ask that you don't ever tell her our secret, for her life which will be so much happier without me. I LOVE YOU. I LOVE YOU!*

"Hey." Walter was stamping out Linda's smoldering cigarettes. "Who was that lady in the Jag?"

"Andrew's mother." Leigh watched Walter look inside of the garbage bag. He turned over the VHS tapes to read the labels. Callie #8. Callie #12. Harleigh & Callie.

Walter asked, "What did she want?"

"Absolution."

Walter threw the tapes back in the bag. "Did you give it to her?"

"No," Leigh said. "You have to earn it."

Dear Reader

Early in my career, I chose to write my novels without marking a particular point in time. I wanted the stories to stand alone without news cycles or pop culture intruding into the narrative. My approach changed as I started working on my Will Trent series and stand-alones, when it became more important to me to anchor the books in the *now* as a way to hold up a mirror to society. I wanted to ask questions with my fiction, like how we got to #metoo (*Cop Town*), how we became so inured to violence against women (*Pretty Girls*), or even how we ended up with an angry mob breaking down the doors of the Capitol (*The Last Widow*).

There's always a delicate balance between writing about social issues and keeping up the driving pace of a thriller. I am at my very core a thriller author, and I never want to slow down or interfere with the rhythm of a story to climb onto a soapbox. I try very hard to present both sides, even when I don't agree with the opposing opinion. With this in mind, I started framing the story that became *False Witness*. I knew that I wanted to incorporate the SARS-CoV-2 pandemic, but I also knew that the story was not *about* the pandemic so much as about how people are managing to live through it. And, of course, my perspective is not just as an American, or as a Georgian, or even as an Atlantan—like everyone else, how I view the world is seen through the lens of who I am as an individual.

As I started work in March 2020, I had to be somewhat of a futurist in trying to predict what life would be like in roughly one year's time. Obviously, a lot changed over the course of my writing. At first we were told to forgo masks so that hospitals would not run out of supplies, then we were told that we should all be wearing masks (then double masks); initially we were told to wear gloves, then we were told gloves offered a false sense of safety; first we were told to wash down our groceries, then we were told they're fine; then there were the variants and so on and so on until finally, thankfully, the vaccines were released, which was wonderful news but also necessitated incorporating their somewhat confusing roll-out into a novel that was nearly finished—though it must be said that these were small hurdles compared to the worldwide loss and tragedy caused by this horrible virus.

As of this writing, we've crossed the devastating milestone of 500,000 dead in the United States. Then, there are the tens of millions of survivors—some of whom are experiencing Long-Covid or whose lives will be forever marked by the disease. Because of the inherent loneliness of a Covid death, our medical professionals have suffered untold trauma witnessing firsthand the ravages of this terrible virus. Our medical examiners, coroners, and funeral homes have endured an overwhelming volume of dead. Educators, frontline workers, first responders—the lists are endless because the pandemic has touched every single person on earth in ways both big and small. The impact of this daily mass casualty event will be felt for generations. Still unknown is how the suspension of grief will eventually seep out into our lives. We know from studying childhood abuse that trauma can lead to everything from depression, PTSD, cardiovascular issues such as stroke and heart attack, cancer, a heightened risk for drug and alcohol abuse and in some extreme cases, suicidal ideation. We have yet to reckon with what the world will look like in fifteen or twenty years' time when Zoomers are raising children of their own.

Though I love my readers, I have always written my books for myself, using fiction to process the world around me. As I set out to realistically incorporate the pandemic into *False Witness*, I looked to recent history for cues. In many ways the evolution of our understanding of Covid-19 mirrors the beginning of what was then called the AIDS crisis, during which my generation experienced a painful coming of age. As with SARS-CoV-2, there were a lot of unknowns when HIV first reared its ugly head. Scientists didn't immediately know how it was transmitted, how it worked, where it had come from—so the advisories changed almost monthly and the homophobia and racism ran rampant. And then of course the way people responded to HIV/AIDS ran the gamut from fear to anger to denial to acceptance to full-on

437

fuck-its. Though AIDS was far, far more deadly than Covid (and transmission was thankfully not airborne), a lot of those same attitudes have been on display in our response to the Covid-19 pandemic. And I should add that during both of these transform-ational tragedies, we have seen remarkable caring and kindness countering what feels like incomprehensible hate. Nothing brings out our humanity, or lack thereof, like a crisis.

As terrible as these last eighteen months have been, the ensuing crisis has provided a foundation for the kind of socially conscious storytelling that has come to define my work. Covid has exposed the ever-widening chasm between the haves and have-nots, spot-lighted the housing crisis and food insecurity, focused attention on the lack of proper funding for schools, hospitals and elder care, exposed a bankruptcy of trust in our government institutions, exac-erbated the horrendous treatment of inmates in our jails and prisons, exponentially worsened xenophobic, misogynistic, and racist hate speech, heightened racial inequalities, and as usual, has grossly over-burdened the lives of women; all topics that I've attempted to touch on within the pages of the book you now hold in your hands. All issues I'm striving to make sense of, to have greater empathy for, with hopes for a deeper understanding.

One of my favorite short novels is Katherine Anne Porter's *Pale Horse, Pale Rider*, which is set during the influenza epidemic of 1918. The main character is stricken with the disease, just as Porter herself was in real life, and we get a firsthand glimpse of the awful effects of the virus—both through the social insecurity of the char-acter's fear of losing her job and being evicted by her landlady, to the four to five days she had to wait before there was room for her at the hospital, to the fever dreams and hallucinations brought on by the lurking presence of the Pale Rider: Death. The last line of the story is both timeless and prescient, and I think it will encap-sulate how we'll all likely feel when we're through the worst of this cruel pandemic and we manage to find our way to a new normal—

"Now there would be time for everything."

Karin Slaughter
February 26, 2021
Atlanta, Georgia

ACKNOWLEDGMENTS

First thanks always goes to Victoria Sanders and Kate Elton, who have known me longer than I have known myself. Thanks to the tiebreakers, Emily Krump and Kathryn Cheshire—as well as the entire GPP team. At VSA, I am very grateful for Bernadette Baker-Baughman, who has seemingly endless patience (or a doll of me that she stabs every morning).

Kaveh Khajavi, Chip Pendleton, and Mandy Blackmon answered my peculiar skeletal and joint inquiries. David Harper has been helping me kill people for twenty years, and as usual, his input was exceptionally helpful, even as he was riding out the devastating Texas snow and ice storms with his cell phone and a set of channel locks. Elise Diffie assisted me with veterinary clinic machinations, though all nefarious workarounds are my own. Also, she might be the only person reading this book who realizes how truly hilarious the name Deux Claude is for a Great Pyrenees.

Alafair Burke, Patricia Friedman, and Max Hirsh assisted me with the legalities—any mistakes are my own (tragically, the law is never what you want it to be). For those of you who are wondering: on March 14, 2020, the Chief Justice of Georgia's Supreme Court issued a state-wide order prohibiting all jury trials "due to the number of people required to gather at courthouses." By October, the prohibition was lifted, but a few days before Christmas, soaring infection rates forced the Chief Justice to reinstate the prohibition. On March 9, 2021, the prohibition was lifted again, citing that the "dangerous surge of Covid-19 cases recently has declined." That's where we are as of now, and I fervently hope it will stay that way.

Lastly, thanks to D.A. for putting up with my long absences (both physical and mental) during the writing of this story. Having enjoyed the quarantine lifestyle for many years, I thought it would be easier; alas, it was not. Thanks to my dad for always being there no matter what. I anticipate a rapid return to soup and cornbread deliveries now that the worst is behind us. And to my sister: thank you so much for being my sister.

Last lastly: I took many liberties when writing about drugs and how to use them because I am not in the business of offering how-tos. If you are one of the many people struggling with addiction, please know that there is always someone out there who loves you.